The Kindreds

Volume One

RAYNE

First Edition

ISBN: 979-8-9920406-1-6

DEDICATION

For those who don't believe.

AUTHOR'S NOTE

On the West Coast of America, there exist ancient ruins whose origins are unexplainable by documented history. Upon exploring these crumbled mansions and palaces, what is believed to be a lady's bedroom was discovered. Within it were the ruined remains of a bedframe, a vanity, and the typical bedroom adornments. There were also chests filled with clothes and jewelry, but most intriguingly, diaries of a young woman named Sada Solares. While old and worm-eaten and stained with strange liquids, the dainty cursive was eligible (some excerpts have been copied into this book). The diaries told a tale that was almost unbelievable with how fantastical and magickal it was. And yet, the discovery of other artifacts, ones unable to be explained by mortal and earthly means, made the diary entries impossible to discount. With the help of these artifacts strewn around the ruins, Sada's story was unraveled.

And now it is written here.

There are names and words mentioned by Sada that are foreign and of a language other than ours, one which scholars believe to have been derived from ancient Greek; a pronunciation key has been included in the back. But if you're like me and you're determined to read the names however *you* deem to sound the best, then forge on, my stubborn reader.

PROLOGUE

Sada's Diary

Dear Jezebel,

I'm sorry. Please don't see this as an excuse, but as an explanation. I only hope that you can forgive me.

P.S. The original broke, but the jewel is the same. Think of me when you wear it.

With all my love,
Sada

THE FIRST

The Brothers

Two mortals walked through an immortal forest, and the forest watched.

"Perhaps we ought to reconsider this," Kartinar Joseph hissed suddenly.

The wind quieted as he spoke, and his whispered tone did nothing to blend the sharp tang of a human voice into the sounds of magick-filled woods. It stood out like a horn on a horse. Though in these lands, a voice in the night was more attention drawing than a horned horse. Kartinar shivered at the thought, but his brother just groaned.

"Stop tryin' to run away at the eleventh hour. Eleven has two ones, and one can't do this alone—*HA!*" The second mortal, Drath Samuel, didn't bother to lower the volume of his voice or his ensuing laughter. The wind blew harder, sensing he was not afraid. "We're nearly there. Best we keep on, less effort that way. Unless thou want to trek back for a month with nothin' to show for it. Trust me Karti, the drifters will lose their tongues when they hear what we've done."

Kartinar nodded along in the darkness, trying to smile and convince his own mind that he agreed with his brother. He started to suck in a steadying breath, but the sound of something rubbing against tree bark drew his attention back into the forest, and the air caught in his throat. He strained his ears, eyes darting around fervently in the near blackness. Unsettled, he just mumbled in agreement to whatever Drath was going on about.

"Oh, I knew it," his brother was saying, chuckling to himself. "Alandra had the right of it, didn't she?"

At the sound of her name Kartinar stopped, abruptly turning to face him. He had to tilt his head up to look into his brother's face, but after nearly thirty decades of doing so he didn't notice the effort or the embarrassment of looking up at another man anymore.

"What?" Kartinar asked sharply.

His brother only laughed all the harder.

"*What* did thee just say about Alandra?" He was so angry that he had lapsed into the broken and archaic speech of their clan, a habit he had worked at for years to break. This only made him angrier.

Drath saw and shook his head, smile fading. "It's nothin'. Let the past have it, as *Om' Modir* would say." He knew he shouldn't have mentioned Alandra's name. The only woman who had ever looked twice at Kartinar, she would not leave his heart even years after she had left his bed. He tried to continue walking but Kartinar stopped him with a hand on the shoulder.

"It art not nothing when it comes to *her*," Kartinar insisted.

The two men stared at each other, both faces too readable for their own good: Kartinar's, sharper and gaunter, was filled with the signs of anger—clenched jaw, flared nostrils—though his eyes told a story of hurt. Drath's, rounder and wider, showed some frustration, but it was mostly pity for an aching heart. Alandra had first entered his and Kartinar's life when they were still young (for mortals) and living with the Troll clan. Alandra and her mother hailed from a neighboring Fae village and often passed through their part of the woods to reach Grandfleur, the Elven City of Flowers, where they would collect nectar for their shop. The people of this world were hospitable, but the Trolls were especially, and the two women were offered rest and succor whenever they passed through. More often than not, they had taken it.

Kartinar had not immediately fallen in love with the pretty young Faery. That was reserved for fairytales, and even in this land those were rare. But it was even rarer for three children to be of similar ages, and so Kartinar and Drath and Alandra were forced into companionship by the elders who understood what a rarity it was. In the beginning, Kartinar had poked fun at Alandra and when the brothers were alone, he would rant to Drath about all the things which made her terrible. Drath would listen with the rapture only a younger sibling receiving attention from their older sibling could experience.

It was later when Alandra had grown and returned to thank their clan's queen for her hospitality all those years ago that Kartinar realized the truth of her beauty and his aggravation became infatuation. He'd summoned the courage to talk to her, and shortly after, he began making frequent stops in Alandra's village. That was nearly a decade ago now. A blink for Alandra in her immortality, but a grueling nine years for Kartinar.

Drath, examining his brother's expression, finally released a sigh. This was not a fight between him and Karti, but between Karti and his past.

"Come on Karti, let's just go." He set his bearded mouth into a grim line. "Oughtn't have mentioned your woman. Looks like the night's playin' tricks on my thinker as well." He nudged his brother with an elbow, chuckling halfheartedly.

"She art not my woman anymore," Kartinar muttered. He dropped his hand, nonetheless. The pair moved on in silence.

As the two men continued their quiet plodding along a starless trail, the forest seemed to get closer to them, and the sounds of it farther away. Kartinar hadn't been able to place why the woods made him so uneasy, but now he realized it was the uncanniness. Immortals were similar enough to mortals that a comparison could be drawn, but just dissimilar enough that the comparison was uncomfortable to make. In the same way, the immortal forest was similar enough to mortal woods that they could be called by the same name; but the stillness of the branches, the silence of the wind as it wove through the trunks, the smoothness of the bark and the lack of fallen or cut trees…The drifters were right, this forest was *alive.*

He knew all forests were: "If it grows, it lives," *Om' Modir*—queen of their clan—used to say as she whispered magick into her garden. But this forest was much, much different. It was as though magick both came from it and died in it. It breathed life in on one side and exhaled death on the other, and perhaps it joined them together as one. Kartinar shuddered to think which side they stood on.

"You know, I'm surprised you agreed to this, Karti," Drath said. He looked completely unbothered by the presence of the forest, swinging his arms and humming beneath his breath.

"What do you mean?" Kartinar asked. He was the one who had struck the deal with the drunk beggar that put them on this journey. "The money was good."

"Jiie. But you usually carry on as though I dragged thou with me by your belt."

"What is this 'usually' you speak of?" Kartinar broke in, exasperated. "This is hardly a customary occurrence."

Typically their excursions involved Kartinar stealing from markets while Drath acted as a distraction, or Kartinar sneaking into an abandoned home in the Border towns after Drath broke the lock on the door. Their life was a motley of thievery and other petty crimes. At first, it had been a way to survive in the strange world they were abandoned in. Then it had become something of a comfort, something they both knew they were good at.

That was hard to come by when the only people they could compare themselves to possessed true magick, and if not magick, then a knack for one or several somethings. Kartinar and Drath had discovered their knack was for crime, and even when they weren't in want of money, they found an excuse to break into a home or a purse. These excursions kept them sane. It was during one such excursion into a drifter's tent when they came across the orb, and the man who owned it. When they began this very irregular journey.

Take it with you, should it please you. I have but one small request…

And much more money to go with it than a drifter should have on him. But it wasn't the money that had convinced Kartinar to accept the old man's request, as Drath thought. It was what he'd told Kartinar when Drath had left the tent to investigate a flash of light. Kartinar's bowels clenched at the memory. He glanced at the satchel his brother wore, wondering if he should just take it and throw it into the forest and be done with it. But seeing Drath so carefree, even in a dark and magickal forest, reminded Kartinar of why he'd accepted the drifter's terms.

"And besides," Kartinar continued, "I'm usually the one pulling you away from your potions and reading to go loot."

They'd taken to calling it looting when they were just boys beginning their career of thievery, and it had stuck. Looting sounded better than robbing, or stealing from unsuspecting people.

Drath waved a big hand. "I'm not talkin' about the lootin'. But whenever we go on adventures—"

"Adventures, truly? Curses, Drath, we aren't children anymore."

"Fine. What else would thee call this? A quest?"

Kartinar shook his head, his short hair brushing the nape of his neck. "That's even dafter."

"Explorin'?"

"That's better, but…let's just hold our tongues. I don't like the way the trees react when we talk so much. It's almost as if they're listening."

Kartinar could have sworn they leaned away from the path at his words, as though trying to appear innocent of their accused crimes. If he were the judge, he would accuse them all of being guilty.

"Oh, spare me, Kartinar, the trees don't give one shred about your voice. You've been spendin' too much time in *Om' Modir's* gardens. The Pixies been talkin' to you, Karti? The plants, maybe?" Drath sneered and Kartinar dodged a jab to his ribs. "If you had any magick, there'd be *Vaisse* knots in your hair—I'd put my ace on it."

The people of Elt had several religions, all of which Kartinar thought to be mildly to greatly imbecilic, especially since they used their hairstyles to reflect their beliefs. Most of the religious folk subscribed to the idea that the world itself was alive, and they probably did think that trees had ears to listen with. Kartinar did not believe that, necessarily, but he did think these trees were imbued with some otherworldly essence, one not seen in the rest of the land.

"My beliefs are of no concern to you. If I were to put my faith in any of these people's religious follies, it would be in the Void. And you don't even know what an ace is!" It almost made him sad, to think of how Drath had been taken from their world before he could learn to play cards. Before he could learn that humans were not rare or less-than.

Drath just chuckled. "Void twists, then."

Kartinar hissed at him to shut up again, then his eyes resumed their darting back and forth across the path, scanning the trees, the trail in front of him, the forest beside him, then the shadows beside Drath…Every step on the rocky dirt was torture to him. He managed to step lightly, but Drath was crunching along merrily beside him, alerting the entire forest to their presence. He ground his teeth together, weighing whether it would be worth it to rebuke him again. Being the intellect of the group was always so taxing.

"Can thee walk any louder?" Kartinar snapped.

"I sure can try."

"The Void you will!"

While they bickered, the forest stretched toward them. The muted sounds had crept in a little closer when they spoke, allowing Kartinar to hear whispers of the things it wanted to tell him. But now it was silent again, and he became aware of the volume of their breathing now, too.

Despite its otherworldly presence, as they drew further away from the Valley of Kings, the forest began to look less enchanted and more normal—more mortal. Mossy ground became rocky, and lush grass gave way to dust and dirt. It reminded him uneasily of the home he'd been taken from. Memories of gravel on cobblestone streets, muddy alleys, dirt roads leading out of the city. Here, dirt had become a marker for him of sorts, telling him how good or downright awful a place might be. The more dirt there was, the worse the place was likely to be.

He gritted his teeth and focused on stepping lighter, drawing his weight up into his chest rather than his legs, just as he'd learned from his years on the outskirts of the city he'd been born in. It was disconcerting how similar this part of Elt looked to his human home. The heaviness in the air may have been born of magick, but the wrongness beneath it felt stained in the way only human touch could manage. Elt was a peaceful world, and even the Border towns were gentler than the alleyways of his birth. Perhaps that was why the drunk drifter had asked Kartinar and his brother to complete this task for him. They were of a world corrupted by wrongness; he was not.

They were far from the Valley now. They had traveled over a month just to get here, and only last night did they finally slink in through the gates and onto the forested grounds surrounding Castle *Te'raina.* Only a few guards remained after its former owner abandoned it, and the brothers had evaded them with potions Drath brewed.

Kartinar had been unsure the cloaking brews would be of any use; the guards were not people, but gargoyles, crafted from stone and brought to life by old magick. They had watched the brothers as they entered, supposedly invisible, through the tall stone walls and iron gates surrounding the castle grounds. But they didn't move to attack. He wondered if that was because of the potions' effects, orders from their master, or simply because the castle and its grounds had been abandoned for hundreds of years. He'd decided then that he didn't truly care so long as the potions worked, but now he wondered if they should have been more mindful of the stony guards.

Now deep into the castle grounds they were at the apex of their journey, and Kartinar questioned his decision to embark on it more deeply with every step that brought them closer to the castle. Even from this distance, where its spires were just sometimes visible through the trees, he was sure its walls were made of dread itself. There was not enough light to confirm or refute his thoughts.

Indeed, there was no light at all. The two men had decided against bringing a light source of their own. Being poor in a world like this left them deprived of many resources, like the floating, spellbound lights that were used in the big cities to keep their constant and otherworldly glow alive. They were left to choose from torches or candlelit lanterns, both of which were not ideal for stealthy travel. Torches smelled atrocious and attracted attention from every direction, while lanterns were too tedious and hard to run with.

The men had opted for travel by moonlight, and most of the time the sky lit their paths brightly. But tonight, it had abandoned them, as did warmth, and sound. Kartinar feared all his senses might be useless here. Even when he sniffed the air, all he smelled was cold. Yet when he shivered, he couldn't be certain it was wholly from the temperature.

"Karti, look," Drath whispered suddenly. "Karti! Stop lookin' at the trees." Kartinar was dragged from his surveillance of the darkness and his eyes followed the dim silhouette of Drath's arm pointing excitedly into the forest.

"I must say, I'm at a loss as to why you pulled me from my tree-watching to look at more trees," Kartinar grumbled. The forest had made him uneasy, and he rubbed his arms as he squinted at what Drath was pointing toward.

"Past them, Beast-brain."

Kartinar strained his neck as he peered above the tree line. He was readying to complain more about how he could, in fact, see nothing but trees, when he was suddenly being lifted into the air and set on his brother's shoulder. Kartinar had to grip his arm to suppress the sudden nausea from the height, but still muttered a thank you as what Drath had been pointing at came into view.

Huge, towering walls rose just on the other side of the trees, halting the forest in its tracks. Some trees on the outskirts seemed to even lean away from the wall, and understandably. It was massive, and thicker than any tree trunk Kartinar had seen. Now he understood why the moon had been absent on their journey: it was held in position above the castle, illuminating the entire building in cold, pale moonlight. Oddly, even in the lilac light of the moon, the castle still appeared to be made of shadows. Or perhaps Kartinar had been right, and the walls truly were built from dread.

He tapped Drath on the arm wrapped securely around his shins in a silent command. His tall brother set him on the ground, then raised his eyebrows in question.

"I marked it," Kartinar answered. "It is indeed as horrid as they said."

Drath grunted in agreement. "I think I felt your stomach drop onto my shoulder." He chuckled loudly, and Kartinar just jabbed his fingers into his brother's ribs, which only stoked the fire of that great laugh.

"Quiet now, we're nearly there," Kartinar hushed. "This is no hour for jest. It's the eleventh, remember?"

"What else am I s'posed to do, Karti?" Drath groaned. "I'm bored to my bones."

"Bored?" he hissed, incredulous. How was it that Kartinar could be so worked up that he jumped like a jackrabbit at every noise, and his brother was fighting off yawns? "Your boredom seems perpetually to be the catalyst for our misadventures. Do keep your attention fixed on *it*."

"What?" Drath asked.

"You know, *it*."

"What's *'it?'*"

Kartinar shifted to glare at Drath, who was trying to hide a smile in the darkness. "Kindly stop trying to vex me. You possess a remarkable talent for achieving such a feat *without* trying."

"I've got it handled," Drath soothed. As if to prove it, he unbuckled the leather satchel that had been swinging at his side. The lines of glowing lavender that had lined the seams of the bag now erupted into streams of brilliant purple light. It shone eagerly, illuminating Kartinar and Drath and a circle of the path around them. Kartinar hissed a curse and Drath immediately buckled the satchel again.

"Well don't go parading it about!" Kartinar said, trying to snatch the satchel from Drath's enormous, blundering mitts.

The big man evaded Kartinar's grabs, swatting his slim hands away. *A watchmaker's hands gone to waste*, as his father had been fond of saying. The thought frustrated him further, and he gave up on trying to steal the satchel from Drath with a curse.

"Ah, to the Void with it! Just leave the cursed thing in there."

"Always you with the final word, Karti," Drath just chuckled in response. He settled the satchel on his hip again.

"Come," Kartinar grumbled, quickening his pace.

He shoved his too-slim hands into his armpits, still thinking of his father's words. They hadn't gone to waste, all right, they had found their thieving knack. His hands knew the contents of every woman's purse and every man's pocket from the Valley to the Border. And some knack it was. He didn't care what anyone said—being human in a world like this was nothing but a curse.

The pair continued in silence, Kartinar stalking ahead, angry at something Drath couldn't place as he meandered along behind his brother. The forest had closed in on them while they walked, and now it opened up again, giving them room to breathe, and to see, as the moonlight finally crept onto some parts of the trail. Now at least there were patches of visibility scattered among the darkness. Though the trail didn't widen, the trees grew farther away from it with every step the men took.

By the time they reached the end of the pathway, three more massive trunks could have been placed between it and the forest before the trees were lining the edges. Kartinar noticed with unease, and hurried his brother out of the forest when they reached the tree line. One would think his mortal fear would have receded by now, after living in such a place his whole life, but… he didn't like forests that moved. The path dumped them at the edge of a moat encircling the entire castle.

Castle *Te'raina* was tall, dark, and indeed dreadful, but he had seen many castles in his lifetime and was unimpressed. What Kartinar was awestruck by was what lay beside it. Stretching from the forest to the distant peaks of the Pinnacle were leagues of scorched earth—it was what gave this area its name: the Dragon's Plate. But nestled in the cracked, black ground beside the castle was a shallow valley of lush, vibrant land. The ground was not dirt, but lava rock, glass of every color, and sand. It seemed the castle was made of black glass collected from this very valley. Pockets of lava still glowed between the vibrant patches of foliage and winding blue streams, leftover from an ancient eruption.

"Spirits above," Kartinar whispered, and couldn't help but step toward the nature-defying valley.

He realized then that they were standing on the lip of the erupted volcano itself, and the valley was inside it. The eruption must not have been as ancient as he had initially thought it to be. Few drifters and fewer city folk had gone this far north-west, but there were rumors of what this untouched land would be like. Piecing together those rumors, he'd thought the volcano to have been dormant for millennia, but he now saw that the trees were still young here, having only just started growing in a once-harsh land now vibrant with nutrients. They were the smallest trees Kartinar had ever seen in Elt. They were just shorter than those in his world, and he was surprised to see that their leaves were like the needles of pines as well, only here they were pink and blue rather than green, and the trunks were black like obsidian.

Drath whistled as he came to stand beside Kartinar. He dropped to a crouch with a grunt and a pop of his knees, found a lava rock, hefted it, and chucked it into the valley. It landed in the nearest lava pool with an indignant sizzle, and a loop of magma popped up like saliva.

Drath grinned and tossed another rock. "Neat."

"This isn't the time for play," Kartinar said, voice still hushed. However, after a short pause, he scooped up a rock of his own and flung it toward the magma. It fell short and lamely dropped into a bush.

Drath's laugh was unnervingly loud in the silence. "Not time for you to play, maybe. Stick to thievin', Karti, I'll do the rock-throwin'."

Kartinar rolled his eyes but grinned anyway. Seeing Drath having fun made him happy—the kind of happy that only a big brother who'd seen his little (giant) brother suffer could experience. By his nature, he wished to urge Drath to stop his playing and get their job over with, to *go go go*. But he made himself push it down for the sake of his brother's happiness. The castle and its moat had been standing watch over this valley for centuries. They could watch a little longer. Kartinar put his hand on Drath's shoulder.

"Tryin' to see if I can make some magma splash onto that rock," he explained, still chucking rocks. "Think anyone lives down yonder?"

Kartinar snorted. "Not in *Torteuir's* fire. We're leagues from that lava pool and you're already sweating like an Elf in an Orc camp. Anyone who dared reside in that valley would die before they could even think to build a house."

"Yeah, but, what about evolution or that rot?"

"I don't think they have that here," Kartinar said. "The Spiritkin's lineage traces back to the Mothers, remember? I believe little has changed between them and the people here now."

"Nah, you don't believe that."

"Sure I do."

Drath leveled him with a stare. "Griffin-dung."

He couldn't help but smile. "Griffin-dung," he agreed.

Kartinar felt as though something had let him go as he'd crossed the threshold of the forest. It was as though the roots and branches of the trees had snuck into his flesh while he walked through the woods and had been dragging him back toward where he'd come from. But now they pushed him out, away. Rather than relieved, he felt bare in the moonlight. With his back to the forest, the black castle on one side, and a valley of fire on the other. None brought him any comfort, and he was unable to go against his instincts to *go go go* anymore.

"Where do you wish to do it?" Kartinar asked abruptly.

He didn't choose himself because while he was the intellect of the pair, this was for Drath. It was his quest. Like a coveted griffin's egg, he had been hatching it since they were boys being treated cruelly by a world that didn't understand them, as hard as they tried to understand it. It was almost as though the drunk drifter had appeared to them in answer to the silent call of his brother's soul.

When Drath was still young, he'd discovered a tome in the outskirts of the Border towns. It was old, damaged by water, and missing several pages, but the cover was almost completely intact. It pictured the symbols of the four elements. Inside were the notes of a mage, detailing his experiments with potions and brews, journaling his transformation from mundane to magical. Kartinar had tried to dissuade Drath from reading the book, and after some initial complaints, he'd agreed.

When Kartinar discovered that his brother had disobeyed his request and not only read the journal but went on to practice what the mage had recorded, it was too late. Drath's talent for crafting spells and elixirs was obvious. It was also apparent that such brews would greatly enhance their success with looting. And so Drath continued practicing made magic, their wealth increased, and so did Drath's desire to become better, more powerful. He turned his sights from mage's magic to sorcery, and it had become his quest to be apprenticed to the last true sorcerer in their world: Amogasanes the Strange.

It was imperative that they kept knowledge of Drath's craft secret from everyone; made magic as an art was hated by all who possessed natural magick, but the actual practice of it wasn't illegal. Not for Spiritkin, the residents of this world. But for humans, it had once been punishable by death. Kartinar didn't want to find out if that was still the case. Yet they'd managed to protect this secret and still discover through secret channels that the only way Amogasanes would take on a new apprentice was if they got his attention with a display so prominent, it was heard of all throughout Elt.

Over a moon past, when Drath had left the drifter's tent, the old man had beckoned Kartinar closer. Warily, he'd obeyed. The man had revealed to him the nature of the orb he possessed, that it was a sorcerer's light—one of the few remaining. He told also the effect he believed it would have on the land as a whole, from the Valley of Kings to the Border towns, and beyond even that. Upon first hearing this, Kartinar felt as though all of the heat had left his body. He'd backed up, ready to get Drath and get the Void away from the old man. But then he'd told Kartinar of what else the orb could do. He'd also told him that there was rumor Amogasanes the Strange sought a new apprentice.

For you, Drath, Kartinar thought as he eyed the sinister purple light leaking from the satchel. *All of this is worth it for you.* Drath didn't know what the orb would do, only that it would have a great enough effect it would be sure to earn the attention and possibly the mentorship of Amogasanes. If he had known, Kartinar knew he never would have agreed. He was not selfish enough for that. But Kartinar cared more for his brother than he did for the rest of the world.

And Kartinar was very selfish.

Drath tossed one more chunk of scoria, stood with another ceremonial grunt and pop of his knees. He glanced around himself before he stalked to the edge of the moat, booted toes hanging over the lip of it.

"Here works," he said simply.

Despite the many castles he'd come across, Kartinar had never seen a moat before; he only knew of their existence from stories. He had been expecting a trench of murky, stagnant water encircling the castle, designed to keep out as many monsters as it contained in its depths. This moat was more akin to a river, with clear, gurgling water flowing and eddying around the grounds like a serpent. There were no monsters to be seen…no animals either, or people. The castle was as empty and beautiful as the crater beside it. He thought of the gargoyles again, their tracking eyes. He tried not to let new—or old—worries surface as he examined the castle's moat. Grass grew thick and green around the edges, and Kartinar dug his fingers into it as he dropped to his knees, pressed his lips to the rushing water, and drank.

"What're thee doin'?" Drath asked. He quickly swung his head around in surveillance as Kartinar sat up.

Grinning, the slender man wiped chilling moat water off his chin and just laughed. At the sight of his typically somber brother, mouth dripping and chuckling, Drath couldn't help but laugh too, though he shook his head at the sight.

"Come Karti, if there's any a time to pay mind, it's now."

Kartinar nodded in agreement and assumed the role of lookout as Drath crouched beside the moat, now emptying a small bag onto the grass. Kartinar kept his back to the castle, facing the forest and valley, ensuring the gargoyles didn't find them, watching for the creatures the moat supposedly kept out of the castle. Nothing moved out there except the wind stirring the grass above the valley. In the forest, the trees had begun to moan.

A flicker of light caught his eye, and his first reaction was to look to Drath. But the satchel was still closed, and the light had been orange, not purple. He saw its source in the valley. Four or five female Fire Sprites had sprung up from the magma and were dancing in a circle, holding hands. Every so often one would throw her head back. Laughter, wraith-like and whispered due to the distance between them, accompanied the sounds of Drath working.

Drath will be happy to know I was wrong. People really do live down there, he thought. And they wouldn't mind being burned up by the heat. They probably generated a good amount of it. He kept one eye on the Sprites and one on the trees as his brother toiled away. It was an unspoken agreement that Kartinar would keep guard while Drath worked, and vice versa; that's how they'd always done it, and that was why they never got caught.

Yet he found himself growing bored in the immobile silence of their surroundings, and Kartinar slid an eye down to where his brother was working. Small trinkets and tools littered the grass beside miniature bottles and tinctures. Most were empty, their contents probably being mixed into the moat that very moment. As Kartinar glanced at the moat, it flared orange suddenly and began to bubble up over the edges, thick foam creeping onto the grass. Drath cursed and upended three tiny bottles into it. The orange water blazed angrily then returned to its original state. Some bubbles remained on the grass, popping silently in the breeze.

Kartinar scowled silently at Drath, and the big man smiled sheepishly. "Sorry Karti," he whispered. "Eyes on the trees. I know it's your favorite activity."

Kartinar just shook his head and continued monitoring the forest.

It was dull, tree-watching. It reminded him of gardening. His adoptive Troll mother had always sent him to *Om' Modir* to help with her garden, telling him that if he didn't have a Boon, he might as well learn all the mundane skills. It was yet another reason to curse being human in an immortal world. He'd had to listen then, being a kid. That was where he'd learned that anything that grows is alive. He glanced at the walls towering above him. They seemed to grow into the cloudless sky as he stared, and he wondered if they could be alive.

The dark stone the walls were made of began to grow lighter as he looked, and if he stared hard enough it even seemed to have a tint of purple. *That could be the moon,* he thought, but it was growing too concentrated to be a reflection of the lavender light. Abruptly his eyes shot down to where Drath was opening the satchel again, light sneaking out of any crack it could find. Kartinar held his breath as Drath flipped open the satchel and glowing light erupted from it, covering everything in pure, concentrated purple.

Even with the thing still inside the satchel, its light illuminated the entire side of the castle that the two men stood beside, its purple tendrils even reaching into the forest before disappearing. The trees seemed to drink in the light, now leaning toward the castle rather than away.

Life goes in on one side, and death comes out on the other. He wondered again which side they were on, and which eternal force the sorcerer's light belonged to. Kartinar thought it was likely the former, the way the forest seemed to be *drinking* the light, the tendrils of color disappearing into the shadows of the trees. But perhaps that was his conscience trying to assuage his guilt.

Though this was Drath's quest, he still looked up at Kartinar for approval before he acted; before he completed the drifter's task and potentially altered the very chemistry of Elt. Kartinar nodded in confirmation; the forest, while eerie, was still safe and nobody approached from the valley.

Drath wasted not a single moment. He was a big, lazy brute most of the time, but these adventures, as he liked to call them, brought out the best in him. This was where he had been crafted to shine, and he did. Quick as a nine-tailed fox, Drath reached his huge hand into the satchel and pulled out a mass of glowing purple light. Both the shape and size of it were impossible to discern—the light was too bright, too great, to see anything but it. It only grew more brilliant and brighter as Drath brought it over the surface of the moat.

As he held it over the water, the current seemed to slow, savoring the presence of the light. Everything was ultraviolet in its presence. Kartinar could hardly see any more than the outline of Drath as he brought the light down closer to the water's surface. If so much light and life went in on this side, what would they cause to come out on the other?

Drath let go, grinning.

Everything became purple.

THE SECOND

Sada

Sada Solares stared at the pub, trying to see through its stained windows. Sullen light revealed marks left by a rag attempting to clean countless weeks' worth of spirits, sweat, and dust from the glass. Behind the yellow panes, shapes could be seen; some hunched inward toward the table where they sat, others had their heads thrown back in laughter. Sada ground her teeth into her lip, then forced herself to walk inside.

As soon as she entered the atmosphere of sweat, the shrill sting of too many voices berated her ears. Yet in her mind they were instantly replaced by one: her father's. If he discovered her scheme, the sound of his fury would be much stronger and much more fearsome than all the voices in all the pubs of Centerton combined. It was almost enough to dissuade her from stepping in further. But the barkeep had found her gaze and was beckoning her, and to leave now would put her manners at stake. Twisting the ends of her hair for comfort, she stepped further into the trap.

The short and stocky man behind the bar whistled as she neared, and her palms began to sweat and prickle as nearby eyes found her. She forced her gait to remain so steady and poised that even her governess in all her strictness would not be disappointed. She almost felt the need to lift her skirts as she waded through the swamp of whistles and smirks. To the left, a woman played a jaunty tune on a rickety piano. To her right she saw a wall displaying the mounted and staring heads of dead beasts, from rabbits to deer and even one bear, who looked like he'd been in the midst of choking when he'd been stuffed. Everywhere else there were people. People at tables, people at the bar. People playing cards, people singing raucously along to the woman's song.

As Sada walked, she hummed along so as not to let her fear send her scurrying out of the place. Music always calmed her. Even in this horrible place. But this is what she wanted, to be able to step out of her title and be a normal person around normal people. She thought that perhaps she would not be treated with such terrible deference by the townsfolk if she wasn't flanked by armored knights at all hours of the day. Her guards could not always be by her side, the optimistic part of her insisted.

Except they could be. And they had been since the day of The Incident, and every day after. It said to the townspeople that she needed more proof, beyond her silks and jewels, that she was better than them; and not only that, but that they were so far below her that she needed protection from them, like they were not people, but animals; beasts. It did not matter, of course, that Sada did not think this herself. It did not matter that the constant company of trained knights was against her wishes. It only mattered that they were there. And so she had ceased venturing into the square and districts where commonfolk frequented, lest she be mocked and shunned. And she had begun to dream of a life unaccompanied by guards where she could simply exist as a person.

But she secretly—shamefully—wished for her guards now as she caught the gazes of the men around her, blurry-eyed even before the sun had time to set. She felt the heat of their hungry stares, and suddenly understood what Jezebel Pérez, who was not only her closest friend but also the crudest, had meant about men being, as she put it, bedroom-minded.

No, listen to yourself, as bad as Jezi! Those are just your nerves talking, she chided herself. Of course they were just curious about a stranger; after all, some of the women were staring too.

"Hail, darlin'! Come on a leettle closer, don't be shy," the barkeep invited. "We don't bite—but I wouldn't mind if you did!" He finished with a phlegm-filled laugh, then spit into a rag that he swiftly tucked away.

Sada shrank deeper into her cloak, the nearest thing she owned to commonfolk garments, but did as he bid. When she reached the bar, she was met with a whistle and a grin from the barkeep. Some of the men he was serving turned on their stools to see what the fuss was about. She sat as far from them as she could.

"May I have some water, please?" Sada asked, then again when the bartender called her a mouse and bid her to speak up. No, there was no deference here.

She waited, face burning, until he returned with the glass of water, which she cupped in trembling hands but did not drink. He peered down at her over the counter, trying to see into the shadows of her cloak. Well, she hadn't come here to continue hiding. After steeling herself with a breath, she pushed off her hood.

"Whoa, lady, what's with the eyes?" he asked immediately, squinting at her.

Her entire face flushed hotly at his scrutiny. "I beg your pardon, I-I do not know what you mean."

Suddenly worried that the makeup covering her birthmarks had somehow been wiped off, she stood and made to leave. Then the barkeep banged on the counter, and she instantly found her seat again.

Yet his rap on the bar wasn't directed at her, but rather at a man two seats down.

"Hey Mick, take a look at these peepers," the bartender implored.

Mick complied readily enough and moved into the seat next to Sada. Before she knew it, his hand was on her leg, tugging her toward him.

"Lemme see those eyes of yours, dear," the man growled. "Mick wants a turn." A knot formed in her throat, and a weight in her stomach. "Best not be rude now, eh?" He snickered.

As though she were being controlled, she turned to face the man. She fought with the urge to touch the inner corners of her eyes and check the makeup was in place. Then a greasy finger lifted her chin up and there was no more choice to be made. Thick eyebrows raised and a whistle blew hot and sour in her face when she looked at him.

"What a pair." Mick turned to the barkeep, his big mouth twisted into an ugly smile. "You don't see colors like that every day, eh, Bobby?"

She released her breath in a few shudders—they hadn't seen the marks.

"I've seen browns, even blues, and one wench whose eyes were so dark they looked black as her soul—what was left of it anyway—"

The surrounding men guffawed loudly.

"—but one dark and one light?" Bobby finished. He shook his drying rag at Mick, grinning. Sada couldn't help but wonder if it was the same one he'd spit into.

"Gotta be rarer than a white rat, ha! But don't worry sweetheart, Mick likes 'em a little different, don't he? Yeah, open those pretty babies wide for me, I wanna get a better look."

His hand squeezed tighter on her thigh, and before concern for her own manners could cross her mind, she leapt up from her seat.

"I must be going now!" she managed to blurt out, and then she was running from the pub with shameful tears filling her eyes.

Laughter chased her out the door as their teases tried to call her back in.

Sada ran through the town until the tears stopped coming. The sun was gone from the sky almost completely before her cheeks were dry.

I shall never make it on my own. Father was right—it's not safe for me to be without guards. I'm destined to be in their company for the rest of my life. And the worst part of it was, she was glad of it.

While she no longer wanted to be in the city alone, neither did she want the company of her guards yet. She found herself in need of peace, not reprimanding. Her father had assigned to her two personal guards, Sir John Martin and Sir Gabriel Hall. Typically it was the both of them who accompanied her into big and busy markets, but when she was just going into the small town that was Centerton, it was only Sir Gabriel. Today, however, Gabe was training at the barracks, so John and his squire, Samuel Morris, had taken his place. Now, working to avoid them, she found her way to the apothecary in the town square and snuck into the bustling stand. There, she buried herself in work.

Herbs were ground into her skin, sticky and soft and pungent. Sada breathed in their clarifying scents as she worked, bathing the back of her tongue in their bright and bitter smells. Green, pink, brown, blue, and other rainbow hues decorated her skin. She did little to clean her hands as she turned from one pile to another. This was a clump of leafy sage stems, some with roots still attached. She absentmindedly brushed the remaining dirt off those roots before she set to peeling each fuzzy leaf off.

The apothecary was a simple stand, little more than wooden counters and a roof. There were no walls, and she liked to look out over the counter as she worked, watching the townspeople go about their daily business.

Summering in Centerton for so many years had acquainted her with all of the minor lords and ladies (there were not many in such a rural town) and many of the townspeople who were active in society, but there were still some she didn't know, or not very well anyway. With these people, she particularly liked to guess the type of relationship they shared with whoever was accompanying them into the square. Were the young man and woman walking past the flower stand siblings, or was that subtle brush of his hand against her skirt intentional, signaling them to be courting? And Father Jacob, at Mrs. Blackwell's tea stand. Was he simply comforting a widow, or was it a secret rebellion being shut down? Oh, it was so fun to guess, to simply watch!

She could see Sir John and Samuel across the square as well, leaning against the inn and talking. Their armor was blinding in the light of the setting sun. They had found her shortly after she arrived at the apothecary. That, she had expected. It was a pleasing surprise, though, when John allowed her to stay. He'd inquired as to her whereabouts, given her a look that told her she'd be hearing his thoughts on the matter later, then Sam had smiled apologetically at her, and they'd gone to wait at the inn until she was finished. She knew they would never let her leave their sight again, for as long as she lived. But they wouldn't tell her father; it was an unspoken agreement she had with both John and Gabriel that if she disobeyed them, it would not be reported to the Duke unless absolutely necessary. For that, she was thankful, and to show her gratitude she tried to avoid as much trouble as possible. Though sometimes it found her anyway. And today, she had sought it out.

John shifted, then, turning in her direction, and she quickly looked away.

"Oh Lord…Sada, what are you doing here this late? The lanterns are already lit!"

Sada looked up from her work to find Jezebel jostling toward her, weaving between hanging herbs and potted plants and messy stacks of papers, most of which were on the floor by the time her friend reached her. Sada made a brief note to herself to organize this room soon, musing at the way Jezebel seemed to knock over everything in her path. If someone ever wanted to find the apothecary's daughter, all they had to do was follow her breadcrumb trail of disarray.

"I'm picking sage leaves off of their stems," Sada said. She frowned at her friend's exasperated sigh. "I thought you hated the stems..."

Jezebel just hid her face in her hand. But Sada could see a smile shining through and she poked at her friend's stomach with a plant.

"Your father will have me hanged for this, you know," Jezebel said, batting the stem away.

Something sharp stirred in Sada's chest, but her smile only grew wider to keep it out of her eyes. She continued to pluck the fragrant leaves.

"Come now, allow me to help. You know you like having me around—you aren't very good at hiding it, I'm afraid." She winked.

"Yes, but…"

Jezebel had put on her shopkeeper's mask to order Sada out of the stand—the steely, commanding guise she donned for relentlessly bargaining customers. If Sada wanted to stay, she would have to barter back.

"Jezebel, you're running yourself ragged with festival preparations. Besides, I've finished my lessons with Governess Brown today and I'd much rather be here than in the sewing room; it's always so dim and dreary. Strange, considering its usages, don't you think?"

Though Jezebel's dark hair was neatly tied back into its usual braid, the orderly appearance could not be maintained past it. She was covered in smears of color from countless poultices and powders, not having enough time to wash between helping customers and preparing for the upcoming festival. Even her clothes were torn in places, no doubt wrought by foraging in the woodlands west of town. The summer-darkened hands she placed on her hips were covered with specks of dried blood from the thornier herbs she worked with, and she was always moving, never stopping to sit or think or breathe.

Sada cringed at the sight of her friend. "At least allow me to offer my help until the festival is over. One more day will do no harm, and you know it is so. It will certainly have the opposite effect for you and your father."

Jezebel looked as though she was going to protest until she took a glance around her disheveled shop. Sada followed her gaze to the customers milling about outside and her father's too-few hires weaving between them, at the endless piles of herbs that still needed to be counted and plucked and cleaned and organized. Jezebel let out a breath instead of a rebuke. She seemed to be in the mood to agree.

Then a frown took over. "Wait, why are you here now, and how? You didn't even say hello. Did Father already let you in without telling me?"

Sada avoided her friend's gaze. Her eyes would still be puffy. "I entered through less formal means," she declared proudly. "Elijah showed me how to come over the stand."

"Ah, that boy. Now I know how Father felt when he was training me. But why did you sneak in? You're not just another customer, Sada, you're allowed behind the stand. Were you avoiding Mrs. Prentice? If she's giving you trouble again, I have just the solution; you know the salve she always buys for her wrist—haggles for, I should say? I plan to replace the willow bark with thyme. Can you imagine?"

"Jezi! You cannot! Mrs. Prentice is not half so bad as she is made out to be. I imagine if we had aching joints, we may find ourselves just as…prickly," Sada said. But she had a grin to match Jezebel's. "I was not avoiding her. It was only that you appeared to be busy. David was practically under your feet, and I felt that my saying hello would most definitely startle him into an injury…or an even more unfortunate position."

Jezebel truly was busy, and the young prentice had certainly been causing tripping hazards in the hectic stall, but it was not why Sada had forfeited manners to enter without greeting the apothecaries. She thought it would also be of bad manners to make an entrance with a tear-stained face and nasally voice. Though, this might have provided a sufficient distraction for the customers, enough to allow Jezebel and her father to gather themselves before the onslaught resumed. Well, your vision was always clearer in hindsight, and when your eyes were not tear-blurred.

For a moment Jezebel did not respond, only watched Sada work. Sada felt increasingly confident that her friend had managed to acquire powers that would allow her to read Sada's thoughts and learn of her time at the bar. She sang quietly to distract herself.

"Are you okay, Sada?" Jezebel asked, her voice unusually soft.

"No, to tell the truth…I'm actually quite dandy!" Sada forced a wide smile and met her friend's eyes. A grin could hide the puffiness of the eyes if performed correctly. "Though it is not you who should be asking. With the number of customers here, I'm quite certain others will be resorting to surreptitious entries themselves, and then none of us will be okay, will we? Unless, of course, you allow me to stay…"

Jezebel pursed her lips stubbornly, but that gave way to a grin.

"Okay. Fine. Help as long as you'd like, both Father and I will love you all the more for it. But if Duke Solares comes calling—"

"Yes, yes, I know. Though he should not, he's away for business. In any case, he would send John or Gabe in his stead. And they aren't half as intimidating, are they?"

"No, not so much." Jezebel grinned, her shopkeeper's mask crumbling. Sada was glad to see it disappear. "Where is the Duke? He usually carts you along on his trips, doesn't he?"

There were several dukes in Califia that Sada knew of, but her father held the highest standing among them, due to his friendship with the king. So now, in both the capital and the neighboring cities, when someone said "the Duke," they were usually referring to Darius Solares.

"Yes, and I admit I'm not certain as to why I was not brought along this time, though you won't hear a complaint out of me. I have all the more time to spend with you!" Sada poked her friend again, earning a swat to the hand.

"From what I know, Father is in Asrich with Prince Aaron. As per the king's usual demand, half the guard went with them to watch over the prince." She grinned. "As though he hasn't been trained in the blade since he could hold a toy sword."

Jezebel snorted. "You would know. I still can't believe you grew up playing with Prince Aaron like he was just some neighbor kid."

Sada laughed, but inwardly her heart squeezed thinking of how the young boy she had once called her friend had been replaced by the young man who was now little more than her political acquaintance.

"So your uncle Beron must be visiting to chaperone you here again, then?" Jezi asked.

"Yes indeed."

Jezebel just nodded along quietly, trying to find something to do with her hands among the piles of uncleaned plants, plucked leaves, and bare stems. She settled on fidgeting with a small clay pot.

"And you have your boys with you?"

"Mhmm. Sir John and Sam, today," Sada said, thinking of the time she'd spent avoiding them. "You know, your absence does not go unnoticed by them and the others. They won't admit it because they're proud, but they like when you tend to them and their many scrapes. Sometimes I think they plot their own injuries just to find reason to call on you."

Jezebel snorted, spinning the pot she held. "It's the touching they like, Sada, not the healing. They're all just greedy for any woman's touch, and they're not so secretive about *that*."

Jezebel wrinkled her nose, leading Sada to wonder which of her recent companions had caused such a reaction, and if it was warranted. Jezebel's friendship came as an exclusive bundle with gossip and dramatics. As of late, most of the men Jezebel gossiped about were Sada's friends, and so she tried not to encourage the stories if she could help it.

Jezebel, of course, did not care. She would probably talk to her reflection if nobody was around to listen to the latest scoop she had on the town folk. "Trust me, Sada," she forged on, "if you knew men like I do, you wouldn't be so fond of them."

"I am not 'so fond' of them! What do you take me for, a lovesick schoolgirl?" she laughed.

Jezebel giggled. "You know what I mean. You see the good in everybody, dear. You're lucky the only men you speak with are the honorable kind. Though sometimes I wonder if even they can be trusted around you, what with the way they flirt with me so shamelessly."

Mick shouldn't be trusted around any woman, Sada thought. But she had heard enough talk about *"those"* men, so she evaded further conversation on the topic.

"Not a fig," Sada said, "they are quite honorable knights. I don't think they could offer such stimulating conversation about your eyes being the color of 'toasted honey' if all their thoughts are as horrible as you say. And we mustn't forget that Jack stopped courting both Rebekah *and* Mary to be with you…that doesn't sound so bad."

"Oh Sada, you're so naïve. Sure they *say* those elevated, romantic things, and maybe Jacky did break court with the other girls…*But* as soon as I bring these men into my bed, they look at me like I'm a piece of meat for them to stab their sword into, I swear it. It's all any man thinks about. As soon as they get the chance, they might make *you* that piece of meat."

The men's voices

(We don't bite…but I wouldn't mind if you did...)

(…Mick likes em a little different…)

were instantly in her head again, their sneers vile in her mind's eye. The lump was back in her throat, and the prickling in her palms. But her guards would never do such a thing. If Gabe had been there, his sword would have been drawn before Mick could flinch.

"I don't think so," Sada defended gently. "The boys have never said a single vulgar thing to me. They won't do so within ten feet of me if they know I'm there and listening. Perhaps you just know the wrong men, Jezi…I know the sort."

Jezebel laughed. "*You* know the sort? Darling, the only men you've been around are those who've been hired to suit your needs, and they're much too scared of your father to try anything. You wouldn't know what to do if you met a man who was truly as bedroom-minded as most are. It's not your fault, dear. All you've known are the walls of your perfect mansion."

Sada ignored the remarks. She'd had the same conversation with her friend many times. Around the time Jezebel stopped visiting Sada at her estate, she also began making sly remarks about her house, her dresses, her jewelry. Sada hadn't understood the reason for the sudden shift; she'd lived in that same house and worn those same dresses and jewelry the entire time she'd known Jezebel. But when she brought it up to Jezebel's mother, Mrs.

Pérez, she only explained that Jezebel's most treasured possession was a rusting yellow ear cuff, as though that would answer everything.

Sada still didn't quite understand how such things affected their friendship, nor why Jezebel became so upset when Sada offered to share her jewelry since she had too much anyway. But she did know that her friend didn't like it when Sada pushed her on the topic, so she didn't dwell on it.

"Whenever Jack talks about you, his cheeks turn pink," Sada said with small smile.

Jezebel's chuckle died off. "What? Are you teasing?"

One of Mr. Pérez's apprentices slipped into the room and Jezebel straightened, clearing her throat. She tossed her chin in greeting to the boy, and Sada smiled at the familiar round face of David.

"Good evening, David," Sada said, and the boy mumbled a greeting around a mouthful of papers.

Both hands full of leafy bundles, he had removed his shoe and was trying to open a nearby trunk with his foot. The two women chuckled at the sight, then Sada stood to help David while Jezebel fiddled with some plants, adjusting the stacks Sada had made. When she returned, Sada continued peeling leaves from stems, creating two neat piles. The stain of the herbs was creeping from her skin onto the cuffs of her dress, long-sleeved still to protect against the remaining spring chill. She tried to roll them up, but abandoned her efforts when the tightly-buttoned cuffs wouldn't budge. The new laundry maid had probably used water that was too hot again, or perhaps that starch stuff.

"Want some help?" Jezebel offered.

"Don't worry yourself over the dress, I'd rather keep pruning." She began to sing softly.

Jezebel began fiddling with the cuffs anyway. "But your dress is getting so dirty," she complained, frowning like a governess as she worked.

"Jezi," Sada laughed, "you're beginning to sound exactly like your mother. Fret not over my cuffs. Look—they are far too stubborn to be bothered."

Jezebel gave up when the sleeves wouldn't budge. "Ugh, I know, she keeps telling me I sound like her too. At least stop wearing your nice dresses down here, for my sake. I squirm when I see how…colorful they become. Your father must be none too happy either, and I can only imagine what Governess Brown says."

"I don't take your meaning, dear," Sada said.

She continued plucking leaves as she glanced at her tight cuffs, noting the stiffness of the fabric, the lack of lace, pearls, and gems. The hem didn't even fall to the ground, stopping just at her ankles, and the neckline was so square. The dress didn't even require a jacket because of how fully her back was covered. She giggled at the thought of wearing *this* to a ball, or even at her estate. Oh, how her father would reprimand her!

"Don't fret, I wouldn't wear my nice dresses here. Father would certainly rescind my allowance; he might never buy me a dress again."

Perhaps now she'd stop her worrying. But Jezebel just spluttered suddenly, and Sada turned, concerned.

"What happened?" she asked, noticing Jezebel's hand on her chest and her bulging eyes. "Did you inhale a leaf?"

"Nothing," Jezebel managed to say. "I'd only thought these were your nice dresses."

"No, of course not," Sada replied, smiling to reassure her friend. "Do you know the lecture I would receive? I wouldn't chance it! I really do need to bring you along to one of Ettedon's balls. They throw proper dances, you know, and then you can see all of the ladies of court in their true finery. My dresses look like sackcloth in comparison to theirs."

"Ah. Forgive my ignorance."

The shift in Jezebel's tone immediately halted Sada's pruning. "Jezebel please don't talk to me so," she pleaded. "There is nothing to forgive."

Jezebel's eyes had already turned cold, and she lowered her head, avoiding Sada's searching gaze. "Yes, m'lady. My apologies."

"Jezebel!" Sada gasped. This was worse than the shopkeeper mask. This was the face of a stranger.

Something in her chest tightened as she watched her friend silently stand and push her way through the disheveled shop, this time running away from her. Her perfectly postured friend had slouched her back against Sada and didn't turn as she called.

She had witnessed such a change too many times and it filled her heart with lead. She despised the way Jezebel stopped talking to her like a friend and started talking to her as though she were something else. As though she were someone to be tiptoed around; someone to be deferred to. It seemed that even without her guards present and even around her closest friend, she would always and only be seen as her title. Sada made to go after her friend, but a light hand on her shoulder stopped her.

"I don't think she wants to see you right now, Lady Sada," David said.

Sada knew he was right. But something tore in her chest as she watched the swinging pots left in Jezebel's wake. As she stared, all she could think of was the bitterness behind her voice, the coldness in her brown eyes. The way she had transformed herself into that stranger.

"Perhaps if I talk to her, clarify..."

This time it was a familiar and bold voice that halted her. The voice of a knight.

"The young gentleman is right, my lady, it appears Miss Jezebel could use some time to herself."

Sada twisted on her wooden seat to find Sir Gabriel Hall standing at the counter behind her, grim-faced beneath his half helm. He had to fold over at the waist simply to see into the shop. Behind him, looking like statues amid the crowd weaving around them, stood two matching suits of green-trimmed armor. From her vantage, Sada could only see their mid-sections, but she knew the men to be Sir John and Sam.

"Oh dear," Sada murmured. "Hi, Gabe."

"Your uncle Ser Beron has sent me to retrieve you, Lady Sada. He wishes to dine with you tonight."

Sada glanced in the direction where Jezebel had disappeared before sighing and turning to Gabriel, her favorite guard. He, along with a second knight, had been assigned to her personally when, as a toddler, she had chosen them from a lineup of her father's men. Her second guard had been replaced several times over the years for various reasons: tickling her too hard, not tickling her enough, making her cry, or failing to address her as Lady in front of her father. But Gabriel had never slipped up. And the one time her father had tried to dismiss him, she had intervened, refusing to let him go. That was the first time she had stood up to her father. And given how things turned out afterward, everyone knew it would be her last time as well.

She bid David farewell and made to slide over the counter as she'd done to enter, but before she could, Gabriel reached over and lifted her up and over it. She was on the ground beside him and laughing before she could protest.

"Gabriel," John chided, glancing around.

Gabe just grinned. "What? Did you think I was going to let our lady crawl over the counter? What kind of a knight would I be then?"

Sam blushed sheepishly, but John just sighed, massaging the wrinkles forming between his brows.

"Whatever would become of me without your aid?" Sada asked Gabriel, and he answered with a smile. She turned to greet the others. "Hello again, John. Sam."

Sam dipped his head in greeting.

"Hello, Lady Sada," John said lightly. "How was your time in Mr. Pérez's apothecary?"

Sada squinted, trying to read the guard's face. Had he told Gabe of her disappearing? Neither of the men looked angry, and she reasoned that she would certainly be hearing about it from Gabe if John had told him. She must be safe.

"Well, it was lovely until a few moments ago," she said.

"Ah! I said the same thing to Sam just earlier today," John said, and grinned. Gabe just raised an eyebrow. John winked at him, but said nothing of the pub.

"Well then, shall we?" Gabriel asked, and he led her away from the shop and toward the carriage awaiting her a stone's throw away. John and Sam followed behind her. "Your attire truly has become quite soiled, my lady."

"Gabe! How much of that conversation were you privy to?"

"Enough of it, little lady. The townspeople have always been strange in the views they harbor towards royalty. Do not let such notions trouble your sweet heart."

"They aren't strange, they're just…" Sada realized she did not have a strong argument. "Well, I'm not royalty, Gabe."

"Close enough, my lady. Had you not been raised in court among the royals, you would see the truth of it. But even if you do not, rest assured that they do."

Gabriel nodded toward the people around them, dressed in cloth too baggy for their bones, with hair falling out of braids and seams popping out of trousers. Sada looked away from them; she didn't like sad things. As they approached her carriage—a bronze one adorned with glittering crystals and streaming with yellow ribbons for her—the sight of it made her chest constrict.

"You look upset, my lady. Would you enjoy some flavored ice before we return to the estate?" Gabe asked.

"Thank you, no. But I do not wish to return yet, either," she said softly.

Gabriel looked to John, who just nodded and gestured to Samuel. The knight and his squire bid their farewells, then went past the carriage to find their horses and return to the manor. Gabe led her in the opposite direction, toward the back of the town.

She knew the carriage would be waiting for them whenever they returned, whether it was in an hour or at midnight. If they stayed out past that time without sending word, the driver would return to the estate to report their absence. That had yet to happen, and Sada wasn't in the mood to test her father's rules further today. Her time at the pub had already been quite enough. Either her father or her charge, such as Uncle Beron, always had to know where she was, even when she was with Gabriel. Tonight, she was happy to abide by protocol. Tonight, she understood why it was in place.

They quickly moved away from the center of town, leaving Jezebel and the shop amidst the rest of the busy stands set up there. Sada had heard tales that, years ago when Centerton was not even a speck on the map, vendors used to sell straight out of their homes. During summertime, they would gather in the town square to set up temporary stands for the season. But one winter had arrived quickly and without warning, piling snow so high it became impossible to disassemble the stands and return the wares to their rightful owners' homes. Since then, vendors had become a permanent fixture in Centerton's square, though they still sold their goods out of basic wooden stands rather than take the time to build stone-walled shops. The vendors had no time or money to afford such formidable structures. It was the only town Sada had seen do such a thing, and she treasured the sight of the colorful clusters of lean-tos and makeshift countertops that made up Centerton's market.

As Sada and her knight left the center of the town and all its people behind them, Gabriel began to drop his regal appearances, swinging his sword to his preferred hip and relaxing his gait. He'd tucked his half-helm under the arm she didn't hold, and his light hair was all wild in his eyes. Sada wondered why he didn't always walk around like this, but she knew if she asked, he would give her the required answer: it was by her father's command. And that was the best explanation either of them would get; nobody received a justification for Duke Darius Solares's commands. Not even his daughter.

For a while they walked in silence, but Sada's mind kept turning over the words Jezebel had said to her, tasting the way she'd said them, drinking them in, drowning in them. Sada hardly knew where they were walking, just that her feet kept putting themselves down in front of one another. The scuffed cobblestone path guided her slippers, but she didn't pay attention to where it led as Gabriel took her around corners and past little houses.

"Have I said something amiss to Jezebel?" she finally said, softly. She kept her eyes on her feet as she talked, hanging onto his heavily armored arm.

Gabriel's gentle concern disappeared as he snorted.

"None but you would concern themselves with such matters, Sada."

She frowned at him. "I don't take your meaning."

"The affront was against you, little lady. Your heart is far too kind, ever assuming the fault lies with you. The occasion of offense is scarcely—no, never a wrongdoing of yours."

"Gabe, I mean it." She didn't understand his remarks. The way Jezebel's eyes had suddenly gone cold couldn't have been because of nothing. "You were privy to our conversation, were you not? You were indeed, do not jest! So please, tell me—what have I said to upset her?"

"If my ears served me rightly, my lady, you merely informed her that you were not, in truth, wearing your finery."

"Why, that cannot be considered impolite, surely…?"

Gabriel grunted, holding back a laugh as he always did when she asked him these sorts of questions—like how to determine north from south and what hair color a gentleman preferred on a lady. He had a strange sense of humor.

"No, Sada, it's not impolite. However, I would suggest that it borders on impoliteness to dictate a lady's attire, especially when she's offering her services in a peasant's—" He cut himself off, casting a sharp glance down at her, but she had already heard.

"Gabriel!" Sada gasped, pulling away. He set his mouth into a hard line. "Jezi is my *friend.*"

Though Sada had grown up hearing townspeople referred to as peasants, one visit to a neighboring town un-chaperoned by her governess had taught her *their* feelings on the word, and she'd never uttered it again, or allowed any of her personal guard to. Gabriel knew this already. There was no point in reprimanding him. Not when Sada knew how deeply he already regretted it from that look he gave her.

"I'm sorry, Sada," he said quietly, and offered his arm again.

Sada looped her herb-stained arm through his shining one and they continued meandering down the path. The silence was taut between them, and she hurried to find something that would break the tension. But they had left the town square now, and all the shops and color and sound with it, and all the things to talk about with that. On the outskirts, only small brown houses accompanied them on their walk. The sight of them didn't stir any conversation, and her mind was empty of any interesting thoughts. It had unfortunately turned back to her time at the pub.

"Did something else happen, little lady? I know you're upset over what transpired with Jezebel, but you seem quiet. Something is different."

"No, I am quite dandy, I assure you."

"I beg your pardon, but I don't quite believe you. But I'll leave it as is unless you wish to speak of it."

She made herself smile. "Truly, I am fine. Thank you, my friend."

Nobody wishes to keep the company of miserable people, Sada, the voice of Memory whispered to her. *And should you find yourself with no friends after one too many gloomy days, it will be by your own volition, having chosen not to be pleasant and happy.*

Your moods are of your own choosing, Sada. Choose joyfulness.

It didn't feel like a choice, but she pasted on her best smile anyway. Gabriel was one of her only friends, and she did not wish to lose him through moping. As they walked, Gabriel told her of what Lucas and Isaac had found on their patrol of the estate, of Jacob's new squire, and of the young lady he'd met while playing aces. They'd been kicked out of the pub together after they began betting with undergarments. The conversation returned to the topic of Jezebel when Gabriel assured her that all townspeople were strange in their own right.

"But she's my friend, Gabe," she argued. "We've been friends for years, since before her father took her on as an apprentice. Do you recall when he trained Jezi and me together?"

Sada smiled at the memory, but if Gabriel or any other onlooker had seen, they would know it was not a happy one.

Her summer estate was lonely, and filled only with her father's hires. With no other children to play with, she'd begun to find companions among the townspeople, but only a few had been allowed to play with her when she came calling. For reasons unknown to her, the others were kept away from her, hidden behind excuses from their mothers. Jezebel had been one of the last townsfolk Sada had met, but also her favorite. They often joked that Mr. Pérez had used an apothecary's magic on them as children to make them such good friends, the way they so easily understood each other. And with the way the man weaved plants and powders into healing poultices, it wouldn't have been hard to accept as truth.

"I know, little lady, yet the fact of your friendship bears little weight. There are disparities between your family and…well, everyone else." Sada frowned at that, and Gabriel matched her expression. "That scarcely helps, does it?"

Sada shook her head no but smiled at his attempt.

"Well, let's see. Ah, an analogy ought to help—Duke Solares certainly puts them to use," Gabe said. Indeed he did. Sada could not count the number of times when her father's tirades had drawn comparisons between herself and circus performers, or even colors and animals.

"Consider a lion and a mouse who come to be friends," Gabriel continued. "Despite their friendship, should the lion find itself famished, the mouse would still provoke its appetite. And should the lion's stomach grumble, the mouse would still be afraid. That's just to say, that even though the two of you are friends, it doesn't change where you come from. Either of you."

"Yes, but Jezebel has always lived in the village, whilst I have always lived in the manor, and only of late has she begun to act strangely. What shifted? Was it me?"

"No, no, see, there you go again. Jezebel has recently come of age, has she not? This means she is now either tasked with overseeing the apothecary's finances or is at the very least well-acquainted with them. It is no light responsibility. My mother would often require an afternoon's rest after tallying our accounts, or else all us children knew she'd turn into a different woman." Gabriel chuckled at the memory.

"I can certainly imagine how difficult a task it must be," Sada said. Despite all her lessons in counting figures, she feared she would never be any more proficient than a girl in grammar school. She shuddered to think of counting *all* of them. "Yet, how do the shop's financial matters pertain to Jezebel and me?"

"In every way. Children think nothing of money. They scarcely grasp its concept. You yourself are barely familiar with it, my lady. But adults must be, and Jezebel has reached womanhood."

"I *am* aware of what money is, Gabe," Sada said, her entire face growing warm. "And I count more years than she does!"

"Of course, you're right," he said hurriedly, "but you needn't work for the stuff, nor do you comprehend the expenditures of those who do, or the value of goods. How much *your* things cost."

Sada scoffed. "Certainly I do!"

"Truly?" Gabriel asked, suppressing a smile. "How much did your father pay for the gown you wear now?"

"Oh quite amusing, Gabe," Sada said, rolling her eyes. "Leah purchased this gown for me."

"Sada…you do know that your lady's maids use your father's coin for your purchases. The vendors have a tab running for his account, and he pays it monthly."

"Oh." She looked down, laughing to hide her embarrassment. "Indeed. Well, I seem to recall that this one cost two pounds…of…silver."

Gabriel's laugh was booming and drew the attention of the one other man on the road. He cast them a quick look, secured his hat, then scuttled away. "If that were the case, then Jezebel would indeed be correct in telling you not to wear such a dress into the shop."

Sada sighed. "Perhaps I do know nothing about money."

"Which is perfectly okay," Gabriel said, patting the hand on his arm. "Your ignorance is well in this instance, little lady. Life becomes far grimmer when you do have to know how it all works, how money controls everything…" Gabriel sighed, and Sada's brow continued to furrow deeper as her confusion grew.

"I beg your pardon, but this explanation is making me all the more confused. I just don't understand how this affects my friendship with Jezi."

Now he was chuckling. "It boils down to mere coin. You can trace any conflict back to money, power, or hatred. They keep the breath in our lungs, you'll come to see."

"Oh I don't like that. I don't like that at all! Why can people not just care for one another?"

He patted her hand with his gauntleted one. "Ah my sweet little lady. I wonder if it's your naivety of the world that keeps you so kind." His eyes were warm as they studied her. "No, I'm sure innocence doesn't deserve such credit. It must be your heart."

Sada smiled at the tall guard, wondering how he held such warmth in his eyes for her when so few others did. But just as soon as she'd thought it, his smile dropped, and his brow furrowed. His brown eyes sharpened and she found that she was not looking into the face of her friend, but of her guard.

"Sada—your birthmarks are showing."

Her face instantly flashed with heat and anxiety poked needles into her forehead and palms, which were already growing sweaty. Gabe immediately turned to scour the street for any observers as she threw up the hood of her cloak. She touched the corners of her eyes as though she could feel the marks there. Of course she couldn't.

Each morning she covered the birthmarks by her eyes with layers of skin-toned powder. Her father had spent pounds upon pounds of silver (this she knew, thanks to his constant reminders) working directly with the finest apothecaries in the kingdom to craft a powder that would stick to her skin and remain in place throughout the day. The apothecary was told only that it was to cover a pale birthmark, and the money answered any further questions. The final product was Sada's present for her eighth name day, along with a command to apply it every morning until the marks faded, whether she left the manor or not.

But they never went away. Nobody, not even the servants, were permitted to see the marks. Her father had covered them himself through other means in her early childhood to ensure that none of the household staff would know of her imperfection. Even the midwife who'd delivered her had been paid to leave the city and kingdom out of her father's fear that word of his daughter's disfigurement would reach any other ears. And if those strange, pale spirals on the inner corners of her eyes—like the swirl on a snail's shell or a curling fern frond—were ever seen by Duke Solares, it was his rage she had to answer to.

The powder had never failed before, and the panic in her chest made it feel as though she were suffocating in it. The familiar feeling of breath evading her set in as her lungs seized then clenched, trapping the air inside and not allowing any fresh breaths in. Pressing her thumb into her wrist, she counted three of her rapid heartbeats

(1, 2, 3)

then she was able to draw in a shuddering breath.

"Did anybody see?" Sada whispered when she could speak again. She could barely hear herself over the pounding of her blood.

"No."

"Are you certain?"

"Yes, nobody is on the street, and all the windows are dark and drawn. We've left the occupied part of town. We passed the last person minutes ago." Gabriel stooped to check on her, touching her cheek. "That's never happened before," he said as though she didn't know.

"No." Her voice was hardly a whisper. Fear held it captive.

"I haven't even seen them, not since that first time."

Gabriel only knew of their existence through an accidental discovery. He had almost lost his title as knight and his position in the household guard over it. She bit her lip, the memory only worsening the weight in her stomach and the tightness in her throat.

"I didn't have the powder then," she said, and then refused to speak of it further.

She didn't know what it meant that her powder had failed for the first time in over a decade of use. She hoped it was a fluke, but she didn't want to think about what that meant if it wasn't. Or of what her father might do either way. She would need to apply many layers of it before Duke Solares returned.

Sada urged Gabriel to continue down the worn cobblestone path with her.

"I don't believe that to be a sound idea, my lady. We'd best return to the manor so you may reapply your powder."

Sada shook her head. "Please Gabe, I don't want to go back yet. The hood will hide my face. See?"

She couldn't see his face from beneath the overhanging of her hood, but she watched as he crossed his arms over his green-trimmed chest plate. Finally he relented, taking her arm once more. Sada could not help but chew on her lip as they walked—it was yet another thing for her father to reprimand her on, but if she did not feel the pain and taste the blood, she feared her nerves would drive her to insanity. Even working away at her lip, the thoughts of her disfigurements would not leave her alone. She needed to talk, lest her own mind lead her to the brink of madness.

"Somebody commented on my eyes again today," she said.

"They're hard to miss. Who was it, John's squire? That boy never seems to shut that thin mouth of his."

"No, only a man. I passed him on the way to Mr. Pérez's shop." The lie felt thick and awkward on her tongue. "I don't understand why there must be such a fuss over them. I can't even leave the estate without wearing a hood if I don't wish to be...*gawked* at like a foreigner."

"You shouldn't. Wear it, that is. Your eyes are exquisite, Sada; I have encountered none that rival them."

Sada laughed, wondering what Jezi would make of that. "Thank you, Gabe," she said at the prompting of Memory's voice.

They walked for a few moments in silence, passing yellow windows and dark wells. They had found the people again, and Sada ensured her face was hidden deep within her hood. A few children were just now hanging lanterns and placing torches in their holders at the archway announcing the way out of Centerton. In the shadows cast by their light, Sada was taller than her knight.

"John tells me you disappeared for nearly an hour."

"Was it truly that long?" she exclaimed, then immediately snapped her mouth shut. He wasn't supposed to know about that.

He raised his eyebrows at her, and as soon as she met his eyes, Sada was filled with shame. She immediately told Gabriel where she had been and how she'd spent hours planning her escape from John and Sam. She recounted her successful getaway, and her efforts to hide from them after her time at the pub. She told him of how she'd hidden in the wine cellar of the Pérezes' neighbors, but an alley cat had nearly betrayed her position. That made him laugh.

"You thought you were avoiding their notice that entire time?"

She turned to him, horrified. "I wasn't?"

"Of course not. If you had, they wouldn't be fit to be called guards, now would they?"

"Oh dear." She pressed her face against his arm with a groan, earning a chuckle.

The embarrassment at the thought of herself hiding in shadows while the knights pretended not to notice was too much to bear. Gabe had been training in the barracks at that time, which was why she'd chosen then to steal away from her guards. John was a fine knight, and Sam a fair squire, but neither they nor any of the others guarded her with such attentiveness as Gabe did. She'd thought as much, anyway, but now it seemed that they were perhaps just better at hiding their vigilance than Gabe was.

When she had been a girl going into the city with her governess or some other chaperone, she did not mind or even think twice about the company of her two guards. She'd enjoyed riding on their shoulders and seeing the city from a giant's perspective. As she'd grown older, she began to notice the looks that two fully-armored knights accompanying a young woman drew. In the capital city of Ettedon where she lived for three seasons of the year, there wasn't so much of this; the districts she visited were typically frequented only by other nobility. But in a small town like Centerton, the reactions were both obvious and prevalent. She noticed the way shopkeepers and the other commonfolk spat her title and bowed mockingly. She heard them call her Lady Convict behind her back, joking that the guards weren't assigned to protect her, but rather to take her to the dungeons. The crimes they invented for her to be accused of seemed to change with each phase of the moon.

Her friends of lower nobility had noticed this as well, and eventually their invitations into the square grew scarce and their refusals of her invitations grew frequent. They never said it was because of the guards, but how couldn't it be? They were small ladies, and their only chaperones had been their mothers or aunts. She didn't blame them for their reluctance to be hated by their fellow townspeople. She may have been the Duke's daughter, but she was still an outsider to Centerton. And as for her noble friends in Ettedon—if they could be called friends—they simply pitied her, and it was obvious whenever she went to meet them, green-trimmed guards following closer than her shadow.

After years of this torment, Sada had begged her father to allow her to go out with only a matronly chaperone like a normal girl. The Duke had wished to hear none of it, however, telling her that her safety was more important than blending into the crowd. *Besides,* he'd said, already angry, *a duke's daughter should stand apart from the flock. Be grateful I've provided you with the means to do so.*

That had led to a long period where she'd simply refused to go out during her summers in Centerton, sending her lady's maids to do her shopping and only making appearances at the most significant events. The only person she saw outside of her family and staff was Jezebel, who would make the trip to the Solares manor to spend the day with her.

A year or two later, Sada had approached the topic with the Duke again, this time asking if the guards could still accompany her but wear normal attire rather than armor. The Duke's answer had been the same as the first time, asking her how she thought they would be able to protect her in civilian clothes, and demanding to know if she truly valued appearances more than her own life. She didn't; she simply knew that the chances of her being attacked and killed in the center of a small town like Centerton, or the luxury districts in Ettedon, were so low that she deemed it an acceptable risk to take.

But she knew her father well enough that two refusals from him were enough to dissuade her from broaching the topic ever again. And so from then on, it was something she simply accepted as part of her life. She knew it would not be changed, and so there was no point in wishing it could be otherwise. But just once, she'd wanted to know what it would be like. To shed her fine silks and the guards that set her apart as

(better than the others)

nobility and exist in the world as a normal person. As it turned out, it wasn't as grand as she'd believed it to be.

"Why did you allow me to remain in my delusion for so long a time?" she asked Gabriel.

The knight just shrugged, seeming to consider his answer. Finally, he said, "A few years ago, I realized that the only way you would truly be able to grow up is if you knew what it meant to be on your own. It was then that I decided I would allow you to go without the company of myself or my men at least once in your life. I wanted you to understand what it's like to be in this world without a knight at each arm or a governess looking over your shoulder. I'd always thought it would be something I orchestrated myself, but you beat me to it, didn't you?" He winked.

"Why?" she whispered.

For a long while he was silent, the only sound being the clink and scuff of his armor scraping against itself or the cobblestone. "I wanted you to learn how to think for yourself," he finally said. And the way he said it was like it was a secret. Sada understood why. Anyone who knew the Duke would.

Gabe met her eyes, and his were stern. "Believe me when I say it won't happen again."

"Thank you," she said.

"Shall I return you home now, little lady?" Gabriel unlinked their arms and offered the other instead as he spun on his heel to face back into town.

But Sada was staring past his arm, looking down the wide paved path they stood on, through the arching stone entrance that was no longer used; she gazed past the stones that used to fade into a well-worn path but were now hidden by needles, over the border of Centerton, into the forest. She stared into its dark depths, wondering at the way the shadows of the setting sun seemed to collect at their roots; wondering what it was saying as it spoke to her.

"Sada?" Gabriel asked.

It was so close. With the last rays of sun on her back, she could feel the chill of the forest and its shadows against her face and arms, as though there were a wall of warmth that ended where the town did. She continued down the cobbled path, closer to the trees. They stretched and groaned toward her, reaching for her. She wanted to reach back. She felt the longing in her chest so strongly she almost gasped as she stared at those endless rows of dark trunks. She took another step into the chill, and her slippered foot found pine needles and dirt rather than pavement. She drew in a sharp breath as the cold assaulted her, filling her lungs with it, cleansing her, raising goosebumps along her arms. But it wasn't simply cold. It was so cold it was hot. It surrounded her and the trees. All she saw was the forest. All she wanted was the forest. She took another step, sliding her slipper into the dry leaves.

"It's coming." She barely heard herself whisper as she made to take another step.

Then Gabriel's cold gauntleted hand wrapped tightly around her arm and she stopped, jolting backward into her guard. She glanced up at the frown that took over his entire face, then looked back into the forest. In that short moment, the beckoning icy heat had been replaced by the usual spring chill and the shadows had receded. Now the forest was bathed in a brilliance of orange and yellow hues as the sun caressed the trees with its dwindling rays. Yet, even though it looked more beautiful, it had become less inviting. Sada backed away from it.

"Come now, Sada," Gabriel said carefully, still gripping her arm. "You know it's not allowed."

"I know," she whispered, still staring at the trees, searching for what she had felt in them just a moment ago. But the forest had released her. She turned and faced Gabriel, brightening her face into a smile. "Are you ready to return home?"

Gabriel just nodded and released her arm. She hadn't noticed how tightly he'd been holding her until she felt the blood flow back into her veins as he let go. She rubbed the feeling back into her arm as they walked.

"I didn't hurt you, did I little lady?" Concern flooded the hard lines of his face.

Sada let her hand fall from her arm. "Of course not, Gabe. You're always so gentle with me," she said as her skin throbbed.

He just examined her as though he might see through the opaque fabric of the dress to the tender arm beneath. But he said nothing further, just shifted the helm under his arm. She wrapped hers around his empty one. Then the pair continued walking, and Sada had to hurry to keep up with her knight's quickened pace.

"Why can't I go into the forest?"

He stiffened under her arm at the question, and stared straight ahead as she searched his face for an answer. But neither his eyes nor his mouth yielded one.

He simply growled, "Nobody can," and then fell silent.

It was the first time in years she'd heard his voice sound like a guard rather than a friend. The first time she could remember where he'd given her a command rather than a suggestion. And though he didn't say it outright, she could feel in the way his muscles had tightened and his posture had gone perfect, the way his chin had lifted, that if she ever asked to go back near the eastern woods, it would be the first time Gabriel would not regard her wishes.

She didn't know why she had asked. Now she wished she hadn't. She knew—everybody in Centerton did, and the locals ensured their guests learned as well. The western woodlands and the southern forest between the manor and town were safe enough; it was the forest to the east, the one beyond the old stone arch, that had been forbidden. After the duchess had vanished into its depths, the Duke issued a written decree, and Centerton's lord enforced it without mercy: no soul was to pass beneath those trees. With how eagerly the townspeople had accepted the new law, she thought perhaps they had reasons to fear the forest beyond her father's own.

As they walked back into Centerton, Sada could still feel the woods at her back, but she didn't dare turn around to meet the darkness again.

THE THIRD

Sada

Some people wakened prematurely from nightmares, or perhaps because of sounds in the night, but Sada wakened to shivers. She hugged her goosebump-covered body tightly as she stood, but her icy fingertips only summoned more of the bumps in their wake. The meek dawn light did nothing to warm her either; its yellow rays provided only the illusion of heat, and when she stood in them, they just blinded her rather than warm her face.

Shivering, Sada mustered up the courage to slip out of her nightdress, her only shield from the cold, and step into a long and loose dressing gown. She was always cold, but after much contemplation—something Jezi called soul digging and which Sada did a lot of—she'd realized it wasn't really the cold she minded. She simply didn't like the feeling of air on her skin, and for some reason, she only felt it when it was cold. She always liked to have something between herself and the air, whether it was a blanket or a gown or a robe. Today it was both a gown *and* a robe.

She then covered the spiral birthmarks beside her eyes with a layer of powder, and then several more layers to be safe. She didn't want Gabe to have to sneak into her room and steal the precious vile again as he had done the night before while she waited, head down, in front of the manor.

Sada then called her lady's maid in to help her into her morning gown and pin her hair up. The Duke had only recently hired her after dismissing Sada's previous maid, Ana, for reasons she had not been made privy to. Sada brushed her hair herself, though—she liked doing it when it wasn't tangled; it wasn't a chore then. Instead of being work, it reminded her of her father's love for her. *Your hair is like spun silk*, he would sometimes say to her when she looked especially beautiful. Any word from her father's mouth was true, and she treasured the good ones because they told her who she was. The good ones were special, and brushing her hair when it was pretty and she saw the spun silk in it reminded her of her father when his eyes were the warm blue of a summer lake instead of the cold blue of fresh ice.

Sada put down the brush, her hair shining, and let the new maid, Sofia, braid it and twist it into an updo that was simple enough for staying in, but elegant enough that she would be presentable for any company who might call on her uncle. Though with her father away, visitors were few and far between.

"How was your night, Sofia?" Sada asked her lady's maid as she pinned the final strands of hair into place. She had been rough with the comb and pins, but it did look lovely.

"Well. And yours?"

"It was just dandy, thank you. Did you have any dreams?"

For a moment Sofia was silent, and Sada thought she wouldn't answer. Then she said, "None fit for a lady's ears."

"Sofia!" Sada gasped, grinning. But her maid did not return the smile, and she finished her hair with her lips pursed tightly.

The morning gown Sofia chose for her was of a thin, pastel silk, suitable to wear while breaking her fast or brunching in the confines of her own manor. The fabric was too flimsy to offer her much warmth, and even beneath the rich robe from Ettedon's markets she still shivered, so she stole the big silken comforter off her bed and wrapped it around her shoulders (it seemed it was a morning for a gown *and* robe *and* blanket). The housemaids would replace it for her before she had time to ask.

Jezebel's voice was in her head before she could stop it: *Of course.* Ladies *need their sheets to be replaced daily. Pretty rich girls can't get mucky like us peasants, can they?* Sada's teeth found her lip, still raw in the places where she'd chewed it the day before. The voice of the memory was a harsh cycle in her head, just fragments repeating nonsensically, but painful all the same.

She made herself listen to the voices of the servants instead as she stepped into the hall. It was always hushed tones and murmurs with them. Sada learned early on that the servants saw, heard, and knew everything, but no information could be gleaned from *them* through spying. They'd learned to keep their voices indecipherable and their faces in the shadows the way their gossiping masters hadn't, and now no secrets were stolen back from them. Sada wondered what secrets they had to talk about.

Save for the murmuring of the servants, the manor was silent. Sada tiptoed down the pine-floored hall quietly, her blanket sweeping behind her, not daring to disturb the calm. Her cold feet whispered across colder floors. As she crossed the upper floors, sneaking down hallways lined with boring portraits of old women and trees, *(They're tasteful, Sada,* Duke Solares would scold her at these remarks*)*, her uncle Beron's voice could be heard floating up the staircase. It was strange how voices did that, she thought as she rounded a corner. How they floated.

Beron was barking at someone, talking *at* them in his typical fashion. Her father said his general's mannerisms were simply one more thing he'd taken home with him from the army. Her uncle often "took things home" with him, from shops he browsed in, houses he visited, women he called on. If their owners ever noticed, he acted just as surprised to find their items in his pockets. But it was his stare that allowed him to persuade them that he could keep whatever he had taken. It reminded them that maybe they hadn't seen him slip the antique coin, which they didn't *really* need, right off the dusty shelf. Green like holly leaves, Beron's stare was well known throughout both their family and the king's army, in which he had once served, and her father still did.

As Sada snuck down the final stretch of hallway, that well-known stare came into view. She watched as it bore unblinking into another man's face, though who he was she could not see. His back was to her and the staircase, gleaming in resplendent armor. The emerald-colored helm and sword hilt indicated that he was one of her father's men. When the man removed his half-helm, Sada recognized the long, orange hair.

"Sir Noah!" Sada couldn't help but exclaim.

He swiveled in a very knightly way to face her, and Uncle Beron's pummeling stare snapped to her face. Both men's gazes softened as she dropped her big blanket at the top of the staircase and ran down to meet them, the cold forgotten.

"Good morning, Lady Sada," Sir Noah Alcázar said, bowing low as he took her hand. He kissed it as he rose, but Sada ignored the formality and embraced the tall man tightly. "It's good to see you, too," he said with a rare chuckle.

"Why aren't you in Asrich with Father?" she asked breathlessly as she released his neck. She hastily remembered her manners and turned to her uncle. "Good morning, Uncle."

Beron dipped his head in response.

Sir Noah unfastened the sides of his breastplate, letting out a breath of relief. "I've just ridden in to deliver a message to Lord Beron."

Beron gestured toward the drawing room where the footmen waited to be called on. The First and Second Footmen stood patiently in the shadows, knowing they served best when they were unseen. Their younger, fresher apprentices perched eagerly beside the table, already clutching steaming teapots and too many plates of pastries.

"Is it a matter of urgency?" Uncle Beron asked politely.

Sada followed Noah and Beron to the adjacent room decorated with plain chairs and couches stiff from disuse.

"No, my lord, there is no present cause for concern nor great haste."

"Allow us to serve you, then. Surely, you're parched from your travels," Beron barked. The sharpness of his voice made for a strange contrast with his elegant speech.

"I would not refuse such an offer," Noah replied. Servants rushed to fluff the cushions in the chair he hovered above, but the knight paused, gesturing to his green-trimmed armor. "Do you mind?"

"Make yourself comfortable," Beron said. "I can instruct the servants to draw you a bath and arrange you a proper meal, should you desire to replenish your energy. The ride from Asrich is a rocky one."

Her uncle settled into a seat across from the knight on the other side of a short wooden table, which the servants were piling with dishes of cakes and empty cups awaiting tea. When she and her father had taken up residence in the country house, it hadn't been occupied by a lord in decades—at least not one of great standing, and certainly not a duke—and everything from the architecture to the furniture was outdated.

The floors and frame were built from polished pine rather than marble, and the walls were plaster painted in a pale blue rather than made of stone and decorated with the elaborate carvings and silk wallpaper that could be found in their Ettedon mansion. When they had first taken ownership of the Centerton manor, there had even been mats of rushes on the floors rather than the woven rugs of their capital residence. Father had disposed of these quickly, seething that they were not horses to be stabled on hay.

Yet he hadn't taken the time to order new furniture to this manor. It was decorated with overstuffed chairs and couches, wooden tables likely to splinter, and short, stubby bed frames. Despite the eyesore that the furniture was, the Duke said it wouldn't be worth the effort to replace it with modern décor when they spent only a few months of the year here. Sada was beginning to suspect that perhaps he liked the old chairs he often sat in before the fire and was simply too proud to admit it.

Most of Sada's life was lived out in the heart of Ettedon to be close to King Abel Castellor, to whom her father had sworn both sword and counsel. They came to Centerton only for the summers, when the younger prince, Aaron Castellor, insisted upon visiting his aunt, who refused to leave her "quaint home among the country folk," as the queen put it. It was a heated topic among the Castellors.

She was Prince Aaron's favorite relative, however, so he could not be dissuaded from his season with her. A few choice members of the Kingsguard accompanied him, as did Sada's father. As one of the king's dearest friends and advisors, only he could be trusted to look after King Abel's dear boy. Sada had always delighted in exploring the little town and looking down at it from the estate, but then she'd met Jezebel, and the Centerton house quickly became her preferred residence. Jezebel made the season less lonely.

Despite spending the entire summer season in the same town as the prince, Sada rarely visited with him. She recalled playing at his aunt's house together when they were younger, and she still saw him at the town's events and at court in Ettedon, but as they'd grown up their hobbies had become decidedly girlish and boyish, leaving nothing to be shared between them anymore. That, and the prince was too young to court her as the rumors said he might, and so they stayed on their own sides of Centerton. Without Jezebel, Sada would have only her guards to keep her company. It wouldn't be so bad, only she couldn't play at sword practice with them, and they wouldn't sing operas or draw with her. That left them with the activity of strolling around the town to look at sights they'd already seen, or taking a carriage through the forest they'd already traveled. The guards were her friends, but they could not be the sort of companions a lady was permitted.

Sir Noah, the long-haired knight who had served beside her father since Sada had been old enough to know what knights were, had begun removing his armor at her uncle's sanction and now set the last piece gently onto the floor beside him. His breastplate had already been taken away by one of the older footmen, and two more appeared now to quietly whisk away his gleaming gauntlets. Noah stretched out into his tall chair, but his posture remained perfectly poised as he leaned into the cushions.

"I appreciate the offer of succor, my lord," the knight was saying, "but I am to ride to meet Duke Solares again once I have finished delivering my message."

"Where are you riding to meet him?" Sada chimed in, just as Uncle Beron asked, "And what might this message be?"

"Apologies, Uncle," Sada said, ducking her head. Beron merely waved her apology away, his piercing eyes fixed on Noah.

The poised knight smiled graciously at them. "Both questions have the same answer. The Duke has concluded his affairs in Asrich and presently makes his return here. I shall hasten to meet him and accompany His Grace for the remaining leg of his journey.

"He would have a bath drawn and a meal of garlic steak, spiced bread, roasted greens, and ale prepared upon his return." Noah said this to Beron, but the butler was listening discreetly from his place at the wall and would see the instructions carried to the kitchens.

"Duke Solares has also charged me to inform you that your oversight of the estate will extend through tomorrow. His Grace will speak with you further upon his return; it shall not be long now."

Something squeezed at Sada's heart, her chest constricting. For a moment, breath evaded her. It wasn't that she had forgotten how to breathe—she knew it was simple, just a matter of push and pull. But that simple ability to pull air into her lungs and then push it out was evading her. She counted three heartbeats

(1, 2, 3)

before her chest was released from the constricting grip that held it. Her fingers had dug into the padded armrest of her chair in her panic. She tried to keep her face even as she sucked a breath in, relishing the air in her lungs once more.

But the men's eyes were on her now, and she didn't know what they had said to her.

"Pardon me?" she asked.

"Is there any word you would have me give His Grace, Lady Sada?" Noah was looking at her questioningly, his dark eyes searching.

"Only that I await his swift return," Sada said softly, and made herself smile over the forced words.

She wondered what matter would keep her father occupied tomorrow, that Beron must remain in charge of the estate.

Sada sipped her tea and kept the men's company with polite interest as they spoke of the matters of Asrich. She tried to pay attention to most of it, as Gabriel would likely find some excitement in the news of lords and knights. But soon her mind was straying to thoughts of Centerton's festival. It would be small in comparison to those she attended in Ettedon, where lords and ladies and earls from across the entire land were invited to attend. Voyagers from distant lands might make their way inland for the markets, ladies from the east would come to dance and bring their jewels to display, and her own king's court would be filled with merchants and jesters and beautiful people.

In Centerton, however, the attendees would be less esteemed. Prince Aaron would be there, of course, after having convinced his aunt to attend. His retinue of guards would do their best (which was not very good at all) to blend into the crowd. The crowd in question would likely be made up only of the commonfolk, the few lesser lords and ladies who resided there, and perhaps a lord or two from neighboring cities like Desdale, come to talk business with each other.

In small country towns like these, festivals were not for introducing foreigners to court or forging ties between outside lands, but for fostering community between the citizens already living there. So far as she knew, it didn't even have a name. It was just called "the festival." Still, how she loved seeing the town come to life. Both the streets and the people would be decorated in lovely colors and their richest adornments, and Sada would be given a chance to wear her finery. Oh, she could hardly wait! Jezebel would be unable to continue in her anger once she saw the dress Sada was planning on bringing her.

Before she realized how much time had passed, Sir Noah and Beron were rising from their chairs. The two men walked side by side back into the foyer, the knight striding along importantly, her uncle placing each step with measured precision. Sada drifted in their prestigious wake like a breeze, delicately weaving around chairs. She didn't like to be loud, with hard footsteps. Men were loud; she was a lady. Behind them all, footmen clutching Noah's various pieces of shed armor, now freshly oiled and gleaming, followed hurriedly.

Sada watched the knight and the retired general for a moment, wondering if her uncle was capable of blinking as he swiveled from commanding the servants to talking at Sir Noah, still staring instead of looking. His too-green eyes were always held wide open, as though trying to take in everything around him—even above, below, and behind.

When Noah was re-dressed in his heavy armor and the butler had opened the door for him, Sada stepped forth.

"Sir Noah—when may I expect my father's eagerly awaited arrival?"

She hadn't asked a servant for the time since she woke, but with how close the sun still clung to the horizon, she assumed it to be near dawn.

"In a few hours' time, my lady. His Grace intends that you accompany him and Prince Aaron to Desdale tonight on a matter of business." Noah Alcázar dipped his orange head in farewell and stepped out of the manor, leaving Sada unable to breathe for three heartbeats

(1, 2, 3)

again. Then the breath returned to her lungs, and she remembered to whisper, "But the festival is tonight."

Though she'd spoken to nobody in particular, her uncle heard.

"You have my apologies, Sada. I know how much fun you derive from attending the village festivals." Beron tried to frown in sympathy, but she wasn't sure his eyes were capable of conveying such a soft emotion. Now they dared her to feel deserving of his kindness. But she didn't want any.

"Pardon, Uncle, but that's not what I am aggrieved by. I promised a friend I'd be there to offer my help." The piece of her heart that had broken at Jezebel's words the day before now crumbled apart further.

"Ah. Just like you, Sada. You've ever been one to befriend the, ah, commoners," Beron barked in that sharp way of his. He began to shine his cuff buttons with the opposite sleeve. "I'm confident this friend of yours will be understanding of your situation. Even the commonfolk recognize the importance of a duke's affairs, especially one of your father's standings."

Once, Jezi may have. Once, Jezi may have even been the one to comfort Sada over the cruelty of being forced to stay away. But now Sada wasn't entirely certain. The Jezebel who ran away angry and called her "m'lady" would not understand why Sada couldn't be at the festival, the most vital night for her father's apothecary. But Sada just lifted her chin and made herself happy enough to smile at Beron.

"Thank you, Uncle. I shall simply have to take a carriage into town today and assist Jezebel in her final preparations. I can only hope it will suffice to compensate for my absence this evening."

She made to exit up the staircase behind her, but Beron's ensuing snap made her pause. "That's reminded me of something, Sada. The festival. A woman called on me this morning."

"On *you?"* Sada asked.

"Don't look so shocked," Beron said. She laughed at his feigned hurt.

He gestured for her to follow and strode down the hallway. Sada hurried after, and they came into the brunching room, the only one in the small, old manor.

"With all the cousins you have running around I'd assumed you knew how many women called on me."

He winked at Sada, then let out a great, barking laugh at her look of horror. With how poised of an appearance Beron maintained, Sada often forgot how vulgar he could be.

"It's only that I was unaware you were looking to add *more* cousins to the family," she teased. Beron just laughed louder at her remark, and she couldn't help but smile.

Her uncle stalked to a cabinet and swung it open, squinting as he scanned its contents. Dismayed younger servants shot each other glances from the shadows. The older ones just shared smiles with each other, no doubt remembering their shocks in the fresh days when they'd learned that Barking Beron was the one lord who insisted on serving himself. Sada trailed her hands across all the wooden countertops as she crossed the room to sit at the single brunch bench overlooking the garden. Beron continued rummaging through the cabinets, young footmen and housemaids hurrying up to him to ask if he was certain he didn't need assistance.

"Don't insult me," her uncle was saying to them. "If I could find a way to whip the brats in His Majesty's army into fighting shape, I can just as well find a decanter." He barked out a laugh at himself that sent the servants scurrying. "But to ease your mind, Sada, I will not be adding any more green-eyed babes to your list of cousins…Intentionally, that is."

With Beron being her father's only sibling and her mother having left her own kin in the north, all of Sada's cousins were fathered by Beron, and there were many of them. He kept no air of mystery about his siring of illegitimates; it was only who their mothers were that was the question. But it was one their family and longstanding associates had stopped asking years ago.

It had stirred up a great many fights when Beron insisted his first natural-born son inherit the family name of Solares along with their titles and a place at his estate. The contrary family members ceased all reprimand after the next dozen children were introduced as having been claimed by him. Now it was just accepted that Barking Beron's…illegitimates…would be accepted into the family. And now there were so many children that Uncle Beron wasn't even sure if all of them *were* his. He'd decided on the rule of green and black to keep things simple for himself and the women who showed up to the estate with the babbling babes: if the children had green eyes and black hair like him, he kept them. If they didn't, they weren't his. Probably.

Finally, Beron discovered the crystal decanter he'd been searching for, and dismissed the servants with a final wave.

"Will you let me tell my story to my niece? I had not thought one needed to ask servants permission for anything, let alone something as simple as this. If you are so keen to listen to us, do so through the walls!" His holly-leaf stare sent them running.

"They only wish to help," Sada offered softly. When her uncle met her gaze, her breathing almost halted and the reprimand that was to ensue instantly blared in her mind:

Do you now presume to remind me of the purpose of my servants? Has a beard sprouted upon your chin in my absence, elevating you to the head of this household? Do you aspire to command legions, engage in battles, employ and discharge staff, earn a livelihood, and bear the costs of your own—

"Yes, well, they can help me pour my tea and set a plate for my crackers. When the time comes that I need help *speaking,* I would only ask that they help lead me into the forest and return only with tidings of a hunting accident."

Sada hardly heard what her uncle had said, only that he was laughing and not yelling—any louder than was typical for him, anyway. *Not every man is Father,* she reminded herself. Then, *You say that like it's a bad thing…* She picked at her lip, wondering if somehow her father had heard her treacherous thoughts from the road.

"That is quite humorous, Uncle," she said, trying to laugh at the joke she thought he might have told.

He waved her off, drinking deeply from his whiskey. "You needn't pretend to laugh at my jests, girl, your mere presence is pleasure enough for this old man. Shall I recount the tale of my caller, or shall we continue to pretend that I might usurp the Royal Jester's position at court?"

At that, she did laugh. "No, no, I would hear this fantastical tale. Who was the woman that called on you?"

The festival had reminded him of it, and she thought perhaps he'd been delivered a formal invitation. That, she believed, would help to convince her father that the trip to Desdale could be put off until after the festival. The rational part of her which learned from the past knew it wouldn't work, but hope is a hard thing to crush.

"I don't recall her name. Pretty thing, though. The housemaids were taking up all of my attention, as is their wont. This time complaining about how the hall boys had stolen their cursed soap. Honestly, I'd mistake them for my own children if it weren't for how cursedly *blonde* they all are. I swear, your father only hires blondes." He made a pointed look at a passing footman, his pale hair flopping as he scampered down a hallway.

"You're right, they are all blonde," Sada mused. She hadn't noticed the overpopulation of yellow-haired servants until then.

Uncle Beron waved his hand. "As I was saying, I only caught a portion of the young woman's message before I had to pass her along to one of the servants, but she did make mention of the festival. And you, now that I reflect on it. It seemed she was under the impression you would be in the town today—"

Sada stood suddenly, heart skittering. *My chance to make amends!* "Oh dear, she hasn't been waiting on me, has she?" *Is it gone?*

She shot a glance out one of the tall windows behind Beron. The sky was still pale from early morning, not yet awake enough to become vibrant. How could her uncle have forgotten to relay such a message?

"This is the consequence of my indulgence in extra sleep," she groaned.

"No, Sada, compose yourself. She expressly asked me to inform you not to come. She said that everything is in order and your assistance is no longer needed. And that is verbatim," he said proudly, tapping at his temple.

The crack in Sada's heart tore deeper.

"I must not have heard you correctly," she said, but Beron sighed, and she knew the message had been heard true. "Was her name Jezebel?"

"I can't be certain. As I mentioned, I do not recall. Yet, the name does strike a chord."

He rose and stretched, then crossed the room, glass brimming with liquor and its accompanying bottle under an arm, and made to leave by way of the door behind her. As he did, he held something small and glimmering up for her to see.

"She did leave this for me," he said, and dropped it into her palm as he left.

In her hand was a small yellow cuff, the copper beneath peeking through, with a single loose ruby in the center. *Her most cherished possession is that little ear cuff she refuses to take off,* Mrs. Pérez had said. Sada was dumbfounded that Beron had been able to get it off of Jezebel, let alone without her realizing.

"You mustn't steal from my friends, Uncle!" Sada called after Beron. But somehow, the fact that he had stolen the cuff calmed her panic.

"It was a gift!" she heard him retort.

Sada slipped the cuff over her ear; if she didn't, she would no doubt forget it someplace. She'd return it when she visited Jezebel today. Her invitation may have been revoked by her friend and impeded by her father, but she wouldn't stay away while Jezi was upset. And what Duke Solares didn't know would not hurt him. She would be back before he arrived. Imagining her venture into the town, Sada returned upstairs to bathe and be dressed for a day in Centerton.

All morning, Sada's mind had been divided between thoughts of making amends with Jezebel, Centerton's festival, and her father's return. And every time she thought of the latter, her chest squeezed itself so tightly she had to pause whatever she was doing to breathe. It had resulted in flurries of servants rushing to her aid throughout the early hours. Normally they were out of her sight, but with the Duke's impending return, it seemed every member of their household staff was about, each frantically rushing to complete one chore or another. Sada felt as flustered as they were behaving.

She spent a quarter of the day in her rooms preparing both for the Duke's return and for her journey into Centerton. First, she bathed, then called in Sofia and spent ages trying on different gowns, matching different pairs of gloves or necklaces or bracelets with them. When the dress was finally picked, she had Sofia take down her hair and re-do it in a more intricate style with more braids and twists. Then she remembered her plan to provide Jezebel with a gown of her own for the festival, and even if Sada could not attend herself she still planned on doing just that.

She and Sofia were still trying to find a dress that would be both flattering on Jezebel and casual enough for the occasion when there was a sudden and light shaking of the manor. A distant rumbling could be heard as the floor trembled for a few seconds. Nearby tables wobbled slightly and a few of the younger, newer housemaids hung onto the walls while the older servants steadied the paintings. Panic alighting in Sada's fingertips, she whirled to look outside. The sky was still the bright color of day—she was supposed to have time!

But she didn't.

Sada's heart had begun to constrict at the familiar sounds, and she began her count of three heart beats,

(1, 2—)

restarting twice,

(1, 2—1, 2, 3)

before she was released from the breathless grip. When she was finally able to take a breath in, she held it in her lungs as the trumpets sounded his arrival and a familiar voice began shouting orders at his men.

The Duke had arrived.

THE FOURTH

Sada

"Hello, Father," Sada said. She was aware of each fluctuation of her voice, the pronunciation of every vowel. "I was most delighted to hear of your early return. How fared your journey?"

She dipped her head, staring at the way her skirts lay on the ground as she bowed, ensuring her knee almost scraped the gravel, but didn't quite.

"What?" he said loudly above her. "You're so quiet I can scarcely hear you. Have we not spoken of this matter?"

"Yes, Father, you're right, my apologies," Sada said, straining to make her voice loud above the cacophony of the dozens of guards and servants arriving behind her father. She wasn't sure why, but around him, her voice always shrank.

Darius Solares, Duke of Altamira and the head commander of the king's armies, hardly deigned to look at Sada as he dismounted from his horse. The stomping, bit-champing warhorse was the unchecked twin to her father's temper, half-rearing and snorting and snapping whenever a servant neared to grab his bridle. Yet Duke Solares did not let more than a flicker of that temper show now as he lifted Sada from her deep bow with a firm finger under her chin.

"You have yet to learn the simple art of curtseying with a straight back," he said. "Was that not the very purpose for which your latest corset was purchased? Why did I even expend the copper? My funds do not materialize from the air, as you seem to think they do." He strode away from the gathering guards and horses, making his way toward the manor.

Sada scurried after him. "My apologies, Father. But was my curtsey sufficiently low this time? I have been focusing on the placement of my feet, just as you suggest—"

"It matters little whether it is low enough if your back is bent and your chin is jutting out, does it? Would you present yourself in such a manner before King Abel? Or even the queen? I should think not, *hope* not—so, then, why should I be subjected to such laxity?" he said as she stared at his emerald-caped back. Walking now was an automatic process; she felt as though her mind was receding further into her body with each step. "I have long held the belief that you were the daughter of a duke and head commander of the royal army, not some lowborn woman like the maids who serve us."

"Yes, Father," her voice said, forgetting to be loud, and she continued trailing after him in his great wake. Face hot with shame, she fought against the invisible claws that were trying to paralyze her chest, which was already being squeezed shut by her new corset.

Her father summoned and dismissed servants as he strode toward the wooden manor in great, important steps. He shrugged his great emerald riding cape off as he walked, revealing a full suit of rich, dark velvet. His full but carefully shaped beard and mutton chops were freshly oiled, and the dust had already been toweled from his face. Even when Duke Solares rode, he refused to wear anything but his finest clothes, always reminding onlookers of who he was and what he was. The Duke's valet, always near enough to hear but not be heard, and see without being seen, caught the cape as it fell. The Duke didn't turn to see what he did with it, just continued on to the few polished steps where Beron was waiting patiently with two pale-faced footmen.

"How did you find the road, Your Grace?" Beron asked, bowing low.

"Rocky as ever. The servants couldn't even manage the simple task of shoeing a horse when Charger threw one. I had to halt the entire caravan, dismount, and show them myself, as though it isn't their very job to attend both me and my steed. The imbeciles put us back by nearly half an hour; they're lucky it wasn't longer." His face was a study in disgust.

Beron grimaced in return and muttered something about how people nowadays seem incapable of performing the simplest of tasks.

Even as his brother, Beron still put on a show of respect for the Duke. If he didn't, he would be outcast from the family, their city, and the entire kingdom, sentenced to dwell wherever generals of the king's armies were sent following a dishonorable discharge.

It wasn't a joke that Beron really had taken more than just a general's mannerisms with him when he'd left the battlefront. He'd always had wandering fingers and hungry pockets, and King Abel often looked the other way in favor of his best battle general and longstanding drinking mate. But stealing Prince Simon's riding knife had been the end of the king's leniency, and Beron quickly found himself without a career, title, or estate, having lived in the king's court since his coming of age.

Duke Darius, with his high titles and higher stacks of coin, had offered his brother a way out. Beron was a thief, but not an idiot; he knew that when someone rescued you from a fate like his, you became indebted to them for the rest of your would-be miserable life. And Beron also knew that the Duke did not believe in second chances—even the first was a rare courtesy. It would not do to jeopardize this one.

"It appears the housemaids have grown lax under your care," her father was saying to Beron, though he turned a hard eye to Sada as he spoke. *Not just the maids,* that look said to her.

They'd gone into the manor, and her father was inspecting the finger he'd just dragged along a nearby vase. He frowned at dust they couldn't see.

Following Duchess Solares's disappearance, the servants and Sada had quickly learned that whatever Duke Solares said was the truth. If he bit into a biscuit one morning and declared it to be cow tongue, Sada and the staff would hastily and eagerly agree. If they did not, punishment would follow.

As she grew older and as the things with which she was forced to agree became more extreme

(*Sada, why do you leave your plates strewn across the house like it's a brothel?* and *Apologies, Father, I was being indolent,* when truly she had not eaten in days)

she began to wonder whether he indeed knew that what he said was fiction and it was all a ruse to see what extraordinary things he could force the members of his household to agree with.

She had not dared to voice her opinion in several years, even if it was to defend herself with the truth, for fear of the yelling and lashings that would ensue for "disrespectful arguing." Yet she grew more fearful each time that one day her father would actually punish her for mindlessly agreeing with something that was so obviously untrue, instead of the opposite. Until then, she and the other members of his household would continue to nod or shake their heads obediently and with the ease of trained actors.

So, when her father showed his

(clean)

dust-covered finger to Beron, her uncle nodded along with a frown and grunted disapprovingly.

"I beg your pardon, Brother," Beron said. Just as disagreeing was not an option when speaking with her father, neither were charming excuses or witty remarks. Not when he was in a mood, which he always seemed to be in

(since Mother)

(since The Incident)

since she became a disobedient child. His anger had once been righteous. To Sada, it still seemed that it was. Even in the privacy of her own mind, she could not disobey her father. But his brother, his men, his servants, and anyone else who saw his true temper knew that the disappearance of the Duke's wife was now a shallow excuse for the raging beast within. Sada ignored that beast because it still wore her father's face. That, and she was incapable of feeling or thinking anything bad about her father. It had been trained out of her since childhood, and evidence of it could be seen in the pale slashes tattooed on the back of her body, which stung when she smelled lemons.

Uncle Beron and Sada followed quietly as her father stepped through the house, inspecting random tables, vases, and windowpanes. After a few more complaints from the Duke, Beron summoned a housemaid to follow along with a cloth. She would reverently wipe away whatever invisible dust Sada's father discovered.

When he was finally—begrudgingly—satisfied that he'd found all the foremost imperfections in the manor, he faced Sada. She tried not to cower before her father's hard, unblinking stare, and his terrible blue eyes. Blue like the ice freshly formed over a lake in the winter, too new to safely walk on.

While Beron's piercing gaze seemed to try and see inside you, her father's eyes kept everyone out. His unwavering gaze was so hard to meet, it kept most from looking at all. No secrets of Darius Solares's would be revealed by returning his stare. And neither would any emotion be relinquished, whatever remained besides anger and disappointment. From his eyes to his shined boots, respect and deference were commanded. It was hard to resist the urge to bow again—and stay there, hiding—as the Duke's hard eyes silently appraised her.

Such a commanding stare.

A small, carefully protected piece of her quietly wondered if he would open his arms, smile, and offer her one of his rare hugs. Maybe he'd even compliment her hair, the way it was pinned up today, or how satiny it looked. She tried to keep herself from hoping for it as the silence stretched on.

"Well? Are you not going to greet your father?" he finally said to her.

Her mouth opened, no sound came out, and she closed it.

Finally, she said, "I'm sorry, Father. How fared your journey?"

Her father did not deign to respond. She had not expected him to. His face just coiled up into disgust as he scanned her from head to toe.

"What are you *wearing?* Please tell me it never made it out of this estate. It never should have entered my home to begin with. Remove it, now." The hope shattered. Sada tried to keep that tiny, wishful piece of herself from crying out as she curtsied to hide her moistening eyes. "I told you *months* ago to stop shopping at your own initiative."

"You did, Father."

"And you chose to defy me?" he said, pronouncing each word with dangerous care.

His blue eyes put up a hard wall between them. He had the tan skin of a westerner and his travels had only darkened it further. It made his eyes look even colder than usual. She couldn't bring herself to look at them any longer, and her gaze dropped to its familiar view of the ground and the Duke's shiny boots. All dusty signs of his ride had been whisked away by a doting servant. *Even my boots are better than you,* they said to her.

"I beg your pardon, Father. I just liked the color."

"What? Speak up. You aren't some meek servant, are you?"

She cleared her throat. "I only said I liked the color, Father."

He was quiet for a moment. "Did you think *I* would like the color?"

"I…I didn't think," she said, choosing her words carefully. "I was being selfish and senseless. I'm sorry."

"This is the consequence of daughters being left to their own devices," her father said to Beron, as though she had bowed so low she'd disappeared. She wished she could. "They regress to the likes of small ladies. I should have trusted my instincts—I knew it was wrong to allow her to play with those peasants."

Sada almost cringed at the way he spat the word. Uncle Beron just laughed along with her father. She tried to remind herself it was his job, but that barking chuckle sounded so real. Red leaked into her face, but she hardly noticed the heat. Her heart was heavy and aching in her chest. Though her mind was distant, the pain always seemed to reach it.

The Duke sighed. "And yet, as always, I just wanted to make you happy, Sada. Unfortunately, if your happiness results in poor decisions such as this, I am compelled to prioritize your well-being over your wishes."

Do you really believe that's what this is? Protecting my happiness? The bitter thought surprised her. She had never contradicted her father before, even within her own mind. It scared her, and she felt her eyes widen, afraid he had somehow heard her thoughts.

"Why are you still bowing?" his too-loud voice asked now. It wasn't barking like Uncle Beron's, but it hurt her ears.

She lifted her eyes to her father's face again, ensuring they were just wide enough to hint at deference, that her eyebrows were furrowed enough to appear apologetic. It worked; he did not yell. But she could still feel the disdain.

His eyes told her.

"Go change."

"Very well. What shall I change into?"

"Dear Lord." He sounded so disappointed. She focused on not biting her lip; he would hate that. "Something that doesn't assault my eyes. If you still need help dressing at your age, ask one of the elder servants for assistance. They are well-acquainted with my preferences…though I had thought the same of my own daughter. Now, I have matters to attend to in Desdale, which I will depart for tonight. You will accompany me. Ensure a servant presents the gowns you select to me before you attire yourself and have your trunks packed."

"Yes, Your Grace," she said, and bowed again though his back was now turned.

She left them to discuss the sightings of peasants on the king's trails as she escaped up the staircase and into her rooms.

✧✧✧

As she slid down the wall to sit on the cold wooden floor, Sada thought of her plans to travel to see Jezebel. She toyed with the scrap of metal on her ear now, running her finger over the little ruby, so small it could hardly be seen. Sada had once offered to have her jeweler in Ettedon craft Jezebel a new one with a bigger ruby, made out of silver rather than copper, or even real gold. That was one of the first times Jezebel called Sada "m'lady." They hadn't spoken for nearly a week after, and Sada was desperately hoping this wouldn't be another of those times.

Yet it seemed her expectations were to be denied in all areas today. For as much as she had tried to suppress it, she'd still secretly hoped that perhaps today it would be her father who returned from the road and not the Duke. The thought was painful, but she was able to suppress it. Disappointment would not help her now. It would be better to turn her thoughts to other matters.

She was trying to do just that as she heard the familiar, slow thud of the Duke's footsteps up the stairs. Then she froze and all thoughts of warm greetings, ear cuffs, and Jezebel fled from her head as those impending steps neared her door, his ankles cracking twice (left…right). Her heart seized; her hands began to prickle. She managed to cling onto some distant hope that he might turn at the last second, heading toward another chamber to inspect instead of her rooms.

She should get up, pretend to be dressing.

BAM. BAM. BAM.

The dreadful knock sounded, shaking the door in its frame, and she barely had time to scramble out of the way as her father opened the door. He looked down at her sitting in a pile of her dress on the floorboards and scowled.

"Why are you on the floor?" he asked. She was just opening her mouth to answer when he said, "Didn't I tell you to take that dress off?"

She nodded quickly. "I—I didn't have time." She knew her mistake as soon as it left her mouth, but she'd had nothing else to say.

The Duke's eyes darkened further. "You do nothing but sit in this manor all day or squander my wealth at the low-born markets. What could you *possibly* have been doing that left you without time to obey my orders?"

"Nothing, Father. I beg your pardon." He gave her a pointed look and she scrambled to her feet, sheepishly smoothing out her dress. When he said nothing further, she began to ask, "Is it time to depart alread—"

"Beron informed me that a peasant woman visited the manor this morning," he said over her. She closed her mouth on her words, hoping it didn't look like annoyance to him. "We discussed this. If you insist on…associating with their likes, it shall be only when you travel into town. I will not tolerate them within my grounds."

Sada felt a sudden flare of heat beneath her skin. That was new, too. New and bad and dangerous. It was quickly replaced by the familiar turning of her stomach and fluttering of her heart.

Keeping her voice even and gentle, she said, "I haven't invited them to our manor, Father. I was unaware that Jezebel would be traveling here."

"It appears you don't exert much control over your acquaintances, Sada."

Not everyone wishes to control their friends as if they were pets, Father, she thought.

"I'm sorry," she said.

"You're not so feeble as to let them dictate your actions and do whatever they will with you, are you?"

"No. You have my apologies."

"You are a lady of high standing, the daughter of a *duke.* Save the prince, you possess more status and authority than anyone in this village does. You understand this, don't you?"

"Yes, Your Grace."

"And you are capable of wielding that power, right? Because you are my daughter, and our blood is not weak. You understand that don't you?"

"Yes, Your Grace."

"All of my acquaintances looked to me as their leader when you and I were of an age. Do you think I would be able to command any army, let alone the king's, if I could not make others obey me?"

"No, Your Gra—"

"I couldn't." Then for a moment he only stared at her, his gaze even sharper than his words. "You are my daughter, aren't you?"

"Yes, Your Grace." For some reason that made her chin tremble. She clenched her teeth and made herself hold his stare.

"Truly? For you scarcely conduct yourself as such." Again, he stared, waiting, testing her. She looked down. "Will you henceforth conduct yourself in a manner befitting my daughter?"

"Yes, Your Grace."

"You shall forsake that ghastly gown and ready yourself for our departure to Desdale before the sun sets. Upon our return, you will seek out this peasant woman and assert the authority you rightfully wield. Remind her of her place and our family's procedures, Sada. I will not suffer her presence in or near my manor."

"Very well, Your Grace," she said softly, and curtseyed.

"No, it is not *well,*" he snapped. "It is wholly unacceptable. You understand that don't you?"

"Yes, Your Grace. I beg your pardon. I did not mean that the situation is well, only that I well-recognize my error. I will fix it with haste."

He stared.

She bowed.

"You will need to remind this woman of our procedures, then."

"Yes, Your Gra—" she began her mindless agreeing again, then realized what opportunity he'd offered her.

She perked up, lifting her eyes. "Actually, I had intended to journey to Centerton this evening. I might remind Jezebel not to trespass upon our grounds when I am present for the fes—"

"We are destined for Desdale tonight."

"I am aware, yet tonight Centerton hosts its summer festival, and I had assured Jezebel—you recall her, the apothecary's daughter—that I would lend my assistance," her mouth said.

In her mind she was screaming at herself: *NO, QUIET YOURSELF GIRL!*

"Might we perhaps make for Desdale tomorrow, Father? I could also remain here with Uncle Beron so you may focus fully on your affairs."

The Duke's glare was withering. "I told you we are to make for Desdale tonight. Or were you not listening?" he said delicately; dangerously.

"No, Father, indeed I was listening. Yet…the festival is tonight…it occurs but once per year."

"Then you may attend next year," he dismissed curtly.

"But Desdale will welcome us at any time—"

"*Quiet!*" the Duke said loudly, and she silenced herself abruptly, hardly daring to breathe. "Have your desires become more important than my orders in my absence?"

"No Father, of course not," she whispered.

"Speak louder."

"Your commands take precedence over all my wishes, Your Grace. You know what is best," Sada said more loudly, but she had dropped her gaze to the floor again.

Her fingers found her hair, tangling it. It wasn't spun silk. It was plain as cotton.

"It matters not that the festival is tonight—*look at me,"* he ordered. Sada snapped her eyes up to his face, cowering under the cold stare. Her fingers twisted more frantically. "It matters not that the festival is tonight, for we shall be in Desdale—*Stop* fidgeting with your hair, you are not a *child*." Her fingers fell away, awkward and bare in their emptiness. *"Is my meaning clear?"*

"Yes, Your Grace," she nearly whispered.

"Why do you look like that? Should you not be joyous that you might accompany your father for such an important matter? Or rather for any matter at all! One would think you should be grateful at such an opportunity. Especially considering your status in court. Well? Why are you not smiling from ear to ear?"

"Of course I am overjoyed, Father," she said even more meekly.

"So this is what you look like when you are overjoyed? Do I look like an imbecile to you, Sada?"

"No! Of course n—"

"Do you think I do not know my own daughter's countenances? Well? Tell me. Why are you not *elated* at such an opportunity?"

"It is nothing, Your Grace. I simply promised Jezi—"

"So you *aren't* grateful and excited?" He scoffed, shaking his head. "After all I've done for you."

"No, Father, it's just that—"

She was a fool for thinking he cared for the truth. Her father slammed a fist down on the dresser beside him, the tall vase on it toppling over. She saw the flowers spill from the glass, watched as a lily dropped neglected to the floor. The sound of the vase hitting the wood was magnified, so loud it hurt her ears. She flinched, cringing away from the sound. Her father's voice put its volume to shame.

"Silence yourself, Sada!" he yelled, and she flinched again.

Her eyes were wide, unblinking. She forced herself to stare at his, but she saw nothing. All she could hear, silent to the world but loud within her mind, were his words on repeat: *Silence yourself, Sada. Silence yourself, Sada—silence yourself, Sada, Sada, SILENCE! Sada, silence yourself, Sada, silence—*

"Yes, Your Grace," she managed to say.

"You will not attend the peasants' festival tonight, is that clear?"

Sada wasn't sure if she could speak. Her chest had become paralyzed again. She began counting her heartbeats.

(1, 2—)

Her father slammed his fist down on the dresser again, restarting the count.

(1—)

"*Is that clear?"* he said again, now through clenched teeth.

His face was so close she could see the sweat on his forehead. Only the area around his eyebrows was the normal color of his skin—the rest was blotchy red. She tried to look anywhere but his eyes. They were cold with rage. He began clapping his hands, right in front of her face, inches from her nose. She flinched, but still couldn't breathe. She felt like a dog being reprimanded by its master.

(Clap…CLAP...CLAP!)

"Snap out of it! Do you need to be *beaten?"* he roared.

(1, 2—)

Sada's entire body was frozen now. Only her eyes moved, darting back and forth in her head, scanning the floor, noticing the Duke's shining shoes, the lacy hem of her gown, the way her hands clutched at the fabric of the dress. So many heartbeats had passed, ever quickening, yet her lungs had still not been released from the paralyzing grip they were held in. The Duke took a step toward her, and then suddenly, by the grace of God, she could breathe.

She sucked in a breath as he closed the gap between them and snapped her head up to look at him, eyes wide and hands shaking.

"Yes, Your Grace, I understand, my deepest apologies," Sada said, and Duke Darius halted.

His emotionless mask had melted to reveal a wrathful, glaring stare. One hand was raised, as though to backhand her. She didn't know if he would have used it. It scared her that she could not be certain he wouldn't.

Those hard eyes were wild with anger, and it was all Sada could do not to run and hide. He was the warhorse in the driveway, rearing and chomping and threatening to dismember anyone who got too close, anyone who looked at him the wrong way. She eyed his arms now lowered at his sides, hairy hands curled tightly into fists.

Briefly she wondered if he would still punish her. She had taken far too long to answer. There were no switches around, but he would find something that would work. The belt around his hips would do nicely; he'd mentioned how heavy it was to her before. If it did not prove sufficient, a servant would always be waiting outside the door ready to retrieve the freshest switch from behind the house where the lemon trees were diligently tended to (never grown in the courtyard, because guests would see them there, and guests couldn't know). But then his fists uncurled, and his mask was back on, face cold and expressionless once more.

"You will be ready an hour past sundown," he said, making to leave. "And I'm having that dress burned."

He left Sada with a slam of the door and she crumbled to the floor once more. The water from the spilled vase crept up under her hem and found her bare legs, but she didn't have the will to move. It was all she could do to stifle her sobs as the pressure built up behind her nose, her chin quivered, and she felt the heat of the tears.

Father will be so angry should he see my eyes swollen up, she thought immediately, but fear of the future could not overcome the pain of the moment. Through lips pressed tightly together to stop her trembling chin, and eyes held wide to prevent tears from spilling over, sobs still escaped.

Silent, gasping, wretched sobs.

A maid found Sada just minutes later, and Sofia hurried into her rooms at the girl's urgent summoning. Sada just let her silent tears fall down her face, only half-caring if her birthmarks were revealed as housemaids cleaned the spilled water and replaced the vase, and Sofia undressed her. She didn't let the maid put a new gown on her, and instead found her way to the bathing room.

Sada sat shivering on the rim of the bronze tub, cold against her bare skin. Sitting there in front of the window, she felt as exposed as her heart did. Conversations with her father always made her feel exposed, made her want to hide. Perhaps it was why she always liked to be covered in a robe or a blanket. But now her mind was so devoid of thoughts she couldn't even bring herself to want to hide. So, she just sat there on the edge of the cold tub, seeing and thinking nothing.

Sada didn't even realize Sofia had filled the tub with hot water and soap bubbles until she was taking her arms and gently guiding her inside. She let Sofia lead her in, rinse her off, wash her hair and soften it with honey, and do whatever else she wanted as she sat there, unseeing and unthinking. Not even Jezebel crossed her mind. That is, not until she watched the sun dip below the tree line out the window beside her bath, tinting the forest orange. That brought her out of her trance. By then Sofia was long gone and the water was cold. Sada felt the horrible air on her skin then, and the gooseflesh surfaced. Then she remembered the festival, and her promise to Jezebel, and what her father had made her promise him.

Do I even care?

She didn't think she cared about anything anymore, now that her self-pitying cry was over. That's all it was: weak self-pity. With it gone, she was strong and numb.

Her fingers felt at the small cuff around her ear again. *I'm sorry, Jezi,* she thought dismally, hoping her friend could hear her.

Then a sudden flash of anger overcame her, and she screamed and slammed her hands into the sides of the tub. The ensuing pain was welcome, and she did it again and again and again. It was born from that new, strange, scary anger she felt toward her father. *Self-pity,* she told herself, *weakness.* But it didn't soothe the hot rage in her chest. She didn't see how her father's business in Desdale could be so urgent that he couldn't wait until tomorrow, or go without her.

He was a duke and commanded Abel Castellor's own army for goodness' sake—he could do anything he wanted. And, above that, he was Darius Solares. He loved bending people to his will more than a smith enjoyed bending steel into a sword. Unfortunately, that also included his daughter.

Sada tried to stifle her frustration but failed. She had promised Jezebel she'd be at the festival tonight, whether they were fighting or not. And, as she'd told her father, it only occurred once a year. That hot anger brewed stronger under her skin the more she thought of it. Sada wasn't sure how to make the unfamiliar feeling go away, but she couldn't sit still with it churning there.

She stood from the bath abruptly, stepping out of the cool water and summoning Sofia with a call. As she walked back into her bedroom and saw the gown she'd discarded at her father's command, that anger flared in her chest once again, feeling too good to ignore.

Her mind was set: she would travel to Centerton's festival tonight, regardless of what her father said.

A ripple of unease washed over her at the decision. She had never truly gone against her father before, and grew queasy at the thought of how he might punish blatant defiance, when he grew so angry at accidental disobedience. He had only once tolerated dissent from his decisions, back when she was a child and his love for her had not yet fully warped into a need to control. It was when she'd told him not to discharge Gabriel from his duty as her guard. He'd relented, but he'd also dismissed half of the household staff in his anger. Her father may have forgiven her, but the Duke did not.

Sada pushed the thought from her mind. She needed to leave room in it for planning.

She would have to go alone, of course. She balked at the thought, and her teeth instinctively found her lip, gnawing at it fervently. She knew her way to Centerton well; she had traveled there nearly every day of summer for almost the entirety of her youth. But without Gabriel, John, or another guard to accompany her, she would be left unprotected from all the bears and wild things of the forest. She briefly thought of her uncle and the belt of knives that was permanently attached to his hip, but he was too loyal to her father to disobey him—as were all the guards and servants. It would also be impossible to sneak one of her horses from the stable without the hands running to tell Father her whereabouts. Sourly, she realized she would also have to make the trek on foot.

The sun had already slunk most of the way below the tree line, and the skies were growing darker with each hour. Soon her father would summon her to leave for Desdale. The thought sparked a jolt of fear in her, and she listened for his footsteps on the pine. But all she heard was the gentle murmuring of servants. Sada blew out a deep breath and, after applying her powder to her birthmarks, summoned her lady's maid once more. She would have to leave within the hour.

Hastily, she had Sofia choose her an evening gown. The maid returned with one of her posher dresses, made of the finest southern silk (of course) with sleeves that hung off her shoulders and embroidery of shimmering thread. Father would be expecting her to dress fashionably for any trip off of the property, but certainly for a visit to a large city such as Desdale. Sada was content with this, as she was inclined to look lovely on any occasion that she had an excuse to, especially for a festival. Her dress would not raise suspicion.

The ladies in Ettedon had begun wearing a more modern style of dress, with a loose waistline and transparent fabric that showed some of the shift beneath. This was a bit too scandalous for Sada. She instead opted for a tailored blend of this new modern style with one she found to be more agreeable.

She slid on a comfortable linen shift and silk stockings, then Sofia helped her into one of her favored corsets and tightened it to fit her waist. At court, the ladies of rank preferred a very stiff and very tight corset to make their waists appear almost nonexistent. Sada's father, however, believed that exaggerating her waist too greatly with a tightly-cinched stay was a disgrace to her natural beauty. This was of no matter to Sada; her softer corsets of preference were much more comfortable.

Once this one was done up to her liking, she donned a plain white petticoat. She considered tying on her pockets but decided that would be unnecessary. She also skipped the hip pads, preferring to let her gowns fall naturally. The one Sofia had chosen was made of beautiful, vibrant silk with the scandalously deep neckline of an evening gown, and fell just above her ankles. It was tightened in the back to fit to her waist, something the women of Ettedon had moved away from, but Sada still preferred.

Then she slid into her slippers, realized they would not do for walking through the woods, and switched to her riding boots. Finally, she buckled the long cloak Jezebel had given her around her shoulders for good measure, noting how the clasp matched her friend's cuff, still secure on her ear. Soon it would be returned. With this in mind to still her nerves, she sat down to have her hair done.

She felt as high-strung as a colt, trying to sit still as Sofia twisted and pinned her hair, and took down the curlers which had been placed in the front parts of her hair and heated. This time she put half of it up in an elegant and elaborate bun and left the rest loose to show she was unmarried. Sada jumped fully out of her seat in front of the vanity when one of the housemaids knocked on the door, thinking it was the Duke. When Rachel slipped in to inform Sada it was nearly time to depart, she had to stoop to help Sofia pick up the pearls which had slipped off the string she was wrapping around Sada's updo.

Sofia believed they were truly going to Desdale, and perhaps that Sada would continue her search for a fiancé while there, and so she dressed and pampered Sada as such. Golden clips in the shapes of butterfly wings were placed near her ears, and she was bedecked in matching jewelry on her neck, wrists, ears, and head.

As her lady's maid finished readying her, she realized she had nothing to take with her on her journey into Centerton. Though it was only half of an hour away walking, she felt bare with nothing to carry in her hands. She would have preferred a clutch, but a glance out one of her windows revealed the darkening sky. There was no time to gather things to bring. She didn't need them for anything other than comfort, anyway, and that was not high on her list of priorities now.

The cloak had one inner pocket, however, just large enough to fit an apple or a good-sized peach. But she had something far more important to bring. She slipped the vial of her powder into the pocket and fastened it. She would take no chances in having her marks revealed. The vial resting beside her heart provided all the comfort she'd needed, it seemed. With a shaky breath, she pulled her cloak closed over her chest and slipped out of her room.

The manor was filled with noise from the servants still adjusting to her father's arrival, no doubt running ragged trying to fix every imperfection he noticed. The cooks were loud, too, the sounds of their shouts and banging pots floating up from the kitchen in the basement. Sada listened for her father's resounding voice through the cacophony and found it as she crept down an open hallway that ran above the foyer. Uncle Beron and her father were below her based on the sounds she heard, though she couldn't see either of the men. She just prayed that they wouldn't see her either as she flitted down the hallway and to the staircase leading to the foyer.

As she crept down the wide steps, the voices of her uncle and father grew clearer. They were talking about a message the Duke had received while in Asrich.

"It must have been urgent indeed to have caused you an early departure," Beron mused.

"The impending death of a city lord is certainly considered urgent…politically, if not otherwise. It is curious how a ducal title alters one's perceptions of importance and urgency." Her father laughed, cold and loud.

"You speak of the Lord of Desdale, then. I had wondered when Judas would finally gift us with his departure from this world."

"He is old, and now failing. The physicians do not expect him to see the dawn. I will arrive tonight so as to be present in the morning, when that fickle heir of his will swear me his oaths and fealties. And God help him if he tries to talk his way out of it."

"I should like to see him try. Prince Aaron will accompany you?"

"He will stand in representation of the crown—and it is time he learned how swiftly loyalties can shift."

Beron grunted. "It is well that you will be present at the time of Judas's passing for more than ceremony. We both know how…fiddly…these successions can be, and Desdale breeds spirited men. No doubt one of them will try to make a claim on the title."

"Precisely," the Duke said. "I will see that no unfounded ambition finds steel to support it."

"I presume this is why you're bringing the girl," Beron said.

Sada felt her palms prickle and her heart flutter at the mention of her.

The Duke said nothing for a moment, then, "It will be wiser to have her within my sight than beyond it."

"A prudent choice," Beron agreed. "One never knows how far the spark from a battle for succession will float. Once one man gets a taste for power, so does his neighbor. When one city takes up arms…"

Sada made it to the bottom of the staircase, now filled with double her original panic. But as she reached the last step, she quickly halted, frozen in her tracks. Her father had rounded the corner and his gaze was on her now, as was Beron's. Both sets of too-sharp eyes drilled into her, and she opened her mouth to blurt some excuse, any excuse.

Before she could say anything, her father scowled.

"From whence do you procure these most unsuitable gowns?" he asked, his lip curling into his mustache. He must not have remembered it was a gown he'd picked himself. Or perhaps he did; he knew it would not matter either way. "Go and change. *Again.* And make haste, we depart shortly."

He must have been in a good mood, for he left it at that.

Sada's mouth nearly gaped at his words. Of course he had no idea she had been actively sneaking out, actively defying him, when he found her on the stairs. Her lack of traveling supplies kept her intentions hidden. She tried not to let her relief show on her face.

"Of course, Father." For once, she was delighted to hear his insulting disapproval. She turned, grinning.

"And change those filthy boots!"

Sada called her acquiescence and scampered back up the staircase before they could pass her. Back in her room and safely away from her father, she let out a laugh of relief. She had not been caught. But should she reconsider her plan to sneak away? She now knew their trip to Desdale was not just leisure. Not only that, but her heart was still racing from the encounter with her father, and she hadn't even been caught. She couldn't imagine how terrifying it would be if she truly was discovered in her schemes. But she recalled how he had yet to tell her he missed her, or hug her, or even properly say hello since he'd arrived back from his trip, and Sada decided that she had no reason to stay and listen. She was not needed to ensure a smooth succession for Desdale's lord. Her only role as a duke's daughter was to marry well, and Lord Judas's son did not quite fit that criteria.

It's final, then. I'm still going to the festival.

The decision made her ecstatic. *Her* decision made her ecstatic. It was a strange feeling, deciding something for herself when her entire life had revolved around obeying orders. And despite the giddiness, it felt inherently wrong, like petting a dog's fur against the grain or taking a little kid's candy.

Have your desires become more important than my orders in my absence? Her father's voice would not be dismissed from her mind. She heard that sentence repeated with every hurried breath she took.

"Just this once, Father, yes they have," she breathed. Saying it aloud felt not dissimilar to disobeying the laws of the king himself, but she somehow found that it brought a great grin to her face.

Resolute once again, Sada silently slipped out of her room. This time as she snuck down the hallway, she made her way toward the back entrance of the house. There were two staircases in the manor, both leading from the second floor to the first (or the first to the second, depending on where you stood) and on opposite ends of the house. The first she'd taken had descended into the foyer. The second let out near the upper kitchens and receiving room. She took this one now. Not only did it allow her to avoid another encounter with her father, but she had also realized that sentries would be lining every entrance to the manor out front. If she slipped out through the back, she could go past the stables and into the forest where a few small paths would feed into the trail to Centerton.

Sada made it out of the house without seeing her father or her uncle, and she stopped for a moment outside, bursting with pride. The night was cool, but she didn't feel like hiding from it. She threw open her cloak, grinning in the face of the wind, in the face of freedom. She only relished in her successful escape for a moment before the scent of lemon sent her hurrying down the sloping lawn and toward the stables.

The citrus trees waved goodbye with their thorny arms. They would know her skin well before the night was over, but for now she bid them goodbye. As she neared the lone-standing wooden building of the stable, she kept to the outskirts of the estate to avoid the eyes of the stableboys, hugging the winding garden paths that led to the edges of the property. Most of the sun's light had abandoned her by the time she reached the forest. The same forest that had beckoned to her so strongly just the day before.

Sada glanced back at the manor, searching once more for any signs that her father had noticed her escape. But there were no panicked shouts, and no guards came running across the lawn to retrieve her, so she slipped into the forest. As she turned, she thought she saw the Duke's silhouette in one of the large windows facing the yard, but she didn't allow herself to turn and look again. Sada started down one of the small dirt trails that would bring her to the festival at Centerton.

The trail led deep into the forest before it ever began leading toward Centerton, and Sada had begun to worry that perhaps she had chosen the wrong path when it abruptly curved to the side at an angle she believed led toward the town. However, her sense of direction could not be trusted. When traveling by carriage or palanquin as she did, you only had to stare blissfully at the sights to be seen with no mind of how you were getting to your destination. And so she only had a general idea of how to get from her manor to the town. Thankfully the route was straightforward, but she didn't fully trust herself not to somehow veer off the main trail and end up taking a side route that led her from the safe southern forest into the forbidden eastern woods.

As she stared into the trees, she recalled the feeling the forest had summoned in her the night before, how cold yet hot it had been, and how badly she had wanted to go into it. Briefly, she wondered if her mother was somewhere in there. Perhaps her disappearance had been something else entirely: an escape from Duke Darius.

If that was so, she found herself pitying her mother in a way that only someone who'd experienced the same circumstances could. But before she banished those traitorous thoughts, that was the extent of the emotion she felt toward the forest and what it housed. She felt no longing for its shadowy depths now, and the air around her brought only a mild chill, the brunt of which her cloak kept away. If she kept going north and didn't veer too far east, she should remain safe from those odd sensations and any other dangers.

She was fairly certain she was going north still.

It was made harder to discern her direction with how dark it was this deep inside the pines; though the sun hadn't sunk all the way below the horizon yet, no light made it through the ceiling of emerald needles. Sada was traveling in near-dark. She should have brought a lantern, she knew, but there was no point in dwelling on it when she could not procure one now. Being without light made her all the more thankful that she had chosen a dress with a short hem; she was too focused on keeping herself from tripping to have bothered worrying about whether a longer one was dragging in the mud. She was focusing particularly hard on keeping herself upright in a pock-holed part of the trail when she heard a noise that did not belong in the forest: the *clink* of metal on metal.

Fear flooded through her, cold and quick. It froze her feet to the dirt. It paralyzed her lungs. When she'd finished counting her heartbeats, thumb pressed into her wrist,

(1, 2, 3)

the source of the sounds could be heard shouting her name. Gabriel and John were doing the calling, but by the sheer number of feet and horseshoes that could be heard colliding with the forest floor, she estimated they had brought with them at least one full squadron of Solares soldiers.

I should wait here and let them find me. Father will be less angry if I go with them and act abashed. What possessed me? I don't belong in the for—

Sada ran, leaving her thoughts behind her. The air was cold and sharp in her lungs, and the rocky terrain hurt her ankles and caused her to stumble more often than not. She didn't think she had truly run since she was a child, and she felt the strain immediately, in the aching of her chest, the pain in her legs, and the dryness of her mouth. She pushed on, swallowing a click in her throat. The horses seemed to have overtaken John and Gabriel, for their shouts fell away and were replaced by rage-filled hoofbeats.

Suddenly a sharp shout sent a new chill across her skin.

"Lady Sada Solares! Return this instant, by the command of your father the Duke."

"Oh no oh no oh no—" Her words were lost in her gasps for breath.

She pushed herself to run faster, but she was only slowing. The light from their lanterns was illuminating the path ahead of her now. She could see her own shadow showing her the way.

"Lady Sada, what are you doing, girl?" That was Sir Caleb Oller, with the accent. He was shouting to be heard over the hoofbeats, but he was close, nearly on her ankles. "Cease this foolishness, allow us to 'elp you! You are aware of how His Grace will react if you continue on in this madness."

"I cannot!" she cried. "You don't understand!"

They would have her soon, and they would return her to the Duke and the pain from the switches would be her closest company for days to come. The brown muzzle of Caleb's gelding drew into view beside her. A single second longer and he would either reach down and sweep her up onto the horse by her cloak or cut her off so that she couldn't continue forward. She veered suddenly off the path.

She didn't realize she was now fleeing east.

The feeling that had overcome her the night before returned to her. It came first as a tickling sensation deep within her belly. Then the cold followed, alternating between a deep chill and the sting of heat. And now the forest was silent; the sounds of the horses had halted abruptly, but she knew Sir Caleb and the others would be dismounting to find her on foot. She could see little of the forest floor anymore with the shadows growing thicker and longer. Roots lined the narrow gaps between the trees and panes of black stretched across them, shifting beneath her feet.

The moon was absent, all sounds belonging to a forest had ceased, and it only smelled of cold. She was no doubt soon to be seized by her father's guards or lost in the woods. But despite her circumstances, Sada was suddenly no longer afraid.

She just wanted *more.*

The air felt thicker here, slower. *No need to make haste,* it told her. *Enjoy this, as I enjoy you.* She slowed to a stumbling trot, then stopped and fell to her knees, gasping for breath. The coldness of the air cooled her skin while the heat warmed her throat and lungs. Unfortunately, she couldn't stay still long. Caleb and his accompanying squadron were approaching quickly, one of them grumbling about not being paid enough for such a task. Another snapped at him to stuff a yam in it and hurry. Sada got to her feet. As she jogged, she found that there was a small path bare of any roots or shrubbery that seemed to reveal itself with each step she took. Yet she couldn't stop herself from looking into the trees beside her.

Something was deep inside the forest, and it wanted her.

And she wanted it.

She could feel her footsteps begin to slow again. It was subtle, but she noticed the way she'd stopped focusing on the self-revealing trail ahead of her, and instead focused on the forest around her. She forced herself to look forward again whenever she noticed, or made herself focus on each step she took, but she always caught herself staring into those shadowy depths again.

The forest seemed to pulse, breathing that heat onto her with each beat. Finally, she couldn't resist it any longer and turned to veer toward its pull, to run deeper into the forest as quickly as she could and find whatever was calling out to her.

She hadn't noticed the lone soldier sneaking up to her. When his hand clamped down onto her shoulder, she yelped and jumped like a jack rabbit.

"I think you'd ought to come with me, leetle lady," Sir Caleb growled in that melodic accent of his. Sada made to dash away again, but his gauntleted hand tightened around her arm. "Ah, ah, none of dat now. Duke Solares will be cross enough as ees, best we 'urry back to ease his temper, wouldn't you say?"

Sullenly, Sada nodded. She had come so far! Was she to be stopped this deep into her journey? Stolen away from her freedom so quickly? She looked dully into the forest, hoping to feel another stir of icy heat. The trees were still and silent.

You called me here, she thought, suddenly angry. *Will you offer me no aid now?*

The forest didn't respond, but a clamor of voices could suddenly be heard. The knights were no doubt annoyed at her antics. Yet she realized with a frown that the voices were unfamiliar: one scratchy but bright, the other dull and deep.

They must be those young squires training under David and Levi...But where are *they?* The voices didn't seem to come from any particular direction. She strained to see ahead, moving up beside Sir Caleb.

Suddenly a flash of color appeared in the corner of her eye and Sada whipped her head around to see what it was. As she did, the colorful thing barreled into her, and she was thrown onto the ground. She heard Caleb grunt in surprise and felt an abrupt heat in her arm where it had been torn from the knight's grasp. The lantern he held swung wildly as he lunged toward her.

There was a bright flash of something purple and blinding, and when it disappeared, Sada was left blind.

THE FIFTH

Sada

Bright pain was hammered into her back and the right side of her body as she hit the ground, and breath once again evaded her. This time the feeling lasted much longer than the span of three heartbeats, though she was in no shape to count. She felt it was a miracle her heart was still beating. It wasn't the pain that was so overwhelming, but the disorientation, as though someone had seized her skull and turned it on its axis. Once she was able to take an aching breath, Sada used it to groan at the throbbing in her skin and muscles.

She then opened her eyes and groaned again at the brightness that met them. It seemed that amidst the pain, her vision had returned.

Regardless of whatever else ails me, at least I am not dead, and at least I am not blind. She knew the former was true because there could be no pain in heaven, and she knew the latter was true because she was looking at something orange. She stared at freshly fallen leaves as big as her face and colorful clumps of moss and realized, still disoriented, that she was lying on her stomach. Her back was hot, probably from the fall, and her front was damp and cool.

My dress! she thought briefly, but she couldn't summon the strength or the will to stand. She reasoned that a little bit of mud wouldn't hurt her. Not any more than that fall had.

"Oh delightful. *Now* look at what thou have gone and done!" a man's voice exclaimed above Sada.

"Hey." It was a dull, deep voice that answered. "At least we're back home."

"Oh *jiie, home,"* the first, sharper voice scoffed. "Most would beg to differ on that account. Truly, I envy thee's ability to forget such."

The voices sounded vaguely familiar, and she thought it might be the men she'd heard talking after Sir Caleb had grabbed her, the ones she thought to be squires. Where *was* Sir Caleb? Had she been left alone with squires? Why had they not returned her to the manor yet?

She blinked, hard, and tried to push herself up, but a wave of dizziness overcame her and she lowered herself to the ground again. It smelled warm. The usual scent of decaying leaves and bugs found in forests was absent, however, and it made some subconscious part of Sada's mind uneasy. All she smelled was moss and the sweetness of sun-warmed bark.

"Thou fancied stayin' in the mortal world? Fine, let's head back then," said the Dull One.

"We cannot, that is precisely my argument," the first snapped. "We ought to have remained. It would have been to everyone's benefit."

"Well, if it eases thou's mind any, 'twasn't my doin' that brought us back, neither."

Sada took a deep breath and managed to push herself to her feet. Pressure immediately pounded in her head, and her view of the forest was abruptly accompanied by pulses of black and grey blobs in her vision. She ignored it, focusing on the two men in front of her, one tall and the other short.

Swaying with nothing to hold onto, she managed to say, "Pardon me," and then she was on the ground again. This time her vision went out completely for a few seconds as she fell nose-deep into moss.

"What in the—*Kindreds' kids,* thee've brought a human with us!" exclaimed the first, angry man.

Sada was rolled over before she could say anything more. Hard roots pressed into her back, and she found herself blinking hazily up at the men. The short one was bent over her, hand still on her arm. Shaggy brown hair to match acorn eyes fell into his face. His features were sharp, but not unkind. She briefly thought he could be Sir Caleb's son, then realized that would be impossible: they probably could count the same number of years. Brothers, then.

"Don't be dull," said the Dull One himself. The man above her was only staring, eyebrows furrowed, and she assumed the speaker to be the taller one behind him. "Humans are supposed to be ugly, aren't they? She's probably Fae. I'd swear it and set my ace on it—they're always where they shouldn't be."

"You still don't know what an ace is," Acorn-Eyes snapped from above her. "Nor what human maidens look like; you were hardly off the milk when we were brought here."

"Well I know, that's why I'm asking thee for."

"It's rude to talk about people like they aren't here," he said, then squinted his acorn eyes. "But look at her ears. Round. Too round to be Fae, or anything but human. Pardon our brashness," he then said to Sada.

She wondered if she looked as confused as she felt. What did they want with her ears? She couldn't help but reach up to feel them. They felt normal to her, but Acorn-Eyes was staring at her as though she were the greatest anomaly to exist. And why wouldn't she be human?

"Alright," the Dull One finally said.

Acorn-Eyes shifted to his knees, peering down.

"Um, hello," Sada said, pulling away from his sudden nearness.

"Are you well?" His bright brown eyes narrowed in a frown at her, and she searched them for anything they might tell her. They looked unfamiliar, so her assumption from earlier must have been correct: he was one of the new squires. He was quite old for squiring, but so far it seemed that everything about him was odd. What was all this talk of humans and *Fae?* Perhaps she truly was still unconscious. She certainly felt woozy enough to be. And you could feel pain in dreams, couldn't you?

Suddenly the man's eyes widened, and he leaned back.

"Void be dark, you might have the right of it," he said breathlessly. He beckoned the bigger man to join him. He did, crouching down with a pop of his knees. Sada couldn't help her flinch. "Look at her eyes—those markings. I've only heard tell of them once before, and that tale spoke of no mortal."

Suddenly her stomach dropped, and her lungs tightened. She didn't bother counting her heartbeats as she snapped up to sitting, her hands flying to her cloak, groping and searching frantically.

Where is it, where is it, where is it? Her thoughts were jumbled with panic, but only one goal was on her mind, and that was clear: find the powder. Her hand finally closed on the pocket, and she unfastened it with shaking hands. She pulled the little vial out, popped its stopper off, pressed her finger to the narrow opening, and overturned it. Her finger came away covered in a thick swatch of powder. She immediately pressed it into the corners of her eyes, then added a second layer for good measure. Then a third for *very* good measure. How had her birthmarks become revealed again? *Twice within one week*...the thought made her throat clench. Finally covered again, she leaned back breathlessly against the tree behind her, still clutching her vial.

She counted her heartbeats, taking in a shaky breath.

What had they asked her? Oh— "I'm well, and I thank you for your concern, sir," she said, eyes closed. "I'm just dandy, so very dandy."

"Huh?" Acorn-Eyes asked. "What in the Void was that, lady?"

She just shook her head and managed a weak smile. "I hope you'll forgive me, but it's a private matter. And I ask that you speak of it to nobody. I'm sure Sir John or Sir Gabriel will inform you of it when your squiring is complete. Just don't tell my father of what just transpired, or you may not be here to see that day." She giggled somewhat deliriously.

She thought she'd managed to say her explanation politely enough through her fright, but both the men were staring at her with confusion.

As she looked, she realized that these men were no knights at all, not even squires. Both were dressed not in emerald-trimmed armor, not in clean common clothes, but dirty, ripped cloth. Dirt was even smeared across their faces. They had no weapons either. In fact, Acorn-Eyes carried no possessions, and the bigger man carried only his satchel, one hand hovering protectively over it. He was sweating like a thief in church, and briefly she wondered if she had been abducted and he'd made a mad dash through the forest with Sada slung over his shoulder while she was unconscious…But his dull eyes were kind, and eyes never lied to her.

Still, fear prickled in her stomach and her palms. She dug her teeth into her lip.

"Well…I'm glad that thou art alright." The acorn-eyed man folded his lips in so that his mouth made a straight line. Sada realized he was smiling, and she managed to do the same.

Who are these people? she was screaming within the safety of her own mind. *Where are Sir Caleb and John and Gabriel, where am I, how did I come to be here? Oh, Father will be so mad!* The thought of the citrus trees and their switches was so overwhelming that she could almost smell lemon. Quickly, she looked around for Gabriel, scanning the forest for his familiar armor or light hair. Sada's throat tightened as she realized he wasn't with her. Nobody was with her. Just these two strange men talking about strange things.

"Pardon my discourtesy," Sada managed to whisper, "but might I ask who you are?"

Acorn-Eyes glanced at his tall counterpart, who was watching her with his head cocked like a big dog.

"We're brothers," Acorn-Eyes said. He stood, brushing off the hole-flecked knees of his trousers. "Simply returning home from our travels."

The taller brother, who looked as though he'd stolen all the height in the family as well as the love for food, bobbed his sweaty head at her. "Good to meet you," he said in a dull voice. "I'm Dra—"

Acorn-Eyes elbowed him in the arm with a sharp glare. "This is Samuel and I'm Joseph," he said, still glaring up at his brother.

Dull One rolled his eyes. "Those aren't our names."

Acorn-Eyes flinched like he'd been hit. "Yes they are…"

"Well, I suppose they used to be," Dull One relented. He turned to Sada to explain. "They're our human names, but nobody calls us that anymore. I'm Drath, and this here is Karti. He's a bit of a jerk, but he's not so bad."

Acorn-Eyes groaned, smacking a palm to his forehead. "Karti*nar,*" he corrected. Softer he said, "Void, Drath, why don't you let me do the talkin' and stop saying what's best left unsaid."

Drath looked as though he wanted to slap his brother upside the head. He gestured at Sada with a thick hand. "What is a—possibly—human woman going to do with our names? *Use* them for Kindreds' sakes?"

"*Yes, precisely.* Should she mention our names to the wrong people…" But now Kartinar looked uncertain.

Drath was chuckling, a comforting sound. "Oh no, we shall suffer horrible deaths now, Karti. I'd forgotten that our names were renown throughout Elt. Surely the knowledge will be used against us. Can thou ever forgive me?"

Kartinar just elbowed him again, but said no more. After Drath adjusted the satchel he wore across his body, he knelt down to her level (she was still sitting on the ground, *oh dear*—what would Father say?), took Sada's hand, grasped it firmly, and moved it up and down. She realized with amazement that he was shaking her hand, as though she were a man!

Drath grinned, misreading her shock as being impressed. "Karti says that this is how you greet each other in the human world. He taught the whole clan when he was little. Right, Karti?"

Kartinar just did his tight-lipped smile again and nodded curtly.

"I must admit I still do not understand what exactly is happening, but we are well met, friends," Sada said. "I am Lady Sada Solares, first daughter of Duke Darius Solares of Altamira."

Drath said something about how that was a cursedly long title to remember, and Sada agreed with a laugh, telling him to imagine how she must feel having to recite it all on the weekly.

When Drath moved back to return to arguing with his brother, Sada stood hurriedly, stepping on her hems which were now brown with mud. Darkness pulsed in her vision once more and almost overtook it, but she fixed her eyes on the leaf of a bush and blinked rapidly until it was gone. As the blackness receded, she realized with sudden panic that it was daytime. When Sir Caleb had found her, the moon was just beginning to rise.

"Skies above," Sada breathed, bracing herself against the smooth trunk behind her. "Was I fainted for the entire night?" Then a new horror washed over her. "I'll have missed the festival!"

"You didn't faint at all," Drath said. "At least, not that I could tell."

"She did," Kartinar corrected, then looked to her. "You may have lost consciousness for a few moments, but certainly not an entire night."

The two brothers glanced at each other uneasily.

But Sada wasn't looking at them anymore; she was looking at the trees, spinning as she took in everything around her. The forest had changed in their midst. In the miraculously pink light that streamed down in beams, she saw the woods had *grown*. Tree trunks that had once been as wide as her were now too large for even fifteen men to wrap their arms around, and the rough bark of pine had been replaced by bark which was as smooth as an aspen's, but rich brown in color. Those trunks led up high in the sky—so high that she had to crane her neck all the way back to see—to a ceiling of great, drooping leaves of orange and yellow and brown rather than boughs of pine needles. Some of the leaves looked like hands.

Beyond the forest's new appearance, the cold had disappeared, the spring chill replaced by a warming breeze. It was all accompanied by a vibrancy obvious to each of the five senses that had not been present when the guards had found her. The sounds of singing animals filled her ears, and the wet scent of autumn was all around, though there was also the smell of spice, as though she was standing not in a forest but in a kitchen where someone had just been baking, perhaps pumpkin bread or hot cross buns. And amidst the sounds of nature, a soft, distant, tune could be heard beneath it all. It was either a lyre or a harp, or both, but Sada couldn't discern which. It was quiet enough that it couldn't be heard over the sound of their talking, but in silence it seemed to fill the air. It was the most beautiful place Sada had ever seen, smelled, heard, or anything, really.

And also one she had never laid eyes upon before.

"What's happened to the forest?" she asked, almost to herself.

Behind her, the two brothers just shared a look. They began muttering to each other and Sada snapped around to face them. Their hushed conversation cut off abruptly, then Kartinar took a step toward her. Sada backed into the tree behind her, clinging to its too-smooth trunk.

"I'm not sure how to tell you this," he began, his acorn eyes scanning her panicked face. But then he stopped suddenly, and his face went slack.

Abruptly, his eyes darted to the trees behind her, and he straightened and held a hand to his lips: *Shhh.* For a moment, Sada strained to see or hear whatever it was he was focused on. Everything had gone quiet and still, save for the sounds of music. She thought she heard the bodiless music grow louder, harsher, the notes now disjointed.

Everywhere else around them, the forest was peaceful. The pink light still drifted down to the leaf-scattered floor in beams, playing with the shadows amongst the trees. The trees seemed to be moving in the light, swaying with the wind and the sunlight and the music of the forest. One of the trees really did move, then. A chestnut piece of it peeled away from the trunk, creeping forward in a shadow. Then another tree separated from the forest. From the corner of her eye, Sada saw another move, from the opposite side, and they advanced toward her and the brothers.

Kartinar swore. "Cursed sharp-ears. Always appearing when they're most unwanted."

"What's happening? Do these trees typically grow legs?" Sada asked, but the brothers just scowled into the forest and at the figures moving through it.

At her side, Drath tightened his grip on his satchel. She didn't miss how he stepped in front of her the way Gabe and John had done so many times before, usually when visiting the city and one of the commonfolk became unruly. Her palms began to prickle with her growing unease.

The figures had broken away from the shadows of the forest now, revealing themselves to be tall, bare-chested men. Each had a longbow either as tall or taller than himself. They wore them slung across their chests or grasped in their hands. Matching quivers were strapped to their hips or backs. Even as they neared, it was still difficult to see them amidst the forest; their rich brown skin was the color of the trunks around them, and the men melted into the trees they stood by.

She saw their mouths move, but only strange sounds came out. There were many rolling R's, and constant rises and falls. It sounded to her the way walking up and down a succession of small hills might feel, but there was an overall flowing quality to it. It was a language, but one she could not understand.

Then someone said, "Known Tongue?" amidst the rest of it all, and suddenly she understood them.

"Why, look at what we have chanced upon," a voice like honeyed tea said from somewhere among the group.

"I had believed to have smelled mortals," another of the men said.

"There can be no doubt—their odor surpasses even that of the elk."

"*Néos.* The elk are clean creatures; this is hardly a remarkable achievement. As for cave trolls, though…"

Their laughter was painfully musical. Sada had been laughed at before—many times before. Each time was painful. It hurt to be brayed at by men, and hurt worse to be laughed at by other noble ladies, with their dainty giggles and pointing gloved fingers. But she was certain that this would surpass even humiliation by the king. These men were more elegant than the highest lords at court, and their laughter said one thing: we are better than you, and both you and we know it.

"Viie," another was agreeing. "The stench of mortals is more powerful even than that of a Beast."

Sada's throat tightened. Once, in Ettedon, she had begged Gabriel and John to take her to the markets outside of the town square. They had tried to dissuade her, saying it was dangerous for a lady to be around needy folk, but she'd insisted. When they went, she was astonished to see the animal dung and mud caking the streets, and the sheer number of citizens curled up on the cobblestone with only a torn blanket to their name and sometimes less. But the discovery of the poor was not the greatest shock she had. As they were leaving a stand selling little straw dolls, a ragged-looking man had grabbed her skirts and put his mud and grease-covered face in hers. He had sneered at her and screeched horrible obscenities, and demanded to know when the queen was coming to marry them.

And then Gabriel was there, pulling her away, and John was hitting the man over the head with the butt of his sword. Later, Governess Brown had told her that the man was a person called a lunatic, one who had probably escaped from jail or the ward, which was a prison for the insane—those who had lost touch with reality.

Upon hearing these men speak about mortals as though it wasn't a term to describe themselves, Sada thought them to be insane people and in need of serious help. But then they drew closer, and the sight of them made her begin to doubt herself. Not on the subject of their insanity, but of their humanity; their mortality.

They had stepped out of the underbrush and were gradually closing in on Sada and the brothers. The tall, strangely elegant men moved in slow, tightening circles around them. Gleaming eyes reminiscent of a wolf's examined them from every angle as the men closed in to form a ring around them. As they settled into their motionless positions, Sada realized just how incredibly tall they were. Even the shortest among their ranks stood eye-level with Drath, who was taller than any man she'd seen before, and the sight of them made her shiver.

They also appeared to have flawless features. Each was muscular as a horse, despite possessing the stealth of a cat. They didn't try to hide it, either. Her eyes trailed up from the bare chests to chiseled faces with strong, straight noses, high cheekbones, and bright almond-shaped eyes. Their features were lupine in their beauty, their gazes assessing and wolf-like. Each had their long hair done in countless braids, hair which was of autumn hues—orange, red, dark blonde, brunette. Some of the hairdos were simple, others were unbelievably intricate, but all were elegant and would draw envy at court were they worn by a woman.

They were the strangest people Sada had ever seen, and yet the most beautiful as well. But despite the otherworldly beauty (or maybe because of it), Sada's palms prickled as the tallest of the group stepped out from the circle and sauntered silently toward them. A crown of gold with gilded antlers extending from it sat jauntily upon his auburn head.

As the king neared, the fallen leaves didn't make a noise beneath his bare feet.

He stopped in front of Sada and the brothers and slid the long chestnut arrow he'd been holding into the quiver strapped across his back. His longbow, gleaming and freshly oiled, swung gracefully to his side. Sada quailed as she realized it meant her small group posed no threat to the men of the forest. Sada found herself wishing desperately for Gabriel, John, or even a squire. But she knew it was in vain…she had no protectors in this strange forest.

"Humans," the tall king in front of her said, and sniffed audibly. "What business do you have within my Wood? Within Elt?" As he glared down at them, Sada saw with a jolt that his eyes were a brilliant orange, like marigolds set aflame. She tried to stifle the small gasp she let out, but his attention fell on her nonetheless and she froze under his fiery gaze.

Eyes were not supposed to be orange.

"We were traveling from the west and happened onto the wrong trail. Such are the troubles of map-reading," Kartinar said with a chuckle. It didn't hide the strain in his voice. "We were merely gathering our bearings before heading back the way we came. Might you be so gracious as to allow us to leave the way we entered, good king?"

The three of them were as still as the men stationed around them as they waited for the king to speak. He tilted his head as he examined them in silence. Every movement he made was graceful and flowing and animal-like. It made Sada feel as though she were a blundering cow rather than a lady of rank trained in the ways of court. But more than that, it made her all the more fearful, and much less certain of his humanity. Perhaps *she* was the one who was insane.

"Do you know where it is that you are?" the king finally said.

Sada felt the familiar prickle of worry in her forehead at his question. Not because of what he asked, but because she had learned that men who responded to you as though you'd never spoken were incredibly dangerous. There were always many wrong answers to their question, and only one right answer, if that. Not knowing it usually meant an unfavorable outcome. The image of her father's cold eyes flashed in her mind, but she found herself wishing that even he could be there to protect her.

Her teeth dug into her lip. She welcomed the pain.

"Yes, we are aware," Kartinar responded.

"You are the delegate, then. Pray tell, how is it that you have arrived in these lands?"

The brothers met each other's eyes for a moment before Kartinar hesitantly said, "We…live here. I know it seems unbelievable, but I assure thee, we do."

The men encircling them chuckled, the first sound they'd made since they'd settled into their guarding positions. The king was not amused. He examined them with fiery eyes, fingering the strap of his quiver. The brothers eyed his motions warily.

"If you know *where* you are, then it should follow that you also know *who we* are. And with that knowledge, then you ought to recognize that *we are not fools,"* he spat. "Tell me how you have come to my lands."

Sada quivered at the malice in his voice, and she noticed Kartinar had curled his hands into shaking fists beside her. But he said calmly, "I understand it may seem incredulous, good king, yet it is indeed the truth. My brother and I were not born within this realm, but it is here that we were raised. Now we wish only to return to our home at the Border."

"It's the truth," Drath jumped in. "We always get this reaction when we tell people we were raised by a Trell woman, but—"

He was cut off as the orange-eyed king reached down and snapped the string of his bow. An ear-splitting crack sounded throughout the forest, disrupting the unnatural silence. Not even the music could be heard above it.

"You dare to deceive me, not once, but *twice?"* the king hissed, hand tightening on his bow. The men encircling them glared.

"We have proof!" Drath said hurriedly, then hastily added, "good king."

She heard Kartinar hiss "*Quiet,*" but Drath just shot him a glance.

"We have proof that we're from Elt," he said to the king.

Those orange eyes flashed at that last word, and Sada briefly wondered where Elt was, and how far from home she'd managed to travel. She had walked for less than half an hour, and there were no cities that she knew of in such a range of Centerton. Let alone one named Elt.

"I await your procurement of evidence," the king said tightly.

Drath gave his brother an apologetic glance then unlatched his satchel. As he undid the buckles, brilliant violet light began leaking out of the bag, and when he reached his great hand into it, he pulled out what seemed to be the very essence of purple. It glowed brightly enough to illuminate the entire forest, and Drath's huge frame disappeared into its unearthly radiance. And as impossible as its existence was, despite the fact that nothing like it existed in Sada's world, it was familiar.

Just after Sir Caleb had found her and just before she'd fallen, she had heard two voices—ones she now knew belonged to Drath and Kartinar—and she had seen a flash of light. It was the same color as the light before her now. The brilliance of it was so intense that tears began to leak down her cheeks; it was no wonder that the first time she'd seen it, she'd thought herself blind once it was gone. Even the predatorily-still strangers encircling them flinched against the light. Sada could hardly see the king in front of them, but his voice rang out easily throughout the woods:

"Stow that away at once!" he commanded, and something in his voice made Drath instantly shove it back into his satchel. As soon as the beaming purple was contained, the men shifted into the offensive.

The king let out a shrill whistle and the strangers surrounding them leapt into motion. In just a few strides, they reached Sada and the two brothers. The absence of the light left black and yellow blotches filling her vision, and she cried out as the strangers were suddenly on her. She reached out immediately for Kartinar and Drath, forgetting they were not her guards. Both of the brothers held onto her nonetheless, moving her in between them so she was shielded from their attackers. The archers were strong though, as strong as her knights if not stronger, and they plucked Sada away from the brothers with one smooth jerk. She cried out as one of them pinned her wrists behind her and held her under a long, muscled arm. She realized with unease that she was eyelevel with his ribs. There would be no escaping the hold of this impossibly tall anomaly of a man.

She heard one of the brothers cry out and hurriedly blinked away the after-images, looking helplessly toward Kartinar and Drath. They were both held captive now as well, and all in the span of ten seconds.

The orange-eyed king looked angry now, and his rich braids flew about his head as he whipped around to look at of them each separately. Sada tried not to flinch as his flaming gaze settled on her.

"You mortals dare to venture into my forest, attempt to deceive me, and then proceed to *steal* from my *lands?"* Sada had to count her heartbeats when his eyes found hers. She could breathe again when his gaze shot to Drath, who was being held by two archers. "*You.* It would have been wise for you to reconsider your actions before you pilfered that item."

"We didn't steal it!"

"*Liar,"* the king seethed.

"We happened upon it in an abandoned burrow, on the outskirts of the Border towns," Kartinar said then. He shot Drath a pointed glare that seemed to say, *And don't say anything else.*

The king snapped his glare to Kartinar. The archers had bent him over with his arms twisted up above his head, but as he spoke, he was shoved onto his knees.

"Silence," the king commanded.

"Free us," Kartinar retorted, and the man holding his arms gave them a jerk.

"Are you quite aware of who I am?" the king asked hotly.

Kartinar grunted, half-smiling now. Sada didn't like the look of it. "Besides a leaf-loving sharp-ears?" he asked. The guard twisted one of his arms and he cried out again, louder this time.

"Karti, shut up for the sake of our mother!" Drath hissed. "Remember what Brumm told us about him?"

"You are aware, then?" the king said. "Perhaps I should grace you with an introduction anyway."

The king's lips parted into a small grin as he set the end of his longbow in the leaves and straightened to his full stature. His bare chest pressed against the braided quiver strapped across his body and he smiled coyly, eyes narrowing into bright slits.

Sada had to tilt her head back to watch him as he met each of their eyes and said, "I am Caprius of Pyrtoxos blood, son to Aphredys hailed from Titian, Guardian of the Seam, and King Over the Elves of the Wood."

As he spoke, the antlered crown atop his auburn head shifted, revealing a tall, slender ear that ended in a point. In that moment, the boundaries of reality shifted. Sada's heart pounded in her chest, each beat echoing the fear that gripped her soul. For now she knew that in the depths of this fantastical forest, amidst the pink sunlight and the dancing shadows, lay secrets beyond mundane comprehension.

Mortals, they had said. And when they said it as though it was not a word to describe themselves, it had not been out of lunacy. For she saw now that all their ears were pointed, all their beauty inhuman, all their grins animalistic.

The king's smile, once smirking and shallow, now held a hint of something darker, something ageless and inscrutable.

Sada was prone to blushing, but now she felt all of the heat drain from her face as she beheld the Elven king.

THE SIXTH

Sada

The Elven archers jostled Sada, Kartinar, and Drath behind King Caprius as he stalked a path through the trees. Sada thought grimly about her wish to be with guards once more, and how you really ought to be careful what you wished for. These Elven guards were certainly not what she'd had in mind; they were no doubt tall, strong, and stoic enough to be guards, but they were too majestic. Sada thought that there was something wrong with this beautiful world if people who looked like kings were diminished to the duty of guarding trespassers. Because if these were the guards, then what did the common citizens look and behave like?

The one who truly was king had confiscated the brothers' satchel containing the strange purple light and now strode in front of them, leading them through the huge forest. The guard who held Sada had his arm wrapped around her shoulders so tightly that her head was squeezed against his ribs, and all she could see was the swishing of the king's flowing pants. Unlike the pure golden tones of the other Elves' trousers, the king's were a sheer fabric striped in autumn colors—though each man wore the same style. All of the pants were opaque around the hips and gradually became more translucent as they went down the leg. It looked very similar to the silk that spiders spun their webs with, the way the light made the silky trap between trees become visible.

All the Elves' feet were bare as well. She'd initially thought that the brothers were only barefoot because they hadn't the money to afford shoes. Then she'd noticed that neither the guards nor even the king himself wore shoes, and at first it had puzzled her, but now it was plain to see why: the woods were breathtaking from the giant trees to the pink sunlight, and yet the most miraculous thing of all was the forest floor. Everywhere she could see, it was carpeted by thick bunches of colorful moss, silky grass, or clover. There was not a patch of dirt in sight. She had no doubt the wood's residents remained clean and unharmed by walking barefoot.

If she were to try such a thing in Ettedon or even Centerton, not only would she be cast strange glances, but she would be likely to step on sharp stones or bits of broken glass; at the least, she would come back tracking mud and dust into her home. Here, she didn't think that was a concern. Her hypothesis was confirmed by a glance down at her guarding Elf's feet, which were free of the stain of dirt. Sada looked at her riding boots then, muddy from her trek through the dark forest she'd begun her journey in, and thought they were probably leaving more dirt on the ground than there was to begin with. A strange sort of shame heated her cheeks, and she suddenly wished to rid herself of the shoes which were certainly befouling the forest.

She was still dumbfounded as to how she'd crossed from a dark and muddy forest into such a clean and vibrant one without realizing it. Something strange had happened, something unexplainable by mundane means, and she thought it was closely linked to the brothers and their purple light. Though she had no real way of knowing, she was nearly certain that this was not only a new forest, but a new world or land entirely.

With as many foreigners that traveled to Ettedon, she had not met any with pointed ears. She was almost certain that Elves did not exist anywhere in the Americas or lands beyond, whether they visited Ettedon or not. The only other realms that she had ever heard talked about were heaven and paradise, and while this place was as beautiful as she knew those divine kingdoms were, she was certain her entrance to them would not be unlovingly met by a wrathful man with pointed ears and a gilded, antlered crown.

Sada realized that there were many things she knew this place was not—Centerton, heaven, paradise…home—but only one thing that she knew it was: Elt. Yet that word meant nothing to her. She also knew that there was no worry of her father's men retrieving her from her escape now. Just a short time ago that would have relieved her; now she shuddered at the thought.

Her guard tightened his arm around her shoulders, and she stumbled. "Hasten your pace, *kora*, lest I find myself compelled to carry you upon my back or in my arms for the rest of this journey," he said.

His voice was gentle but stern, and he did not offer a wink or grin to indicate that his comment was a jest. Sada trotted along beside him in order to match his long strides. Three of her steps made up one of his.

"I'd thought Elves of the Wood were said to be friendly," Kartinar muttered as they were escorted along the pathway. He was still bent over at an awkward angle by his guard, contorted so that he could see nothing but his own bare feet. He was panting as he said, "I suppose leaves are the only things you love, huh?"

The king did not laugh. "All people of Elt will proclaim our kindness and know it to be true. Yet the distinction lies there…You are not of Elt."

"How many times must we say it?" Kartinar said. His guard was kind, and did not punish him for his impudence.

The king either did not hear him or he chose to ignore him, and continued his dialogue. His light voice struck clearly through the stillness of the forest, which was still eerily silent, as though all the creatures it housed knew there were strangers in their midst. The birds sang no more, and the squirrels no longer chattered. Every so often, Sada caught the gleam of eyes watching them through the foliage, yet the wildlife was still and shy. Distantly, the harps or lyres or both continued to play.

"Trespassers, deceivers, thieves, and other miscreants hold a distinct perspective on my people that is greatly contrasting with the views of true, devoted citizens of the Valley. It is a rare occurrence for us to cross paths with such degenerates within the Valley of Kings; in most of Elt, truly. Our societies have evolved to recognize that conflict is superfluous," King Caprius said.

"Someone might tell that to the blood vermin," her captor muttered above her.

Though he'd spoken quietly, the king still heard him. He bobbed his crowned head in agreement. "*Viie.* Some Spiritkin seem to hold a more…*mortal* view on such matters. It is they who know the wrath of the Elves of the Wood. They undermine the very principles that have enabled us to maintain peace in our lands for centuries. Consequently, when we do encounter individuals of this nature, they are handled very…exclusively, particularly mortal strangers invading our lands. Though we have not been treated to such an incident in many, many centuries."

Some of the Elves chuckled at that, and Sada's guard squeezed her tighter against his side.

The king looked back at them again, his brilliant orange eyes gleaming. "I trust that your time in Elt, though brief, will remain memorable. Should you attempt such an act in the future, I recommend journeying through regions inhabited by Spiritkin who consider themselves to be…what was it the Druids have begun calling themselves?" he glanced at one of the men trailing just behind him. "Specifists?"

"Pacifists, my king," he said with a dip of his head. But King Caprius had begun whistling a melody in time with the harp-lyre. It seemed he had grown bored of the conversation.

"The Nymphs would have extended their kindness to both of you," one of the two Elves holding Drath said. He wore his hair in braids like the others, but then those braids were plaited as well to form a single thick braid like a rope.

"All three, even. They have tongues for many tastes," added another who had beautiful eyes and two pale, almost golden scars making an X across his strong nose. They did little to mar his beauty. A few more sniggered at his remark.

"Indeed," King Caprius agreed. "You ought to have considered venturing through their parts of the Valley."

"The Nymphs have never much liked my brother. They prefer shiny things, and everything about him is rather dull," Kartinar said. Sada and

Drath exchanged a glance, and she flushed remembering the mental name she'd given him upon their introduction.

At Kartinar's remark, the king whipped around, crown sliding out of place, and their parade halted. Sada's hair caught in her guard's elbow as he jerked her to a stop, and she let out a small cry.

"You speak to me of Nymphs as though I do not know the ways of my very own people," King Caprius snapped, stalking toward Kartinar.

Kartinar's eyes were blazing, his face a study in repressed satisfaction. "No, my good king, I only did not wish to presume that a monarch such as yourself would partake in the coming-of-age rituals practiced among the smallfolk."

The king slapped Kartinar. It was so fast that Sada only saw King Caprius's hand lift, then Kartinar's head snap to the side. He did smile, then, and spat blood onto the pristine forest floor. One more insult to the king.

"The both of you seem determined to affront me, do you not? You, the scrawny one, must have conceived of the notion to venture into our domain and trespass upon my lands, and you are unquestionably the most adept liar among your companions." He glared at Kartinar, then at the blood staining the moss.

Drath was led over to the king as he spoke, and his guards (he required one to hold each arm), forced him to one knee before His Majesty. Sada had the idea that despite his size, Drath would be unable to escape their strong grips, and certainly be unable to outrun their arrows.

The king glared at him. "And as for you, little Giant, you possessed the light. Did you steal it as well? No, your hands are too large, your movements too inelegant; any attempt at thievery would be a laughable affair…It was the girl, then."

Sada paled as the king's flaming gaze rested on her. He walked to her silently, a small smile playing on his lips. Elegant fingers, dangerous fingers, played with the string of his bow, releasing ominous twinges of sound. She reached for the ends of her hair to tangle her fingers in, but her movement caused her captor's hold around her arms to tighten, and she was rendered immobile. She bit into her lip instead.

"Did you think you could avoid my attentions simply by holding your tongue?" King Caprius asked. "You may have thought yourself wise for it, yet by doing so you have marked yourself as the most deceitful of your companions, more so even than the little man."

"She had *nothing* to do with it," Drath said abruptly.

"She was brought here from the mortal realm when we dropped the light," Kartinar said. His acorn eyes were alight with anger. *"It wasn't her choice.* King Caprius, I beg you—spare the girl from whatever designs you have for us."

"Ah, he begs!" The tall king chuckled lightly, still grinning.

He stopped in front of Sada, and her guard pushed her out to meet him. He was examining her with a frown. For a moment, it seemed as though he wouldn't speak. He stared at her eyes, unblinking.

My birthmarks! Has the powder come off again?

Her heart thudded sharply at the thought, and she reached up to feel at the corner of her eye. A jab in the ribs from her guard's bow—thankfully not on the sore side—stopped her before she could. It didn't hurt, but still tears threatened to well up in her eyes.

You only just applied the powder, you shouldn't touch them anyway. And besides, it couldn't have come off in such a short period of time. It was just her eyes, then, and she couldn't go and put powder in them. Though Lord knew she'd wished she could countless times.

Ugliness and oddities often draw attention, the voice of Memory whispered. She thought of Mick and the bartender, and tried to hide her eyes with shuttered lids.

As she did, the king finally spoke. "Well *kora*, will you permit this deception on behalf of yourself? Or will you find yourself wise enough to provide me with truth?"

Her guard shoved her, and she stumbled forward.

Sada tried not to focus on the way her heart raced, tried to ignore how cloudy her mind felt. Words were failing her, and she wasn't sure if the truth would keep her safe or further endanger her. It had never bought her favor when it came to her father. But some things had…Years of training and critique from the Duke snapped her body into motion then, and she didn't have to think as she curtsied, low, even lower than she did for her father or the king in her lands, however far away they were. When she rose, she prayed that her lessons in court would not fail her, and obeyed King Caprius's command.

"I would not presume to lie to you, Your Majesty. I have no doubt you would see through it, in any case. And so I shall confess to you the truth: Less than one hour past, I was in the forest outside of Centerton, trekking through mud. I still do not know how it is I came to be here. All I wish now is to return to my own world, but I fear that I have no means to do this myself." She hadn't meant to say her "own world," and yet the words felt natural as she spoke them. Some part of her knew that this truly was a different realm, one she did not belong in.

When she lifted her chin again—still shuttering her eyes—the king was smirking smugly. She recognized the look; she had seen it not on the face of her father, but on the faces of noblemen who were easily fooled by false courtesies and flattery. Her manners had pleased King Caprius.

"Mortal curtsies are just as lovely as they are written to be…Who trained you in the customs of court to result in such a charming one?" he asked, eyeing her mud-stained dress.

She resisted the urge to pull her cloak back over her shoulders, which had shifted to expose not only her dirty gown, but her chest and arms as well. She also resisted the urge to flush, though her face did not yield to her desires.

"My father holds a prominent position with my homeland's king, Your Majesty, and so I was fortunate to be brought up in his royal court. I have found that it is quite challenging to live amongst monarchs without acquiring the proper decorum."

He grinned at that. "Indeed, you say it true. I'm rather fond of this title you have used for me as well—Your Majesty. Don't you agree, *andrótes*?" he asked his archers. They obediently nodded their agreement. "I believe I shall keep it."

Despite the prickling in her palms, Sada put on her best smile for the towering man—or rather, Elf. "I am pleased this title finds favor with Your Majesty, though I must confess it is not of my own creation. It is the proper form where I come from. If I may venture to say, it describes you well."

"And what is this kingdom which you speak of hailing from? What court bred such customs?"

"I hail from the kingdom of Califia, whose royal court resides in our capital city, Ettedon."

"Intriguing," King Caprius murmured. "And which lands do you come from?"

"The Americas, Your Majesty."

Drath looked to Kartinar then, but the shorter brother was staring intently at Sada. His lips were moving slightly, like he was mouthing a word or words, and he was frowning so hard it looked almost painful. King Caprius didn't notice. He just tapped at his temple, his nail *tink tink tinking* against the metal band of his crown.

"The Americas…interesting. I would know more of these lands. Where are they located?" the king asked.

Sada's face grew hot. "Well…I know great seas surround us on three sides, and we are settled near the leftmost one, but I admit this is the extent of my knowledge. The study of geography was never my strength," she said with a laugh. "Yet now…I do not know how far away either my lands or my kingdom are, nor even in which direction to search."

The king appeared thoughtful, though his eyes, which seemed to be ever-burning fires, were hard to read. He was nodding, arms crossed over his chest and one hand on his temple, repeatedly lifting his crown up and letting it slide down his braids again. He wore more than any of the others, and they gleamed in the sunlight like cords of deeply-burnished copper.

"Unless you are a remarkable liar..."

The king bent forward then, dipping his head down to her neck. The scent of leaves and moss washed over her as he leaned in, then the spiced scent of his forest, and then...lemon. She froze completely. She didn't even dare to breathe as his braids grazed her shoulder and she heard him sniff twice.

Then he pulled away, the cold metal of his crown brushing her temple, and said, "No...you bear the scent of fear, not wickedness. A human maiden adorned with the perfume of both fear and virtue, a true rarity indeed.

"You, on the contrary..." The king strode away from her, and she granted herself a moment to draw a trembling breath. He came to a halt before the brothers, and a sneer graced his lips. "I need not even approach to catch its scent; the stench of miscreancy guided me through my forest to you."

"Yes, good ki—Your Majesty, we *are* thieves, but we didn't steal the spirits-cursed light!" Kartinar snapped. He was rewarded with a cuff over the head, but it did nothing to dull the rage in his eyes.

However, they certainly appeared dull when compared with those of King Caprius. It seemed that fire itself had been born in his eyes, the way he was glaring down at Kartinar. Drath looked on meekly, finding wisdom in silence. Neither brother's response (silent or not) stilled the king's wrath. She thought that nothing could have swayed his decision, in any case. The favor she had found in him had been purely by luck alone, and perhaps aided by her father's training and her courtly demeanor.

"I have long grown weary of your echoed lies and affronting remarks. Your retribution shall be determined in the court, and I will hear *no more* from you until you are *invited* to *speak*." King Caprius was nearly snarling as he snapped at the brothers.

At his whistle, the Elves holding the men continued forward, more roughly now, and Sada's stomach clenched with dread. But the one guarding Sada didn't make to move. Neither did the man standing beside them, the one with the scars on his nose. Somehow that short, wavering whistle had conveyed a different message to the two of them than it had to their companions. She turned to glance up at her guard, but his dark green eyes were locked on his king.

"Shall I follow them?" Sada asked hesitantly.

"*Néos*. That will not be necessary. My guards shall escort you to the Seam so that you may return home," King Caprius said.

She should have kept her silence if she'd learned anything from her years under her father's rule, but she couldn't help it. Her tongue could hardly be stilled. "Why?" she asked. "Why myself and not them?"

King Caprius paused, seeming to think, and looked off into the trees. The streams of pink light coming down through the leaves were thinning. The sun was setting, or would be soon. Standing in the path of one beam, he looked almost like a boy. With not even a hint of peach fuzz on his face, Sada suddenly thought he might be. But neither her own guard nor those of the brothers had facial hair of any kind either. And it couldn't be possible for all of them, with their great height and stature, to be youths.

After a few moments where Sada began to wonder if the king had not heard her, he finally responded.

"Would you deem it truthful if I say that I am uncertain why I place my trust in you and not your companions?" He didn't turn to her as he spoke, and she knew that he did not expect nor want an answer. "The scent of dishonesty can be masked through many means, but I feel within the braids on my head that it is not so with you. Somehow, I believe in the truth of your story, *kora.* Yet that of the human boys…no, they must face trial."

The king returned to stand before her, and Sada felt as though the elegance radiating off of him was almost palpable. Still, his instant shift in demeanor toward her, from reproachful to kindly candor, made her uneasy. It reminded her of her father in distant days when his anger was less frequent but also more spontaneous; more dangerous. She stiffened as King Caprius gently took her hand, but she managed to look at his too-majestic face. They both stared silently as the king was captivated by her strange eyes and she by his strange beauty.

Finally he blinked. The spell was broken.

"May the spirits walk before and behind you, mortal girl," he said in that light voice.

With that the king walked away, his autumn hair burning in the pink light of his strange forest. In front of him, the brothers were still being herded down the trail by their guards, deeper into a darkening forest. Kartinar twisted to look at Sada and she made to wave, but the green-eyed Elf that had been guarding her put a huge hand on her shoulder. She flinched and he just smiled at her. She couldn't tell if it was meant to be comforting or threatening, so she just let him and the other who had stayed behind lead her back the way they had come and away from the brothers and the Elven king.

Kartinar

When Kartinar turned to wave at Sada, he saw one of the Elves guarding her, tall and strong and tan, tug her more tightly against his side. Shortly after she was turned away, Kartinar was rewarded for his efforts of bidding the girl farewell with a jab to the ribs. Though equally as harsh as the ones passed between him and his brother, it was more painful when delivered by a sharp-ears, especially one of Caprius's.

Still he watched as she was led away, disappeared into the trees by strange Elves, and thanked the spirits (which he of course did not believe in) that at least one of them had been allowed to escape.

Caprius

Caprius had lingered between the two groups—to be imprisoned and to be freed—thinking of the girl. That gleaming hair, free of the prison of braids, and so long that most Elves could only hope to grow such locks unrestrained. He thought of her smiles, so sweet and yet halting. But mostly he thought of her eyes. One light and one dark, both wide with hope and joy and reverence as she looked upon him. It made the tips of his ears tingle. She made a king feel like a king, as he believed all women should.

He also found himself wondering if she was not somehow of Fae descent. Of course, she stank of the sweat of mortals, but she had the short stature of a Faery, if she was not as shockingly thin and hollow-boned as they. He had noticed, of course, what peeked out from beneath her cloak, and it was not the slender body of a Fae woman, to be sure. Caprius had spent much of his interaction with the girl trying to steal glimpses of the tips of her ears to find some indication of a long-lost lineage.

He tried to imagine a tale that would suit her circumstance. As they'd walked, the human brothers had told a story of being born in the mortal world and brought to Elt. Perhaps the girl had been born in Elt and brought to the mortal world. They looked like humans and smelled like Eltics; she looked like an Eltic and smelled like a human. How delightfully ironic it would be if it were true! It was also possible that the Spiritkin imprisoned during the third Realm War, the Harvest War, had not all perished or escaped; that the Eltics' reconnaissance mission had failed. She of course had no wings, but not all Fae did. If her Fae relatives had been lowborn, there would be no wings.

But imagine as he might, he could not convince himself that it was at all true. As pretty as the girl was, it was only by human standards. Caprius reasoned he probably only found her beautiful because all the drawings he'd seen of humans had depicted them to be as homely as Dwarves. She wasn't as plain as their women, but neither was she as shockingly beautiful as any of the fairfolk, lowborn or not.

Of course, she may be a child to one of the Felled, Caprius thought. That sobered him entirely. He tried to convince himself that it was impossible for her to be such a dirty creature, that at the worst she was simply a unique human girl. It took his train of thought in a direction he did not want it to go, and so he put the thoughts from his mind altogether, resisting a glance over his shoulder. Yet as he closed the distance between himself and his prisoners, he gave in. He looked back and caught the sight of brilliant hair swishing as the girl turned her head in wonder, and glinting in the pastel sunlight.

Kartinar

Kartinar watched from the corner of his eye as the young king caught up to them with long, urgent strides, and then overtook them. Once safely at the head of their group, his pace slowed and so did that of Kartinar and Drath's captors. Kartinar had the thought that if someone looked up to or well-trusted by Caprius—perhaps his prudish sister he'd heard rumors of—were to tell him that true kings took up the rear of a party, Caprius would be behind Kartinar and the others before he could think to adjust his antlered crown. He adjusted it then, pushing the great thing too far back on his head which was too small for such a trophy. It looked positively idiotic slanted back so far on his braids, about to topple off, but Kartinar figured that it looked better there than hanging halfway over his brows and eyes.

He chuckled at the thought, earning himself another jab from his captor, the beast of an Elf. Then Kartinar had the great sense to call out to the king. Drath shot him a glare. *What in the name of the Void are thee doing?* it said. But Kartinar was already wondering that himself, and he didn't have an answer for either of them. Except that he wanted to see if the Kid King would at least be honest, if not merciful.

Or perhaps you believe yourself deserving of a crueler punishment than the one he's already set upon you, is that it Kartinar? he thought grimly. *At long last, you shall receive the treatment that all in Elt deem fitting, and their condemning whispers will cease. When it is done, you may say, "See, Caprius treats me unjustly, too. I am one of you now. Spare me your scorn, for I have already received punishment for the crime of merely existing."*

And punishment for what he and Drath had just done. Not that Drath could be blamed. He didn't even know what he'd set in motion. He supposed it was punishment for that, too, tricking his only brother and companion. Even though it was all for him.

And what of the effects it will have on Elt? Kartinar thought. *From the Valley of Kings to the Border towns and even beyond,* the drifter had said. That's how great of an impact the purple light, channeled by the moat and the rivers it connected to, would have on the world. The old man had refused to tell Kartinar of exactly what that impact would entail, other than the fact that it would set in motion a "new age" for Elt. Whether that was benign or malevolent, Kartinar could only guess. All that had mattered to him was that the drifter had believed it to be a great enough event that it would cause Amogasanes to take notice of Drath and accept him as an apprentice.

Now, that didn't even matter. How could his brother apprentice under the last true sorcerer in Elt if he was locked in Caprius's dungeons, or worse, killed in them?

They were slowly nearing the unofficial capital of the Valley of Kings: the fair city of Titian. Except these days it was anything but fair. The city that seemed to be eternally preserved in autumn like a fly in amber was supposed to be the sanctuary where all Eltics came to do business, visit, and even live. It was a romantic idea, and had seen success for perhaps a century or two during the final years of the former King of the Wood's reign. Now, the idea that outsiders could live in Titian was laughable. The Elves thought they did well at masking their disgust toward the homely folk of Elt, but it showed in the tightness of their smiles, the hard looks in their eyes. It also showed in the dwindling numbers of foreigners living in the city.

While Caprius's father ruled, Titian had truly been a bustling capital home to residents hailing from across the land, no matter their race, religion, or amount of magick. Now, even Elves of the Wood native to other cities besides Titian counted themselves lucky to call the Autumn City their home. And then, of course, there was the economy. Kartinar didn't truly think the residents to be lucky, but Titian was still considered to be paradise within paradise, if Elt could be called such anymore.

The kingdoms were becoming corrupt, and the rest of Elt would be likely to follow suit. The sorcerer's light would either encourage the corruption or work against it. It was certainly powerful enough to do either. After the deed had been done, Kartinar had felt the earth tremble as though a great snake had left the moat, slithered beneath his feet, and into the forest. Drath had sworn that when he plucked the light from the water, it had been so cold it was hot, and his hand didn't stop buzzing until hours later.

When they had met Sada.

Kartinar didn't want to curse her, but, well, it seemed that their trouble had begun once they'd found themselves acquainted with her. No, even before that. He was old enough to have stopped dreaming that humans could possess the magick that certain Eltics did, but there was something about the girl. It seemed some part of her was so strong, so magnetic, that in an effort to reach her, the sorcerer's light had somehow pulled Kartinar and his brother from Elt and into the mortal world without them so much as touching the portal that joined their realms.

And then there were those markings beside her eyes.

Almost as soon as the thought formed in his mind, the forest's music became suddenly disjointed, as though the bodiless instruments momentarily lurched out of tune. Everyone looked up, but the music returned to its normal harmonics almost instantly. King Caprius narrowed his eyes and glanced behind them, but said nothing.

Gooseflesh rose on Kartinar's arms as they continued walking, and he quickly turned his mind from such thoughts. Sure, he was the thinker of the group, but if he thought of this, he would fry his brain and then he would be thinking no more. Except he had a strange feeling that such a fate awaited him whether he thought of the human girl and the purple light or not. His captor was not known for his even temper or his mercy, and apparently his unnatural love for humans had been nothing but a rumor.

Good job, Kartinar. You've potentially altered all of Elt more dramatically than you can even begin to imagine, and it will all be for naught.

Caprius still hadn't responded to his hail of greeting, and so he called out again, even though it got him a cuff over the head from his guard.

"Your Majesty, I beg a moment of your time."

"You have been commanded to hold your tongue, *agor,"* Caprius said.

Kartinar bristled at the name. Despite the number of years he may be able to count, Caprius was ten times the child Kartinar was. And he would do well to remember that, or…

Or what? said his voice of reason. *What will you, a lowly mortal boy—or man, if you like—do to an immortal king surrounded by his equally immortal guards?* That thought quelled some of the dangerous irritation prickling his neck, and he sighed the rest away.

"A wise command, Your Majesty, and I give my word I will abide by it henceforth. And yet I must beg one question, to settle my mind and my tongue."

His guard's hand had switched from his shoulders to his neck, and now it squeezed tightly, pinching at the raised mole his mother had called a beauty mark. (*That's for girls,* he had always protested.) He fought the urge to slap the Elf's hand away.

"I shall give you a means to settle that tongue of yours, seedling," the guard growled.

Yet Caprius raised a hand, shadowed in the dwindling light, and the guard released Kartinar's neck. The king turned lazily in his direction, and they all stopped before him. When Kartinar said nothing, he gestured impatiently, waving his hands like a toddler.

"Well? I wish to reach my capital before dark. We concurred you shall endure in silence *after* this comment, not prior to it, *viie?"*

Kartinar ground his teeth together. Caprius adjusted his crown which had shifted to cover his eyebrows and the irritation poked more strongly at his neck. Yet he put it all from his mind as he had done with thoughts of the girl and asked his one question. He could feel Drath's eyes on him, wondering, scolding even, but he looked only at Caprius, at his captor.

"This is not a trial, is it? What we are led toward is death… *Viie?"*

The young king, his bare face made younger by dusk, chuckled merrily. If he was offended by Kartinar's use of his native tongue, he did not show it. He even laid his hand on Kartinar's shoulder.

"In the end, seedling, death is what we are all led toward," he said.

Then he turned and they resumed their march toward the all-but-fair city of Titian, where all were welcome and yet only autumn-complexioned natives lived. All the while, they were accompanied by the eerie, endless sounds of harps and lyres, and an unshakable sense of dread.

THE SEVENTH

Sada

As Sada was led further away from the king, the brothers, and their accompanying guards, an invisible string began tugging at her heart and telling her to run back to them. With each step she took, it grew more taut. Now it was such a painful urge she thought she might cry out. She knew that she walked toward freedom while her newly-met companions walked toward imprisonment, trial, and no doubt everything but freedom. Somehow, she felt that with her acceptance of liberty came their condemnation to punishment. That if she turned and ran and caught up to them, then fell to her knees in the dewy moss and begged King Caprius to release them, he would do so. And if she did, they would all link arms and happily return to their world together.

Yet she continued walking, and that line attached to her heart grew thinner and tighter. Soon it would snap, and guiltily she realized she would welcome it. Then the decision would be made for her, and it would worry her no more.

She drew some comfort from the knowledge that her guards would not allow her to make it more than two steps before one restrained her, perhaps even slung her over his shoulder like laundry to be taken in for the rest of the trek. She tried not to think about what would be done to the young men, but she did not think their trial at court would be fair. It often wasn't. That made some small anger stir in her, but what could she do? She was just a girl in a land belonging to peculiar almost-humans.

The ones walking with her certainly were strange. Though they were extraordinarily tall and possessed more strength than she'd felt even from her father's guards, they made no sound as they moved through the forest. Even as they stepped on leaves which rustled noisily beneath Sada's feet, their own steps elicited only a whisper. They didn't speak to each other either, and Sada squirmed in the silence, chewing her lip.

"What a lovely forest you call home," she said. Neither of the men escorting her responded. They didn't even glance in her direction. Perhaps they hadn't heard her.

"Pardon, but—" she began again.

"You have been heard, seedling, what is it you want?" It was the Elf behind her, the one with the brilliant eyes and scars across his nose. Heat flowed to her cheeks.

He reminded her of a pirate. She'd never met one, of course; she didn't know if they were even real, though Uncle Beron claimed they were. But she'd heard tales and had seen drawings, and she'd always, for some reason, fancied them. She imagined them to be handsome, fearsome men who feared nothing and who tamed the sea. They would also, of course, have both a parrot on their shoulder and scars on their face. This man had no parrot that she could see, but the scars fit her mental depiction. It was not his scars that stood out to her, however, but his eyes. They were the color of honey or caramelized sugar. They were bright among the darkness of his features.

They were the eyes of a wolf.

She jumped when he poked her in the back with his bow.

"Apologies," she said sheepishly. It appeared her training in conversation and small talk would not serve her with these men. She would be direct, then. "May I ask where it is that you're escorting me?"

"To the Seam," was all he said.

"What is the Seam?"

"The place where our two realms meet."

So they are two different worlds!

"My realm…and Elt?"

Neither of the men spoke, but the one next to her nodded his head. Once. His long brown hair, woven into dozens of braids, cascaded around him like a cloak at the movement. All of the Elves' hair was braided, but his braids were made up of four and five strands instead of three.

Sada tugged her own cloak back around her shoulders. It tried to flutter open with every step she took.

"Will the brothers be punished?"

"They must be."

"Yet not I. Simply because I told the truth?" she asked. "I committed the crime of trespass as well, didn't I?"

"With purpose?" the Elf beside her asked.

At the same time, the man with wolf eyes laughed, asking, "Do you wish to be imprisoned as well?"

"Not a fig! No!" she exclaimed. "And no again! No to both!"

Mr. Wolf chuckled, but the other was not amused. Finally he looked down at her, his eyes brilliantly bright. They were as green as pine needles in the shade. "The king is aware of this. And Elves of the Wood do not punish innocents."

That meant the Elves believed the brothers to truly be guilty of the crimes they'd been accused of. Well, Kartinar had admitted to them being thieves.

"Oh. Well, that is very kind," Sada said. He turned away and continued his silent march. She had to stop herself from giggling at the stern frown tattooed on his brow. "What is your name, sir?"

He laughed drily. "Sir is not a title used in Elt. We train not in the ways of knights. They are a brutal and unforgiving species."

Sada thought of Gabe, how he called her little lady and offered to buy her flavored ice when she was sad. She then thought of John, and the way he'd carry her around by her ankles when she was a girl. Sada thought the Elf had known the wrong knights, if he'd known any.

"Have you met any knights before, si—" She had to press her lips together abruptly to stop from saying it. "Have you met any knights in your time, kind stranger?"

The two men laughed lightly. Mr. Wolf had moved up to walk in stride with the green-eyed Elf, and he raised his sharply arched eyebrows at her. "Many, in battle," he said. "Though not by choice."

"Viie," agreed Pine-Eyes.

"Pardon me if I am being impolite, but is battle not brutal and unforgiving, whether those fighting in it are knights or not?"

"We do not fight," said Pine-Eyes. His voice was stern and cold as iron.

Sada felt as though she should stop herself from continuing on, but curiosity loosened her tongue. "Dear stranger, I know little of battle, but from what I have studied of the histories, it seemed to me that such an event requires the participation of *both* parties. How is it possible to go to battle, refrain from fighting, and survive?"

Pine-Eyes sighed, as though he were trying to teach a child her letters and she could simply not figure out how to write an *i*. It sounded awfully like the creaky groan of Governess Brown. "To fight is to draw blood with eagerness. It is to choose battle and bloodshed. We cannot claim to have fought. We defend, and not with iron or steel as your *knights* wield. Such a distinguished title is too noble for someone who uses the bones of their world to inflict pain upon its residents."

His sharp jaw was set, eyes narrowed into slits. He looked like a cat who had decided playtime was over, and was now about to trap your hand with sharp claws and teeth the next time you reached in for a pet. Sada decided that this time she would mind her tongue. She thought that "someone who uses the bones of their planet to inflict pain upon its residents," was quite a unique way to describe a knight. She had been raised to see them as valiant and honorable protectors of the kingdom, of lords, and of ladies like herself. And what were the bones of their planet? Swords? She didn't think that the world had a skeleton of swords and knives hiding below its earthen surface, but what did she know? She had also thought that to have a battle, it required two fighting sides. Apparently, that was wrong.

"Very well. What if we strike a deal? I'll refrain from calling you 'sir,' if you tell me your name!" she said. Pine-Eyes didn't return her smile. "Or perhaps another title you would prefer? My name is Sada Solar—"

"Girl, the King Over the Elves of the Wood has just spared your life and freedom. That is enough mercy to last the rest of your short lifetime. Do not press your luck seeking kindness elsewhere, especially where it has not been earned." Her green-eyed guard glared at her for two seconds that felt like ten, and she had to clench her jaw to keep it from trembling. Her eyes began to grow hot and moist, and she looked at the floor, her tears following her gaze.

They walked in silence after that.

He's so mean, he's so, so mean, she thought as she cried, hoping that neither of the men could see her do so and wishing all the while that her hair was down to hide her face.

No he isn't, whispered the voice of Memory in response. *He speaks truly, and not unkindly. Must you be catered to in order to consider a person kind? Will you cry whenever you are not deferred to? I'd thought you to be the daughter of a king's commander, and yet look at you…*

She forced herself to stop crying then, and to hum through the tightness in her throat. To help distract herself, Sada tried to make her own footsteps as quiet as the Elves', drawing her weight up higher into herself as she had done to sneak across her manor, but she failed miserably. She did, however, quickly forget all about the insult—real or imagined—as she tiptoed through the forest.

As they walked, the moss beneath her feet began to give way to something else. She could see a path beginning to form between the trees ahead. It was made of something smooth and glossy, with a warm, golden hue that both captured and reflected the sunlight. It was as if the earth there had turned into a river of honey, frozen mid-flow, with the sun's rays trapped inside.

She bent down to examine it when the moss and grass fell away completely. Up close, she could see that it was nearly translucent, and the color of toasted honey. And where the sunlight was illuminating it, she could even see whole ferns and leaves deep within it, perfectly preserved.

"What is this?" Sada breathed, running her hands over the glassy surface of the path. The sunlight it trapped emanated a gentle warmth.

"The Road of Ages."

"Oh what a lovely name! Though I wondered about the material it is made of."

The Elf with the wolf eyes had stopped to wait for her, and he chuckled. "Have you never seen amber, seedling?"

"So, this is what amber is! I've heard tell of it before—how it preserves flowers and leaves and even insects for centuries. Yet I still cannot fathom how it is done. But truly, it is a marvel to see it in the flesh!"

He frowned. "Insects?"

"Indeed! It saddens me to think of, though."

"And why does this aggrieve you?"

"To think of the manner in which they died to be preserved in such a way."

To her surprise, the Elf actually agreed with her, looking solemn even. "We must only hope they found no pain in their death," he said.

They aren't all as cold as Pine-Eyes, then.

"Come now, seedling. Daylight is not eternal."

At his urging, she stood and continued on to catch up with Pine-Eyes, who was waiting impatiently and twirling an arrow in one hand.

"You know," she said as they walked. "Your eyes look an awful lot like amber themselves." Mr. Wolf didn't answer, but she caught him smiling out of the corner of her eye.

As the moss yielded to the amber, it became hard to look at the path directly; the brilliance of its glow made her eyes water. When they reached the green-eyed guard, Sada saw he was standing at a small wooden structure that looked to be built straight out of a tree itself. The counter and roof were overhanging, but when she looked inside, she saw into the hollow of the trunk. There were wooden chests in there, closed over any treasures they might hold, as well as stacks of large, rectangular sections of some yellow papery material. There was nobody manning the stand.

"What is this for?" Sada breathed, poking her head inside. It was cool and dry and smelled of wood.

Pine-Eyes pulled her back, still scowling. "Come. And walk faster. You as well," he said, turning his glare to Mr. Wolf.

Mr. Wolf said something in a different tongue, probably the same they'd been speaking in when she and the brothers had first met the Elves' group. The two shared a glance, looked at Sada, then Pine-Eyes rolled his eyes quite dramatically and continued walking.

Mr. Wolf gestured for her to follow. She thought that if she asked him what the building was for, he would answer, but she didn't want to get him in trouble with his colleague. She managed to hold her tongue.

The trees were still just as unfathomably large, and she still stopped to gape at them every so often, but they grew sparser as the Road of Ages grew wider. Now it was so wide that three or four people could comfortably walk abreast (Pine-Eyes still stalked ahead of them despite this), and the trees were dozens of yards apart. She saw the merchant stands, then.

They looked so much like the ones in Centerton that her excitement for the festival was instantly renewed (as well as a little guilt at how late she'd be, but Jezebel would *have* to be understanding of this! She ought to take a souvenir so she would believe her). Some were colorful and decorated with scarves of silk, or giant feathers as tall as Sada. Others were simple in their design, and made only of wood. Even the wooden planks of this world were strange; they didn't look like planks at all, but rather flat, nearly perfectly rectangular branches. There were no splinters or wood grain to be seen. Some even had the hand-like leaves growing from them.

Running her hand over a stand made from such planks, she felt that the wood was as smooth as the bark of the trees, and wondered how they could possibly craft wooden planks with the bark still on them. She'd never seen it before; though neither had she seen a path of amber, in the woods or anywhere else. Some of the stands were made of stone, and they had bits of the amber scattered throughout. She'd thought all would be empty of any goods, as she saw no merchants tending them, but there were stacks and piles of wares in every stand.

"Do they not fear thieves?" Sada asked. "In Centerton, all of the merchants take their wares home at night, lest they be stolen."

Mr. Pérez had once been able to leave his stores of herbs in the apothecary overnight. After all, who would steal herbs, when they had no idea of their properties, no means to turn them into tinctures? As the years went on, he came to see that the answer was many people, and eventually he had to do as the other merchants did and cart his merchandise between shop and home each day.

Mr. Wolf nodded. "You live amongst humans. We do not. We are separate for a reason, seedling."

"Oh." Were humans truly the only ones who stole and fought, as these Elves made it out to be? She thought of asking, but didn't think she'd receive a fair answer from either of the men. They seemed to despise her people. "What are the stands here for? Are markets not typically found in cities?" she asked instead.

"They are, though it is merely because not all may be situated near the Seam. Yet King Caprius has graciously begun to allow a few select merchants to trade here, as he is now graciously allowing visitors of the capital to view the Seam."

"Oh, how dandy! Are they there now? The visitors?"

Mr. Wolf shook his head, dark braids dancing. They fell nearly to the middle of his back. "*Néos.* Only during the brightest times of the day are visitors allowed at the portal. But you are more than a visitor."

"Indeed," Sada murmured, thinking of the brothers.

The merchants seemed to be selling everything imaginable from their stands. She saw wooden cups and barrels, clay cups and jugs. There were other stands filled with crates that she could not see into, but when she walked past, she smelled the scents of bread and sugar and other delightful things. There were shops overflowing with crates of fruit of every color, from pink to turquoise, and in shapes she had never seen. She thought she even saw an apple in the shape of a rabbit, and it was so detailed that she almost thought it might begin to hop away. There were stands filled with things she had never seen before, too, like crystals that glowed in the shadows and vials of metallic liquids, and bits of bark with black sigils singed into their surface.

Pine-Eyes had drawn ahead again, and when she asked after the wares in these stands, Mr. Wolf explained to her what they were.

"The merchant who sells here," he said, pointing to the arrays of glowing gemstones, "claims that these crystals are infused with the power of the Seam itself." He shook his head, laughing.

"And I would assume by your reaction that they are not?"

"Of course they are not. Nobody in Elt possesses the magick required to channel the Seam itself. Except perhaps one. But even if it were possible, it would be strictly forbidden."

"Why? Would it create more portals?" Sada asked.

"I cannot begin to speculate. But the Seam's magick belongs only to Elt and the Kindreds. We are not to wield it."

"Ah, I see. What are the Kin—oh wow!" she broke off as she saw a counter displaying bowls filled with pale glitter. It looked like the shavings off a star. "What is this?"

"Dust gathered from the edges of the Seam, where visitors are not allowed to tread. It is said to be filled with tremendous power, and will grant a magick-user a surge in abilities if consumed in the correct manner."

"Magick, truly?" Sada gasped. Then she caught his eye and saw he was smiling. "You are such a trickster!"

He laughed. "If you think I am a trickster, I would take great joy in seeing what you think of the Pixies or Fae."

They continued on, Sada asking after the strange goods displayed in some of the stands, and him answering. Sometimes truthfully, sometimes not. Eventually, though, Pine-Eyes grew impatient again and turned to whistle sharply at them. Then Mr. Wolf stopped smiling and joking and prodded Sada in the back until she was nearly running and they caught up to Pine Eyes. She didn't ask any questions about the merchants or their merchandise after that, but they found the edge of the market soon after, anyway. As soon as the stands stopped, the path of amber began to give way back to moss as well. Soon, there was no sign that there had been any market or any path at all.

✧✧✧

Off the path, Sada's boots seemed to find every twig to snap, and in the surrounding quiet it was the loudest noise in the woods. The birds had taken up their song again when she'd parted ways with the brothers, but as night drew closer, they grew quieter. She resigned herself to scanning the great trees for any pretty birds or fuzzy animals, but she found no movement amidst the chestnut-colored trunks. No gleaming eyes stared out from the clumps of ferns and plants. Not even the ceiling of orange and red and yellow leaves was stirred by the flight of birds.

Save for the strum of the harp (or was it the plucking of a lyre?), the forest was quiet and still, and seemed to grow even quieter as the Elves led Sada into the depths of the wood. As they went, the moss and clover grew in an even thicker blanket, the coverage only broken by small ponds and puddles scattered throughout the trees. Huge loops of roots erupted from the ground in some places, like the humped back of a serpent surfacing from the sea of moss. Sada could walk beneath some of these without trouble, and for others, Mr. Wolf lifted her over, easy as you please.

The trees were spaced widely, and the three of them were able to walk in a nearly straight line through the wood, only breaking away from their clear-cut path to round the occasional huge trunk or waist-high clump of fern. It was incredible how big everything was, from the people to the foliage and fauna. She even thought she caught a glimpse of a huge, bird-sized butterfly from the corner of her eye.

Sada couldn't help but stare wide-eyed in wonder, mouth parted into a smile that quickly grew into a grin as she beheld the beauty. Her guards didn't stop her as she moved away to investigate miniature mushrooms growing on the trees, or spin in slow circles as they walked, trying to see every bit of the forest. Mr. Wolf even smiled as he watched.

"Is it not remarkable?" she cried out, when the beauty of the forest in the pink sunlight seemed almost too much to bear. "It's like I've stepped into a painting, and you have the joy of living here, day after day!"

It seemed she couldn't stop exclaiming how incredible it was with every other breath she took. Sada had never heard of a place like this. And in all the nursery rhymes telling of faraway lands and people, none came close to describing the world she now trod in. Where the stories talked of great monsters and blood-sucking creatures, Sada walked alongside grandiose Elves of indescribable magnificence.

It was hard to even look at them for too long; her eyes kept trying to find imperfections and failing. Even scars looked like art on an Elven face. It left her cringing at her own human appearance, with her mud-spattered dress and mussed hair. She absentmindedly twisted her fingers into the pieces that had come down from the pins as they walked, needing something to occupy her in the awful quiet. She had never been fond of silence, always needing to fill it. Lessons of when to be silent were the only ones of the governesses that had always failed her.

She was about to ask the Elves about the braids they wore when they stopped suddenly and rested the ends of their longbows on the ground. Pine-Eyes leaned on his bow, gesturing at the cluster of trees in front of Sada.

The forest looked different here. The bushes and plants had grown scarce, but the trees were thicker, and much taller. The branches alone were as big around as Sada herself, and she had the idea that she might be able to wrap herself up completely with just two or three of the leaves. Just off to the side stood a ring of trees, their trunks so thick and near together that they almost appeared as a wall of bark. That is, until you traced their trunks into the sky to the great leaves sprouting from them. Pine-Eyes pressed his longbow flat against her back, moving her toward the ring of trees.

"Is that it?" she asked.

The men nodded. She couldn't tell if what she felt was apprehension or excitement.

"What should I do?"

"Enter the circle of trees ahead," Mr. Wolf said. "Within it you shall behold what appears to be a pond, though it will be much more striking than anything you have yet to see. Leap into the heart of it with both feet. Should you merely wade in, it will not work. Or so the tales say."

She took a step then faltered, glancing at the two strangers. They made no move to follow, and her throat suddenly tightened at the thought of being alone. What if she did it wrong?

"Will you not accompany me?"

"We shall remain to ensure your safe passage. The denizens of our realm harbor no warmth for mortals," Pine-Eyes said.

"Oh. I see. Thank you."

He pressed the longbow into her back again and she started forward toward the circle. As she walked away from her escorts, the air grew colder and heavier. With each breath, it felt as though she were breathing in a mouthful of mist, and it didn't quite fill her lungs. Here the air was more akin to Centerton's than Elt's. She wondered if that meant she was nearing her world, if the fabric between her realm and this one was thinning. She hoped so.

Don't I?

The Elves were silent, and she briefly wondered if they had left despite their promise to stay. Nerves flickered in her belly but a glance over her shoulder revealed the two tall men to be staring unblinking at her, unmoving.

Like unarmored sentries, she thought. Sada slipped between the massive trunks, still staring at the strangers. She lifted a hand in a wave. Neither of them moved. Part of her was glad when their unearthly beauty disappeared from her view.

The space inside the circle of trees was small. She and another human could stand abreast, arms spread out, and each easily touch one side of the ring. A single Elf could probably come close to doing the same. It was rocky here too, and the sight made Sada realize that the rest of the forest had been entirely free of rocks. Now she climbed over small, smooth boulders to get to the center of the ring. There in the middle, protected by the great ring of trees, was a silver pond.

Sada immediately fell to her knees upon seeing it. Its surface gleamed and swirled with something that looked like starlight, and she couldn't help but gasp at its reflective beauty. It looked like someone had taken all of her silver jewelry, and the gems it held along with it, and melted it down. There were also glimmers of something that reminded her of diamond dust everywhere her eyes looked.

She leaned over the pond, admiring the way it shimmered and rippled. Though Sada hadn't touched it and the wind was still, it began to swirl gently, moving in lazy circles that nearly hypnotized her. With each undulation of the liquid, more of the glittering stuff was revealed, more extravagant even than the queen's jewelry. It was all Sada could do not to plunge her hands into it and sit there staring at its swirling surface for all of eternity. Her eyes watered at the beauty, and greed bubbled up in her chest.

Yet she remembered Mr. Wolf's instructions, and she was not one to disobey. Sada forced herself to look away from the molten starlight and instead climbed onto a nearby boulder, reminded of her days as a child in Centerton spent climbing trees with Prince Aaron. Those days were long gone. The rock hung over the edge of the pool, and when Sada stood on it she was able to look down into its silver depths. It had begun to swirl faster now, as though anticipating Sada's leap.

It was time to go home.

She wrestled off her boots and stockings and let them drop to the rocks, absently wiping the mud from her bootheels off on her dress. Then she unclasped her cloak and let it fall too; she didn't know how deep the magickal pond was, and didn't want to be weighed down by the heavy fabric if she had to swim. Goosebumps appeared instantly on her bare arms. The air was frigid now. It smelled of the blank scent of cold. The forest was completely noiseless as well, even from the sound of music. All Sada could hear was the rhythm of her own pounding heart as she gazed into the portal, which was almost too bright and beautiful to look at now. The last thing she thought of was the fate of the two brothers, and as she leapt, the string connecting her heart to theirs snapped.

Sada squeezed her eyes shut and fell into the swirling starlight.

THE EIGHTH

Sada

Something so cold it burned swirled around Sada, seeping into her every pore. It wasn't just around her; it was within her—filling her lungs, threading through her veins, numbing her limbs to all sensation other than *it.*

The Seam.

The pain was sharp and all-consuming, yet she did not awaken to it. Her eyes remained wide open, staring blankly at the silver and starlight pulsing around her in waves, each beat synchronized with her heartbeat. Yet her mind slept, shielded from both the beauty and the pain.

In a place so remote and veiled that her own consciousness could not reach it, something else stirred. Awaking with a slow, deliberate exhalation, it stretched within her, whispering a greeting to the darkest recesses of her mind. It did not seek control—yet. For now, it merely observed, its essence a faint shadow beneath her own thoughts. The sensation was fleeting, almost imperceptible, but it left a subtle trace, a whisper of something foreign and unfamiliar within her. As if something long dormant had simply shifted in its sleep.

As it did, a slow grin spread over Sada's face beneath wide, unseeing eyes. She began to laugh.

Sada stood from the pond. For a moment the strange feeling attacking her skin froze her in place as she blinked the liquid out of her eyes. Then she woke up to the pain and her reflexes took over. She tried to cry out as she scrambled out of the water, but she ended up choking instead as her body fought between coughing up the liquid in her lungs, trying to fill them with air, and screaming from the pain. As she frantically dragged herself onto a nearby stone, glittering, molten silver trickled off her legs, each stream leaving a trail of icy pain in its wake.

OH GOD HELP ME—

Finally she was able to scream. No alphabet could replicate the sound she produced.

Tremors seized her body; her clothes were soaked in the burning liquid. Sada tore off her dress and petticoat and threw them to the rocks. Then she sat there coughing and shuddering and hugging herself with eyes squeezed shut until the pain began to recede and she was able to move.

She collapsed back against a boulder. She had made it home.

It took a while for the pain to leave her completely. Like a foot waking up from being asleep, she would think it was gone and then she would shift slightly, and bright stabs of pain would pinch her skin. Even when she didn't move, her lungs ached with each breath, no matter how shallow. So she let herself lay there, eyes closed, imagining Gabe's reaction to her homecoming.

Surely the men would still be in the forest looking for her. She believed this so completely that every time she heard the rustle of wildlife, she flinched, and her stomach released a wave of tingling anxiety that rolled up her chest, thinking the guards had found her. But even when she was certain that she had been found and was about to be taken captive, lectured, and brought back to her father to be lectured further, she did not sit up to look around.

They will find me when they find me, she thought. Now that she was home, she was not so eager to see her guards. Now that she was safe, there was more fear of her protectors than longing for them.

Yet even though the wriggling worm of nervousness continued to grow in her belly, feeding itself with every rustle of the undergrowth, she had a feeling that since she had been gone for so long, her punishment would actually be lesser. Yes, Father would likely punish her both with words and the switch (which was worse, she would never be able to say) but he would be relieved that she was home, and the punishments would be more perfunctory than angry. She actually smiled at this, now fantasizing about the thought of her father hugging her.

She was so absorbed in her daydream that she truly felt as though she were seeing her father. She watched as he stood up, a frown etched on his face, and then, before he could open his mouth to lambaste her, he would hold out his arms instead. She would run to him, then. She would hug him tightly and she wouldn't let go, not ever, or at least not until he pushed her away or someone pulled her off of him.

This thought made her so filled with joy that she actually squealed a little. Then she was so excited at the prospect of seeing her father and Gabe again that her eyes flew open and she sprang to her feet.

Still grinning, she looked around for familiar surroundings. She was terrible with anything having to do with geography, but she'd traveled through this forest for years. There would be pine trees, of course, and short bushes of holly and maybe even blackberry bushes. There were also small, sharp rocks and sprinkles of obsidian. She thought she'd seen a fallen tree just before Sir Caleb had caught up to her, but of this she couldn't be certain. She'd been in a sort of trance, and it was hard to remember anything from that moment. In fact, everything after the moment she decided to escape to the festival felt like nothing short of a dream. But now was real.

Yet although she had a general idea of what markers she'd see in the forest, she saw none of them. The portal seemed to have deposited her in a ring of trees and boulders exactly like the one in Elt. Even the trees themselves were the same huge, chestnut ones that had encircled the Seam. She tried to peek out of the openings between the trunks, figuring she would glimpse the pines of Centerton's forest outside of the ring, but it was too dark to see. However, as she looked, she noticed something dark and soft poking out of the rocks beside her. She leaned over and grabbed her cloak from where she had thrown it before she jumped.

Her excitement at her return turned into stone in her stomach. Sada scrambled to her feet and wrapped the cloak around her half-bare body as she whipped her head around, searching for mundanity. The air was no longer icy, but she shivered nonetheless; everything looked exactly the same as it had in Elt—the rocks, the trees, the clumps of moss.

Sada frantically clambered over the stones, slipping in her hurry, and raced to the border of trees separating her from what she desperately hoped was the dark forest of her home. But as she slipped out from between the huge trunks, Sada's heart dropped. Though the forest was dark, it was unmistakable that it was still made up of the great, towering trees of Elt's woods. The same thick blanket of moss covered the ground, and the ferns and flowers grew much taller than they ever should be able to in her world. She smelled not pine, but moss and the spices of fresh baking. Panting in her panic, she heard something she had hoped to never hear in the forest again: the distant sounds of what was possibly harps or lyres.

"Oh no no *no*," she moaned.

The Elves! The thought was bright and full of hope. They had said they'd ensure her safe passage, and that meant waiting until her crossing was done with. She looked around wildly, scanning the trees for the archers' unnaturally still bodies, hoping when she couldn't see them that it meant their bare chests had simply blended into the colors of the trees again. But they were gone. She ran to the other side of the tree ring, slipping on mist-slickened rocks, and hung her head out of the trees on that side. Nobody looked out from the forest at her. She did the same at every opening between the trunks, desperately hoping that perhaps one glance would reveal what another had not. She didn't stop until she was breathless, cold with sweat, and utterly without hope. Then she finally admitted to herself that she was alone.

And the forest was dark.

The pink light had dwindled as Sada walked with the Elves, and now it had been replaced completely by the purple light of a strange moon. The woods were illuminated by it, but in the night, their vibrant colors had become all lavender and black, and she shivered at the eeriness of it. Then the sound of any creatures and wind dwindled away and fell silent, and Sada was left only with the company of the music. It had changed as she looked for the Elves, she realized. It had been as subtle as dusk bleeding into night, but she heard them now. Not lyres or harps, but the eerie thumping of drums.

War drums, she thought.

The sound caused Sada to recall Pine-Eyes's warning: *the denizens of our realm harbor no warmth for mortals,* he had said. She could feel her heart thundering in her chest in discord to the drumming, and some terrified instinct told her those

(monsters)

denizens could probably hear it and smell the blood it was pumping through her veins. She backed into the ring of trees again, their tight circle the only comfort she had against the terror of the night and a strange, possibly unfriendly forest. Hastily, she made her way back to the center of the circle. Perhaps she had jumped wrong, or hadn't landed in the heart of the portal as the Elf had instructed. She scrambled back atop the boulder she had jumped off and prepared herself to leap into the painful silver water again, but when she looked down all she saw was a pond. It wasn't eddying or swirling, it didn't hypnotize her as she looked, and it wasn't even silver. It was simply a plain pool of water, darkened by the disappearance of the sun.

"No, no, no," Sada whispered to herself.

She tore off her cloak again and jumped anyway. Perhaps the dark was creating an illusion, perhaps the pond was still filled with the same molten starlight as it had been before. But as she landed with a splash, no icy hot liquid burned her skin, and she could see the warped shape of her bare legs beneath the clear surface of the water. Around her feet she saw sand billowing up in clouds at the impact. Dread weighed heavy in her stomach, but she wouldn't let herself consider her reality. Instead, she just climbed back atop the boulder and jumped again. When still nothing happened, she did it again.

Then again.

Then again.

She kept going until the water had become cloudy with sand and clumps of loosed moss floated on the troubled surface.

Sada pulled herself from the pond for a final time, wet and defeated. Dressed only in a soaked slip and corset, she curled herself up against one of the rocks near the pond, wishing that the water streaming off of her would begin to burn again. Even the strange and horrible pain would be more welcome than what this meant: that she was stuck in a strange world of Elves and burning silver water and people that called her "mortal."

I know that they aren't human. But if I'm known as a mortal, what does that say of them?

Worst of all, she was stuck in a world without Gabe, her father, or Jezebel.

As she lay there shivering in the warm breeze, she couldn't help but think of Jezi. Sada's promise had been broken, and she'd abandoned her friend. She hadn't even been able to apologize, and now she might not ever. Sada's stomach twisted at the thought of never being able to see her again. Gabriel would be in the woods or in Centerton searching for her now, thinking she'd just run away like the silly young lady she was. Her father would no doubt be pacing the manor, perhaps looking out the window that oversaw the orchard where she'd thought she'd seen his face as she snuck away.

She almost laughed at how stupid she was to have been afraid of them finding her at the festival. Now it would be all she could give to have Sir Caleb and Gabriel and John show up here leading their lines of knights, to see her father's scowling face and his cold blue eyes, citrus switch in hand. She even allowed herself to fantasize that Uncle Beron had seen her sneak away and followed her; he'd always been one to seek out trouble. Sada's fingers drifted up to the cuff on her ear that he'd stolen, and she felt the tiny ruby encased in it. As she felt how small it was, barely big enough to be discernible from its casing, the crack that had been forming in her chest split apart and huge, unladylike sobs escaped from her body.

Part of her feared it would attract the attention of the unfriendly residents she'd been warned about, and part of her hoped it would bring the Elves running. But neither thought mattered. She was no longer in control of her body, and it wept and blubbered and screamed without her instruction. Sometime during her crying, she fell asleep, though in her dreams she still cried. She had to watch as Jezebel and Gabriel, Beron and her father, and even her faceless mother were hunted down in Elt's huge forest and killed by a shapeless creature with huge teeth. Then as the dream ended, she realized the monster was her. Though she slept, Sada wasn't sure she rested at all.

Gabriel

Gabriel stalked through the darkened forest with his head down and jaw clenched. The moon seemed to have decided to hide its face this doomed night, but he didn't carry a lantern. One of the new lads, Benny he was called, had tried offering him one, then followed at Gabriel's side when his offer was refused. In his anger, Gabriel had shoved the boy aside; he'd seen him fall and the shame came instantly to his heart, but he stalked ahead, nonetheless.

He wanted to blame Caleb for this mess. John had been the one to notice the little lady's absence, and he and Gabriel immediately set off into the forest, not wasting time to saddle and mount up. Caleb did take the time to do so, and quickly overtook them along with his best men, promising with a grating wink that he would return the "leetle brat." Gabriel had run even harder at that comment, planning to pull the devil of a man off his horse and take the mount himself. But even at his panting speed, he had only caught up to Caleb's riderless horse, cropping grass while his squire Andrew held the reins. Upon Gabriel's fervent interrogation, Andrew had pointed him into the woods where Caleb had apparently taken off after Sada on foot.

"She's fast for a lady, I'll tell you that," Andrew had said, whistling. "Caleb's got some legs on 'im but I won't lie and say that I'm sure he'll catch her."

"Then what in the good Lord's name are you doing just *standing there?"* Gabriel had roared. He started into the forest then turned back. "How long have they been in there?"

Andrew just shrugged, calm as you please and chewing on a piece of grass he'd plucked. "Five or six turns o' the minute, I s'pose."

Gabriel had snatched the stupid piece of grass from his worthless mouth before turning and sprinting into the forest.

He hadn't needed to run far. The path was still close behind him when he came upon Caleb, head down and eyes grim. His gauntlets were covered in gritty mud and there was a streak of the stuff in his blonde hair. He seemed to have lost his helm somewhere along the way. All Gabriel saw was that he was alone; the little lady was nowhere to be seen. Resisting the urge to slap the man (he was still Gabriel's senior), he took Caleb by the shoulders and shook him hard, then leaned into his face.

"Where in damnation is she?" he spat.

Caleb just shook his head. "I don't know."

"What do you mean you don't know? Isn't that why you came out here? To know?"

"I mean what I say, Gabriel, *I don't know.* She just…disappeared." Caleb waved his hands in some idiotic motion conveying dust puffing into the air, and then Gabriel did slap him.

"You devil-loving wretch," Gabriel spat. "You had one job coming into these woods: bring Sada back! How hard is it to catch her? She's only a *girl* for God's sake. *She's only a girl!* Now you tell me she disappeared?" Gabriel shook him again. "What worthless kind of an excuse is that, Caleb?"

He hadn't felt this much rage in years. He hadn't been so overcome by anger since his days of barfights. He'd told himself he would never feel this way again, let alone act on it. But Caleb's next words took away every ounce of control he had left. He didn't even notice that the Spaniard man's accent had slipped back in almost completely; if he had, maybe he would have realized that meant Caleb was telling the truth, and worse—that he was terrified and in shock. But probably not.

"I do not know what to tell you, Gabriel," Caleb had said. "She deed not slip away from me, I deed not lose sight of her. One moment she was there, the next she jost *wasn't.*"

Then Gabriel's gauntlet was swinging through the air and something crunched as it landed in Caleb's face. Looking back, he realized that it wasn't what Caleb had said that had made him break. It was how he'd said it, with that *who cares, really,* kind of attitude. Gabriel hoped he knew exactly who cared now, and that anytime he forgot, his broken nose and missing teeth would remind him.

Gabriel had gifted him those reminders, armor against skin, all the while crying, *"She's just a girl she's just a girl she's just a girl!"*

Remarkably, Caleb hadn't fought back. Now, his anger cooled by that blissful sensation of numbing apathy, Gabriel wished he had. He also knew now that it wasn't Caleb who could be blamed. The senior knight walked some distance behind him now, with John in between, probably in case Gabriel decided to do something stupid again. But he knew he wouldn't. He knew that he and Caleb and all the knights trudging or clomping along behind him would likely be waving goodbye to Duke Solares's manor by the morning, if they didn't depart from this world by the swing of the Duke's own sword tonight. That idea was more sobering than cold water. Gabriel wished to wash it away with a lukewarm glass of beer in the pub.

Why did you have to go in there, Sada? he thought grimly. For he believed that her decision to "sneak" into that bar was what began all of this. Sada had never been one to do anything except mind her father, governess, and guards, and be happy doing it. Yet that day she had wanted to do more; do something she was told not to. And only a day later, she was escaping into the woods alone. If only she had asked him to come along. He would have gladly done so and accepted punishment from Duke Solares rather than endure this: this wondering of where she was, if she was safe, if someone had taken her and stolen her away.

He thought of her mother's alleged disappearance, and how similar it was in nature to this. How rather than a disappearance into a dark forest, maybe it was a planned escape from the duke to whom she was married, and the life that came with it. If that was the reason, he couldn't fathom the logic behind it. If he were the duchess, he would have done whatever was necessary to remain with the status and wealth granted by her marriage to the Duke. Regardless, he thought she had stuck around long enough to have her daughter, and then she was free as a bird to do as she pleased. Duchess Solares, at least, had guards with her. Sada had nobody, not even him.

Yes, it was Gabriel who was to blame, not Caleb.

They had searched for what felt like hours, lanterns swinging, torches sputtering to dark before being re-lit. The men with mounts had gone to Centerton and come back. His throat was raw and hoarse from screaming Sada's name, and he knew that some of his men wouldn't be able to talk tomorrow, if they even could now. Yet in all their searching, they had turned up empty handed.

They had all seen the patch of mud where the shoeprints of Sada's riding boots obviously stood out, but none could discern the meaning behind the frantic footwork and the imprints of two other bare feet: one pair small, the other large. The marks of Caleb's heavy boots stopped less than a foot away from this scuffle, and no prints led to or away from it. Gabriel had the horrible vision of bandits dressed in black dropping from the trees, scooping Sada up after a frantic scrabble in the mud, and then clambering back up the jigsaw bark of the pines. Yet he knew it was an illogical notion.

Now they trudged back to the manor without hope, and without a lady.

The manor pulled into view much sooner than Gabriel would have liked for it to. Its old shape was foreboding in the dark, with only a few window panes brightened by the yellow light of lanterns and candles. They looked like hungry eyes, and the garden path leading up to the back of the manor was a tongue. For a moment Gabriel had the idea that he should run away and never enter that manor, for a dark and horrible fate waited for him there. Yet Sir Beron had trained him better than that, and he faced his duty with a grim sureness.

Gabriel entered the manor first, followed by his squadron, then John and his men, then Caleb's men, and Caleb brought up the rear. Duke Solares was waiting for them, hands clasped behind his well-dressed back, looking at them lovelessly. He noted Caleb's mangled face and Gabriel's bloody gauntlets, but said nothing. His eyes were cold and hard, and in them Gabriel saw his own feelings reflected. Anger and a little bit of despair ruled there. Then the Duke blinked and there was only anger. Once those hard eyes had scanned the muddy troops, they landed on Gabriel.

"Speak, boy," Duke Solares growled. "By the state of Sir Caleb's face, I can discern that he is in no shape to offer me a report. As my daughter's most trusted guard, the duty now falls upon you to explain why she is not in your company."

Gabriel did not speak.

"I suppose she is not tucked safely into bed, is she?"

"No, Your Grace," Gabriel muttered. "Lady Sada is—"

Duke Solares's mask of calm shattered so abruptly that the squires and even some of the knights staggered back in a clamor of armor. *"Where is my daughter?"* he roared. "I dispatched you worthless soldiers to retrieve her, and I distinctly commanded that you were not to return unless she was with you. I don't very well see her, or have I fallen blind? I thought not. *Now where in damnation is my—*"

"She is not with us, Your Grace!" Gabriel roared. His voice surprised himself, and Duke Solares as well. The stony man blinked, mouth still opened in rage, foamy spittle stuck in his slate-colored mustache. "You say true, Lady Sada has not returned with us. We searched hours in that dark forest and another in town and saw nary a sign of where she went."

He knew he was digging his own grave with each word he spoke; he saw it in the blue fire of Duke Solares's eyes, but he could not stop.

"Where she is, I know not. I wish with every shred of my soul and honor that I did. Unfortunately, I saw nothing of the incident. I came upon the place of your daughter's disappearance when she had already gone. I have only returned to inform you of this news, and to give you what little solace it may afford."

Gabriel was panting, but Duke Solares was now standing calmly, his hands clasped behind his back again. "You saw nothing of her disappearance, Sir Gabriel?"

"No, Your Grace. Only her tracks in the mud. I was not there when sight of her was lost."

"Who was there then, sir?" he said coolly.

Before Gabriel could dishonor himself further by naming Caleb and offering him up for his surely impending punishment, the senior knight stepped forward himself. His face was remarkably bloodied, but his blonde hair was recognizable. As he knelt, he dipped his head, and those locks fell forward to shade some of his messy face from their duke.

"'Twas I, Your Grace," Caleb said. He knew the punishment he faced better than all of them, but his voice was strong regardless. "I chased your daughter down on horseback and on foot. In the end, she escaped me. In the end, it was I who lost her. Do with me as you will; I shall accept any punishment gladly and with acceptance in my heart."

For a moment, Duke Solares said nothing. Caleb remained with his head bowed. A bead of blood dropped onto the perfectly polished floor. Gabriel thought Duke Solares might have Caleb's nose cut off for it, but he seemed not to notice the blemish. Behind him, Gabriel heard the clinking of tired guards shifting in heavy armor. Duke Solares did not look up for this either. Finally, he unclasped his hands and held one out, palm up.

"Your sword, sir," he said to Caleb.

Everyone in the room froze.

Without so much as a word of protest, the knight unbuckled his scabbard from his side and placed it in Duke Solares's hand, ready for execution. Their duke drew the sword, gleaming, well-cared for, and threw aside its scratched scabbard. The only noise in the manor came from it smacking against the floor. He examined the blade, turning it in his hands, admiring it.

"Tonight marks a day of despair," Duke Solares said as he studied the blade. "You are all at fault, and yet my daughter has taught me something of mercy and of kindness. To honor her, I shall take her lesson to heart. Only one of you shall die today—he who holds the greatest portion of responsibility on his shoulders."

Gabriel heard the silent sigh of relief spread out behind him. He felt the weight lift in his own heart, like removing a full set of armor after a day of duty. None dared to speak, not even to thank the Duke for his kindness, lest it be revoked. Something in Gabriel's heart squeezed at the sight of Caleb, the eldest knight, kneeling so meekly before the Duke.

Go, take his place, his heart told him. *This isn't right. Kneel beside him.* Yet he didn't move. The guilt could not overcome his relief at being spared. Duke Solares took the pommel of the blade into his hand, preparing to strike.

"I shall accept any punishment gladly and with acceptance in my heart," Caleb said again. This time he whispered it, as though to remind himself. Gabriel watched as his eyes squeezed shut, and when blood dripped onto the pine floor this time, it was mixed with tears.

"You may have lost my daughter, Sir Caleb." The Duke turned from the kneeling knight. "Yet it was you who loved her the most."

Duke Solares swung.

Gabriel didn't have time to register the gleam of the blade before it was buried in his neck and his head was flying across the room. He didn't feel the pain. Nor did he see the pain in John's eyes, or the pleasure in Duke Solares's, as he unknowingly accepted punishment for Sada's disappearance.

And he hadn't even needed to kneel.

Sada

Sada awoke aching and sore. She found herself lying on something hard and warm, and briefly she wondered if she'd managed to fall asleep on the floor and escape unnoticed by the servants. But why would she go and do that? The only person she'd regularly seen sleeping on the floor was Uncle Beron, usually with the smell of whiskey blanketing him rather than a quilt; the bottle would have been silently swept away by a servant as soon as he was no longer conscious to protest it. *I should banish the drunken scum from my estates,* Duke Solares grumbled whenever a wide-eyed housemaid would whisper to him her discovery of a slumbering Lord Beron lying dead to the world on the floor. Yes, "drunken scum" were the ones who fell asleep on the floor, but not nice young ladies.

Especially not those who call Duke Darius Solares their father, she thought. She opened her eyes to soft sunlight coming down between large leaves and trunks to warm the rocks which surrounded her, and a knot in her stomach reformed with familiarity. There were no servants to wake her here, and no drunk uncles either.

The hearth of panic was gone from her chest, and now it was a subtle sense of unease that resided somewhere deep in her throat and gut. It prickled at the palms of her hands and forehead. She thought she would be unable to speak if she tried to, but she didn't need to speak. There was nobody around to hear her, and as Governess Brown said, only lunatics like the man in the street spoke to themselves.

Well, if I'm not a lunatic yet, I may very well be close to earning the title.

Sada pushed herself to her feet and reached for her cloak, which she found lying across some rocks, the ends soaking in the pond. The boring, blank pond. As she bent forward, her skin screamed in protest and she gasped, laying back gingerly. She had fallen asleep in just her slip, and the sunny pink rays of the forest had found her skin and marked her; one side of her body was sore to the touch like a bruise, and hot, too. A clean line separated the burnt skin from that which had been covered by her dress or pressed safely against the rock.

Sada had never been burned before. Her nurses and nannies had always rushed her inside before the sun was able to scorch her, or she was sheltered by so many scarves, hats, and parasols that the evil sun was powerless against such protection. The part of her that was more imaginative than rational believed the burn was a magickal effect of Elt. Perhaps she was turning into an Elf or another Eltic creature. The thought didn't scare her, but that was because she knew it was unlikely. Still, the effect of the burn seemed fantastical, if not otherworldly, and she poked at her arm, staring in fascination at the brief change in color it caused. Then she pressed on, past the point of fascination, unwilling to admit it was because she didn't want to look up and see the world she had tried to leave.

Yet the game could only distract from so many things, and thirst was not one of them. Suddenly water was the only thing on her mind. She scrambled for the pool, ignoring the tight pain it brought to her one sunburned knee. She briefly wondered if the water was safe to drink, then decided that she would rather not know and brought mouthful after mouthful of it to her dry, cracked lips. It was warm from the sunlight, but tasted as clear as the water from a well. The last few mouthfuls were gritty with sand that had been stirred up in her frantic splashing, but she hardly cared. Finally, face dripping and thirst sated, she sat back.

Seeing the pretty trees with their hand-like leaves again made the morosity sink back in, like the water settling uneasily in her stomach.

Sada stood and gingerly adjusted the long velvet cloak around her shoulders, then stumbled across the uneven ground to find her dress and skirts. As she walked—and tripped—she watched the pond from the corner of her eye, hoping desperately she would see the mystical swirling silver again. But the water was clear, the sand settled serenely at the bottom of the pool once again. It made her feel like crying, so she focused on her feet—one now a different shade than the other. She found her dress lying half-hidden in the rocks. It was dry now, but the strange liquid of the Seam had dried with the fabric, leaving shimmering silver webbing on the gown from the hem to the bodice.

She had the sudden thought that this dried portion of the Seam would be enough to transport her home. She couldn't quite jump into it feet-first, but perhaps she didn't need the full portal. She hurriedly pressed her fingers against the raised surface of the portal's leavings, hope flickering in her chest.

"Ah!"

She drew her hand back almost as soon as she made contact. Though solid, the stuff was hot to the touch, yet cold at the same time. Just like the feeling in the eastern woods. Except this time it hurt, almost as badly as a wasp sting.

"That wasn't very nice," Sada scolded it.

She was quickly distracted from her chastising as a shock of electric tingles filled the palm of her left hand. She gasped, staring at her hand. Other than the new sunburn and a broken nail (*I'll need to find a file,* she thought absently), it looked normal. She looked back to the rivulets of the Seam frozen on her dress. Were the remnants of the portal what had caused the sensation? The pain was still lingering in her fingertips, but curiosity was stronger than fear of worsening it. She touched the silver again, wincing at the burn. A buzzing sensation immediately filled her left hand again and slowly worked its way up to her elbow even when she pulled her fingers away. That was strange because she had touched the stuff with her *right* hand. She then tried touching it with her left hand.

The sensation was so sudden and strong, her vision disappeared for a moment. Immediately upon contact, it felt as though every particle of her left arm, from fingertips to elbow, had begun vibrating at an impossibly fast speed. That, accompanied by an overwhelming feeling of heat so brilliant it was cold, had caused her arm to freeze up and her vision to shut down. When she regained control of her body, she threw the dress away with a prolonged screech that grew louder as it continued. Then, clutching her forearm with her good hand, she panted and gasped from the pain, squeezing her eyes shut and clenching her teeth.

Finally, it was gone, and she drew in a shuddering breath. She never wanted to touch the dress again—even the parts that weren't contaminated. Briefly she wondered if she could manage in just her cloak, but it flicked open with every step she took, exposing her slip, and that just wouldn't do.

With much reluctance, she retrieved the gown, ensuring she only touched it with her right hand.

Though rudely painful, the Seam's remnants were incredible. Sada admired their gleaming beauty in the light, noting how even dried, the silver seemed to swirl. But the dress was ruined. Her father had taught her of fashion, made it a rule in his household, and despite the beauty of the silver, the dress was now the equivalent of one of her father's paintings being finger-painted on by a child. Even if the paint was the most beautiful color in the world. With thoughts of her father's imaginary scoldings in her mind, she gathered her garments from the nearby rocks and gingerly dressed herself.

The clothes were warm from lying in the sun, and when she put on the cloak, she may as well have been in a heated manor. But the forest around her resembled no part of her home, and the reminder sent her fingers to find the tips of her now-tangled hair. Most of it had fallen from the elegant updo it had begun in. An updo fit for a festival. Now it was fit for a bird or mouse to nest in. She tried not to think about how tangled it was, because if she thought about that, it would make her think about how she had no brush to fix it, and if she thought of that, she would think of how she had no way of getting to her room to get a brush to fix it—and if she thought of that, she might cry.

And so Sada tried not to think at all.

It wasn't hard. Whenever Father yelled at her, she went into a strange sort of trance. It was a halfway state between waking and daydreaming, the kind where you didn't really think of anything, but you didn't really see anything from the real world either. When he began to yell, her brain took her there. It was almost as if she left her body, gave control to some other part of her which was always there but did not always make itself known. It knew when to make her nod, how to make her eyebrows scrunch so she looked apologetic, at what times she should agree or fervently shake her head, when she should lower her eyes or meet the Duke's.

That part of Sada came out now. It saw that she was alone in the woods, truly alone for the first time in her life, and it put her mind to sleep. And so she went back to the middle of the tree ring, far from the evils of the forest where only strangers lived, and sat. She sat unseeing, unthinking, unknowing.

If the Elven guards or the denizens of the realm that they had spoken of had been around to see her, they would have seen a young woman alone among the rocks. At first, they would think she was completely still—almost as unnaturally still as one of their own immortal kind—but then they would see her hands, twisting restlessly in her hair, tangling it, breaking it, abusing it. Then they would see her face and wonder if she was asleep: her jaw would be completely slack, her mouth slightly parted. But then they'd see her eyes, which were open, and realize she couldn't possibly be asleep. She hardly blinked, and her eyes did not move to track the world around her; they simply stared, wide open and with no emotion—only a blankness, an emptiness. Like a dead thing, they stared.

And stared.

And stared.

At nothing.

So then her observers might conclude that she was daydreaming, lost in her own world, and turn away, because it was almost unnerving how she seemed to be sleeping while awake. But they would be wrong, because to daydream assumes your mind is active, but Sada's was not. There was only one image burned into her brain, and she could not look away:

Her father's eyes. Blue and cruel and dangerous like fresh ice, daring her to feel sorry for herself.

I'm not, Father, she told him in her empty mind. *I'm strong. I know this is my fault. I know I shouldn't have run. But I did, and I will deal with the consequences.*

Just not yet. For now, she would only sit and do nothing. Empty save for the image of the Duke, and her whispered responses.

It took a long time for Sada to "wake up" again, to rise from the trance her mind had put her in to keep her safe from reality. The transition was slow. She'd begun it by daydreaming. Her father's fresh-ice blue eyes had turned to the pinecone ones of Jezebel. Sada had imagined going to the festival, returning the ear cuff, making up with her friend. They'd spend the rest of the night selling Mr. Pérez's wares and Sada would return home tired but happy, now escorted by her guards, trading jokes with Gabe and laughing with him at Sir Ryan's permanent scowl. The fantasy ended when she thought of hugging her father.

He will never hug you, she thought, and it was a bitter one. But it was good, reminding herself of that. It made her come back to her body. For the last hour she had not moved even an inch. Toward the end she had wanted to, because the outer two toes of her left foot had grown numb, and there was a stone poking into her right hip, but she had been physically unable to even shift her body. At that point even her fingers had ceased to fidget with her hair and her lower lip had been free of her teeth's bite. She had truly frozen, in both mind and body. But now she was thawing, and the daydream was receding, and so she forced herself to move, first her left foot, then her right. She shook out her arms, took a deep breath, and let it out in one of those shuddering sighs that only come after a deep stress or sadness.

And then she was okay. Not good, of course, but okay.

She methodically buckled her cloak, found her boots and pulled them on. She pulled the remaining pins out of her hair (they were doing more harm than good), gathered her hair behind her shoulders, tucked it behind her ears out of habit—only to untuck it again, with Governess Brown's scolding about beauty taking precedence over comfort ringing in her mind. She was still relatively devoid of thoughts, and her chest felt strangely hollow, the way it did after you finished crying. She welcomed it, because at least it was not fear.

Finally she looked through the ring of trees and into the forest. It was brilliant, of course. It was beautiful in every meaning of the word, and looking at it made her want to scream or squeal or sing because such beauty should not be possible. Yet she did none of those things. Instead, though she did not want to, she stepped into Elt.

The only thing settled in her mind was the goal of finding her way back home. It was not a question of "if" for her. Because no matter what, she was a Solares, and she was the daughter of Duke Darius. She *would* find her way home, no matter how long the journey took. She knew this as surely as she felt the ground beneath her booted feet when she stepped into the woods.

The air shifted as she did, as though the circle had been a small realm of its own. Like a child reluctant to leave the light and step into the darkness, she glanced back at her safety. But she knew she could not stay there. The portal had rejected her, somehow, or she had broken it. Either way, she was not welcome there, and either way, it would not take her home.

Out in the open forest, the air was dancing with a soft but warm breeze, and the pink sunlight gently warmed the skin on her hands and face. The forest smelled of the sweetness of leaves, moss, spices, and sun-warmed things. It was so unlike the dim and muddy forest Sada had gone into the night before.

And never returned from, she thought as she imagined her father sending his men to look for her. She saw Gabriel's face and wished desperately to be hugged by his armor-encased arms. She almost began crying again at the thought, but the voice of Memory prodded at her. *It is not the ladies who cry that find themselves with a place upon the throne*, it told her. Sada had always refused to acknowledge the other part of the saying: *It is the ladies who make others cry that wear the crown*. Sada would not make others cry, no matter how crownless it made her. She did not want a crown anyway; ruling did not suit her. She could hardly order servants around without feeling guilty.

But the crown was where she needed to go now. The Elven king had treated her kindly—mostly—and who better to go to with your troubles than the king?

I could think of a few better people, actually: the emissary, an advisor, a courtier, the queen...The king was in fact the last place she would go to for help in Ettedon. Even her own father would scold her for coming to him before trying the servants or Governess Brown first.

But she could only hope that rulers of Elt were more concerned about their subjects than the rulers in her world. King Caprius had known what to do the first time; there was a good chance he'd have an idea of how to help her now, too. And even if he didn't, he was the only native to this land that she knew. What other choice did she have? She briefly thought of the two brothers and wondered at their fate. She should have tried harder to have them returned home with her.

Though it didn't do me *much good,* Sada thought dismally as she looked back at the ring of trees. The wooden circle seemed to mock her.

As Sada drew away from the Seam, the change in the forest was almost shocking. It was no longer eerily silent, but rich with the trilling and singing of birds. Critters rustled the leaves of the fern clumps and bushes, and she heard a snort or sniffle every so often that made her jump. There was even the distant barking and bugling of foxes and elk alike. But the creatures making their noises remained hidden from her. And amidst the sounds of nature, that soft, distant tune could be heard underlying it all. Much to Sada's contentment, the scary drums had been replaced by the lyre-harp, though she still didn't know which it was. She had never mastered manmade instruments.

As she walked, she began to sing. It was a folk song she'd heard many times from Governess Brown (though she sang a very butchered version that made Sada giggle) and a few times from her father. He denied any ability to sing, but Sada knew the truth, and it was a beautiful one. As a girl, she'd ask him to sing the song again and again for her, and when he finally gave in, he would always dramatically roll his r's to her delight. He said that her mother had required him to learn the language of her people before they could marry, and so he had learned it that very *eméra* ("day" in her mother's tongue). That had made Sada giggle too.

She heard the story-song less and less as she grew older and her father grew colder, but though it had been years since she'd heard him sing it, his voice and his rolling r's were still strong in her memory. Singing the folk song from her mother's home calmed the nerves in her stomach and helped her think.

"Véla tou druómou thélei sé órcheistai—
The view of the forest makes you want to dance—
Arktós bruné, éthimos? Órchesthai metá mou!!
Brown bear, ready? Dance with me!
Fónai tou druómou thélousi sé gelân—

The sounds of the forest make you want to laugh—
Lýkos grisé, éthimos? Gelân metá mou!
Grey wolf, ready? Laugh with me!"

Sada had set off in the direction she thought she'd come from with the Elves, though she'd been more focused on the beauty of the forest than on remembering the path they walked. That had always been Gabe's job, and in her mind the Elves had taken up that duty in place of her lifelong guard. Though Sada did remember that they had gone in a straight line from the Road of Ages to reach the Seam, and so she followed a line of trees straight through the woods. Hopefully when she reached the path, the merchants would be there, and they could take her to King Caprius.

Sada glanced up at the ceiling of broad drooping leaves, searching for the sun. The autumn-colored canopy opened up farther ahead, and when Sada reached the spot, she could see the sun peeking up over the heads of the towering trees. She gasped as she realized it was pink. She had thought the color of the sunlight was a trick of the forest. Something about the wonder of it made her laugh in delight despite her circumstances.

Sada continued on, singing softly and grazing her hand against the strangely smooth bark of the trees. It ignited a gentle buzzing in her left hand. She still marveled at the way their bark was free of any bumps and gnarls. A few of the trees had scratches around their bases, though, and she wondered which creatures put them there. As she sang, the sounds of the forest grew, and the music seemed to get louder. It was then that she realized how truly loud this forest was.

The woods of her home were rarely filled with the sound of anything but the voices of insects; other than that, it was silent. Here, the bugs were the only things that did not sing, but their songs were replaced by those of bigger, furrier, and more feathery creatures. And even when they were silent, still the harps and lyres played their tune. Now both they and the voices of the wildlife were so great she could hardly hear her own footsteps. Sada smiled—the forest was singing with her! She slowed the speed of her voice to match that of the lyre-harp sounds.

"Phíle, élthe kaí véle!
Friend, come and see!
Esti panégyris en tó druómo!
There's a party in the forest!
Élthe kaí véle, élthe ný!
Come and see, come now—"

Sada stopped in her tracks.

All around her, there were eyes.

Some peered at her through bushes, others peeked around trees, and even more still looked down from the canopy above. No matter their location, they were all staring at her. Some belonged to elk or moose looking at her below racks of antlers as long across as she was. One pair belonged to a lynx, panting and crouched below a bush. A few bunnies, eyes wide and noses twitching, hunkered at the bases of trees. Above them, clutching the wide trunks, perched fluffy squirrels as big as cats, and some, she saw, had three tails.

Her voice faltered at the sight, and when she blinked the creatures were gone, the undergrowth rustling. The music had died back down to its soft lilting tune again and the chatter of the woods was once more resigned.

"What in the criminy crackers…?" she whispered.

Sada looked around for more eyes watching her, but seeing none, she hesitantly continued forward. A jolt ran through her from fingers to scalp, tickling her skin and making sweat form on her palms. It was a bright mixture of fear and excitement. She'd always loved animals, but she'd grown up with warnings of how the wild ones would gouge her belly out or give her soap-mouth or other diseases.

Seeing all those creatures had been incredible, but she wasn't sure what she would have done had they gotten closer. Soap-mouth was one of her greatest fears. The doctors called it hydrophobia, because it made you scared of water. It came from angry animals, and the townspeople named it "soap-mouth" because the animals who had it looked like they had just eaten a bar of soap. The thought of a livid, foamy-mouthed squirrel biting her made her nauseous. She scanned the forest as she walked, now alert for any signs of potential attackers.

But as she did, she got to imagining what they'd look like, and she couldn't stop picturing a raccoon nibbling on a bar of soap. She giggled, then quickly covered her mouth, lest any potential observers think her insane.

Sada began to sing again, softer this time, to calm her nerves. Where had the animals come from? She hadn't heard any of them growing closer to her, though to be fair she hadn't truly been paying much attention to her surroundings. The sky had been so beautiful, and she had been focused on *flipping* her r's instead of *rolling* them, as her father had taught her was appropriate.

Apparently, nagging Duke Solares on his pronunciation of her language had been Duchess Solares's favorite pastime. Father had taken up the hobby with Sada as his victim after her mother's disappearance. Sada rolled and flipped her r's as she walked, thinking of the strange incident that had just occurred. She pondered whether the hobbies of Elt's animals often included people-watching. Perhaps they knew she was a stranger to their land, and they wanted to observe her.

The denizens of our realm harbor no warmth for mortals. She wondered if these shy, furry animals were included in the denizens the Elf had spoken of. She didn't think so. Other than the lynx, with its half-fearful and half-reproachful gaze, the creatures had been nothing short of adorable. If she'd had food with her, she might have offered them some, hoping one would be daring enough to eat from her palm.

But the soap-mouth…and so many other diseases that Governess Brown's friend, Mrs. Havens, told you of. Right. So probably she wouldn't. But it was a romantic idea.

Her stomach growled. She hadn't eaten in ages, and the spiced scent of the forest and the smell of fresh baking did nothing but sharpen her hunger. She supposed she would have to wait until she reached the Elven king to eat, or until she came across a house made of candy like in the stories her nursemaids told. But the pains of hunger were so distracting that it was all she could think of. Her hunger fueled fantasies and visions of stumbling into a village of chocolate, or a cottage made of cheese. It would be devoid of any residents, and she would take a huge bite straight out of the wall. She would eat and eat until the whole house was gone.

She was wondering what sorts of food King Caprius might have in his palace when she spotted a bush weighed down by whole clusters of bright berries. She went to it, and saw the fruit resembled the shape of blackberries, but they were bright blue rather than black, and the bush had no brambles.

She plucked a berry free to examine it. Her left hand immediately began to prickle, but she hardly noticed. The berry was the size of a peach pit and looked tantalizingly juicy. It certainly looked edible, and the brilliant color made her stomach rumble in anticipation. She tried a nibble. Sweet, icy liquid gushed over her tongue, and she gasped at the cold. It was as though the berry was frozen, but…soft? She popped the rest of the fruit in her mouth, running her tongue over it as though she could test it for poison that way.

Governess Brown had told her of a reaction that some people have to certain foods, usually nuts. When eaten, their throat would close in on itself and they would be unable to breathe, and usually they died. Sada ate the berry with this in mind and after she swallowed it, her throat felt tight for one panic-filled moment…then it went away. She waited a few seconds and nothing horrible happened, so she plucked another berry and ate it, relishing the way the icy juice cooled her parched throat.

She continued on until she was full with no regard for ladylike appearances. When she was done, there was a bare spot left on the bush where she had stolen its fruit. She wished she could save more for later, but the only pocket her cloak bore held her powder, and she had forgone tying her pockets onto her dress.

Of course, had I chosen to wear my pockets, then I wouldn't have needed them, because that's simply how the world works. So really, it is the pockets' fault that I am stuck here in this fantastical world. That made her giggle at herself again. Well, she wouldn't bother chiding herself for her lack of foresight; the moment was done and gone. She wiped her juice-covered hands on the moss and continued on her way.

As Sada walked, the air began to grow warmer. She thought that perhaps it was mid-day already or the ceiling of leaves had thinned to let more of the heat through, but when she looked up she didn't see the sun overhead, and the treetops were just as tightly clustered together as they'd always been. She decided that the world here was simply strange, and she didn't know its laws of nature. But it was becoming unbearably hot, and her face was flushing.

She switched to carrying her cloak when it grew too warm, but removing it did little to combat the heat. And now her gown was sticking to her armpits and her corset was sticky on her stomach and back. She tried to hold up her hair which had begun to stick to her face and neck, but the effort was too great in the heat. She had to slow the pace of her walk lest she begin panting like the lynx she'd seen.

Sada reached a large, shady trunk and leaned against it, nearly gasping now from the intensity of the heat. Her eyelids were drooping and the fire encasing her skin seemed to be sapping all of the energy from her. She felt herself slide down the trunk of the great tree, and there was little she could do to stop it. She reasoned that if she was going the right way, she should reach the merchant path in just another hour. Resting for a moment would make her journey quicker, she told herself as her eyelids fought to close.

Waves of heat were crashing over her body now, and she feebly tried to pull down the sleeves of her dress or unlace the back. If she could just *breathe* for a moment, perhaps she'd be able to cool down. Her heart was pounding concerningly against her ribcage, and worry prickled sharply at her forehead. Yet it did nothing to combat the drowsiness the heat exhaustion had brought on. Her eyelids drooped further, and the vibrant colors of the forest blurred. She vaguely thought she could see the eyes of curious creatures begin to appear around her again and one more worry of soap-mouth lit up her mind, then her own eyes closed, and she saw no more.

Sada awoke in a panic and her eyes flew open to take in the forest around her. She had fallen asleep in the middle of the day. If the Duke found out, she would be yelled at or lashed. Her chest was already paralyzed, and she tried to gasp but was unable to. Heart fluttering, she squeezed her eyes shut and counted three of the panicked beats

(1, 2, 3)

then her lungs were released from the paralyzing hold, and she drew in a huge breath.

Father isn't here. The citrus trees aren't here. I'm safe.

As her heart slowed its racing tempo, Sada glanced around herself. It was still light, she was still alive, and she seemed to be unharmed. She looked down to make sure of the latter, and when she did, she saw an antlered head lying across her lap. Each breath from its great nostrils stirred the folds of her silver-webbed gown. Sada's frightened gaze took in more fuzzy shapes clustered around her legs, and something resembling a fur scarf was draped across one of her shins.

The panic in her chest surged and Sada couldn't help but stiffen and yelp at the sight. As she did, the huge elk sleeping on her lap shot to its feet and galloped away with a bugling cry. The other creatures started at that too, and they all scurried into the forest, wide eyed and chittering. Sada was left with a pounding heart as she watched the animals disappear into the underbrush.

"What in the heavens above and the earth below…?" she wondered aloud, hand pressed tightly to her chest. Her heart pounded beneath her fingers.

The creatures were so friendly in Elt! Even friendlier than her geldings—and *much* friendlier than her mares. It was nothing short of a dream, waking up to wild creatures asleep on and around her, and she had sent them off in fear! Thoughts of foamy mouths flashed in her mind, but these wild animals had looked cleaner even than the pets of her world, certainly not diseased.

She determined that the next time one of the animals got close to her, she would pet it and not be afraid.

Smiling at the memory of the weasel lying across her ankles, Sada drew herself to her feet and brushed bits of moss off her gown. As she did so she caught a glimpse of blue and realized her fingers were entirely stained with the juice of the berries she'd eaten. The heat was gone from her body now, despite the light that still pinkened the forest.

Well, my throat didn't close up, but I certainly had some *sort of reaction to that fruit!* she thought uneasily. No matter how hungry she grew in the time it took to walk through the woods, she would not let herself eat any more of the vibrant fruits.

Looking back up through the opening in the leaves, she realized the pink of the sun was no longer above her. Just how long had she slept? She chewed at her lip. The day was melting into night again already, the forest quieting. Sada picked her cloak up off the ground where it had fallen but didn't put it on—soft sunlight still made its way into the forest to warm her. She continued walking, urged on by the fear of the dark.

Sada traipsed through the forest for what felt like an endless amount of time, nothing to occupy her mind but her singing. As she walked, she noticed a pair or two of bright eyes looking at her from the trees. She found the stares typically came from furry elk with huge antlers, foxes with multiple fluffy tails, or rabbits with four ears. She'd even spotted a stray chicken, but when she made to approach it, making poor attempts at clucking noises and crooning in the tongue of the north, it disappeared.

By the time the sun set, Sada was still walking. The forest darkened, the bright eyes of the animals began to disappear, retiring for the night. Sada knew she should too, that it was dangerous at night, but she couldn't bring herself to stop walking. It meant she had to face the now undeniable reality: she was utterly lost. She should have reached the amber path long ago, and since she hadn't, it meant she'd gone in the wrong direction.

"Please, please, please," she kept whispering. *"Please, please, please."* She didn't know who she was begging, or what she was pleading for. Probably God, and probably for many things: *Please let me not be lost. Please let me find the Road of Ages. Please tell me this is a dream. Please let Mr. Wolf or Pine-Eyes find me or appear suddenly. Please let me go home.*

Please, tell me what to do.

Please, please, please…

If her father was here, if Gabe was here, if John or Sir Caleb were here, she would not be afraid. Even if they were lost forever, she would not fear. They would know what to do. They always knew what to do. But Sada never did. And she was never alone. Now, she didn't know how to be.

Fear was creeping in steadily, and she worried that if she stopped walking, she would be frozen again and retreat into her mind, left defenseless against the creatures of the woods. And so she kept walking, toward the setting sun, figuring that walking in the same straight line was better than wandering aimlessly in whatever direction her heart desired. As Governess Brown often recited to her, *the human heart is the most deceitful of all things.* It stuck in her brain, and so she began singing frantic nonsense about the heart's deceit and of how it had betrayed her in telling her to run away to the festival and of how it had caused her to become lost, and she sang in a panicky falsetto until she felt her fear transform into a great beast inside of her, making her twitch at every noise and imagine every possible worst-case scenario, and then she began to sprint.

She tried to run from the fear that was within her. She ran as hard as she could, eyes wide and frantically searching the forest for any hidden danger and also for any sign of the amber path that she knew she wouldn't find. She ran until she stumbled over a tree root hidden by moss and shadows, and then she sat where she'd fallen.

Her voice and mind were suddenly as tired as her body. She told herself she needed to get up and keep going, that moving in some direction was better than just sitting on the ground, that if she just kept walking a little further, she'd find the path… but she didn't truly believe that.

"You're lost, Sada," she whispered to herself. "You cannot deny it. You should have found the merchants and the path by now. Lost you are, lost indeed, and in need of a new plan. But not tonight. The night is dangerous, in this place even more so; the Elves themselves warned you." Saying the word "Elves" aloud made her pause and laugh at the sheer unreality of it all. "Elves, Elves, Elves. Inhumanly beautiful men with pointed ears, four-eared rabbits, and portals fashioned of…molten…starlight are…real…"

It was then she realized her mistake. She'd been searching for the Road of Ages and the merchants who would be working in the stands that lined it in hopes of finding someone who could take her to the Elven king, when in reality, if she would have stayed put at the portal, they would have come to her. The portal, where Mr. Wolf said visitors went. She could have simply stayed put, and someone would have come to see the Seam and inevitably found her there. That realization, and the following realization that every single decision she'd made by herself the past two days had led to her being lost in a world where human was not the norm, made her laugh. She laughed loudly and hysterically, so hard she began to cry.

It was the only sound she could hear.

The forest had gone silent once the sun set. The abrupt synchronicity with which all the animals stopped rustling, chirping, and chittering had been more than unsettling. They were not unlike those wind-up soldiers the village boys played with, who went marching across the dirt with a few twists of the metal knob in their back before falling still once more. As the toys were powered by that metal knob, it seemed as though the animals were brought to life by the sun, and the life drained from them as the light drained from the sky.

Finally her hysterical laugh-sobs stopped as well.

Now as Sada sat in the still forest, all she could hear was the distant playing of the mystical instruments. Once the animals had stopped making noise, she had realized that it wasn't just a lyre or a harp playing, but both. The drums also began again at night, their distant thrumming almost eerie. When the moon rose, the other instruments fell away and left only the thudding rhythm. It reminded Sada of the war drums she'd heard.

It was the only time she had been anywhere near a battlefield, before her father had been elevated from his position as Captain of the Kingsguard to serve as head commander for King Abel. Her father had been leading a battle charge against a throng of "scheming scum" as he'd called them, a group of men in Desdale who had taken to pillaging the poorer towns.

The battle had gone well, but it was on their journey back to the capital when the other boot dropped, the soldiers of a minor lord galloping in from the west without warning. She had heard the war drums of Califia then, their dull thudding so unearthly low it hurt your ears and made you want to scream.

Her father had bid Gabriel take her back to the castle on his horse. The drums had followed them long after the view of the battle had dwindled out of sight.

Sada had never forgotten the haunting rhythm of those drums, and she was reminded of them now. The ones in this forest, however, just had a gentle lulling to their drumming. They almost enticed her to sleep, despite the fright-filled memories.

But she wouldn't let herself sleep. It wasn't that she thought staying awake would somehow make her less lost than she truly was. She had accepted that truth; rejecting it would do nothing for her. After her little self-lecture (and ensuing breakdown), rational thought had returned to her, and it was rational thought that kept her from sleeping now.

Gabriel had once told her that if she ever found herself lost in the wild, she couldn't fall asleep until she'd found somewhere safe to hide. The forest was all fun-filled and pretty during the day, but at night it became cruel to young maidens, he'd said. He'd also told her that the sun always rose in the east and set in the west, as though knowing the direction she was getting lost in would help her at all.

Thanks, Gabe, she thought, and made herself stand and search. It felt like the hardest thing she'd ever done. *I only wish you were here to tell me in person.*

The forest was bright with that lovely lavender moonlight. Sada let it guide her, following the bits of it that pooled up on the floor where the hand-shaped leaves were sparse above. Through blurry eyes, she saw that the trail of moonlight led her to a large tree with a hole in the center of its trunk. As she neared it, the strange tingling she'd felt earlier returned to her left hand. She rubbed at it absentmindedly and peered inside the trunk, but the moonlight didn't reach the hollowed center of the great tree. The shadowy depths made worms of fear wriggle up in her belly.

Bears, diseased raccoons, fist-sized spiders, the fear-worms said, *they all hide in there.* But she was too tired to give in to their wishes to flee. She couldn't hear anything moving around inside the tree, so she hiked up her dress and made to step inside. That foot she stepped with met not moss, dirt, or wood, but empty air, and she tumbled into open space with a squeak and a drop of her stomach.

The fall dumped her into near total darkness. She landed on one leg, which collapsed almost immediately at the impact, but she was not hurt.

She immediately sat up and waved her hands around blindly, suddenly filled with panic. She felt no fur (or worse, skin and cloth) indicating another occupant, however. All she felt was the roughness of dirt. That calmed her some.

Wow, true dirt! she thought with some amazement. It was the first of the stuff she'd come across in this world. Smooth, thick roots snaked across the packed surface. A few feet above her was the moonlit gap she'd stumbled through. No evil denizens of Elt peered down at her, and her panicked heartbeat began to steady.

Satisfied that she was safe—or as safe as she could be in the wilderness—she wrapped her cloak around herself and huddled down in the little dirt cave to sleep. The tingling in her hand faded as she did so, and a feeling of gentle peace took over.

In her own, open bedroom, she slept with a lantern constantly lit. When her father had discovered this, he'd demanded to know when she'd "let" herself become afraid of the dark. She hadn't been able to answer this, because she couldn't remember ever *not* being afraid of it. No answer would have pleased the Duke, anyway. She didn't remember the one she'd given him, but after she'd said it, he'd ordered her not to use the lantern again. He also sent his valet to check each night and ensure she'd obeyed.

She spent the next couple of weeks sitting awake in her bedroom, wide-eyed, palms sweating, her breaths coming in rapid and shallow pants. Her eyes would dart between every corner of the room from the moment she went to bed until the sun lit her room enough that she could see there were no monsters hiding in the shadows and finally sleep.

After nearly two weeks of this, she'd finally started sneaking out into the parlor to sleep on the couch there. It smelled of the dank sweat of their guests—and it was in their Ettedon residence, so it was prettier than it was comfortable—but there was light from the lanterns in the kitchen where the cooks worked late into the night and began again early in the morning.

It was safe.

After a week of this, she was allowed to use her lantern again, though only after hearing an hour's worth of criticism on her choice to be weak. It was the first tirade that didn't affect her. She was so filled with relief from having her lantern back that she didn't feel the typical shame that came with the Duke's reprimands.

Now, sitting alone in the hollowed-out trunk of a tree in the middle of the woods, the thought of a lantern did not even cross her mind. Despite being in near total darkness, she was not afraid. Maybe it was because she could feel all the walls if she just reached out her arms, or because of the calming scent of the wood and earthen walls, or because she was out in nature as humans were meant to be. Regardless of the reason, Sada basked in the blissful peace and let the distant drumming guide her to a dreamscape. Its booming rhythm resounded through the forest floor, and she could feel it vibrate against her back where she lay cradled by the earth.

She was beginning to think the Elf's warning of unfriendly creatures was unfounded; this forest was the most peaceful place she'd been in.

THE NINTH

Sada

"You nicked dizzy juice from the sharp-ears again last night, didn't thou?"

"What's their wine gotta do with it?"

"There's notta scent of human *anywhere*, Groll. Come 'ere!"

The conversation was interrupted by the sounds of scuffling.

"What in the name of the Kindreds art thou doin', wench?" cried the second voice.

The two voices were coming from above her, just outside the tree: one was high and whining, reminiscent of a bee buzzing; the other was low and strong. Sada had awoken with her entire left arm ablaze with that intense vibrating sensation from the day before, and she didn't move from the position she opened her eyes in. Something instinctual told her she didn't dare. As the strangers argued above her, she tried to still her breath, afraid that if she so much as shifted in the wrong direction the man with the deep voice would smell her again. The thought of a creature that could both speak like a person (if quite strangely) *and* track her by scent alone made her breath hitch.

"I'm tryna smell the dizzy juice on yer breath, that's what!" exclaimed the woman. "Now hold still, *wench.*"

"I ain't no *fe*-male!" The man sounded like the folk from the south-east she'd met once, come to Califia in search of new land. They were slow talkers and even slower walkers who often brought strong drink called milk punch that made men very loud and *very* vulgar when they partook of it. It was unseemly for unmarried women to drink fermented beverages, but Sada would not have wanted to try the stuff even if she had been allowed. The unseen voices above her sounded quite similar to those of the people who brewed it.

The voices were silent for a moment, and the only noise was the snuffling of what sounded like a pig. Then he hawked and spat loudly.

"There, I dost thought it right. Only thing to be smelled 'round here is the wine waftin' on up from yer big'un belly! Ain't no human, Beast-brain."

The man grumbled. "Thought I dost sniffed one."

"Maybe if we call for it, it'll come. Hew-man!" the one with the high voice called. "Heeere, redblood—come out ya little thang!"

The woman broke off sniggering and Sada heard shuffling above. A big leaf floated into the opening of her tree cave, and her stomach dropped further: they were very close.

"Shush, woman," the man grumbled. "The rain must've covered its scent."

"Yer tellin' me that yer the Mudhands' best tracker and thou can't even follow the smell of a *human* in the rain? If one was here, even Flink would be able to smell it. Skies, even his cursin' snooty would. An' anyway, some Beast would've gobbled it by now."

The man just sniffed noisily. "That's enough outta you. You couldn't even smell the ones with the Elves."

That must have been the brothers and me! Sada's panic rose into her throat for a moment before settling back into her belly.

The female creature quieted at that. After a moment, she spoke again, grumbling. "Let's get on back, we left Flink. The snooty's prolly like to lead him off a cliff near soon here."

It was the man's turn to snigger now.

Sada listened as they shuffled away, her hearing sharpened by fear, waiting to move until their voices grew distant. By the time they were out of earshot and only the sounds of critters could be heard, the tingling had faded from her hand and arm. Now that she thought about it, the tingling seemed to start when she was in danger of being hurt, or when something of significance was about to happen.

She had never felt it before, but then, she had never been in true danger before. Maybe happening into this realm had granted Sada the ability to feel her instincts as a physical sensation. Or perhaps this was an ability that everyone possessed, and which had remained dormant in her until it became necessary. She didn't much like the idea that it signaled danger, as it would mean both that Pine-Eyes's warning had been correct, and that it applied to the people she'd just heard.

She distracted herself from these unsettling speculations with thoughts of asking Gabe where he felt his instincts—was it always in the left hand? Her daydreaming, as usual, served to almost completely dismantle her fear and soon, Sada dared to uncurl her stiff legs and stand. She tiptoed to the opening in the trunk, which was just above her head, and used the roots in the wall to climb to a spot high enough for her to see out. After slipping a few times, she managed to brace herself long enough to look outside.

At first, she saw only trees and bright sunlight. Then movement caught her eye. Two squat figures were walking away from her tree—or rather, waddling. They were short and cute in an ugly way, and looked nothing like anything Sada had seen before. She watched with both fright and wonder as the round creatures the colors of dirt and rock shuffled away from her, one scratching at the moss on its head.

"Can't we leave 'im there a little longer?" the male creature (and scratcher) was saying. "He's so *slow*."

"He's slow in the leg, yer slow in the head, what's the difference?" The one which Sada presumed to be the woman chuckled and the man shoved into her. He was bulkier with larger limbs, but she was strong herself. Her sturdy form didn't budge, but she jabbed him back with a pudgy hand, nonetheless.

Briefly, Sada wondered if she should run after them in hopes they knew how to get to the Elven king. But with the way they had been talking about her, she decided to stay hidden until they were far gone. At first, she listened to her good sense. The creatures were out of sight within minutes, and when the forest was empty, she climbed out of the hollowed trunk.

Sada pulled herself up onto wet leaves and recalled the little male creature mentioning it had rained. Indeed, the woods were sparkling with the shimmer of water. The sight of it made Sada realize she hadn't had anything to drink since she'd left the Seam, and the near encounter with the strange creatures had made her mouth go dry. She desperately scanned the woods for any signs of water.

Before she took a step, though, she pulled out her vial and covered her birthmarks. Then she set off.

She soon came upon a clear puddle hidden between tree roots and ferns. She dropped down to her knees to drink it, relishing the chill. As she was lifting mouthfuls to her lips, she heard those drawling voices again and froze. She looked up, brightening with both fear and excitement. All she saw were trees, looping roots, moss, ferns—there! She spotted the round creatures again. Yet now a third accompanied them.

That will be Flink, Sada thought, *the slow one.*

He was clad in a torn cloth shirt, and walked just behind the first two. A cat-sized opossum who was nearly as tall as he was trotted at his side. The two in front, Groll and the woman, were arguing again, but Flink walked silently behind, stroking the opossum's shoulder and humming off-tune to himself.

Sada's hand was buzzing with her newfound *instincts* once more, though the sensation wasn't nearly as strong as it had initially been, and it was almost pleasant. The group disappeared around a tree. So, Sada did the only reasonable thing for a girl lost alone in the woods to do: she stood and followed.

She didn't know why such an idea had taken hold of her. The humming in her hand protested, and so did her good sense, but this time she did not heed either. The forest brought something to life in her, something that had only been able to take form as relentless curiosity and barraging her elders with questions at home, but which now could be realized through *adventure.* The forest brought out her curiosity. Delicate as the cat who was killed by it, she crept after the little group, a delighted giggle trapped in her throat.

She followed them for quite a long while. Often, they were in her line of sight. She ensured that she stayed far enough away that the one with the good nose, Groll, would not smell her. Sometimes Flink's opossum would stop and glance around and Sada was afraid she had been discovered. She would either stay perfectly still, holding her breath and clutching her skirts, or she would quickly scamper behind a nearby trunk or tall patch of grass. Then either Groll or the woman would snap at Flink—who had stopped to wait for the animal—and they'd both come running, the boy wringing his little hands.

When Sada couldn't see them, she would use her *instincts* as her guide. It was strange trying to use them as her compass, playing hot and cold with her own hand. She'd never needed instincts before. Gabriel had always been her guide and guardian, leaving no room for Sada to need sense or city smarts. Yet in Elt, her newfound ability proved quite useful to point out the danger she would otherwise be oblivious to.

Though it doesn't always happen around a threat. The first time was when I touched that bit of the Seam on my gown. She didn't think there was much danger to be had there. Other than the danger of pain, but even that was not so bad. It seemed that her *instincts* alerted her not to threats, but to things that were…different, and not of her world. Perhaps even powerful.

Whatever system the ability operates on, I'm thankful for it.

The three little creatures had been out of her sight for a long time now, and she was wondering if she should just give up on her quest and return to following the sun. Sada thought it was now somewhere to her left rather than at her back where it should be. As she was musing over this, her hand was suddenly filled with the tingling, and she gasped loudly before she could think to stop herself. The little people were nowhere to be seen, but in front of her, the trees suddenly stopped.

There was a thick cluster of big-leafed bushes the color of autumn just an arm's reach away, and when she stepped forward, her toes hung off the lip of a steep hill. To her left and right, the bushes extended in a curving shape, creating what looked like a rounded hedge wall if you looked at it the right way. Sada plunged her arm into the hand-shaped leaves and tried to pry a gap into the wild hedge. She managed to with some effort, and poked her head into the opening she formed. The sight made her breath catch.

The trees hadn't disappeared, they'd simply started to *bend.* She realized that the edge her toes hung over wasn't the edge of a hill, but the lip of a valley. Thick trunks bent at steep, unnatural angles to form a dome over it. The pattern looked like the top of a latticed pie. She realized also that the bush she was half-buried in wasn't a bush at all, but the top of the tree from across the valley. Each bent tree laid its head on the opposite side of the gap, forming what appeared to be a ring of bushes guarding it. Sada gazed on in rapture before realizing that she probably shouldn't have her head stuck in the leaves if the creatures reappeared.

She had just managed to extract herself from the treetop when she felt a sudden pressure on the toes of her boots. Her *instincts* roared all the way up to her elbow and she had time to make out four toddler-like fingers of stone on her feet before they were yanked from beneath her and she was on her butt. She tried to pull away, but then there were tiny hands on her ankles, and rough palms digging into her calves as well. They heaved and suddenly her butt and back were over the lip of the valley. Sada threw out her arms to catch herself on the branches above and around her, but then her hands were taken into custody by her miniature captors as well. With a cry and a few grunts from her attackers, Sada was pulled beneath the leaves and sent skidding down an earthen path.

Duchess Solares had not been loved by all, but those who did love her had done so intensely. Governess Brown had been one of those people. And so, she had thought it prudent that a large part of Sada's instruction be on the topic of the duchess. More specifically, her heritage.

Sada was a woman of the west through and through, but her favorite tales had come from the north along with her mother. Governess Brown told her everything she remembered from Duchess Solares's storytelling and singing, which was much. Yet according to the governess, there had been even more she had brought with her from her home, but didn't have the time to share. Sada had loved the tales but forgotten many, as her later schooling had been more focused on calligraphy, singing, practicing the piano, learning the grueling histories of Ettedon, and of course the more practical (boring) histories of the north and her mother's people.

Yet one legend came to her now: one of Trolls.

They were ugly creatures, in both spirit and appearance, and had sharp teeth for opening the throats of livestock—and sometimes people. They lived among rocks and roots and dirt, and enjoyed solitude but could be found dwelling with their sisters and mothers, who were also their wives. Humans had few kind words for the Trolls, but the creatures described themselves as guardians of the wood and friends of seers and sorceresses. If they could speak, it was only in rhymes and riddles or half-formed sentences. Some looked like people; some looked like bits of forest. Some were said to be tall and stupid, others short and quick of both foot and mind. Despite the varied accounts, all who encountered them agreed on one thing: they loved humans only in stew.

As Sada looked into the curious faces of her captors, she knew them to be Trolls. It was a fact that came to her with the same spontaneous surety as the fact that she was in a different realm than her own had. These Trolls were of the short variety, as she'd seen earlier in the forest. Atop their heads grew piles of greenery in place of hair. Some had the stuff on their stomachs and arms as well.

They looked as though someone had tried (somewhat unsuccessfully) to shape a fat toddler out of the earth, then had brought it to life with some dark magic. Their skin seemed to be made of stone or clay. Yet their hands were warm and alive where they'd touched her, and they had no sharp teeth, nor did they speak in rhymes.

Sada's *instincts* were painfully strong in her arm, buzzing frantically, and she winced as she grasped her wrist to try and will it to stop. The Trolls skittered back at her movement, wide-eyed and open-mouthed like children witnessing a miracle. One poked her with a stick, and a young one who looked to have been freshly molded from clay ran up and tugged her hair before hurrying back to the safety of the pack. It did not seem that these particular Trolls enjoyed solitude. There were perhaps twenty crowded around her now.

One approached. A man with a long beard of lichen swinging between his stone legs. Atop his head perched not only moss and lichen, but clusters of mushrooms and small plants as well. Ferns sprouted thickly from his ears, and Sada wondered if he could hear through the mess. Then she wondered how creatures made of rock could hear at all. He halted his shuffling at her feet, and when she tried to cringe away from him, he whacked her shin with the stick he held in a chubby, four-fingered hand.

"Ow!" Sada cried.

He did not look sorry. He only looked. He looked at her face and her arms, examined her boots and her cloak. He poked at the soles of her shoes and tugged on her laces, making little muttering noises. He turned and swept his squinting gaze over the people gathered and they just shrugged. Nodding, he returned his gaze to her.

"Vi'sh nau Troll," he said. He spoke gutturally and harshly, and in a language she, of course, did not understand. Yet he looked as though he expected her to.

For a moment she only stared, then she remembered how her encounter with the Elves had begun.

"Pardon, um, Known Tongue?" she said, eyes darting around the surrounding creatures.

A collective murmur rolled through the crowd, and they shared glances with one another. The man only frowned and sighed. He grumbled something more in his native tongue, and then when he spoke again, it was in her own language.

"Thou art not Troll," he said. His voice was still deep and gravelly, and he spoke as though he were chopping the words like her father's cooks did to onions, but she could understand him.

He raised an eyebrow of lichen, as though expecting confirmation or denial of his statement.

"No…I am not a Troll," she said slowly.

He nodded looking pleased, and a gentle murmur went around the crowd. He lifted his staff and the murmuring stopped. A hand went to stroke his beard.

"Not a Troll, but a…?" he questioned.

Again, Sada stared. She had been asked questions like this before, only then they were in written form and posed to her by tutors. Fill-in-the-blank questions, made to test her knowledge on history and grammar. *King Thomas II began his rule over Ettedon in the year of* ____ was one example she knew well.

Maybe they do speak in riddles, she thought. She was opening her mouth to answer when Pine-Eyes's warning came to her. She pursed her lips to stop from betraying her secrets, and eyed the man. He was certainly a denizen of this world, as the green-eyed Elf had warned her of. Yet he did not look dangerous. Already the *instincts* were fading from her palm. And in any case, he had a kind face. He looked like one of the village grandfathers she and Jezebel used to beg stories from in trade for administration of herbal remedies.

Sada tried to stand so she might curtsey politely before answering, but the old Troll smacked her with his cane again.

"Ah!" she whined.

I was only trying to be courteous! Childlike tears found her eyes.

"Not a Troll, but a…?" he prompted again.

But Sada was too offended by the smack to speak, and then someone else was answering his question for her.

"Groll thinks it art a mordal." The voice came from the front of the little crowd. It was the woman Sada had been following. She was scratching at the bits of moss on her round belly.

"Mortal," Groll corrected.

"Yeh, that's what I said. What art you on about?"

"Thou said mor-*dal,* it's mor-*tal,"* Groll said. He pressed a finger to his nose in frustration, then sighed. "Never thee mind, just be silent and let the old man about his business."

The man with the staff squinted, and a contemplative groan came from beneath the beard. It was followed by a fart. He raised his eyebrows and glanced around suspiciously as though looking for the culprit. When he found none and the giggling of the little ones had died down, he returned his gaze to the Troll woman.

"Thee know this how, Bacha?" he asked. "Mortal, mordal, *how?"*

The woman, Bacha, looked ashamed. The Troll didn't blush; Sada didn't think her stony skin was capable of such a delicate expression. But she seemed to look everywhere but at the man with the staff.

Finally she spoke, but it was in muttered tones. "Groll smelt the redblood. Then…well, we led thee on back here." Bacha kicked at the valley floor.

"Smelled like a human. Smelled like somethin' that could die," added Groll. Sada looked for good humor in his gaze, but his watery eyes were blank with indifference. *Well, it's true,* they seemed to say. Truth or no, the way he said it made Sada want to draw her knees up against her chest and make herself small. But she didn't want to be smacked by the cane again.

The old man was frowning, stroking his stringy beard. Clumps came out on his rough, porous fingers as he did, but he just shook the loose strands off and kept at his contemplative caressing. He groaned again, but thankfully he didn't pass air this time.

"Led back…" His frown said that it took much effort to hold his thoughts together long enough to string them into words. "Why?"

"Why what, *Gom' Brodir?* I can't tell thou why the human art in Elt." Groll turned to Sada, raising his voice as though she were deaf. "Why art you in Elt, mor-tal?"

Sada was spared having to answer the man, as *Gom' Brodir* brought his cane down with a crack on Groll's mossy head. Despite being made of stone, Groll jumped, squinched his eyes and teeth together, and grabbed at his head.

"Yachow!" he screeched. He grabbed Bacha's thick arm for comfort, then glared at the old Troll.

Bacha just looked at Groll indifferently and sniffed. *"Fakta.* Forgive thee, *Gom' Brodir.* The fool doth be drunk."

Gom' Brodir was glaring right back at Groll. "Why. Thou. Lead. Thee. Back?"

Still glaring through drooping eyebrows, Groll lowered his hands from his head. "We've all heard the stories," he growled. "Told to us by the old women. The cubs know 'em better'n me, but I still remember well."

The *Gom' Brodir* muttered something in another language. "Stories, *jiie—stories.* Troll not eat flesh."

Sada's breath caught. Then, as though he hadn't just said something utterly heart-stopping, the old Troll tapped Groll lightly on the head with his cane.

It made a dull sound, and he chuckled. "Empty."

Orla

Orla was standing in the offshoot of Old Mother's cell, the birthing cell, and the view of the scene below was unfortunately spectacular. Surrounded by pots of dirt containing freshly birthed Trolls too young to surface, she watched the exchange with a mixture of annoyance and worry. She bit on bark-like nails as the Old Brother whacked Groll on the head. Groll was growing angry, and Old Brother didn't look too pleased either. That was spectacular. Orla had thought the ancient Troll too stupid to know anger.

There was a girl with them as well, who could have been an Elf or Faery cub. *No, too ugly for that. But too pretty to be from most of the other kingdoms*...And too tall to be a Troll, of course. Examining those long limbs, Orla wondered how such tall creatures could manage. They looked like deer. Though this one certainly wasn't as graceful as one. She was covered in patches of brown from her tumble into the valley.

Loose hair. No Boon, then. Who and what is thee magick-less creature?

Myths and folktales floated into her mind. Tales of mortals that bled red and died within a century of birth. With thin skin in different shades of bark, and the ability to speak in hundreds of tongues. She had heard of the Seam, of course. Every Spiritkin had. Though Kindreds knew only those pompous Elves of the Wood ever got to lay eyes on its beauty. But there had been whispers that the new ruler of the Elven Wood, King Caprius, might allow the citizens of the Valley to visit the Seam.

So far as Orla knew, that had never been allowed in history. Only the Keepers got to see the elusive portal. She had also heard that through the Seam lay another land. An ugly land filled with war and famine and pain. Their wolves did not keep the counsel of Druids, but listened to the commands of men and licked grease from their fingers. Cats were as small as rabbits, and rabbits were as small as gerbils. It was said, too, that the land contained trees no older than a few hundred years, no bigger than saplings. It wasn't lack of time that prevented the trees from growing full and large, but the mortal residents of the world. The land was scarred, and the trees murdered by those mortals: humans.

She art one of them. It was something Orla had no way of knowing, yet she was certain of it nonetheless. Dread seeped into her skin, cold and uncomfortable. She scraped at the dirt beneath her nails, then switched to biting them again, the grit grating against her teeth. Humans should not be in their land. They must have found the Seam. Were they invading once more, as they had all those centuries ago when Elt was younger? Did it mean war between their realms was afoot again? Were the old histories coming to life before her eyes? This one did not look to be a warrior: she was soft, and armed with no weapons of steel, wood, or stone. Perhaps she was a scout, or a messenger. Trolls knew little of espionage, but Orla thought that perhaps this human did.

Spy—dirty human spy, she thought bitterly. Then Groll knocked away Old Brother's staff, which had landed on his head again, and pointed furiously at the maybe-human. Orla's eyes widened with the human's, and she ran to find the clan's mother. This was getting out of hand.

She was sitting in the queen cell where Orla had left her. Trolls surrounded her, each vying for the honor of feeding her. Old Mother smiled patiently at all of them, accepting a spoonful of custard or a bite of cake from each in turn. One dipped a bit of pie into sugar-paste before carefully lifting it to the queen's mouth. The Trolls each fed her different foods, but they all fed her with reverent care. The room was silent, and the thoughts they communicated were gentle as well. They reached Orla's mind as she neared, but the calm could not penetrate her anxiety. Orla disrupted the peace. She burst into the small cell, shoving her sisters aside and causing a hum of angry comments to fill the warm air.

The food, the food, they cried. *Someone guard Mother's food!*

When Orla reached Old Mother, she fell to her knees in a deep bow. Wordlessly, her mother touched her neck, the place of weakness, allowing her to rise. When Orla lifted her face, tears streaked her cheeks.

"Old Mother," she said, suddenly breathless. "Thou need to come. There art a disturbance in the valley. Groll and the Old Brother are—what art you doing?"

Orla suddenly forgot about the human girl, of Old Brother and Groll fighting. In the time she had been gone (*I should never leave her alone so long!*), the youngest cubs of the hive—those not still in the dirt, that is—had filled the queen cell. Orla hadn't seen them amidst the throng of her elder siblings feeding Old Mother, but now they were all she could see. Over a dozen cubs, so young their bodies were still soft, crouched around their mother. Some stared reverently, others looked around stupidly, watery eyes wide and staring.

Old Mother caught Orla's look and dismissed her older children. Orla saw the wave of her cracked hand, but she was not included in the commanding thought the queen sent to the other Trolls. Old Mother was the only Troll in the clan who had been gifted with a Boon, and it was one all Trell queens possessed: one of silent speaking. Typically it meant that only the one with the Boon could communicate through thoughts, but Old Mother's magick was strong, and she was able to share it with her daughters so that they could all speak with their minds if she desired.

The women left wordlessly—though Orla imagined some protested with their mental voices; Shoda certainly would—guarding the platter of royal food closely. Five different Trolls had a hand on it, all ready to catch the tray if one of them slipped. The food was easy to make, but the royal custard necessary to sustain the queen was a valuable commodity. They wouldn't waste a drip or a crumb. One of Orla's sisters, Welda, made to grab the white jar tucked away on one of the few shelves in the room. The queen just shook her head, sent a silent command, and Welda left empty-handed.

Orla and Old Mother were left alone with the children.

"Mother, what—" Orla began.

One of the cubs looked up at Old Mother suddenly, round cheeks puffed out and mouth drawn tight to hold in the saliva trying to seep out of her lips. She waved frantically and made little noises at the ancient Troll, trying to get her attention. Mother just smiled at the little girl, then pointed at the clay jar Welda had tried to take.

Bring it to me, my Orla, Old Mother thought to her. The familiar sound of her voice in Orla's head calmed all panic that had been building up in her.

Happily, she retrieved the jar and brought it to her mother. It was made of a special type of soft white clay, which was mixed with the ash of animal bones, white sand, and a glittering stone called quartz. When it hardened it became a beautiful near-translucent material. Once, their people had specialized in the craft, but now the cave of clay held only tones of grey and red, and the quartz was a rare mineral, one they had lost the knowledge which handling it required.

The one remaining porcelain jar was reserved for the use of the queen only. It had been holding royal custard since before Orla was born, and would continue to for many centuries. The Trolls all handled it delicately when it was their turn to hold the jar, and now Orla gingerly passed it to her mother. The queen held it to the cub's mouth.

"Spit," she ordered gently.

The cub would understand mental commands more easily than spoken ones, but if they began to rely on the silent speaking too early, they would be unable to learn how to speak verbally later in their development. Orla had met one of these verbally stunted Trolls when she was foraging; Troll clans often crossed paths in Grandfleur. The mute Troll was brought along everywhere with her sisters, but it was obvious to everyone, and probably to she herself, that she was unwanted. Orla would hate to see her sisters live such a life of pity and barely-masked hate.

With obvious relief, Orla's little sister opened her mouth at their mother's command. A pale yellow liquid like milky honey dribbled out and into the jar. There was already some at the bottom as well. In time, it would congeal and darken into a golden custard used for baking the queen's food. When the cub's mouth was empty, Old Mother moved the jar and held it out to the other children gathered around her.

"Dost anybody else need to spit?" she asked.

A few nodded eagerly and as she passed the jar around to them, Orla followed with a clump of rabbit down that had been balled up tightly to serve as an absorbent cloth. She wiped the cubs' dribbling mouths with it.

Orla didn't speak for a moment. The feeling of peace that came with hearing Old Mother's voice in her mind was fading, and it had been replaced by anger. She had thought herself a favorite of her mother's, and yet the queen had gone behind Orla's back, planning her

(death)

retirement without her. Without even telling her! Finally Old Mother set down the jar, much fuller than it had been, and faced Orla.

"Thou art angry," she said simply. Orla's hands curled into fists and she nodded, sharply. "Because I did not tell thou?"

Orla wanted to simply stew in anger, but looking at her mother's kind, gentle face, the smile that never left her cracking lips, it all burst forth.

"Thou dost not need this much royal custard!" she cried suddenly, gesturing to the cubs whose mouths were filling as she spoke. "We *never* have this much custard. It can only mean one thing, an' I don't like it! Old Mother, I need thou—the clan needs thou…please don't go."

Old Mother set her hand softly on Orla's cheek. She leaned into the warm caress, that gentle peace filling her chest again. She fought it. She wanted to stay angry. If her mother was going to choose to die, she would not let her do so feeling forgiven.

"I'm old, my sweet cub. I know you art scared. Try not to shout among the children. And besides, they will produce royal custard for me always. Thou knows it's all I can eat." She swept her hand in an arc. "This doth mean nothing."

Orla jerked away from her mother viciously. "Don't go lyin' to me!" she cried. "I'm not as simply-minded as thou's other children. I tend the cubs every day; I know how much royal custard they make. This is more than three days' worth. It's 'nough to feed a *new* queen. A young'n who can't give birth to her own cubs to make more custard." Her voice dropped to a whisper. The anger was quickly being replaced by sadness. "I know they make more when a new queen is gonna be born."

Old Mother just smiled her soft, sweet smile. Then at another muffled cry from a cub, she picked up the jar again and began to pass it around. Orla took it from her, not gently. She had been tending the children since she was a young Troll herself. She wouldn't allow her anger to stop her from her duty. She held the heavy jar at the mouth of each cub, wiping it when they had given up their mouthful of the custard that would turn a newborn cub into the next queen: the Young Mother. Tears threatened her eyes. She would only ever know one Mother, and she was sitting behind Orla peacefully.

When the children had deposited all the custard they held, she set down the jar. Their bodies were still soft, and some had stupidly chosen to sit on their rears like Old Mother rather than crouch on their feet as she'd taught them. Orla scolded them as they stared up at her, wide-eyed, then she went around helping each of the little ones, not yet six inches tall, to their round little feet. Some of their legs were flattened and mishappen from their time on the floor. She had to mold them back into the proper shape. Her work was crude and left fingerprints, but that was their own fault. In any case, time and gravity would smooth out what she did not.

She discovered one little girl whose belly had been flattened into an odd shape. With one hand, Orla held her under the armpit; the other pressed and kneaded against her belly. Her little sister leaned against her, making muffled baby noises.

As she worked, Orla summoned the courage to ask the question that had been heating her tongue. "Hast thou chosen her yet? The new queen?" She avoided looking at her mother, spending longer than she needed reshaping the girl cub.

"No. She has not yet been laid. She is here."

Old Mother waited patiently for Orla to turn around. She smoothed out the legs and rears of a couple more children, then, finding no more distractions, faced the queen. Old Mother took her daughter's hand and placed it on her belly. Troll bellies were always round, but the queen's was positively rotund. Yet Orla knew there was life inside not from the size, but from the warmth emanating from it. Old Mother's stone skin was hot to the touch.

Fresh tears prickled at Orla's eyes, but these were ones of joy. Old Mother's emotions seeped through her skin and into Orla, forcing her to feel the joy only a mother could.

I will never feel this for myself. The thought made her want to hug Old Mother forever, so she could always feel the excitement of preparing to bring a new life into the world.

"Soon?" Orla whispered, her hand still on her mother's belly and feeling the warmth of her unborn sister.

Old Mother nodded. "Yes. Thou art right about the cubs. Their bodies know a new queen is forming, and they are preparing her food. Soon I will die, and then your sister will become your Mother."

No she will not, Orla thought stubbornly. Only the queen was capable of reproduction and birth. Every Troll in the clan was her child, and they were all each other's siblings, save for the males who had come from other clans to father some of Old Mother's cubs. The males were the only ones who left their clans. The new queen would be Orla's sister as well, and though she would adopt the title of "Young Mother" when Old Mother died, she would never be the clan's true mother until Orla and her siblings all passed and were replaced with the Young Mother's own children.

"Has the new queen cell been made yet?" Orla asked stiffly.

"It is being constructed now. Your sisters have been working hard all day… I am sure thee will want drink and food soon."

Orla ignored the unspoken question (she would *not* serve the traitorous fools*)* and looked out the window Old Mother had been staring through all morning. If only she had looked sooner, she would have seen. A dozen

Trell women stood on a ledge extending from their mother's cell. They were covered in the pale smears of clay. Some hauled huge cartfuls of the stuff from the tunnel in the valley wall which led to the cave of clay. Circles of grey where the Trolls had stepped led between the cave and the dwelling. Others patted handfuls of soon-to-be terracotta onto the walls and floor of the new queen cell that was already taking form, protruding from the ledge the women worked on.

Orla turned away in disgust.

Old Mother took up her hand. "Thou will care for the Young Mother, as you have done for all thy other siblings all these centuries?"

Orla didn't want to, but she nodded. Once. She felt a long breath go in and out of her mother's body. For a moment she was worried it was her last, and that she would die right then. But then the queen lifted Orla's chin and met her gaze. Old Mother's eyes were not as wet as they should be. Their inky blackness was foggy at the edges, growing as milky as new royal custard. Yet her face was kind. It was so kind, and Orla almost broke out into sobs then.

"Something is wrong, Orla."

"What is it, Old Mother?" Orla frantically grabbed at her mother, touching her arms and shoulders and face, feeling for any cracks that were too large, looking for any seeping pores or rotting lichen.

Old Mother laughed, grabbed her daughter's hands, and held them firmly. "Hush now, hush." Her countenance sobered. "Something is wrong with the clan, and I believe it extends to all of Elt. I want thou to know that I am not doing this because I want to leave thee. I do it because I am afraid."

Old Mother's voice had dropped to a whisper. She had always been soft-natured, but now she sounded frail as well. For the first time, Orla sensed her mother's weakness. Her most primal instincts told her to attack, to destroy her weak, ancient mother. A queen should be disposed of if she was frail. Then Old Mother's grip tightened on her hands, and her gaze grew steady. The scary feeling passed.

Ashamed, Orla looked at nothing but her mother's eyes, willing herself to see the strength there, and feel it herself.

"Why art you afraid, Old Mother? I will keep thou safe. Me an' my sisters will."

Old Mother smiled; she even laughed again. "Sweet cub, I know thou will. Yet this is something evil that you cannot protect me from. Perhaps if you Wielded a Boon…" She frowned with stony eyebrows. "But no, not even then, no. I feel it by the knots in my hair. This force is dark, something only our Creator or the Kindreds can save us from. Verily, I have tried once already to make a new queen, when the evil was only stirring."

Orla tried to pull away after hearing this new deception, but Old Mother held her firmly, and held her gaze even more strongly.

"She died inside of me, Orla. Such as has never happened before. The evil is already in my womb, child, dost thou understand? I fear as well that it has infected my Boon, or perhaps the minds of my children. I have found some of your sisters doing strange things, and when asked, they told me I had commanded them to do so with a thought. Yet I had never sent them such an order. And the anger…do you not see the anger? I feel it working, even in you my sweet Orla…oh, sweet, sweet cub."

Old Mother released Orla's hands and hastily placed her own on her pregnant belly. Orla felt numb. The shameful feeling of anger was gone, but she thought this was worse. And what was this talk of death in the womb? She had never heard of such a curse, a new life born with no breath—not a birth of life at all, but of death? She shuddered, and realized Old Mother had fallen silent. She was looking down at her abdomen, at the life quickening there.

I only hope this one survives to see the light of the world. I cannot save thee. But perhaps the Kindreds can—may a vessel be found worthy soon.

Orla believed that thought from the Old Mother was supposed to be private. But she had heard it anyway.

This is something evil, she had said. *I fear as well that it has infected my Boon, or perhaps the minds of my children...This is something evil…*

Orla set her fingers on her mother's chin and lifted her head up to look her in the face. Mother was scared, and so Orla had to be strong for her. She understood now. This was not selfishness from her queen, but the opposite. Orla would not let her die, especially not believing her daughter was angry with her.

"Come, Old Mother, there is something you must see."

THE TENTH

Sada

Groll batted the cane away when it came toward his head again. His lip raised to expose round, yellow teeth.

"Thou can't punish me, *Gom' Brodir.* I art *savin'* us. The clan's gettin' weak, and so's Elt. Our rituals don't cursin' work. Makes me think to myself, maybe we need to go back to the older ways. We didn't go hungry then. The cubs didn't grow too slow then." Groll turned to Sada, wiping the moisture from his eyes; they were black and hungry. "Maybe to save the clan, we need to do as the stories said: eat mortal flesh."

Sada felt the blood drain from her face. She didn't like the way some of the Trolls were eyeing her, as though assessing a fine cut of meat at the market. *3 coppers for the thigh, 5 for the liver; buy two arms, get one half off.* Groll even licked his lips, and Bacha didn't look too opposed to the idea. Most, however, looked apprehensive. Women lifted little children onto their backs, and Flink hugged the opossum around its neck.

"I don't wanna eat the red-blood, Groll," Flink whined. He looked small in his tattered clothes.

"Shut it, Flink. Dost thou want the clan to die like *Om' Modir?"* Groll snapped. "You'll eat thee. I'll drain her blood for thou and cook it into a stew so you don't have to bother with chewin' the tough bits…but she doth look soft and tasty, dothn't she?"

Sada was beginning to think that she should probably hike up her skirts and run. She drew her knees up, preparing to do just that, when all the Trolls buckled over and grasped at their heads. They moaned in chorus.

"Fool!" The voice was new, and sounded like sand being ground against rock. "You art so quick to bury me, when I stand living before you. I am not dead yet, and I shall certainly not die with this mad talk living in my clan. If thou wish to eat mortal flesh, Groll, then I shall cast you head-first into the Seam, and thou can see how you fare in a world of humans. Try eating one then, *grot!"*

Sada followed Groll's angry eyes to see an extremely round and (relatively) tall Troll woman standing atop a boulder. The boulder looked like the upper body of a large Troll, its lower half buried in dirt. Its features held an uncanny similarity to the woman standing atop it: round cheeks, big eyes, distinct knots of lichen for hair. The woman wore no crown, but she stood and spoke with an air of authority that marked her as a leader over these people.

Still, Groll spoke against her through gritted teeth and with clenched fists, struggling to stand up straight. *"Om' Modir,* thou have felt the wrongness in the clan! We hafta do somethin'. Cubs art young for too long, and some don't even come out of the dirt now. The others act strange. Look—Flink even wears *clothes* now, like he's one of the cursin' fairfolk. Tell me nothin' is wrong, and I'll shut my chomper."

Om' Modir was not impressed by his angry speech. She waved a little hand. "Bah. Flink is just strange: he's always liked clothes and creatures. I don't deny your fears, my child. But we shall not partake of human flesh, and that is final. If thou wish to use your teeth to eat more than nectar and bread, then chew on some leaves!"

With that, the queen climbed down from her boulder. The gathered Trolls seemed to have been released from the spell of pain and were looking at Groll uneasily, scratching the moss atop their heads as they muttered to each other. Flink ran off to play with the opossum, who was chasing its naked tail. The other children, bored of the adult conversation, threw one more look at Sada and then scampered to join the boy and his animal. Groll stalked away, dragging a protesting Bacha by the arm; the remaining Trolls parted as he left. After he had gone, they lingered spread apart, looking toward the boulder.

Sada was trying to follow their gazes when she felt a tap on her ankle. She looked to see *Gom' Brodir* prodding her—gently this time—with his staff, which was splintering from the repeated blows to Groll's hard head. When he got her attention, he motioned with his hands for her to stand. When she did so, Sada could see the round *Om' Modir* approaching. There was something regal in her waddle, and as she neared, Sada conceded to *Gom' Brodir's* frantic gestures and grunts, and curtseyed to the knee-high woman.

She rasped a chuckle and laid a hand on Sada's neck. *Gom' Brodir* tapped her shin again. When Sada rose, a smile spread across the woman's face, her cheeks like two grey apples. She was further distinguished from the others by the fissures of age spread all along her arms and legs and around her mouth where it curved in frequent smiles.

And then Sada saw she had been mistaken in her earlier assumption: the woman did indeed wear a crown, just one of foliage rather than gold. Atop her head grew what seemed to be an entire forest in place of the mossy hair that most of her people bore. Sada saw clumps of ferns and lichen which seemed to be woven into knots, and bushes the size of small apricots, and clusters of brown and white mushrooms. She even spotted a small tree the size of a twig. Beneath it, Sada thought she saw a beetle crawl—or was it a tiny Troll? A little stream ran through it all, keeping the greenery alive. Sada could have stared for hours, grinning at the miniature world she wore as a crown. But she forced herself to meet the queen's eyes. Save for the milky signs of age, they were as black as the others'—but hers were filled with pure joy.

"Ah, little cub," she sighed. "It's been many a year since I've seen a human. Do your people still harbor as much anger as they once did?"

Sada was taken aback by the question. She had expected a response to her presence similar to Groll's or the Elves', not a beaming smile and questioning of her people's mannerisms. Sada couldn't help but laugh.

"I am unsure how to answer such a question," she admitted. "I suppose some do harbor anger, yes. But at the same time…some do not. Is there any place where people do not hold some ire in their hearts?"

"*Jiie.* Once." The queen's eternal smile flickered. "Come, come—your hands, dear cub, give me your hands. I want to feel their warmth."

Sada sank to her knees and proffered her hands. She blushed when she saw the dirt now covering them from her scramble down the valley, but *Om' Modir* paid the mess no mind. (Her people were, after all, made of rock.) The queen sighed when she closed her stony palms around Sada's first two fingers.

"As warm as a quickening belly," she murmured with closed eyes. The Troll beside her, who behaved like a guard, sniffed. "What art thou called, cub?"

"Oh—I am Lady Sada Solares, if it please Your Majesty. And thou art called *Om' Modir,* yes?"

The archaic speech felt strange on Sada's tongue. She'd never been trained in it and had met only one man who spoke in such a manner. The children called him Sir Art, but his true name had been lost to the ages. He was older than Ettedon itself, some said. He certainly looked to be that way, and his use of the Dead Speech did him no favors on that account.

"*Jiie, jiie!*" the queen said through childlike giggles. "Thou say it true. You art a clever cub, are you?"

Sada blushed. "If I may ask, what does it mean?"

Om' Modir released Sada's hands to wipe at her eyes, which had become as watery as the youths' from her laughter. "Old Mother, it means. They tell me I am the queen of these people." She winked, and Sada giggled. This old woman reminded her of her uncle in some ways. "Come with me, Sada. I would hear your story and share my home with you. It has been long since I've broken bread with a redblood."

Om' Modir would not let her satisfy her and her Trolls' curiosity until Sada had been fed and her belly warmed with something they called mead, which was supposed to be sweet but tasted as bitter as wine. It reminded her of the southerners' milk punch once again.

When she discovered it truly was wine, just made from a special nectar, she nearly spat it out in anguish. It was only her first hour of meeting these people, and she had already disgraced herself as a lady! Sada immediately switched her drink to water, though she was red-faced for a long while after, and her condition was not helped by the cup of the devilish liquid that she had drunk.

Sada learned that the Trolls ate no meat—something that was unheard of in Califia, and probably across all of her world. The woman Sada had thought to be the queen's guard, Orla, simply squinted at Sada and harrumphed when she asked about the strange diet, but a mossy woman named Edri happily volunteered that most Spiritkin who lived in the Valley of Kings refused to kill living creatures or eat their flesh. The squat woman said it with a bright smile, but Sada thought that when it was put in such a gruesome way, nobody would want to eat meat. She was suddenly thankful that there was none on the table.

All but a few of the women helped to make the food for the feast. When Sada offered to assist, she was abruptly ushered back to her seat on the floor in what they called the central cell. She learned then that the men, women, and guests of the clan had very distinct roles. The clan was fairly small, consisting of perhaps fifty Trolls, and they were called the Greenheads—they naturally grew more moss than the other Trolls in the area. All but four were women.

The few men were called wanderers, and all were from other Trell clans, both distant and neighboring. The only exception was *Gom' Brodir* (which meant "Old Brother" in Trell), the resident male of the Greenhead Clan. The wandering males stayed with a clan for a few months, catering to the queen, and then left to find a new clan. Sada was not told of the activities the men took part in while with a clan's queen, but she did not think she wanted to know either.

While the feast was prepared, Groll and the other male Trolls sat around *Om' Modir,* looking upon her reverently and making strange humming noises. Some even danced while *Om' Modir* looked on with a smile.

Sada tried to avert her eyes. She preferred to watch the women work, anyway.

The female Trolls had much more distinct and numerous roles in the clan. Some were outside the dwelling where the Trolls lived, which was an asymmetrical but artfully crafted clay structure consisting of several angular rooms called cells. These women were working on a new cell, but Sada wasn't told what its function would be, and when she asked, her hosts just smiled and talked of something else. A few other women were in a cell a few rooms apart from the central cell, and were tending to the children, whom they called cubs. They would be asleep soon, and then the women would leave to attend the feast. Most of the female Trolls were in the food cell, preparing dishes for the banquet. Sada had watched with amazement as they turned three or four ingredients into a plethora of dishes.

Trolls subsisted on a diet of nectar, pollen, tree sap, and a few select herbs for flavoring. *Om' Modir* had said with a laugh that their teeth were simply for decoration, as all the food was soft. The women of the clan turned baskets full of crumbly pink and golden pollen into countless food items, more than Sada's cooks could make with sugar, flour, salt, and whatever else they cooked with. She watched with rapt fascination.

First, a handful of the pollen crumbles was taken from the basket and put into a ceramic dish. A ladle of water was added (if it was food for the queen, a milky-yellow substance was substituted) until it became a paste. Then a Troll or two worked it with deft hands until there were no more lumps or grains visible. This paste was passed on to the next Troll station, where they would stir in thick blobs of nectar straight from the flower, or pour in fermented nectar from a jar until the paste thickened. At the next station in the relay, a woman would add butterfly milk or fresh herbs and flowers for flavoring. The smells made Sada's mouth water unbidden.

Once the batters were separated by flavor and more pollen or nectar was added for texture, they were shaped into various food items. The batter that was more pollen-heavy became bread, while the herb-laden pastes turned into cakes and muffins. Tarts and pies were made by using a rolled-up leaf to pipe jelly made of petals, nectar, and squished fruits into hollow dishes lined with thick batter. Once the pastries were formed, they were taken outside the dwelling to a clay oven. Thick white smoke wafted up from it, and hunger began to pain Sada's belly. Thankfully, the food didn't need to cook for long; the Trolls baked it simply for taste.

The queen was served first. She ate the same types of pastries as the rest of the clan, but hers were made with that milky-yellow substance the Trolls called royal custard, which somehow sustained her queenly abilities. Again, questions of what these were had been met with sly smiles. While the queen was fed by adoring young daughters, the rest of the clan was served. First, the nurses who cared for the cubs. Next, the flower girls—they would be venturing out of the Trolls' valley to collect more pollen and nectar soon, it seemed. The men had moved to their own cell to dine, and a couple of cooks brought them their share. The women who had made the food took their portions last, when all the pastries and breads had been cooked.

Sada was served only after all the Trolls had taken their choice picks. It was not dissimilar to the customs of court in her own kingdom, and mostly she was only happy to eat. But a small part of her stirred in anger at the idea that they thought themselves to be more important than her. This whisper of a feeling was so quiet that she hardly recognized it. And yet, it was there.

Sada scarcely remembered to say a thankful prayer before she was diving into the pastries in quite an un-ladylike fashion. They were bland without salt, but not lacking in sweetness. And the herbs offered a gentle brightness. To a mouth that had been deprived of sustenance for so long, each dish was manna from heaven. With every other bite, Sada thanked the cooks. She learned only later that this was disrespectful, since cooking was seen as a duty and gratitude was used only sarcastically to hint at the idea that they had done their job unwillingly.

The Trolls did not talk while they ate, but once glasses of filtered nectar and mead were served and the pastries taken away for fermentation (this was the proper way to eat the bread and cakes, but they'd had none prepared when Sada arrived) the central cell came to life with chatter. As the Trolls talked, their eyes darted to where Sada sat at the end of the table, opposite *Om' Modir*.

She felt their stares pull heat to her face, but then their queen stared sternly at them, and they all paused for a moment, looking, but not seeing. Their eyes unfocused, their mouths slackened at the corners. The sounds of drinking and conversation ceased for less than a second, but the pause was noticeable. Then suddenly everything resumed and the Trolls snapped back to animation, continuing whatever they had been doing as though nothing had happened.

But they didn't stare after that.

Sada sipped at her drink uneasily, but did not inquire as to what had transpired.

"Art thee ready for your travels, my cubs?" *Om' Modir* was looking at the group of women seated at the middle of the table—the flower girls. These Trolls had blossoms growing atop their heads amidst the moss, and Sada thought their arms and legs looked slightly longer and more elegant than the others'.

One such woman was licking a flowery tart filling from her fingers, but looked up at *Om' Modir's* question. "Yurt. Me an' Tolsa think some of the cubbies art ready to come with us on this forage."

"Oh? Which girls art thou thinking of?"

The sticky-fingered Troll listed off a string of one- and two-syllable names, all beginning with G's and ending in vowels. It appeared that none of the named girls were at the table.

Orla, who sat at *Om' Modir's* elbow, shuttered her eyes and sniffed contemptuously, as she seemed prone to do.

"Gruna an' the other G's just barely left their pots, Tilla. I dunno if they should be set to work yet," Orla said. She glanced at the queen for approval, but Her Majesty was sipping mead with a smile on her face.

Sada did the same with her water, happy to have food in her belly and conversation to listen to.

Tilla shook her shoulders, as though shaking off the comment. Sada had seen other Trolls do the same to express their indifference. "They art gonna be fine. Quit yer whinin', Orla, an' tend to the cubs still in their pots. Tolsa already gave me the go-ahead."

Orla turned in shock to stare at Tolsa, who was sitting with the other nurses. She just shrugged, though her ears flattened slightly.

"I'm still wipin' dirt from their heads!" Orla cried.

"Hush, girl. I don't like it neither, but…" Tolsa dropped off, leaning in closer to Orla. "Times are a-changin'. Less and less cubs—"

"Hush now." *Om' Modir* silenced the girl with a touch. The smile didn't waver, but her black gaze was stern. "Let's not bother our guest with talk of the children. Tilla, when do you plan to leave for the forage?"

Tilla seemed fairly unbothered by the entire exchange. She belched loudly and shifted on her grass mat, stretching out her round, full belly.

"Affer the next rain, I should think. The petals will be fresh an' the sun is always stronger the next day. Means the newer buds are like to open up," she explained to Sada, gesturing with her hands.

"Where do you find the nectar? I haven't seen many flowers here." Truly, Sada hadn't seen any at all. Not even the yellow wish-flowers that grew rampant in every part of the kingdom. She thought that was strange for such a beautiful world, but perhaps it was winter here. A very warm, very leafy winter.

"Grandfleur, redblood. Grandfleur," explained Tilla, as though that would answer all her questions. She stretched her arms up and stood with a groan. "S'cuse me, I hafta find myself a bush."

When she left, a woman across the way from her smiled apologetically at Sada. "Excuse my sister's manners. I would be happy to answer your questions instead, flesh-cub."

Sada smiled awkwardly at the nickname. *Flesh-cub?* She recalled Groll's talk of eating her with some horror. But this woman did not look as though she wanted to eat Sada. She hardly looked as though she wanted to eat Troll food: she was the thinnest of all the clan, and her belly hardly bulged. It was even completely flat on one side, but the woman wore a belt of flowers that did a fair job of concealing it. She raised her stony eyebrows expectantly at Sada.

"Thank you, I am grateful," Sada said hastily. "I only wonder at what Grandfleur is…I have not yet heard the name."

Sounds of surprise went up around the table, and *Om' Modir* giggled gleefully. "A sure delight indeed," the queen said. "Tell thee, Nore!"

Nore smiled indulgently at her mother. "Grandfleur is a city that some of the Elves of the Wood live in. It's in the Blooming Vale, the branch of the Myriad Wood that's got more flowers than trees."

"And flowers big as trees!" said Flink. He was the only child at the table, and the only male as well. Sada assumed he must be a favorite child of the clan because nobody argued over his presence.

"Hence the name," added a woman with a square nose.

"There ain't many flowers here, and the ones we do have aren't big enough to get pollen from. And that's a right shame. Imagine how much food we'd have then! There'd definitely have been fermented cakes for thou to try if we had our own poppy fields here. But the journey ain't too bad with how rarely we make it." Nore paused to sip at her nectar.

In her silence, another girl who was nearly vibrating with excitement took up the tale. "The flowers art as big as thou, flesh-cub! Even bigger—as big as an Elf!"

"Big 'nough for the Elves an' Fae to live in 'em," added Flink. He turned to Sada. "I ain't never been but that's what Bacha says."

Nore nodded in agreement. "The flower forest is beautiful. We go there to get the nectar n' pollen, me an' my sisters. The crumbles are as big as Flink's head!" The little Troll giggled delightedly at that. "An' one flower has enough nectar for a full day of eatin'. But we hafta get it from outside the bounds of the city. The sharp-ears live in the real big flowers, an' they don't make pollen nor nectar, bein' houses and all."

"That sounds lovely!" Sada breathed. Her imagination was running wild with visions of little people curled up to sleep in huge bluebells as big as she was. She saw the Elven king stepping bleary-eyed out of a giant rose and couldn't help but giggle.

"'Tis." Tilla had rejoined the feast, and sat down heavily on her grass mat. Flink crawled eagerly into her lap and she tugged on his big ears.

"How do you collect the nectar and pollen? With the flowers being so big, the task seems difficult," Sada said.

"Maybe for the cubbies, but it gets easier with the centuries," said Tilla.

Nore voiced her agreement. "All the flower girls go together. We bring lots of baskets for the pollen an' jars to hold the nectar. After that, it's pretty simple. Some of us stand off to the side and keep the buzzers away, and the rest of us collect. We just pull the flower down to drain the nectar out, 'cause it's all pooled up in the bottom of the bud, you see. Once it's dry, we get the pollen. Usually it's two to a flower; one girl holds the stem down so we can reach the cursed thing, and the other girl goes right on inside and fills the basket with pollen crumbles. Nothin' to it."

"That is wonderful," Sada said.

She wondered how much she would be sneezing if she had to be the one to collect the pollen. There was a beehive at their Centerton estate, just behind the stables. Sada used to watch the little bees fly in and out of it. Once, one landed on her finger. Terrified of being stung, she had been paralyzed with fear before finally shaking it off. As she stared panic-stricken at it, she saw its legs and fuzzy butt were coated in yellow dust.

"Are the buzzers what you call bees?" she asked. Tilla raised a quizzical eyebrow. "Fuzzy creatures that fly around? They're yellow with black stripes and sometimes they sting people."

"Ah, *jiie, jiie,"* Nore said. "Never heard 'em called anythin' but buzzers."

"Sometimes bumblers!" Flink added.

"I dunno 'bout them stingin' folks," Tilla added, "but them harassin' and flyin' away with the cubbies happens, sure as the Kindreds' return."

There were a few murmurs of *"Jiie"* and "Yurt" at that.

"They sure as skies ain't gonna be no vessels," added one of the cooks. At this, laughter erupted.

Kindreds? As in kindred spirits? Her mind went straight to Mrs. Pérez, who didn't worship God, but the world around her. She often said Sada and Jezi were kindred spirits bonded by a soul tie. And vessels made her think of ships rocking in the harbor. Somehow, she didn't think these Trolls were speaking of either. They were still giggling at the woman's joke.

Sada smiled politely at the cook before turning to Nore. "Did you say something about keeping the bees away from the flowers, Miss Nore?"

The Trolls exchanged glances with each other at Sada's question.

"It's just Nore, cub," Tilla said.

"Oh, I only meant—" Sada started, but an explanation would do no good. These Trolls did not know the titles of respect of her world, and she did not feel like explaining the different terms and usages. She just smiled instead. "Pardon me. Nore, then."

Nore sipped her mead to clear away the last traces of laughter, then nodded and tapped at her head, at the moss and little flowers growing there. "That's what these art for. The striped fools don't care 'bout nothin' else when these are around."

"One sprinkle of pollen on your head and *yahoo*—no more buzzers in the way!" Tilla exclaimed.

Now Sada did chuckle along with Flink and the queen's hoots of laughter. She thought that some parts of *Om' Modir* were as young as the boy Troll.

"I should like to see such a thing someday," Sada said. Then an idea suddenly sprang to mind, and she sat up excitedly, turning to Nore. "You said the Elves of the Wood live in the flower forest, yes?"

"The Blooming Vale," Tilla supplied.

"The Blooming Vale, thank you," Sada said. "Might I go with you on your forage? I seek the Elven king, but I fear I am lost. I am certain that if I travel with you, my journey will be far easier than it has been thus far."

Nore looked uncertainly at *Om' Modir.* Sada waited expectantly, but when she saw the smile on the queen's face sadden, her heart sank. *She'll say no,* she thought morosely. *I should never have asked.*

"I'm sorry, Sada. I fear we cannot help thou in this," *Om' Modir* said gently.

Sada stifled the tears that wanted to come to her eyes. *Stupid girl.*

"I understand, Your Majesty," she said. "I hadn't wished to overstep my boundaries as a guest in your home and valley. I apologize."

"No, dear, no!" said *Om' Modir* quickly.

"It ain't that!" Tilla said hurriedly. "It's just…"

"Thou art speaking of King Caprius?" asked *Om' Modir*, interrupting softly.

Sada nodded.

"Grandfleur is one of the Elves of the Wood's principal cities, but it is only one of three. King Caprius calls the Autumn City, Titian, home."

"Oh. I understand," Sada said. "That must be their capital."

"I'd take you there myself, but…I don't know where it is," Nore admitted, glancing at Tilla.

Tilla shook her head. "We only been to Grandfleur. I ain't never even met a Titian."

"Well, there was that one," Tilla started.

Nore shook her head. "That was a Druid, Tills, remember?"

"Oh…yurt. The shiftskin, sure. Same color skin though," Tilla said with a shrug.

"And anyways, you can know for sure that none of us have met King Caprius," Nore added, addressing Sada. A few of the Trolls smirked or snorted laughter at that.

Flink, oblivious to Sada's dejection, turned wide, beetle-black eyes to her. "Yeah, what's he like, Sada? I heard his braids art made o' fire!"

"An' he rides a fee-nix instead of a big-deer!" chimed in another flowery Troll, her voice brimming with excitement.

That name she did know—phoenix. Governess Brown refused to tell any tales that didn't originate in the north, but Jezi's mother often spoke of all the legends of the world, from that of the fire-bird to fish-tailed merfolk residing in distant seas. She even claimed to have seen a one-horned horse called a unicorn.

Sada couldn't help but smile. "None of that, unfortunately. Well—His Majesty may indeed ride a phoenix, but not on the occasion that I met him."

The Trolls were typically silent when others spoke, but all of their voices rose in excitement with talk of the Elven king. *Om' Modir,* ever smiling, lifted a cracked hand. Their eyes went blank and their mouths hung open for a moment, and then they all fell silent. Once again, it was just evident enough for Sada to notice, but not quite enough that she was so uneasy as to ask about what had happened. And her *instincts* hadn't alerted her to anything amiss either, so she just sipped her nectar until they turned to her again.

"I think it is time for thou to tell us your tale now, Sada," *Om' Modir* said.

And so Sada did.

When it was done, all the Trolls were wide-eyed with amazement. They had never met the King Over the Elves of the Wood, but many tales were told of the Drake, as he so called himself. She told them of his auburn hair and the fiery temper that matched his eyes. As best as she could without bordering on disrespect, that was. She didn't talk of how he had made Kartinar walk doubled over with his arms over his head, or the way the king had screeched when the purple light was revealed.

Actually, she didn't mention the light at all, though she hadn't omitted that detail on purpose. Sada bit her lip as she waited for *Om' Modir* to pass judgement on Sada's tale. Perhaps *Om' Modir* would call her a liar, trespasser, and thief as well, and banish her from the forest as King Caprius had.

Finally, after an agonizing moment of silence, a grin split *Om' Modir's* face. "That 'twas the most exciting story I've heard this century!" she declared. The other Trolls voiced their agreement.

Sada smiled softly, but her mind was still infested with worry. "What of the Seam, *Om' Modir?* Where did it go? I fear I have broken the portal, and I know not what to do! Will King Caprius imprison me?" she cried. "Oh, I just want to return home!" She couldn't help it. The words had spilled from her lips as the tears were now doing from her eyes.

Suddenly, the Trolls were all around her. They hugged her as best they could, pressing their surprisingly warm bodies against her. Some hugged an arm, others embraced her feet (now bare so as not to dirty the dwelling), and Flink even clambered onto her back and wrapped his little arms fiercely around her neck. *Om' Modir* joined the embrace last, taking two of Sada's fingers into her hand, but by then Sada was laughing rather than crying.

"Thank you, my friends," she said with a small smile. They held her for a moment longer before releasing her.

"Thou have done well, my cubs. Please leave Sada and me for a moment," *Om' Modir* said to the gathered Trolls. They left, dipping their heads and shaking their bodies in farewell as they passed their mother and queen. She cupped Flink's cheek as he left, and then they were alone.

"Your children are very kind," Sada said. She wiped the remaining moisture from her eyes, still sniffling.

"Jiie, they are. So are you, little cub. But it seems that thou art also plagued with many worries. Fear not for the Seam. The portal is moody and

unpredictable. It changes locations without warning, so that not even those who guard it know where it will appear or when."

"Truly?" Sada asked, hardly able to believe it. "Do you know how to find it in its new location? Can you take me to it?"

That sad smile was back. "I cannot, sweet cub. You said it true when you told us that King Caprius is who you must find. He and his people are the guardians of the Seam, and only they have the means of finding the portal now."

Sada drew a deep breath and let out a sigh. It was shaky, but her sorrow was gone, replaced by determination.

"Thank you, *Om' Modir*. It will be an exciting journey that will in turn become an exciting tale, don't you agree?"

The old Troll laughed, a sound like dry leaves crunching. "I do! Indeed, I do! My children do not know the location of King Caprius' city, Titian, and I am too old and too pregnant to make the journey. Yet I have been there once, and I can point thou in the right direction."

"Would you?" Sada asked excitedly. She scrambled to stand, careful to mind *Om' Modir's* big belly. "If I leave now, how long do you think it will be before I reach the city?"

"No, no, that will not do."

"But I must—"

"No." Neither her voice nor her gaze invited argument. "Thou shalt leave on the morrow. The journey should take less than three days with those long legs of yours. Tonight, you will rest. I will hear no more on the matter. *Jiie*?"

Sada nodded, smiling. *Is this what it is like to have a mother?* If it was, she thought she might like to have one.

"Good girl. Orla will show you to a room. There are not many males staying with us this season, and so there are a few empty cells." Then, as an afterthought, "They may smell of dirt and Trell men, though. Dost thou mind?"

"No, I have slept in dirt itself recently." She gestured at her filthy gown, and *Om' Modir* laughed. "As for the men, I don't believe I know what they smell like, so I can't very well be opposed to it, can I? I thank thee for the hospitality, *Om' Modir*."

"And I thank thou for the story."

Om' Modir offered Sada one of her eternal smiles, and then she left, waddling, with Orla taking her place.

Orla didn't talk much, and only communicated to Sada with rough gestures and glares. If Sada made a wrong turn or went the wrong way on one of the ladders that connected the upper and lower cells, she would snap, "*No,*" but then she was silent again. Sada tried to meet it all with good grace and managed to restrain herself from conversation after the first few attempts proved unfruitful. That was hard, but her exhaustion made it easier. The day had been long, and her legs ached from sitting for so long on hard clay flooring. Mostly, her heart was tired. It had been dragged through fright, excitement, wonder, joy, hope, sorrow, and more in the span of one day, and both she and it needed rest.

Finally, Orla led Sada down a ladder made of sticks tied together with long grasses and gestured at the corner of the room. There was a grass mat in place of a bed, thankfully thicker than the ones they had sat upon to eat supper. The room smelled mostly of dirt, with a faint hint of mildew, which Sada assumed was the scent of Troll men that *Om' Modir* had mentioned. It felt familiar in a distant, aching way, though she could not place how. This cell was on the outer side of the Trolls' dwelling, and a slit of a window opened one clay wall to the warm night air. It smelled of sap and rain to come.

Sada thanked Orla and made her way to the window above the pale green mat. It was too small to stick her head through as she wanted to, but she dropped to her knees and slipped her fingers over the sill. It was powdery beneath her hands.

There was a shuffle, and Orla cleared her throat.

"Thou won't be stayin' long, will thou?" she asked curtly.

The harshness brought Sada's fingers to her hair, but when she turned, she had a smile on her face. "Only for the night."

Orla nodded, glancing around the room. "Just don't want thou takin' advantages of my mother's hospitability is all. She has a lot on her mind, but she's too kind to say so…"

"I would not think to overstay my welcome nor ask your mother for any more than she offers me. I thought it rude to refuse her invitations to supper and a room."

Orla scoffed aloud. *"Shore*—not wantin' to be rude when thou look like one of them fairfolk princesses *Gom' Brodir* warns the cubs about. They sure look pretty an' fair 'nough, but their hearts art cruel an' takin'. Anyway, that's just what the old man says—what do I know?"

How to be cruel, Sada thought, but she held her tongue, bit it even. The pain there masked the pangs in her chest. *Switches and stones may make me groan, but words shall never harm me.* Was that the way the saying went? Sada thought that in reality, it was reversed. *Bring forth the switches, but keep your harsh words from me,* she thought dully. She made herself smile at Orla, forced her throat to open and speak.

"I am no princess. If I were, perhaps I would have a gown to wear that is not caked with dirt and grime." She laughed lightly, but Orla seemed to find it as humorless as she did. "And by the morning, perhaps even before you wake, I will be gone."

"Thou and thou's fancy speech. I'm too dirty to be a princess, that what yer sayin'?"

"No!" Sada cried, "that's not—"

Orla sneered. "'Fraid of a little dirt? I'll be workin' in it 'fore *you* wake, fair lady. Mayhap I'll even sew thou a *gown* of it, would thou like that? No, too fair for it, much too fair. I hope you art able to find some enjoyment in this men's room, but it is far from a princess's way o' livin' ain't it?" She sniggered and clambered up the ladder of sticks, leaving Sada to stare after her.

"I am no fair lady," she whispered when the girl had gone.

Suddenly the view of the forest through the little window was no longer beautiful, and the gentle breeze was now harsh on her skin. She shivered and dragged herself to the corner to huddle against the clay wall.

Switches and stones, switches and stones, she thought morosely. *It is not the ladies who cry that find themselves with a place upon the throne…Why do you let yourself be so weak?* the voice of Memory tickled her mind, and it did nothing to calm the aching in her chest.

I am weak. Orla will wear the crown, as ladies who make others cry do. I, the princess, will be serving her in my muddy dress. She sighed. *Maybe I was a fair lady in Califia, but it matters not, now. For I will be stuck in Elt forever, and here I am nothing but a flesh-cub.*

As Sada sat there, she finally realized what the smell of the room reminded her of: Gabe. The guards when they met her after training in the barracks. John when he took off his helmet and let his sweaty hair down. She never thought she'd miss such a scent, one she'd covered her nose at before. But now it made her feel so close to them that she realized just how far they were. Sada fell asleep with tears on her cheeks and sorrow in her heart. The worst part was, she liked it.

Om' Modir

Old Mother sat peacefully in her queen cell. The new cell was almost finished being constructed, and she watched her daughters work happily, one hand resting on her warm belly. The life there was growing quickly and strongly. Soon, her abdomen would become misshapen from all of her daughter's kicking. She only prayed that the Kindreds would allow this Young Queen to live.

The last child had been a terrible sight, one to make not just a mother shudder, but anyone unlucky enough to see. It had kicked inside her until it hadn't. Then it bit and clawed with hands too big for its body. Trolls were born soft, but this one had been stony and cracked from the moment it slithered from her womb to the dirt. The birth had been painless, and that at least had been some small blessing. But when she held her daughter—the new queen—up to the light, Old Mother's eternal smile had flickered and her face drooped.

The little Troll was long-limbed and as lanky as a Faery, with hands that ended in claws rather than chubby round fingers. The legs were skinny, unable to support its round body. Its face was half-formed, but what was there had been twisted into a sneer as it glared at its mother. And the color. The cub was black and purple like bruised fruit, and its insides oozed out of cracks that were too big, in the way old Trolls oozed when they were dying. In the way Old Mother herself would soon die.

The eyes had perhaps been the most awful part. They were not black but purple, with gleaming irises like one of the fairfolk. And within their sickeningly beautiful depths shone evil. She was certain it was not a cub who was looking at her, but something on the other side of the world, using it as a vessel in the way Kindreds might use Spiritkin as theirs. Old Mother hadn't been able to bear touching the thing anymore, and she threw it down with a groaning cry. It kicked once, said "Omma," then died.

Yet even thinking of it now, she rubbed her belly with a smile. The life here did not feel evil. She had kept herself mostly constrained to the insides of the Dwelling so that she wouldn't expose herself to whatever dark force had certainly infected her womb. She also refused to use her Boon unless the command was either short or necessary. Now she called her daughters working on the new queen cell into her own. When they entered, she touched her eldest daughter, Aba, releasing a new command and manifesting her Boon into something physical and separate from herself in the way only Troll queens could.

The command was *sleep,* and it manifested into a pleasant scent of wildflowers and dreams that clung to the earthen skin of her daughter. Everyone she passed would immediately receive the command of their mother and queen.

Aba's eyes grew moist and droopy with fatigue. By the time she and her sisters had bid Old Mother a restful night and the blessings of the Kindreds, they all had the same look in their inky eyes. They trudged from her cell, buzzing mildly and bumping into each other as they went, to spread her command and then follow it themselves.

Old Mother smiled after her cubbies, then she waddled to the circular clay chamber at the end of the room. The blossoms had been freshly changed, and white petals welcomed her in. Old Mother crawled into the cell within her cell and followed her own command to sleep, wondering if the human girl was doing the same.

THE ELEVENTH

Sada

Sada had expected to sleep late, considering she'd woken early and in a panic the previous morning. Unfortunately, she woke to the same feeling today. There were no strange voices to upset her dreaming, but the panic was there all the same. She shot up from the grass mat, wet with sweat and cold with dread. It was not an unfamiliar feeling: Sada woke from fear as often as she woke from a chill. Fear of nothing; fear of everything. It mattered not the source, as there often was none. It was terrible each time.

She righted the grass mat and stacked the smaller ones the Trolls had given her in place of quilts, which they did not use. A peek out of the slitted window revealed the indigo of night. She should have returned to sleep, but the idea scared her. So she exited her cell, and after several minutes of wandering and trying every ladder or archway that might lead to freedom, she finally came across a room filled with sleeping Trolls. In the corner was another hole in the floor, but coming from this one was a welcoming breeze that tickled her bare toes. There was no ladder. Sada slipped out of the opening and onto cold, wet grass.

Then she walked.

Her feet took her across dry dirt and grass patches as she made her way around the dwelling. She passed the small clay oven, which still smelled of char and faintly of bread, and saw the newly constructed cell high above. The dwelling was as tall as her Centerton manor, yet half the length. The shape was asymmetrical, but not without design. It looked like an angular wasp nest. Sada was suddenly glad the Trolls did not have stingers.

She wandered all around the valley, stopping only when she reached the mouth of a cave. It yawned wide, shadowy and scary, but her *instincts* didn't come to life. She poked her head in. The cave smelled of wet earth, of rain and of the mud which accompanied it, and of the empty rooms of the dwelling. Sada pressed her hand to the wall nearest her. It was soft and malleable. She pulled away a chunk that stained her hands grey. Squishing the clay in her fingers, she retreated and wandered back to the dwelling.

The sky was still dark and bruised, but some of the stars were winking out. It was almost time to resume her journey. She would bid her farewells to *Om' Modir* and her other Trell friends first, but she also imagined the queen would force upon her a final meal. The thought made her smile.

Sada found her way to the big mossy boulder that *Om' Modir* had used as a podium. It was indeed a sculpture of the queen, from the smiling cheeks to the round belly. Her legs were buried in the dirt, but her arms were free and resting in the grass. Sada sat in the crook of one elbow and leaned against the sculpted queen's smiling face, playing with the bit of clay. She planned to sit there in the grass and watch the sky lighten, waiting for the Trolls to wake so she could bid them farewell. But within minutes she was asleep again.

It was Bacha who found her and alerted the rest of the Trolls with a shrill cry. They had thought Sada had made a run for it, maybe because of what Groll had said the night before. Sada assured them she had not, and that she wished them to see her off. Bacha grumbled something about needy redbloods, but Sada thought the Troll looked happy.

Om' Modir had indeed prepared another feast to send Sada off, and she did not dare to refuse, despite Orla's glares. The cakes from the night before had fermented, and the cooks told her they were still not as they should be eaten, but perhaps better than the night before. Indeed they were. The pastries were sweet and flaky as they had been before, but now each bite was accompanied by a tang that paired vividly with the herbs baked into the pollen-dough.

Sada ate more than she would on a typical morning, or even a typical night, and she ended the feast with her belly near bursting. She thought she might not be able to walk a step with it so full, but she didn't know the next time she would be able to eat in this forest of poison berries. After a round of nectar and mead for the Trolls, and water for herself, the fullness had settled to something manageable, and the Trolls and their queen led Sada out of the dwelling.

The air was warm with sunlight coming down through the latticed ceiling of the valley. Tilla sniffed deeply and declared it was also heavy with the promise of rain.

"Yurt—the forage will happen on the morrow, and perhaps we'll see thou in the flower forest," she said as they walked.

Many of the flower girls, some of the cooks, a couple of the nurses, and as many children as were allowed led Sada up the path which they had dragged her down only the day before. She recalled the fear she had regarded them with upon that initial encounter. Looking around at their smiling stony faces, at the dimples in those grey cheeks and the laughter in their big, black eyes, she wondered how she ever could have felt such fear for them. Now there was only a warm glow in her heart.

Flink and his opossum chased each other up the path, sending sand to cascade down onto the rest of them. Some of the nurses scolded him and the other children who followed in his wake, but it was good-natured. Once she reached the top, the children even worked together to help her scramble over the steep lip. The Trolls were round and chunky, but surprisingly agile when it came to navigating their valley. Even the old queen was nimbler than Sada when it came to this.

Outside the valley, Orla sent all the children back to the dwelling, save for Flink. Many of the other Trolls accompanied them. Sada peeked through the leaves enclosing the valley and waved goodbye to the Greenhead clan—a gesture which they copied with some amusement and wonder.

Now she stood facing *Om' Modir* outside the valley, who was flanked by Flink, Groll, Bacha, Nore, Tilla, and Orla. Flink, dressed in his tattered clothes and wringing his little hands, looked as though he might cry. All the Trolls' eyes were watery, but Sada had come to know that was natural for them. Hers, however, were not designed to water constantly, and when the first tear escaped past her eyelashes, she couldn't help but laugh. She had known the people for a day! Though that didn't truly mean much; she had also cried when a guard she had known but an hour was discharged. Her heart held on strong and fast to those she came to care for, and already the Troll clan had rooted itself there.

Sada descended to her knees as *Om' Modir* approached. The old woman was smiling still, but it was a sad smile. Sada's was as well.

"I thank thee for thy kindness, food, and hospitality. I shall not forget thee nor thy clan, and will think of thee often," Sada said.

"Oh, *bah," Om' Modir* said, shaking her shoulders in that dismissive way. But her smile broke into a grin as she took Sada's hands. "I thank thee for the story and the returned smiles. May thy journey be swift and fruitful, and may thee find favor within the Kindreds' hearts."

Trell goodbyes did not linger as those in the human world often did. Nore showed her how to bid them farewell in the way of their clan, and Sada replicated this by holding up her hand, then pressing it gently against each of the Trolls' palms.

Then she stood, and *Om' Modir* gifted her several pastries and slices of bread, which she slipped into a flexible sack made of woven tallgrass that Tilla had gifted her.

"Art thou sure you won't stay for the forage? After, we would have much more to offer you," *Om' Modir* said, but Sada caught Orla's eye and any thoughts of accepting fled as soon as they formed.

"I am certain. You have been so good to me already. Perhaps if we meet again, I may return the favor."

Sada waved farewell and walked in the direction they had pointed her, almost opposite of the way she had been going the day before. When she glanced back, the Trolls were still there, standing on the lip of the valley. They had all fanned their arms out in a T position, even little Flink, and they were gently rocking side to side and singing. The sight made Sada solemn again, and she turned around once more and didn't look back until she could no longer hear their gritty voices.

The Troll clan had told her to use the sun's path as her guide: she should keep the sun on her left in the morning and on her right in the evening. *And in three days, I will reach Titian. If my legs do not give out on me before then.* Sada had awoken with her legs stiff and aching, and it had hurt so badly to take even one step that she had been very inclined to take up *Om' Modir's* offer and stay with the clan for one more night. Yet something in her heart and her left hand told her that if she stopped now, she would never get up and go again. Or by the time she did, it would be too late.

Elt was beautiful, but it was not home.

Home was Jezebel and the apothecary in Centerton; home was the sneers hidden behind laughs and the insults cloaked in compliments at the court of Ettedon; it was Gabriel calling her little lady; home was in the sting of the lemon tree switches and her father's cold eyes. Once again, she was reminded of the saying: *switches and stones may break my bones, but words shall never harm me.* She would take the stinging of thorns on her skin over this relentless aching in her chest any and every day. That was what drove her on to find the Elven king, despite the stiff pain in her legs and feet.

That, and the guilt.

This was a motivation that she hardly dared to give thought to: the fact that her desire to return home was driven less by her love for the people there, less by the familiarity of her Ettedon house, and more by the guilt. Guilt for upsetting Jezebel, for Uncle Beron stealing her friend's beloved ear cuff, for abandoning her guards and subjecting them to the Duke's wrath…but most of all for abandoning her father; for disobeying him so starkly after everything he had done for her.

His booming voice reverberated in her head: *are you truly so ungrateful as to cast aside my wishes,* simple *as they are? All that I do, I do for your sake, and yet these are the thanks I am met with?*

The thought alone made her belly stir, and her chest squeeze tightly. She saw the Duke's eyes everywhere: in the two blue berries set apart from the other clusters on the bush; in the dark whorls on a stone; in the reflection of the sun on a puddle; in the brilliant blue glare of a fox, watching her from the shadows of a tree.

The animals of Elt did not only come with extra ears and tails, but also brilliantly colored eyes and fur. The elk of this world were not confined to varying shades of brown, but ranged from black to white and many colors in between. The prey often had dark eyes, but not only brown ones. Rabbits also had mossy green eyes, and the does' eyes sometimes seemed almost purple. The predators, like the blue-eyed foxes stalking her with her father's eyes, possessed irises of sky, sage, gold, and sometimes even lavender.

Sometimes she felt as though her father had somehow managed to recruit them to his personal army, or take possession of their bodies so that he might watch her even here in this different world. Those delusional thoughts that her father might have eyes in Elt did not bring her comfort. Instead, it incited tingles in her stomach and prickles in her palms and dispelled any and all traitorous thoughts—

(What if I ceased my efforts to return home?)

(What if I abandoned my quest to find the Elven king, turned back to Om' Modir, *and took a place among the Trolls?)*

(What if I made a home high in the trees and spent my days in the company of the forest's creatures and spirits?)

—that sometimes crept into her mind when she wasn't standing guard. When they did, the glimpse of the Duke's eyes in the forest reminded her of her treachery, and she found herself walking faster toward King Caprius, and in turn, home.

She also found her thoughts turning to the Elven king quite often. More often than she'd like, perhaps, but they served to entertain her while she journeyed. There was little else to break the monotony of her days except for the persistent ache in her legs. Daydreams had always filled the idle hours of her life in the city residence and court, and here they served the same purpose.

She would be walking and singing along to Elt's music and then, unbeknownst to her, her voice would falter, her mind pulled entirely into thoughts of Caprius. She pictured their last moment together; his auburn hair smoldering in the evening light, as though someone had slow-roasted the sunset or managed to weave the darkest flame of the fire into thread. She pictured his eyes, two embers burning for her and her alone, as he first caught sight of her.

Most of all, she replayed the memory of him leaning in, his braids brushing her collarbone while his scent, the essence of autumn itself, embraced her. She wondered what an embrace from the king would feel like. How well might those arms protect her? How fiercely would he defend her? With his sharp tongue and blazing gaze, nobody would dare hurt her.

Not even the Duke, her treacherous mind whispered.

It was when her face flushed and her stomach fluttered that she would abruptly pull herself from the reverie, embarrassed. Clearing her throat, she would begin to sing again. But just as a river conforms to the shape of its bed, so too did her thoughts inevitably return to daydreams of King Caprius.

Perhaps life in Caprius's palace would not be as dreary as life in her father's mansions. Perhaps the Titian court would not be as harsh as

Ettedon's. Perhaps by the end of the year, Sada might even find herself queen. Was that such a fanciful notion? She was, after all, a noble lady of the highest rank. And so, it was this—perhaps even more than her guilt, or her dwindling desire to return to her bleak cage—that drove her ever forward.

Sada was happy to find that after walking for the time it took to sing but two songs, she felt limber and energized again. Each step was easier than the last, and her legs carried her swiftly through the trees.

The rain began to fall shortly after her second wind came.

Tilla was right, she mused as she held out a hand to catch the droplets. They were scarce; most were caught on the leaves overhead before they could reach her in this dense part of the forest. She thought that was amazing since the trees were so far apart. Perhaps two or three carriages could line up between each one, nose to wheel. Hitting the leaves high above, the rain sounded like the rattle of the drums that the costumed performers played at Ettedonian feasts.

Part of her thought the water would be warm to match the hues of the forest, but it was cool and bright on her skin. It felt somewhat similar to her *instincts* when they were just beginning to prickle at her fingertips. As she walked, the birdsong picked up in excitement at the rain, and some swooped between treetops, pausing on branches to shake off the water. The puddles dotting the forest floor grew deeper, and their leafy reflections were upset by the drizzle that was slowly increasing to a true rainstorm. Spotted fawns and four-eared rabbits peeked out then excitedly began to splash in the water. The mothers gave a few distressed bugles and squeaks before they, too, joined. Sada passed a puddle encircled by little creatures that looked like lilac wish-flowers with legs. The little ones, not even as big as an apple, would take turns jumping in and splashing each other by kicking up the water. Delighted, Sada stopped and crouched beside them.

But the soap-mouth, the diseases! the scared part of her mind cried out.

Oh, hush, replied the other. The part that delighted in this adventure, the possibility of danger. The freedom. *Soap-mouth probably doesn't even exist here, girl!*

The mother of the puffballs looked at her with wide, white eyes, pupils becoming pinpricks, and began to squeak frantically, jumping up and down.

"Do not fear, I mean no harm," Sada tried to soothe, but as she was speaking, one of the little ones splashed her with water. She blinked through droplets to look at them and saw they were all frozen still, looking between Sada and the one who must have splashed her, waiting for her to attack or run.

Sada attacked.

With a grin, she dipped her hand into the puddle and splashed the little one back. Then the game commenced, and despite the mother's frantic squeaking and bouncing, Sada and the little puffballs relentlessly soaked each other. When the mother saw this was not a dangerous attack by the wild flesh-cub, but truly was a game, she even joined in, splashing her little foot in the puddle. When it was drained and Sada's face was wet with both tears of laughter and rain, the little ones gave one final splash and then were herded away into the bushes.

The rain was coming down hard and fast now, and though the sounds of the lyre-harp had picked up into a frenzied melody with the torrent, even their music was now drowned out. She realized she had forgotten to ask the Trolls what the instruments were, and who played them. She had heard more of the drums than anything in their cozy little valley, but she had seen no drummers. She thought that the Trolls could have used their big bellies as drums, especially the men, and that made her giggle. She brushed her dress habitually as she stood, but then realized it was soaked through. Even if there was dust in this forest—outside the Troll valley, of course—the gesture would have been useless.

She continued walking in the direction the clan had sent her off in, though she could no longer see the pink sunlight as a marker. The forest colors had dulled with the rain, and everything had a cast of grey to it now. The birds had stopped their singing as well as their flitting between branches, and the deer and rabbits had retreated into the bushes with the fuzzy fellows Sada had been playing with. She was alone in the forest, and the rain was coming down in fat droplets that left her hair and skirts dripping. She spun and skipped in the downpour and tilted back her head to catch the rain, but she couldn't enjoy the activity for long; she was freezing.

I need to find shelter, Sada thought, and looked around for it. Bushes, trees, ferns, roots…there were no hollow trunks to hide in now. She had the sudden idea that she could make herself a lean-to like the horses in the village were provided, but there were no planks in the forest, and no fallen branches to gather either. She thought an outcropping of rock might do nicely to hunker under while the storm passed, but there were no rocks in this wood, either!

Sada glanced up at the tall trees around her. If she could get up higher, she'd be able to see more of the forest and perhaps find a tree with low branches, or a root large enough to duck under. But she could not gain a higher vantage point, as the trees here had no branches for her to climb; the lowest ones were so high up on the trunks that she had to cock her neck back to see them, and she didn't think even the Elves could reach them. So she continued walking and trailing her hand across the trunks of the trees she passed, marveling at the way the icy-hot *instincts* came to life in her hand as she touched them. Sada's hand caught on something as she reached one especially skinny tree, about the size of a typical pine in Centerton. She paused; it was the first gnarl she'd felt in the forest.

Yet as she looked at the knot her hand had found, she realized it wasn't a gnarl at all, but a small wooden wedge jutting out of the tree. Above it and below it were others, circling all the way up the trunk and down to the roots like steps. What sort of world was this to have shelves spiraling up trees? She pressed down on one of them and found it to be sturdy; it appeared to grow straight from the tree itself. So Sada did the only reasonable thing to do in this situation: she drew up her gown and began to climb.

The steps were just large enough to fit the sole of one foot, and there were no other handholds besides more of the ledges above her, so she had to hug the tree (this one was small enough for her to get her arms most of the way around) and sidle around it to climb. She stopped to check her progress and saw she'd climbed high enough to make her hands sweat and prickle, but she still couldn't see anything more than trees, so she kept going. When she resumed her tree-hugging climb, she didn't see the small creature poke its head out of a hole in the trunk just above her and flit down to her shoulder.

"What a novel way to use the staircase! Novel indeed!" a tiny voice said in her ear.

Sada started with a squeak and twisted to find the voice, but as she did, she lost her footing and fell a few stomach-dropping seconds to the ground. She landed with a groan, gasping for the air knocked from her lungs.

"Oh dear! I meant for a tickle of the tummy, not a fumble of the feet!" the tiny voice said in her ear again.

Sada scrambled to sitting, looking around, but nobody was with her. The rain was the only noise. In her hand, her *instincts* were making themselves known. Then she felt something like a bird alight on her shoulder, and something like a wing brush her cheek. She turned slowly to see a tiny person staring at her, as tall as a sparrow and dressed in a short gown cut and sewn from a leaf. Beautiful yellow wings like a butterfly's draped down the little woman's back, shimmering with what looked like crushed starlight. Sada couldn't help but marvel at the vibrancy of their color, like the silks brought by merchants from the east. Her wings fanned excitedly when Sada faced her, and her bright pink irises widened in tandem with Sada's.

"Bright days to you, star child. How does the rain find you?"

"Wow, hello," Sada breathed. Her breath rustled the small woman's bright pink hair, and she brushed it out of her face with a tiny hand, waving the other one dramatically.

"Mind where you're blowing!" she whined, but it was quickly followed by a giggle. The little woman then pinned her wings flat together so as not to catch a draft and be pushed away. "Wow, your eyes are *amazing.*"

"Oh *dear*—I didn't mean to blow on you!" Sada exclaimed. At this, the woman clapped her tiny hands over her tinier mouth and erupted in fits of laughter. "I've…never spoken to someone so…small."

"That doesn't surprise me the bittiest, oh-no-oh-no! You smell all about mortals, and only you Faery people are curious enough—and reckless enough, shall we be honest?—to search out the *humans.* And your people don't visit here. *Still.*" She sighed dramatically. "But I won't be a bitter-butt. How did you get to the mortal world? Well, you must have used the Seam, but how did you get past the guards? Oh, you *must* tell…me…?"

Trailing off, the little woman moved out of her view and began playing with the hair by Sada's ear.

"That tickles!" Sada cried, giggling.

"Kindreds above—round ears? You weren't just visiting the humans, you *are* one!"

She heard a soft whisper like the pages of a book scraping together, then the slight weight disappeared from her shoulder. She reappeared in the air in front of Sada, her wings vibrating so quickly they were just a blur of yellow-green.

"How did you come here? *When* did you come here? You are from the human realm, right? I thought Caprius's men would have stopped you, since…you know."

The barrage of questions left Sada feeling as stunned as when her tutors surprised her with a quiz. Yet she smiled nonetheless—she hadn't had the good fortune to meet someone so talkative in years!

"I must confess, I am not entirely certain as to how I came to be here. I was in the forest in my world, um, traveling to a festival, and I fell. Then when I stood, I found myself not in the wood where I fell, but in *this* strange and lovely world. It's a longer story than that, but that's the essence of it."

"Mm. Mhmm…Yet you *are* a human, right? Redblood, fleshling, mortal, child of death, bringer of war and destruction?" She blinked sweetly, petal-pink eyes wide and curious.

"Pardon?" Sada asked. "I am a human, yes, though I do not claim to be all the rest of that!"

The tiny woman seemed not to care for Sada's objections. "Amazing," she breathed. "It's been years upon years since a human foot has stepped in these forests, oh, I say. *Oh,* how I wish my brothers were here to see this! They won't believe me if I tell them I met a fleshling—*in the flesh*—" she giggled, then continued brightly, "I must bring them proof, that's what I'll do! Proof by name. What do the other redbloods call you, dear doe?"

Sada was grinning. "I am Lady Sada Solares, first daughter of Duke Darius Solares of Altamira. It is unfortunate that we have no chaperone here to properly make our introductions…yet might I inquire as to your name and lineage?"

"*Whew.* Titles o' titles, a sure sign you're talking to one of the highborn fairfolk—or a human too, so it seems!"

The winged woman had been flying in loops in the air, dodging the raindrops which were becoming scarce again. Now she settled on Sada's knee and sketched what must have been her form of a curtsey, which was a ballerina's arabesque—wings splayed out.

"I have no lineage to speak of—my paterwing flew off with some blue-winged skimpsy soon after he saw I had no twists in my hair—but the name's Cidinen Everdance, and I'm your local Pixie! Of course, most Pixies here are local. But I've lived here the longest, and if Trea Woodsworth tells you any differently, *don't* believe her. You can't trust a Pixie with dull wings." She fanned hers out in demonstration to the contrary, displaying their brilliant colors.

"Oh, how dandy! I've never met a true fairy!" Sada exclaimed, thinking of the fairytales and bedtime stories her nurses had fed her dreams with; Governess Brown would be so shocked to see she had been wrong, calling them make-believe and—

"Not a *Faery!* A *Pixie!*" Cidinen cried, looking incredulous. She clutched at her bosom as though she'd been pierced there by an arrow. "Don't wound me so, new friend."

"I beg your pardon! I knew not the difference. Then it is an honor to make your acquaintance, Miss Cidinen, *Pixie* of Elt."

Cidinen was nodding appreciatively. "The same to you, bright days, bright days! Though just Cidinen will do fine. It's so pleasing to the ear, don't ye say? Oh—this is how to say, 'nice to meet you' the Pix way." Cidinen crossed her legs, then bent to the side at the waist, displaying her wings. She made them shiver, sending the light playing across them and pinpricks of water vibrating off.

"Ooh, wonderful!" Delighted, Sada gave a little clap.

"The pleasure is my own."

"I must say, after meeting the Trolls I expected other people of this world to speak in a similarly archaic fashion. Yet your own speech is very modern."

"Archaic…as in old?"

Sada nodded emphatically. "*Thee, thou, art,* and such."

"Oh sure, sure. To call that old is to speak true; we haven't spoken in such a manner in many o' many a century. But the Trolls think it makes them sound smarter. More *refined*, I think Avidi said. Nobody wants to tell them it isn't so. Or that it doth art not so, as they might say." The winged woman tried and failed to trap a giggle behind her hands.

"I must admit, it was difficult to understand upon our initial meeting. The common people of my world talk more similarly to you than the clan, and even in my lessons on courtly mannerisms, I believe my tutors only spent one day on archaism."

"Are there Trolls in your world, then?" she asked, eyes wide. "Oh, I can't believe humans are real! I'd thought you all to be legends! We all wondered what happened to you after the second war, anyway."

"Which war do you speak of?" The Elves had mentioned something similar. "Do you know our history?"

"Ahh…never mind, never mind, dear. You were telling me about the Trolls in your world?"

"Oh, okay. Unfortunately, we do not have Trolls in Califia, or anywhere in the Americas so far as I know. Nothing so exciting as them. It's simply that my people once spoke in a similar fashion, and learning the ways of history is important," Sada explained.

"Oh. Why?

"Well…" She frowned. Why was history so important? She wasn't quite sure, and so she recited what Governess Brown had told her. "To do away with the bad and imitate the good."

Cidinen nodded along thoughtfully, then smiled, and Sada did the same. The explanation sounded fair to them both.

"I can't say I see why you'd want *Trolls* in your world. Pixies, sure, we're nice to look at and talk to, but…the waddlers? Humans are strangelings, strangelings as you are fleshlings."

Sada nodded in agreement. "To be sure. Yet *Om' Modir* and her clan were very kind to me. Every kingdom and city can do with kindness, no matter the realm."

"That may be so, but…" Cidinen had been flitting merrily in the air, now free of rain, but she suddenly dropped to a dead hover in front of Sada, and her pretty face grew sober. "This place is dangerous for your kind, maiden. Lots o' Beasts waiting to gobble those purty eyes right out o' that fleshy skull of yours. You shouldn't stay here any longer than you must."

"Thank you, Miss—I mean, Cidinen. I've been told this by another, yet I must say that I have begun to wonder as to why. Above all, I wish to know what this place you call home truly is. The Elves have named it Elt, but I confess this knowledge did me no good other than to give a label to the object of my thoughts."

Cidinen blinked, her wings pausing in their fluttering for a moment. "Say you what? You've met the Elves already?" Sada nodded. "And you still managed to come through the Seam without being cast back onto your side like a stone into the pond?"

Sada nodded again. "I wish they *had* cast me back onto my side…but, alas. I met them quite a distance away from the Seam."

"Yet still you met them. And still you wander around out here like a lost fawn, dear?" Sada nodded sheepishly again, and Cidinen let out a loud breath. She began to flit around again, pacing in the air. "Which kind of Elves did you meet? Well, you're in the forest, of course you met the leaf-lovers. Don't be *dumb,* Cidinen. But *which* leaf-lovers*?* The Elves of the Wood are as different from each other as a hippogryph is from a griffin."

Sada didn't know what to make of that, only that it sounded similar to something *Om' Modir* had said.

"I don't know about hippogryphs and griffins, but the king only said he ruled over the Elves of the Wood, but the Trolls—"

"You met the *kingling*, and he let you go? I thought you just ran into some leaf-loving limp-ears!" To demonstrate, Cidinen put her hands up to her ears and bent them at the wrists in imitation of a dog's floppy ears.

Sada didn't know what that meant either. Were leaf-lovers like some of the eccentrics in her world who scolded woodcutters for felling trees? *And what are limp-ears?* She imagined King Caprius with the ears of a beagle and had to stifle a laugh.

"His Majesty's ears did not look limp to me," Sada said. "They were extraordinarily pointy! But you make it sound as though there is more than one kind of Elf."

Cidinen rolled her eyes. "They're the only Spiritkin that have different races within their race. Sharp-ears are so tedious. Really, it's the fault of the Mother Elf; they say she was *quite* promiscuous, if you follow where I'm flying." She winked.

First limp-ears, now sharp-ears, and that word "Spiritkin" again.

"What is a Spiritkin?" Sada asked.

Cidinen blinked at her.

"The mortals really are as ignorant as the stories say. Tales be true, for they both begin with T," she murmured. "A Spiritkin is what I am, what all the Pixies, Druids, Goblins, Elves, and all the others are. I suppose it's a name for all the smart beings in Elt. You redbloods have a similar term, don't you? Persons? People? Something of the P-variety?"

Sada giggled. "Yes, we call ourselves people."

"Well, there you have it! People are just your world's version of Spiritkin. It's told that in the mortal world you live among humans and animals. Here in Elt, we have Spiritkin, animals, and Beasts. So I guess the word Spiritkin is just a way to distinguish us from the mindless Beasts of this world who just want to eat and kill.

"Though we do also call ourselves people. But don't tell the rest of your mortals we stole it from you!"

"Your secret is safe with me," Sada laughed. "Besides, I think you're definitely still a person, even if you aren't human."

"I think so too! Especially because our Granddams were!"

Sada's jaw dropped. "Your *grandmother* was a human?" She forced her expression into a more polite one. "I apologize for my brashness; it's only that I can't exactly imagine how that is possible."

"No, silly! The *original* Granddams were human, not *my* granddam."

Sada's confusion must have been evident on her face because the little woman sighed.

"Okay, sharpen up—it's time for a history lesson.

"Centuries upon centuries ago, Spiritkin were born from human women joining with immortal beings of some sort. It was so long ago we don't even know what beings the Grandsires were anymore, but lots of folk believe they were angels—do you know what those are? Oh, jolly, I wouldn't have been able to explain. Well, our human Granddams that I mentioned birthed the Mothers, and then the Mothers birthed us—the Spiritkin."

"Oh!" was all Sada could say.

"*Whew!* I feel like a priestess from all that teaching!"

Sada had heard of angels and humans having children that grew to such gigantic stature they were named for their size, but their race had died off long ago. To be in a world where not only Giants, but potentially many other fantastical beings existed made the fairytale-loving parts of her scream in childish delight.

"Then you are partly human?" she asked.

Cidinen laughed at that, loud and clear. "No, not at all, not the bittiest! The *Mother* Pixie was part human, and that's how my people were created. But that was centuries ago. Now I'm just a Pixie."

"Then you're not human, but you have souls as we do?" Sada asked. The name intrigued her. "Spiritkin…What a curious name. It sounds as though you're some family of the spirits."

Cidinen's face lit up, and she began chattering excitedly again.

"Human, person, Spiritkin. Doe, fawn, deer. Maybe you have the right of it, and we are distant kin! Maybe you're my mother! No…that wouldn't work. I heard that humans only live to be a couple hundred years, and I'm nearing my fourth century. But *I* could be *your* mother, sure, little fawn."

"Your *fourth century?"* Sada whispered. Her eyes were so wide she could feel the strain of them bulging. When she realized what she'd implied, she threw her hands over her mouth. "Oh—I don't wish to be rude! Certainly, you look as young as a maiden."

Cidinen giggled. "You're in a world of immortals, youngling, where wisdom and magick grow with age. That is not the insult you seem to think it is."

Sada laughed again, simply because of the incredulity of it all. She couldn't even comprehend a lifespan so long that one still looked young after living for centuries. The little woman hovering in front of her could have been Sada's age, yet here she was claiming to be over sixteen times as old as her. She really shouldn't be accepting these things as easily as she was, but what else could she do? Everything she learned here defied all she'd known before, and yet what could she trust if not the eyes in her face and the ears on her head? Reality was being redefined right in front of her, and Sada was simply an observer.

"Oh—you were asking about the Elves! I got us so sidetracked; I always do that."

"That's okay, I'm just the same. And I appreciate the knowledge!" Even though it made her head hurt.

"Oh joy! Ode to the brightest of days! My brothers never let me talk this long. Now listen up, hear me well, little dear. There are the Elves of the Wood, with whom you've made an acquaintance—however strange that may be—then the Elves of the Deep. They live, you guessed it, in the ocean; there are the Elves of the Pinnacle, though I'm beginning to wonder if they're really just legend, I've never met one; and then there are the Blood Elves." Cidinen's eyes darkened at the last name.

"Blood Elves?" Sada murmured.

When Cidinen stilled her fluttering and landed on Sada's knee, something like fear was sketched on her face, and her fair skin was raised in tiny goosebumps.

"They're as dreadful as they sound. You'll want to stay far away from them; bad, bad fellows, I say, worse than dull-wings, worse than the Titians. I would have warned you to stay away from any of the kingdoms, yet it sounds as though you tickled King Caprius's fancy. As a norm, he and his folk don't tolerate outsiders."

She thought of the way the king's fiery gaze had scoured her from head to toe; how he had leaned in close to her neck, smelling of the forest, to breathe her scent. Heat brushed her cheeks.

"They did make an effort to send me back," Sada said quickly. "Back to my own world, that is."

Cidinen laughed again, and it sounded like someone had played a few keys of the piano. "And yet you're still here. Did those bare-chested chaps enchant your mortal eyes and render you unwilling to go? You know what they say about the Kid King's fancies. Well, you don't, but I do." She popped into the air again to fly in close to Sada's face.

"No!" Sada blushed furiously. "Nothing of the sort! I did try to leave as we both wished, and yet it simply…didn't work."

Cidinen frowned, and her fluttering wings slowed, though she did not fall. "What do you mean it didn't work?"

"I'm not certain. I followed the Elves' instructions, yet when I jumped into the portal—the Seam—it just turned into a regular pond."

"What was it before?" Cidinen whispered.

"Something beautiful…It was silver and sparkling and hypnotizing, like starlight taken from the heavens and molten into liquid. But now…" Sada sighed. "I only hope the Elves don't grow angry with me. I'm trying to find them now to once again request their aid. I was told that King Caprius holds guardianship of the Seam, and that he will know its new location, or else have the ability to find it."

Cidinen did not chime in as she usually did, and Sada saw that all the color had drained from the little Pixie's face. Her brilliant eyes were fixed on the hem of Sada's skirt, the place where the liquid of the portal had hardened into a silver web on the fabric of her dress. She flew down to the ground beside it. Sada suddenly felt the great urge to hide it or run, but did neither of those things. She let her fingers tangle in her hair instead.

"The Seam," Cidinen whispered, sounding distant.

She reached out with a miniature hand and touched one of the veins of glittering silver, looking almost as if she were in a trance. As soon as she touched it, Cidinen snapped her hand back, and just as quickly seemed to snap back to reality. Her wings began to flutter so quickly that Sada couldn't see more than a bright blur behind her.

"I must go. The ones of old were right in banishing your kind from our wonderful world. Only pain comes with your wretched visits. You never should have come to this world, you of the cursed flesh." Cidinen glared at her so sharply that Sada flinched, then the Pixie flew away before she could respond.

The rain began to fall again, first sparingly and quietly, but it quickly began to pound on her skin. Sada hardly noticed, and she certainly didn't care. She deserved the discomfort.

Sada was left with the company of the trees, fingers in her hair and teeth digging harshly into her lip. Something had shifted in Cidinen as soon as Sada mentioned the Seam and its change. Sada had known something was wrong with the portal, and that worried her for her own sake, but the Pix woman had looked truly panicked. Scared. And the way she'd snapped at Sada…it made tears threaten her eyes.

The horribly metallic taste of blood was on her lips and tongue now, but it distracted her from the more horrible feeling crushing her chest: guilt. She tried not to let herself feel bad for making Cidinen so terrified; she hadn't purposefully done anything to the pond that was the portal between their worlds. And if what *Om' Modir* said was true, then she and King Caprius simply had to find its new location. She had just been present for one of its naturally occurring relocations, that was all. It was nothing more than unfortunate timing.

Yet now all she felt was worry prickling sharply at her forehead and stirring up bubbles in her belly. If the Seam really was broken and not merely in a new location, how would she get home now? The thought had her chest beginning to seize up, and she took a few breaths to calm it, pushing the worry from her mind. If the portal really was damaged, there was certainly nothing *she* could do to fix it. She of the "cursed flesh." She was better off continuing on her quest to find the Elven king and allowing him and the other Spiritkin to work out a way to send her home.

If what Cidinen had said of humans was true, and if the Elves behaved in the same manner they had the first time they found her in their woods, they should be more than happy to help.

Sada considered climbing the Pixie's tree again, but all she'd seen the first time was more sprawling forest, and the rain was now a torrent that made the steps look wet, slick, and dangerous. Instead, she looked to the sky, so dark it was almost colorless, and began walking in the direction she had been going.

Or so she thought.

THE TWELFTH

Sada

Sada had, in fact, *not* continued the way she had been going.

The rain had gone on for over a day, but the trees provided a fair amount of cover when she walked near their trunks. She'd forced herself to continue onward whenever it was light enough to see, though it was hard to determine day from night in the storm. She stopped to rest at one point and fell asleep, though she wasn't certain how long she'd slept or if it had been at nighttime, because it was still storming when she'd woken and continued walking. When the sun finally made its appearance, it became obvious that she had been traveling with the sunrise to her right rather than her left. This realization had done nothing to dampen her hopes or mood, however. She'd just accepted the fact calmly and reoriented herself, all the while singing a childhood song. She'd noticed a change in herself during her time in the forest.

(Away from him.)

She felt it first in the quiet moments, the ones where the wind stopped moving and the trees stood still, holding their breath, waiting for something. She wasn't scared anymore—not the way she used to be. She'd spent her whole life knowing every choice was teetering on the edge of disaster, that one wrong move would send everything crashing down. It wasn't a hyperbolic way of thinking, either, fueled solely by fearful imaginings, but rooted in the reality of life with the Duke. But here? Out here in the wilderness, away from it all, she wasn't afraid of making her own decisions. She wasn't afraid of being alone. She no longer feared simply existing, unlike when her entire life had felt like a test she was destined to fail.

What scared her now was the realization that she might actually like being lost.

The idea was still small, just a sapling searching for water, but it was growing with every droplet of choice she fed it. That tiny voice, the one she barely let herself hear, was getting louder every day. A part of her didn't want to find the Elf King or the portal that would take her back. Back to where she couldn't get lost, even if she wanted to—even if she thought she had. To where even the smallest things, down to what dresses were acceptable to wear in the seclusion of the manor, weren't hers to decide.

At first, her stained dress had been a source of embarrassment. Now she grinned whenever she saw the stains, because they meant she was in a place where no one would scold or hit her for having them. No, here she had freedom, raw and untamed, and she wasn't sure if she could give that up. The thought twisted inside her, unsettling as it was, but there it was. A small part of her, growing like a weed in the cracks of her mind, didn't want to go back at all.

She couldn't think about this too long, though, or guilt and shame would torment her. She had a perfect life, and a perfect father, and to wish to escape that was being as ungrateful as she could possibly be. She deserved a lashing for such thoughts.

But it wasn't only those thoughts that allowed her to accept her situation so easily. She had also simply exhausted herself of worry over being lost. It was really not too bad. So upon seeing the sun, she'd spun about and started back in the right direction.

The animals had watched with blank stares, then continued following her at a distance. With the brave ones, she'd shared bits of her food. One porcupine had even followed her for the better part of a day. Sada had decided that in a world inhabited by the children of mystical beings, soap-mouth was the least of her concerns.

Her primary concern was her complete lack of skill in navigation. She would begin walking in the correct direction, but it seemed that every time she checked the sun, she was going the wrong way. Whether that was because walking around trees and foliage had ended up shifting her direction ever so slightly until she was turned completely around, or whether it was simply due to her poor navigating, she did not know. Either way, it was becoming frustrating.

But so far today she'd managed, more or less, to keep on the correct path. But when one worry abated, another arose: the food from the clan had been reduced to crumbs some time ago. Now even the crumbs were gone; too hungry to be concerned with manners, she'd wet her finger on her tongue and pressed it against the little morsels until they stuck, then sucked them greedily off. Only then did she leave the satchel hanging on a branch, where she hoped someone else would find it and make use of it.

Already, her hunger was fading as her body realized she wouldn't be eating anytime soon—she would certainly not be trying any more berries. Instead she felt weak…hollow…though her legs no longer ached while she walked. They had accepted their fate and become numb to the pain of exercise, and now dutifully toted her along without a word of complaint. It was at night when the pain set in, when she stopped moving. But if she fell asleep quickly enough, she usually didn't notice it.

It seemed to her that fruit-bearing bushes were becoming more frequent in this area of the forest. Some of them were quite…unique as well. Apples grew in the shapes of flowers, leaves reached for her as she walked by, and some berries even whispered when she neared. If her experience with the icy berries hadn't been enough to scare her away from eating any of the forest's fruit, these oddities would have.

Since she was still strong enough to continue trudging on, she avoided the vibrant fruits she came across…mostly. She did eat one of the many pink cherries, and that night her dreams were so vivid that when she finally awoke, she'd thought that was when she'd actually begun dreaming. Then the animals that now regularly kept her company in the night had skittered away in their typical frightened fashion, and the illusion was dispelled. She didn't want to eat leaves, either, but she wasn't sure what else there was as an option.

She certainly couldn't *hunt.* Even if she'd had a bow or knife with her, the thought of actually killing and eating a wild animal sent her hunger fleeing. Who could know what diseases she might contract from eating them! Mrs. Havens, one of the Centerton elders, had told her that even breathing around dead birds could be fatal; she wouldn't have that anywhere near her mouth.

And imagine the trouble it would be to pluck all their feathers…

Even if she managed to overcome this fear, then catch and kill something, how could she cook it? It did not grow cold in this forest, but one night her aching legs had kept her up, and so she had tried to make a fire. She loved to sit before her fireplace in her rooms in the Ettedon house. But when she tried, she realized she had no idea how to do it. She'd seen her servants make them, and of course knew the flames required wood, but how did they *create* the fire? Where did it start? No matter how hard she tried, she could summon up no memory of how it was done.

She thought about leaving the branches out in the sunlight so the heat might start a flame, but then she realized that if that was all it took, all the trees in the forest would be burning. She gave up on the whole attempt within the hour because it just made her feel ignorant, being unable to make fire when even the maids and cooks could.

So instead of eating, she resigned herself to continue plodding on all day, settling into a routine: resting when she felt weak, drinking water when she grew too hungry, reapplying her powder when necessary, and trying not to lose hope that she'd ever make it out of the woods alive.

There was still the undertone of music ever present along with the sounds of the forest, but now the harp and lyre had been joined by something akin to a wind chime. The drums still beat at night. Sada had yet to stumble across the source of the music.

She was singing along to it as she walked when suddenly all the animals that had gathered to watch her (as they had taken to doing when she sang) disappeared. One moment she was being followed by elk and rabbits and birds; the next, they and their bright eyes were gone. The forest was silent. Her *instincts* pricked at her left palm. Now uneasy, Sada continued on, stumbling across the grooves and bumps hidden by thick orange moss and dark green grass.

The footing had grown uneven in this part of the forest, with small gorges and hillocks decorating the earth. Sada's knees had become bruised from stumbling so often that she had to begin carrying a long stick to use as a walking staff. The end had been nibbled on by a fat and slightly stupid squirrel, but it still served her well enough. She was using it to help herself over a particularly large chestnut root when a squeal split the newfound silence of the woods.

She jumped back with a squeak, heart flying into her throat. Then she froze, glancing around for the source. There was no movement in the forest save for the shadows playing with the sunbeams.

Another animal scream pierced her ears. Sada's head snapped up. Her throat closed as though halting her breath would halt the possibility of danger as well. Just ahead of her was a thicket of innocently dancing ferns and some of the whispering berries, and she went to it with both growing fear and a strange urgency.

It may be some of those little squirrels I saw the other day playing with each other, she thought. Maybe even one of the tree cats. But she didn't really think that was true. As she walked, the icy fire of her instincts grew stronger, spreading up her left arm. She heard a louder cry followed by a growl come from the thicket. Sada paused dead in her tracks at the blood-chilling snarl. Besides Groll of the Trolls and a panicked deer that charged at her the other day, Sada had encountered nothing particularly scary. But this Beast sounded dangerous, and it made her hands go cold. She began to back away from the rustling thicket, but just as another squeal rang out, her arm alighted in a blaze of painful tingling.

She took another step backward.

The pain increased. She hissed a breath through her teeth.

When she moved forward, it regressed to an uncomfortable vibrating sensation. Something within her was telling her to go into that thicket, and when she tried to fight it, she was met with the unbearable feeling that she was making a terribly wrong decision. She bit her lip. Her free hand found the tips of her hair. Then, before she could gather enough sense to go against the morality residing in her heart and manifesting in her left hand, she steeled herself and rushed into the whispering and sunlit brush.

When she stumbled inside, she froze, and a scared little groan escaped her lips. Directly in front of her was a bright blue filly. It had wings like an angel and a spiraling horn growing from its forehead…Directly in front of *it* was a big, drooling fox with black fur and nine tails bristling behind it. The fox had to be as big as a dog—not a tame house dog that begged for scraps, but the kind that the farmers kept to scare off bears. The kind that looked to be part bear itself. The sight of its bared, gleaming teeth made Sada's heart pound. She instantly regretted her decision to go into the thicket. Unfortunately, it seemed that it was too late to change her mind. The fox had heard her loud entrance, and its terrible golden eyes were locked on her now. It licked its wet teeth and seemed to grin: it had found an even tastier meal.

And then it spoke.

"Hello, pup," it growled.

Sada froze, and all her fear collected into a hard blockage in her throat that made it impossible to breathe. Her lungs froze along with her feet.

(1, 2—)

Oh those horrible eyes—

(1, 2—)

I shall die here before I can say farewell to my family!

(1, 2, 3)

Her chest surged with breath.

The black fox lunged into a sprint.

With it snarling and racing toward her, Sada had no choice but to flee, fight it, or faint.

She very nearly succumbed to the latter. Then the Beast leapt for her, blue foal forgotten, and Sada cried out and scampered to the side. She felt a rush of air and the prickle of her *instincts* as the fox sailed through the air beside her. As it landed, it spun and immediately lunged for her again. Her knees buckled, she cowered down, and she lifted her staff up to shield herself, squealing like a mouse caught in a trap. Eyes squeezed shut, she felt a jarring impact as the animal's teeth found the stick instead of her face and dug into the thick wood. Sada wrestled with the Beast for a few seconds, feeling as though there was no strength in her arms, that this was a dream, and that the branch would snap and it would take her throat in its jaws and it would all be over.

The fox let go and she whimpered. *Just let it be done with.*

It struck again.

Sada barely had enough time to swing her staff out. The attack surprised both her and the fox. It connected with the immense creature's chest, and it let out a squeal similar to her own and fell, backing away with its belly against the ground. Sada stumbled away, panting. The Beast only paused for one breath before it was running toward her again, its nine huge tails bristling behind it. As it bounded toward her, Sada swung her staff. She missed, and the Beast leapt, paws outstretched. She hardly had time to register how massive its claws were before it was raking them down her exposed side. She felt flesh tear away and she grabbed at her ribs, somehow remembering to hang onto her staff. The gasp she let out was more from surprise than pain. Shock had numbed the wound. Shock that she had actually gotten hurt. Wasn't that just for nightmares and stories?

Her attacker was crouched low to the ground, licking its claws. The ones it had used to scratch her. When it lifted its muzzle again, it was russet with blood.

"Red blood. Delicious," it said in a feminine voice that sounded far too human.

"Th-that's mine!" Sada said incredulously. Then the fox flared its tails out and growled a warning. "Lord, watch over me," she whispered.

Its eyes gleamed with satisfaction. The Beast was enjoying this. Yet that didn't make her as terrified as it ought to have. Now that she had been wounded, the whole interaction became much easier to accept. It was as though the fear of getting hurt had weakened her, but now that she knew what the pain was like, that it wasn't fatal….

The fox dove again and she shoved her staff out to meet it, baring her teeth at the fiery flare of pain it gave life to in her side. The animal whined as it was hit, but didn't pause for long before striking again. This time she was ready, almost eager. Sada shoved her staff out again. When she used the blunt end of it to meet the fox midair, she was able to keep the Beast away.

It leapt again, and she countered.

Leap. Jab. Whine.

Leap. Jab. Whine.

Without realizing it, Sada had begun to grunt out the beginnings of a battle-cry with each thrust of her spear-like staff. Somehow, the shouts seemed to fuel her. She began to understand why Gabriel enjoyed his work so greatly, why her father craved the days of battle. Yet despite her constant parrying of its blows, the Beast did not cease its assault. Sometimes it would try to circle around her and jump from a new angle, but she resisted the urge to whack it on its dark head, opening herself up for injury, and waited until it jumped.

Leap. Jab. Whine.

She continued fending off its attacks with increasing confidence, but her strength was waning quickly. After only a few minutes, it was an effort just to raise the staff high enough to meet the fox in the air. And the great nine-tailed monster didn't seem to tire in the slightest.

She had just struck it hard enough that it lay on the ground for a few seconds before getting up, but when it rose again its yellow eyes were more bloodthirsty than they had yet been. The Beast wiggled its tails behind itself as it prepared to jump, and Sada realized with newfound horror that it was just *playing* with her. Playing with her the way her father's hounds did with the rabbits on the estate, even after all this time and all these blows. The creature had probably been feigning its whining, wanting her to think it was tiring so she'd let her guard down. Yet she didn't have to. This wasn't a mental game for her, but a physical test. And for a girl who'd spent most of her life within the walls of one grand building or another, it was one not likely to be passed.

The fox sprang again, and it took all Sada's strength just to lift her staff up to connect with the animal. But she underestimated the height of its leap, and it sailed over her stick, the end of it just grazing its stomach. That was the only white part of its body.

My blood will stain it red, she thought.

Then it landed with its claws dug into her shoulders, and she fell into the tree behind her with a cry.

Sada managed to lift her staff up and push against the creature's neck, but its claws were deep in her shoulders, and the pain made her weak. The Beast's jaws snapped closer as her arms began to give out, feeble from days with no food and little rest. It seemed to grin again as she whimpered out of pain, fear, and exhaustion.

What are you doing? the voice of her father suddenly asked. *I am head commander of King Abel's own armies ...this weakness is* not *in our blood!* Yes—he was head commander, and her uncle had been a general, once upon a time. If the men of her family could lead and take on armies equipped with gleaming steel and whistling arrows, Sada Solares would not dishonor her family name by giving up a fight—

(A fight? Ha—this is merely a skirmish! her father's voice corrected)

—against a woodland animal.

Sada spluttered as some of the thick drool pooling in the fox's mouth dripped onto her face, warm and stinking and horrible. It was even worse than the wound on her ribs. It was more horrible than anything she'd ever experienced. As the drool leaked into her own mouth, an overwhelming, all-consuming wave of vigor flooded her, beginning in her arms and ending in her legs. She gagged, then screeched so loudly it made her throat raw. Then she took the rest of her strength and that newfound energy fueled by disgust and fear and put it into one final surge. She shoved her staff up between the fox's jaw and its neck and pushed as hard and fast as she could, at the same time kicking her legs up into its belly.

The animal jerked back with a gurgling wheeze escaping its crushed windpipe, and its claws ripped free of Sada's shoulders. They took with them shreds of flesh. She gagged again and spat out the drool, then gasped in relief, but it was short-lived. As soon as she pushed herself up to sitting, the fox leapt again. It latched onto Sada's ribs, and she shoved it with the staff again, causing its claws to rake down and across her side. She cried out and the fox snarled, seeing Sada's moment of weakness. The Beast tore the staff from her hands, and it landed somewhere out of sight. Weaponless, Sada had to wrap her hands around the fox's great neck in a desperate attempt to fend it off.

But she was so tired. The fear was gone, and now only exhaustion remained. She could feel the blood pumping out of her with each heartbeat, warming her sides and coloring her dress red. And the mossy ground felt so nice to lie on.

I can't believe this is possible. I'm truly going to die. I never imagined it would really happen, she thought. Yet her body kept on fighting even as she inwardly made peace with her death. As she tried to choke the big monster, it snapped its gleaming teeth in her face, golden eyes swirling maliciously. It dug its claws into her ribs once more and Sada cried out reflexively against the pain, her vision pooling with red and black. Just as her grip was loosening around the fox's neck, it let out a loud, blood-curdling and hair-raising shriek that seemed to silence the entire forest, and the pain of its claws disappeared from her sides for the final time.

Sada's eyes flew open wide, and she scrambled to sitting, whipping her head around to look for the fox and its nine-tails. She saw the bushiness of them just off to the side. The Beast was lying beside Sada, jerking and twitching, and bent over its belly was the winged unicorn. As Sada scrambled to move the little animal away from the fox and out of danger, it lifted its head and pulled its spiraling horn free from the fox's side. Purple-brown blood dripped onto the foal's blue nose. It nickered, tossing its head.

Sada scrambled away from the creatures, heart pounding. The fox was still twitching and whimpering, despite the gash on its side. Sada saw but didn't register that, beginning at the wound, its black fur was turning white. The foal bent to sniff at the Beast's side, lipping the exposed flesh.

It's still alive! It could attack us!

Without another thought, Sada stood, grabbed the foal, and sprinted from the ring of bushes.

The fox's whimpers followed Sada as she ran, and it was all she could do not to run back and help it in some way, even if that meant killing it. Yet she knew that blood loss would kill her for doing that if the fox did not. And so she ran, putting as much distance between herself and the dying Beast as she could. Before she could get far, though, her sides began to pulse with lightning-strikes of pain in time to her rapid heartbeat and she had to stop, gasping, and fall to the ground. The foal spilled from her arms with a snort.

Sada pressed herself to the green and pink moss and tried to slow her breathing. Each gasp of air caused spikes of pain and heat to shoot across her sides. Her arms were heavy and weak from defending herself; her shoulders throbbed; even her head and throat ached from her screaming. The shock had been a blessing, but now the threat was gone and so was the numbness.

Sada had never been in such pain. The worst injury she'd ever suffered was wrought by falling off her horse while riding; she'd scraped the skin off her knee and banged her head a little. The pain she felt now was so terrible that she couldn't feel a part of her body that didn't hurt, and every time she moved, the stains of blood on her dress darkened. It didn't take an apothecary's training to know that the things hidden beneath the skin were supposed to stay there, including the red blood she was known for in this world. She also thought she ought to keep moving, though she didn't know where. She was faint, confused, and tired, but the thoughts swimming through her head told her to get up.

Move, move! You'll be stuck here forever, in the land of talking foxes and Trolls and men with bare chests and pointed ears! Find the king, find the Seam! Just MOVE. And so she dragged herself as far as she could before she collapsed between a couple of big tree roots.

Sada awoke, and with fumbling fingers unclasped her cloak as she'd meant to do before falling unconscious. Lowering the sleeves of her gown, Sada groaned as she saw the state of her wounds. Her stomach began to churn with worry once more. It wasn't even the pain that was the source of her upset, but the knowledge that something was wrong in her body. Even if she hadn't been trained in the ways of an apothecary, one glance made it obvious that if she did not treat her wounds, they would be fatal. Her shoulders were only slightly marred with round punctures, but the marks across her ribs were long and deep and oozing blood.

She knew that the first thing she needed to do was to keep herself calm and suppress any thoughts—

(My bones are exposed, that's white, that's my bone, bone shouldn't show, oh God please help me I'm going to die, I'm going to die, I'm going to—)

—that would cause her to panic. But bits of flesh still hung off her sides where the fox's claws had torn away from her. How could she not panic at that? Not yet in full possession of her wits, Sada tried to pick some of it off the way she tore the skin off her lips with her teeth. But this flesh was still attached by sinews of living skin, and the pain was too great to handle. Instead, she just pressed the cloak into her wounds to soak up the blood. Each touch of the fabric made her cry out, and she hated the noise—

(Why are you choosing to be weak? It is a choice; you know that, don't you? said Memory's voice)

—but it couldn't be helped. Eventually the panic of knowing that something was horribly wrong with her body became so great that she grew nauseous and woozy, and so she tied the cloak tightly around her sides and resigned herself to counting her breaths until they slowed, and she didn't feel as though she might dirty her dress further with bile. If she couldn't see the wound, then she couldn't worry about it…as much.

Eventually she fainted again, though the part of Sada that housed her drive to live kept her half-awake in case the smell of her blood attracted any unwanted attention. As she dozed, the awake part of Sada heard quiet steps and the sound of snuffling, but the sounds blended into her dreams, and she continued to doze. Distantly, she felt something warm curl up beside her. She'd awoken to animals sharing her sleeping space nearly every night since she'd come to the forest, so this didn't alert any alarms within her mind. Her *instincts* tickled her left palm, but it was nothing compared to the fiery throbbing in her sides and shoulders. Then something soft began nuzzling her ribs, trying to get under the cloak she'd wrapped around herself.

That was enough to wake her.

Sada jolted awake to see a small blue shape curled up beside her. But unlike the deer and ferrets that ran away in a panic whenever she awoke to find them sleeping with her, the winged unicorn just lifted its head from her side and snorted softly. Its coat was long, fluffy, and not horse-like, especially since it was the color of the cerulean water lilies that the queen liked to have set out at the smaller feasts. Its mane was a resplendent tumble of fluffy golden curls, with a tail to match. The wings, she saw, were a mix of that cerulean coat color, the gold of the mane, and brilliant white. And there was the horn, golden and covered in the blood of the fox. In her disorientation, Sada thought it was a guardian angel.

Then she looked into its eyes—its *human* eyes in an animal head—and all her panic over her wounds strangely receded. She saw in its eyes the eddies of mystery but also serenity, and somehow, she knew then that she was going to live.

"Oh, good, you're okay," Sada said. Panic over her own condition had consumed her foremost thoughts, but in the back of her mind she'd harbored worry for the foal. It released with a sigh at the sight of the little animal.

Sada held out her hand, noticing how it trembled. The foal lifted its little muzzle to her fingers and sniffed noisily, nostrils flaring. Smoother than velvet, it tickled her skin. Its touch made her *instincts* do the same. Appearing satisfied, it nickered softly and Sada couldn't help but smile. It was curled close against Sada's side, its brilliant eyes shuttered lazily. Satisfied. Sada decided it would be safe to pet it. She reached out a hand to stroke its furry side, but as soon as her fingers felt the softness of the fur, that icy hot tingling shot up her entire left arm and shocks of words and images flashed through her brain.

Frightened…evil…danger, she heard a panicked voice whimper, and she saw flashes of golden eyes and nine dark tails. Then it was *aid…protection…guardian,* being whispered and suddenly Sada saw *herself* standing in front of the fox, bloody and panting but fending it off. She barely had time to register how strange it was to see herself from another person's perspective when the image faded. It was replaced by gruesome images of the fox twitching in the leaves, and then the warm taste of blood filled her mouth. When it came from biting her own lips, it made her tongue draw back reflexively. Yet this time, she *liked* the taste. She had no time to register that realization. No panicked words accompanied this image, and when it faded it wasn't followed by any others.

Sada jerked her hand away from the foal with a gasp, the taste of blood instantly fading from her tongue. The Beast appeared surprised as well and blinked wide eyes at her.

"What in the skies above and the earth below was that?" Sada whispered. She stared at the winged unicorn, and the filly stared back.

It shouldn't be possible, but it was as though Sada had seen the foal's memories…felt her feelings. In that moment, Sada had also realized that the little animal was a girl. Sada's hand pulsed with the receding vibrations of her *instincts,* but that was hardly anything to think twice about now. It was becoming familiar. This, however…

She wondered if she had accidentally eaten another of those pink dream cherries. Perhaps the battle with the fox of nine tails and this encounter with the winged unicorn was part of some tragically wonderful dream. The filly snorted softly, the warm air eddying on Sada's skin. That did little to convince her of her wakefulness. She reached out to touch her lovely blue coat again.

There were no flashing images. No breathless words of thought.

She was losing blood, on the edge of consciousness, and coming down from the heights of panic—that was enough to convince a rationally minded person that she had imagined most or all of her interaction with the fantastical horse. And yet Sada was not a wholly rational person. She dreamed of implausible fantasies and had believed every fairytale Governess Brown and her nurses told her as a child.

And after feasting with people of stone and talking to a woman the size of a bird and with the wings of a butterfly, I might be insane if I didn't believe this filly just spoke to me.

Besides, the body often recognized reality before the mind could, and she couldn't discount the visceral chills that ran through her when she remembered the hope-filled words that had accompanied the image of herself: *protection, guardian.* Then the thought of the fox took over, bloody and dying, and the rush Sada had felt disappeared. But not the feeling that it was real.

With the excitement over, her sides were throbbing in pain again. Sada winced as she untied the cloak and peeled it off her sides. She didn't want to look, though she was fairly certain the wounds were bleeding less, but she made herself check anyway. She was right that the blood flow had slowed, but it did little to calm her nerves. Even in the dim light of dusk she could see how angry and deep the gashes looked. It began to stir her stomach as the panicked thoughts returned, but she had years of unofficial training under Mr. Pérez, learning the ways of an apothecary, and this time she managed to still both her mind and her stomach.

"I need to tidy this wound," Sada murmured, half to herself and half to the little creature curled up beside her. "You can watch if you don't try to lick my blood." Half-delirious, she giggled.

Sada thought of the process she and Jezi used to treat the town boys who staggered in from street brawls, or even her own guards who returned from sparring with ugly marks to show for it. First, they would rinse out any debris, then disinfect the area with an alcohol solution. If it was a deep wound, Jezebel or Mr. Pérez would sew it up. Next, they would apply an ointment of comfrey and animal fat, then wrap the wound with a clean cloth.

But that was all to treat scuffs and small cuts. Someone with the severity of wound Sada had would be sent to a physician in one of the larger cities like Ettedon, not to the apothecary. Mr. Pérez was incredible, but he specialized in home remedies for ailments and aches.

Well, what other option do you have?

The answer was none. And so, her assessment complete, Sada immediately broke the first rule given to a patient with a serious wound: *don't move.* She made to stand, planning to search for water before the growing dusk became dark, but the filly snorted and put her head across Sada's lap. She froze, preparing for another volley of vibrant images and shouted words, but they didn't come. The winged unicorn just lay there looking up at her.

"I must find water to wash my wounds," Sada said to the foal. Then she made to stand again. This time the animal nickered deeply and shoved her muzzle into Sada's stomach.

"Ah!" She winced. The foal just stood up and nudged her again, harder this time. Sada leaned back against the rocks, trying to get away from her strong muzzle. "Stop, you're hurting me," she said to the filly as though she could understand her.

But she did stop her shoving. She then lowered her head to the wound and sniffed. Sada's heart fluttered; the foal had done the same thing to the fox after she stabbed it. She felt a ripple of fear go through her body and tried to scoot away from the Beast, but she snorted and glared at her with those human-like eyes. Sada froze, and the filly dipped her head back to her side, sniffed across the entire length of the wound, and then began to lick.

After removing her cloak and makeshift bandage, Sada only had on her undergarments and corset; but those were torn beyond repair, and so her wounds were raw and exposed. She cried out, anticipating pain, but it never came. In fact, the gashes grew numb. But Sada was terrified of the infection that the foal would give her, and she made to move away. Again, the foal snorted sharply and this time she nipped Sada's leg as well. Every time Sada tried to move away, the filly would glare at her, protest with a snort, or nip her. Eventually she gave up and just prayed to God that the otherworldly creature licking her wounds wouldn't pass on an infection that would hasten her death.

The horrible experience went on for countless minutes. At one point, Sada looked down and saw the creature nibbling at the flesh hanging off her side like it was grass. She noticed Sada's look and turned up wide, innocent eyes as she chewed away Sada's skin. This made her stomach turn so viciously with unease that she had to look away simply to avoid vomiting.

Just as Sada's dread was growing unbearable and she was ready to jump to her feet and sprint away despite the pain, the foal stopped her licking. She moved away from Sada, smacking her lips, and Sada tried not to cringe at the sight of her own blood on her muzzle, red mixing with the purple of the fox's, as if she'd just finished gorging on marionberry pie.

Once the Beast had moved far enough away that it couldn't nip her anymore if she tried to move, Sada made herself look down at the wounds. She braced herself for the sight of how inflamed they'd be after being touched and irritated so much, afraid to see the damage. Some farmhands thought the best remedy for a gash was to allow their dogs to lick it, but that farmer's tale had been dispelled by wise apothecaries and physicians long ago, and Sada knew it would only result in worse infection.

Yet when she looked, the gashes on her ribs were gone. Not just the blood, but the wounds themselves. In place of the bloody claw marks were four long, red scars on each of her sides. No blood oozed out, and the surrounding flesh was no longer puffy and sore, but smooth and flesh-colored. Tentatively, she touched the marks on either side of her ribs. They were tender, but the touch didn't cause her to cry out.

She turned wide-eyed to the filly. "Was this you?"

The filly, of course, said nothing, but she held Sada's gaze steadily.

Sada couldn't help but laugh. Without thinking, she leaned over (now painlessly) and hugged the winged unicorn around her neck. This world was as incredible as it was strange. Jezi and Mr. Pérez would be so envious of this winged unicorn's ability to heal. Sada was, despite her unease, and she wasn't even a true healer.

"Thank you," Sada said to the little creature, pulling away. Sada didn't care if she understood her or not. But something in the way her wonderful eyes blazed made Sada think she did.

THE THIRTEENTH

Sada

Sada awoke sometime between late night and early morning with the little winged unicorn sprawled across her lap. Looking at her, she recalled a lullaby one of her nurses had sung to her as a child. It mentioned a horse with the wings of an angel. He carried heroes into and out of battle, and everyone who rode him was victorious. He was called a pegasus. Looking at this filly with both wings and a horn, Sada thought she seemed to be a mix of the legendary pegasus and the unicorns Mrs. Pérez spoke of. Sada wasn't sure what name such a creature deserved. Regardless, this little unicorn-pegasus shouldn't exist outside of lullabies and nursery rhymes.

Sada was delighted that she did.

The typical blanket of animals she had grown used to waking to was gone from her lap. Her heart sank when she noticed, but a quick glance up revealed their ensemble of sleeping bodies scattered just a few paces away. None were sleeping on the side where the unicorn-pegasus lay.

Last night, after Sada had made certain that the wounds from the fox really were healed and it wasn't a delusion, she made herself get up and find a better shelter further from the dying Beast. The marks on her shoulders were still throbbing and inflamed, but the wounds weren't deep or bleeding. Still, she worried about infection. There had been no discernible yarrow or comfrey to make a poultice with, so she settled for wrapping her cloak around her shoulders and curling up into a hollow in the ground.

The filly had followed her through all of it until Sada lay down to sleep. Then she disappeared, and Sada thought with some sadness that it was the end of their short companionship. But now the filly was here, warming her legs. Sada smiled, stroking her silky neck, and leaned back to rest until the sun was fully up.

Sada was overjoyed when the filly followed her again as she set off later that morning. She even waited patiently when Sada got stuck in a patch of sticky bushes, their leaves and blossoms oozing what felt like honey. Now she traipsed alongside Sada as she searched for a stream or pond large enough to rinse herself and her blood-stained clothes in. Only her shoulders seeped blood now. Her ribs were still fully healed, a miracle she had to keep reminding herself of with frequent touches to her sides. Each time she did, she grinned at the filly and thanked her again.

They had been walking for a time when the foal nickered suddenly. Sada rubbed her arm when it began to prickle with icy heat in response.

"What is it, Lady Blue?" Sada asked her.

She had taken to calling the foal that, as she had no idea what to name a winged and horned horse. Neither unicorn nor pegasus felt right, and that would be like calling a dog, "Dog," in any case. She had also taken to speaking aloud to Lady Blue, either singing or telling her the many thoughts that bounced through her head. She wasn't sure if she was imagining it when the winged unicorn would snort and whinny as though responding to her.

To this question, Lady Blue just huffed in response and cantered away, and Sada watched in confusion as she disappeared over a ridge. Having no better sense of where to go, she followed her. The hill on the other side wasn't steep, but the ferns and moss decorating its slopes were slick with water. Sada realized why when she descended into the thick, cool mist spawning the moisture. She managed to walk a few feet before the fog obscured her vision and she had to resort to half-crawling down the slippery hillside. But even that tactic soon failed her. She missed a foothold and slid the rest of the way through the cold fog with a yelp.

The hillside deposited her into a wide gorge. The walls were fuzzy hills of pink and yellow and blue moss, speckled with miniature flowers that leaned toward her when she moved her hand over them. Small waterfalls fell from hidden nooks in the moss. There were few ferns or other forms of foliage here, though there was an abundance of sand. It led to the center of the gorge in little paths, where several of the waterfalls ended their journey in a gurgling pond.

Sada brushed herself off, thanking the Lord that these woods were scarce of rocks and sharp things. When she stood, there was a ceiling of mist overhead. To her left she saw several pools, some calm and others bubbling, before her view was cut off by a wall of fog and mist. To her right was another wall of moss like the one she'd slid down. Rainbows filled the air like vibrant clouds, suspended in time and space. There was also the sound of distant singing mingling with the instruments of the forest. It sounded as if it was coming from behind the fog. Sada paused to marvel at it until she heard a familiar whinny and found Lady Blue standing in one of the pools. Sada picked her way over the damp sand and wet moss, and joined the foal at the pond.

Dipping her fingers in, she found that the water was warm, just as the humid air was. Already she was beginning to sweat, and that was certainly saying something considering she existed in a constant state of cold. She glanced around to ensure there were no other visitors in the gorge, then threw off her cloak. She peeled her tattered and stained gown and once-white petticoat off her body, then wrestled her way out of her corset. Though she was almost certain she was alone, she left her shift on.

Once her shoes and stockings had also been tugged off, she walked to Lady Blue through the pond, using the colorful stones ringing it as handholds. She was stamping her hooves in the shallow water and squealing delightedly. Sada laughed along with her excited whinnies.

The sandy bank looked like her vanity before her maids had a chance to clean it: a necklace, a few bracelets, a string of pearls, and even a pearl comb were scattered across it. She had time to wonder who they belonged to before a splash from the filly distracted her. She splashed her back, grinning. As Sada reached the center of the pool, she noticed swarms of little white fish streaming around her and the winged unicorn's legs. Gemstones also glinted beneath her feet. Sada followed the rapid path of the fish over the edge of the pond, which cascaded over a short ledge into another, bigger pool. Sada stepped down into this one and sank deeply into it.

She sighed as she floated onto her back, and the water caressed every part of her body, melting the aching and stiffness of her muscles. Her body may have grown used to walking, but it certainly wasn't used to fighting; every limb was aching from her battle with the fox. But the heat of the water wrapped around her and seemed to whisk her pains away in its lazy current. To Sada, whom Jezebel often joked was literally cold-blooded, this seemed to be a small grove from paradise.

After her eyelids had become droopy, Sada made herself stand from her blissful floating. As she did, she noticed with horror the pink tint her blood had given the water. She desperately hoped she hadn't ruined the drinking hole of any creatures of the forest. Hopefully they wouldn't seek her out to exact revenge for tainting their springs, either. But it was already bloodied now, and there was nothing to be done about that. She retrieved her garments from the side of the pond where she'd left them and began to clean them.

As Sada was scrubbing her tattered petticoat under the water and trying to figure out how her servants had washed her clothes, the current of the big pond began to swirl harder around her body. She paid no mind to it and just switched to a wringing method on her skirt. It seemed to get more of the blood out, and was gentler on the rips the fox had decorated it with. Then the current pushed forcefully against her, and her feet were swept up in the water and her head plunged under.

She spluttered as she stood, combing her hair out of her face, and squinted into the water. She saw nothing. She glanced down at her legs instead to see if the team of white fish had returned, but gasped when she saw hair floating beneath the surface of the water.

Her first thought was that she had stumbled into a watery graveyard, and the hair belonged to a disembodied head.

Then a woman rose out of the pool directly in front of her, skin as blue as a sapphire, dripping water, and very alive.

And very beautiful. Her lips were full, her features elegant and sloping. Her hair looked as though it were still under the water, gently weaving around itself and floating away from her skin as though it was almost weightless. This stranger was one of the most beautiful people she had ever seen.

Sada screamed.

"Oh dear!" she cried. Then, remembering her manners, she said, "Are you well…miss?" All the while, she was scrambling to cover herself. Even in the company of another woman, it was terribly improper to be seen in a shift alone. Sada wasn't sure what else to say as the woman just smiled. Her aqua eyes lit up.

"Hello, lovely," the stranger said. Her voice was like the tide. "What has you wandering in my springs?"

The blue woman glided through the pond toward her as she spoke, moving as fluidly as the water around her. Sada took a step back at her nearness.

"You have my apologies if I've intruded on you," Sada said, keeping her eyes averted. It was the most she could do to restore some dignity to the situation. "I would not have come if I'd known this spring was occupied—I wish not to be impolite."

"This entire glade is occupied," the Nymph said in that mesmerizing voice. "But feel free to be impolite anywhere in it. Haven't you ever met a Nymph before? We never were ones for rules—and the ones who are will forgive you for breaking them."

A Nymph! These were the people—the Spiritkin—that Kartinar and the Elves had mentioned.

The woman giggled as she stood, dripping, from the water. She looked like one of the women in the paintings that decorated the king's dining halls—the ones where the ladies were always being fed clusters of grapes. Her long hair, decorated with jewels of every color, continued to ripple around her as if it were caught in a gentle current.

Sada backed away from the woman, half-swimming and half-stumbling toward the shore. "Thank you for allowing me to bathe in your spring. Unfortunately, I must return to my travels now," she said hastily.

She turned to swim away, but as she did, the stranger gasped. "Oh my!"

She felt a soft hand encircle her wrist. Something sharp dug into her skin, and she thought it might be the points of long and jagged nails. The Nymph tugged softly, but it was enough to pull her easily back through the water.

"What pretty jewels you wear on your fingers…" She trailed a nail over Sada's hand.

She jerked away from the touch with a half-scream, and the Nymph giggled. The sound made panic seize Sada's limbs.

"Where are you going, decorated like this? Surely you belong with my sisters and I, sparkling as you do."

"Oh—um, thank you. I would love to stay and meet your sisters, but unfortunately, I have business elsewhere," Sada said. She tried to back away again, but the Nymph hissed softly. She froze in her tracks. The woman smiled.

"Hmm, so scared…you must be young, then, to be so naïve." She pulled Sada's wet hair away from her neck, tapping at the sapphire hanging there. "Young is a nice change; the old shiftskins and sorcerers can make themselves look pretty…but they don't have the same bite to them." She snapped at the air beside Sada's ear.

Sada tried to laugh, but it got caught in her throat.

The Nymph chuckled as Sada began to twist and pull at her hair, unable to do anything but that as she willed her feet to take her far from here. She just stared at the water in front of her, watching the Nymph's blue fingers poke and prod at her rings and bracelets as her throat tightened. She kept sniffing at her skin, and Sada was beginning to wonder if the stranger was planning on eating her.

The Nymph dragged her closer to peer at the gold and bejeweled rings on her hand. Sada could smell the scent of fish and moss on her.

Father always warned me not to wear my jewelry in the busy markets, lest someone try to rob me of it. I had always imagined my attackers to be masked men, not a woman who—

"You can have them, if you'd like," Sada blurted. Realizing this might be her path to escape, she moved to pull off her rings. The woman growled, digging her nails into her palm, and Sada faltered.

"*I* will do it for you, darling. No need to trouble your sweet self." Her soft voice was at odds with the predatory gleam in her eyes.

Still, Sada did not protest as the Nymph twisted off Sada's rings and transferred them to her own hands, pausing now and then to stare at them, their reflections gleaming in her dilated pupils. When she reached around Sada's neck to unclasp her necklace, the prick of her nails sent horrible shivers skittering across her skin. The woman paused as she pulled it off, scanning Sada. She held her breath.

Don't look at the cuff. Anything but the cuff. She resisted reaching up to touch her hidden treasure.

Sada released a shuddering breath of relief when the Nymph pulled back, and satisfied, clasped the necklace around her neck. Her skin rivaled the stone's beauty.

Please, Lord, say that it is over now.

Sada made herself smile, worried the slightest show of rudeness would eradicate her chance at escape. "I must say, they look much better on you."

"Do you think so?" The Nymph smiled sweetly at her, then her eyes darted to the golden bracelet on Sada's left arm. "Oh! A morsel almost escaped my notice." She brought it up to her nose to sniff it.

"Please, take it as well! The gold will look lovely with your—ah!"

Sada broke off as the Nymph licked her wrist and the bracelet there.

"Oh my," the woman said with a gasp, and her mesmerizing voice turned enraptured. Her fingers tightened on Sada's arm as she whispered, "You're not just young and naïve, are you? You're mortal. I wonder how I didn't smell it on you…though I thought I'd tasted something exotic in your pretty blood…Now I see, it wasn't pink at all, but red…"

The Nymph's grip tightened on her flesh. Her nails dug in more sharply, and Sada thought they might be drawing blood. A low rumble started up in the woman's throat. Some fear-filled noise escaped Sada's own, for as much as she wished it was not true, the Nymph sounded hungry.

Sada wished more desperately than she'd ever wished in her life that she could just scream, or move, or do something. But her fear had paralyzed all but her racing heart. Just as she thought she might die at this stranger's blue hands, a squealing whinny ripped through the air. The sharpness of the sound was enough to shock her into movement, and she lunged backward with a gasp.

As she did so, the Nymph hissed. The blue woman was crouching down into the water, eyes wide and panicked and staring at something behind Sada. She spun around in newfound fear, but it was replaced by sweet relief when she was met with the sight of the winged unicorn standing in the pool above and stamping her golden hoof. Lady Blue whinnied sharply again, tossing her golden mane as the Nymph hissed. The mist and sunlight came together over the foal to illuminate her twisted horn and the purple blood still encrusting it. The sight was horribly beautiful.

"*Caelicorn*," the Nymph snarled. Her captivating voice had become animalistic at the sight of the foal.

Lady Blue neighed again; not the soft nicker Sada was growing used to, but a loud and piercing squeal that summoned goosebumps. If Sada hadn't been healed by the little animal, the sight of her horned head tossing wildly would have terrified her as well. The Nymph was scared without question; she had slunk away from Sada and Lady Blue and was climbing warily onto the shore now. The woman's eyes didn't leave the horned foal until she reached the sandy bank, then her gaze flashed back to Sada. But it was only for the merest of seconds. As soon as her eyes shifted, Lady Blue reared with an ear-splitting whinny.

As she reared, head tossing, she fanned her feathered wings out, displaying an underside of brilliant gold down feathers, like sunlight captured in physical form. Their golden hue reflected the misty sunlight so brightly Sada had to shield her eyes against the brilliance, and behind her she heard the Nymph hiss again. It was too bright for Sada to see as the blue woman snapped her teeth at the winged unicorn for a final time and disappeared into the mist across the hot springs. The singing coming from behind it suddenly sounded eerie rather than beautiful. Once she had gone, the foal tucked her wings back to her sides again, and Sada lowered the hand covering her eyes.

"Bless you, Lady Blue! That was *astonishing*!" Sada said to the filly, running through the water toward where she still stood on the pool's ledge. She hopped down with a splash to meet Sada halfway, and she couldn't help but fling her arms around the foal's neck. As she embraced her, her forearm erupted in tingling and Sada felt the connection alight between them again.

She gasped at the flood of pictures that ran through her mind:

Mushrooms.

Ferns.

Squirrel.

She smelled something hot and delicious that made her stomach growl. Then distant murmuring sounded behind her, and everything instantly became a blur of color. Within seconds, Sada was seeing images of the hot springs. Heat splashed onto her legs as she leapt into the first pool, then the heat turned to anger and became part of her blood as she saw herself again from a third-person view. She was wet and cowering, trapped as the blue woman neared her.

Sada didn't have time to even feel ashamed of her paralyzing cowardice, for the final few images of the encounter with the Nymph were accompanied by a torrent of uncontrollable rage that consumed Sada's mind. She cried out somewhere in the physical world, cringing against the onslaught of terrible emotions, and then her mind was blank again. Save for one word burned into her mind and echoing in her ears like a whisper:

Caelicorn.

Sada was released from the attack of memories, and she fell into the water, gasping. She looked at the foal: her human eyes, her brilliant wings, and the twisted horn of gold still stained purple.

"Is that what you are? A caelicorn?" The word felt strange and slippery on her tongue, but as she said it the foal's eyes widened and her nostrils flared, and she knew it was true. "Thank you for saving me. I am indebted to thee." The archaic speech felt right in this moment.

The caelicorn snorted and looked behind her, perhaps ensuring the Nymph hadn't come back. Sada's stomach knotted as she recalled the hypnotic way she'd talked, the mesmeric gleam in her eyes. What would her fate have been if Lady Blue hadn't appeared when she did? She thought of the memories that had somehow been shown to her, the way the filly had immediately returned when she'd heard Sada's voice. It seemed she had earned the little creature's friendship.

Sada let out a shuddering sigh she hadn't realized was trapped in her lungs. The heat of the water suddenly felt anything but blissful, and the warm air above was now cold against her skin. She wanted to leave—immediately. Especially before the Nymph could return, possibly with her friends this time. She collected her petticoat from the water, preparing to leave, but when she retrieved her gown, which she had not had time to clean, she knew she wouldn't be able to wear such a filthy thing and still call herself the Duke's daughter.

She sighed, wishing she could cast aside her propriety and knowing she couldn't. Then she quickly scrubbed the clothes that were still dirty and wrung them out a few more times until the water ran clear from the fabric. The whole time, she expected more hair to billow up in the water around her feet. As she worked, memories of her interaction with the Nymph—that nail trailing across her skin, the sound of her teeth snapping in the air, her hungry eyes—plagued her mind ceaselessly. The hollowness of her belly had been replaced by the familiar nausea of anxiety. It only worsened with every noise she heard, and every few seconds she was looking over her shoulder to check for signs of the Nymph's return. Finally her clothes were as clean as they would get (or so she told herself) and she threw them to a mossy part of the bank.

She's gone, Sada, she told herself harshly. *Stop being such a coward. Would Father be proud of you in this moment? No. And do you wish for your wounds to fester? Also no. So cease your worrying and clean yourself if you wish to leave this place!*

"Fine, fine," Sada muttered to herself. But she cast one more glance toward the fog.

She found a thick clump of moss growing nearby and used it to scrub herself down. She paid careful attention to her shoulders, rinsing them as best she could. The flesh around the punctures was red and tender, but not yet infected. She thought it would be okay if she could find something to make a poultice out of, or if she found King Caprius within the next few days. The rest of the dried blood was concentrated on her stomach and sides.

When she washed it, the miracle of the filly's healing became undeniable. Where yesterday there had been deep, potentially mortal wounds, now there were only twin scars. In the time since the healing, they had lightened, and now there were four pale lines on each side of her ribs, as though she'd had them for years. She had to force herself to look away, or she thought she might go crazy trying to figure out the healing properties the filly somehow possessed.

Magick is what it is, she relented. *Simple magick, don't you know that, Sada?* Shaking her head, she forced herself to move on to washing the rest of herself.

Her hair was greasy and heavy with oil from days without having it shampooed, and she looked for any herbs Jezi had told her that soaps were made of. There were no soap nuts growing at this spring, though she hadn't expected there to be; that would have been yet another miracle of this world, and too many were just not possible. Yet she did discover a pile of blue flowers beside a comb of crystal. The petals produced suds when crushed and mixed with water.

Sada knew they probably both belonged to the Nymph, but she reasoned that all the jewelry was fair enough payment. So she made a nice lather from the petals and scrubbed her head.

When she finished, her long hair was squeaky from the soaping and tangled from far too many days without brushing it, and now she had no honey to condition it with. She settled for combing through it with the crystal comb. When she pulled the loose hair out of the comb's teeth, a huge, colorful bird immediately snatched it up off the bank and disappeared into the ceiling of fog with it.

Once her hair was detangled to the best of her ability, she braided it as tightly as she could. It was the only way long hair could be kept relatively manageable without a softener, or someone to put it into updos daily. Fortunately, a simple braid was something Sada could do—Jezebel had taught her, so Sada could braid her when they worked in the apothecary together. Though it was much easier to do on a friend than it was to do on herself.

Once she had finished her own grooming, she called Lady Blue over, who had been splashing in one of the shallower ponds. At Sada's call, the caelicorn cantered over to her, still squealing happily as she kicked up the warm water. Sada smiled at the little animal. Despite her fierceness, she was still a baby.

A baby that can kill foxes the size of wolves, Sada thought as the caelicorn neared and the blood on her horn became visible. *And who eats the flesh off your wounds…*

When Lady Blue stopped beside her in the shallow end of the pond, Sada knelt in the water to the filly's hooves. She shied away uncertainly, eyeing Sada, but she crooned to the little horse and sang in soothing tones until she stilled. Then she set to work untangling the long hair feathering her golden hooves. Sada thought they might truly be made of gold itself. She tried to rinse off her coat as well, but that was when Lady Blue's cooperation ended. She stamped her hoof indignantly—and childishly—

whenever Sada neared her wings with water. Instead, Sada tried to detangle her glorious sunny curls. This didn't happen as easily as she'd hoped it would, so they were left a tangled yet beautiful mess.

When Sada finished the filly's mane and tail, she tried to wander off to stomp and splash in the shallower springs again. Sada let her play for a while, and splashed her back a few times. Every time her mind tried to recall those memories of the Nymph, she thought of her father instead, and of what his reprimand would be. She also managed to convince herself that if the caelicorn had sensed the danger of the Nymph from outside of the valley and come to protect her, she would certainly alert her to any danger a second time. And she wasn't in a hurry, after all. She was already lost beyond belief. A wasted day she would worry over, but not a few minutes of fun. When it had been had, she beckoned the filly to her side and cupped water in her hands.

"Put your head down," Sada instructed. Lady Blue eyed her, but listened.

When she dipped her muzzle, Sada wet her hands and rubbed the blood off her horn. It was smooth like marble, but surprisingly warm. As she washed the spiraling horn, the tingling returned to her left hand. But no images flashed through her mind. Instead, a deep sense of friendship and gratitude invaded Sada. It was as though someone had planted the feelings directly into her chest; she knew they did not come from her own heart, but she felt them even more strongly than if they had. This time Sada didn't pull away from the foal, allowing the tingling in her arm to grow stronger. There was nobody else around from whom the foreign feelings could have come: it had to be the caelicorn.

Verily, Sada thought.

Except it wasn't her own thought. It was as though someone was whispering into both of her ears but neither of them at the same time. The feeling incited the icy-hot tingling again, but this time it was inside her mind and all around her head as well as her left hand.

"Hello?" Sada said, glancing around herself uneasily.

But she'd already known that she wouldn't find anyone there. The hot springs were empty of all life—Spiritkin, Beast, and animal alike. It was filled with mist and rainbows, and the sound of gently cascading waterfalls and trickling streams. Sada met the caelicorn's golden eye, and within its human-like irises she saw the truth. And she'd heard it as well.

"It's you speaking to me, isn't it?"

Sada's heart quickened as the foal's eye widened in agreement, and the voice said from everywhere but nowhere:

Yea, verily.

How is this possible? Sada thought, and just as she was about to speak the words, the voice tickled her mind again.

It is but the way of my kind. The caelicorn's voice sounded like the earth itself was speaking to her, and she wondered if what she was hearing was the essence of Elt. She also wondered how such an ancient voice could come from an equally youthful body. *Verily,* the voice continued, *as it is possible for wings to sprout from mine own body and for this horn to grow from mine own head, and as it is possible for me to mend thee, and for thee to mend me, so too is it possible for the two of us to talk without speaking.*

"Wait, what do you mean *I* mended *you?"* Sada asked, then thought, *Why, she sounds not unlike the Trolls!* Only the caelicorn spoke in the archaic tongues properly, while the Trolls did not. Coming from them, it was endearing the way a dog chasing its own tail was. From the filly, it was awe-inspiring and commanding of respect.

Yet as curious as the way she spoke was, Sada was more curious about what Lady Blue had said. As far as she'd been able to tell, the caelicorn had been unharmed when Sada had found her with the fox. Sada had a good idea of what a healthy foal looked like; she had been fast friends with those at their Centerton stables. The stableboys first tried to shoo her out, scared Duke Solares might do away with them if he discovered they had allowed his lady daughter into the animal pens. But upon her insistence (and Gabriel's, who could hardly refuse her) she had been allowed to feed the colts apples and comb the fillies' manes. None had been so curly and resplendent as Lady Blue's. And, of course, their coats were not quite so blue. The caelicorn filly was also slightly smaller than the foals she'd seen in the stables, but healthy, nonetheless. No ribs showed, and while she still had the fuzziness of a foal coat, it was satiny soft.

Upon our meeting, I was unable to fly, Lady Blue explained in her silent but powerful form of communication. *My wings had been sundered and then had healed too hastily, and in the wrong position. It was to my astonishment, I confess, that after sleeping beside thee, I was able to fold them aright. Now, some time thereafter, I find that I can spread them open once more.*

The caelicorn fanned her wings open again to demonstrate. As she spread them, their gleaming golden undersides were revealed, and Sada had to turn away from the blinding light again, shading her eyes. It was not dissimilar to staring directly into the sun—the one in her own world, that is. Elt's sun was much pinker than the golden glow her sun and the filly's wings gave off. The foal shifted beside her, and when the glow disappeared, she lowered her hands and opened her eyes again.

"How amazing that your wings are healed! Though I am unsure I can take credit for such a miraculous transformation as the one you describe. I am certain, however, that you did indeed heal my own wounds, and for that I am grateful."

Lady Blue stamped her hoof. *It was thou. Dost thou place no trust in me? We have been bonded by blood; I can discern the source of my mending as well as thou may discern the source of thine own.*

Sada was taken aback by the stern certainty in the little caelicorn's voice. *I do trust you; I apologize—*

Thou art a healer within thine own realm. It was not a question. Somehow the knowledge had been drawn from Sada's mind and into the filly's. She absentmindedly touched her temple, as though feeling for what was taken. Or rather, shared, for the knowledge remained with her.

Despite what Lady Blue said, Sada was not truly an apothecary. She merely aided Jezebel in her work during the summers in Centerton, and Jezi had only just finished her own training. If anyone was a true healer, it was Mr.—

Apothecary, perhaps not. Nevertheless, a healer, certainly. If not by trade, then by nature. It was thine essence that mended my wings, Sada. Not herbs and poultices—nay, they would have aided me naught. Yet thou…yea, I know it by the wisdom of my mothers and the horn upon my brow. And thus, I offer thee my gratitude. Wilt thou accept it?

"Without hesitation!" She felt a strong urge to curtsey, the way she felt the urge to bow before her father. Yet she thought it would be quite against her birthright to bow to an animal. "I believe I understand what you are saying," she said. Though truly, she did not understand, and she feared the uncertainty in her voice was obvious.

Before the caelicorn could chastise her for her lack of trust once more, Sada asked, "Do you think you will be able to fly again soon?"

She waited for a response, but the unearthly voice didn't come. She looked patiently at Lady Blue, but the foal just blinked her brilliant eyes at Sada and snorted. Still, no voice tickled her mind, and despite all the fantastical things she had experienced in Elt, she wondered if she had somehow imagined the exchange. Governess Brown had always scolded her for her vibrant and "dangerous" fancies. They'd earned her more than a few lashings over the knuckles.

"Can you still hear me?" Sada asked hesitantly, then repeated it in her mind. She thought of translating it into the archaic tongue: *Canst thou still hear mine voice?* Then she decided that was silly.

If the caelicorn heard any of her thoughts, she gave no sign. She just nickered lightly and walked away, leaving Sada feeling a bit foolish. And now that she wasn't actively enraptured in her mental conversation with Lady Blue, her unease over the situation with the Nymph returned. She stood from the warm waters and retrieved her clothes from the moss and stones on the bank.

Holding the limp, tattered garments, she couldn't help cringing at how ugly they had become from her time in the forest. Her father would be appalled if he saw her wearing these within his own home, let alone outside of it where others might see her. Beyond the tears and ugly maroon stains, the water had done nothing to rinse the silver webbing from the Seam off her gown. Only the cloak from Jezebel remained undamaged, and dark enough to hide the bloodstains.

Perhaps commoner clothes should be the more expensive ones.

With a regretful sigh, Sada began to dress, buckling her damp corset. She pressed her hands against her chest so that when Sofia tied the corset, it would be settled in the right place—

Why would Sofia be here? There are no servants here, she realized quickly when no hands began pulling at the lace. Heat filled her cheeks even though she was the only one to witness her foolishness. Then she laughed. It was the only thing she could do. How could she have possibly thought for a moment that there would be servants in the middle of the forest into which she had been magickally transported? She erupted in very unladylike laughter once more. That was just it—she hadn't thought. Not even for a second. She had merely assumed that what had always been would continue to be.

"How spoiled you are," she told herself, and with no small measure of amusement.

For a moment, she fumbled with the laces behind her back, trying to figure out if it was even possible to do the things up by herself. She thought she could turn the corset around so that the laces were in front, but then it wouldn't be stiff in the right places, and it would be impossible to sidle it around to the right position again once it was sufficiently tight. She was very close to giving up and resigning herself to returning to the forest, improperly dressed with no corset beneath her gown, when she was yanked backward.

She squealed, clasped her hands over her mouth when she realized the noise she'd made, then whirled around expecting to find another Nymph behind her. Her eyes landed on Lady Blue. When Sada noticed her, she stretched out her neck, chomped at the air a few times, and wriggled her lips. She looked like the horses in the stables when they could smell the apple slices Sada held behind her back. Her first reaction was to giggle at the display, but she quickly realized what the filly wanted when she butted Sada in the belly.

Sada turned around once more, and she felt something nuzzling into the small of her back. Then there was another forceful tug. This time she held herself steady. The corset tightened. Lady Blue tugged again, and it cinched closer around her waist. After one more tug, the pulling stopped, and Sada managed to tie the laces into a bow. The corset wasn't as tight as it should have been, and it was more than a little out of place, but Sada was quite pleased with how it had turned out. Lady Blue nickered in a very self-satisfied-sounding way.

Sada thanked her (aloud and in her mind, just in case the filly was listening) then finished dressing. She twirled so that Lady Blue could admire their shared work. The foal nickered again, and she giggled. Once she had clasped her cloak around her shoulders and reapplied her powder, she gathered up her boots and joined the caelicorn on the other side of the springs, then the two of them climbed out of the gorge.

Out of the warm mist of the hot springs, the air felt cool in comparison. Lady Blue cantered off once they reached level ground, and Sada followed at a distance. She had come to accept that she was lost in these woods and had given up on aiming in any specific direction. She would begin the day with the sun to her left, but by the time it set it would often be anywhere but on her right. When it had become obvious that Lady Blue planned to lead her in a relatively steady course, she'd decided that a creature born of this world had a better chance at navigating it than she did. Now she sent a thought to the filly: *Find the Elven king.* Then she decided that fate would have its way with her.

Holding her boots and stockings and walking barefoot in the moss, she fell back into her usual rhythm. Sada began to sing as she watched the caelicorn kicking the air and flapping her brilliant wings. Hidden between the trees and undergrowth, an ensemble of animals began to follow along, keeping their usual distance. Sada smiled at the company and let the distant music of the forest guide her song and her step as she followed the little blue caelicorn through the woods.

THE FOURTEENTH

Sada

Sada and Lady Blue had been walking for a while, moving slowly through the undergrowth as the woods changed around them: the trees had begun growing closer together, and the space between them was filled with bright bushes and foliage all decorated with vibrant flowers, fruits, or berries that Sada had to resist eating. Some of the trees also had swirling patterns seemingly engraved into each of their trunks. The pale whorls had begun appearing on the odd trunk the day before, but here, almost every tree was marked with them.

She told herself it was certainly a coincidence that they looked like her birthmarks. *It's a common enough pattern…right?*

Besides the flora changing, even the ground was different. In addition to the thick roots that now webbed the forest floor, it had become even more irregular. Grassy hills like submerged Troll heads and mist-filled gorges decorated the surface of the earth, and Sada had to pick up another walking staff in order to stop herself from tripping as she traveled.

She navigated the forest more easily with no shoes on, but she'd become too nervous that someone might see her barefooted, so she'd stopped to pull on her stockings and boots. At least the stiff sides of her riding shoes kept her ankles from twisting too badly on the hillocks. Lady Blue, unhampered by the bumpy terrain, had taken to cantering off ahead of Sada and returning every so often for a few moments of walking.

As Sada's time in the forest grew longer, her journeying grew less hurried and more meandering. Now she stopped often to touch a branch or a flower, which always incited a wave of *instincts* rippling through her left hand. There were also many beautiful paths of sunlight branching off from the main route they followed, and Sada sometimes followed them for a time before returning to Lady Blue when she whinnied.

There were many Pixies in this part of the wood, and she also left Lady Blue's set course frequently to follow after them, just for a little while, trying to catch the glimmering powder that fell from their wings. One had stopped to talk to her, but left when he realized she was the mortal that Cidinen had warned him of. Sada came to see that word of herself and her breaking of the Seam had traveled quickly through the local Pixie families, and most seemed wary of or hostile toward her. This saddened her greatly, but not enough to stop her efforts to speak to each of the little people she saw.

Only a short time before, she'd found one such miniature Spiritkin perched on a chestnut branch, seated on a clump of yellow moss. He was dressed in pants and a coat made of leaves, and wore a tiny hat upon his bright hair. His wings were lime green, and his eyes equally so. When Sada neared, he'd flitted up into the air, though she didn't think he'd seen her. She followed, hand outstretched to catch the glimmering sparkles he shed.

Lady Blue had whinnied unhappily when she noticed Sada meandering off their path. The filly was eager to explore, but she was also determined to travel in a mostly straight line toward their destination, it seemed, and she grew upset when Sada veered too far off course. Sada dismissed her snorts as dramatics and continued after the Pixie. It was only when Lady Blue grabbed the fabric of her gown in her teeth and yanked her backward that Sada stopped her pursuit of the little man.

When she looked down, she gasped, for she saw a drop-off into a deep crevice. Sleeping in it was a large, man-like creature with yellow skin and huge tusks, and only the tatters of a leather skirt around its waist. Above her, the Pixie was sniggering behind his little hands. He zipped away laughing when Lady Blue whinnied indignantly at him, and she saw with some horror that he had landed on the ear of the monster and was tickling it with a feather. As the Beast began to stir, grumbling unhappily, Sada and Lady Blue sprinted in the opposite direction. In the distance, the yellow Beast's roar could be heard, and the caelicorn didn't allow her to stop running until his footsteps were no longer audible.

Lady Blue taught her that this was a Beast known as a cave troll. They were opposite in almost every way from Woodland Trolls—like those of the Greenhead clan—who were their Spiritkin counterparts.

Sada's thoughts returned to this unfortunate encounter when she saw a beam of sunlight lying a path through the forest, off to the side of Lady Blue's own path. She thought that somewhere at the end of it she could see an Elven maiden dancing with hummingbirds, but she couldn't be sure it wasn't a trick of the light. She bit her lip, looking off in the direction the filly had gone. Perhaps she wouldn't notice if Sada just started down the path…after all, Lady Blue was nowhere to be seen now. Sada glanced back at the translucent pink path laid upon the moss, and at the dancing woman at the end of it. Was that an Elf, or was it just branches and leaves in the shape of a face? Sada wanted to see for herself. She tiptoed toward the sunlight, giggling at her own antics as she went.

The music of the forest began to rise as she followed the light, and her *instincts* prickled with a lovely vibration. The path of pink was lined by saplings, a rare sight in this forest, and bushes of whispering berries and peaches dusted with starlight. The voices told her that she was loved, and beautiful, and she thought one particularly motherly voice told her that her hair was like spun silk, the richest silk that could be purchased by a lord or lady.

At the end of the path was the Elven woman. She was definitely a maiden, not a bit of branch at all. Sada didn't know how she could have thought such a thing. She was young and beautiful, and clothed in a prettily flowing dress of glittering satin. Her hair was long and glorious and unbraided, falling almost to her ankles. It looked to be made of starlight itself, glimmering so brilliantly that Sada had to shield her eyes. The Elf was dancing, arms outstretched, among tiny and colorful hummingbirds. Even a few Pixies flitted in the nearby air. She laughed as the little birds alighted on her arms. Then, when she turned, her eyes fell on Sada.

Sada paused, breathless at the beauty before her. The woman's hair fell around her like a cloak of the most brilliant thread. Her eyes, silver and upturned like a cat's, but wide like a doe's, gleamed as they took Sada in. She stretched out an elegant hand, then curled her fingers in, beckoning Sada: *come to me, darling girl.*

Sada started forward, breathless and entranced. The woman began dancing again. Sada wanted nothing more than to dance with her. To take her hand, become acquainted with her, and run away to the giant flower in which she and her equally lovely sisters certainly lived. They would all be the best of friends, sipping nectar-sweetened tea as Pixies braided their hair and hummingbirds danced in the air at their command. Grinning, Sada began to run toward the dancing Elf. Her entire left arm was alive with ice and fire.

Just as she was reaching the beautiful clearing, Lady Blue burst out from a clump of flowers, wide-eyed and snorting. The woodland animals that had been walking alongside Sada at a distance scattered as they always did when the filly reappeared. So did the Elven woman. One moment she was there, dancing and laughing, then Sada looked to Lady Blue. When she looked back, the Elf was gone, as were the hummingbirds, the Pixies, and the sunlight. She was left standing beside the caelicorn and staring at an empty clearing decorated only with moss and a tree that looked uncannily similar to a woman's face.

"Where did she go?" Sada whispered. The only answer was a tiny and distinct chorus of giggles. It worsened the aching in her heart at the loss of a companion. Confused, she thought it might have been Jezebel who was dancing in the clearing.

A muzzle of velvet pressed into the hand dangling limply by her side.

The work of Pixies, she thought suddenly. It was in the voice of the caelicorn. She looked down at Lady Blue, whose golden eyes were unusually warm with sympathy.

"A farce?" Sada asked quietly. Lady Blue nodded emphatically, stamping a hoof. "They love me not."

Lady Blue didn't have to send an agreeing thought. Sada already knew it to be true. She sighed, then turned to the filly and forced a smile onto her face.

"Thank you for coming to my rescue. It seems that once again, I am indebted to you."

Thou dost not owe me. Would thou owe a mother any favor for bringing thee into this world? Nay. And so, neither dost thou owe me for rescuing thee; with thy rescue comes mine own.

What do you mean by saying your rescue is bound with mine? Sada thought, alarmed. *While I would be enormously thankful, you are under no obligation to accompany me into perilous situations. Please, don't think that if I am to stumble into danger you would be compelled to follow. I should hate to see any harm come to you for my sake.*

Lady Blue responded with a disdainful snort. *I lack the words to fully explain—for the present. The recollections of my foremothers return to me slowly, but return they do. All that I may say is this: the bond may elude sight, yet it exists, nonetheless. Dost thou not sense its tension, stretched between thine heart and mine own?*

Sada tried to feel what the filly spoke of, but all she felt was the fading of the *instincts* in her palm and the hollowness of her empty belly. Yes, she cared for the filly, but she felt no invisible bond tying her heart to the foal's. Finally she gave up her searching and shook her head.

"I beg your pardon," she said regretfully. "I feel no such connection; only a deep care for you."

In due time, it shall be unveiled to thine senses. Thine mortal nature writhes in conflict with it, I fear. Yet time shall bring resolution to this matter.

The response left Sada feeling more uneasy than she had even when the dancing Elven maiden was revealed to be a prank of the Pixies. Yet even upon her insistence, Lady Blue would say nothing more on the matter. Their invisible bond, which she could not feel but the filly claimed the existence of, had fallen silent, and none of her efforts could reawaken it.

Lady Blue led her back onto the deer trail they had been following, then after ensuring Sada would follow, she ran off to explore on her own once more. Sada was left to consider this bond between them. *Like a thread,* the caelicorn had said. Yet Sada felt nothing of the sort. She imagined some glittering golden line like the silk of a spider stretching between her bosom and the filly's, slanted to accommodate the height difference.

She resigned herself to waiting for time to reveal it, as Lady Blue had promised would happen. But she wondered at her mention of Sada's mortal nature being in battle with it. Did she mean mortality as in her ability to die, or as in her humanity—as in the essential difference between her and the Spiritkin? In the latter case, she wasn't certain she wanted her mortal nature to lose the battle. What would that look like?

Sada and the caelicorn continued on in silence. But Sada's mind was filled with enough of her own thoughts to make up for the absence of the filly's. When darkness fell, Lady Blue found a tree with low-hanging branches for them to sleep beneath. Despite the full day of walking, Sada found her mind was too active to sleep. Whenever she closed her eyes, she saw blue skin. And so she stayed up as the moon rose and tried to make a container to carry water in out of a leaf and sap.

By the time the moon was high enough that the entire forest was alight with a lavender glow, her back was aching and her hands were sore, and the wounds in her shoulders were throbbing. Her efforts to make a container had failed, and she was left with nothing but sticky hands and aching muscles. Defeated and tired, she finally laid down against Lady Blue in their usual position. The curve of the filly's back fit perfectly into the arch in Sada's, as though they had been crafted to match. They slept beside each other, and sometime in the night, the animals of the wood joined.

Elt's climate was revealing itself to be wonderfully moderate, and without the familiar noontime heat beating down, it was only by glancing up at the sky that Sada knew it to be midday. At Lady Blue's behest, they stopped to drink from a stream alongside birds the size of a thumb. One hopped forward to peck at the caelicorn's horn, which was met with an appalled snort. Not all of the creatures, it seemed, were afraid of Lady Blue.

The water was cool, and the ground was soft, and Sada didn't want to leave. But she knew she must, and one look from the caelicorn was enough to tell her that her new friend would not allow her to give up even if she was nearly ready to herself. And so she forced herself to go on. Looking for herbs and trying to identify the plants she came across helped to keep her mind off the rapidly growing idea that she would never escape this forest.

Though she was beginning to think that she had entered a new forest. *Now I have two to escape from.*

The woods had changed again as they'd walked that day, and the change was so abrupt and so drastic, she felt almost as though they had crossed some sort of border. It happened when they walked down a short slope, entering into some shallow, woodland valley whose end she couldn't see. The flat carpet of moss had shifted from dark green and orange to a lively lime, and it shared its territory with thick clover and grass, all covered in dew. It was softer beneath her feet than any rug she'd walked on, maybe softer even than her bed. Flowers brought color to the greenery, speckled throughout the forest's flooring and the leaves of the trees, which were of every kind.

Before, the trees had all been of one species—those tall brown ones—with fruit-covered bushes sprinkled throughout. Now, she saw pines, weeping willows, eucalyptus, and cherry trees all growing together; beside them were white dogwoods and flowering plums, purple jacarandas, and crepe myrtles. There were trees with dark bark, trees with pale bark, and trees with red bark. Some of them grew the needles of evergreens, others leaves of varying shades of green, yellow, and red. Some seemed to wear only crowns of flowers, of white and pink, blue and purple. And weaving throughout them all was a fine, soft mist. It reflected the sunlight to cast rainbows everywhere—on the trees, the clusters of flowers and ferns; against Lady Blue's wings, and on Sada's skin.

As they walked, following tendrils of mist that sometimes wrapped gently around her wrist and tugged her or poked her lightly in the side, they came across many a spring. They were small enough to hop over, and didn't disturb their journey, but they were frequent enough that she and Lady Blue could stop to drink whenever they wished. The water was cool and sweet, just as the air was. The whole forest smelled of life and growing things, and of sap and nectar.

There was also fruit. There had been bushels of berries in the forest of orange and red, but here it seemed that almost every other tree bore colorful berries or apples. She saw many trees bearing wild plums, apples, and pears, and peaches with skin shimmering like a Pixie's wings. The undergrowth was scarce, but growing in the spacious gaps between the tree trunks were bushes of elderberries, pink cherries, and small, translucent berries that sang when she drew close. Wrapped around the big humps of roots were silver, thornless vines. Upon Sada's first few investigations, they appeared to bear no fruit. Then as she'd walked by one such plant, a beam of sun had hit it at just the right angle, revealing a new sight: growing on its vines were ripe, pale grapes glowing faintly. They disappeared when a cloud passed over the sun.

After their break for water, Lady Blue had disappeared into the thick clumps of shadows decorating the forest. Sada hadn't seen her for quite some time, but she hardly noticed. All she could think of as of late were stories of her mother, for some reason. Not the ones of her people in the north, but of the duchess herself. Governess Brown had said Duchess Solares had pale skin like the original settlers, now so rare in the east. It was told that her hair was light as sand, and her eyes were blue like the Duke's. But where his were dark, hers were the light to match them. Or combat them.

Now, as if on cue, the filly's bright blue muzzle poked out from around a tree.

Blue, everything is blue! Sada thought. She smiled, giggling somewhat deliriously to herself. It had been far too long since she'd eaten, and water was not scarce, but she found that she often forgot to drink it, or simply did not want to stop walking to do so. As with earlier that morning, she did not want to get up to continue walking if she did. When she did stop at puddles and streams, she could not drink too much of it at once or her stomach would be twisted in cramps for the next hour. But she didn't think it was the lack of sustenance and hydration that was breaking her mind.

It was the fact that she had never been alone for so long in her entire life.

More than that, she had never needed to rely on herself ever before. With every decision she had to make, she found herself hesitating, as though her father or Gabe would appear and decide for her. When she realized they wouldn't, she had to stop and consider what they would want her to do. Would Father tell her to stop now for a break, or to continue on a little longer? Would he want her to shelter under this tree with the low branches, or that one with the tall roots? Would he tell her to leave behind her boots so she could more easily navigate the uneven ground, or keep them on for propriety's sake? She never considered what her own choice would be.

The weight of making so many decisions, and also of constantly wondering if she had made the wrong one, was burning out her mind.

"Everything is blue, Lady Blue," Sada said to the filly. "See? Even you! You, too, are blue, Lady blue. Anyone can be blue, if they so choose!"

The filly's wise eyes watched Sada laughing to herself from beneath that beautiful horn growing from her brow. Sada felt her chest squeeze at the magnificence of the little animal.

Sada sighed. "I'm sorry. You're probably tired of my ravings, aren't you? Well, I tire of them myself. I should think you'd like me better if you knew me as I am at home."

Lady Blue nickered as she neared, loud and long, and Sada had to cover her ears against the sharpness of the noise. When she reached her side, she stamped her hoof and tossed her head.

"What is it?" Sada asked. "What has you so spirited, my darling friend?"

The filly just snorted and poked her muzzle into her side in greeting. As she did, an overwhelming sense of hunger overcame Sada. She frowned at the strange onset of the sensation, pressing her hands to her belly. Her stomach had grown used to the hollow feeling of starvation and she no longer found herself hungry, except during the nights when she dreamt of jam and bread and honeyed hams. Her stomach rumbled then as the caelicorn whickered.

"It is lovely to see you again as well," Sada said as she climbed over a patch of rocks and boulders. She cringed and muttered an apology to the forest after seeing the chunks of pink moss her riding boots sloughed off.

She continued walking when she dropped down to the other side, but Lady Blue, who had hopped over gracefully, stood in front of her and stamped her hoof. Then she poked Sada's stomach again and the jolt of hunger seized her once more. It held on for a moment before beginning to fade.

"Pardon me, my lady," Sada teased.

She did not move out of the way, just nudged her again. It incited another wave of hunger, and the feeling in combination with Lady Blue's reluctance to move brought on a moment of irritation. Sada crossed her arms impatiently, staring at the wide-eyed filly. She suddenly noticed how bleary her typically bright eyes were, how her head hung forward out of its typical craned posture.

A small realization dawned on Sada then and she hesitantly reached her hand out to the foal's nose. She pushed her muzzle into Sada's palm, and that ageless voice breathed into her mind again. It whispered one word: *food.* Then the caelicorn pulled away and watched her with those unnervingly intelligent eyes. The voice and the icy hot tingling in her mind disappeared as she did so.

Sada swallowed hard; the strange connection with the filly still unnerved her. She thought of the thread again, and was reluctant to encourage the battle between it and her mortality. But Lady Blue was waiting patiently for her to respond.

"I, too, am hungry," Sada said. She knew it was true, even if she did not feel the urge to eat any longer. "However, some if not all of the fruit in this place is dangerous, and I am unwilling for either of us to suffer its effects. It would be wiser not to eat yet—to exercise patience and wait until…to wait for…"

Sada trailed off as she realized she didn't know what she was waiting for anymore. Indeed, it had once been the rediscovery of King Caprius. Yet she'd been wandering in the forest for a countless period of time with no trace of the Elven king, his kingdom, or any of his people, save for the illusion of the Elven maid. Perhaps it was time to stop waiting for him to rescue her.

Certainly, she would continue her search, but when a pang of hunger unsolicited by the filly's touch struck her, she admitted to herself that it would be more unwise to abstain from eating than to risk the discomforting effects of the forest's food again. Yet it hurt to accept that it might be a long time yet before she happened upon King Caprius again. Sada sighed. She hated that she was beginning to accept she might not be returning home. Lady Blue was watching her through her dilemma, and Sada finally relented.

"Very well. I shall try to find us some food," she said.

A sense of defeat tried to creep into her heart, but she forced it out and replaced it with excitement. No longer must she suppress her inclination to eat the tantalizing fruits of this forest! Out of fear, she had passed them over. Yet now, she could pick from their offerings without restraint. She wondered if they would taste like the fruits of her home, and if the caelicorn's diet would be similar to that of a horse's. There was no hay or alfalfa here to be seen, yet there were apples and grass aplenty. She set off with a happy heart, dreaming of the basket of fruits she would collect, and choosing not to recall that she had no basket with her.

Lady Blue stayed with her as she walked this time, leading her through the flattest parts of the forest. As they walked, they passed many bushes covered in vibrantly-gleaming fruit, but her left hand tingled in what felt like a warning whenever she neared them. So they continued forward, passing over the many shrubs decorated in beautiful berries. Sada's stomach had begun rumbling again once she made the decision to find food, and it became hard to pass over such succulent fruits just a reach away.

But she made herself keep on walking until she came upon a tall tree covered in those whirling patterns. The branches grew very high up on the trunk, but they were thin and hung down all the way to the ground. Sada saw that this was because they were laden with heavy bushels of what looked like crimson grapes. Her mouth watered at the sight, and when her hand didn't prickle in protest, she approached the tree. It gave off a flowery scent.

"Look!" she said. "We may just find our food closer than I believed."

Sada reached out to the leaves, but pulled back with a yelp when she noticed two wide, dark eyes staring out at her. Lady Blue sniffed at her in concern, and she put a steadying hand on the filly's mane. Before her was a child clinging to the trunk of the tree. At least, she first believed it to be a child. Yet upon further inspection, she realized that the little creature only appeared to have the features of a human, but at the same time seemed to be a part of the tree.

Its skin was the same rich brown of the trunk, and its hair was a fluffy cloud of bright green leaves. Its face was dappled with pale freckles from the cheeks up, and on its chest, shoulders, and arms were what looked like the shadows of small leaves, only they were light brown rather than black, and did not dance in the light. The hands and knees which clung to the tree trunk also seemed to be melded into it—or growing from it. And yet it had the face and body of a human child.

Sada's first instinct was to run away screaming; her second was to rush forward and pull the little child from where the tree seemed to be consuming it; her third was to utter a greeting. Yet all that came from her mouth was a whispered:

"Hshw…what?"

Her fingers dug mercilessly into Lady Blue's mane, and suddenly a sense of calm and understanding filled her. *Sprite,* she suddenly knew the little creature to be. *Tree Sprite,* more specifically. He was a spirit of the forest, connected to this very tree's essence and destined to guard it with his life.

The boy was not being suffocated or consumed by the tree, yet growing from its heart. Soon, they would be separate entities, yet still connected in spirit. Sada's breathing calmed, and she managed to smile at the wide-eyed child of the forest. Through her connection with Lady Blue, she also knew that she would have to ask this Sprite's permission before taking anything from its tree.

Sada curtseyed politely to the boy. "Greetings, young one. How do you do?"

The Sprite blinked at her, and Sada exchanged a glance with Lady Blue. Was this normal Sprite behavior? Her friend offered her no advice, so Sada just smiled and continued on.

"My companion and I seek food, and your lovely tree seems to offer positively *splendid* fruit. Would you be so kind as to share some with us?"

He blinked solemnly at her, wide eyes round and dark. Then, in a whispered voice, he said, "No."

Sada's smile faltered. She had been asking only as a courtesy. She hadn't truly expected a child, no older than the age of seven by his appearance, to refuse her, a lady of rank. Did the silk of her skirts, however dirtied, not show her status?

What is wrong with me? she suddenly thought. *He can keep the fruit if he wants—it's his, for goodness' sake! Who do I think I am?*

Then the Duke's voice was in her head. *You are my daughter, aren't you?* She saw those cold eyes, demanding subservience. *Will you henceforth conduct yourself in a manner befitting my daughter?*

She clenched her hands, and she felt her chest tighten.

Not if this is what it means, she thought, looking at the Sprite's grave face. She forced her father from her mind, and his anger from her heart.

"Pardon me?" Sada asked the boy. She kept her voice warm, refusing to let her moment of arrogance win.

"You can't," he said faintly. Sada had to step in closer to hear his weak voice. "We are ill. To take from us would mean our death."

"What does the child mean?" she asked Lady Blue in a conspiratory whisper. The tree appeared to be in full health, its leaves vibrant and its berries round and ripe. Though its branches were drooping, she had assumed that to be the nature of the tree, or simply due to the weight of the large amounts of fruit. She waited patiently for Lady Blue's response, yet it was not the caelicorn who answered.

"Our spring left us. I don't know where it went. One day it was there. But now…" the Sprite child broke off, and he looked near to tears. His wide eyes were glistening, and he clung closer to the tree. "It—it ran away! Where has it gone? My spring! My spring…"

At the sight of the little boy crying, Sada felt a pang in her own heart. Hesitantly, she stepped into the shade of the tree and placed a hand on the child's back. He was clothed in stiff bark, which seemed to meld directly into his skin. Sada stroked his back and leafy hair, trying to suppress the shudders running through the little child's shoulders.

I'm comforting a tree, she thought to herself.

"There, there. I see no cause for tears, my little one. The leaves of your tree and the ones on your head still look vibrant and springy. Were you truly unwell, I would expect to find many fallen leaves around you. Yet all I see here is moss. I know your spring is gone, but your tree does not seem to be in want of water. So what troubles you?"

Her voice was kind, yet inwardly she thought this to be a child's dramatics. She had seen many among the younger housemaids and the town girls whom Jezebel nannied while their mothers worked in nearby shops. Most had been resolved with simple solutions that Sada would have expected the child to be able to resolve on their own. Yet she'd learned that typically what they sought wasn't a solution, but comfort.

Yet when she offered it, the Sprite boy spoke to her as though *she* were the child, unable at all to see the problem at hand.

"Not in want of water!" he cried. "Not now, no. The animals that come to eat our fruit water the ground. But if *you* take the fruit, will *you* leave water? I don't think so. The Spiritkin who wear clothes don't give back what they take. But I can't stop you…not until I'm fully sprouted. But look! I can already take one hand off of my trunk. Soon, I'll be able to guard my tree. But now all I can do is cry while I watch you kill us."

Sada was mortified. She drew back in horror, eyes wide.

"Kill you! Never a fig! My dear, if it is water you want, then water you shall have. My friend and I will bring it for you. Enough to last several days, in fact! Won't we, Lady Blue?" She turned to the filly, who was looking bored and lipping grass. She stamped her hoof and nodded her head emphatically, nonetheless.

When Sada turned to leave, determined to find water for the child, he called her back with a whisper.

"Wait…would you tell my spring to come back instead?"

"…Pardon?"

"Find the spring for me. Then you can have all the berries you want!"

Sada opened her mouth to respond, then closed it, unsure of what to say. She wasn't certain she would be able to procure an entire spring for the little boy. Yet those big, solemn eyes fueled her on and she agreed ardently.

"Of course we will find the spring and tell it to come back!"

The boy simply smiled and laid his head against the trunk. Sada waved and ducked out from beneath the trees drooping branches, beckoning to Lady Blue. When they were out of range of the Sprite's hearing, she placed a hand on the filly's neck in hope she would open her mind to conspire with Sada. Thankfully, she did.

"Pray, how might we find a spring and persuade it to return to a tree?" she whispered, forgetting that the caelicorn would hear any thoughts she had.

We shall not. Springs have no ear for commands, just as they have no power to flee from yonder tree.

"You are right, to be sure. I thought the same, yet I wished not to say it in front of the child…Do you suppose there was ever a spring to begin with?"

She snorted. *Verily, without question.*

"And yet it has run away…"

Nay, certainly not, Lady Blue said flatly.

Sada glanced at the little filly, who was looking very bored with her half-shuttered eyes and swishing tail. "It appears that you are not inclined to help this child, Lady Blue. Is this true? I have no desire to cause you offense by asking. No, never mind me, I'm sure you are eager to offer your aid."

It doth not offend me. The child indeed indulges in theatrics. Yet, my kind are guardians of this realm, and Sprites are of Elt. Hence, by my very essence, I am inclined to aid him, even beyond what thy nature prompts thee.

Sada wasn't certain that could be true. Even from childhood, she had been tending wounded animals, and she was known to ask her nursemaids for any servants with scrapes to be ushered straight to her. Not that they ever obliged this request. Yet Lady Blue sounded fixed on the matter, and so she wouldn't argue. Certainly, two helpers were better than one.

"Well, where might we discover this spring? And how?"

I know not its location, but as for the method of discovery, I can readily explain. We shall track its course to its present abode. Indeed, child, the spring hath not fled elsewhere. It is more likely to have been hindered by some obstruction. Trees are not cut in Elt, and their collapse is infrequent, yet it does occur. Perchance a tree hath fallen across the path of the spring's flow.

Sada laughed. "Very well."

Lady Blue slid her gaze to Sada. *Why dost thou laugh, girl?*

"Pay me no mind," she said, still smiling. "It is only…Well, the way you speak."

Yes?

"It does not match your appearance. You look like a filly, but you speak like…like, well."

You think I speak like a granddam? the caelicorn thought, sounding incredulous. Aloud, she snorted.

"I did not say such a thing!"

And yet, I hear thy thoughts.

Sada sighed. "I had hoped you wouldn't. It's a compliment, if you consider it. You're wiser than you look!"

Hmm…alas, you are not incorrect. I speak with the voice of my mothers, and their mothers before them. My body may be young, but my memories are as old as Elt.

Before Sada could interrogate Lady Blue on the topic, she moved away from her hand. The filly led her to the dry streambed, just a pale mark in the surface of the earth. Hugged by moss, it was a sandy scrape, appearing as though a large cat had drawn one claw through the ground. It held no water, but the sand was still damp with moisture. They followed the riverbed away from the fruit tree, looking for the source of the blockage.

"Did you happen to notice any fallen trunks on our walk to the tree?" Sada asked, for they had come along this path (only going toward the tree instead of away from it, then) when they happened upon the Tree Sprite.

Lady Blue shifted so that her back was beneath Sada's hand. *Not a one,* her eerily near and yet distant voice said. *Still, we shall seek, for at that time I did not seek fallen trees, and mortal vision is feeble.*

"Ah…indeed."

Sada's thoughts turned to the Sprite again, then. She couldn't seem to understand how a creature could grow from a tree like a plant, but look like a human. And it was a child, yet also the guardian of the tree? Were she and the tree one being, or were they separate?

They are separate beings of the same origin, Lady Blue explained. *Both are born of Elt.*

Sada's immediate thought was: *Has she no mother?*

Nay.

"How inconceivable…" Sada murmured.

Yet thou can conceive that an ordinary tree hath no mother.

I suppose so, Sada thought. *Yet trees are not speaking beings…*Then, with some alarm, she realized that Lady Blue was probably young enough to still need her mother. Yet Sada had found her alone in the woods. She hadn't even thought to ask why she was by herself, or how she had gotten there. An even more panicked thought arose then.

"Lady Blue, please tell me I did not steal you away from your family..." Sada chewed her lip, looking at the little filly. "Where is your mother? Do you know?"

The caelicorn did not answer.

"Lady Blue?"

When Sada looked down at her friend, she saw that those golden eyes appeared troubled, and she felt a strong feeling spreading through her, originating in that place where the two of them spoke without words: a feeling of uncertainty. Lady Blue moved out from under her hand.

The rest of their search went on in silence, save for Sada's random comments about the foliage and animals they passed. They walked for a few more minutes, Sada examining the nearby trees for more fruit they might later eat and Lady Blue stopping to smell at the ground every so often. It didn't take long to find what they were looking for.

Just ahead was a glint in the path of the dry streambed. It was small but clear, and stopping it in its path was a collection of smooth and mossy rocks. They were fashioned in the sort of dam that the Centerton children might lay across a stream, making the little fish there easier to catch.

"Ah! We've found it!" Sada exclaimed, delighted at their discovery.

Lady Blue was in the opposite of spirits. Upon seeing the nature of the blockage, she stamped her hoof and tossed her head.

"What is it? Why are you so troubled?" Sada asked. "We've found the spring, and now it can be returned to the little Sprite."

She didn't even need to touch Lady Blue to hear her angry thoughts.

This obstruction is not of natural origin, as I presumed—it hath been wrought with purpose!

"Yes," Sada agreed; that was clear. One stone may have rolled into the way of the river on its own, but four? Certainly not. "Children often engage in jests and tricks, and the nature of some even border on wickedness. Even the Pixies of this realm appear to behave similarly. You witnessed such firsthand; why are you surprised now, Lady Blue?"

To lead strayed wanderers deeper into the woods doth suit the mischievous nature of Pixies. And vile pranks are common in the realm of mortals, that much is certain, yet in thine own realm, such should remain! This is not the way of the Eltics, and assuredly not the fairfolk. I cannot fathom that one of Elt would seek to extinguish the life of a Sprite—especially one still sprouting. Yet such was the aim of the perpetrator behind this obstacle. Her eyes were wide and blazing with golden fire. *Evil doth linger within these stones, Sada. I know it by the wisdom of my foremothers and by the horn upon my brow.*

And Sada believed her. The caelicorn only swore by her mothers and her horn when she was truly certain about something. She'd only heard it happen once before, when speaking of her wings healing. Even Sada's own *instincts* blazed with cold fire when she reached out to the stones. Yes, there was something wrong with them. Not the nature of the stones themselves, but lingering from the person who had placed them. Sada looked around uneasily, wondering if they were still nearby. She fervently hoped they were not.

Lady Blue was pacing agitatedly, and so Sada bent to move the stones herself. Then, with a sudden worried thought, she pulled back.

"Is it catching?" she asked Lady Blue.

The filly just stared at her blankly, her answer obvious in her eyes. *Art thou daft?* Sada imagined her saying. *Nay, it is not catching; naught can be caught from a stone!*

But Sada would not move until Lady Blue spoke the true answer into her head, saying, *Nay.*

Her *instincts* bit deeper into her flesh when she touched the rocks, but they were not so strong as to be unbearable. Yet even when the stones were moved and the stream began to meander back toward the Sprite and its tree, a lump still blocked her throat. She tried to smile at Lady Blue, pointing at the now-flowing stream, yet she didn't feel the happiness she was trying to force into her smile. The caelicorn only spared a cursory glance at the spring, then started back toward the tree. Sada followed, uneasy in her friend's troubled company.

For a while Lady Blue said nothing, and after several failed attempts to break the silence, Sada refrained from saying anything as well. Then, when they were nearing the tree once more, the caelicorn shifted beneath Sada's hand. One thought floated into her mind, and it did little to calm her nerves.

Evil festers within the flesh of Elt. The flat and dark tone in which Lady Blue spoke caused a shudder to run up Sada's neck, and she flinched away from the filly's touch as quickly as she could. The forest around them was beautiful, but she couldn't help but notice oddities and wrongness when she looked deeper into the trees now.

Beside certain trunks, the clumps of shadows looked too thick, or seemed to be pointing in the wrong direction. The gaps in the leaves appeared in the shapes of screaming faces, and the whorls in the trunks looked like eyes when glanced at from the corner of her own. Rather than giggling nonsense, the whispering berries told her to climb up a tree and leap from it. Even the music of the forest sounded haunting and foreboding, and it made Sada want to whirl around, checking behind her back and over her shoulder with every other step she took.

Yet when they reached the Sprite, it was obvious that he shared none of Sada's foreboding. Upon seeing the stream that now flowed beneath the drooping branches of his tree once more, his face lit up with delight. Now two of his hands were free to move away from the trunk he clung to, and he waved them delightedly. Seeing the child's glee dispelled some of Sada's distress. After all, he was grown from Elt itself, and he seemed to sense none of the evil that Lady Blue did.

"My spring! My spring!" the Sprite cried giddily. "It's come back to me! What did you tell it to make it come back?"

Sada couldn't help but smile, and then all of her worries were vanquished. "We told it of your longing, and it was most eager to return to your side," she said. The child let out another delighted squeal.

"Take as many berries as you want! We can always make more. Maybe leave a couple of bunches for the deers, they're very nice to me. But the rest you can eat!" He looked down at his spring again and crooned to it some more in childish tones. "I missed you."

"I'm very thankful for the berries," Sada said. "They look absolutely wonderful."

Still smiling, she plucked one of the ruby-red bunches off the tree and examined the plump cluster for danger. It was heavy in her hand. The fruit didn't appear to be poisonous, but neither had those icy blue berries she'd eaten during her first day in the forest. She didn't believe the Sprite would purposefully mislead her, and her arm wasn't tingling in warning, so she popped one into her mouth. Sun-warmed juice gushed over her tongue, yet no unbearable heat alighted in her skin.

"What do you think?" She held the cluster of fruit out to Lady Blue. She just sniffed the berries and snorted, looking bored. "Do you suspect they may be poisonous?"

Lady Blue just met her eye and then walked away, curly tail flicking. Hastily, Sada grabbed another cluster of the berries off the tree, taking from the low branches. Reaching overhead made the wounds on her shoulders ache. She took only a couple of handfuls of the fruit, wishing again for her pockets. The branch she picked from sprang up from the ground when she did. She hoped the "deers" could still reach it at its new height, but if not, there were other branches to eat from, and now a spring to drink from as well. She curtseyed and thanked the Sprite again, who was distracted by the return of her spring, then left to follow the filly. The crooning of the tree Spiritkin followed her.

The forest had become lush with thick grasses, and the foal now found a patch of moss amongst the verdant flooring to lay on. It was pink as watermelon, speckled with very small white flowers the size of lemon seeds, and smelled of roses. Sada joined her on the ground, for a moment just turning her face to the sun and relishing in its warmth.

The sun of Elt felt gentler than that of her own world; not lacking in warmth, only harshness. She wondered how she had even been burned by it upon waking that first day in Elt after trying to leave. Perhaps the sun was only harsh to those not from its world. Or perhaps it was punishing her for trying to leave. That day felt so long ago now. Sitting here in the rosy sunlight, she nearly wished she didn't have to leave such a lovely place. If only her father, friends, and estate could be transported here instead!

For a while, she sat there imagining what she and her family's life would be like in Elt. But it was just a distraction. She found she was almost reluctant to fill her stomach when it had been empty for so long. It felt pure this way, clean. But with food now within reach, her stomach loudly disagreed, and finally, she ate. She chewed happily on the crimson fruit, growing more eager for the food with each saccharine bite.

She offered a berry to the caelicorn. She just turned her head to nibble halfheartedly on some grass. Sada tried splitting the berry open before holding it out, but still, Lady Blue showed no interest. Even when Sada squeezed some of the bloody juice onto her fingers for the filly to lick off, the only response was one of disdain and disinterest.

"I don't understand," Sada said hopelessly. "It was you who begged for food, and yet now you refuse it. Are the berries dangerous, or do you simply wish not to eat them?"

Sada was not granted a response.

Sada finished her fruit quickly, but without satisfaction or enjoyment. The filly looked positively dejected now, lying with her chin on her foreleg, and Sada found that she had little appetite with her friend looking so downcast. Every attempt she made to offer Lady Blue fruit was rejected. Eventually she gave up, standing and flicking imaginary dust off of her cloak. She left the uneaten berries laid out on the moss, not wanting to carry them with her. The animals would finish them. Now that she knew some of the forest's fruit would not harm her, she would be more apt to eat straight from the tree in the future.

Sada did this as she and the caelicorn continued walking. She first came upon a lovely peach tree, whose trunk was covered in the same thin dusting of gold that its fruits were. When she bit into the fruit, the dust was slightly sour, offering a delightful contrast to the sweetness. She also allowed herself to eat of the whispering berries, whose voices were unsettlingly silenced upon chewing and swallowing the fruit. She had only a few of these. She knew the fruit wasn't alive (thought so, anyway), but it was too disconcerting to pop one into her mouth as it was whispering, *How do'ee do Madam? And jolly, jolly, raccoon folly!* and then to hear it slowly fade away before cutting to silence as it was swallowed.

"Quite perturbing, isn't it?" she had asked the caelicorn about the hushed voices. "Do you enjoy berries? I've always been fond of blackberries, but I find raspberries to be too tart. What do you think?"

She was not answered.

Next, she moved onto the oranges dangling from fragrant yellow leaves. When peeled open, the exposed fruit emitted a faint golden glow. She was also delighted to see that these citrusy fruits were not coated with that horrible white webbing which she had to pluck off before eating the fruit it encased.

All of these fruits she presented to Lady Blue. Yet the filly turned her nose up at each. The peaches she offered a perfunctory sniff, but the end result was the same. After Sada had eaten her fill and was feeling guilty over the fullness of her belly when the filly's was surely empty, she threw a glowing orange to the ground in exasperation.

"Is there anything that will please you?" she cried. But still, Lady Blue would not answer in that voiceless whisper of hers. She only turned to continue on through the woods, tail swishing and hooves rustling in the grasses.

Sada was left with no choice but to follow dismally. The fruits did not sustain her for long. After just half an hour of walking, her stomach was rumbling with a greater fervor than it had for her entire journey thus far. It seemed that eating had only awakened her appetite; once dormant, it was now an angry, roaring thing. As she followed Lady Blue's golden tail, she crossed her hands over her growling and gurgling stomach.

I wonder if there is any food in this forest besides fruit.

As the sun had just set to that perfect height which painted everything in a glow—usually golden, but in this world it was a soft rose—that made it ten times as beautiful as it typically was, Sada and Lady Blue reached a part of the forest decorated in vines. Each trunk was wrapped in a tight robe of them, like Sada on a chilly morning, and they hung from the high branches in lovely green drapes. Growing from each braided strand were clusters of little pink and lemon-yellow flowers. The vines were so thick and numerous that she could not see beyond an arm's length at any given moment, and she had to walk with a hand on Lady Blue's neck so as not to lose her when the emerald curtains swished closed behind her blue flanks. Sada's eyes watered at the beauty, and when she trailed a hand across the striking plants, her *instincts* lit up with delight.

"I think the beauty may be too great for my heart to bear," she whispered to the filly. She was looking at her own arm, captured by a beam of light and bathed in pink and brightness. Each little hair that stood on end in her awe was illuminated in it, and every pore it grew from could be seen as well. As for Lady Blue, she could hardly stand to look at her. Sada's heart was one of both an artist and a romantic, and when she saw the beauty of the caelicorn in the afternoon glow, she felt only desperately tragic that it could not be captured with a brush and paints, or with words of a poem on paper. She released the aching in her heart with a song instead:

Daughter of the sky, o' Lady of Blue,
How your hide is a cruel shade of beauty.
Don't wound me so with this splash of azure,
For the pain is pointless when the sight is so fleeting.

If I cannot capture it, let it not be so
My heart cannot stand the torture.
Your golden curls are like an angel's hair
On complementary wings, I would be brought to my closure.

In that perfect light which made all things beautiful, those which already were became nearly painful to look at. The caelicorn's long, cerulean fur looked like the finest of silk, and that which decorated her feet looked so perfect it must have been sewn in place. Her golden curls shone so brightly, Sada truly could not look at them. If she did, her eyes throbbed with a blissful ache. And the horn. The horn was a thing of magnificence. With perfectly crafted spirals, it looked to be carved from a solid golden ingot. Something terrible and greedy in Sada's heart wanted it for her own. But the feeling was fleeting and not of herself. For when it passed, her heart ached in joy not at the beauty of the caelicorn, but that the two of them should be friends.

Through their inexplicable connection, Sada sensed that Lady Blue felt all of this transmitted through the hand that was placed just behind her ears. She twitched them appreciatively. Sada didn't consciously realize that part of her bliss was coming from the caelicorn herself. Yet suddenly all of their glowing happiness was shocked by a jolt of surprise, and the brief static of fear. It was like a lightning bolt suddenly coming down on a serene lake.

The caelicorn halted in her steps, snorting and pawing the ground. Sada was more silent in her apprehension. Her fingers curled into the filly's mane and her gaze darted around, eyes trying to find the source of her friend's startle.

What is it? I see nothing, where do you sense—

Then she saw. The orange ears of a fox, that elegant swoop of the nose, and those cunning dark eyes. The grin set into that muzzle. Immediately the image of the nine-tailed fox and its evil golden gaze was behind her eyes. She saw its dark muzzle wet with blood. Then she saw the caelicorn's memory of it: the furry body lying dead on its side in the moss and ferns, not a bloody muzzle but a bloody belly from which she fed—

Suddenly the fox's thin muzzle lifted into the air. Its lips pulled back as it sniffed once. Those colorless eyes slid to Sada. Beside them she abruptly noticed the two wider but just as colorless eyes of a rabbit. Finally the third pair of dark orbs turned to her, these belonging to a raccoon. Her throat tightened.

"They're only animals," she told Lady Blue, who was still standing stiffly beneath her hand. But even though she tried to make herself sound calm and comforting, her stomach turned with unease.

Something is amiss, the filly thought. Sada soon saw what that was.

The fox raised a paw in greeting. Cuffed just below the brown pad of its foot, buttoned tight around its thin russet wrist, was the tweed fabric of a suit. The fox grinned a sickeningly human grin, and it began to wave, its entire upright body rocking as it did. Sada's stomach turned. Lady Blue's own sense of foreboding entered her mind as the filly thought, *Creator above and Elt below…*

Is this the same as the evil we sensed at the Sprite's spring? Sada thought.

Nay, this is not evil, simply…wrong.

Sada agreed. Her left arm was vibrating within itself, and her reflexes screamed at her to get away from this unnatural…*uncanny*…creature, like a doll come to life. She moved to back away, to turn and run, but then the fox-man called out.

"Hail, friends!" he said in a chirping and accented voice. "Hail to a lovely afternoon!"

THE FIFTEENTH

Sada

The fox was jumping as he waved, all his yellowed teeth bared in that smile.

There is still time yet to retreat from this wrongness, Lady Blue was saying to her, but unfortunately Sada's arm had already raised itself in greeting, and her hand was turning in a ladylike wave. Her mouth was stretching into a ladylike smile, and then the fox was brightly beckoning them over.

Never mind it. Honor calls us to respond, the filly thought darkly.

Sada groaned inwardly. *My apologies, I know not what I am doing—*

But then her feet were walking her toward the talking animal dressed in human clothes.

When she reached it, it stuck its arm straight out in front of itself, elbow locked, and she realized it was very awkwardly trying to take her hand. She placed hers in its tiny paw, awaiting an equally stiff bow and a respectful kiss from its muzzle. It didn't come. The fox just clasped her hand between its two paws and began moving them up and down.

He is trying to shake my hand as well, just as Drath did! she thought. *What is it about me that causes the men of this world to treat me like I am one of them? The dirt on my dress?* At this greeting, Sada let out a noise somewhere between a scoff and an amused laugh.

"What is it? Have I done it wrong?" the fox asked. His smile disappeared, and he darted furtive glances between her and his companions.

Just beside him stood a large rabbit (this one had the typical number of ears) clad in his own suit, though his was a rich blue. He stood up on his back legs like the fox, and seemed to look more at place that way, balanced on his haunches. In one of his paws he held a handkerchief that matched the color of his suit. Behind both of the suit-clad animals huddled a raccoon in a pink dress. It had a billowing skirt and was trimmed with lace, in the old style Sada had just brought herself to move away from. Seeing the style of dress which she so loved made her heart do an excited little skip. The lady raccoon looked terribly afraid, and was clasping the hat on her head—which was decorated with fruit—with both hands, as though she feared it would blow away at any given moment.

They all stood in front of a table set with various pastries and china sets. The sight of the animals wearing human clothes and using human implements made her uneasy, to say the least. It looked like a scene straight out of a fairytale…she hoped this was the kind with a happy ending, and not some bleak moral lesson.

Though the fox looked to the pink-dressed raccoon for his answer, it was the rabbit gentleman who responded.

"I believe you have offended her, sthir. You thee, she isth a lady. The hand is to be kisthed, not shaken."

When he first began to speak, Sada didn't know at all what he was saying. Then she realized he had a lisp, and shame bloomed on her cheeks. Thankfully, neither he nor his foxy friend seemed to notice.

The fox's face lit up at the answer. "Ah! Kissed! Yes of course, why didn't I think it? Your hand, lady?"

Sada hesitantly replaced her hand in the fox's grasp. This time he let it balance on the stiff pad of his paw then brought his muzzle to it. His whiskers and breath tickled the back of her hand, but she stifled the urge to pull it away until after he kissed it. Yet he did no such thing. Instead, his pink tongue darted out and he licked it, once.

Sada jerked her hand back with a startled squeak. The fox immediately flinched backward, smiling nervously. To Sada, he looked ready to attack her with those yellowing teeth.

"What is it? Have I performed non-respectfully?" Again, he looked to the shy raccoon for confirmation or denial.

"*Dith*-rethpectfully," the rabbit corrected with a twitch of his nose. He wiped it with his kerchief.

Sada, completely on edge but still just as completely concerned with manners, immediately cried to respond in the negative.

"Not at all!" she blurted before she could be stopped. "That is…merely the response of a lady to the greeting from a gentleman."

The rabbit seemed not to believe her. "A thcream?" He and the fox exchanged looks. "Isth thisth not typically done in fear?"

"Fear? No, no. Well, sometimes yes. But also in…greeting." She smiled in what she feared was a terribly awkward manner. What was she doing? She was a terrible liar!

The fox, however, appeared appeased. He clapped his paws together in the same manner that her uncle Beron did after settling a dispute between servants. "Ah! Well, then, shall we all scream together?"

"No!" Sada blurted again as he was opening his mouth in preparation. When the animals looked to her quizzically, she said, "It is only custom for the *ladies,* you see."

Quiet! she chided herself. She could almost feel Lady Blue's certain exasperation.

The animals nodded, murmuring their understanding. Then the fox instructed the raccoon lady to scream at Sada in greeting. Unfortunately, this could not be stopped by any amount of her nervous blabbering. The raccoon released a shrill shriek that startled several birds into the air and forced a pained smile onto Sada's face. When finally the awkward introductions were over, Sada was trying to think of a good way to excuse herself from this situation so she and Lady Blue could flee and discuss what in the world had just happened, when the fox's face broke into another grin.

"I should invite you to join us for tea now, shouldn't I?" he asked. She wasn't sure if he was looking for confirmation that, yes, this would be the polite thing to do, or if he wanted her to agree to tea. Either way, she was inclined to answer with a strong *no.* The tea table behind them looked inviting, to be sure, but she was still uneasy about the encounter.

Before Sada could decline, the rabbit's eyes settled on Lady Blue. "I darethay, that isth a *fine* looking horsthe you have there!" he said, half-hopping and half-walking closer to squint at the filly.

At being called a horse, which Sada supposed to be some sort of insult, Lady Blue tossed her head and stamped her hoof so hard into the ground she exposed soil.

"Ah…" Sada began, shooting a worried glance at her outraged friend. She could feel the indignation radiating off of her without even making contact. "My friend here is actually a caelicorn, sir. And I agree she is very fine. Unfortunately, we have an appointment with the king and must decline—"

"Thaecilorn!" the rabbit exclaimed.

"Lovely name, lovely name," the fox said, nodding his head appreciatively. "We must have you and Caelicorn for tea, ma'am…?"

For a moment, Sada didn't register his question for what it was, only smiled politely. When she did realize, her eyes widened in surprise.

"Oh— I am Lady Sada Solares, first daughter of Duke Darius Solares of Altamira." She said this and then curtsied automatically and without thinking.

"What a long name," the hare-man said under his breath. Then he wiped his wet nose with his handkerchief and sketched a curtsey of his own. Sada had to bite her lip to keep from laughing. Lady Blue looked amused as well. "I am Guyle, Madam Lady. I am pleathured to make your meeting."

Sada returned this sentiment, then looked to the fox for his introduction. He stepped forward, one hand placed over his heart as though about to take a vow. "And I, Madam Lady, am known by the name of…the name of…" he paused then, muzzle propped open, and his eyes darted to look at Guyle. His voice dropped to a whisper, and he leaned in toward the rabbit conspiratorially. "What is the name of the boy who showed you how to…you know…" He mimed buttoning up a shirt.

"Ah, yeth, the name wasth *Tom,* I hope," Guyle whispered back. The two of them shot Sada a glance, then stood straight again.

The fox-man cleared his throat, replaced his hand in the vow posture, and grinned. "I am known by the name of *Ton—"*

"Tom," hissed Guyle.

"What?"

"Tom, not Ton."

"Ah, yes. My name is Tom, pleased to make your meeting Lady Ma'am Sada." Then he bowed, stiffly, though at least it was not a curtsey.

Sada expressed that she was pleased to meet both of the sirs, and began to excuse herself and Lady Blue once again, when Tom reminded her that the lady still had to introduce herself. Sada at first thought he was referring to herself, and was going to remind them that she had been the first to make the introductions. Then the suit-clad creatures shifted and Sada saw and remembered the raccoon in the pink dress. She was sitting at the tea table quietly, hands still clasped to her fruit-covered hat.

Sada looked politely at her along with the fox and the rabbit, awaiting her introduction so she could just as quickly leave. The raccoon said nothing, just shuffled her fingers along the brim of her hat. She opened her mouth, but only a pitiful little wheeze escaped. Then she closed it and covered her snout with her human-like hands.

"Oh, dread," Guyle muttered.

Tom grinned at Sada in his usual fashion. "Excuse the lady if you would, she has more trouble with the language than—" he made a series of squeaking and barking noises that made Sada's eyebrows raise in surprise, "—I mean, than *Guyle,* and I." He grinned again, then turned to the raccoon. "Get off of that chair, sow. You know it is easier when touching the ground."

Sada tossed Lady Blue a puzzled look at this, but the caelicorn was not looking up at her. She was staring hard at Tom.

The raccoon clambered obediently down from the wooden chair she sat upon, one hand clutching the hat, then faced Sada with a huff.

She took a long, deep breath then in an adorable and chittering voice said, "I...am...Mary! *Miss* Mary!" She threw both of her little arms into the air as she exclaimed this, like a child who has just won a game. Then she bent to all fours, heaving audibly.

"Ah, Mary...sthrange choicthe," Guyle said, eyeing the raccoon.

Sada just curtsied, and once Mary caught her breath, she returned the gesture.

"Well, now you have met mine and I have met yours. I would say it is time for tea then, is it not?" Tom asked.

"I thank you again for the invitation, Mr. Tom. Yet my friend and I have an appointment with the king and must make haste...I am sure you know how kings do not like to be kept waiting." Sada tangled her fingers in her hair as she stared at the fox, those unreadable black eyes staring back.

The grin stretched wider.

"Ah, yes. *King,* what an atrocious name. We find that most people with unfortunate names do not like to be waiting," he said in his screechy voice.

Sada did not know what to make of such an answer. Had they never heard of King Caprius? She supposed that when it came down to it, they were only animals. As if to prove her point, the fox-man suddenly dropped to the floor, lifted a back paw, and began to violently scratch at his ear.

"You animal!" Guyle said reproachfully. "Where are your mannersth?"

Tom immediately hopped to his feet again, wobbling as he found his balance. "Apologize," he said, bowing again. His tail bushed up behind him, and Sada once again found herself repressing a giggle.

"Accepted. As you said, the king would not like to be made to wait. It was a pleasure meeting you, yet now we must depart." Sada sketched a curtsey, then turned to leave.

"Leave!" cried Tom. "Yet you have not had tea! And look at how badly Mary dreams to serve you."

The raccoon lady had climbed back into her seat while Sada spoke with the gentlemen. She now held a beautiful teapot between both of her toddler-like hands, and was looking hopefully up at Sada, like a kitten waiting to play. Her heart crumbled at the sight of those big, watery eyes, so much like the Trolls'.

She bit at her lip, looking between Mary, Tom, and Guyle. Finally, her eyes landed on Lady Blue. Her friend's eyes were just as unreadable as the animals.

That's what she is, too, when it comes down to it, Sada thought, then chided herself. Lady Blue was completely unlike these creatures pretending to be human. She placed a hand on her friend's neck, opening up that line of communication.

I wish to stay, only for a moment. I have not the heart to refuse them, Sada thought.

A sense of strong curiosity flooded her mind just behind her eyes, then, but no words accompanied it. *Why is it that sometimes she speaks to me, and sometimes she does not?* Sada thought. But the feeling that Lady Blue had sent was enough agreement for her.

She turned to accept the fox's invitation.

The table was square and plain, covered in a lacy and yellowing cloth. Sada had seen one of a similar style in the house of Jezebel's grandmother. Only she didn't have the fondness for tea that these animals seemed to. Just gossip. There were four chairs at the table, one at each side. Upon it was set an array of china—too much for the company present—and even more food. The sight of the various pastries—*human* pastries, made of flour and not bee pollen—nearly made Sada forget her manners. As the others served themselves and explained to Sada what each of the pieces of silverware were called (fork, sthpoon, and kniff) she had only a mind for the food.

Would she eat the lemon tart first, or the croissant? Perhaps she would try the scone, or the strawberry cake. Finally, they reached a point where manners deemed it appropriate for her to eat, and she said a prayer of thanks then sunk her teeth deep into the lemon tart, eating half of it in one bite. The tartness of it brought a flood of needles to the back of her mouth, as always happened with food that was extremely flavorful. Yet the uncomfortable sensation was a welcome one, and she closed her eyes to enjoy the food.

"Do you cook your own food, lady ma'am?" Tom asked her. Sada nearly spit out her pastry in laughter. She managed to cover her mouth before her unladylike grin could reveal the food that was inside it.

"I do not," she said when she had swallowed. "Do you?"

She would have thought it silly to ask a fox if he cooked his own food, yet here one sat at a table dining not only with her, but alongside his typical food itself—a rabbit. Tom had a small pie balanced on his claws so that it would not touch his paw pads. His lips pulled back in a grimace as he nibbled at the crust.

At her question, he and Guyle shared a glance, then they both grinned.

"Why, in fact, we cooked this very meal ourselves," the fox said proudly.

"Helped to, anyway," Guyle amended.

Sada had not paused to wonder at where the food had come from, but this answer was one she never would have expected.

"How incredible!" she exclaimed. "It tastes amazing!"

"The memberth of the Learned have many talentsth," Guyle said airily.

Tom was staring aghast at Mary. "No, *sow,* that is what the kniff is for! The kniff is used for cutting, the spoon for eating."

"That is typically how it is done," Sada said with some amusement.

The raccoon was sawing at a muffin with the edge of her spoon, knife held at the ready to spear a chunk. She thought she should mention that muffins are typically not eaten with spoons, but decided that Tom's chiding was enough for the lady to deal with.

"Ah, see? Even the person agrees, and should we not trust her on *person* matters?"

"Though are Sthpiritkin to be trusted on matterth of the human?" Guyle muttered.

"Certainly! One society can learn much about another through war," Tom said.

Sada frowned, but didn't get a chance to ask what either of the creatures meant by their comments, thanks to Tom's continued exclamations at Mary.

"See how much easier it is? I daresay!" the fox was shaking his russet head, looking truly baffled. "Thank you, Ma'am Sada."

Sada smiled behind a napkin. "I'm happy to help, of course. But I believe your lady was doing just fine without my input."

"My…my lady? *Mine?*" At this, Tom barked a laugh, and Mary covered her nose, shaking her head.

"You thought they were *mated?*" asked Guyle incredulously.

"No!" Sada exclaimed. Her face was filled with unbearable heat. "I only…I'd thought the two of you to be in courting, perhaps, or…oh, never mind me. I apologize at my impropriety." *I never should have opened my cursed mouth!*

Despite her embarrassment, she suddenly felt like laughing. She immediately knew the source of this unwelcome feeling and shot Lady Blue a glare.

"Ah, courting! We know of thith, Tom," Guyle said proudly. Tom snatched away the rabbit's kerchief to dab at his nose, which had grown wet as he laughed.

"Indeed! I simply find it so amusing," Tom was saying, "that you think I would court one of the green-eaters." He giggled rather girlishly, and Sada felt some of her embarrassment dispelled.

"Ah, I see. I suppose I would also be uncomfortable in your situation, considering…you may have…eaten, ah, one of her relatives at one point." At this comment, Sada wished to bury her face in her hands and run away to hide in her shame.

Yet the animals burst into laughter, even Mary. "What a delight, to truly experience the humor of the talkers!" Tom cried. He laughed squeakily.

She assumed those were humans and Spiritkin. Sada wondered if all the Spiritkin spoke one language. Then she recalled her encounter with the Elves, how they had been speaking a strange language before one said, "Known Tongue." Then Sada could understand. She thought the Elves, perhaps all Spiritkin, knew many tongues. She thought she would too, if she were immortal.

Mary chittered something in raccoon, and Tom paused to lean in and listen, fuzzy ear twitching. When she finished, he straightened. "The lady compliments your gown, Ma'am Sada. She wonders if the style is new."

At this, Sada was able to offer a true smile. This gown was one of her finest. It had been, anyway.

"Yes! You see, the simplicity is of a new trend. Yet the form-fitting bodice is of my own design, drawing inspiration from past fashion. I prefer it greatly; truly, my heart belongs to the style which Ms. Mary wears."

Mary smoothed out her dress, black eyes gleaming happily.

"And are the, ah, rips a part of the design as well? I can't say I have seen others of your kind wearing anything similar."

"Oh, these…" her face grew hot again and she tried her best to shift and cover the tatters. "No, I don't believe the tailor designed it to be customized in such a fashion. Pardon me…but did you say that you've seen other people?"

"Certainly," Guyle said, and spread his hands out. "You sit beside them now, how could we not have seen them?"

"Oh, ah…" What was the word they had used? "Talkers, I mean. You've seen them?"

"Well…" Tom shared a glance with Guyle. "That is a story for another time."

"Indeed," Guyle said. "Another topic, then!"

"Agreed! No talk of talkers!" Tom said, and clapped twice before taking up his pie again.

"Very well." A little uneasy, Sada cleared her throat. "Your suits, I must say, I have been admiring as well. They appear to be of a high-quality material, and are very fashionable indeed." The fox grinned. The hare nodded. "Did you make those as well?"

The two men laughed.

"Nay, lady, nay. It is pastries only, for us," Tom said.

"I must assume that the same people who made the suits made Ms. Mary's lovely gown as well. I would call on the makers to design me a dress. Where did you acquire it all?"

At that, Tom stopped smiling and Guyle stopped nodding and chewing. The two exchanged a glance. They looked at Sada. The silence stretched on, but they did not make to answer.

Her fingers found her hair.

Mary offered her more tea, though her cup was already full.

Finally, Tom broke the silence. "The Learned have fine taste in fashion as well."

"Indeed," Sada said nervously. She chewed on her tart. Silence may have been the better option, but she could not still her tongue. "Who are the Learned, may I ask? Or what is it? A group or an organization?" Some part of her expected to be met with more silence, but the animals were more enthusiastic to answer her on this topic.

Tom nodded. He had nibbled off half the pie's crust, and now set to work on the other half. "We are the gifted ones. The ones who study the languages of the talkers."

"Ah. Indeed, your knowledge of the Known Tongue is very fine," Sada said, earning a toothy grin from Tom. Guyle just nodded along as though this was well known. "May I inquire as to how you learned it?"

"'Twasth a thimple matter, really," Guyle said. He had started into a slice of pie as earnestly as Sada, and his grey muzzle was covered in purple, as were the cuffs of his blue suit. He dabbed at his nose with his kerchief, which did little in the way of cleaning. "Oncthe we were exposthed to the language, it wasth easthy to understhand."

Sada was nodding indulgently, but through the hand she rested on Lady Blue's neck, she felt a desire coming from the filly for Guyle to stop saying so many words with S's in them…or in his case, Sth's. Sada mentally chided her, but also found herself suppressing a giggle behind a napkin.

"Well…" Tom began. "Let us not give ourselves too much credit, Guyle. We were plenty exposed to the and the Known Tongue in the Before, yet we did not learn it until After.

Guyle stiffened in his seat, shooting Tom a sharp glance. He tugged on his suit, adjusting it nervously. "Let us not talk of the Before, Tom," he muttered.

Sada was dreadfully curious about what this Before was, yet Guyle seemed quite upset by the topic of it and so she did not inquire. Tom agreed amiably enough not to speak on the matter any longer, and the four of them went on eating in silence. It was terribly awkward for Sada, but the animals didn't seem to mind. Guyle nibbled quickly through his pastries, and Tom smacked on them noisily, seeming hardly able to tolerate the experience, but determined to soldier through. Sada had finished more pastries than she would have been willing to admit to anyone, and when she finished her tea, Mary looked up excitedly. She seemed to be keeping a careful watch on Sada's cup. Seeing it was empty, she beckoned for it with both her hands.

"Oh," Sada said.

Mary was gesturing so vigorously that her fruit-laden hat slid over her ringed eyes, and a grape rolled off the brim. Sada was truly becoming concerned for the little raccoon's well-being, and so she offered the cup to be refilled though her belly was pushing brutally against her corset.

"Okay. Thank you," Sada said.

It had only been a matter of minutes since Guyle closed the discussion of the ambiguous Before, when Tom cheerfully took it up again.

"So, Ma'am Sada, what were you doing in the Before?"

Guyle's ears flattened, but Tom was looking at her expectantly. Sada looked between them, then asked, "Pardon, but what is the Before?"

Guyle sighed as this were the most tedious question she could have asked. Tom and Mary shared a quizzical glance.

"Is this not common knowledge?" the fox whispered at the raccoon. She lifted up both her arms, palms up: *I don't know.* "Well, we Learned are privy to more than most can claim to be."

Then Mary turned to Sada. "Cold. Hot…Awake?" she said. She looked to Tom questioningly, dark eyebrows furrowed beneath the brim of her hat.

"Not quite, my dear," he said, then looked to Sada. "The Before is what happened, well, before the surge of magick ran through Elt. At least, that is what we believe it to be. There was Before, and then the ground turned both cold and hot, and now…now it is the After. Now, we can understand the languages of the talkers, and speak them as well. Now, we wonder what else we can do…"

"Oh, I see. Ms. Mary said something about being awake?" Sada said. She chose to ignore the ominous gleam the fox's eyes had taken on at that last sentence.

Tom nodded. "That is how she describes the feeling of the transition into the After. For myself, it was more like opening my eyes all the way." He demonstrated theatrically.

Guyle grumbled something, his lisp so strong that Sada could not understand. He dabbed at his nose and shot Tom another glare.

"Many of usth cannot remember the Before very clearly. There are theoriesth about what it was, but none can know for a thertainty. All we have now isth the After, and that isth all we need."

"Yes, well," Tom began cheerfully, but the jostling of the table as Guyle shoved away from it silenced him. "Leaving so soon?"

"Yesth. There isth the meeting to be had. *Your* attendanthe isth not required," the hare said, looking between Tom and Mary, "but I muth attend. I will be thpeaking to the Learned about human artifacths. Apparently full underthanding hath ethcaped thome of the…meat-eatersth. If I will be excuthed, then."

He curtsied to Sada, snatched his handkerchief off the table, then bouncily strutted into the woods. Moments later, he could be seen bounding away on all fours, kerchief streaming out behind him from where it was tucked into his blue suit collar.

Sada realized that this may very well be a good time to excuse herself, but also realized that she was much too curious to do so.

"Guyle thinks himself very important to the Learned. As though he were the one to discover the potential in the humans and their speech," said a new voice, deep and dark and flat.

Sada whirled in her seat to discern the newcomer, but there was only Mary and Tom. The former blinked sweetly at her. The latter grinned his foxy grin, and Sada felt a new roll of unease settle into her belly.

"Very important indeed," Tom said, and it was in that strange voice.

"Mr. Tom…pardon, but your voice sounds different."

The grin stretched wider, exposing molars. "Indeed. I have found that as my time spent among humans increases, so too does my full understanding of their kind. Not only does my ability to speak their language grow, so too does my ability to speak *like* them; to *act* like them. Say, Lady Sada, you appear to dress very similarly to those belonging to the race of man. Might this be because you and they are one in the same?" His stare was now not only unreadable, but exquisitely cold. He bit harshly into a muffin, still grinning, still chewing with that grimace that said he could not bear the taste but would go on eating anyway.

Sada tried to swallow her nerves, but they only lodged in her now-dry throat. Lady Blue shifted closer to her, every muscle tense beneath her lovely coat. Sada did not want to tell this fox the truth, did not want to tell him anything at all. The thought of lying crossed her mind, but she knew she would not have been able to formulate one of any believability. The caelicorn may have been able to, but she was either unable or unwilling to speak to Sada in this moment. Her only choice, then, was to tell the truth, and hope that no harm came to her because of it.

She forced a sweet smile. "You say true, Mr. Tom. I am of the mortal realm."

The fox grinned.

THE SIXTEENTH

Sada

"Ah, I believed this to be the case," Tom said in his gravelly voice. "You might have passed for one of the fairfolk, but their clothes are not so concealing as those of you humans. I must say, I am growing to prefer the latter. You say you are off to see the king. I have heard only of two kings thus far; the king of the Fae, and the young king of this forest, and neither are near. If you wish to reach them, you will need knowledge of this place; protection from it."

He tapped his claws together. Sada thought that the birds should not be singing now, but they were, and just as cheerily as ever. She wondered if they, too, wore tweed suits.

"I can offer you this, but in return I would ask something of you," he continued. "As you may have gathered, I am curious about your kind. Tell me what I wish to know of your people, and I will tell you of the world you now reside in."

Sada reached out with both her hand and her mind to Lady Blue, hoping for guidance on how she should proceed. Yet the filly was silent. She only stood beside Sada twitching her ears and tail. The fox seemed highly uninterested in her, and Sada wondered if that was a good thing. In any case, it seemed she would have to guide herself in this matter. If only Father was with her.

She thought it safest to go along with what the human-sounding fox wanted until she was able to leave. She didn't think he would harm her, but her arm was also writhing with the frenzied pangs of her *instincts,* and she knew that she should not linger in his company any longer than she needed.

"Very well," she agreed. "What would you know?"

Tom waggled his orange paw in the air. "Ah, ah. I wish you to know that I am a man of my word. And so, a question of your own will be answered first. Let us begin with the one that went unanswered. You wished to know how we encountered your people."

He did not wait for Sada's agreement. She had been curious about such, but now she was too nervous for much curiosity to remain. Nevertheless, she sat politely as he explained. She thought Father would tell her to learn as much about him as she could. If he wanted to talk, she would let him. Usually she found that when the Duke went off on long tirades, it was not for her ears but for his own—to hear his own voice and to relish it. The fox's eyes reminded her of her father's. She thought Tom might be similar to him in other ways as well.

"I had not yet met the rabbit, Guyle, in the Before," Tom said. "I believe I was hunting one of his kind when the surge happened. As I described to you, Elt shuddered—not physically, but energetically—and then the ground became so hot it was cold, or so cold it was hot. Either way, the feeling was unbearable. Fortunately, it was gone as suddenly as it had come. But it had left something behind in me, and a few others. I didn't feel the difference in myself immediately. I told you that it felt as though my eyes had been opened, but that feeling was slow to come. All I knew was that my prey had been scared off, and so I moved to find a new meal. As I was walking through the forest, the smells began to change. There was now not only the smell of living things, but of *life*. Of *people*.

"Of humans.

"I recall a sharp pang between my ears, then reality seemed to…quiver. I do not know how else to explain it. It was more of a sense of knowing that it had happened than a feeling. The pang brought with it a brief moment of blurred vision. When my eyes cleared, so did my head. I believe I had thoughts Before, but now I was aware that I could think. I was aware that I was hungry, and I was aware that I wanted a rabbit, rather than a squirrel or a mouse. I was also aware that I was not in the forest I had grown up and lived in. I was no longer in Elt.

"Around me there were not only trees, but strange structures made of trees, and rock, as well as what I came to know as glass. I will admit, this was terrifying to behold, and my first instinct was to run. Yet as I told you, I had recently become aware of my instincts and actions, and I was able to suppress this one. I made myself crouch there in the shadows and watch. I saw people. More people than I had ever thought could exist. I had never considered the people that I'd interacted with, but I did know that the ones I had suddenly become surrounded by were not the same as those of Elt. They smelled more sour, and duller. Yet when they spoke, I was charmed. As I sat there watching, some young boy came up behind me and grabbed my tail. I couldn't suppress my reaction to this: I bit him, and then I ran.

"When I stopped running, I found myself at the edge of the wood. This wood was unlike the one I'd grown up in; it was dark and smelled of rotting things, and coldness. Yet among the trees was something that smelled familiar. It was Guyle, yet at the time, I saw only a rabbit of my world. My instincts from Before took over, and I had no reason to suppress them, and so I hunted Guyle. Yet when I pounced, he begged me to spare him. I figure that many of my prey must have begged this of me in my life, but I never knew it Before. Yet this time, I understood him. It was so shocking to me that even though my teeth were at his throat, and I was moments away from tasting that first gush of blood—which is the best, by the way—

I was able to pull away. I tried saying something to him. He understood me."

"Were you speaking the Known Tongue then, or in fox? How did he understand the language of your species?" Sada asked.

Tom paused, mouth half-open, and looked at her with simmering eyes. *Father's eyes.*

A jolt of nerves shocked her belly. Indeed, he spoke to hear his own voice. He did not want to hear her questions.

No more of those, she thought.

"I did not speak in *'fox.'* Do you speak human? No. We speak in different dialects of the same tongue."

"Oh, I see. Please, continue."

Tom looked like he had a sour taste in his mouth, but he went on. "It went against both of our instincts, but we stayed to talk to each other. Not everything was easy to communicate, but most of it was. We learned that we'd both experienced something similar to one another. We also knew that we were curious about this world, and determined that we would try and learn more about it. We stayed in the forest that night, but the next morning, we went into the city to watch its inhabitants.

"It was incredible. They were so noisy, and so *different.* And more than that, they were evolved. Seeing them build was phenomenal. Both Guyle and I had never done more than dig holes, to remove substance to create a home or a place to hide. These creatures created from, rather than take away from. We watched them communicate with such specific details and information that we were boggled that we had never thought to do the same. We did not realize that Before, we simply didn't have the ability to. Their food was also a splendor. It was on a day when I had stolen a loaf of bread from the open door of a bakery that Guyle and I discovered Adam.

"He was only a boy. It would have to be a child who taught us, we learned later on. The adults were too afraid of us, of our abilities, to even consider doing more than killing us. Yet children and animals are similar; they are curious. Adam began leaving me bread from his mother's bakery. At first, I would take it and run it back to Guyle. Then I would bring him along and we'd eat it on the porch, as well as drink the water left out for us. After some time and more trust, we followed Adam into his room below the bakery.

"It was there we learned to speak."

Though Tom's voice was just as deep and just as scary as it had been when he started his tale, Sada found that as he talked, she'd relaxed. Now her curiosity had found room in her mind alongside that nervousness, and she leaned forward expectantly.

"Is that the end of the story? How did Adam teach you? How long did it take?"

Done with his tale, Tom grinned indulgently, leaning back to pick at something between his fangs with a claw. Mary, still as silent as before (and perhaps Before), poured him tea.

"Thank you dear," he murmured to her. Then his dark eyes returned to Sada. "The boy taught us the same way I am sure you and all other humans learned the language. Point. Speak. Repeat. I'd bring him an object, he'd name it, I'd repeat it. Though our abilities certainly served to increase the speed and ease at which we could learn."

"How so?" Sada asked.

"As an example, after we were taught one rule, others came to us through, shall we say, instinct." He tapped his claws on the table. "I caught on particularly quickly. Guyle caught on slower, but still faster than some." His eyes drifted to Mary, and she lowered her gaze, clutching at her hat.

"Yes, I admit I was curious about that," Sada said. "If the surge of magick granted you the ability to speak the Known Tongue, how is it that some of you can speak better than others?"

"That is where you err. The magick granted us the ability to *learn,* not to speak. Something in the way Guyle and I are created allows us to speak certain words with more ease than others. My kind, as well as the wolves, and the cats, are quite adept at speaking the talker words. Whereas the more silent types—the green-eaters—find it to be more difficult. Guyle is merely an exception to his species, yet I'm sure you heard in his lisp the difficulty he still has. You may have heard it mentioned earlier, but being in contact with Elt helps us to speak better."

"Yes, I did hear this," Sada said. "Why do you suppose that is?"

"As you said, the magick granted us some ability. Without it, we would be like the animals who still cannot understand a word of the Known Tongue, who have no idea whether they are having thoughts or not. The magick and the ability came from Elt when it surged; of this I am certain. Of course being near to the source enhances the ability." Tom sipped on the tea, the handle of the cup hanging off one long claw. When he set it down, his eyes were glimmering. "Now, lady, I would hear your tale. How have you come to be in my world?"

Sada told him. As she spoke, he drank his tea and nibbled on pie crust. Mary seemed to listen, but Sada couldn't be sure how much of it the raccoon lady understood. In the time it took for her to tell her short tale, Lady Blue hung her head to rest. The sky turned purple with the onset of dusk, and the sound of the drums grew louder than the other instruments of the forest. All the while, Tom listened intently. When she finished, he was grinning.

"It sounds as though the surge sent you to my side, as I was sent to yours," he said. Sada agreed. "Do none of your kind know of Elt, then? Adam did not, but again, he was young."

Sada shook her head. "I believe not. I had never heard of your world or of the creatures—Spiritkin and Beasts—that inhabit it. Some are told of in my fairytales, but not all. From my encounters with the Spiritkin, however, it sounds as though knowledge of my world and of the Seam is common."

"My kind are not common among the humans, then?"

Sada laughed and Tom grinned with her. "No, they are not." His cheerful grin seemed misplaced when compared to his deep and monotone voice. Yet it had seemed perfectly agreeable with that first voice of his. His real voice? Or was this voice now the true one? "Mr. Tom, your voice changed once Mr. Guyle left us. Is this your true voice, then?"

"It is."

"Then I have to wonder why you were modulating your voice in his presence," she said, frowning.

She thought there would be some secrecy to his answer, but he gave it to her freely. "There are many aspects of myself that Guyle is not privy to. He thinks himself to be leading the Learned into some sort of revolution." At this, he and Mary chuckled. "Yet he knows little of the true purpose of the Learned."

"And you do?" Sada asked.

"Oh, verily. Verily, indeed. I have great plans at work for my people." He grinned again, teeth shining with spittle. "Tell me, human, how is society governed in your world?"

Immediately, her thoughts turned to her father. She thought of bowing before him as he dismounted his war horse. She thought of the way the servants followed him with a rag, ready to wipe away invisible dust. Yet the fox would not want to hear of her governing, but society's as a whole.

Is there truly a difference? she thought. She decided that there wasn't, not in any way that mattered.

"Well, foremost there is the king. He rules over all of our land, from shoreline to shoreline to mountain."

"His rule is great," the fox noted.

Sada nodded. "Yes. Yet from my understanding, he does little by way of ruling. The king's advisors are those who truly govern. They seem to make the laws, then he enforces them through the army, and sometimes speaks to the citizens of Ettedon about their problems. The king can create laws and repeal others, but typically he only holds feasts and balls." At this, her hand flew to her mouth, and she automatically looked around for any of King Abel's men who might have followed her into Elt. "Oh, but I am speaking out of turn. Forgive me."

The fox just tapped his claws. "Hmm…The king and his advisors are the only ones who hold power over your society, then?"

"Well, there are others beneath their stations. There are earls, and dukes—my father counts himself among the latter—along with lords of varying ranks. Each possesses a measure of influence and governance, though to speak candidly, I confess my knowledge of their doings is rather scant."

Tom was nodding, and steepled his fingers together to rest his chin upon them. "It is your turn to ask a question," he said.

Sada thought she should ask him something that may help her in her quest to find the king, perhaps even ask for a guide, but curiosity bested her.

"Why do you suppose there was a surge of magick, Mr. Tom? And do you believe it has something to do with the disappearance of the Seam?"

He looked to Mary and uttered something in those squeaking, barking tones of a true fox—one who did not wear tweed suit. Mary responded in the endearing chittering of a raccoon. The conversation was short, and when it ended, both animals looked to her.

"Mary has been nursing a theory. She believes that the surge of magick is related to a legend of the Spiritkin. This surge would have happened multiple times throughout history, making this one something that does not deserve our concern. However…I have reason to believe that this particular surge of magick is different from the past."

"What legend do you refer to?" Sada asked.

Tom looked to Mary, then lifted a clawed finger. "Mary knows the legends of this world better than I. I specialize in the human aspect of things. One moment."

They conversed in their animal chatter once more, Tom nodding and picking thoughtfully at his teeth. Mary's eyes were wide with excitement; she had even forgotten to clutch at her hat.

She turned to Sada, fuzzy eyebrows raised. "Kin-dreh! Kin-dreh!" she exclaimed, seeming to vibrate with excitement.

Sada smiled indulgently. She felt as though it was a toddler speaking to her. Tom was grinning at the raccoon as well.

"She means to say *Kindred*, you see."

At the word, chills ran over Sada's skin.

"We appreciate your patience. I typically encourage her to practice her speech whenever possible, but now is not the time." Tom glanced to the sky, where the lavender moon was replacing the sun. "Our moments together are dwindling, and we each have much more to learn. So I will tell you briefly of the Kindreds, the legend of the Spiritkin, and the basis of all their region…" He paused, cocked an ear toward Mary who was chittering at him, then looked sheepishly back at Sada. "*Religion,* excuse me. L's are difficult for my tongue. Though not as difficult as the S is for Guyle to pronounce."

He grinned, then with one more sip of his tea, Tom explained to her the legend of the Kindreds.

They were two spirits as old as Elt, and by their very nature were in possession of incredible powers. Every few thousand years, they returned to Elt. Some said they were the ones who originally coupled with humans to create the Spiritkin, but this was merely speculation about what was already legend. As Tom said, these ancient spirits influenced nearly all religion on Elt: do you believe, or do you not believe? To what extent do you believe? And so on. The more radical worshipers also practiced rituals and sacrifices, some involving dark magic and others involving fervent worship, in hopes to usher in their return.

"Of course, none of them could. If the Kindreds are real, and I have reason to believe they are, then they are powerful beyond imagination, and so, of course, powerful beyond control. Their return cannot be predicted or orchestrated, but there are certain signs that point to their nearness: impending war, tensions among Elt's creatures, famine or plague. Ms. Mary believes the surge of magick was Elt welcoming the return of one of the Kindreds."

Sada had been oohing and aahing and gasping delightedly throughout the story. Yet now her arm became ablaze with *instincts* and she grimaced, clutching at it in hopes it would stop. Tom noticed, ears swiveling.

"Your arm pains you so? Does this always happen when you hear a tale?"

He grinned, but Sada only managed a grimace in response. "Pardon, no. Sometimes it pains me, but there is no cause for concern. You said that there were signs pointing to the return of the Kindreds, such as war and famine. Has Elt been experiencing these?"

Tom shrugged. "Mary and her scouts have reported such tensions; they spend most of their time observing the Spiritkin. But I'm sure I do not know. Recall, I have only recently 'awakened' to reality. I know not what goes on in the kingdoms of the fairfolk, or even in different parts of the forest. Soon, I hope to, but now, no."

Powerful beyond imagination, she thought. Why, if these ancient spirits were as old as Elt, and potentially sired its inhabitants, perhaps they could fix the Seam, or even create a new portal through which to send her home.

"Mr. Tom, What would it mean if these Kindreds had returned to Elt?" she asked lightly.

He must have sensed the hopefulness in her voice, for his ears perked up at that. "You wish to meet the Kindreds, little lady?" At hearing that nickname, her heart seemed to constrict. "So many questions, so much curiosity! I deplore it, and yet in the same vein, I adore it. Ah, I know little of the Kindreds, and even Ms. Mary does not know as much as she one day hopes to. Though from what we gather, your desires are not misplaced. Now, I daresay it is my turn to ask a question."

Sada nodded. "I do believe you are correct. What would you know?" she asked. But her mind had drifted from their conversation to the idea of aid arriving in the form of powerful spirits. Perhaps she would not need the Elven king after all. Indeed, she could do without further ridicule from him. Yet some part of her still desired to see him again…

Tom leaned forward, grinning. "Tell me, Sada, what are the most cherished values and beliefs among humans in your world?"

She had lifted her teacup to drink, much to Mary's delight, but halted as a giggle burst forth. "Values and beliefs? I had thought you would ask about current fashion, or methods of craft!"

"I have great plans for the Learned, Lady Sada." His face was stern. "Greater than any Guyle can imagine, that is for a certainty. They will not stand on a foundation of the latest cuffs or mortar."

Sada's grin faded, the laughter dying in her throat. Tom looked terribly serious, his dark eyes not containing even a spark of humor. "As you will," she said lightly, then chewed her lip, thinking. "Well, I suppose humans pride themselves on strength, and power. As we discussed, there are several titles of power in my realm, from duke, to viscount, to knight. Even within households, there are layers of power…It seems inescapable."

Tom cocked his head, ears twitching. "You speak of humans as though you are not of their race. Humans pride *themselves* on strength and power, you say."

"Oh, I hadn't noticed that," she said with a nervous laugh. "Perhaps it is because I disagree with those values. I believe we should value compassion and honesty above all—and I suppose some of us do. The world cannot go on without it, and we certainly do our best to encourage it through laws and justice."

"What do you mean by this? How do you enforce compassion and honesty? How can you make a person act in a certain way?"

"Why, we can't force anyone to act or think in any way!" Sada exclaimed. "And we would not want to. Instead, we discipline people who act without it—those who do harm to others."

"An example?"

"Well…take the criminals. Thieves and killers are not left in the city to continue their thieving and killing, but are locked up. Liars are punished less severely, but nobody would trust a liar, and I believe that is punishment enough."

Tom tapped his fuzzy chin with curved, black claws. "But is punishing those who act or think in the ways you dislike not forcing them to act or think in a certain way?"

Sada's face was heating beneath the scrutiny. "Certainly not!"

"But why not? How not?"

She opened her mouth to respond but realized she didn't have an answer. When he said it in such a way, it truly did seem like they were forcing everyone to act in the way they wanted. But that wasn't bad, was it? Should killers be allowed to go on killing, just so they could claim freedom to act in the way they wished? And as she was thinking that, the answer came to her.

"Have you heard of free will, Mr. Tom?"

"Will, as in the ability and desire to make a decision?"

"Indeed, or to take an action. Everybody—animals, humans, Spiritkin—has the ability to choose their actions. Free will means that anyone can do anything they wish. Someone inclined to steal a bracelet from a jeweler, for example, has the unrestricted ability to do so. Nobody is going to bind his hands behind him so that he can no longer take the action to steal. However, he has been informed that *if* he steals the bracelet, he will be punished for it. Free will allows him to know this and either decide not to steal, or to know this and decide *to* steal.

"I believe…I believe that when free will works alongside justice, that it means people have the right and the ability to do anything, and are informed of the consequences for each of their actions. They can choose to set them in motion, or not."

Sada felt as accomplished as though she'd just taught a lesson in ethics, and she sipped her tea happily. How proud her tutors would be of her! She expected a compliment from Tom, or even a shocked look, an expression of epiphany, but he only cocked his head, his eyes still that unreadable black.

"Do humans value justice, then?" he asked blankly.

The pride faded. "Yes, of course. Evil must be punished, and good must be rewarded. We could not call ourselves human if this was not so."

"Why do you feel so strongly on this matter?" Tom asked. He sipped his tea, which was more of an inhale combined with flicking his tongue into the cup.

How could she explain it? There was no why, it simply was. The way her blood boiled when Jezebel told her of a customer who was allowed to speak to her in the rudest fashion simply because Centerton's lord favored them. Or how her heart physically hurt when she saw city kids pulling the tails of stray cats and throwing rocks at them in the alleys. It was not something to be put into words. The simplest explanation was to say it was the Lord. But while it was true, Tom would not understand. Besides, Sada found it to be intellectually lazy, reducing something beautifully complex into a phrase recited by clergymen when they had no wish to explain further.

"It is simply something that exists in us all. I don't think it is a thing that can be explained. It wouldn't be dissimilar to asking me why I wish to go on living."

"I see. And do all humans feel this way?"

"I believe the good ones do," Sada said delicately. "Even if it is not manifested as a deep, inherent feeling in them as it is for me, I am convinced that, at the very least, they hold such a feeling because it is what permits us to function within society."

"Why do you say so?"

Sada sighed. She knew the answers to these questions, but she'd never had to put them into words before. She found the process to be decidedly tedious.

"Justice is the upholding of good, and the punishment of evil. Evil is detrimental to society, hence the existence of the king's justice, and the dukes' and lords' justice below him. If those who commit wicked deeds were permitted to act without punishment, society would soon disintegrate, wouldn't it?

"Were murderers allowed to kill without consequence, society would cease to exist as a whole. On a lesser scale, if thieves were left to steal, liars to deceive, and cheats to swindle, who would wish to leave the house? I believe that even if society managed to endure, everyone would be wretchedly unhappy, don't you? Thus, justice guards not only human life and society but also our happiness."

She waited for the fox to ask another question, but he only looked at Mary thoughtfully. They conversed in the animal tongues, and Sada allowed herself a deep breath and a drink of tea. Her palms were sweating, though she did not know why. Perhaps it was because she had grown up certain. Certain that the way she lived was right...*just.* Yet under this wild animal's scrutiny, she felt his questioning began to leak into her mind. Did justice truly make sense? Were they forcing people to be good? Was that bad? But what, then, about free will? She decided that she had answered well, and had represented her people well, too. She would not trouble herself over these what-ifs, especially if she was not even in the world where they existed.

Are humans the only ones who value justice? she thought with alarm. She was beginning to wonder if this was so when she remembered how King Caprius had been eager to punish the brothers because he thought them to be liars and thieves. At least the Elves, then, had a sense of justice. But that was not very comforting to her, for she did not believe the brothers to be deserving of their punishment. Even if Kartinar had admitted to thieving, and certainly he could not go unpunished for that, he claimed that he and Drath were not guilty of the crime that the king had accused them of. And what good was justice when it was carried out against the just?

"This has been quite an enlightening conversation, Lady Sada," Tom said. He pushed away from the table, straightening his tweed suit as he stood. He offered Mary a furry hand to help her out of her own wooden chair. "Unfortunately, it seems that night is almost upon us."

Sada pushed away from the table, knocking over her tea in her haste. "Pardon, Mr. Tom, but didn't you say that if I answered your questions, you would in turn aid me?"

He pivoted to face her. "Oh, but I did, didn't I? I could have gifted you clothes, though they certainly wouldn't fit one of your…stature. I might have given you a knife to use for hunting, or a basket for gathering fruit. Even a map to find the young king." He grinned, displaying wet, yellow teeth. "But what I have given you is much more valuable than any of those temporary tools: I have given you *knowledge.* But I do not expect your thanks. We have made a trade, and gratitude is not a commodity I find to be valuable. Good evening."

"Knowledge? Wait!" Sada said. "I must ask before you leave, or I will surely regret it—where is the location of the portal that allowed you to step into my world? Was it the Seam, or a different portal?"

The fox and the raccoon shared a look. "Why, you are standing on it now. It was in this very location that we entered the human realm. It was a rip in the fabric between our worlds, like the ones in your dress. But it is gone now, as you can see. A few days ago it began to quiver and chitter. We were able to drag this table through it, and then it was gone, like sand into the wind."

"Like nev'r here," agreed Mary in her whispery voice.

Sada tried to keep the disappointment from her voice. "Ah, yes. I see…I wonder if there were any other rips."

"It would seem that the existence of two should be unlikely enough. How curious that we, the creatures who happened through them, managed to encounter each other." The fox cocked his head, keen gaze piercing. "A curious twist of fate indeed. And yet, fate is seldom random. There must be a reason you were drawn to our realm, and I to yours."

Sada frowned. "I wish I knew," she confessed, her voice barely above a whisper. "All I know is that I must find my way back home."

Tom's expression softened, a hint of sympathy flickering in his eyes. "Home…A powerful anchor indeed. But sometimes, the path home lies not in retracing our steps, but in forging new ones."

Sada blinked, caught off-guard by the fox's cryptic words. "What do you mean?"

Tom regarded her solemnly, his gaze unwavering. "I mean that perhaps your journey here was not a mere accident…Perhaps there is a greater purpose to your presence in our realm…

"The lady and I must leave you now. The moon is lifting higher, and I fear that the longer Guyle preaches his stupidity to my people, the farther they stray from our goal. Well met, Sada of the humans. You were more intriguing than one would guess at first glance." He turned to go, but stopped after a few steps. "Oh, and it is not polite to lie to strangers, dear. Ms. Mary's voice will probably be hoarse from that scream for days to come. With all that talk of justice and compassion, I would have thought you to hold yourself to it. Well, that is humanity for you, isn't it?" He grinned humorlessly, then went into the woods and left Sada with a face hot and full of shame.

"Oh dear," she said and sighed. "I'm sorry for tangling us up in that predicament, Lady Blue."

The caelicorn snorted. She didn't seem to be too upset with Sada over the detour she'd caused them, but when Sada made to leave the clearing, Lady Blue stayed behind. She stood beside the tea table and stamped her hoof. Sada returned, frowning.

"What is it, Lady Blue? Truly, I did not mean to engage us in such a detour."

The filly just pressed her nose into Sada's hand and she felt a sudden urge to tidy up the table, which was a mess of crumbs and disarrayed pastries.

"Oh, yes. I suppose we ought to clean up if they don't intend to," Sada agreed. "Perhaps Mr. Tom was correct in saying that I need to practice the ethics I preach, wasn't he? Well, it appears I have you for a tutor now instead of Clergyman Sanchez."

When she thought of telling the short, balding man of how she found her ethics being corrected by a winged and horned blue foal, she burst out laughing.

If I told anyone of a single event I've experienced as of late, I would be locked up before I could finish a sentence! Clergyman Sanchez would be the first to call for her arrest, too. He'd been her religious tutor since she was a girl, but she'd never managed to make him her friend. She and Jezebel joked that the hair had chosen to flee from his head because it could have more fun on the ground. Still giggling, she righted the teacup she'd knocked over and tried to sop up any remaining liquid, but she found she didn't know what to do after that. She'd never stopped to watch the servants clean. Where did the plates go? And the remaining tea? Should she water the bushes with it?

"Don't…worry of…the mess."

The voice came from the trees to her left and Sada started with a squeak. Mary was crouched at the base of a tree trunk, hat clutched in her little hands.

"Pardon, Ms. Mary, I didn't see you there! We just thought to tidy up before leaving. Oh—I promise, I had no intentions of taking anything!"

The raccoon waved a hand dismissively.

"Take if want…Came to talk…without…fox." She cleared her throat and beckoned Sada over. Before she went, Sada met Lady Blue's eyes. The filly nodded once, and she went to crouch beside Mary.

"Without Mr. Tom? Is everything well?"

Mary began to nod, then shook her head, then just waved both of her hands, looking exasperated. "Listen!" she said, and Sada shut her mouth. "I come…warn you, Sada; if the…surge…was really signal…of…Kindreds' return, then something…truly…terrible…must be in Elt. That we can…not yet fully see the…s-igns of it, even more concern…than if could."

Mary paused, panting and frowning. She looked the way Sada felt when trying to do the arithmetic problems her tutors gave her. Sada put a hand on the raccoon's shoulder. Her dress sleeve was puffy beneath her palm.

"Take your time, if you can," Sada said. "You're doing well."

Mary shook her head: *no time.* She looked over her shoulder sharply then, listening for something Sada couldn't hear. The forest was dark and empty of life. The animals were silent in their sleep. But Sada still felt the sense that someone was in there, between the trees. And she felt just as strongly that the someone was wearing a tweed suit and a humorless yellow grin.

Mary looked back to Sada and leaned in, eyes wide and bright in the moonlight. "I warn you—be on guard…defend trust with…sharpest blades. I…can't…ch-arge our people to…watch over you: they busy…with…T-om, and won't…go with…stranger. Yet, I will tell them… not bear any ill…will toward you…or companions." Mary grinned, then, and her eyes gleamed in the final light. "Lest justice…fall…upon them."

Mary looked over her shoulder once more, then curtseyed, low and gallantly. Sada stood and did the same. Then Mary turned and ran into the bushes where Tom was surely waiting, clamping her hat down on her head with one hand. Sada looked after the raccoon lady, feeling that she had risked her well-being, maybe even her safety, to give Sada that warning.

My third warning since I've come here, she thought. Goosebumps broke out on her legs and arms. She thought she saw two shapes in the wood, lit by a moonbeam. One tall and one short. In the dusk, they did not look nearly so terrifying as they had upon their introduction. In the darkness, they could just be a fox and a raccoon, not dressed in human clothes, but clad only in fur as nature intended.

Sada felt strangely alone after Mary left. She was not human, but at least she could speak her language. She looked to Lady Blue, who had lifted her head to watch the animals depart. Now she blew air softly through her nostrils, watching Sada with those intelligent eyes.

"Do not worry, you are the only friend I need," Sada said with a smile. The caelicorn brushed her muzzle against her arm, and a feeling of companionship filled her.

Sada went back to the table, eyeing the pastries. Her belly was now so full that her corset felt too tight, something she hardly experienced after years of living in one. Yet she would not unlace it until she was in the privacy of whatever sleeping place she chose for that night. She considered Mary's offer to take some of the pastries with her, recalled again that she had no pockets, and decided she did not want the sugar and crumbs all over her hands anyway. Governess Brown would tell her to eat fruit instead. Being away from home was not an excuse to let herself go. So it was empty-handed that she and Lady Blue left the clearing.

In a forest of pine, it would have been too dark to navigate at this late hour. Yet in this part of the wood, the leaves were slit with beautiful designs and let in plenty of purple moonlight to see by. Lady Blue led her over the parts of the wood that were not so treacherous for an uncoordinated lady, and she had taken up a walking stick to help her if she still managed to find uneven footing. It was late and she should be sleeping, yet her mind was still awake with thoughts of her conversation with Tom. She wondered if Guyle was still talking to the Learned, who he thought were learning from him, but who truly awaited Tom's instruction.

What greater plans does he have for those animals who can now understand and copy the ways of people? she wondered.

"What did you think of Mr. Tom and Mr. Guyle and Ms. Mary?" Sada asked Lady Blue.

The filly only snorted in response and continued walking, her hindquarters swaying dramatically as she did.

"I thought them to be quite lovely." Lady Blue looked skeptically in her direction at this, and Sada grinned. "Truly, I did! If not a little strange…" *And unsettling.* "I wonder if the return of the Kindreds is truly what granted them their ability to speak. Or rather, to learn. Do you believe it is what sent me over here?"

Lady Blue did not answer. Perhaps she didn't know, or perhaps such conspiracies were beneath her. It was curious, the way she only sometimes spoke to Sada. It was never in any discernable pattern, either, but seemed purely up to the filly's whims.

"You don't always answer me. Is there a reason for this?"

An enigmatic eye met her in silence, but the stare was long, and Sada knew that even though she was not speaking, Lady Blue was listening. She turned back around and led Sada to a flat patch of grass beneath a drooping tree, set in the arms of its great brown roots.

She is correct, Sada thought, looking up at the rising lavender eye in the sky. It watched as she settled into nature's cradle. *I must sleep…and she must eat.*

The filly had settled down beside her and was nibbling at a tangle in the feathers of her foot, trying to work it out. It seemed to be doing just the opposite of that, however, and Sada laughed at her. The filly responded by wiggling her lips, and it was in such a horse-like manner that Sada giggled delightedly again. Then she took the foal's foot and began working at the tangle.

"You may be wiser than me—and more ethically sound—that I do not intend to contest. But I have had much more experience at untangling hair than you have."

The caelicorn just blew out air in either agreement or contentment, and watched Sada work in silence. The tangle was deep, but her nails were long. She didn't look at the filly; her mind was troubled and she didn't want her friend to see. Yet finally she had to voice her worries.

"You will not eat the fruit I offer, nor the scones and creampuffs. Eating grass seems not to sustain you, only to offer you some strange amusement, because I always see you spit it out after pulling it from the ground. Yet I know you are hungry, for you told me so yourself, and even if you hadn't, you are just a baby. What, then, should I feed you? I will not see my one friend in this world go hungry."

She looked up to meet the caelicorn's eyes. They were unreadable in the shadow of the tree, but she seemed to be studying Sada. Deciding if her words were true?

Finally, the ageless voice swirled up through her arm and into her mind and she heard it say, *The fruit here is unpalatable. You must find something else.*

Sada was unable to stop herself from flinching away at the power in the voice. Sometimes it sounded like that of a child, soft and delicate. Other times, it sounded as though the eldest and most powerful queen to ever rule spoke to her. Now was one of the latter times. When Sada spoke, she was surprised to find her voice near to trembling.

"What else is there to eat?" she asked.

She touched the foal's leg again, but no voice tickled her mind. For that, she was grateful. Instead, she saw a single image floating in the blackness behind her eyes, only visible in flashes of color when she blinked. She closed her eyes and the image solidified: A four-eared rabbit sat in the tall grass, nose twitching and eyes wide. It looked strangely like Guyle, minus the suit and plus an extra pair of ears. It smelled of warmth and a hunger satisfied. She felt the warm gush of blood over her tongue as she looked at its quivering pink nose.

Sada's eyes flew open at the taste of blood. Saliva had filled her mouth. She hastily pulled away from Lady Blue and thoughts of soap-mouth and worms wriggling out of the rabbit's flesh instantly replaced the vision.

"I cannot eat a wild rabbit," Sada said hurriedly. "And neither can you! Horses eat grasses and grains. And in any case, I have no means to kill it."

As soon as the words escaped her lips, the filly had pressed her hoof against Sada's leg, and she saw another image. This one was of herself, or so she believed. Sada was hardly recognizable in the image the caelicorn showed her: the pictured lady was just a stiff carcass of skin loosely wrapped around jutting bones. She lay limp across grey tree roots. The vibrancy of her silken skirts was the only color in the image. Even most of her hair was gone, lying in clumps around her. Spun silk to be made into a fabric.

She had seen a similar image once before, only on a card made of bone and decorated with deep engravings. She and Gabriel had once had their fortunes read at a carnival in Westmere. The young, smiling woman had told Sada that she would soon come into great fortune. Yet when she had Gabriel pick from the cards, facedown and only showing their bleached backs, he had drawn three. She only remembered the final card, depicting a woman with pointed ears, lying dead in the forest and surrounded by dead animals. The fortune teller said that Gabe would fall in love, but he would surely die. Though the woman tried her best to scare them (and succeeded in doing so with Sada), Gabe had burst into laughter as soon as he'd left the tent.

Yet this vision…it spoke only of death, with no laughter to be had. It felt as though all the blood had drained from her body as she thought of herself withering up from starvation, left to be finished off by the wild things of these woods. Perhaps the troll the Pixie had led her to would gobble her up when she became too weak to crawl away. Maybe Groll would find her with that skillful nose of his, and finally be able to return to the old ways, using her as the first sacrifice.

Sada jerked away from the foal. Lady Blue just tucked her leg back into her side and looked at her with wide eyes. Now rather than seeming to be filled with wisdom, they showed the filly's true age. She was only a baby, perhaps weeks old at the most. Separated from her mother and left to follow Sada around aimlessly throughout the woods of Elves who seemed unwilling to show themselves. Lady Blue blinked those wide eyes, and suddenly they appeared to be brimming with tears. Sada hadn't thought horses able to cry. But then, she also hadn't thought it possible for them to be equipped with wings and a horn.

She had to look away from the pitiful sight to give her answer.

"I will not do it. We will grow sick," she said firmly. And yet her voice trembled.

She tried to lay down to sleep, but it felt like a pile of dirt was heaped within her belly. Steak was perhaps her favorite meal, but the thought of actually killing the animal herself…the illnesses she could contract…

No, that is not what upsets you so greatly, she realized. *Lady Blue licked your blood and ate bits of your flesh. You wanted to believe all she was doing was cleaning your wounds, but she enjoyed it. And now she wants more blood and flesh to soothe her hunger. Perhaps if you do not give it to her, she will take it from you.*

No unicorns, pegasi, or horse-creatures of any kind, no matter how fantastical they were, should eat meat. Sada looked at the filly beside her. She seemed to have fallen asleep. Sada lay her cloak over herself and squeezed her eyes shut, trying to do the same. Yet every time she did, she saw the image of herself wasted and dead. Or she thought of the caelicorn, muzzle dark with Sada's own blood, and smacking her lips to savor the taste.

Finally Sada descended into sleep, but her dreams were filled with terror. She would walk through a beautiful sunlit forest before suddenly collapsing. There she would lay, dying and wheezing for help. Lady Blue would come to rescue her, but when Sada reached out a hand, the filly only nuzzled beneath it and sunk her teeth into Sada's exposed ribs. She tore away chunks of flesh, dangling ribbons of silk and skin, before gulping it down. Sada watched as she was eaten to death by her only companion.

In her sleep, Sada shuddered as the filly took another bite.

THE SEVENTEENTH

Kartinar

The Elven king's dungeons were nicer than anywhere Kartinar and Drath had ever lived. Their chamber was nicer than the cells of their clan, nicer than the abandoned drifter tents and burrows they took over residence of, nicer even than their home in the mortal realm, of which Drath remembered nothing and Kartinar remembered little. But he remembered enough to know that it had not been comparable to this.

It was hardly a dungeon cell, but a small suite, with two cushioned beds stuffed with feathers (certainly not griffin feathers, but any feathers at all beat the living Void out of a grass mat or plain dirt) and blanketed with quilts sewn from the great tiche leaves of the Titian forest. He and Drath were sharing the space, but it was not cramped; Drath could probably lie down and fit three times between one wall and the other. There was no pool for bathing. They had yet to be afforded that privilege, and Kartinar assumed that it would be something communal they shared with other prisoners—if there were any. But there was a private latrine that was cleaned daily and a basin of water for washing their faces. There was even a barred window, though it only looked out between tree roots at ground level. It did offer a splendid view of passersby's feet, however.

Sometimes he and Drath spent their time trying to guess the person's race based on their feet alone. The fact that most Spiritkin went barefoot helped greatly, as skin tone was a great indicator of an Eltic person's race. Thus far they had seen the robes of seven priestesses, the tan feet of twenty-three Titians, the green feet of one Goblin, the hairy feet of one Dwarf, and the small, pale feet of either a Grandfleurian Elf child or an adult Faery. These were all their guesses, anyway. There was no way to be certain they were correct on the matter, or even that each similar-looking pair of feet didn't belong to the same person walking back and forth. But it was a fun enough game to pass the time. Sometimes Kartinar even tried to reach out and poke the passersby, but he'd only succeeded in lightly brushing the ankle of one unfortunate Titian man. They knew their guess of his race was correct because he'd immediately dropped down, put his tan, glaring face to the window, and cursed at them in the as Kartinar and Drath sniggered shamelessly.

Other than this, there was little to do to pass the time, and there was much time to pass. They had already been held for a long enough period that Kartinar had given up keeping track after the first two days, with no indicator as to when their imprisonment would end—or when their trial would occur. But at least they hadn't been separated. And at least the rooms were comfortable.

The dungeons were so hospitable because it was one of the Titian kings of old—one of the Titian kings of honor—who had designed them. This was in the days before they had grown to be haughty sons of Beasts, and were still as compassionate as their reputation claimed them to be. Today, the Elves of the Blooming and Verdant Vales still upheld that reputation for the Elves of the Wood, but the Titians made that task harder for them every day.

Kartinar was just thankful that Caprius hadn't pronounced a royal decree that the dungeons be redesigned to be less hospitable. It was likely that he simply hadn't visited a place as lowly as a dungeon, and so never had the chance to see how truly nice they were, or else he would have remedied their state. For Kindreds' sakes, Kartinar and his brother were fed better here than they had been since living with the clan!

Servants brought in large meals in the morning and at night, and smaller meals in between. They didn't speak, or look at them other than to glare, but Kartinar didn't much care. He'd tried getting answers out of one blonde woman who looked less glaringly at him than the others, but she'd threatened to take his meal if he continued talking, and so he'd opted for silence henceforth. Drath was eating his meal now, one of spiced bread, various fruits and vegetables, and some fluffy grain Kartinar had never seen before. Kartinar had given his brother his own share, too. He'd said it was because he wasn't hungry, but he knew within the privacy of his own mind that it was really because he felt he didn't deserve it.

"Why do thee look so down for?" Drath asked him around a mouthful of the grains. He'd split open a gourd-like fruit and dribbled the juice on them, and Kartinar couldn't help but grimace at the mess of slop he'd created and was eagerly devouring.

"Apologies if I'm somewhat sullen over the fact that we've been imprisoned by some of the least loved Spiritkin in Elt," Kartinar grumbled.

Do not direct your guilt toward your own brother, he chided himself. But it didn't matter. The frustration remained.

"At least it weren't the Blood Elves who took us hostage."

That did absolutely nothing to improve his mood. How could Drath speak of those creatures so lightly?

"Wasn't," Kartinar corrected sharply.

"What?"

"'At least it *'wasn't,'* not 'weren't.' How many times must I remind you? The fairfolk shall never take us seriously if we speak like—ah, to the Void with it, never mind. We're in the royal dungeons now; what in *Torteuir* does it matter anymore how seriously the cursed fairfolk regard us?" He laughed hysterically, shaking his head.

Drath rolled his eyes. "Spirits above, ease up Karti. That old fart of a drifter told us the sorcerer's light would cause enough of an impact to get Amogasanes the Strange's attention, didn't he?"

From the Valley of Kings to the Border towns, and beyond even that, he'd said. But Kartinar didn't wish to repeat that message, which had felt so laced with dread when he'd heard it.

"Indeed."

"Then there art nothin' to go on worryin' about, now is there?"

"Pardon, brother, but I don't take your meaning," Kartinar grumbled, still stormy.

"Well, I don't wanna be cocky. That ought to bring me bad luck. But all I'm sayin' is that even if Master Amogasanes doesn't want me as his apprentice, he still ought to come down here and at least *investigate* a potential student, oughtn't he? I mean, thou said the old man thinks he might be lookin' for one." Drath shoveled his last bite of mush into his huge mouth. He'd finished both their meals within perhaps five minutes.

Even being his brother, Kartinar still found himself amazed at how truly large Drath was. From his bear-like hands to his Orc-like stature. Even knowing they were born of the same parents, Kartinar still sometimes wondered if perhaps the Spiritkin were right in naming him half-Giant, or quarter-Giant, or any amount of Giant. The man was enormous, by all rights. It was a wonder he'd been called to the art of sorcery, instead of something more fitting, like smithing. Not that the craft existed in the Valley. And the Border smiths were sorry imitations of the true metalworkers. Had Drath been raised in the Orc tribes or the Dwarves' mountains, perhaps he would have found himself called to the anvil. As it was, they would never know.

And as it was, his brother's love of sorcery had led to their imprisonment. *That's unfair,* he reminded himself, because it was really Kartinar's love for his brother that had led to them being here. It was a stupid plan. He truly did hope that what Drath believed was correct, and the master sorcerer Amogasanes would investigate the potential of a new apprentice and come to rescue at least Drath, if not the both of them. Kartinar knew the man held incredible sway over the kingdoms of Elt, and believed that he would be able to convince Caprius to release them if he so desired. But hearing the way Drath spoke of him, calling him *Master* Amogasanes, believing so whole-heartedly in this man he'd never met—

(and not in his brother, who is right in front of him, who has never let him down)

—enraged him much more than it should.

"And what if your precious little sorcerer does not come to your rescue, what then, Drath? Hmm? What shall you do if the great Amogasanes fails to appear? Or better still, if he arrives only to discover that you are but a mere human, forbidden by law itself to practice his craft? What then?"

Drath's patience truly deserved applause. He simply set aside his plate and held Kartinar's gaze, dull and calm against bright and irate. He swished water around his mouth. He picked some food out of his teeth. All the while Kartinar glared at him, for no good reason, he knew, yet he glared anyway. It felt good to be angry. Because at least it wasn't guilt. At least it wasn't fear.

Finally Drath took a deep breath and let it out. "Firstly, it's *we.*"

"What?"

"If my 'precious little sorcerer' doesn't come to *our* rescue; what will *we* do then? I ain't leavin' without thee, Karti." Drath leveled his gaze at him, but Kartinar just scoffed and turned away, looking at the wall of wood where a door would appear when it was time for either their next meal, a latrine cleaning, a bath (finally) or for their trial. It was a roulette of the door.

"I mean it. We're brothers. And secondly, sorcery is basically illegal for everyone. No one in Elt condones it except those who practice it. Not even the Spiritkin with no magick for themselves like sorcery. So it oughtn't matter on that front. And thirdly, I don't know what *we'll* do if Master Amogasanes decides he doesn't want nothin' to do with me. I guess you'll figure it out then, won't you? You always do, that's how we made it so long."

"I'll figure it out?" Kartinar asked. That was a splendid idea, considering him "figuring it out" had landed them here.

"In case thee haven't noticed these past, oh, twenty-three years, that's how it works. You figure and steal, I break things and make potions from the recipes in the dusty old diaries of dusty old sorcerers." Drath stood with a pop of his knees. He crossed the room and Kartinar watched him warily. His brother sat down beside him, knees popping again. "If it weren't for you, *Om' Modir* might never have taken us in—"

Kartinar scoffed. "Spare me. She would have taken in even an Orcen child without a second thought, had it appeared at her door motherless and hungry."

Drath grinned at him. "Mayhap thee have the right of that one. But, mayhap you don't. And regardless, what would've happened to me after the raiding if thee hadn't taken us to the Border? If you hadn't gone out looting that first day, or convinced me to come later, when I could count more years?"

"I speculate we would have been prisoners to death rather than the Kid King," Kartinar muttered. But the anger was quickly fading.

"Jiie. See? Your thinker is still thinkin', you'll be able to figure us up a plan if the old sorcerer can't."

Kartinar sighed, leaning back against the wall of their cell. The wood was cool against his head. He hoped their guards would allow them access to the pool soon; his hair was growing incredibly greasy, and incredibly itchy. And perhaps while they were bathing, Kartinar would be able to find a way to escape, or a guard to bribe. He chose not to think about the fact that they were moneyless. Some people were stupid enough to bribe simply with the promise of money.

"I do hope he is more to you than just some old sorcerer, given that seeking his attention is the very reason we now find ourselves imprisoned," Kartinar said.

Drath's face fell. "I'm really sorry about that, Karti. Is that really the only reason you agreed to it?"

"No, no," Kartinar immediately said, facing his brother. Concern shone dark in Drath's eyes. He shouldn't have brought that up. "I told you, it was all for the gems. And in any case, it's not thee's fault. Had we not wandered into the leaf-lovers' forest, all would've been well…perhaps even then we might have managed, if not for that girl…"

"No, it ain't her fault," Drath said sternly. "Don't go draggin' little Sada into this, not now and sure as the Void not durin' our trial. It was *us* who dragged *her* into this—literally. And thee knows it."

"Yeah, you're right. And I won't."

There was no sound as a door was opened in the wall to their left, but Kartinar saw the movement out of the corner of his eye as the wood began to expand and contract and melt away. Kartinar snapped his head up, hitting it against the wall with a wince, and Drath followed suit—though he managed not to nearly concuss himself. They watched as a tall gap opened, revealing a Titian man and woman. The man had dozens of braids, marking him as a magick-Wielder, and a powerful one at that. Far too powerful to be merely a guard of the dungeon, even if it was a royal one. The woman wore only a few braids; Kartinar recognized her as one of the chambermaids. She dipped her head to the man and stepped out of sight.

The Wielder entered their cell.

"King Caprius has declared that your trial shall take place today," the man announced. "I had thought you may wish to bathe before presenting yourself before His Majesty."

"How incredibly generous of you," Kartinar muttered, but he stood. *They're still using that ridiculous human nickname for him?*

"You thought right," Drath said, heaving himself to his feet. "Thanks Elfie."

The Elf glowered. "Call me this, and you will find yourself with no bath today and no food for the remainder of your time spent here."

"Sorry, sorry," Drath said.

Kartinar just met the man's glare. He looked familiar, though Kartinar couldn't place how. His braids were dark, and he had two scars in the shape of an X across his nose. Those were what drew Kartinar's attention. Where did he know this Elf from? Then he saw the golden *haiséthra* on his bicep, and he knew. *Om' Modir* had told him of such a mark. It was a blood-mark in the shape of the Pyrtoxos sigil—a flaming bow and arrow—signifying he was a member of Caprius's Kingsguard, the Gilded Ones. And he was likely one of the archers that had been with Caprius when their group had been discovered.

He led Kartinar and Drath out of their cell and two women wearing only a few braids each immediately rushed in to clean it. Even being servants, they looked down on Kartinar as they passed. It wasn't that he was shorter than most Elven women, though that certainly helped them to do so—it was that they were immortal, and he was mortal. Even the immortal help was better than a mortal king. And Kartinar was far lesser than both of those. He was a mortal thief, a peasant—even worse than an animal, because at least they were beautiful. He was surprised the servants didn't spit on him. He wasn't certain he'd even be angry if they did.

As soon as they stepped out of their cell, they were in the common area. The dungeons were in the base of the Tree of Titian, the giant tiche that the entire city sprouted from, and which the royal family resided in. Kartinar had been through the dungeon commons once before when they'd first arrived, but his guard had had him doubled over (probably because he wouldn't shut the Void up) and he'd only seen the earthen floor. Now Kartinar was able to look up at the domed ceiling where all the roots making up the walls—each as thick as a house—sprouted from.

It was strange knowing that Caprius readied himself just a few hundred feet above them. Only a few floors separated him from the Elven king. Except where Kartinar would be bathing in cool, used water, Caprius would soak in a heated bath filled with oils and herbs and tinctures to make him not only look like royalty, but smell like it, too. Kartinar and Drath would dress in their dirty and tattered rough-spun cloth, and above them, Caprius would slip into never-before-worn silken pants, and maybe even a shirt if he decided the occasion was formal enough for one. Kartinar felt the grimace on his face, curling his lip. It couldn't be helped. The differences in their lifestyles were glaring and disgusting. He couldn't even imagine what he would do if he had the coffers of a king.

I'd start by payin' that cursed sorcerer to train Drath, is what I'd do. Then I'd hire an army to attack the Kindreds-cursed, spirits-cursed, Void-and-Torteuir-sentenced Blood Elves. He was nearly shaking with anger now, thinking of the Spiritkin who had ripped apart his life and spat on all that he loved. But they were all the way across Elt; there was nobody to be angry with except the figments of his thoughts. He clenched his fists and repeatedly hit at his thigh to distract himself.

"Karti, come on," Drath leaned down to whisper.

"Yeah," Kartinar said. He shot one final glare toward the ceiling.

Caprius's royal guardsman led them through the common space, which was floored with packed sand, and past a short table where more servants sat. These ones were folding towels. They looked up to glare at the brothers before returning to their work. They might think themselves better than him, but at least he found joy in his work. These Elves showed no emotion on their perfect faces, but he reckoned they thought themselves to be above the task. They certainly couldn't find joy in folding towels. And all Titians probably thought they deserved to be King or Queen Over the Elves of the Wood, in the secret spaces of their hearts.

There was little else by way of decoration in the common space, but Kartinar did see a few chairs. They were unoccupied, but on the end tables beside them were perfectly stacked tomes waiting to be read. Were they for the guards, the servants, or the prisoners? Kartinar thought it might be the latter. As strange as it was to think prisoners might be given reading material, the guards and servants surely had their own quarters and greater selections of tomes.

He'd seen many servants, but only a few guards. There had been none outside his and Drath's own cell, though that was probably because the marred Gilded One who now escorted them far outranked them, and they'd been dismissed when he'd arrived. He did see one guard posted across from their cell. The doors would not be formed until they were needed, but there were plaques with words of the seared into them spaced evenly along the walls, and he assumed they marked each cell.

The archer beside one such plaque stood stiffly, not moving even to shift his weight between his feet. His brown pants stirred around his ankles, but that was only because of the breeze sneaking in between the gaps in the roots above. Other than that he was motionless. He only blinked. Kartinar didn't understand why immortality came with the ability to remain motionless for extended periods of time. Perhaps they experienced time differently. Or perhaps it had nothing to do with their lifespan, and only to do with the inhumanity of their ancestors. That, he thought, was more likely.

The Gilded One walked before them with the grace of some animal, not a human. And when he stopped beside the pool, he waited silently for Kartinar and Drath to catch up. The pool was indeed in the very center of the common area, though Kartinar didn't believe it was to shame prisoners into submission. The old kings had been too kind for that, and if they were to make their prisoners comfortable within their cells and offer them tomes to read, they would be unlikely to humiliate them only when bathing. He thought it was more likely attributed to the fact that most Spiritkin, and certainly the Elves, were simply not ashamed of nakedness. It was evident in the minimal clothing they wore, and it was evident in this public bathing area. It was likely that Kartinar and Drath were the only prisoners who would find anything strange in the concept.

And yet, strange they found it. Kartinar shared a glance with his brother as they beheld the pool. It was not only public, but plain and wrought of stone, and did indeed look cold. Their guard seemed not to notice their apprehension, and ordered them to strip.

"I shall be close by in case you take it within your head to orchestrate some sort of escape."

"Aw, don't worry, we won't cause trouble for you. Wouldn't want thou to hafta mess up those pretty braids of yours."

"That would be quite alright by me, for I could do with a bit of excitement," the Wielder said. "I only ask that you refrain from taking any of the women hostage and, if you must attempt an escape, that you do so while not entirely unclothed."

"Not entirely unclothed?" Kartinar asked, pulling off his shirt. It was so weighed down by dirt and sweat that it clung to him like a sad lover. "I'd been under the impression that your people celebrate nudity."

The Gilded One laughed, revealing canines that were just a little sharper than they ought to be. "I do not wish to celebrate *your* nudity, mortal. And certainly not whilst I am wrestling you to the ground."

The servants within earshot sniggered at that, and Kartinar offered them all glares. Even Drath was chuckling.

"Now disrobe," the Elf ordered. He retreated a few steps, but he did not turn away.

"What, do you plan to stand there and observe?" Kartinar asked. "Did you mean you'll only celebrate my nudity with your eyes?"

"I didn't think you Elves were into that," Drath added.

The guard let out a long-suffering sigh. "Someone must keep you in their sights. And I shall not force the poor women to endure such a burden. *Now,* disrobe."

"Hey, thou ought to tell us your name before we get naked for you," Drath said.

"You truly make demands? You ought to recognize this bath as the courtesy it is, human. Should you wish to behave as unruly as a hippogryph, I can very well escort you to the throne room as you stand, though I would most earnestly advise against such folly."

"Fine," Kartinar said.

"You goin' first?" Drath asked.

"Sure."

Kartinar undressed and went into the pool. It was shallow; he could stand flat-footed and only his shoulders were submerged. Drath would have a harder time bathing in here. The Elves had left out soap pearls and he used them on his hair and skin. He had planned to wash his own clothes with them as well, but once he'd taken them off, a single-braided servant had silently appeared to take them away. She left Elven clothes in their place. Typically, Kartinar would have found reason to be upset by this. But even he had to admit, his clothes were disgustingly filthy. It would be a favor to everyone, including himself and Drath, to just accept the sharp-ears' clothes.

Kartinar toweled off while Drath bathed. Though a prisoner, he was given a towel made of loomfly silk—even if it was of the rough variety—rather than quilted leaves. Yet another remnant of the Elves of old and their respect toward all people. Then he dressed in the brown pants and shirt he had been provided. The clothes were in the same style that the Elven men wore, opaque around the hips and growing more sheer as they went down.

Most Elven men opted not to wear any shirts at all, but Kartinar was thankful he had been given one. He didn't know if he'd enjoy being bare-chested in a world of humans, but surrounded by immortals with nary a physical imperfection, going without a shirt was not a torture he wished to subject himself to. Even if it was entirely sheer. Seeing it on Drath's huge frame made Kartinar burst out laughing, and even the Gilded One had to try and hide a smile.

"You look rather like a Giant attempting to masquerade as a Faery," Kartinar said.

Drath elbowed him so hard he nearly fell into the pool. "I'll hear none of it. At least it ain't covered in dirt."

"It might have been all the better if it were," Kartinar said, still grinning. He dodged Drath's next swing.

"Come, mortals, King Caprius awaits you," the archer said. That sobered Kartinar, and he walked silently alongside his brother as they were led toward the trial that would decide their fate. "You may call me Boonlord Agathon," their guard said as they walked.

"I think I'll stick with *Vo* Agathon if it's all the same to you," Drath said.

At the same time, Kartinar said, "Agathon? That's rather short for an Elven name."

"I must entreat you to use the proper titles when addressing my people whilst you remain within our kingdom. It may not earn you favor, but it shall certainly help in sparing you from punishment. If you will not name me Boonlord, then use the title 'Syr.' As for my full name, I have no reason to even speak it—for we both know that you will be unable to remember it, let alone pronounce it."

"That's the cursed truth if I ever heard it," Drath grunted.

"You may have the right of it," Kartinar agreed.

All Elven names were long and full of vowels. He'd heard it was because they each had a specific meaning that couldn't be expressed in less than four or five syllables. He thought the Elven tongue was just more complicated than it had any right to be. He liked the way the Trolls named their young: all one-, maybe two-syllable words. Each generation began with a certain letter: Kartinar had been of an age with the K-generation, and Drath with the D-generation, which was why they had been named as such. It was nice and orderly, as all things were with the Trolls.

Kartinar's true name was Karti, as Drath called him. But as a teenager, he had determined to make himself worthy of the fairfolk's respect, and had demanded he be addressed by a name more similar to their own. As an adult, he regretted ever disrespecting *Om' Modir* and his Trell mother by refusing the name they'd chosen for him, but it was too late to change that now. Still, thinking of the Trolls made his heart constrict.

If this works, I'll be able to avenge them.

That was enough to steel his nerves as he and his brother were led to face King Caprius.

Caprius

The King Over the Elves of the Wood paced at the head of the throne room, stalking back and forth beneath the empty throne that hung suspended from the ceiling by the roots it grew from. Created from one defining element of each of the Seven Central Kingdoms—wood from his, sand from Mar Belleza, gold from Gizletras, bone from Nyphtos—it was supposed to remind them of the importance of their unity, and their compatibility. *If even one aspect is removed, the entire throne crumbles,* Woia would say. But without the Druid queen there to remind him of this, and without the other royals of Elt to murmur their agreement, it simply looked stupid.

Caprius flicked his long, golden cape dramatically as he spun on his heel; occasions like these were the only times he would cover his body with so much heavy fabric. Though the spun loomfly silk could hardly be called weighty, it still felt restricting. As did the amber shirt he wore beneath it. Everything was heavy compared to air. He preferred feeling Elt's breath on his skin. Being separated from it made him feel disconnected. He rolled his shoulders and plucked at his collar, trying to make the fabric fall more naturally. It was no good, it still felt just as disgusting on his skin. He needed a distraction.

"Servant!" he called, snapping. "Bring me a scrysi."

One of the women waiting along the wall immediately went to do so. She returned with a rather small one, only as large as his torso, but it would have to do. He bid her to hold it up so that he could look into it. A scrysi was a frame of wood or stone or some other material—this one was of gold, of course—with a sheet of water suspended within it by magick. When one looked into it, they could see their own reflection, like bending over a puddle. It was quite a marvelous invention. One of the only human ideas that the Spiritkin had chosen to retain, though they had improved upon the mortals' design, of course.

As Caprius waited for his prisoners to arrive for their trial, he looked into the scrysi, admiring his reflection. It was wonderful, of course. None would deny it. He adjusted his crown so that it sat just behind his frontmost braids. Typically, he wore them loose, but for the occasion he'd had one of the servants tie back the top half. They had insisted he leave a couple of braids out to frame his face, and he admitted, if only to himself, they had been right on that front. It looked very elegant; very kingly. And it displayed the length of his hair, and therefore his power.

It was very good indeed. He could not wait to see the faces of the mortal brothers when they beheld him, their judge, captor, and potential executioner. He almost wished his council would be here to witness their trial. The old Spiritkin had certainly vied to be included, but Caprius knew that they only wished to meddle, not observe. They were too used to his father's rule, too set in their ways, the old ways. He really ought to replace them.

They were ancient and therefore wise, and yet they also viewed him as too youthful to rule. He knew that half of them would have voted to rule in his stead if the choice were theirs. He was lucky they held to the law so strictly, and that the laws of the monarchy clearly stated that Caprius, as the late King Aphredys's only eligible heir, inherit the throne immediately upon his father's death. And so, he had—and so, the council members could go on whining and mumbling about his age. Though if they kept at it, he might order them removed from his council. Or their heads from their bodies.

That notion was amusing, but he knew he could never do such. He thought he could fight in battle if the need arose, and certainly he was skilled with his bow—it was what he was known for across Elt—but killing someone in cold blood was different. As much as he desired to do it when he grew angry, he knew he would never release the arrow he held at the ready in his mind. He did not agree with his father that a good king was temperate—passion was necessary for all things, most of all rule—but he did hold to the belief that a king should not murder unnecessarily. He would be no better than the Orcs or the Blood Elves if he did.

Filthy creatures.

"They have arrived, my king," his herald announced from the entrance to the throne room.

Speaking of filthy creatures, Caprius thought, grinning.

"Send them in," he called, dismissing the servant and the scrysi as he strode purposefully toward his throne.

Now this…this was a throne, not the one hanging above him. It was large and crafted of the Tree's roots, brought up through the trunk and woven into a seat for the first King Over the Elves of the Wood. At some point, the throne had been gilded, and sigils had been carved into the gold, as had been done throughout the throne room. When Caprius had taken it up as his seat, he had ordered antlers to be formed from the wall behind it. Now, when subjects or visitors or prisoners like the ones he now received looked upon his throne, they looked upon antlers as tall as the room itself crowning him, twin to the crown upon his head.

"And herald," Caprius said, sitting. "Address me as 'Your Majesty.' I have told you, things shall be different under my rule—unlike the reigns of those who came before. Therefore, I myself must be different. My predecessors were merely kings. I tell you now, herald, I am not just a king, I am not just royal; I am majesty."

At his signal, the herald placed his hands on the wall Caprius sat across from. Now it was just a muraled wall depicting old kings and the battles they had fought in. There was no discernable entrance because there was no entrance at all. Then at a touch from the herald an outline began to form, splitting apart the faces of past monarchs and their fearsome caelicorn steeds. Caprius watched as his father's wooden face began to ripple and melt, and the wall split apart to form an opening.

Caprius grinned at his prisoners.

Kartinar

"Enter, mortals," King Caprius called.

Kartinar looked once more to Agathon as he went in. The royal archer dipped his head almost imperceptibly before retreating. The brothers entered the throne room.

It was in the center of the Tree of Titian, and so it was huge, and it was circular. It was also tall. Murals, brought out of the wooden walls of the tree with magick, could be found on every surface of the lower halves of the walls. Kartinar was surrounded by beautiful and intricate depictions of the Elves of the Wood's history. There were sharp-eared kings, mostly, but some had their wives at their side. One wall depicted a meeting between each of the monarchs in Elt, displaying more peace than a true meeting between the royals could hope to boast.

Above the murals were tall windows formed in the tree by Wielders. They followed the trunk's natural curvature and appeared to twist in some areas, lean in at others, and lean away in others, still. Extremely sheer sheets of golden silk had also been hung between the frames, giving the illusion there was stained glass there, though Kartinar knew the Elves didn't believe in making such a material. The made it so that light was allowed in, but an orange glow was given to it.

The brothers walked through puddles of it on a floor blanketed by a huge, wine-colored rug sewn from various types of silk and down feathers. It was soft beneath Kartinar's bare feet, and he couldn't help but think of how he trod on more money than he would ever hope to own. Just one swatch from just one of Caprius's rugs would sell for enough to keep food in his and Drath's mouths for the rest of their lives. And yet they walked across it as though it was merely dirt.

Peeking out from beneath the borders of the rug were the great rings of the Titian Tree, marking its centuries-old age. Kartinar knew it had housed nearly all the generations of royalty for the Elves of the Wood. He wondered if the sorcerer's light would affect the great tree. He hoped it didn't, if the orb and its effects turned out to be something malevolent. The Tree was too beautiful to be destroyed.

Also bordering the great room were servants, clinging to the walls like the murals. The only reason he knew they were servants was because they stood as far out of sight as possible, and their eyes were always on the master servant, whose eyes were on the king, always awaiting orders. Were he to look only at their clothes, he would have thought them nobility.

They wore the fine, colorful silks of the rich Elves, not the rough spun clothing of servants. Kartinar also noted that none of them even had the limp ears of common Elves, but the tall ears of nobility. It made his upper lip twitch, wishing to curl. It wasn't the servitude that disgusted him, he knew the servants were paid well. It was the fact that Caprius held so much power he employed nobility—however distant down the line they were—as his servants. So far as he knew, all Titians believed themselves to be above all others, but not even the common-born Titians could hope to serve the king.

Beast spawn, Kartinar thought as he stalked toward Caprius. He was lounging in his chair like a cat, already smirking. And his crown was already slipping down over his pointed ears. He was wearing a full wardrobe today, as Kartinar had suspected. As were the members of his Kingsguard. All in amber and gold, the colors of the kingdom.

The Elves stood in a V-shaped formation, beginning at the engraved steps leading up to the throne's dais and fanning out from there. There were nine Gilded Ones of the Kingsguard, three masters for each of the three classes of Boon-Wielders, with the king himself making up the ninth.

Kartinar had come to know that numbers had great significance when it came to the Spiritkin and their magick.

The powers of some were obvious: one guard with dark blonde braids stood within a beam of sunlight so brilliant that it made his entire body look as though it was encased in gold. Then Kartinar looked up and saw that the beam did not fall as light should, but was bending at an angle to get to him. The nature of others' abilities was not so obvious. But the magnitude of their magick was—each of the men wore countless braids, setting them apart as some of the most powerful magick-users in the realm. And all their eyes were on Kartinar and his brother. It raised gooseflesh on his arms. Once he had wanted to be one of them. Not a member of Caprius's Kingsguard, but a magick-user. A Wielder. Then he had grown to despise them for possessing what he could not simply because he was human.

And now, standing before them, he feared them.

He hadn't realized how truly powerful a master Wielder was. But now, though none of them even used their powers, he could sense it. Even to his human senses, it was palpable in the air, like the tension between enemies, the static before a storm, the fear that came when you messed up and you knew your mother knew, and you were waiting for her to deliver her punishment. Kartinar tried to avoid their stares, but they followed him until he stopped before them, just feet away from the outermost Gilded Ones.

And despite his hatred toward Caprius, despite the fact that he respected a random elk more than the arrogant young king, Kartinar did not have to be told to kneel. Because he didn't want to give any of those Wielders, including the one on the throne, a reason to use their magick against him.

He dropped to one knee and hung his head. Staring at the wine-red carpet, he heard Drath do the same.

"Very good," Caprius said. He spoke like they were puppies who had just managed to sit when asked. "I had not thought you would comply so swiftly, least of all you, little man."

Kartinar ground his teeth together, hating the noise but hating the sound of Caprius's voice more, and said nothing.

"Very well, you may rise," Caprius said. They did. "Must you wear the garb of my people? First, you trespass upon my lands, and now you seek to claim our style of dress as well? Is there no end to human greed?"

Kartinar clenched his jaw to keep from retorting that the clothing had been given to him against his will, and that no person or people could simply own an entire style of it, either. It was just a combination of silk; there was nothing special or holy about it. Given the same materials as the Elf who had invented the style, anyone else could have designed the same style of garment. Why should the Elves lay claim to it simply because they had done it first, or made it the most popular?

But the king would not listen on that front. He seemed to think that some people, some Spiritkin races, were inherently deserving of certain things while others were not. Certainly, humans were deserving of none of it. Kartinar looked past the eight Wielders to meet the king's stare, hoping stupidly that Caprius would see the hatred in his. The orange of the king's eyes was obvious even from the distance.

"Well, what calls you here today?" Caprius said. "Ahh, I jest, merely jesting. What is this, not a word to say? You were so eager to talk but a day or two ago."

"Speaking out of turn did me no favors then. I've since learned my lesson," Kartinar said. *And it was much longer than a day or two.*

"Oh?" Caprius asked. "And what, pray, does that mean to you?"

Kartinar ground his teeth again, hating the enjoyment in the king's eyes. "It means I shall speak only when asked or commanded to do so." He could see Drath looking at him from the corner of his eye, monitoring him.

Don't worry, Drath, I won't screw this up for us, Kartinar thought bitterly.

Caprius was grinning his insolent grin. "I cannot say whether I am glad or disappointed. It certainly made for quite the spectacle, watching my men deal with your insolence. Wouldn't you agree, *andrótes?"*

The eight members of the guard nodded. Some muttered agreement. A few nearest to Kartinar and Drath—those with the most magick, the most power—chuckled or grinned. At the back of the V, standing beside the dais, Kartinar saw a familiar face smirking. Agathon, the man with the scars. How he had gotten from the entrance to the throne room and into formation without Kartinar noticing, he did not know. Kartinar caught his eye and scowled. Agathon betrayed no emotion.

A fine performer, he thought bitterly. *Pretending to do us favors offering us baths and fresh clothing, even a name. And now, smiling fondly at the memory of my punishments.* They had not been serious punishments, only a twist of his arm here and an elbow to the ribs there. But the Elves were strong, even if they didn't intend to be, and the bruises were still fading, even now.

"Well." Caprius clapped his hands. "I suppose we could while away the entire afternoon trading jests, but that would pale in comparison to the amusement I have planned for us! Shall we begin, then? My council wished to attend and offer their insight into your story and sentence, but I decided their input to be rather unnecessary. They are old, but age alone does not make one wise, does it? I thought a…fresher opinion would be more preferable, considering this will be a fresher age for my kingdom. What do you say, boys?"

Boys.

Despite being called the Kid King, Caprius was decades older than both Kartinar and Drath. Yet he looked like the only boy in the room, with his bare face, light voice, and a countenance which altered between pouting and grinning as quickly as a flame was relit or blown out. Kartinar just smiled a tight-lipped smile. It was the best he could offer the Elven king.

"As you say, Your Majesty," Kartinar said.

"Let me see…how ought we proceed? My father never held trials; to speak plainly, I am not sure the man ever bothered with prisoners at all. But as I said, this is a new age for the Kingdom of the Wood. So, how shall we begin? I suppose I should start by informing you of the crimes for which you are being held."

"A fine idea, Your Majesty," Kartinar said.

"Very fine," Drath echoed.

Caprius narrowed his eyes. "If this is mockery, be warned, I shall tolerate none of it."

"'Tis not anything of the sort, Your Majesty. I apologize if something I said imp—"

Caprius waved one hand, adjusting his crown with the other. "Never you mind, never you mind. Just control that tongue of yours, youngling."

"Yes, Your Majest—"

"*V'* Drath of Samuel blood, *V'* Kartinar of Joseph blood," the king began, raising his voice much more than was necessary. Then he paused, frowning. "I had thought you to be brothers, yet you are of different bloodlines? Another falsehood?"

Kartinar exchanged a glance with Drath. His brother looked ridiculously calm standing there, tapping a rhythm out on his leg. He looked so calm it was as though he wasn't entirely certain where they were or what they were doing. That was fine, it was better if Kartinar acted as delegate.

"No, Your Majesty, I beg pardon for the confusion. Joseph and Samuel were the names given to us by our human parents. In the clan, we were known by the names we now bear. As for our surname, I fear I have long since forgotten it," Kartinar said warily.

"Sir-name? What is this thing? You were once knights?"

"Apologies, Your Majesty. That is what humans call the name of their bloodline."

"Ah, intriguing, you mean to say your bloodname. You have none?"

"None that I recall," Kartinar admitted. "Though we certainly had one once, I have long forgotten it. However, we were raised by the Stonefoot clan. Perhaps that may serve as a stand-in."

Caprius began to summon bright flames to his fingertips, then dismiss them as soon as they formed. He went on like this for a few moments, appearing to think. "I do not entirely trust your word on the matter of your…Trell associations, but it matters not—I have a fair idea." He straightened, smiling.

"*V'* Drath and *V'* Kartinar of red blood, you stand accused of the following crimes: violating the treaty between mankind and Spiritkin through your use of the portal between our realms, the Seam; trespassing in Elt, and specifically in the forests of Titian, which lie within the borders of the Kingdom of the Wood; stealing a sorcerer's light from a citizen of Elt; your self-confessed thievery elsewhere; and attempting to deceive me, Caprius 'the Drake' of Pyrtoxos blood, Guardian of the Seam and King Over the Elves of the Wood."

Kartinar and Drath shared a glance. *Are half of those even laws?* that glance asked. *Is it illegal to lie to a king? And when did humans sign a treaty with the Spiritkin?*

Despite the circumstances, Kartinar had to try his best to reign in a grin. Seeing his own bafflement reflected on his brother's face was too much to handle. He prayed Caprius wouldn't notice as he looked back to the king.

"Well? Do you admit your guilt in these matters?" Caprius inquired.

"Your Majesty," Kartinar began, "I am unfamiliar with the laws of your kingdom—"

"Ah, so you admit guilt in the final charge, then, do you not? You and your brother claimed to be residents of Elt; should you not be well-versed in its laws?"

"Pardon, but my brother and I—"

"Pardon, *Your Majesty,"* Caprius corrected sharply.

Kartinar took a deep breath, clenched his fists and released them. "Pardon, Your Majesty, but my brother and I were raised by a Troll clan. We have not claimed to have lived in any of the fairfolk kingdoms."

"Trolls, certainly. You say, then, that you have never set foot in my kingdom? You say that you have never paid visit to the Gilded Streets in Titian?"

"Well, perhaps we visited the market once, but—"

"Ah!" Caprius clapped. "Then you ought to have taken the time to acquaint yourself with the laws of Titian, should you not?"

"For but one trip to the market?" Kartinar exclaimed.

The Gilded Streets were home to the second-largest market in Elt, and of course it happened to be in Titian and controlled by the Elves of the Wood, and therefore Caprius. Kartinar wasn't certain there was a single Spiritkin who hadn't visited the market, but he *was* certain that there were Spiritkin who didn't have Caprius's laws written on the insides of their eyelids. He didn't see all of them on trial around him.

"Karti," Drath hissed.

Kartinar clenched his fists to keep himself from speaking further, but he knew he'd already spoken out of turn. Caprius's eyes glinted. Whether it was with anger or delight, he could not be certain.

"Careful, mortal. I thought you had claimed to have learned to leash your tongue, did you not? If you have not, I have eight Wielders at the ready to leash it for you, in one manner or another."

The Gilded Ones closest to Kartinar grinned. He tried not to look at the eagerness that was bright in their eyes.

"You have my apologies, Your Majesty."

"Hmm. Regardless, you need not know my laws to tell me if you are guilty of the charges, youngling."

Kartinar tried not to let his disdain of the name show. "If I were to admit to my possible guilt, I presume my brother and I would remain imprisoned?"

"Something of that nature," Caprius replied.

"And if I claim to be innocent…?"

The king sighed. "Should you choose to tread such a fruitless path, you will be required to provide evidence of your innocence."

Then he was right in that it was fruitless. What ways did he have to prove his innocence with no witness but his accomplice? Even if another person had been present at the various events they were on trial for, he saw no way to hunt them down. And then even if he managed that, he had no reason to believe a Spiritkin of any kind would testify on behalf of a human, especially if it would cast them into disfavor in the King of the Wood's eyes. Regardless, Kartinar saw claiming innocence as his only option. He would not falsely declare guilt.

"I only ask, Your Majesty, because I have yet to hear mention of a treaty between my people and yours."

Caprius shrugged, toying idly with his crown, his expression one of boredom. "That is no fault of mine. Careful, boy, your eyes betray your insolence."

Kartinar tried to calm the ire he felt, or at least keep it from his eyes, but it did him no good. How could he claim innocence or guilt in regard to a law that he wasn't even certain existed? And spirits be cursed if he thought the king was going to walk him through a history lesson to explain to him the origins of the supposed treaty, what it entailed, and whether it had an expiration date.

"Well, what shall it be? My boredom grows with every passing second I spend watching you attempt to think." Caprius chuckled.

Kartinar eyed the king. If he declared himself and his brother as guilty, he was potentially sentencing the both of them to a lifetime of imprisonment at best, and death at the worst. He doubted they would find themselves lucky enough to be exiled back to their own world. That idea was laughable. But if he claimed innocence, he would be forced to provide evidence that was un-procurable. How did he prove his honesty, or the fact that the sorcerer's light was traded, not stolen? He looked to Drath. His brother was looking at him not with fear, not with resignation, but with…hope? Confidence? He looked like a man who knew his older brother would talk them out of a messy situation, as he'd been able to do for their entire lives leading up to this point.

I don't know if it'll work this time, but I sure as the Void am gonna try, Kartinar thought. He hoped Drath could read it in his face.

He faced the king again.

"King Caprius, I profess my innocence in all crimes save for two: trespassing in the forests of Titian and the aforementioned thievery. And I profess my brother's innocence in all crimes save for the former."

King Caprius's orange eyes darkened, and he thought he saw pale smoke drift out of his nostrils. Several of the Gilded Ones smirked.

"Foolish mortal," Caprius growled. "Now you must prove your innocence on all relevant accounts. Are you prepared to do this?"

Kartinar leveled his stare at the king. "Indeed, I am."

THE EIGHTEENTH

Sada

Sada awoke with a beam of warmth on her cheek, and smiled at the pure bliss of it. The air was cool and fresh, and smelled of living things and morning dew. Curled up at her back was her friend and companion, keeping her warm, and—

Sada suddenly jolted upright, scaring away the hedgehog that had been cuddled into her belly on the opposite side. Around her, the other animals of the wood followed suit, a family of mice squeaking noisily as they left. Lady Blue only blinked bleary eyes at Sada, and whickered a sleepy greeting. Sada smiled back, but despite herself, she felt her hands checking for injuries given to her in the night. There was only the soreness in her shoulders and the subtle rise of those scars on her ribs.

The ones that she healed for you, she reminded herself coldly. *Yet at the same time…how much flesh is gone because she ate it?*

She had been plagued by nightmares of the filly transforming into some horrible Beast the past couple of nights. She always awoke in a panic, as she sometimes had at home when she realized she had slept too late, or had accidentally fallen asleep during the day and could therefore expect a haranguing and perhaps even a switching to look forward to. There was nobody to yell at her or switch her here, yet still her heart beat madly in her chest and her hands shook. She had to take a few moments to remind herself it had only been a dream before she was somewhat calm again.

When Sada had stood, tightened her corset (something she was becoming very adept at doing herself) and began walking, Lady Blue whickered again and bumped her nose against Sada in her traditional greeting. And seeing the filly greet her so giddily before running off, fanning her wings and kicking the air, she felt shame color her face. How could she be afraid of this little creature, who found so much joy in pulling up grass and spitting it out, or catching sunbeams on the undersides of her wings and flashing them at Sada?

She knew the caelicorn was right in the meaning behind her message. Sada was growing weaker every day she didn't eat true food, and in a forest full of creatures that could kill her even if they *weren't* magickal and immortal…It would be stupid to forfeit her survival out of fear. Fruit wouldn't sustain her for long. And not only that, but now her heart ached with a painful mixture of guilt and sympathy for the little filly. If Sada was hungry, how hungry must she, a growing filly, be?

Now she called Lady Blue back to her with two sharp whistles—one low and one high. Whistling was a skill Sada had finally picked up as she traveled. Lady Blue immediately burst forth from a blackberry bush, leaves scattering in her wake.

"Don't play in those, you'll get scratched by the thorns!" Sada fretted.

But running her hands over her long coat, she found no wounds. That fur of hers was extraordinarily thick. She took a deep breath, then knelt so she was eye-level with Lady Blue. The filly stretched out and lipped Sada's nose, making her draw back in laughter.

"Stop that, I'm serious. I'm going to hunt now. I'll bring you back something to eat, okay? You won't have to be hungry while I gorge myself on fruit and pastries anymore."

She grinned as the filly nodded her head enthusiastically. As she stood, she felt gratitude, strong and deep, take root in her heart. It was what stopped her from changing her mind.

"Stay here," Sada said to Lady Blue. The caelicorn just whickered at her back as she turned to find something to kill.

Recalling how the other animals seemed to hide in the caelicorn's presence, Sada put some distance between herself and the foal before she began to truly look for any animals. She had also left her cloak with her friend: If she was to hunt, she'd need to be quiet, and the less flowing fabric on her, the better. The lords Gabriel escorted on hunts were anything *but* quiet, with their drunken laughter and clanking armor—armor that was never used for more than decoration. And that was why they hardly returned with any game unless Gabe or John shot it themselves, or tied up the buck so the lords could slay it. Sada would be like her knights, not the lords who pretended at hunting to soothe their egos. She wanted—needed—to be successful.

Even without the extra belongings making noise, her boots still snapped every twig and crunched each leaf they stepped on. So she stopped to unlace them and left them sitting on a big tree root to be retrieved on her way back. The long grass was soft between her toes, and the thick moss cushioned her footfalls; she was nearly silent without the boots, if she avoided the leaves.

This must be why the Elves walk around barefoot, she realized as she stepped soundlessly over roots and rocks. But she still wasn't as quiet as the Spiritkin, and her gown snagged on the bushes she passed, seeming to rustle the entire forest. After a few minutes of adjusting and readjusting her posture and gait, she finally settled into a half-crouch that she found to be the least disruptive and continued forward with more confidence.

And with excitement.

As a girl, she'd always wanted to accompany Gabe in his training, whether it was for sword fighting and archery, or hunting and sparring. As she'd grown older, those dreams had faded as she kindled her interest in singing and piano. But now the excitement she'd felt at imagining the thrill of the hunt and of sparring returned to her as she snuck through the forest.

Mr. Tom and I have switched roles, she realized. *Now he eats pastries like a lady, and I hunt like an animal.*

But her hunt didn't truly begin until she rounded a dark trunk and nearly faceplanted when her foot slipped into a hole in the ground. When she picked herself up, she found she'd stumbled upon a small, bright clearing, pink with sunlight. In the center of it was a four-eared rabbit. The sight was eerily similar to the vision Lady Blue had shown her, and goosebumps rose on her arms.

Sada crept toward it, then realized she didn't have a weapon to kill it with. The thought of ending the little creature's life made her stomach clench—it was easy in imagination alone, but seeing his fuzzy little nose in real life was a different story. She made herself push the emotion down. Lady Blue needed to eat, and for whatever reason, she couldn't hunt for herself. A quick glance around revealed a few stones nearby, as well as a jagged fallen branch. Sada decided on the rocks and quietly picked up a few of them. Should she sneak up and hit it over the head? No, she would have a much better chance if she attacked from the shadows, even if her aim was so bad that Gabe teased her for it. The rabbit was still sitting in the clearing, chewing on grass, when she lowered herself into a crouch and pulled her arm back.

Sada's heart raced, and the rock became slippery in her grip as her palms began to sweat. She couldn't do it. She couldn't kill an animal, especially one who hadn't done anything to her, who was just sitting and nibbling on clover. It had been hard enough hearing the dying whimpers of the fox who had been trying to *kill* her, let alone a bunny with its back turned. It looked so much like Guyle, save for the four ears. Sada's arm began to drop but then she remembered the vision of herself lying lifeless and malnourished between the trees. She pictured Lady Blue there instead, whickering for help. It was enough. She forced herself to shove her apprehension deep inside as she readied her arm to throw again.

She flung the rock at the rabbit. It ran before the stone hit the ground. Without thinking, Sada took off after it. She crossed the clearing in a matter of seconds. Then she leapt over small bushes and rocks as she followed the hare through the forest. Its four bouncing ears guided her between trunks and through thickets of undergrowth as she sprinted after it, heart racing. Adrenaline fueled her and her legs pumped quicker than she'd ever asked them to as she chased her prey.

The rabbit disappeared into a cluster of bushes and flowers and Sada saw her opportunity: rather than follow the bunny through the bushes, she darted around them. The rabbit burst free of the leaves in a blur, but Sada was already in front of it. It noticed her through eyes white with fear, but before it could change direction, she leapt at it.

The rabbit squealed as she landed on top of it, grasping for its fuzzy body in the grass. But despite being the size of a large cat, it was so slippery she couldn't get a hold on it. She had part of it trapped under her knee, and she twisted to wrap her hands around the animal, but it squeaked and bit down on her hand, hard.

I'll get soap-mouth! she thought immediately, and she jerked her hand away with a yelp of her own. But a sudden anger came over her at the pain, stronger than her fear of infection and disease. Red flashed across her vision and lit up her entire body for one potent second. She bared her teeth. She pinned the rabbit between her legs then maneuvered around so she was sitting on top of it before she could even form a coherent thought.

It was much bigger up close, more akin to a jackrabbit than a bunny. It used its huge hind feet to pummel her legs as she held it down, but Sada could hardly feel the scratches through her adrenaline. The rush of victory was crashing through her veins and something foreign and powerful was rising up in her chest at the sight of the animal trapped between her hands, unable to get free; unable to do anything but squirm and struggle to get away.

Absentmindedly, Sada felt her fingers curling around the animal's warm neck, digging into its flesh and pressing against its pulse. It squealed, but all she could focus on was the sight of its eyes rolling wildly, the way the band of white around them grew with its fear. She could almost smell it, the pure terror pouring off the animal. The strange feeling in her chest was swelling with every second she held the animal down, telling her to squeeze harder, to lean in closer. She didn't just want to kill it, she wanted to make it *suffer.* She felt as though she'd pulled away from the physical realm and was accessing some distant part of herself.

She wasn't sure if this was some foreign entity possessing her, or her true self finally emerging. Her *instincts* were bright in her palm. Then they shot up to her elbow. The feeling was so strong and sudden that she cried out, but it was not in pain.

Sada squeezed harder, hardly feeling her own eyes widening with the rabbit's. The creature began to let out frantic, feeble noises, little squeaks that made her blood rush with each one. A groan of pleasure escaped her lips. She didn't notice her drool dripping into its fur. Its mouth was open in a silent scream now, its pink tongue visible as it panted and gasped for breath.

Die die die die die, she thought greedily. Just as its kicking was slowing, a sharp snap split the air and Sada's head whipped around to find the source of the noise.

There crouched a bobcat, as small as the rabbit was big. Its fangs were bared and wet, its eyes hungry. It was ready to pounce, to steal *her* prey. Typically, Sada would have been scared at the sight of those long fangs. Now only anger surged in her. The red flashed in her vision again and that foreign part of Sada *hissed* at the bobcat. Her fingers curled deeper into the rabbit. The bobcat stepped forward, but Sada released something between a growl and a screech, and it flattened its ears and retreated, eyes never leaving Sada's.

Her own were wide and her mouth stretched into a grin as her victory was realized. She turned back to her prey when the competitor had left. To her disappointment, it had died while she was distracted. She slowly released its neck, stroking its fur to smooth it back into place. She crouched lower to the rabbit to study it, then lifted it to the air. In death, its eyes hadn't changed. They were still glossy and black. She wondered if human eyes would dull in death, if animal eyes didn't.

Eat, that foreign part of her growled.

She listened.

She raised the rabbit to her teeth and bit in. The fur was a terrible taste on her tongue. And try as she might, she couldn't get past that dry and fluffy stuff to the meat beneath. It was then, as she was trying to, that she fully came back to herself. She was suddenly aware again of the moss beneath her knees, pressing into her skin. She smelled the musk of the rabbit, felt its limp body cooling in her hands. Her stomach suddenly lurched and she tossed the corpse away. She dug her fingers into her mouth, scraping out the fur, trying to claw out the taste. It was all she could do to keep from retching on it.

She was cold now that the—

(torture)

—hunt was over. Cold and ashamed. She couldn't stop looking at the rabbit. The rabbit she'd not only killed, but made to suffer. In her mind, she heard only its suffering squeaks, its breathless panting. She saw only those helplessly darting eyes, that pink tongue as it opened its mouth as wide as possible to get a breath, now purple from the pressure she'd put on its neck—

The torment of the memory was unbearable. But she deserved this agony. Not for killing the creature, but for enjoying it. She sat there telling herself that for what felt like countless minutes. Finally, when her mind felt as empty as her heart had in that moment, she remembered her purpose in the task. Lady Blue needed to eat, and she didn't think she would enjoy a cold meal. She picked the hare up by the tip of its ear with the tips of her fingers, then walked dejectedly back in the direction she thought she'd come.

She generated no thoughts of her own as she went. She only saw over and over the image of the rabbit as she choked it, tongue popping out of its mouth. She only smelled the scent of its dead body. She only felt the texture of its dry fur on her tongue as she tried to eat it before it turned cold. Over and over, the memory tortured her.

And the guilt. It was all she felt.

Lady Blue met her somewhere between where they'd parted and where Sada had gone to hunt. That was good, too, because Sada had realized she was walking in the wrong direction. Lady Blue was holding Sada's cloak in her teeth, tripping over it as she proudly pranced to her friend, but she dropped it with a squeal of delight when she saw the hare. Sada threw it at her hooves.

She'd already decided that she wouldn't eat the animal, or any others she might catch in the future. Even if what she'd done—

(She grinned as she choked the animal, her drool spilling onto its fur as the fox's had onto her face, rejoicing in its suffering)

(Its fur was dry on her tongue, the warm and musky scent of the rabbit thick in her throat)

—hadn't spoiled her appetite, she had no idea how to make a fire to cook it, and she wouldn't have it raw. Who knew what terrible diseases those wild animals might have? Governess Brown had lectured her enough for simply petting the wild deer, let alone eating them. So she would eat her fruit, no matter how little sustenance it provided, and she would bring the filly meat.

"I hope you enjoy," she said numbly.

She put her back to a trunk and her head between her knees, seeing images of the hunt. The sound of Lady Blue chewing and ripping at flesh made her stomach turn again—

(that could have been you making those noises if your teeth had been sharp enough to get through the fur)

—but she did not vomit.

Finally, the filly was done. Sada was too sullen to be startled when her muzzle was suddenly pressing into her hand. The abrupt absence of throbbing pain where the rabbit had bitten her hardly registered. She didn't feel the wetness of the rabbit blood on Lady Blue's nose, either; only the gratitude and contentment that came from the touch. She smiled. At least her friend was happy.

Wordlessly, Sada stood and went to the remains of the rabbit. Lady Blue had left only the ribcage, a half-chewed ear, and some fuzzy ball that she quickly realized was a tail. Apparently, most of the bones were to her liking as well. Sada knelt and methodically picked up the remains, then carried them away. Lady Blue began to follow, but she told the filly that she wanted to be alone. She wasn't upset with her friend (many creatures ate meat, why shouldn't the filly?) but with herself. She didn't want to be seen. So she walked for a while, letting her feet take her wherever they wished. She still could not think, but at least she could walk. She knew that Lady Blue would find her if she was lost.

At the base of a random bush, she dug a grave. She was putting the bones into it, prepared to cover them with dirt, when suddenly her *instincts* alerted her to the presence of a stranger. She had no time to turn before they spoke.

"What in the name of the Creator do you think you are doing?" said a shocked and female voice.

Then the sullen swell in her chest died instantly, only to be replaced by fear. Oh, how she welcomed the distraction.

Sada whirled around to face the voice, both alarm and the strange, fiery cold prickling at her skin. Crouching in the branches of a nearby tree was what at first glance Sada thought to be a woman. Then, after using a staff she held to brace herself and hop to the ground, Sada saw that the stranger could not be defined so easily.

She landed on feet like a human, but her ankles were long like a deer's. Her eyes were like a doe's as well, and two furry ears the same olive brown as her skin stuck out from long, free hair strung with vibrant flowers.

And, of course, there were the antlers. Slender and tall, they sprouted from the top of her head and extended upward like a crown wrapped in flowering vines. She wore no clothing other than dark brown feathers to match her hair around her chest and hips, and all of these things together made Sada feel as though she wasn't talking to a person, but a spirit of the forest, perhaps one even more powerful than the Sprite.

"Who are you, to come into this Dell and dare to taint its floors with the stain of bloodshed?" the deer-woman snarled as she stalked toward Sada. Her voice was unlike anything Sada had heard before, with her flipped R's, her too-round vowels, and hissed S's. But though the accent was strange and foreign, the message was clear.

As she neared, the woman's height became apparent—though she was as slender as a noble lady, she was almost as tall as most human men, and Sada looked up in fear as she scrambled to her feet. Her antlers made her appear even taller, and Sada could think only of stories of men being gored and killed by bucks as she regarded the stranger. Her eyes did not look so doe-like glaring down at her beneath brows of feathers.

"I—I apologize," Sada stammered, and the heat of shame filled her cheeks. She seemed to be apologizing to every person that she met in this forest. "I didn't mean to disgrace your Dell!"

The antlered woman just snorted as she came to a stop in front of Sada. It sounded strangely similar to the snort of a horse, or of a caelicorn.

"Why else would you be hunting here?"

Sada's *instincts* began to prickle stronger in her hand at her nearness, and she wondered if it meant she should be afraid.

"I—my friend needed to eat. I didn't mean to cause any harm…" She trailed off as she realized how stupid the words sounded; she had killed an innocent creature, and if that wasn't harm, then what was? "Not any more than I must, that is."

"Indeed, every creature must eat. Yet to come here with intent to kill, in the only one of Elt's domains where it is expressly forbidden…" The woman struck the ground with her staff, her brown eyes bright with fury. "There are fruits and berries on every bush in this Dell! Are they not enough for you? Will only spilled blood satiate your hunger?" She was nearly growling by the time she finished, and Sada was taken aback by her outburst. The tingling in her hand flared in warning.

"I am sorry, truly…Lady Blue told me the fruits were inedible."

"And who is this 'Lady Blue' you speak of? Another Nymph pretending at nobility?"

"No! That's simply my nickname for her. She's not a Nymph at all, she's a caelicorn," Sada said, twisting fervently at her hair.

At the last word, the tall woman froze. The anger burning in her eyes darkened to something unreadable. The stranger stepped forward into a crouch, her antlers inches away from Sada's neck. Sada stepped backward and felt her heel sink into the grave she'd dug for the rabbit's bones, as though even Elt were reminding her of her crime.

"I do not know who you believe yourself to be, but you do not belong in this Dell, and neither do your tasteless jests." The deer-woman's voice was dark, and terror sparked in Sada's skin.

She took another step forward and Sada retreated a few more; the way the woman was crouching as though about to spring, one hand gripping the staff, made Sada wary. She fumbled for the words that would untangle her from this mess.

"You're correct, but I didn't come to be here purposefully," Sada said hastily. "I'm trying to find my way home, I just stopped to…"

"To *hunt.* Hunters are not welcome in the Dell of Druids."

Well, that had not been the right thing to say. "The Dell of Druids?" Sada asked instead.

"Do not play coy with me, *all* know of this Dell. Certainly the residents of our neighboring kingdoms themselves do." But she frowned. "Yet you dress in such a strange manner. You cannot be a neighbor, then. Do you truly have no idea where you are, girl?" When Sada shook her head, the stranger asked, "How young *are* you?"

"Old enough to marry, young enough to be a maiden since I haven't." It was a phrase she'd heard her father regurgitate any time a bachelor or their father inquired as to Sada's age.

At that, the woman threw back her head and laughed. The sound was strange and inhuman, like the chirping of birds and the bleating of goats. "If you were old enough to wed, girl, you would not be asking me what the Dell is."

The woman frowned with feathery eyebrows and leaned forward to sniff the air between them. Sada was immediately reminded of the Nymph in the hot springs and tried to back away, but the stranger's hand shot out and grabbed her wrist. In a motion too quick for her to fight, she twisted Sada's arm, held her wrist to her nose, and sniffed. Then she dropped Sada's wrist and beheld her wide-eyed.

"How did you come here, mortal?"

Before Sada could answer, the prickling of her *instincts* doubled in strength, and she gasped at the sudden uproar in the icy burn.

"Are you well?" the woman asked. Then her gaze shifted behind Sada, and she hissed suddenly, eyes widening. She dropped into a crouch, staff readied. "Get behind me, human!"

Sada obeyed, fear alighting in her skin, then turned to see what the stranger had suddenly become so frightened of. She relaxed as she saw a familiar blur of blue fur, then the little horned head that poked out of the trees. Again, the cloak was clasped in her teeth. Sada smiled. But the woman was not so happy to see the winged unicorn.

"Divine wrath!" she hissed. "A caelicorn…but that is simply not possible." An unearthly growl began to rise in her throat and Sada gasped as long claws suddenly sprang from the woman's fingers.

"Wait! She won't harm you!"

Indeed, Lady Blue was regarding them calmly from a few feet away, her enigmatic gaze switching between the two women. She dropped the cloak and nickered.

"You know not what you say, human. The eradication of caelicorns was not without reason." The filly snorted at that and the growl in the stranger's throat grew deeper.

"No, I swear it," Sada said, hardly noting the strangeness of the woman's words in her alarm. She stepped around her to go to the filly, but a clawed hand shot out and grabbed her wrist.

"Do not be foolish, girl. Stay behind me and I will protect you."

Sada just pulled away and hurried to the foal's side. She whickered softly in greeting and Sada put a hand on her neck, feeling almost protective of her caelicorn friend. As she touched her, her *instincts* blazed and the caelicorn's voice whispered, *Druid,* everywhere in her mind.

Is that her name? Sada thought to herself, but that felt wrong. *Is that what she* is*?* she corrected. As she did, she felt a resounding sense of *rightness* in her body. It was as though she had never been more certain that she was correct in her lifetime. Not a Sprite or a forest spirit, then, but a Druid. As Sada dropped her hand, she glanced down at the caelicorn to show her she understood her message, though she wondered if the filly knew that the word meant nothing to her. Sada was still so ignorant of this world.

The exchange had all happened in a heartbeat, and she tried not to let evidence of it show in her expression as she smiled at the Druid in front of her.

"See? She won't hurt you," Sada insisted.

She watched the woman's eyes dart between her and the caelicorn, a frown deepening between her eyebrows.

"That is a dangerous Beast, girl," the Druid said warily.

Sada shook her head. "Not her. She healed my wounds." But as she spoke, she recalled the image of Lady Blue pulling her horn out of the fox's side.

She was protecting me, Sada thought to herself firmly.

"An unbonded *caelicorn* healed you—a mortal?" the woman asked, eyes not moving from the filly. She laughed drily. "By choice?"

Sada nodded. "She's been traveling with me for some time now, and all she has done is help me. Truthfully, I'm indebted to her at this point."

The filly whickered in agreement.

"Creator be kind: Elt really is changing." The stranger looked to the sky, murmuring something under her breath. When she looked back to Sada, her gaze was resolute. "You must come with me to see the Mother of Druids. Humans are not meant to be in Elt. We will need to learn more of how you came to be here, and which others accompanied you, before we return you to your realm."

Sada perked up at the last line, stepping forward. "We would greatly appreciate your help—"

"No," she said sharply enough to make Sada flinch. "Not 'we.' Any tale involving a caelicorn has never ended in anything but bloodshed. It will remain here, and I will summon one of my kin to resolve the problem of the caelicorn."

Sada dug her fingers into Lady Blue's mane. "Forgive me, but I cannot let that happen. Lady Blue will remain with me." Her face grew as hot as her sunburn had been and her voice shook on the last few words, but she was resolute. She would not leave the filly now.

The Druid clenched her jaw before closing her eyes and taking a deep breath. Opening her eyes, she said, "Then you will both accompany me to the Mothervale, and your fates will be determined together."

"Pardon me," Sada said, "but would the…Mother Druid…utilize the Seam to return me home?"

"I cannot speak for the Mother," the Druid woman said slowly, "but I imagine she would."

Sada took a deep breath. "Then I must decline. However, this need not worry you, because my end goal remains the same as your Mother's. I seek King Caprius, the Guardian of the Seam."

Sada's heart felt like a caged bird in her chest. She wasn't sure if she could go on, the way the Druid was staring at her. This felt as horrible as speaking out of turn to the Duke. Before she could falter, a feeling of peace seeped into her mind.

Continue. She may be of help, Lady Blue said. Sada dug her fingers deeper into her mane and went on.

"As you can see, I have become somewhat turned around." When Sada laughed, it was shaky, but it was easier to speak now. "If your offer to escort both me *and* my friend still stands, I would greatly appreciate it—but I must beg that you bring me directly to King Caprius, considering the Mother of Druids would have me end my journey with him, regardless."

For a moment, the Druid only looked between Sada and Lady Blue. Then she glanced to the sky again, as though consulting the heavens. Perhaps she was. Finally, she met Sada's eyes again.

"I do not even wish to know how you are aware that Caprius is the Guardian of the Seam…You seek to return to your world?"

"Yes," Sada said, nodding eagerly.

"Spirits above," the Druid muttered. "By all rights, I should bring you to Mother Woia, but…tell me this: how many other mortals accompanied you to this realm?"

"None!" Sada said. "I came here alone. I promise."

That isn't a lie, right? The brothers grew up here.

"A mortal's word does not go far in this realm, girl." She glanced behind her, tapped her claws on her staff. She was going to decline, summon her people, imprison Lady Blue and perhaps Sada. Had she truly come this far just to end up facing the same fate she had already narrowly escaped?

"Please," Sada said, surprising herself. The deer-woman looked back, something closer to surprise than sternness in her eyes now. Sada took it as her sign to continue.

"I've been lost here in your world for who knows how long with no true shelter, and no idea where to go. Every time I begin my day walking toward Titian, I end it walking away. I can spend time answering your Mother's questions, but I think we may agree that what I truly need is to go home.

Your world is beautiful, but I don't want to be here, please…" Sada didn't know what else to say, but she couldn't have gone on anyway. Her chin was beginning to tremble, and her eyes were hot and moist with the onset of tears.

Don't cry, don't cry, don't cry, she told herself. *Your birthmarks might show. And in any case, Father will be so angry if he sees your swollen eyes.* She didn't even realize that the Duke wasn't there to see the effects of her tears.

Sada balled her hands into fists and bit into her lip, hoping the pain would stop the tears. As she tried to stop herself from crying, the Druid woman tapped her staff, eyes switching between Sada and the caelicorn beside her. After what felt like eons of silence, she finally let out a sigh.

"Why must I have been born a Druid?" she groaned, looking to the sky. But she finally retracted her claws. "Very well, girl. You ought to consider yourself lucky that Druids serve as guardians to *all* beings within Elt's realm. Mother Woia would not be so happy with me if I denied you that guardianship simply because you are not *of* the realm, so…I suppose I will escort you out of the Dell, find you some food that is not capable of thought and emotion, and then I will decide how much farther to guide you. Do not look too excited yet—I have a condition."

"Name it, please," Sada said.

"You will answer my questions of your arrival and actions here since you will not answer Mother Woia's."

"I would be glad to!"

"Very well. We head north, then. The caelicorn, however, may not be allowed to roam free. I must warn my people of this so they may take it into custody before it harms an innocent."

"She won't harm anyone, and she won't roam! She stays by my side now, and I wouldn't let her hurt a soul."

The woman snorted. "You would need all the luck of Elt and the blessings of the Creator to be able to control one of those Beasts."

But Sada didn't want to control Lady Blue. She just knew the little filly would never harm a person.

"She won't be a threat," Sada said. "If she so much as levels her horn at someone, we will both come with you to Mother Woia. I know my word may not mean much, but I promise. Besides…you would be able to smell the deceit on me, wouldn't you?"

The Druid raised a feathered brow. "I am going to choose not to answer that. But very well, I accept your terms, if only because it remains a foal. However, I will employ the creatures of this wood to keep it under watch."

"Oh, thank you," Sada breathed, her knees nearly going weak with relief. "I'm indebted to you until you call on me."

The woman just shook her head, the flowers in her hair rustling as she did. It looked more akin to a horse's mane, with the flora and feathers braided throughout it. The flowers were of every color, but Sada noticed that many of them were tulips. She found that endearing for some reason.

"No, you are not. This is the way of the Druids. Do not insult us by offering compensation for aid."

"Oh, I'm sorry, I didn't mean to offend you." Sada's cheeks threatened to blush.

For a moment, the Druid just stared. Then she cracked a grin. "You have not…*yet.* So do not. Come along, then. And tell that Beast to keep its horn away from me."

The Druid's long legs paired with the fact that she moved like a deer meant that Sada found herself having to speed up to a trot every few steps just to keep pace. Sada was considering asking her to slow down—though she would never actually voice the request, especially considering she had already so rudely negotiated with the woman earlier. It was then that Sada noticed she didn't know the woman's name.

"Excuse me," Sada said.

"For what do you need to be excused?"

Sada felt heat stain her cheeks. "I was only trying to be polite."

The Druid chuckled. "I know, girl, and I was only trying to make you squirm."

"At least one of us was successful."

She laughed again, bleating like a goat and chirping like a raccoon. "Go on then, what were you excusing yourself for?"

"I realized I don't know your name. If I may ask, what is it?"

"The others call me Dedrei."

"They only call you that? Then what of your real name?"

"Is Dedrei not real enough for you?" The Druid glanced over her shoulder, grinning when Sada began to stammer. "Hush, I know what you mean, girl. I was not born with a name, nor given one at birth. My people come into their names differently than most."

"And which way is that?" Sada asked.

"Curious little thing, aren't you?" Dedrei murmured.

"Forgive me if I'm prying. I just like to know the stories of my friends."

Dedrei's horse snort quickly turned into a chirping laugh. "You speak like one of mine own or a Verdelorian, claiming us to be friends already. You are curious in more ways than one then, human. But I will relent. Your mother probably gave you your name at birth, yes?"

Sada's heart beat faster at the mention of her mother. "Yes. Or soon after, I imagine."

Dedrei's head bobbed in a nod. "My people do not grow up with mothers. As soon as a child is born, they are left in the woods to be raised by Elt."

"As an *infant?*" Sada interrupted in shock. "How can you survive in these woods alone as a child?"

Dedrei's only explanation was, "Elt does not harm itself." Then she went on. "Once the child grows old enough and finds their way back to our Dell, they are given a place among our people, but still they have no name. After the youngling has been living with the tribe for a while, we begin to refer to them by words of our tongue that describe them.

"It can be in reference to anything from the way they walk to the sound of their voice, or especially the skills they possess, if they have any of a unique nature. But one name always stands out among the others, and eventually all of our people begin using it to refer to the youngling, and only then do they have a name."

"That's amazing," Sada breathed. She wondered what name she would have been given if she'd been raised in such a way. No doubt it would be something about her eyes. It seemed that only her closest friends could look past them. "What were you named for, Dedrei?"

The Druid giggled. "Would you believe me if I said my startlingly good looks?"

"Oh, of course! I would not be surprised," Sada said.

"What about if I said the particular way my hips swish when I walk?"

"Certainly! Jezebel and I used to practice our hip-swishing as girls, until Governess Brown told us it was unseemly."

"And what about the magnetism of my personality?"

"I'm certain you're the most magnetic of your people!" Sada gushed.

The Druid sighed. "Well, it is only so much fun if you agree along with me. Alas, I do not think I will tell you the origins of my name. It will be more fun that way."

"How can that be more fun?" Sada cried. "Now I will be wondering all the while!"

Dedrei threw a wicked grin over her shoulder. "I never said who it would be fun for, girl."

Sada chuckled. "Hmph. Well, I'm determined to figure it out. And in the meantime, you'll need a nickname, of course."

"A nickname? What is this?"

"You have never heard of a nickname?" Sada exclaimed. "It is a name that you call your friends! Typically it is a shortening of their name, or it can be a word that is similar to their name, or just something that reminds you of the person."

"How intriguing…you have yet to tell me even your full name, though."

"Oh! I am Lady Sada Solares, first daughter of Duke Darius Solares of Altamira."

Dedrei turned to raise her eyebrows in disbelief. "Please tell me that *you* have a nickname, so I need not repeat that sentence every time I wish to address you."

Sada laughed. "Just Sada will do."

"I can manage that, I think. *Sada.* A lovely name; a strong name. What were you named for? I have heard little of modern human traditions."

"As you said, I was named as an infant. In my realm, children either inherit the name of a family member, or another important figure."

"Such as…?"

"Well, sons are named after fathers, and daughters are named after grandmothers. Many boys are given the name of the king, as a symbol of luck. Others who don't take the name of another are named for symbols of strength, or beauty, or sometimes simply because their parents liked the sound of the name."

That caused Dedrei to chuckle again. Sada enjoyed the company of people who could laugh easily. It reminded her of Gabe.

"If your names are always recycled, you will never have more than a handful to choose from! Ah, humans. And you, girl? Were you named after your grandmother?"

Sada smiled, fingers in her hair. "No, my parents held to the same opinion as you've just expressed. It was just a nice word, I suppose."

"With a strong meaning, too," Dedrei said.

"You know its meaning?" Sada asked, brightening. "Even I do not."

"Certainly I know it, it is of the Fair Tongue." Sada felt her *instincts* prickle as Dedrei turned over her shoulder to meet her eyes. The Druid's gaze glittered with something unreadable. "Sada means 'eternal,' or 'life.'"

The two women walked in silence for a little while. Between avoiding tripping over her skirts and trying to keep pace with the Druid, Sada had neither the focus nor the breath to make conversation. Dedrei didn't have such a problem navigating the Dell, of course.

Up closer now, Sada could see that the nature of the Druid woman was even stranger than she'd first thought. She'd noticed the feathers covering the areas that required privacy, and at first, Sada had thought them to be a style of clothing. But walking behind the Druid, it became obvious that they were growing *from* her, as surely as her antlers were.

And her hair, which was wavy and thick like a horse's mane, had several braids throughout it adorned with tulips, but Sada noticed that the flowers stayed in the hair that was unbound as well. She almost believed that they were growing *from* her hair, rather than having been placed in it. That should be impossible, but so should a woman bearing the ears and ankles of a deer. For all the characteristics she shared with a doe, Sada was surprised that she didn't have a tail as well.

The caelicorn had been trotting alongside the women, cantering ahead every so often as she usually did. She liked to fan her wings when she ran, and as of late she'd managed to hover off the ground for a few beats before returning to her run. Though Dedrei was still wary of Lady Blue, the filly seemed taken with her. She pranced alongside the Druid as she guided them through the forest. But the filly's time alongside her was cut short when she leaned over and tried to nibble on the tulips sprouting in Dedrei's hair and the Druid banished her to walk beside Sada.

She couldn't help but giggle at the tall woman's fury.

"The flowers in your hair are mostly tulips," Sada said.

"How observant you are."

"Well I was just wondering…Is there a reason?"

Dedrei shrugged. "I am sure the Creator has one, but I do not know it."

The floor of the Dell was covered in dew and spotted with puddles and ponds alike. As Sada hiked her hems up to keep them from dragging in the water, she realized she'd forgotten her boots in the bushes where she'd begun her hunt.

"Oh, criminy crackers!" she said abruptly.

"What's wrong?" Dedrei asked, glancing back at Sada.

"Not a fig. I just left my boots behind."

"Oh." Dedrei waved her off. "You do not need those here. Even your soft feet will be the better for it. Contact with Elt is good."

She was right, of course. It had always felt wrong to separate herself from nature with shoes, especially in these woods. Elt felt alive, and not just in the way all nature was. Sada had begun to imagine that the drums beating at night were really the world's heartbeat. The disembodied music was its voice.

"I agree, but my gown is too long without the extra height of the boots. It drags in the water now."

"You mortals and your tedious clothing," Dedrei chided, but she slowed to a stop. "I can mend that for you, if you do not mind me further ruining your dress."

"*Further* ruining?" Sada asked. "It looks perfectly acceptable to me."

Dedrei met her stare blankly, then the two of them broke into grins.

"You find yourself too funny for your own good, girl. Though my elders say the same of me," Dedrei said, then knelt in the colorful moss. Sada started as her fingernails grew into sharp claws again, and she used one to cut into Sada's gown and begin to slice the hem off. "Do not worry, I will not use them on you," Dedrei murmured as she worked.

"I believe you. It's just shocking, is all." She was admiring the curve of those long talons. "How can you do it so effortlessly?"

"Would it be less shocking if it required effort?" Dedrei glanced up through her slender antlers to grin at her.

From that angle, it became incredibly apparent how unlike a human Dedrei really was. While she was undeniably a person, her features were deer-like, from the shape of her chin and nose to the daintiness of her mouth. Her eyes were definitely those of a doe's, too, round and deep brown, like the bark of a pine tree after a rain. Though seeing her up close, Sada saw that her pupils were diamond-shaped, not circular.

"My people are what others call shiftskins, changelings, form-takers."

"Like a shapeshifter? I've heard legends of those. Though in my stories they were rumored to be very ugly and cruel."

"The stories had it true, then."

"Not at all! They describe the opposite of you, Dedrei."

Dedrei just chuckled. "If you insist."

"I mean it, truly. Your people are called Druids, correct?" Dedrei paused for an almost imperceptible second, then nodded and continued slicing. "What else can you shapeshift into?"

"Any creature, and any part of any creature—I am sure you have noticed the feathers I wear. Just not other Spiritkin; only Beasts and animals."

"The feathers are a form of clothing, then?" Sada frowned. "I'd thought them to be as much a part of you as your hair. Oh—forgive me, I've spoken out of turn."

"Mentioning an observation is speaking out of turn?" Dedrei shook her head again, smiling. "No, you thought correctly; perhaps I misspoke. I only say I wear these feathers because we choose to grow them where you see them. They are a part of me, though a voluntary part—does this make sense?"

Sada nodded. "Can you choose to grow the hair on your head as well?"

"Strangely enough, no. We cannot shift outside of the constraints of the natural form. I cannot lengthen the fur of my elk form, just as I cannot withhold or lengthen my hair in my Spiritkin form. I do not believe I have been asked such a question before."

Sada was opening her mouth to say she'd heard that more often than she could count, when Dedrei stopped her cutting.

"What is this?" the Druid asked as she held out the scraps.

"Do you mean my hems?" Sada teased, grinning.

Dedrei was not amused. "*This.*" She pointed at the silver webbing of the Seam stuck to the gown's fabric. Sada's *instincts* prickled at the sight.

"Oh. When I jumped into the Seam…" Sada recalled how Cidinen had flown away when Sada had told her of the portal. Now she was hesitant to tell Dedrei about how the sparkling quicksilver had turned to mundane water at her touch. "It dried on my dress after I climbed out, and now it won't come off. I believe it stained the fabric."

Well, it wasn't *completely* false.

"The elusive portal between realms...stained your clothes?" Dedrei mocked. Sada blushed and the Druid just chuckled darkly. "You exited the portal here in Elt," she said, picking at the webs with a claw. "Where did you enter it?"

Sada swallowed hard. "Umm, here as well...at least, the second time. I don't believe I went through the Seam originally."

Dedrei just raised an eyebrow, then used a nail to peel a piece of the Seam's silver webbing off the gown. She held it up for Sada to see. In the rainbow-tinted light of the Dell, it gleamed magnificently. Sada sucked in a breath at the brilliant sight and the Druid offered for her to hold it. As she took the bit of silver lattice from Dedrei's claw, it turned to quicksilver in her hand.

Sada drew her hand back with a gasp as her skin erupted in a blaze of both icy and fiery tingling. Unlike the sensation of her *instincts* that she often felt in her hand, the prickling was like the essence of pain itself. It was the same as when she'd touched it her first day in Elt.

"Ahhh," Sada whined, and hastily wiped the rest of it on her cloak. "I knew that would happen—why did I do that?"

Dedrei just watched it all with narrowed eyes.

"Sada," she said finally. "What happened to the Seam?"

Sada grimaced. "Must I tell you?" she asked. Dedrei nodded, and nothing in her gaze invited refusal.

She sighed, still rubbing at her hand, and recited the story to Dedrei. The Druid listened in grim silence, not even speaking once she had finished. Lady Blue seemed to grow bored and pranced off into the trees while the women stood in the mist.

Finally, Dedrei spoke, dark eyes somber. "Elt has been changing in ways unexplainable even for our world. There is something terrible looming in the space between our two realms, Sada. And you, girl, are stuck right in the middle of it."

Sada couldn't help but feel as though Dedrei was completely right.

THE NINETEENTH

Kartinar

First, Caprius demanded that Kartinar and Drath prove their residence in Elt. And so Kartinar did so in the only irrefutable way he could think of: with history.

Kartinar did not remember much of his life in the human world. He remembered his mother's face—tired, soft, framed by thick and coarse brown hair—and he remembered his father's voice—chastising, sharp, always chasing him. He knew his father was a watchmaker and that he had always wanted Kartinar (Joseph, then) to be the same. But eight-year-old Joe had not wanted anything to do with watches, and what eight-year-old would? He wanted to play in the muddy streets with the other boys, make fun of the girls, spit at the nobility that walked beneath the eaves of the buildings he climbed atop.

He knew that his parents were poor, and he also knew that he didn't mind being poor. He was skinny, but all the kids he knew were, and so he thought nothing of it. Sure, he was hungry more often than not, but if he kept his mind and body occupied with play, he didn't notice it too badly. And his mother always reminded him that he was small; he didn't need as much food as the others, anyway. So he was always happy to halve his shares with her or, when she wasn't looking, with little Sam.

He remembered nothing of the Seam. He wasn't certain it was even where he and Drath had come through and into Elt. All he remembered was stumbling across a walking and talking boulder with arms and wide, black eyes. Her name was Esda, and she became his ma—she could not be his mother, because a mother gave birth to you, but she was his ma when his own mother was not. Somehow, Esda had convinced Kartinar to bring his brother (Drath was only two or three at the time) and come along with her to the Stonefoot clan to which she belonged. Knowing his ma, she'd probably bribed him with sweet cakes, or something of the sort. It might have taken days, or she might have convinced him on the spot, but however long it took, Kartinar had agreed.

He'd met the Stonefoot clan's queen, *Om' Modir,* and after they'd talked for a little while over food, she'd declared that the clan was to take him and Drath in. Most of the Trolls were smitten with them. All but a few accepted them. Trolls were good Spiritkin, and they harbored no ill-will toward Kartinar and his brother despite the fact that they were human children. Esda was a nurse, and so she was well-versed in raising children. Though she quickly realized that raising human boys was quite different from raising Troll girls. Kartinar often thought back to how lucky he and Drath were that she had chosen to take them in as her children. Even if she had raised her younger siblings, only Troll queens could be mothers, and while *Om' Modir* had approved the adoption, it was something that had never been done before. Regular Trolls simply could not be mothers. Yet she learned, and she was patient, and she was kind. She raised Kartinar and Drath well, and she taught them of right and wrong, and she taught them of Elt and of the Spiritkin so they might have knowledge of the world in which they'd been abandoned.

Esda loved them both. And they both loved Esda. They loved the entire clan, who had all gone against what they were raised to believe about humans and taken in two strange ones. Kartinar had come to think of all the Trolls as his family, especially those in the K- and D-generations, and he knew Drath felt the same. They couldn't do the work of the typical male Trolls—the drones—because their purpose was to travel between clans to mate with the queens. And so he and Drath took on the traditionally female roles.

It wasn't strange for them, to work among their sisters, but the visiting drones from other clans always had a laugh at them. Men preparing the meals, feeding *Om' Modir,* building new cells and repairing old ones. He'd spoken to Drath about it once to ensure it wasn't going to his brother's head—he was sensitive, a heart that big could only be so—but they'd both agreed that the drones could go sit on a stinger. And so they went on building and repairing cells and feeding their *Om' Modir* and preparing food for the clan. Sometimes they even went foraging with the flower girls.

He wished they had been doing any of those things the day the Blood Elves had come.

Instead, Kartinar had been visiting Alandra. And he'd agreed to let Drath come. It was probably only the second time he had ever agreed to such a thing. Normally he didn't want to have to look after his little (huge) brother while he was visiting his woman. But he'd been in a good mood that day, and so he'd relented. The three of them had spent the day exploring the markets of the Fae kingdom, buying tricks-in-a-bag and playing them on each other or innocent passersby, and tricking older Fae into buying them fermented nectar. It was an incredible day. Not the best, but pretty cursin' near.

Kartinar and Drath had returned to the clan drunk. But what they'd seen had instantly sobered them.

The first thing they'd come across was a basket left abandoned on the ground, pollen crumbles strewn across the moss. Kartinar's heart instantly twisted; his throat felt like it would close. His palms became sweaty and he lost the ability to speak or move. Attached to the basket's handle was a chubby stone hand. There was no body attached to the hand.

He remembered saying, "Oh," as though he'd just realized something. And he had. He'd realized that one of his sisters was dead, or at least injured. Healthy people did not lose hands.

Drath had thrown up. Kartinar hadn't even waited for him. He'd just walked numbly, now in a daze, into the grove of trees where their clan's dwelling was situated. The grove was typically peaceful, filled with giant butterflies, singing birds, four-eared hares, and three-tailed squirrels scampering between the ferns. That day it was morose, and it was empty. Typically, the grove smelled of grass and wet bark and sweet things. That day it smelled of smoke and of dying things. And as he neared, he heard not the soothing and hollow tones of the wind chimes and flutes that played in the grove, but moaning. And whimpering. And ceaseless, eardrum-bursting screaming that made you want to slam your hands over your ears and yell for it to stop.

But Kartinar couldn't. He could only walk, closer toward what he already knew awaited him. He wished he would have just turned around, taken Drath, and left then. He'd known he would only find death ahead, and no closure in it, only pain. But still his feet took him forward, because he heard the moans and the wails and the horrible screams, and that meant that not everyone was dead yet. And it meant that he might be able to save the ones who weren't.

And so he pushed past the screen of honeysuckle that sheltered his clan and he saw the smoke he had smelled, and he saw the people he'd heard moaning.

Their bodies were everywhere. Littering the ground like discarded branches or leaves tossed down by the wind. There was hardly empty space to walk. Half of the dwelling still stood, but its innards were exposed, the comb-like lattice of cells open and displayed for the world to look into. Naked, but empty. The Blood Elven reavers had torn his siblings from their home, from their rooms, from their gardens, and tossed them to the ground. And there they'd killed them with either magick or knives or swords, metal stars, hammers, teeth—he knew that anything that could be imagined had been used on them, simply because of the identity of their killers.

And he knew it had been the reavers simply because of the scale of the destruction. But it was confirmed by the single silver nail cuff lying beside one of his sister's bodies. It was the only shining thing amidst the dull bodies of clay.

He stepped over as many severed limbs as he did whole bodies. In the middle of the massacre sat a mountain of clay, formless, waiting to be shaped. At first, he'd thought the Blood Elves had scraped it from the clay deposit and left it there, maybe to return and sculpt a sigil or calling sign. Then he saw a small arm, sticking out of the mound. And a nose, half of a foot. And he realized that it wasn't clay waiting to be shaped, but clay whose shape had been destroyed.

The adults had been hacked to bits. But the children, still soft and malleable, had been crushed.

Kartinar had fallen to his knees, then, shaking and seizing, not crying but just staring blankly at the mound of his siblings, too defenseless to even fight against their attackers. And then he'd seen the woman lying at the base of it. Shielding it with her body, trying to save even one baby from its doom, trying to nurture as she'd done her whole life.

He rolled his ma over so he could look at her face one more time, and then he'd wept so long that his tears dampened the clay her face had been formed of and it, too, became an unrecognizable lump of grey.

"Stop," Caprius said. His jaw was clenched, his eyes dark. He looked away. "That is enough. I have heard…The incident was reported to me, nearly a decade ago. I recall it."

"That is sufficient evidence, then, Your Majesty?" Kartinar said. His tone was too sharp, but he was afraid that if he made it soft, his voice would break. Beside him, Drath was silent. But the tears were loud on his cheeks.

To his surprise, Caprius didn't reprimand him. "Yes. I am sorry for your loss. Your clan now treads above the sky."

Then the king, all eight of the guards, and even the servants along the wall lifted one hand with all their fingers curled save for the pointer and middle finger. Then they turned their hands sideways and spread the two fingers apart so that one was closer to the ground and the other closer to the sky.

Kartinar nodded. The only times he hoped that the Spiritkin's religions (at least one of them) were true was when he thought of his family. They didn't deserve to float endlessly in the Void, whether they were conscious to experience it or not. They deserved a seat beside the Kindreds at the highest table, to dine with the spirits and the Creator and live in blessing for the rest of eternity.

The moment of compassion was gone as abruptly as it had begun. Kartinar was almost thankful for it. It felt wrong to be comforted by an Elf.

"Well…had I known that would be such a melancholy tale, I would have saved it for the end. Regardless, we must carry on. Servant?" Caprius clapped. "Bring me nectar. Chilled this time. I have no idea why you insist on serving it half-warm."

A servant promptly knelt, opened a hole in the floor, and descended down a ladder to retrieve the king's drink.

"Now, then, what crime shall we explore your guilt in next? Any suggestions?" Caprius looked between them expectantly.

"Uhh," Drath said, glancing at Kartinar.

"Do you wish to address the crimes of which we are guilty last, or would you prefer to settle them now and be done with it?" Kartinar asked.

"Hmm. Last, I suppose. Ah, good." The servant returned with a goblet and a pitcher of nectar. Caprius dipped his finger into the pitcher, nodded (apparently it was chilled to the correct degree), and took the goblet when the servant filled it. "What else was it you claimed to have been innocent of? Deceiving me?" He chuckled.

"Yes, Your Majesty," Kartinar said.

"You do understand I did smell the deceit on your very skin…"

Kartinar was still not entirely certain he believed that. *Om' Modir* had also claimed to have been able to smell when he was lying, but he'd always believed it was fear she'd smelled, not deceit. How could you smell deceit? Though in the same vein, how could you smell fear?

"To tell you truly, I am not certain how to prove my innocence in this matter," Kartinar admitted. "Might I inquire how you distinguish the scent of fear from that of deceit?"

"You may not. It is not something that can be explained, only understood." Caprius sipped from his goblet. "It reeks."

So it's sweat, then, Kartinar thought grimly. He had very little hope of refuting the king on this matter.

"Then is there no way to prove my innocence?" Kartinar asked.

Caprius grinned, and opened his mouth to, Kartinar presumed, say no, there was not, when one of the Gilded spoke.

"I can."

Caprius's head whipped to the side so quickly that his braids snapped through the air and his crown nearly slid off his head.

"Who spoke?" he asked, using his free hand to hastily shove his gilded antlers back into place.

One of the Kingsguard stepped out of line, stiff-backed, arms tight against his side, jaw clenched. It was Agathon. He held Kartinar's gaze for a moment before turning to face the king.

"I did, Your Majesty."

"Ah… *V'* Agathon. You were one of my father's favored, did you know? Well, I am sure you did. He was never shy in his affections."

"Indeed, Your Majesty. King Aphredys treated me well." Agathon dipped his braided head.

"You are one of the Manipulators, are you not? Remind me of the nature of your Boon."

"To Manipulate a person's desire to tell the truth, Your Majesty."

Caprius smiled lightly. "Ah, I recall now. Father always called you the Judge. It seems you are perfectly suited for the task, are you not? Very well. Must you be in contact with the human, or can you do it from where you stand?"

"I can accomplish it from here, Your Majesty—

"I should hope so, considering your position in my Kingsguard and the number of braids you wear."

"—though contact increases the potency," Agathon finished.

Caprius looked as though he was about to speak, but he smirked instead. "Potency, you say? Well, *V'* Kartinar, what say you? Do you wish to experience the effects of a master Wielder at their fullest strength?"

Kartinar's stomach instantly flipped; his palms grew slick. He'd thought Agathon had been doing them a favor in offering his assistance, but after hearing what Caprius had said and seeing how he'd smiled while saying it, now he wondered if the guard had simply wished to inflict pain on him. His power may have been manipulation of the desire to speak truly, but the way the two Elves said "potency" made it seem as though Kartinar would not be made to *want* to tell the truth, but simply made to tell it.

"No, I-I don't believe that to be necessary, Your Majesty, I believe I can comprehend the full extent of—"

"Full contact it is!" Caprius cried, still grinning. He drained his goblet and called for more nectar as Agathon moved away from the dais and walked soundlessly toward Kartinar and his brother.

"I implore you not to use any of your fanciful tricks, *Vi* Agathon. I have no wish to linger here all night," called one of the Kingsguard.

"Indeed. For the love of the spirits, refrain from any needless theatrics," agreed the Elf cloaked in sunlight.

"Rest assured," Agathon replied, "I shall Wield my Boon in the plainest manner possible."

Spirits be good, Kartinar thought as the Elf stopped in front of him. He had to tilt his head back to look him full in the face. Agathon didn't speak, but Kartinar thought he read something in his eyes, beneath his stern frown. He held his gaze for a long moment before he reached out to Kartinar's shoulder.

Kartinar flinched, bracing for whatever potency he and Caprius had spoken of. But there was no pain. Agathon's palm was hovering just above Kartinar's shirt. If he even breathed too deeply, they would make contact. Hesitantly, he met his stare again.

Do not move, it seemed to say. *Play along.* Kartinar was all too happy to obey the wordless command. He wasn't certain what the full effects of the man's power were supposed to feel like, but he thought that it wasn't supposed to be pleasant. So he balled up his fists and screwed up his face, just in case Caprius or the other guards could see him.

"V' Kartinar of human blood, you will now speak only the truth. Is this understood?" Agathon asked.

"Yes," he said through gritted teeth.

"What is the color of your hair?"

"Brown." The answer was automatic. He couldn't even think of lying because he had no time to think. He didn't even know he was going to speak until he did.

"What is the color of my hair?"

"Brown."

"Where are you?"

"In Elt, in Titian, in the Tree of Titian, in the throne room of the Tree, beside Drath, in front of—"

"That is enough."

Agathon had asked the questions rapidly enough that Kartinar didn't have time to formulate a lie. He didn't necessarily feel Agathon's power physically, but he knew that he was not fully in control of his answers. It was almost similar to a sneeze. Once it got to that tipping point, your body's desire to sneeze became so strong that even if you wanted to, you could not stop it. So it was with Agathon's magick. He not only felt a strong desire to speak the truth, but he was also powerless not to. It also felt like a surge of energy was released as soon as he truthfully answered the question. Almost like a reward.

"Now, then, are you prepared to answer King Caprius's questions?" Agathon asked. Still his palm hovered just above Kartinar's shoulder.

"I don't know," he blurted. Caprius and some of the Kingsguard chuckled.

"Your Majesty, what is your question for the mortal? The more precise your inquiry, the more accurate and concise his response shall be. Answers grow quite long-winded when the questions prompting them are too broad."

"Indeed, I recall. I suppose I may as well pose all my questions while you have him thus. *V'* Kartinar, did you trespass upon my forests?" Caprius asked.

"Jiie, but not on purpose," Kartinar immediately said.

Caprius looked to one of the servants nearest him, frowning. *"Jiie?"* he asked. The servant looked equally baffled.

"Uh, it's Trell for *'yes,'* Your Majesty," Drath offered.

"Ah. How quaint," the king said. "What do you mean by this? Did you or did you not know that you were within the Titian wood?"

"I knew, but I didn't know it was against the law to walk in the Titian wood. It's a forest."

Kindred's spit, he thought, cursing his mouth. He hated that he couldn't censor himself, and even more so that his Trell accent was slipping out. Along with being unable to lie or omit the truth, he had no time to modulate his tone of voice, nor his vocabulary.

Caprius muttered something unintelligible. "Very well. You trespassed nonetheless, regardless of your knowledge of the law, or lack thereof. Let us proceed. You have confessed to thievery; I take it this is indeed true?"

"Jiie."

"And what have you stolen, and when?"

"Various items: food, clothing, tents, possessions, joy, and more that I forgot, and since our clan was destroyed, up until we left the Valley of Kings and entered the Dragon's Plate."

Drath groaned beside him, burying his face in his large hand.

Just be glad we had no chance to steal in the Plate, Kartinar thought at his brother.

They probably would have stolen from any homes in those scorched and barren lands, had they not been so aptly named. The Dragon's Plate, home to Castle *Te'raina*, had been devoid of civilization since the Beast Wars. Once, each Spiritkin kingdom had possessed responsibility over one species of Beast. But for some reason—because of a curse, some thought, or because of a woman, others said—many of the kingdoms had risen up against the others in war, riding their respective Beasts into battle. The terror-instilling, fire-breathing dragons had been one such species of Beast, and had laid waste to a patch of land nearly as large as the Valley of Kings. Then the volcano had erupted somewhere between then and now, leaving the land nothing but the ruins of a dragon's breath and Elt's scorching vomit.

Save for the crater, and its anomaly of beauty.

Caprius smirked. "At least you are forthright in this regard. Now, to more pressing matters—did you steal the sorcerer's light?"

"No."

Caprius looked taken aback. "No? Then how did you come into possession of it?"

"I traded for it."

"And what did you trade?"

"Supplies and a favor."

Caprius frowned, his brow furrowing. "Supplies and a favor…for whom?"

"A man who said he was a drifter, but I think he was really a sorcerer."

"And for what reason do you believe him to be a sorcerer?"

"Because he said he used to be apprentice to the last true sorcerer in Elt, Amogasanes the Strange, once upon a time."

Caprius had been lounging in his chair throughout the trial but now sat up, leaning forward in his seat like he was watching a play. Beside Kartinar, Drath looked on with a frown. Kartinar wished he could tell him all was well.

"Describe to me the appearance of this man."

"He was old, with long, free grey hair, brown eyes, light skin. He wore a dark blue cloak so I couldn't see his body." It felt like his mind was heaving to vomit. He didn't even think he'd remembered these details, and yet his mouth continued spewing them. "He had a big, hooked nose, kinda full lips, and drooping eyes. He was sittin' down but looked the same size as a leaf-lover, maybe a bit shorter. I couldn't tell if he was fat or thin." Finally he stopped talking. It seemed like it was done. The surge that released from his body after saying that particular truth was powerful enough to raise goosebumps on his arms.

Caprius waved his hand, leaning back in his throne. "Enough, enough. If your…suspicion…is somehow correct and he was truly a sorcerer, he was likely in some guise—even as meager a sorcerer as he must needs be. Very well. It appears you had been more truthful than one might have initially believed. Rare indeed for a mortal, though perhaps the Trolls deserve some credit for instilling such virtues in you. They are technically Spiritkin too, after all."

Kartinar was very glad that Agathon's power didn't force him to tell the truth unless it was prompted, because if it had, Caprius would not be happy at all with what he had to say in response to his final comment.

"Are there any further questions I might assist with, Your Majesty?" Agathon asked.

Caprius tapped his chin thoughtfully, then his eyes brightened. "Now that you mention it, just one remains." He looked back to Kartinar. "You have either confessed or disproven guilt to all my original accusations, save one. So I ask you, mortal—have you attempted to deceive me?"

Kartinar barely had time to register the jolt of fear that ran through his limbs before his mouth was answering, and possibly betraying him.

"Yes and no."

Caprius grinned. "Yes and no. And on which topic or topics have you attempted to deceive me?"

"On my respect for thou, my likin' of you, and the effects of the sorcerer's light."

Caprius's grin was gone almost as quickly as it had appeared. His eyes were shuttered and flames came to life and went out on his fingertips, promising pain if Kartinar spoke further out of turn. Except Agathon was still manipulating his desire to tell the truth, and so he had no choice but to do just that. Kartinar met the guard's eyes, and he thought the man looked almost remorseful.

"I would warn you to be careful, mortal, but it seems you cannot be, can you?" Caprius stood, flames now encasing each of his fingertips.

"Ah, griffin-dung," Drath muttered.

Kartinar could only watch and fight the urge to run as the Elven king stalked between the walls of the Gilded Ones.

"And what, exactly, are the effects of the sorcerer's light?" Caprius asked.

Then Agathon must have realized the king's nearness meant he would notice the ruse they'd conspired in, and he pressed his palm against Kartinar's shoulder.

A surge of energy spread through Kartinar so strong that his muscles began to flex and relax without his permission, and he fell into a seizure. Agathon went down with him. And like a demonic presence being exorcised, the truth—and potentially his condemnation—was expelled from his body.

THE TWENTIETH

Sada

Dedrei had nearly decided to return to her tribe once Sada relayed the story of her encounter with the Seam. She'd only stayed to escort her out of the Dell because "There is no vow a Druid can break." Sada did not know why her tale upset both Dedrei and Cidinen so greatly, but she had a guess. It was likely for the same reason she herself had been upset upon seeing its glittering surface change, its waters becoming mundane: the magick of the Seam was gone. And based on the reactions of both the Druid and the Pixie, this was not a normal occurrence. It had either rarely happened in the past, or never at all. It was perhaps a permanent change, possibly a detrimental change, to the Seam or to Elt as a whole. And Sada had been the one to cause it.

Om' Modir had been the only person who had not seemed distressed over the Seam's disappearance. In fact, she had told Sada that it was in the portal's nature to move. But surely Dedrei knew this if she knew of the Seam at all, and she was certainly not calmed by this fact. Sada could only wonder if that meant the Troll queen had been mistaken in thinking that the Seam's change was normal. She wished desperately to confirm with Dedrei that this was not so—not only to fuel her own hope of someday returning home, but also to assuage her guilt over potentially altering an important aspect of the Spiritkin's realm.

But Dedrei would not speak of the portal.

So the two women continued their journey out of the Dell, albeit more awkwardly. They'd hardly even spoken the rest of that day, and when they found a place to rest for the night, Dedrei had refused to sleep unless Lady Blue was at least ten paces away. Sada had gone to lie beside the caelicorn. It broke her heart to see her curled up alone in the grass.

In the morning, Dedrei had been less curt and more conversational, and had also slowed her pace to one that Sada could easily match. But even now, as they continued their journey beneath the sun high in the sky, Dedrei still refused to speak of the Seam. Any time Sada brought it up, or even if the light simply caught its webbing on her dress, the Druid's deer ears would flatten and the flowers in her hair would wilt. So Sada stopped asking about it, and instead tried to distract her new friend with talk of other things, inquiring about her tribe and her people. Dedrei, however, only seemed interested in Sada, and how a mortal had managed to survive alone for so long in this world of immortals.

"Now that we have been companions for a time and you call me a friend, tell me true—had you sincerely not endeavored to hunt with the intention of killing within this Dell?" Dedrei asked as she held back huge clumps of ferns so Sada could pass.

"Well," Sada began sheepishly. "I did indeed seek to hunt…and yes, it was with the intent of killing. Yet I had no desire for it! And I swear to the skies that I was certainly and entirely unaware that such an act would bring dishonor upon the land of your people."

Dedrei snorted. "Swearing to the skies will not get you far here, girl," she said.

"Oh, well, it doesn't serve me much in my world, either. Governess Brown says it all the time, and I suppose I must have picked up the habit. But what prompts you to say that?"

"It is a swear of the *Vaisse*—the Spiritkin who practice *Vaisse'ulism.* It is not a religion practiced within the embrace of these woods."

"*Vigh-seh*?" Sada tried. The word felt thick and awkward on her tongue. Or rather, her tongue felt thick and awkward on the word.

"No, *Vigh-eh-suh,"* Dedrei corrected, and in a much more beautiful and elegant accent. The words sounded far back in her throat, something Sada could not replicate no matter how hard she tried. "It means 'vessel' in a language long lost to us."

"Vessels of what?" Sada asked. It sounded like something Mrs. Pérez would talk of. *We are all the world, and the world is us,* she liked to say. Perhaps the *Vaisse* believed themselves to be vessels of Elt's energy.

Dedrei cleared a tall root, leaping up as gracefully as a cat and sweeping her legs over it. When she dropped to the other side, she used her staff to prod at bushes and move aside vines as they walked. She'd told Sada earlier that she was looking for signs, though she didn't say of what.

"They desire to be vessels of certain…beings. Spirits." Dedrei paused to squint at a tree, then continued on. "It is a complicated matter that we need not delve into."

"Do you speak of the Kindreds?" Sada asked.

Dedrei snapped her head around, frowning. "How do you know of their legend? Does their legend exist in your world as well?"

Sada shook her head. "No, not specifically. Though I have heard that some speculate they might be a kind of angel, and such beings do exist in my realm. At least, *I* believe them to."

Dedrei had crouched to examine a beautiful white boulder, and now frowned up at her from where she hunkered.

Sada had thought the boulders to be giant pearls at first, and the thought was accompanied by visions of huge, land-dwelling clams. But Dedrei told her the person-sized boulders were not pearls but pure opal. Apparently, it was abundant in both the Dell of Druids and in the Elves' Verdelore forest, which shared a border. Sada was still awestruck that such a lovely gemstone could occur in such a large size and quantity. She absentmindedly pressed her hand against the one Dedrei squatted by now, delighting in the rush of *instincts* it brought to her left palm.

Lady Blue, who had been trotting happily ahead of them, noticed the two women had paused, and pranced to rejoin them. She bent her head to sniff at the boulder, and then at Sada's and Dedrei's faces in turn. The Druid waved her off with a playful hiss, then whickered like a horse (or a caelicorn) as though to let the filly know through her own language that it was all in good humor. Looking at the two of them face to face, Sada noticed with a shock that Lady Blue seemed to have grown overnight. Her chin was at a height with Dedrei's head as she squatted—and the woman was obviously tall even when crouched down as she was. When she had first met Lady Blue, the filly's back stopped just at the middle of Sada's hip. Now, if they were to stand side by side, the caelicorn's back would be closer to level with the very top of Sada's hip.

Did the rabbit alone do so much for her? If it had, Sarana had been right in pressing Sada until she gave in and hunted it. She didn't let herself think of the matter further, for fear of the gruesome memories which would resurface with the line of thinking.

"How did you hear of Eltic tales, such as those regarding the Kindreds?" Dedrei asked.

"Oh, my friend mentioned it—Mr. Tom."

Her frown, which had returned with her question, now deepened. "That is not an Eltic name."

"I believe Mr. Tom's name was inspired by my people. It's a long story, one I shall tell you later…perhaps over tea."

Dedrei and Lady Blue shared a skeptical (and fairly judgmental) glance as Sada giggled to herself.

"Very well. The idea of an Eltic possessing a human name makes me uneasy, though, I will have you know."

"I must agree," Sada said. "But I fear I have veered terribly far from the topic. May I ask why Druids do not practice *Vaisse'ulism?*"

"Certainly," Dedrei said. She stood and continued leading them through the opal-dotted forest. They walked for nearly a minute in silence, Sada wondering to herself if the answer was so complicated that the Druid needed a moment to gather her thoughts.

"Pardon, but…are you going to tell me, then?" Sada asked when Dedrei still showed no signs of answering.

Dedrei grinned impishly over her shoulder. "All you had to do was ask…"

Sada scoffed through a smile and poked Dedrei in the side. "You knew what I meant!" Dedrei batted her hand away, and something in the gesture made her smile falter. Just for a moment.

"We respect the Kindreds' existence and power. Yet my people do not go so far as to revere them as gods or rulers. It is possible they gifted us our Boons—yes, I shall tell you of these later, now close your curious mouth, child—but they certainly did not gift us life. And even if they had, my kin and I would not dedicate our lives to becoming no more than a...*container* to be possessed by their spirit, or essence...whatever you shall call it." The Druid's brown eyes were suddenly sharp with fury. "It is a *waste* of this gift that we call existence."

Yet Sada was imagining what it would be like to be possessed by such a being. "Is that truly what happens?" she breathed. "Do they replace one's spirit with their own? Do they control the person's body like a driver controls a carriage?"

Dedrei waved a hand. Her talons had come out as she spoke, but now—to Sada's relief—they reformed into a much safer shape.

"No, it is—" she began. Then, registering what Sada had said, she frowned. "A *care*-itch?"

Sada smiled. "Not quite. *Keh*-ridge," she said, sounding it out as Dedrei had done for her earlier.

"Carriage," Dedrei said, slowly. It sounded like a made-up word in her accent. "What is that?"

She has probably never ridden in one, if she was raised by the forest.

"They're lovely little vehicles pulled by horses. It is a much more convenient mode of travel, I must admit, though not nearly as enjoyable as riding. Unfortunately, my father won't permit me to travel in anything other than a carriage or a palanquin."

Dedrei's expression was so comically baffled that Sada couldn't help but laugh aloud.

"You laugh at me, yet it is your world that is strange beyond imagination," the Druid said.

"My world? It is yours that possesses talking berries and pink sunlight!" Sada cried.

"And what other color should sunlight be?"

"Yellow!"

"Yellow?" Dedrei's eyebrows rose even further somehow. "A sun the color of lemons?"

"Indeed!"

"Now I know you are playing a trick on me. You are no better than a Pixie or a Faery, girl." Dedrei shook her head, but she was grinning.

"I swear I am not jesting. To the skies, I swear it," Sada said, still giggling.

"Well, yellow sunlight or no, the process the Kindreds use with their Vessels is not so dramatic as what you described. Forgive me for embellishing. It is said that the body—the vessel—is shared by the original spirit and whichever Kindred has taken it over. Though you will hear a different story from each religion, and different details from each member of it. I myself admit I am unsure of the specifics, as we all are. Records of the Kindreds never survive the centuries between their Descents. This disappearance of relevant documents is so consistent that I must believe it is by the will of either they themselves or our Creator that we have no evidence of their presence."

"I wonder what they're like," Sada mused. She looked to the sky, trying to imagine glowing beings descending from the clouds. Perhaps riding a chariot or pegasi made of clouds themselves. Or sunlight, even. "I hold the hope that perhaps they may take me back to my realm in case the Sea— in case King Caprius cannot."

Her fingers fled to her hair as she glanced at Dedrei, waiting for her features to turn stormy. Instead she merely coughed out a bleating laugh. Her smile was dark.

"You are both young and mortal, and you cannot be expected to understand the ways of immortals. But allow me to tell you something, youngling." When she turned to face Sada, her face was a study in cold ire. She saw the Duke's eyes there suddenly. "Immortals rule this world, immortals of every race. Were a citizen of common descent to come knocking on one of these rulers' doors—supposing they even *made* it to the door—the ruler would not deign to open it, let alone listen to or attempt to solve the problem presented to them. Perhaps once, but now?" She laughed dryly. "And the Spiritkin are infants when compared to the Kindreds. Hope all you want, but if it were me, I would not count on beings whose existence dates back to the beginnings of Elt to help you, girl."

"Hope is a fleeting thing. If you grab onto it, you might just soar away with it," she whispered.

"What?"

Where had that come from? *Someone said that to me once…*

(In the forest?)

*…a long time ago…*Sada smiled. "Nothing. I suppose we shall have to wait and see."

"Hmm. Are all humans this cheerful in the face of darkness and doubt?"

"Oh, it is not so dark. See how the sun shines?"

Sada paused in her walking, lifting her face to the sun. It seemed brighter in this forest. The rocks were always sun-warmed, and the sweet, fresh smell of the grass and moss was brought out by the heat. Lady Blue, soft and sun-warmed, slid beneath her hand as she stepped up beside Sada. Her *instincts* tickled her arm, and behind her eyelids formed the image of herself, head tilted back, smiling into the sunlight. She laughed, her smile growing wider as she watched herself do so.

Dedrei paused with her for a moment before they both continued on. The caelicorn followed with a squeal of delight, kicking moss up into the air. Dedrei muttered something about disrespecting the hair of Elt, but a smile curved into the corner of her mouth.

What a beautiful world Elt was. Jezebel would love to see the opals glittering between the trees. By now she probably would have discovered the properties of the strange and colorful Eltic leaves as well. Perhaps she would have a theory for why trees of so many different species could all grow together in one Dell. Maybe Dedrei would know.

The Druid was ahead of her, and she used her staff to vault over a wide puddle. "Why do it if you did not want to?"

"Hmm?" Sada asked. "Do what?"

"Hunt. Kill."

"Oh…"

The memory of Lady Blue showing Sada the vision of herself dead, hollow, and starved resurfaced behind her eyes. In the image, her body was quickly replaced by that of the filly. Sada glanced at her, now sniffing at a thicket of leaves ahead of them. Were her ribs showing, or was her fur just laying in a strange way?

"I tried to eat some of the berries I found growing here on my first—well, second day in the forest, but they made me feel strange, and then I fainted. I thought I shouldn't risk eating any more after that. Then I found Lady Blue, and she convinced me to eat so that I wouldn't starve. But really, I set about looking for some so that *she* wouldn't starve. She's just a baby, after all.

"I tried some more berries, but when I offered them to her, she said they were inedible. She showed me two visions. At least, I believe that is what they were. One was of death and hunger. The next was of the solution…" Sada trailed off at the memory of the rabbit squirming beneath her hands, the way she hadn't been able to stop squeezing its neck. How she had tried to eat it. She shuddered.

"This is why you can never trust a caelicorn," Dedrei said, eyeing the filly. "All of the fruit in this Dell is safe to eat. It is what my people live on."

Sada frowned. "But the berries I ate made me horribly sick. My entire body was on fire."

"You ate them upon your arrival in Elt?" When Sada nodded, Dedrei continued. "You told me that King Caprius is the one who found you, yes? Those were berries of the Elves' forest, girl. You are in different woods now."

"Truly?" Sada asked, eyebrows raising. "How far did I walk?"

"Far enough to walk yourself into another domain," the Druid said. She turned to glance at Sada. "Caprius's Elves are nearly on the opposite side of this valley, the Valley of Kings."

Sada's chest tightened at Dedrei's words. If she'd crossed the Valley to the opposite side, it meant she had been walking in the opposite direction of where she needed to go nearly since she'd arrived. But hadn't the Trolls told her the direction of Titian? And hadn't Lady Blue been leading her in that same direction?

She told Dedrei this, frowning all the while. "I have been traveling for long enough in the direction of the Elves that I should be nearing them now, not only just crossing out of the domain of the Valley opposite to them. How can this be? How am I still so far away?"

Dedrei bleat-chirped a laugh. "Well, you should not trust the advice of Woodland Trolls to the extent of surety. And as I have said before, the caelicorn is sure to lead you astray to benefit its own goals."

"I cannot imagine she would ever do such a thing," Sada said softly. "And the Trolls were kind and hospitable…they would not purposefully lead me astray."

"I never said it would be with intent…not concerning the Trolls, anyway."

"Mm…I'm not sure…"

Dedrei tossed an amused glance at her, but Sada's eyes were trained on her bare toes. Her face was hot, and she hardly noticed her teeth tearing at her lip. She was lifting her fingers to the tips of her hair when Lady Blue's swaying back slipped beneath her hand.

Peace.

The caelicorn's voice was strong and sure in her mind. *The ways of Elt are amiss. Perhaps it was not the fault of yourself or the Trolls that you were led astray from Titian.*

What else would it be? Sada thought with surprise.

Yet Lady Blue did not answer. She just remained beneath Sada's palm, radiating calm. Still, it was hard not to let herself imagine how much sooner she may have gotten home had she only decided to travel the other direction coming out of the ring of trees surrounding the Seam. But Dedrei was here now, she reminded herself, and soon she would be home again. She brushed the dim thoughts away and looked to the caelicorn again, wondering why she hadn't eaten the berries if they were safe as the Druid said. If Lady Blue heard those thoughts, she gave no sign other than a typical flicking of her tufted ears.

Sada would ask Dedrei instead, then. "She refused to eat any of the ferns or fruit I picked for her, and she only sometimes nibbles on the grass. Why do so, if the vegetation is safe?"

"Caelicorns are not lambs or fawns, human," Dedrei scoffed. The word somehow felt like an insult coming from her. "Did you not notice that horn on her head? It is not used for picking berries."

The image of the caelicorn pulling her horn from the fox's bleeding belly flashed in the front of Sada's mind. Suddenly the warm air felt cold, and she shrugged her cloak closer to herself.

"I'd thought it to be a last resort," she said, half to herself. "…But you're saying that she…prefers meat?"

"Indeed. What did I tell you, girl? They are not innocent creatures; they are born with weapons in their very skulls."

"Then why did she ask me to kill the rabbit instead of hunting it herself?" Sada asked.

Dedrei pointed with her staff at the filly now prancing ahead once more. "She is still a foal. Caelicorns are not raised by their mothers, but by their *Hédras*, their Spiritkin Rider. Since she has yet to find hers, it is likely she sees you as her temporary caretaker. Which means that she will be expecting you to find food for her while she is with you. And kill it as well."

"I can't!" she exclaimed, face contorting with revulsion.

But you did, said a dark whisper. When Dedrei turned, her eyes seemed to say the same. Lady Blue turned at her exclamation as well, gazing evenly at her, as if to ask what the fuss was over. Sada herself had reasoned that many animals and people kill to eat—it isn't inherently bad. *But they don't understand,* Sada thought, thinking of the taste of fur. *They don't know what I did; what I might do again.*

"What will I do?" Sada asked.

Dedrei just shook her flowery head, the vines on her antlers swinging. "It is a difficult decision. Some might say impossible. Do you let her go to find her *Hédras* so that they may raise her and kill for her? Or do you keep her by your side so she remains unbonded and cannot bring more of her bloodthirsty kind into this world?

"If you decide the latter, you then must choose again: Do you kill for her so she may live, or let her die so your hands remain clean of blood? It is a question of both morality and the strength of your soul."

Dedrei's words made Sada shiver. But some of what she said didn't make sense.

"I can't let her go if I'm not forcing her to stay."

"Hmm?" Dedrei asked, glancing over her shoulder.

"I'm not keeping her here," Sada said. "She's been following me without my asking for days, and always sleeps by my side at night. How can I let her go if I don't hold her here?"

Now it was the Druid's turn to look puzzled. "That is confusing," she admitted. "Caelicorns have only been known to show loyalty to their *Hédras*, and nobody else. Though she is the only one of her kind that has been seen in centuries. She should not even exist. Perhaps she is an anomaly in more ways than that."

"She *is* different," Sada said firmly. "She healed me." The Druid just nodded and cleared their path with her staff. But glancing down at the cerulean filly, an uneasy thought invaded her mind. "She didn't…accidentally make me her *Hédras*, did she?"

Dedrei's eyes were ignited with something unreadable as she turned to Sada. Her diamond pupils flared. "That is impossible. You are human."

Sada froze mid-step at the intensity in the Druid's voice. "I apologize! I didn't mean to suggest—"

"No, hush, child. I spoke harshly." Dedrei's gaze softened. "But my words are true. The caelicorn has not bonded to you. Not in the formal, magickal sense, anyway. There is nothing to worry over."

Sada nodded and Dedrei took the lead again, but she found herself too absorbed in thought for further conversation. As she followed Dedrei, she watched the caelicorn prancing in the mist. The pink sunlight made the blue of her coat gleam so brilliantly it was impossible to imagine the little filly killing and eating another creature. But she had. *As do people and cats and dogs and half the animals in the world.*

But it wasn't the filly's carnivorous diet that made her hands prickle. Sada hadn't seen her devour the rabbit, but by the crunching of the bones and the time it took to reduce the creature from animal to bits of skin and bone, devour was exactly what Lady Blue had done. And there was the way she'd licked the blood off of Sada's side…perhaps the healing of her wounds was only a side effect of the filly's true intent. But then why had the caelicorn stayed with her?

Because she found a hunter.

"Just because they eat meat doesn't mean they're evil," Sada said. Though she spoke to Dedrei, it might only have been to remind herself. "Half the animals in the world eat meat. Humans eat meat, and not all of us are bad."

The tulips in the Druid's hair rustled as she nodded her head. "Not evil, no. But dangerous, yes. There was a time when caelicorns were the most fearsome steeds on the battlefield, before Elt fell into peace, when wars waged for centuries at a time. They were respected and coveted. Then their violent nature became too intense to control, only fueled by the slaughter they aided us in. The foals only grew more bloodthirsty with each one born. Soon nobody could control them, not even their Riders, and the future of Elt's people came into jeopardy."

At the words, Sada recalled what Dedrei had said upon first seeing the caelicorn. *Their eradication was not without reason.*

"That's why they were all killed," Sada realized aloud.

Dedrei's features were expressionless. "It was terrible, but it was necessary. Caelicorns were among the wisest creatures in Elt, but there came a point when their craving for violence outweighed their wisdom. Then it was done, and we have not seen any of their kind in centuries." The Druid glanced up at the ceiling of leaves as she spoke, squinting at something Sada couldn't find. "Elt truly is changing."

Something uneasy stirred in Sada at her words, and she wondered why; she had no attachment to this world, yet the thought of its balance being thrown off made her queasy. The icy fire of her *instincts* began to build in her palm as she wondered what Dedrei meant when she said her world was changing. It flared brighter when she recalled something else Dedrei had said to her, too. That there was something terrible in the elusive space between Sada's human realm and Dedrei's immortal one. *And you, girl, are stuck right in the middle of it.* Sada couldn't help the gooseflesh that spread over her skin.

But she didn't dare upset Dedrei again by asking what she meant by Elt changing, or anything concerning the Seam. So instead, she focused on the little caelicorn, wondering if it was safe to have her around. Was Sada only a means for killing and providing the filly with food so she didn't have to bloody her own horn? The thought made her cringe, especially when Lady Blue returned to butt her nose into Sada's side. As her velvety muzzle brushed against the scars marking Sada's ribs, her *instincts* flared brightly in the area for just a moment. No mental message brushed the depths of her mind this time, and after a few gentle jabs, the filly returned to explore the wilderness ahead of them.

"Dedrei," Sada began, then paused as she noticed something. "Dedrei, Dedrei," she murmured under her breath.

"Hmm?" the Druid called.

"One moment," Sada said, then resumed her muttering. "Dedrei…Deh-drei…*Dee*-drei, dee-drei, dee-drei. Rei? No." She was on the cusp of something, she could feel it. But just what it was, exactly, still eluded her. "Deh-dree, dee-dree, dee—*Oh!*" she exclaimed suddenly. "DeeDee!"

"What in the world is going on back there, child?" Dedrei asked, turning to stare at her.

"Your nickname!" Sada scrambled to catch up to the Druid, grinning. "I've finally figured it out!"

"My nick—oh yes, you told me of this tradition upon our meeting. I had not realized you have been spending all this time attempting to invent one."

"I haven't," Sada said, frowning. "They must come naturally, otherwise they're no good. And naturally has this one come! You're DeeDee!"

Dedrei blinked. "Dee-dee? How did you get that from 'Dedrei?' Those sounds aren't even in my name!"

Sada grinned. "But it sounds so right! So, what do you think?"

Dedrei looked as though she wanted nothing more than to command Sada to never again speak that group of sounds together in her presence, but the Druid must have noticed her excitement, for she only sighed, shaking her head as she liked to do.

"If the name brings you such joy to use, I suppose I can…tolerate it."

"Oh. Well, I needn't use it if it upsets you," Sada said.

"No, no. It is a fine nickname, Sada." Sada grinned while Dedrei shook her head. "What were you saying before you interrupted yourself?"

"Oh, I was going to say that—oh!" Her voice jolted as she slipped on a slick root. She wind-milled her arms to catch her balance and the motion sent a shock of pain through her shoulders. *"Ah."*

"Are you alright?" Dedrei asked, eyeing her.

Sada nodded, holding her right shoulder. Her sunburn had finally faded after paining her for days, but that pain had been replaced by the aching from the punctures on her shoulder. The wounds were worse on the right side than the left, and pulsed with her heartbeat beneath her fingers. She tried to ignore the fact that the skin was incredibly tender to the touch, and that the soreness seemed to be spreading. *Infection,* her mind whispered, and nausea roiled up in her belly in response. But she forced herself to push the thought from her mind as she smiled at Dedrei.

"Sore shoulder," she said. Dedrei's nostrils flared almost imperceptibly, and though she looked skeptical, she nodded and continued walking. "So…you seem to know a lot about caelicorns…*DeeDee.*"

"Hmm." The tall woman's staff hit the ground with a steady rhythm as she walked, the sturdy beat to her melodic voice. "Druids know the tales of all Elt's creatures," she explained. "That, and my people were great friends with their Grandsire species, the pegasus."

"I've heard of those," Sada said. The elegant, winged horses were perhaps one of the only true stories she had been told of fantastical creatures, though she hadn't known them to be anything but fairytales at the time. "Did they also have the…abilities caelicorns possess?" she asked hesitantly.

She wasn't sure how to phrase the question without outright saying she believed the filly was sending her thoughts. That sounded crazy even to her, who had experienced it.

"If you are referring to their unmatched ability to kill and harm," Dedrei said darkly, "then no."

Sada cringed at the venom in her accented voice. "Do you have anything *good* to say about caelicorns?"

The Druid just chuckled softly. "They are quite magnificent, are they not? Their horns, their wings, the vibrant colors of their fur. Caelicorns come in every color of the rainbow…but she is especially beautiful." Dedrei pointed with her staff to the cerulean filly flapping her wings and snorting happily. "This one would find its *Hédras* among royals. In the time of the caelicorns' glory, Spiritkin might even have held tournaments in an attempt to activate the bond with one like her."

Sada's eyebrows lifted at the remark. Lady Blue certainly was gorgeous, though Sada hadn't imagined how coveted it would make her.

"She is blindingly spectacular," Sada murmured, her question forgotten as she stared at the way the filly pranced.

"What is her name?" Dedrei asked.

Sada realized with a jolt she'd never given the filly a true name. She'd only thought of her as *Lady Blue,* or *the filly*. That was strange; for her, nicknames were what solidified a friendship. It was her favorite part of meeting someone new. Why had she not given the filly a name?

"I call her Lady Blue, but I suppose she doesn't have one…Oh, I can't believe I never gave her one!"

The Druid stopped in her tracks, staring blankly at Sada. Then her lips spread into a grin and she doubled over laughing. She braced herself with her staff as she let out that musical bleating and chirping sound. At the eruption of noise, the filly trotted back to investigate. She paused at Dedrei and pushed her nose through the screen of hair that fell as she bent to laugh, sniffing her face.

Then Dedrei stood and actually spoke to the caelicorn. "Did you hear that? She thinks she gets to name you."

The filly angled her head at Sada then, one of her bright eyes regarding her as though she understood what the Druid had said and was equally amused. Sada's cheeks were hot with embarrassment by the time Dedrei finished laughing.

"In my world, we name our animals," she defended, but it did little to calm the warmth in her face.

"We name our animals, too," Dedrei said, wiping tears from her eyes. "But not Beasts."

"So is there a difference? I keep hearing of these Beasts as though they are different from animals. But in my world, they are simply the wild and dangerous ones."

Dedrei nodded as she moved on through the Dell, the caelicorn remaining by her side. "There is a difference, indeed. You know what animals are. I found you burying the bones of one just yesterday." Sada blushed harder at the memory, but the Druid just continued. "Beasts are something between animals and us, Spiritkin."

"I've been taught what Spiritkin are. It is an interesting concept."

"Is that all we are?" she mocked, but still she nodded in acknowledgment. "We have never been able to fully understand Beasts. We believe they were created in a way similar to us, though rather than a human Grandmothering the species, it was an animal or a Spiritkin." Dedrei's lip curled. "Abominable as it is. What resulted was a sentient creature, intelligent enough to know of our separate domains and kingdoms, but wild enough not to care."

Sada recalled what Cidinen had said to her of the creatures. "They just want to eat and kill."

"It appears you have heard the saying. But it is not entirely true. Many Beasts are incredibly intelligent, kind, and respectful, but they are bound by a theroid form, and so they do not create societies of their own. Whether that be from lack of desire or ability, I cannot say. But many coexist within Spiritkin societies as our companions and assistants."

"Wow. Elt is like a fairytale come to life! So Beasts have their own names, then?" At Dedrei's nod, Sada frowned at the caelicorn. "How do you find out what it is?"

"In the same way you learned mine, of course."

Sada scolded herself for the obvious question and stopped, going to her knees beside the filly. Then she held out a hand as an invitation. Rather than rest her muzzle in Sada's palm like she expected, the caelicorn lowered her nose and touched the tip of her glimmering horn to Sada's forehead. Just the light brush of contact was enough to make her *instincts* roar to life.

She gasped as a sudden space opened in her mind, like taking a deep breath after holding it without realizing. It felt as though a bubble formed not in her skull, but in her mind itself, expanding, building in pressure, before popping like a sigh and releasing it all. It was as though another mind had joined hers, or a new space had been unlocked within her own. One that she hadn't known existed.

Once the initial shock of awe faded, she spoke into that space within her head, sending her thoughts floating across to it. She watched as they drifted over and were received:

What is this?

How is this possible?

It's so bright!

She grinned at this new experience, then forced her thoughts into compliance.

What is your name? she asked, and distantly she heard the filly snort. Wherever Sada was, it was a space set aside from the physical world she knew she was kneeling in, but couldn't feel.

As Sada silently spoke into that new, airy space, she felt something like a bridge close the gap between it and the rest of her mind. Now it wasn't a space separate from Sada, but an entirely new piece of herself. And in that foreign Mindspace that was now her own, she heard one word whispered in that enigmatic, ageless voice:

Sarana.

Her left palm tingled at the spoken name, and she jerked away from the horn at the sudden burn of cold and heat. But the new space within her mind remained, and it was as though she could feel the breath of the caelicorn tickling her mind through it. Sarana said nothing further, and Sada slowly got to her feet. Dedrei had been eyeing her curiously throughout the interaction, and now poked Sada with the butt of her staff. The ribbon tied to it tickled her arm.

"And what did you discover?" the Druid asked.

"Her name is Sarana," Sada said distantly. She was still probing at that new Mindspace, searching for anything within it. It reminded her of how after losing a tooth as a child, you'd prod and poke at it with your tongue, feeling the new gap in the flesh. It felt similar to that, only she hadn't lost something to gain the space.

"A name fitting for a royal caelicorn," Dedrei said. Her sharp gaze flicked to Sarana, and the filly just whickered before disappearing into the brush again.

"How does it work?" Sada blurted. Suddenly she needed to know everything about what her connection with the caelicorn was, and how it was even possible. "When she speaks to me in my mind, and understands the thoughts I think in response…what can that be? I merely think something, as anyone would, and if I'm touching her, she seems to hear it and responds! Such a thing shouldn't be possible!"

"That, girl, is partially why caelicorns were so sought after," the Druid said. She veered off to the side then, scanning the trees as she spoke. Sada hurried to follow. "The ability to communicate with one's steed in battle was a war-winning advantage. It eliminated all miscommunication between Rider and mount. And, of course, their Riders had access to the caelicorns' seemingly infinite knowledge. It made for a very deadly pair to come up against in battle, especially when the counterpart to the caelicorn was a Blood Elf."

Just the name made Sada's skin and *instincts* prickle. She couldn't figure out why, though. She had yet to even meet a Blood Elf. Dedrei beckoned for her to quicken her pace and held aside ferns and tall flowers for them to pass through as they journeyed into the thick of the Dell. They had to go through it to come out on the border shared with Verdelore, another Elven city.

"It is only mind-speak between a caelicorn and a person," Dedrei continued. "Some Wielders have the—"

"Wielders?" Sada said.

"Magick users. Do not interrupt, girl."

"Pardon. Magick is real, then?"

Dedrei looked at her flatly, annoyed at the disruptions. "I think you know the answer to that already."

Indeed. She was speaking to a woman who had antlers and could change her form at will. "You say true. Go on."

"Will you allow me to this time?" Dedrei asked. When Sada nodded, she said, "Some Wielders possess the mind-speaking ability themselves. It is only truly special when a bond forms between a caelicorn and its Rider. That is a connection that cannot be broken, even by death. Once a Spiritkin joins with a caelicorn, their very essences are linked, and what kills one kills the other. But it also creates a channel of power between Beast and Spiritkin, a channel that either one can tap into. You must keep this caelicorn close to you, if only so she cannot find her *Hédras*. Once she does, we will be unable to stop her, and then she will have a foal, and caelicorns will prowl Elt once more."

"By stop her, do you mean…" Sada trailed off as Dedrei nodded, her mouth set in a grim line. A horrible realization dawned on her then as well and she let out a small gasp. "If a caelicorn and their Rider die together, then that means when all of the caelicorns were killed—"

Dedrei cut Sada off with a low growl. "I need no reminder of it. It was a terrible sin, one regretted by all who took part in it. Which is why it was vowed that the mistake would never be repeated, should caelicorns come into existence again."

Something terribly sad glistened in the Druid's deer-like eyes as she recounted the tragic history of the caelicorns. Sada couldn't help the pang that seized her own heart at the pain that shone there. Sarana had re-emerged from the trees while they talked, and Dedrei watched her now, frowning.

"In all my centuries, the only caelicorns I have known have been bloodthirsty slaughterers." When she turned to look at Sada, her eyes were glossy with tears. "I can only hope that you are right about this one, Sada."

Sada just set her hand on the Druid's shoulder. Beneath it, miniature flowers and leaves tickled her palm. "Death is a hard burden to carry—but so is fear. Even as the caelicorns are not evil, neither are the Spiritkin who were responsible for their eradication."

Dedrei just smiled and used her staff to jab Sada in the side.

"I did not choose to accompany you thinking it would be this somber of a journey," she said lightly, but when she turned, Sada caught the fall of a tear. "Take off your cloak."

Sada started at the sudden command, but did as the Druid bid. She had stopped in a space where the trees grew closer together than in the rest of the Dell. No rocks or opals marked the ground here, only a thick layer of clover broken up by pads of colorful moss of all shades and hues. A trickle of a stream ran through the small clearing between the thicket of trees, and Sarana began splashing in it as soon as she discovered it. Sada stepped around the stomping filly at Dedrei's beckoning. When she stopped at the Druid's side, she pointed toward the base of a tree with a dip of her antlers.

"Lay your cloak here," she said.

Sada did as she bid. "Are we stopping to rest?"

"Yes. For the night," Dedrei said. "Tomorrow, I will teach you how to forage for food the Druidic way."

THE TWENTY-FIRST

Sada

"Is your stomach upset right now?"

"...No, Sada."

"And does your head pain you?"

"Does my head—? No, it does not. What are you going on about, girl?"

"Well, have you ever noticed that when your stomach is upset or your head does ache, you can never quite remember what it feels like to be well? No? Truly? Well, given the manner in which you were glaring—"

"I was not glaring."

"Given the manner in which you were flatly staring at me...I'd thought perhaps you didn't agree. But you have noticed, then?"

"Yes, Sada. I have noticed."

"Well, then, I thought that I ought to remind you to take notice of how it feels to have a settled stomach and a clear head, that we might properly cherish such while it lasts."

"Thank you, Sada."

Dedrei shook her head as she finished her work, but she was smiling. She was tying the bandages she'd crafted onto Sada's shoulders. They were made up of long, soft leaves held in place with flexible vine. Beneath them, a poultice of herbs was packed onto her shoulders. When they'd gone to sleep the night before, Dedrei had demanded Sada show her the injuries on her shoulders. Sada hadn't wanted to see them herself, knowing what she would find if she looked. But finally, Dedrei had convinced her.

When she pulled down the sleeves of her dress, four angry, red punctures on each shoulder greeted them, just as Sada had known they would. That was the extent of the wounds on her left shoulder. But on her right, they were also seeping a disgusting whitish-yellow liquid, and the redness around the punctures was steadily spreading.

Sada had immediately grown nauseous, her forehead and hands prickling, and had to pet Sarana—she was still getting used to the name—for comfort so as not to pass out from the panic the mere idea of an infection brought her. Dedrei declared the wounds to be in need of treatment, then scolded Sada for waiting so long. Dedrei had asked Sada to relay the story of how Sarana had healed her other wounds, and after she did, Dedrei beckoned the filly over. She asked if she'd heal Sada's shoulder wounds, but Sarana took one sniff at the infected area and backed away, lip curled. Sada was glad of the refusal; she didn't want to risk Sarana getting sick. Even Sada didn't want to be near the wounds and the foul smell that was beginning to emanate from her right shoulder. Unfortunately, her head was attached right next to it.

Sada had awoken the next day to the familiar smell of bright, pungent herbs. Her eyes had flown open, heart racing with excitement at what it might mean that she could smell the apothecary—and distantly did she hear Jezebel's voice?

But when she sat up, she was not in Mr. Pérez's shop, but in the forests of Elt; the herbs were not being ground in a mortar and pestle, but on a rock near where she had slept; and it was not Jezebel's voice she heard, that had been her mind's fancy. Instead, Dedrei was humming and chirping as she worked. Sada quickly forced herself to dispel the disappointment; it had just been a dream, and pining over what could be but was not would do her no good. So she'd fiddled with Jezebel's cuff on her ear, then forced herself to go to Dedrei and learn. Nothing distracted her like learning.

Dedrei had told her about the herbs she'd used for the poultice. Many had names she didn't recognize, and most were not green like the ones in her world, but some shade of blue or yellow. But she did recognize the white flowers of yarrow, and thought she smelled something like lavender. Some of the flowers, Dedrei had even taken from her hair. She didn't pluck them, just held her hand beneath one until it fell readily into her palm.

Dedrei willingly answered all of Sada's questions about the plants, describing their properties and uses. The Druid admitted that when it came to some of them, she didn't exactly know the details of how they provided aid, just that she had an "intuition" that they would. It reminded her of how Sarana simply knew things without explanation. Dedrei seemed certain in her knowledge, and so Sada was certain in Dedrei.

She reminded her of both Jezebel and Gabe in ways she couldn't exactly put into thoughts. But it made the fading dream less painful. When Dedrei had finished, using her saliva to mix the poultice *(It is not as powerful as the caelicorn's, but it will do more good than water,* she'd said after seeing the look on Sada's face), she'd sponged off Sada's injuries using a wet clump of moss, then spread the poultice on and wrapped it in the leaf-and-vine bandage. Now she stood, admiring her work, and went to rinse her hands.

"Thank you, DeeDee," Sada said when her friend returned. "Oh, forgive me. I quite forgot that thanks do not hold the same meaning for you as they do for me."

Dedrei smiled, then bent to pull Sada's sleeves back into place for her. "I appreciate the sentiment. But I did not aid you solely out of Druidic duty, girl." She didn't explain further, and Sada didn't ask. "You are still calling me by that name of nick?"

Sada giggled. "Yes. I like it. And it means we're friends. You will have to come up with one for me, next."

"Will I?"

"Certainly! Would you assist me with my corset?" Sada asked. Dedrei raised an eyebrow, examined the laces, and sighed. But she agreed.

"Why do you constrict your body so? It is strange enough that your people insist on covering every inch of your skin from Elt's caress, and now I come to find out that you also implement minor formshifting?"

Sada giggled at that. "We do not shapeshift!"

"No?" Dedrei asked, tightening the laces. "Then what purpose does this serve?"

"Well, I suppose some ladies use it to alter their figure. But it also supports posture and preserves modesty," Sada said. "Would you tighten it a touch more?"

"And my point has been made for me," Dedrei retorted, and Sada relented that she might have the right of it.

"Isn't it much easier with two people?" she asked when it was done.

"I could not say, Sada. I have neither done it, nor seen it done, with just one person."

"Oh…right." Sada smiled sheepishly. "I'll tell you then, it is much easier with two people."

"There you have it. Are you ready to continue, then? Did you drink your fill of water?"

"Yes, I'm ready." She gathered her cloak and whistled for Sarana.

After the first day, Dedrei had set a slow pace for their journey, saying they shouldn't rush given how much Sada had already exerted herself. She said one ought to travel as a stream did—meandering and guided by Elt. As much as Sada wanted to hurry, she begrudgingly heeded the Druid's advice. And she had to admit, her body thanked her for it. With Dedrei as her guide, they walked easily and rested often, whether it was to admire a flower or stop to try a fruit that looked good. And so it was that they meandered through the Dell, this time with Dedrei pointing out the names of different creatures and plant life they passed.

"If time allows, I will fashion us a water carrier and a basket for our fruits. Until then, we shall have to eat them straight from the bushes and trees."

"Just like the animals!" Sada exclaimed. "Oh, how thrilling this is! Did you know, when I was but a girl, I always longed for an adventure in the woods?"

"I could not have known that," Dedrei said, looking upwards. She checked the sky, the feathers of her eyebrows fanning out over her eyes to shade them from the glare, then started walking just to the right of the sun.

"You are full of sass! You remind me of Jezebel. She had the same spirit. Well, I'll tell you, I always dreamed of getting lost in the woods, befriending the woodland creatures, and stealing apples from my father's orchard or pies from the kitchen whenever hunger struck."

"Have you not been lost in the woods for a quarter moon now? I believe your dream was realized long ago," Dedrei snorted.

"Well, yes. But I'll tell you, it is *quite* different with company. Company that can speak, that is. I enjoy my journey far more now that you are here with me."

"I suppose I am pleased you can find some enjoyment in this, strange though you may be for it." Dedrei turned to wink. "Yet I wonder as to why you wished to lose yourself in the woods as a child. I did not imagine that to be a dream often dreamt by city-dwellers. Tell me, Sada, are you secretly a Druid pretending to be human?"

Sada laughed, then smiled recalling the days of her childhood. All she'd wanted to do was explore, and do the things she could not like jousting, jumping her horse, sparring with Gabe, feeding the wild animals. The constant refusals and warnings of the dangers that came with such activities had turned her dreams into fears. But she still remembered what it was like to hope for the things she once had hoped for, rather than dread them.

"I believe I wished to find my mother, when I was very young. She vanished into the woods when I was but a child, and after that, Father forbade anyone from entering that part of the forest. Even now, decades on, the ban remains. But as I grew older, I think I simply sought some respite. From all the rules."

Dedrei nodded. "You never knew your mother?"

Sada shook her head. "Aside from the tales I've heard of her, no. But my father did all that she could not, in her absence. I would be nothing, and nowhere, without him."

"And yet, it is from him that you wished to run."

"Pardon?" Sada exclaimed. Her heartbeat instantly increased and she scanned the forest, not realizing that she was looking for a pair of cold blue eyes to leap out and reprimand her for the disrespect, the lack of gratitude. "No! Never!"

"Ah. Somebody else enforced the rules over your life, then," Dedrei said. She rolled her eyes. "We need not speak of it if you do not wish to."

Sada took a shaky breath. "I would never run from Father. He does everything for me. All he does is for me."

"Okay, Sada," Dedrei soothed. "That is fine. There is one thing I am curious about, though."

Sada was absorbed in memory. Not of anything specific. It simply seemed her mind had swallowed her up. She thought she smelled lemons, and all she could see were her father's eyes. Her legs only kept moving because it was what they had already been doing, but she felt as though she weren't controlling them. It was like she was a layer removed from reality.

"Hmm?" she asked, not really knowing what she was responding to.

"I told you that your name means 'eternal,' or 'life.' Did your mother name you, or your father?"

Sada realized the irony and chuckled, then the scent of lemons was gone. "My mother did. Isn't that funny? She gave me life, made me life, and then left mine."

Dedrei seemed to realize that Sada was lost somewhere in her own mind, for she didn't speak after that. Sada was glad to have someone to follow in the wilderness. She hadn't realized it when she'd been alone, or even only with Sarana, but it was exhausting being alert all the time, and thinking all the time, and making decisions all the time. She'd never had to do such a thing before, and it was like trying to use a muscle that had atrophied, or running after being still your whole life. Now that Dedrei was here, leading her through the Dell and remaining alert for danger on behalf of both of them, Sada could allow her mind to wander.

She found that it went to thoughts of her mother. She saw flashes of her pale blonde hair and eyes so light an azure they looked almost colorless, like the winter sky when all the blue seemed to have drained out with the warmth. She wasn't certain if the images were from her own memories, or memories of the one picture she'd seen as a child, or purely imagined depictions based on Governess Brown's descriptions of her mother.

She had the beauty of water, or of ice. If there ever was an angel come to earth, it would have been your mother, the old woman had often said. When Sada asked if that meant she had been sweet and kind, her governess had laughed. *Her beauty may have been of ice, but her spirit was of fire.* Apparently, the duchess was spirited, funny, and had quite the mouth, with an impish sort of humor that manifested as a gleam in her eye and a wild grin on her lips. But she had not been a cruel woman—on that front anyone who would speak of the duchess agreed. Sada used to be able to get her father to speak of her, but that had stopped with his singing of her lullabies. It was as though his anger had replaced his willingness to speak of his lost wife.

Sada had often been told she looked like a perfect combination of her mother and her father. She wasn't certain if she was glad of it, or if she despised it. However, she did think that once she got older it had become one of the reasons her father seemed to scorn her. As much as he claimed that he hated punishing her and that it was out of love, Sada didn't think you could hurt someone you loved as badly as he had hurt her.

She thought she smelled lemons again, and her mind went blank for a few peaceful moments. It was Dedrei's voice that brought her out of her revery. It felt similar to being submerged in the bath, looking up through the water at your ceiling, everything slightly blurred but still visible, then coming up and breaking through the surface, taking a deep breath, and realizing how blurry it really had been.

Sada blinked away the memories as she might blink away bath water. She nearly ran into Dedrei, not realizing the Druid had halted mid-step.

"What are you—" Sada began to ask. And then she realized that it hadn't been Dedrei's voice she'd heard. Her friend was utterly silent.

Dedrei was frozen in place as well, standing in the defensive position she'd taken upon seeing Sarana: half-crouched, chin tucked, and antlers lowered. Fear immediately jumped through Sada's body, doing frantic circuits within her limbs.

Upon seeing Dedrei's stance, she expected her friend to be facing a terrible monster, like a dragon or a giant wolf, or something far more terrifying than her own imagination could hope to procure. And so when Sada followed Dedrei's line of sight to a little tan-skinned and brown-haired girl standing amidst the bushes, the fear in her was replaced by surprise and then confusion.

"Oh! A little child! Do you see her moth—"

"Hush," Dedrei said, and nothing in her tone invited Sada to do otherwise.

So many questions burned in Sada's mind: where was the child's mother? Why was Dedrei acting so strangely at the sight of her? Did a monster hide behind her that Sada could not see? Was the girl a Druid—though she looked like an Elf, with her pointed ears and elegant features—and they were interrupting the ritual of her people that said the children were to be raised alone in the forest?

But Sada asked none of them. She thought that if Dedrei had hackles, they would be raised. While she did not have fur, it looked as though the brown feathers that grew to cover her glutes were bristled up, and she'd elongated her nails into claws. Sada didn't like that. It meant that either Dedrei was about to attack a helpless Elven girl, or there was some danger that Sada wasn't privy to.

Sada bit into her lip to keep herself from breaking Dedrei's command and speaking, but she didn't think she would last long. Thankfully, the Druid broke it herself before Sada could.

"Something is amiss," Dedrei said softly.

"What is it?" Sada whispered. "I see only an Elven girl."

"Indeed," Dedrei said, still eyeing the child. She looked to be about six or seven, and her eyes were puffy from crying. Tears that somehow seemed tinged with gold leaked down her face, her sniffles and shaky breaths doing nothing to halt them.

"Oh, we must go to her!" Sada said, but she didn't move. Her instincts were growing stronger in her hand. She hadn't realized the tingling had begun at all, the onset had been so gradual, but now she felt it creeping up her left forearm. "DeeDee?"

"Where is the caelicorn?" she asked abruptly. And as soon as she did, the fear returned to Sada's belly, stirring it like a cook stirs a pot.

"I'm not certain," she said, scanning the forest. "Do you think she's ok?"

She saw nothing other than bright green foliage, lime- and lemon-colored moss, giant trunks, and the Elf girl. There was not an animal to be seen, including Sarana. Sada fought the urge to whistle for her. If there truly was a danger to be had, she wanted the filly away from it, even if her deepest instincts told her to keep her within sight at all times. Instead, she tried to call to her mentally, speaking into that new space within her mind.

Where are you? Sada asked. There was no verbal response, but Sada felt a sense of safety fill her mind. The filly must have picked up on Sada's emotions as well, because a deep sense of concern probed at her next. Sada didn't have time to answer Sarana's unspoken question, and that was just as well, because she wasn't certain what she would have said. *Was* something wrong? She didn't know.

Dedrei didn't give her time to consider it further.

"Come, Sada," the Druid said, reaching back with one hand while keeping her eyes on the Elven girl, her antlers leveled at her. Sada thought the prongs looked sharper. It raised goosebumps on her arms.

"Okay." Sada wasted no time taking Dedrei's hand and allowing her to lead her forward.

The girl watched the two women as they walked past, head turning to track them, never ceasing in her sniffling. Sada felt almost spazzy with nervousness. It wasn't a pleasant or unpleasant feeling, just a barely-containable one. She felt as though the very particles of her body were bouncing on their toes. Her eyes were held wide with adrenaline, and she suddenly didn't feel the need to blink. She held the Elf's green stare as they walked by her. But once they had passed, that lively edginess receded almost immediately along with her *instincts* and Sada halted, making Dedrei stop and face her.

"Will we not go to her aid?" Sada asked. "She cries ceaselessly, and I see no signs of her mother. She is but a child, Dedrei, and she does not appear to me to be one of your people."

"You have the right of that," Dedrei said. Her voice was guttural, as though even her vocal cords had shifted to become more animalistic with her fangs and claws. "But that is no mere child. As I said, something is amiss. I mislike the energy I feel emanating from the thicket in which she stands." Dedrei gestured with her antlers. "Do you see her legs?"

"No," Sada said. Only the girl's upper body was visible, as though she was crouching in the bushes. "What ails them?"

"I do not know. I cannot see them either."

Dedrei's stare was hard. She couldn't close her mouth all the way for the sharp canines now protruding from her lower and upper teeth, and her lip was ever so slightly curled to reveal her gums, which were slightly orange. Dedrei had never looked human, but she had looked humanoid. Now she truly looked half-animal, and as wild as though she really had been raised by the forest.

"I'm scared," Sada said. Dedrei just nodded. Sada wasn't certain if she knew that she'd meant she was scared of *her,* not the Elf. Sada wriggled her wrist free of the Druid's grasp, which had become constricting. She backed up a step, not intending for it to be toward the girl, but it had been.

"Sada, wait!" Dedrei exclaimed.

Sada heard the sound of leaves rustling and turned to see the Elven girl standing up. Sada's face immediately slackened, and her stomach seemed to drop out of her body completely; her *instincts* surged up to her elbow as the girl stood from the cover of the bushes.

Her torso came up from the thicket, but it was not attached to two legs as a child's torso should be. Instead, it appeared as though it had almost melted. Then the head of a deer came up from the foliage beside her, a leaf balanced between its ears. The innocence of that leaf contrasted sharply with the look of the neck, which was longer than any deer's neck should be, and which also became deformed at the base. Finally beside the deer's head surfaced one of a tree cat. Its lips were pulled back in a snarl, its striped face the depiction of hostility. Where its shoulders should have been was only a twisted and malformed trunk of flesh. Each of the heads—Spiritkin, deer, and tree cat—connected to an elongated and deformed neck-torso. And each of those neck-torsos melted into a single scaly, four-legged body.

Sada couldn't scream. Her voice had abandoned her along with any self-preservation. For all she did was stare. She felt as though she was going to throw up, not the contents of her stomach, however, but her heart or her soul, or something else vital within her. Fear was too weak a word to describe what she felt in that moment. It was closer to a combination of disgust, horror, and unreality.

The creature, if such a horror could even be called that, stepped forward with one scaly and clawed foot, and once again, Sada found herself thankful that Dedrei was now with her. As Sada was staring helplessly, Dedrei grabbed the collar of her dress and yanked her backward.

Then she said, *"Run,"* and that was all Sada needed to hear. She spun on her heel and took off at a dead sprint, fueled by pure terror and perhaps something supernatural as well, for she ran faster than she'd ever thought herself able to. She didn't look at where she was going. Her body navigated the wood for her, leaping over streams and hillocks, dodging trunks and stones. She felt as though she had an endless amount of energy, and even if she sprinted for a day, so long as the monster was on her heels—she could not hear its footsteps so much as feel them, sending tremors through the earth to chase her—she would not be able to expend it. But this flat-out sprint was the best she could do to try and rid herself of the energy.

At some point, Dedrei told Sada to get on her back. Then she shifted into what Sada thought was an elk from what she could see in her peripherals, and ran beside her so closely they nearly touched. She hardly even noticed the Druid, other than the brown flashes of her coat, and the tawny glimpses of her vine-strung antlers. And though the rational part of her mind knew that an elk was surely faster than her human self, she could not obey her friend's order. Firstly, she felt as though she was simply incapable of ceasing her sprinting; she was still so full of frantic panic that if she stopped moving, she thought she might truly go insane. And secondly, the irrational, fear-driven back of her brain trusted nobody but herself (for the first time in her life) and would not allow her to place her life in the hands of anyone, even Dedrei. And so she ignored the Druid, and she continued to run.

She truly wasn't certain how long she sprinted for. She never tired, even when her breaths began to come out in short, barely-there gasps and sweat was dripping cold down her spine, the back of her thighs, and her chest. She was in some sort of survival trance, and the only thing she could think was *run.* She only stopped when Dedrei bounded ahead of her in her elk-form, turned to the side, and stopped dead in Sada's path. She barely had time to slow before she was careening into the Druid. Her face met a wall of chocolate fur and then she bounced backward and to the hard ground. Sada immediately tried to stand so that she could continue running again, but her legs would have none of it. Realizing the feeling of rest, they collapsed beneath her, and then began to shake and tremble so spastically that she could not even bend her knees to try and stand.

Sada didn't see Dedrei shift—she was too busy looking around for signs of the monster—but then the Druid was kneeling in front of her in her Spiritkin form, concern etched deep into her face.

"Are you well, child? Hush, breathe deeply, not so shallowly like you are a cat."

Sada just frowned at Dedrei, still panting as rapidly as her heart was beating, which was to say, much too rapidly. This was no time for concern nor rest. Her face must have expressed as much because Dedrei shook her head.

"We have succeeded in outrunning it. How, I cannot say, but you ran nearly as swiftly as my elk form. But we shall marvel at this later. For now, take comfort in the knowledge that we have outpaced the chimydra greatly enough for you to recover the breath you have spent."

Sada trusted Dedrei, but the part of her that was driven purely by the need to survive was still activated, and she looked around for herself to check for any signs of the Beast before accepting that it was not in their vicinity. She could not even feel the tremble of its steps in the ground. Sada nodded. The energy had faded quickly from her body, and now she felt the extent of her exertions. Her face seemed to be filled with the essence of heat itself, her thighs burned harsher than any acid, and her left arm throbbed where her *instincts* had scourged her.

"Interesting…creature," Sada said between pants. She frantically fanned at her face. It did no good, but even a worthless gesture like that made her feel better than just simply sitting and waiting for the monster to catch up to them. "What…is…it? Chim…?"

Dedrei chuckled dryly. "Interesting is certainly one way to describe it. I believe it to be a chimydra, though it is unlike any I have seen in my lifetime. It is small, still young. It must have been born with its defects, though what may have caused them…" She shook her head, and the flowering vines wrapped around her antlers swung with her hair. "I believe that is due to something beyond just a physical defect."

"Like the spring," Sada said. Her breathing and heartbeat had slowed some, but she still felt as though all the blood and heat in her body were coalesced in her face.

"The spring?" Dedrei frowned.

"Tell you of it…later. But Lady Bl— I mean, Sarana said…was evil there."

"I see. Yes, I fear we shall soon witness signs of its influence spreading throughout the realm." Dedrei's eyes hardened, then, and she locked her gaze with Sada's. "Once you have caught your breath, we will move. I must eradicate this abomination. Were it but an ordinary Beast, hunting us for food or sport, as some Beasts do, I would suggest we leave it be and outpace it until it lost our scent or its interest in us. But as things stand, I cannot, as a Druid and as a resident of this realm, permit such evil to exist and corrupt our world. I fear I am being called to eradicate it wherever I find it, beginning with this chimydra.

"Hear me now. Not far from here is a hollow where a family of foxes dwell. If I mark you with my scent, they will take you in until I can retrieve you. You will be safe with them."

Dedrei stood and held out a hand to help Sada to her feet, but she wouldn't take it.

"Why are you saying that?" Sada asked with a frown. "It would be difficult, if not impossible, for me to aid you from the den of a fox, would it not?"

"I have no time to waste in debate, Sada. I cannot call myself your guardian and willingly send you into danger. Come now, before the chimydra closes the distance between us."

She extended her hand once more, but Sada folded her arms stubbornly. "No," she said, raising her chin. "I will come with you. I can travel beside you or follow in your wake, but either way, I will come. You are not only my guardian, you are my friend, and I cannot call myself your friend and leave you to face danger alone."

For a moment they held each other's gaze, Sada fighting the urge to chew her lip. But she refused to back down. It was not something to even be considered. She had fought one Beast before, but she did not see this as a qualification to fight more. Rather, she saw it as her duty as a human being to do as Dedrei said and fight evil, in whatever form it may come.

She had the idea that her body was too tired to register any fear that ought to come along with that decision, but that mattered little to her. She was determined to help her friend. Even regardless of her personal disdain for evil, she would not allow Dedrei to fight any creature alone.

Finally Dedrei sighed, rubbing at her face. "Your stubbornness is something to be studied. Why you wish to accompany me to face the spawn of evil, I fear I shall never understand. Yet I see that you will not be swayed. Very well, girl, you have won this battle," she muttered. "Let us be off."

"Thank you," Sada said triumphantly. "But first, if it is not too much trouble, I must know where Lady Blue is. Will you keep watch for the...what did you call it? A chimydra? Will you keep an eye for it while I try to find her?"

Dedrei narrowed her eyes, scanning Sada's face for a moment. "Very well. Just make haste; it draws near. And do not stray too far."

Sada smiled, but it was a tired one. "I won't." First, she tried whistling, once low and once high. When their agreed upon signal didn't summon Sarana, she closed her eyes and reached into the Mindspace.

She didn't see anything other than the reddish-black color of the back of her eyes. Then, when Sada focused on it, thinking of her connection with Sarana, a pinprick of white light formed in her vision. Whether that was her physical vision or the vision of the elusive third eye Mrs. Pérez spoke of, she couldn't be sure. And though it had never happened before, the sight of that light didn't surprise her. She had a deep and sturdy feeling that it represented Sarana, or their connection.

Sada wondered where Sarana was, still watching that light. It wavered as she focused on it, the edges shifting from blurred to clear. Her thoughts weren't in words, as they were when she thought to herself, but more of a formless curiosity about Sarana's location.

The light seemed to shiver and grow clearer, then she heard, *North of your location. You are safe.* The latter thought was accompanied by relief that seemed to begin at the top of Sada's head and fall over her body like a cloak coming closed.

Yes, Sada thought. But again, it wasn't in words. She simply knew that her being safe was the truth, and her knowledge of that truth was conveyed to Sarana. *You are as well?*

Indeed. I shall return to you presently to aid in your battle against the chimydra.

Panic instantly rekindled in Sada in frantic jolts.

NO! she thought, and flashing images of the filly being gouged by those reptilian claws or torn apart by the tree cat's jaws jumped through her mind as well. They must have entered the Mindspace, though she hadn't intended that, because Sarana was instantly shushing her. Her voice was that of one thousand mothers.

You underestimate my strength, child. My body is young and my horn soft, yet I have centuries of knowledge regarding both battle and Beasts such as the chimydra. Perhaps I may aid you and the Druid with my wisdom, if not with my strength.

Sarana, Sada began, but she sensed that the caelicorn was finished responding to her. The light began to grow larger—closer—then she felt Dedrei's hand on her arm. She opened her eyes to the brightness of the forest, coming back to herself and the discomfort in her body from her sprinting. Despite the near-certain fact that the Beast must be closer to them now, Sada felt only a resounding calmness and surety in her mission.

"Is it near?" Sada asked, looking at Dedrei. She appeared focused as well, her diamond-shaped pupils narrow and sharp.

Dedrei nodded and reached down to help Sada up again. This time she let her. The Druid brushed her dress off for her then took her hands.

"Come. Listen to me now," Dedrei said, and she told Sada her plan.

Sada listened, entirely focused on her friend's every word. She had never seen Dedrei's eyes so serious, brightened with the intensity of what she imparted. Her features were no longer animalistic, but that quickly changed. Once she'd instructed Sada, she stepped back.

And she began to shift.

All in the same moment, Dedrei's nose broadened and flattened, her canines grew sharper and protruding, her claws lengthened and thickened, her antlers receded. Dedrei's long, brown hair shortened and thickened into a lion-like mane, her hands broadened into paws, and a tail sprouted above her glutes. Then Dedrei was curling over to stand on all fours as her body grew, her legs lengthening and thickening as slabs of muscle developed on her flanks, shoulders, neck, and back.

Her skin became fur spotted like a leopard, and her feathers, which were a rich brown in her Spiritkin form, filled out along her flanks and legs and took on hues and patterns of every color—green, blue, yellow, striped, spotted. Her tail, which was as long as she was, filled out and feathers sprouted from it as well. In just a matter of seconds, Sada was no longer staring at a tall, supple woman with antlers, but a feathered leopard as tall as her chest. The only remainders of Dedrei were the flowering vines, which were still tangled in her mane, and her brown eyes like pine bark after a rainstorm with their diamond pupils.

Despite the impossible transformation she'd just witnessed and the fact that there was a chest-high leopard staring at her just feet away, Sada felt no fear. She nodded to Dedrei, then after holding her gaze for one more second, a second weighted with an unspoken urging for her to be safe, the Druid bounded away on silent paws. The chimydra had drawn near to them in the time Sada had rested, and she could once again feel the vibrations its clawed feet sent through the earth with each pounding step. Dedrei would now follow those tremors, along with the stench she claimed the Beast to have, until she met it in its path. Then she would serve as a distraction while Sada searched.

Sada had confidence in her friend's strength, especially in what seemed to be such a powerful form, but a part of her felt guilty for allowing Dedrei to run headlong into danger while she ran about gathering supplies. Had Father been there, he would have been fighting the chimydra before they could stop to formulate a plan. But she was not her father. And she knew that if he was there, he would also tie her to a tree before allowing her to go anywhere near the Beast. And so, she reasoned, doing as Dedrei asked was doing a great service, one greater than the Duke would allow her to.

I'm sorry, father, she thought, and then she went away from where Dedrei had gone.

Dedrei

Dedrei did not bother with silence as she went to the Beast, though she made little noise in this form regardless. The leoteryx was one of her strongest forms in both senses: she had spent nearly a year with a family of them, learning their ways and customs, and it was an easy form to adopt. The big cat was also known for its stealth and ferocity, especially when defending its young or its pride. And so it was with complete focus and confidence that Dedrei tracked the chimydra as it tracked Sada.

She had not liked the girl upon their initial encounter, and that was now something she berated herself for. She had acted in the same manner that fairfolk acted toward the rest of the Spiritkin, with haughtiness and arrogance. It was true that her identity as a Druid compelled her to aid the girl. But her duties did not require her to converse with Sada, nor answer her strange questions and entertain her strange comments, like those ones about her head and stomach, or when she asked what Dedrei's favorite leaf was. And they did not require her to care for Sada.

And yet she found herself doing all of those things. It was also true that her identity as a Druid compelled her to reconcile this evil presence in their world. But that was not what fueled her forward with such urgency, and such anger. Instead, she found herself urgent to reach this Beast because she feared what would happen to the girl if she did not.

The Mother of Druids, Woia, taught of balance and peace and love, even toward humans. All Druids knew Elt's history with the humans and their realm, but still they were called not to hate the mortals. Woia taught them this specifically. To begin with, humans were fellow creatures with the breath of life in them. But more than that, they were distantly related to all Spiritkin, and one should not hate kin.

And yet Dedrei and a few others had found themselves harboring disgust for the human race and their evil actions; the corruption and harm they had once brought to Elt, and still brought to their own world and each other. But—even though the dirty part of Dedrei despised herself for it—she found her companionship and time with Sada erasing that disgust. Sada could certainly talk too much, and she had no true concept of how the world worked, but she was a light in a world of darkness. Even in a balanced realm like Elt, she shone.

This chimydra sought to put out her light, and so Dedrei sought to put it out of its misery and end its abominable existence.

She smelled the stench, one of rotting flesh and mildew, before she saw the Beast. But it came into view shortly after. It no longer ran—it had grown too tired; it was still a baby after all—but it carried on in Sada's direction all the same. Each of the heads swung around madly, as if they all sought something different. But the body they were all conjoined to had one purpose: to kill Dedrei and Sada. And it seemed that none of the heads were powerless to stop that. Perhaps they all wanted it.

The abomination of a head saw Dedrei first, and when its watering green eyes locked onto Dedrei's, she immediately stopped, sank into a crouch, and snarled. It was less of a decision and more of a visceral reaction to the monstrosity. The tree cat whipped around to face her next and matched her snarl, its hackles raising around its striped face, made even angrier at the sight of another wildcat. Then the deer stared at her blankly, nostrils flaring. It was a wonder it did not die of panic at or soon after its birth, being situated next to the head of an animal who by nature wanted to kill it. Oh well, Dedrei would take care of that.

The Beast stilled its pounding walk, claws sinking into the soft earth. Dedrei's gaze switched between the three pairs of eyes—green, brown, green. Her nostrils flared against the stench of corruption. The Elven girl smiled pitifully and the tree cat hissed.

Dedrei leapt.

THE TWENTY-SECOND

Sada

The adrenaline had left Sada, replaced by calm. She had been given careful instruction, and now she had a purpose. She would be able to complete it without fretting. She even sang as she walked to do Dedrei's bidding: *Seek out a large leaf or a hollow piece of bark—mind that it is without holes—and then find yourself a pond. The caelicorn, should you chance upon her, can guide you to one. Gather as much water as you can and then return to me. Go slowly so that you do not spill; there is no need to rush out of worry for me.*

Sada had found Sarana quickly. Or rather, Sarana had found her. As she walked along a path adjacent to the direction Dedrei had gone, she'd seen a blur of cerulean between the trees, the gleam of the filly's golden horn, and then she was whickering softly to Sada. A sense of relief radiated through her, made stronger by the share of it coming from Sarana.

Sada had dropped to her knees and hugged the filly, then a sense of urgency filled her mind, and she quickly stood, brushing off her dress, and continued through the forest. She had updated Sarana on her quest, not certain that the connection they shared would inform the filly of such information; she certainly was not aware of all of Sarana's thoughts. The filly understood her unspoken request immediately and moved off at a trot, glancing back with a watchful eye every few moments to ensure Sada was following. She was, and it was only by dropping all ladylike appearances and scrabbling over roots and rocks on all fours that she managed to match Sarana's pace.

She could no longer feel tremors in the ground signaling the chimydra's hunt for her, but she heard its cries every so often. They were typically the yowls of the tree cat, sounding more defiant than agonized. Every so often the deer would raise its voice to scream alongside the feline. She never heard Dedrei's voice, whether it was a cry of pain or a shout of rage, but she knew that her friend lived because the chimydra did not advance, and Sarana never quickened her pace or turned in that direction except to swivel her ears every so often.

Sada already felt close enough to the Druid that she believed she would feel it in some way if her friend met death, or found herself with a grave injury. Logically, this was not likely; there was magick in Elt, but she possessed none of it, and even if she did, she didn't know if it worked in that way. But still, the idea was enough to keep her from worrying overmuch for her friend. She followed Sarana's golden tail through the forest, mind set only on finding water and nothing else.

They came to a puddle shortly, and Sarana stopped and pointed to it with her horn, just in case Sada had not seen it, she supposed. It was only when she dropped to her knees beside it that she realized she had neglected to find anything to collect and carry it with.

"Oh, fiddle a farrier!" she cried. "I've forgotten the most important bit of the instructions!" But as she was getting up to search for a leaf or piece of bark as Dedrei had told her, she saw something strange.

Standing nearly eye-level with her on a loop of root to her right was a short mushroom. At least, she'd assumed it was a mushroom, because it was the same shape and size and color as one, with a brown cap and a tan stem. But it had chubby arms and short legs, and black eyes peeking out below the cap. It gaped at her, wide-eyed and open-mouthed, and Sada gaped right back at it.

"Hello," she finally said, and she was so close that her breath rustled the large, black-and-white flower it was holding, nearly blowing the mushroom fellow off the root. He made a few squeaking and grunting sounds, and somehow his eyes widened even further, then he thrust the flower forward at her. "Is this for me?"

The mushroom person said nothing, only shoved the flower forward again. Gently, so as not to frighten him, Sada took it between two fingers. As soon as she lifted it away, the little creature stumbled backward and with a squeak, fell off the root.

Sada sucked in a breath and leaned over, searching for her little friend. She saw him among the leaf litter, lying on his back with a hand to his mushroom cap head, looking dizzy. Two other mushroom people were crouched around him, and they stared up at Sada with the same expressions of absolute bafflement the first one had given her. Sada reached down to help the fallen creature up, but he flinched away and one of his companions batted at her fingers with tiny fists. She withdrew, whispered a thank you, then went to the water.

The flower she'd been given was large and shaped like a bell, with a hollow space inside. She thought it looked similar to a honeysuckle flower, only ten times as large and spotted black and white like a cow. Sada still felt no real panic, but the sense of urgency was strong in her mind, urging her to hurry back to Dedrei, and she hastily dipped the flower into the puddle. Sarana was ready and waiting to lead her back to Dedrei, and as soon as Sada stood, she made off at a trot in the direction the Druid had gone. Sarana never stopped to scent the earth or cock her head and listen, and Sada wondered how she was able to track their friend. She would have to ask later. For now, she put all her focus into ensuring the water never spilled from the flower.

Sarana had briefly explained the nature of a chimydra to Sada as they'd sought the water. The chimydra was a Beast that was a combination of several animals with multiple heads of different species, and while they were not friendly, they were never so abominable as the one they now faced. When Sada asked, Sarana had said that the thing which made this creature so evil was the fact that it had a Spiritkin head. It had never before been seen on a chimydra, because chimydras were Beasts. Beasts and Spiritkin did not mix. It would be the same as animals and humans mixing. The fact that this chimydra had somehow been born with an Elven head was the reason both Dedrei and Sarana were so eager to destroy it. Sarana's disgust didn't need to be conveyed in words: it emanated so strongly through the bond that Sada felt almost as though it was borne of her own heart.

The way chimydra were defeated, Sarana had said, was by targeting each of the animal heads' inherent weakness. If cut off before this happened, they would just grow back, and become fiercer with each regrowth. Only after defeating each aspect of the chimydra would its body as a whole be destroyed.

Sada assumed the water was for the tree cat, considering cats in her world did not like water. The Eltic felines were probably not so fond of it either. How they would destroy the other animal aspects, Sada did not know. She did not even think to consider it. Dedrei would take care of that. All Sada needed to do was bring the water, and then she would receive further instruction from the Druid, and she would then obey it.

She and Sarana worked their way through the forest at a trot, and despite the fact that Sada stared only at the flower as she ran, taking care not to jostle her arms, she managed not to trip. They reached Dedrei quickly. Even if Sada had not had the filly to lead her, she reckoned she probably could have found the Druid and Beast by herself—the tree cat's yowling could be heard even from the puddle, and only grew louder and scratchier as they neared. When the monster drew into view, the screeching was so loud that it was all Sada could do not to drop the flower and cover her ears. Instead, she ran straight to Dedrei, her face contorted in a cringing wince all the while. Dedrei was crouching before the monster, feathered tail swishing.

Before Sada could get close enough to the Druid to ask what to do with the water, Dedrei bared her long, yellowed fangs and growled. The sound was feral and guttural enough to stop Sada in her tracks. She skidded to a halt in the moss, cool water splashing onto her hands. But she hardly noticed in light of what was taking place before her.

Dedrei was a fearsome sight to be seen in this form, one which Sarana had told her was called a leoteryx. With her hackles raised and her mane bristling, she was the size of a bear. Her claws dug gorges into the earth, and her eyes were brilliant with fury. Sada thought that if she were standing in place of the monster, she would probably faint at the sight of Dedrei as her opponent. The chimydra did not seem intelligent enough to feel such fear, however. There were deep, wet gouges across its dark chest and forelegs where Dedrei's claws had marked it, and yet it danced before the Druid as though it had not been harmed, and faced no threat of further injury. As the Druid growled and roared, the tree cat yowled defiantly back. Yet its screech was pitiful when compared with Dedrei's.

But it was not the tree cat or the leoteryx that Sada watched.

Beside the cat head, the deer was wide-eyed with panic. Its nostrils flared so widely she could see the red of its veins lit by the sun. Its brown eyes, so unlike Dedrei's now, were ringed with white and rolling every which direction like the wheel of a carriage, and its mouth was open and panting and foaming white. Yet Sada knew it was not from soap-mouth, but rather a much deadlier disease: fear.

As if to demonstrate Sada's very thought, the deer head began jerking back in any attempt to flee from Dedrei. But the lizard body and the other two heads were stubborn—the chimydra held its ground despite the deer head's panic, even going so far as to swipe at Dedrei. When it did, the Druid snapped her powerful jaws at the outstretched lizard hand, and the Beast immediately jerked it back. If Sada hadn't known better, she would have thought Dedrei looked disappointed that she had not been quick enough to snap off a knuckle or claw. The chimydra tried to dodge to the side, then, to reach Sada, but Dedrei cut it off easily and it retreated. The tree cat snapped its puny teeth, but Dedrei had eyes only for the deer. Her lips curled upward in what looked like a gruesome feline smile as she growled again.

This time, it was not a roar or a yowl, but something low and dark, so deep it was felt more than heard. Sada cringed against the sound. It vibrated in her eardrums and her skull, making her jaw tickle and ache. The deer was even worse for wear than Sada was. At the sound of the huge leoteryx's growl and the sight of it crouching almost leisurely, tail lazily flicking back and forth in the air, the deer head lurched backward. In an attempt to flee the predator, it swung into the cat head and Elven head. The tree cat turned and snapped at the deer, drawing blood from its cheek, and the deer squealed. It was panting wildly now, and making pitiful bleating noises. Sada doubted it could see at all with the way its eyes were constantly rolling, more white than brown showing.

Then Dedrei took a single, stalking step forward. The deer, it seemed, had had enough. With a final scream, it began to jerk away from the leoteryx, so violently that Sada heard tendons cracking and a sound like bubbles popping. It rammed into the tree cat head again and its feline counterpart snapped at its neck and jaw. Its flailing movement tore the wounds open wide, skin pulling apart, blood gushing and squirting out, muscle stretching. The tree cat's biting in combination with the deer's frantic jerking was a truly deadly combination. Dedrei growled again and with one final jerk, the deer head ripped itself away from the chimydra body. The head separated halfway from the neck-torso with a sickening popping and ripping noise like that of a shirt tearing. It died before it could completely free itself, and, tongue lolling, its head slowly sank forward so that it was hanging down over the chimydra's scaly chest.

The Beast hardly seemed to care that its head was dead. It only reached up and batted at it with a scaly paw. The tree cat did its best to lean down and sniff at the exposed and bloody flesh, but its torso was too thick to be flexible and it could only get close enough to flick its tongue out for a taste.

Sada stared, eyebrows raised and mouth open, at the chimydra and the red blood dripping off the deer's ears. She turned to Dedrei and barely noted that her friend had shifted. She shook one paw until it turned into a hand, and then she was fully in her Spiritkin form again.

"Did you see that?" Sada asked, gesturing to the chimydra.

Dedrei didn't answer her. "Bring the water. This is not over."

Sada did as she was asked, still staring in amazement at the dangling head. Sarana stepped up beside her, regarding the Beast with a cocked head and perked ears. The chimydra seemed distracted by its dead head, and Dedrei whistled to get its attention.

As soon as it turned, it lunged, though by this point the chimydra was tired and its attack was half-hearted. Even in her Spiritkin form, Dedrei's agility was evident, and she easily side-stepped to avoid the reaching claws and snapping jaws. It leapt and she dodged again, and the chimydra ended up facing Sada. Without thinking, she moved in front of Sarana, closer to the Beast's claws. When it swiped, she had to dodge its foot to avoid being clawed. She hopped away, and for some reason a giggle escaped her, almost delirious in nature. The monster growled and batted at her again, but Sada dodged once more, spinning away this time, still grinning and squealing when the claws came close enough to rip through her dress.

She knew that she faced true danger, and yet she could not help but feel that it was all some game. This felt nothing like her battle with the fox, where she'd feared for her life so greatly she had almost *wanted* to die just so the worry of it would be over. Dodging the chimydra's attacks wasn't exactly fun, but still, she laughed and squealed and grinned. Dedrei was whistling and yelling to get the Beast's attention, but it was either more entertained or more irritated with Sada as an opponent than it was with Dedrei, for it ignored the Druid. It crouched, preparing to swing a paw out again, and Sada made to dodge once more. But Sarana hopped out in front of her, stamping down her front hooves and squealing. Then she opened her wings and angled them so that they reflected the sunlight into the tree cat and Elven girl's eyes. As the chimydra winced, its entire large body recoiling, Dedrei tossed the water into the feline head's face.

Immediately, it yowled, hissing and clawing at itself in an attempt to scratch the water off. It gouged its own neck and torso but didn't seem to care in its confusion, and again, Sada wondered what controlled the chimydra body if not the individual heads. Did they have minds? Souls? If not, then was it animated purely by magick? The cat head jerked, then, trying vainly to escape the touch of the horrible water. It must have moved at the wrong angle, though, because Sada heard a distinct *crack* like the pop of the Duke's ankles, only louder and much more disturbing. The cat froze mid-yowl, its eyes suddenly going wide as it realized something was terribly wrong. Then a low whine began to escape from its half-open jaws along with a string of drool, and the head slowly slumped forward, like a tall lump of clay folding in on itself atop the pottery wheel. As the cat head came to rest beside the dead deer head, the whine stopped. Sada watched expressionless as the drool began to pool up in the grass.

"What happened?" Sada asked.

"Paralysis," Dedrei said simply.

"Ah. It's still alive, then. Shall I kill it?"

That time, both Dedrei and Sarana answered her, and both responses were a resounding *"No."*

Sada was still spazzy with adrenaline, as on-edge as she had been upon first seeing the Elven girl. She even bounced in place, feeling as though she had to dispel the energy bundled up inside her in some way. She felt like the embodiment of the static in the air before a storm. She thought she ought to feel bad for the chimydra, but she couldn't, not yet. So she just looked with a disconnected curiosity at the limp heads, and the final able one, as she bounced on her toes.

This Beast is much enfeebled: the Druid shall fare better if we remain safely aside, removing ourselves as cause for concern, Sarana said.

"Oh," Sada said, and as her bouncing slowed, she realized she was somewhat disappointed.

It *had* been fun dodging the big creature's attacks. Perhaps because it was as Sarana had said, and it was not a true threat. Or perhaps it was the resurfacing of the young and reckless aspect of herself; the aspect that had wanted to joust with Gabe and hunt with John, which Governess Brown and Father and her guards had buried and replaced with fear. In Elt, there was nobody to keep her from what they had called reckless danger, and what she had thought of as *living.* Yet she heeded Sarana's advice out of concern for Dedrei, and retreated to stand with her back against a tree, but ready to leap forward if the monster somehow gained the upper hand.

After noting with a quick glance that Sada had moved out of harm's way, Dedrei dropped into a crouch to watch the Beast with narrowed eyes.

The chimydra swung its final head around helplessly. The Elven girl's eyes, still ceaselessly watering, continued on an endless loop looking between the fallen heads, Sada and her friends, and the forest.

The big lizard body shifted on its feet as though unsure of what to do. It didn't seem likely to attack anymore, but Sada didn't feel as though that made it any safer for Dedrei to approach. Despite the fact that the chimydra didn't seem like much of a threat, the birds still didn't sing, and the deep-rooted instincts in Sada told her that meant it remained a threat, no matter how weak. The only sound to be heard was the child's sniffling, which had neither slowed nor increased throughout their altercation. Finally the Beast fell onto its haunches and the girl began to wail.

Dedrei stood. Weaponless and clawless in her Spiritkin form, she approached the chimydra. It regarded her somewhat sullenly with its final head, the body shifting to face her. Sada saw its shoulders tense, but it made no move to attack. She thought it was more likely to flee.

"Take care, DeeDee," Sada said. Fear for her friend overpowered any lingering excitement she had felt.

Dedrei nodded, but did not answer. She was near enough that if she only took a few more steps, she would be able to touch the Beast. That was where she stopped.

Sarana spoke no words into the Mindspace, but Sada was reminded of the knowledge that a chimydra having a Spiritkin head was an abomination, whether it sought to attack them or not. The evil it represented, and perhaps harbored, would not be bested until the head and the creature it belonged to were deceased. She met Lady Blue's golden eyes and nodded her understanding. The sheer amount of energy coursing through her put not only her body on edge, but her concern for her friend as well. She bit her lip, still shifting on her feet in an attempt to expel at least some of the nervous energy, as she watched her friend.

Dedrei

Dedrei's heart clenched as she looked into the eyes of the Spiritkin head, seeing something achingly familiar in its tearful gaze. The eyes, though set in a monstrous form, reminded her of the gentle gaze of a child lost—one who had barely known the world before it was ripped away from them. She took a shaky breath, feeling the old wound tear open once again, but this time she embraced the pain. It was the only way forward.

"I…I had a child once." Stepping closer to the chimydra, she spoke softly, hesitantly. "A daughter, called Shiual. She hardly saw three springs before she returned to Elt. So small, so fragile. She was too delicate even to be taken out of the tribe to be raised by the forest. I had thought that keeping her alongside me as no Druidic mother is able to would be a blessing, but in the end, it was a curse.

"She had a laugh that was like the first birds of spring, and big, beautiful green eyes…somewhat like your own. She could not shift into any animal form, for she never had the chance to spend time with their families and learn their ways. But she was talented. She had the blood of old royalty, and she taught herself how to wear a tail. Always a fox tail." Dedrei felt herself smiling, despite the familiar pain. "I watched her take her first steps. Her tail caused her to lose her balance, but she refused to go without it. Eventually she took to wrapping it around her little waist so that she could still wear it but not stumble. I thought I would see her grow into someone strong, someone brave. I thought I would be able to ask her why she chose a fox tail rather than one of a cat or wolf. But…I never had the chance."

She could feel the tears threatening hotly in her eyes, but she pressed on, refusing to look away from the Elven head, whose sniffling had started to falter; its own eyes still glistened, overfull of golden tears that now fell silently. The lizard body seemed to droop, no longer shifting or searching for ways to flee: the remaining head was wholly in control now, and captivated by her story. Dedrei continued, knowing that Sada was hearing all of it and hoping that it did not affect her in the way she aimed to affect the chimydra's child head.

"I have made myself forget as much as possible about the night she was taken from me, but I remember the darkest parts. Yet I cannot bring myself to burden you with those—you have suffered too much already. All I will say is that sickness came like a shadow, and there was nothing I could do to fight it. I held her in my arms as she faded, and I begged the Creator to take me instead. But while I was heard, my abominable wish was not heeded. I have carried that ache every day since, knowing I will never hold Shiual again, never hear her voice, and never ask about the fox tail that she died wearing."

Dedrei could see the Elven head trembling now, its face a mirror of her own anguish. The tears streaking down her cheeks were so torrential that her entire face was wet with translucent gold. For a brief moment, the monstrous creature before her looked more Spiritkin than ever, vulnerable and haunted by sorrow. She felt her own tears fall, but there was a clarity in her heart—a grim resolve that this was the only way.

"I do not know what brought you here, or why you are trapped in this twisted body," Dedrei whispered, "but I can see your pain, and I am sorry for it. Maybe, in another life and another body, you were someone's child, too. And I hope you knew love then. Perhaps once you were mine. And if that was the case, then I can say with a certainty that you were loved."

As she spoke those final words upon which her voice cracked and shook, she had grown one nail into a long and sharp point. The child head's lip trembled, unaware of what Dedrei planned. The chimydra lunged forward suddenly, and distantly Sada cried out. But the Beast did not seek to attack her. With one arm, Dedrei embraced the Elven torso as it sobbed into her hair. With the other, she slid her nail into its chest and pierced its monstrous heart. The creature let out a shuddering breath as it slumped against her.

Dedrei went down with it and knelt there for a long moment, her hand still pressed against its scaly breast. Her heart was heavy but certain. She felt the Beast's own heart slow and weaken in its pulsing around her claw. The monster did not fight its death; she thought it even welcomed it. As the child had reflected Dedrei's sorrow, perhaps Dedrei had reflected to it the chimydra's monstrosity. The heart stilled and she withdrew her nail, thick with purplish-black blood.

Bowing her head in prayer, she saw its tears mingling with hers on the ground. The sight of those golden Elven tears only confirmed the Beast's monstrosity, but it did not lessen the sting of what she had done. It was still a child of Elt.

I have returned you to where you belong. Perhaps you can heal in Elt's embrace, Dedrei thought. She stroked the dark brown hair of the Elven head once, trying and failing not to imagine that it was Shiual instead.

Sada

Sada watched numbly as Dedrei knelt with the fallen Beast and prayed. Her language was beautiful, sounding more like birdsong and the babbling of a brook than any human language. Although Sada couldn't understand what she said, the sullenness of it was heavy in the air. She, too, had cried as Dedrei told her story, and she hurried to wipe the tears, now cool on her cheeks, before her friend could see. She didn't want her sorrow to take precedence over Dedrei's grief over a lost child.

After hearing of Shiual, Sada realized as well why Dedrei's companionship felt so familiar and novel at the same time.

Dedrei stood and Sada tried to smile softly at her. Sarana went to the Druid and dipped her head. Dedrei bowed back. It was the most respectful interaction she had ever seen between the two.

Dedrei led Sada and Sarana away from the chimydra in silence. They went in the same direction they had once run to flee from it, and Dedrei stopped to pick up her staff before continuing on. Sada glanced back to look at the dead monster more than once. To be certain it didn't get up again, or out of hope that it would, she didn't know. She wasn't certain if burials were custom in Elt, but Dedrei did not instruct them to do anything with the body but leave it there. Perhaps because it was an abomination, as she'd said. It was quickly left behind in the forest, and then Sada and her friends were alone with the trees once more. The birdsong had returned, as well as the chitter of animals. She thought she'd heard a fox and thought of Shiual, and wondered if Dedrei did too every time she saw one of the animals. She wondered if her memories were still painful, or if they were long enough past to be a source of joy yet. It had certainly seemed like the former, and that made Sada's sorrow for her friend even deeper.

The nature of the chimydra's death still bothered Sada. Sarana had told her that each head had to be defeated by its own weakness before it could be killed as a whole, but she had never told Sada what those weaknesses were. Based on what she'd seen of the deer's gruesome ending, its weakness had been fear; the cat's had evidently been water. But the Spiritkin head...It had been weakened by grief, or sorrow, but not its own. The grief of another, of a stranger. And that meant that the Spiritkin weakness was empathy, compassion—care for another being. And likely it was the human weakness as well.

Sada had grown up hearing that she was too sensitive. If ever one of the horses or dogs was injured on a hunt, Gabe and John instructed the others not to speak of it near her, for she would demand to see the hurt animal, then weep inconsolably over its injury and impending death. She cried when she found birds with broken wings, or sometimes when she visited the commonfolk's district of the capital and saw the conditions in which they lived. Once, she had even cried because she'd stepped on a fallen leaf that was still green. The Duke's tirades often ended with her in tears, which would only result in stronger punishment. *I had thought you were my daughter,* he would say, *but Solareses are not weak. What in damnation are you crying for?* And he would threaten her with a switch until she admitted that she had no reason to be crying, and somehow forced herself to stop.

She had been raised to view empathy and care as a weakness. Now she realized that some secret part of her had thought that view to be one of the things that—while the Duke wholeheartedly believed it—was not actually true in the real world. Seeing the Spiritkin head debilitated by compassion angered her. How could it be wrong to hold care in your heart for another living being? How could it be wrong to feel others' emotions as strongly or more strongly than your own?

Sarana must have felt her anger through their bond, for she moved beneath Sada's hand to calm her. The contact was not necessary for their connection, only for physical comfort, but it came with a message.

Though it be a way thou may be harmed, it follows not that it is wrong, Sada. Thy skin is tender, and may be easily pierced by blade or claw, yet were it hard as stone, thou wouldst not feel the wind upon thy cheek, nor the grass beneath thy feet, nor my coat betwixt thy fingers. Weakness is needful; it is the mark of life itself. And often, it is our frailties that make us who we are.

Sarana's comment was wise, but it did not soothe Sada's frustration alone. That came from the caelicorn in a different avenue. She felt it as a cool stream pooling in the Mindspace and seeping into the rest of her body. She could not feel it physically, only mentally, and yet the physical effects of her anger—clenched jaw, nails repeatedly poking into her palm, harsh heat in her chest—dissipated as Sarana's peace overcame her. In a few moments, she was as calm as still water. She smiled softly at the filly.

Would you do the same for DeeDee? she asked, but the caelicorn shook her head.

'Twas anger thou did feel, and anger serves none. Yet it is sorrow that the Druid doth feel. Sorrow may lead to reflection and change, and it must not be dismissed or shunned.

Sada nodded. She had come to accept that the caelicorn was wise beyond her years, and what she said made sense. She still wished that Dedrei didn't have to suffer.

Even were I to desire it, Sarana said gently, *I could not. I share not the bond with the Druid as I do with thee.*

When Sada inquired as to what Sarana meant, she only regarded her coolly with a golden eye, and said nothing. Sada wasn't certain if it was because their connection was not strong enough to continue the conversation or if it was because Sarana simply did not feel in the mood for conversing any longer, but she didn't press the issue. She had felt from the beginning that their Mindspace was unique to the two of them alone. She hoped to explore the extents of it soon, perhaps when she and Sarana were alone with each other once more.

The thought of being without Dedrei's company incited a sting in Sada's heart and she suddenly felt as though she had to close the gap the Druid's long strides had put between them. Perhaps if Sada stayed very close to her, Dedrei would not remember that she intended to leave once they reached Titian.

They walked ceaselessly until the pale pink of Elt's sunlight began to turn rosy with dusk. She thought the Druid was probably too lost in her memories to think of stopping, or of gathering fruit as she'd told Sada they would that day, but Sada didn't mind the walking. If they didn't stop, she didn't notice her tiredness; or her hunger, which had returned once she'd eaten the Sprite's fruit.

The music rose and fell in great, slow arcs, as though Elt itself was sighing. There was no breeze, but still the trees seemed to dance, their leaves rustling and tickling each other gently. All around them, lovely flowering bushes of all kinds, looking like bouquets put together by Pixies and Sprites, were bathed in the pink. Stargazer lilies glimmered like they were painted in stardust, and the purple of the foxglove brightened so that its vibrancy hurt her eyes. They perfumed the air with scents of lilac, candied apples, and other sweet things. The rose bushes, which had been thornless during the day, were just as lovely, but they shivered as wicked thorns slid out of their stems to fend off the creatures of the night.

Elt was breathtaking as usual in its beauty, but most of all Sada was struck by how *clean* the forest was. The fallen leaves on the ground never dried into colorless husks as they did in her home's forests, but remained soft and colorful even in death. She wondered if that meant they were not dead at all. And not only were the woods of Elt lacking in dirt and dust, but also dead and fallen branches, and rotting wood.

She had seen a single fallen trunk, and it had been a giant of a tree, so large that even lying on its side, Sada could not reach up to touch the highest point of its trunk even on her tiptoes. Its leaves had all remained green as well, even though it had fallen so long ago that it was covered in moss and flowers like a Forest Giant's blanket. If there were insects, they didn't bother her, Sarana, or Dedrei. It was the same for spiderwebs; if they existed, they were too far up in the branches to be seen or felt.

The creatures of the forest were spotless as well, and the picture of health. She saw not one mangy deer or skinny squirrel as were common in her world. All had thick, shining coats and were plump, bordering on downright fat. Sada watched as round four-eared and two-eared rabbits alike bounded to their hollows in stones, logs, and bushes to sleep for the night, and as sleek grey- and russet- and yellow-haired does gathered up their white-freckled fawns to find a clearing to lay down to rest in. Sarana watched from beside her, seeming almost wistful to Sada. She often wondered if she wished to go among the other creatures without scaring them away. Sada often felt the same about the people of Centerton and Ettedon. She put a hand on the filly's neck as they walked, trying to send her comfort as she often sent to Sada.

When purple joined pink as the moon began its ascent, Dedrei stopped at a small clearing, so suddenly that Sada wondered if she had been snapped out of her reverie by the sight of it. The clover-speckled grass was flattened in a circular area in the space between trees, and tufts of white and brown and grey fur hung on the surrounding bushes. Sarana immediately went to investigate the area, scenting the perimeter and the snagged fur. When she'd pronounced it acceptable, she tossed her head and stamped her hoof, but Dedrei had already settled against a root with a sigh.

"Deer once took their rest here," she said, running a hand over the grass. "Some say that my people's *Antýchos*, or immortal Grandsire, was a deer spirit, because of our cervine features. I always liked to believe that perhaps he was a being who simply loved deer, and that manifested in his descendants as doe ears, long ankles, and delicate features." Dedrei smiled at Sada. "Perhaps that is foolish."

Sada shook her head. "I don't think it is foolish in the least. Governess Brown—oh, she is the woman who taught me all I know of courtly matters and society. In many ways, I suppose, she raised me—but she once told me of a woman she'd met whose people believed that each beauty mark and freckle marked a spot where a spouse had kissed you most often in a past life. I thought it quite charming, though I told her it would mean my spouses must have had some rather peculiar tastes indeed."

Dedrei grinned at that, evaporating any lingering sadness from her eyes. "Do you mean to tell me, Sada, that you have freckles in strange places?"

"Oh, certainly! There is one upon my ankle that comes to mind most readily. And—" Sada began, then hesitated. "Oh, I shouldn't say, it would be most improper."

Dedrei rolled her eyes. "Humans and fairfolk alike are forever preoccupied with propriety—it speaks volumes of your kinship, even distant as it is. Tell me, girl, you have already begun to."

"Oh…very well, then." She leaned forward to whisper conspiratorially. "There is one on my *belly button!*"

Dedrei just blinked at her, then she burst into bleating laughter. "That was the impropriety you spoke of? We all have navels, child. And that is certainly not a peculiar place for a spouse to be kissing."

Sada recoiled. "It *isn't?* But…why?"

Still laughing, Dedrei shrugged. "You will have to ask the man who becomes your husband, I suppose."

Sada crossed her arms and harrumphed. "*My* husband shan't be kissing any of *those* freckles."

Sarana lipped half-heartedly at the grass for a while, and inspected the tufts of deer fur left on the bordering bushes, but as Sada and Dedrei settled into the crooks of roots to rest, the filly joined them to curl up against Sada's side. Tonight, Dedrei didn't insist that Sarana sleep away from them. She even whispered something to her in Druidic before rolling onto her back to pray and prepare for sleep.

The stars had come out, poking brilliant holes in the fabric of the night sky to reveal the heaven of light behind it. After praying, Sada listened to Dedrei chant her own prayers in her strange language. While it usually sent her well on her way to sleep, tonight she lay awake, thinking of nothing in particular, but awake, nonetheless. Whenever she closed her eyes, it felt like a monumental struggle to keep them shut, and when she lost focus, she would realize they had popped open again to give her a view of the trees, limned with lavender.

"DeeDee," Sada whispered when the Druid had fallen silent.

"Hmm?"

"Does tea exist in Elt?"

Dedrei snorted softly. "No, we have not yet stumbled upon the marvelously advanced notion of soaking leaves in water to draw out their flavor. Truly, only humans could contrive such brilliance."

Sada scowled, though a smile played at her lips. "Well, you have not discovered the invention of carriages," she teased.

"This is quite true. I am certain that no Spiritkin mind has ever even *dreamt* of such a thing, oh wise human."

Sada rolled her eyes, grinning. "Might we have tea, then? Perhaps tomorrow morning? I confess, I know not how to start a fire. I attempted it some time ago, and the results—well, the lack of them, rather—were most embarrassing. But if you could start a fire, I am certain I could find some herbs for our tea."

"I possess no control over the elements required to *'start'* a fire, as you put it. My people are without magick—at least, the usual sort. And Fire Sprites are not known to dwell in forests, nor are we near any Druid tribes. In fact, we have avoided the ones that lay in our path," she said. "And, in any event, we have nothing to heat the tea in, do we?"

Sada opened her mouth then closed it, repeated this, began a stammering question, then stopped. "You have mentioned so many foreign terms and concepts that I know not even where to begin," she finally said.

Dedrei chuckled lightly. "I would assume you wonder about the Sprites."

"And about the magick, too. I did not know there was a traditional or untraditional sort. But we might begin with the Sprites. Sarana and I encountered a Tree Sprite."

"Did you? Then that is a fine place to start, for explaining all the magick of our world would consume the entire night and a large bite of tomorrow as well," Dedrei said, and Sada giggled.

They lay side by side, separated by Sarana who was sleeping soundly, and looked at the stars together as the Druid taught Sada of Elt.

"A Sprite is a race of Spiritkin, tied to some aspect of nature. You met a Tree Sprite, but there are also Water Sprites, Wind Sprites, Fire Sprites as I mentioned, and many others.

"Most fairfolk refuse to alter any aspects of Elt permanently, but fire is an exception, for it is naturally occurring and its by-products remain useful to Elt and its creatures. Ash alone makes a fine fertilizer. Yet as I said, my people do not possess the magick needed to summon fire ourselves. Instead, we call on the aid of Fire Sprites to do so on the rare occasions that we find it necessary."

"I see," Sada said. "You do not use fire often, then?"

"No. It is usually reserved for the brewing of tea, as you mentioned, which we drink only during ceremonies, rituals, or larger gatherings. Or, of course, on especially cold nights when even the fur of a snow bear form cannot keep us warm."

"How interesting," Sada breathed.

"All Druid tribes welcome Sprites of every kind to dwell amongst us. We often find ways to aid one another. There is usually at least one Fire Sprite within each tribe, which is why I mentioned this earlier."

"I recall. But you said also that we've been avoiding every tribe we might encounter. Why should we do such a thing? I cannot imagine your people are at some sort of war with one another."

Dedrei chuckled. "Indeed we are not. Such a notion is truly unimaginable."

"Then why avoid them?"

Dedrei sighed. "It would lead to far too many questions and complications—ones I have no desire to address at present. It is time to rest, Sada. Tomorrow, there will be ample time for more talk."

Dedrei rolled over and Sada did as well, trying to heed her friend's advice. Still, she found her mind awake. She let her mind drift, seeing visions of Fire Sprites dancing in the flames below a cauldron warming stew, or a pot of tea. Soon those visions became dreams, and she slept. In her mind, she became a Fire Sprite, and she visited the Druid tribes in her dreams.

THE TWENTY-THIRD

Naexa

Somewhere deep in Elt, a little girl awoke in the woods. At least, she appeared to be a little girl to anyone who might glance her way. But as she walked through the small, disheveled cabin she'd found and looked into a mirror stood up against one of the walls, a woman stared back at her. She passed by, uninterested in the cracked, dirty thing. As she left the cabin, she shifted her short, bouncing ringlets into the beautiful dark hair she'd seen in her reflection and began to braid it.

As she braided, she felt her legs and torso lengthen and she grew to the true height the mirror had shown her, though that was not much taller than the child's height. Her knees popped as they settled into their new sockets, and she could feel the tendons and fibers weave around each other, fighting for space as they stretched. The skin on her back began to stretch and split as something tried to emerge, but she bid her body to keep that part of her hidden, and then her flesh stilled. She filled out the long gown that had been loose on her child body, but now hugged her slender hips and waist. Her eyes remained a magnificently deep purple.

Once she had resumed her (nearly) natural form, Naexa took up her basket and cloak, then left the sparse woods to continue her journey.

She slept in child form because children recover quicker than adults. But while she traveled, she needed her abilities at their greatest strength, and that meant traveling in her true shape. She had little to her name besides her power, and she did not need much more than that. She walked now with nothing but the larkfruit-filled basket and her hooded cloak, pulled over her head to hide her conspicuously violet-sheened hair. She lowered her gaze, too, keeping her chin tucked as she walked. This far away from the Valley of Kings, the roads were unmarked and would be littered with thieves, killers, and people killing to thieve. Fairfolk were not uncommon beyond the Border, but those with fair morals to match their looks certainly were. It was best not to draw unwarranted attention, and without dipping into her power by taking the form of an ugly man, the cloak would have to do.

The trail she followed was narrow and rocky, evidence of its lack of travelers. She passed only two carts pulled by huge, woolly mountain sheep, whose vast twisting horns she had to sidle out of the way of to avoid being gouged. She managed to snatch a bundle of blue-grey crag flowers from the back of the cart, which she added to her basket to elaborate on her disguise. As she walked, she was careful to hunch herself over and shuffle to hide her proud stride. In towns outside of the Valley, a straight back and sure step drew just as much attention as beauty.

Masquerading herself as a poor woman traveling to sell foraged goods had proven over the years to be one of the most reliable disguises in areas like these. Naexa had learned that the most convincing lies were those rooted in truth: while she didn't come to these towns skirting the Valley with the goal of selling flowers, she did pocket every gemdrop she earned. Usually she only received opals, drops of the lowest value. But in the Border towns, a good number of drops, even of opals, was still enough to purchase new clothes to replace her tattered ones, or new baskets to replace those which were constantly stolen.

But Naexa never purchased a meal.

Her diet in the wild had begun with unripe berries and bitter leaves, but she'd realized quickly and harshly that vegetation alone did not suffice for a grown woman—certainly not a Faery. Her needle-like canines were designed for ripping into flesh tougher than that of oranges. Fruits were meant to supplement the Fae, not sustain them. But wildlife (any life) was scarce in the Wilder, the unclaimed lands of Elt, and she'd had little choice.

Once the months in those harsh and undomesticated lands had stripped her of the little fat she'd had stored on her thighs and waist, and after she'd sustained a crippling injury from an ogre, she'd had to turn to carrion. At that point, though she'd made her way to the Border towns, she'd had no strength left to steal—those living beyond the Border guarded their possessions fiercely, and taking them was no small feat. The rotting corpses she'd been forced to scarf down had left her stomach roiling, and the meat tended to find its way back up her throat before her body had the chance to sift any nutrients from it.

But fresh animal corpses were rare to find in a land of Beasts. So, once she gained a small amount of strength back from the dead meat, Naexa had forced herself to learn how to hunt. She'd proven to be an unskilled huntress despite the sharp eyesight, agility, and fangs her people possessed, and failed to bring down even a four-eared hare. She attributed the lack of success to her weakness, but it might have been due to the time spent away from her people, and the time spent hiding their attributes. If you spent too long pretending to be someone else, you eventually became them.

Due to some twist of fate, the sorcerer who would become her master had found her not long after she set out to become a hunter—he who wore the cloth crown of blue: Amogasanes the Strange, last true sorcerer of Elt. He'd taught her the art of sorcery, and now the rotting corpses littering the forest floors were her leftovers, and it was the Beasts who scavenged amongst her leavings.

Fires in the forest were too dangerous this far outside of the protection of the Valley, drawing too much unwanted attention from the prowling creatures, both Beast and Spiritkin. And so Naexa first had to eat her kills raw from the bone. She had found she'd liked it, so even when her power grew great enough that she could keep a fire without fear, she had never cooked her meat. Now, nearly two decades later, she still did not cook her food, despite being strong enough to burn entire forests to the ground along with any inhabitants who may try to stop her.

The thought of warm, rich blood on her tongue made her salivate, reminding her of her lack of breakfast. She glanced at the larkfruit rolling in her basket, but fruit had become unappetizing to her over the years. One look and it quelled the hunger rising in her throat, and she set her eyes on the roofs of the town she strode for.

It was a small town by the name of Thymenos, inhabited by thieves, tinkerers, bounty hunters, and tradesmen, as most Border towns were. It was plain in every way, from its coloring to the goods it had to offer. The buildings were an unaesthetic mix of brown stone and sun-faded timber, which spoke to the lack of magick in these parts. Shutters hung crookedly from hinges that hadn't been repaired in years; the people of the Border had other worries, none dealing with beauty. Dust clung to every surface, swirling into the air whenever a cart rolled by or a heel kicked the dirt, giving the town a near-constant haze.

The contrast between Thymenos and the town she had traveled from was as stark as the difference between spring and winter. Crielune was an Elven city as beautiful as its people, with homes and edifices crafted from opal and tiche wood. Set in the Autumnal Vale and on the outskirts of Titian, it was nestled in a shallow valley of red and gold, guarded by tall trees of autumn and eternally caressed by gentle sunlight. Naexa missed its beauty, temperate weather, and easy roads—but she did not miss the society, which she had left some days ago.

As Naexa had traveled out of the little town of Crielune, following a latticed path made of dark roots, she had been wondering if her schemes were truly necessary when she came upon a sight that confirmed they indeed were. Off the road had stood two muscled Titian guardsmen, each armed with full quivers and gleaming longbows. To her surprise, one even held a short sword, though he and his partner both looked disgusted at the sight of it—Titian bones themselves were probably made of arrow shafts. Between the guards cowered two men: a Fae man on his knees wearing a mien of defeat; the other a Titian man lying prone in the moss, a slate knife clutched in his tan hand.

Instantly, Naexa's tranquility had been replaced with a mixture of disgust at seeing a peaceful realm so overrun with crime, and curiosity at what, exactly, had transpired. With the lapse in her hold on her emotions also came a lapse in control over her magick. She hadn't realized that her spirit had slipped out of her body. The shift was ever so slight, but it was enough to make her noticeable to the beings of the spirit realm, and also to allow them access to her.

"Do you wish to know what happened?" a dark, lulling voice asked as she watched the guards begin to wrestle with the Faery.

Naexa immediately whipped around in search of the speaker. His voice had caused gooseflesh to raise on her arms and make the fire in her blood flare—a reaction that no Spiritkin had caused in her in centuries. She found the source of both the voice and her unease peeking around a tree just to her right. One clawed, grey limb hugged the trunk, and she thought she could see the tree decaying at his spectral touch. His gargoyle-like head tilted playfully to the side as he studied her.

"I wish to know nothing from you," Naexa snarled. In her surprise she had forgotten the first rule Amogasanes had taught her once she'd gained access to the spirit realm: do not engage with it, unless you wish it to engage with you.

The spirit—she didn't think it was a demon, because if it were she would have felt utter, mortal fear rather than unease—seemed to realize this and grinned, his eyes becoming black slits.

"Are you certain? I can sense your curiosity," he purred. But he did not move, which meant that her protections still held him at a distance from her. Still, he would not leave her alone until she completely rooted herself in the physical realm once more.

Naexa closed her eyes and forced herself to breathe deeply, dispelling any lingering nerves in a few shaky breaths. Then she drew her spirit fully back into her body until she could feel Elt's hold on her once more. She disliked the heavy feeling, which was why she often allowed herself to sit slightly above the physical realm. She hadn't realized even the fairfolk towns were becoming infested with spirits now. There was evil in Elt, but with how new its presence was, the good had always purified the land of the bad. Beings of light resided around the homes and bodies of worshipers of the Creator, and the religions were so popular in the Valley of Kings that there hadn't ever been room for dark spirits to nest alongside the good ones.

Now, it seemed, there was room. And she was likely standing beside some of the people who had invited them in—unknowingly or not.

Fully anchored once more, she opened her eyes to find the dark spirit gone. Elt looked the same now that she was returned to her body, but it was more overwhelming. She could feel everything completely—the slight breeze, the subtle vibrations from bird song. And she could hear the voice of Elt at full volume now, lilting along in the background, as she could hear the guards growling commands and insults at the Faery who now seemed to be their prisoner.

The party who had stopped her journey had moved down the path, back toward Crielune. The Faery, whose blonde hair was striped like a tiger's, was being dragged by the guard who'd held the short sword, which presumably belonged to the Faery. It was now tucked into his quiver strap. The other guard was pocketing the shale knife she'd seen. He didn't even glance over his shoulder at the Titian lying between the trees. The party simply left him behind.

This is behavior that would be witnessed past the Border, not in the Valley of Kings, Naexa thought bitterly. The corruption of the kingdoms was spreading, and quickly. She'd known it to be prevalent in Caprius's cities, but she had thought him cunning enough to remain subtle about it, exercising his cruelty through the high taxes and prejudice he favored. Not in leaving citizens dead or dying beside public roads.

Naexa stalked in pursuit of the trio, transfiguring her appearance as she went. When she reached the men, she cast her hood off, then reached out with a now-brown hand to grab the shoulder of the rear guard.

"Halt, men," she said in a voice that now had the timbre of a man's.

When she transfigured herself, it wasn't just an illusory change in appearance. She altered her very anatomy to match the person or creature she wished to become. The guards who spun around now faced an incredibly tall, and incredibly well-muscled Titian man. She could not alter her clothing, and would have to hope that her knowledge of Elven military and a little sternness would make up for the purple cloak she wore. Thankfully it had been too large on her natural form and fit this one well enough.

"On what charge do you intend to apprehend this man?"

The guard holding the Faery was just shorter than her, and his eyes were so vibrant that she wondered if he had yet to reach his hundredth name-day. Yet he wore braids where the other, older Elf didn't, which more often than not would place him in a position of command.

He has the look of a man who enjoys commanding people. Her thoughts were confirmed less than a breath later.

"What concern of yours is it?" the youngling asked.

Naexa let her eyes narrow. "This is how you speak to your superiors, then?" she growled, and she shifted so that the brown braids she'd transformed her hair into would tumble around her shoulders.

The braidless Elf widened his eyes, and he turned to say something to the young one, but the Wielder just held up his hand.

"I am Rhaelion'Pyrithos of twelve braids, five decades into my second century, and lord over the Twelfth Russet Squadron of the Earth Sect. This is one of my men, *V'*Nikaros."

Rhaelion's expression was cool as he regarded Naexa, waiting for her response. Their Fae prisoner muttered something about Elven politics, but hastily shut his mouth when Rhaelion nearly jerked his slender arm out of its socket. Nikaros shot him a look out of the corner of his eye, but said nothing. Subordinate to both his captain and Naexa, he would not speak unless spoken to.

Since Naexa was older than Rhaelion and acting as a superior who possessed a stronger Boon, Elven custom would only require her to provide her name and the honorific he should address her with. Yet seeing as she did not wear the uniform befitting her pretended position, and considering that Rhaelion clearly possessed the arrogance of his people, she decided to forego typical protocol and respond in the full formal manner.

"Viie. I am Phalios'Vasadini of twenty-one braids, four decades into my fourth century, lord over the Gold Unit of the Snow Sect. You may name me *Jei* Phalios."

She hoped there wasn't really a Unit Lord Phalios in the Host of the Wood. She had just pulled that name out of the Void, but it certainly sounded Titian. She hoped also that the men before her didn't know the true identity of the lord whose unit she named, but she had chosen a position that was higher than theirs, yet still low enough that it wouldn't be well-known among the soldiers.

The older guard, Nikaros, bowed stiffly to her, but Rhaelion remained straight-backed. He shifted to lean on his bow, chewing the inside of his lip as he looked up at her. Naexa did not break his dark gaze, did not even blink as she tried to will him to accept her lie without using her magick to do so. Already she had used more than she had wished by transforming herself so drastically. Rhaelion fingered his bowstring and for a moment she thought he would recognize her fallacy.

Certainly if she was in his position, she would question why a unit lord of the king's army was wearing such a ridiculous outfit, let alone walking weaponless and alone in the middle of a rural wood which he didn't have jurisdiction over. Yet she was well-versed enough in Elven politics that her disguise was not only in her appearance, but also her speech and mannerisms.

Rhaelion finally accepted her with a bow. "Apologies for my insubordination, *Jei* Phalios."

Naexa's ensuing sneer wasn't solely in the name of disguise. "See to it that you answer my question, then. Unless it is your wish that I report your impertinence to your unit lord…"

Rhaelion's jaw clenched and his prisoner sniggered, likely believing himself to be near freedom. Naexa wasn't certain this situation would end that way, but it might. First, she wished to know the man's crime.

"Certainly not, *Jei!"* Nikaros said hastily. His voice was strangely squeaky.

"We will answer," Rhaelion said stiffly.

"Then I will repeat myself but once. On what charge do you intend to apprehend this man?"

"Defending oneself from murder," the Faery muttered.

Rhaelion jerked him forward and bent so that he was glaring in the man's face. "One more word from you, and it will be the last, bird-bones." He shoved him away for Nikaros to catch.

Rhaelion straightened and adjusted the quiver across his bare chest. Naexa was surprised to find many thin, pale scars there which belied his youth.

"I chanced upon this Faery as he was sliding a blade into the gut of a Titian citizen. He must be conveyed to the capital to face charges of murder," Rhaelion said roughly.

The Faery glared up at him through loose, striped hair. "Not going to tell him that your noble citizen was about to stick me with a dagg—"

Before he could finish, Rhaelion slapped him across the face, sending his head snapping to the side. Naexa's nostrils flared along with her magick, but she squeezed her nails into her fists to keep both tamed—for the moment, at least.

"He will have his say," she managed to say with an even voice. She crossed her arms, trying to look bored, but wasn't certain she achieved it. Both of the Elves were regarding her suspiciously. "This town is dull enough—allow the fool to provide me some meager amusement."

"As you will it, *Jei,*" Rhaelion said, and turned smirking to the Fae prisoner. "You have heard the unit lord. Do tell him what it is that you believe occurred."

"What I *know* occurred, is that I was heading for Crielune, when this man," the prisoner pointed roughly at the dead Titian behind them, "jumped down from that tree next to where he's lying. I thought it was just Titian antics, you know, until he drew that dagger. He lunged at me and only missed my heart because, well, everyone knows Fae are quicker than Elves—"

"Save us the trouble and come to the part where you ran him through with your blade," Nikaros said.

"Fine. He turned around to try and stab me again, so I unsheathed my sword and stopped him before he could kill me. And now I'm being imprisoned for preventing my own death!" He threw his hands up then, laughing hysterically. "Mother was right to tell me never to leave Aisathas."

"You witnessed the entirety of these events which he relays?" Naexa asked Rhaelion.

He grunted. "*Viie.* A pitiable spectacle indeed, to witness a fellow Titian bested by a cursing Faery."

"Then you are aware that the Faery acted in his own defense, rather than in any spirit of offense?"

Rhaelion shrugged. "He came into the spirit of offense when he stabbed our man."

"He was a fellow guard?"

"I mean to say that insofar as he is a Titian, he is one of our own." Rhaelion's brown eyes narrowed sharply. "What are you aiming at, Unit Lord? Are you to escort us to the capital for a formal report?"

Naexa clenched her jaw, looking between the Fae man, hardly half the size of even Rhaelion—who was short for an Elf of the Wood—and the two guards. The Faery's left cheek was swelling where he'd been slapped, his traditional, flowing clothes were out of place and torn, and the fiery look of his people was slowly draining from his yellow eyes.

"He will not be taken to the capital," Naexa decided.

The guards shared a look. "You wish to execute him here, yourself?" Rhaelion asked.

"It is against protocol," Nikaros said uneasily. As an older man, he would be keener to follow the written rules. The youngling, however, seemed only to desire that the Faery was punished. His only regret would be that he couldn't slit the man's throat himself. "Would it not be prudent to bring him to the capital, *Jei?"*

Naexa slammed her fist into a tree beside her, unable to contain her frustration. "Do you not see the grievance I harbor in this? A man is set upon and, in his desperation, wields a weapon to defend his life. Yet it is not the assailant who faces justice, but the innocent defender, compelled to protect himself because the very guards charged with that duty proved either incapable or unwilling!"

"There was no foreseeing that the man would have slain the Faery, left unobstructed," Rhaelion said, eyes darkening. "He took a life without cause."

Naexa laughed dryly, but thankfully was spared from forming her growing anger into coherent language that the imbeciles before her would be capable of understanding.

"Was I supposed to wait until he drew my blood, first, then?" the Faery asked. "Would that have given me sufficient cause to draw his blood in my defense? Or would I have to stand there and wait for him to mortally wound me in order to justify my actions? Because at that point, it is not self-defense, it is reven—"

This time it was Nikaros who slapped the prisoner. And this time the Faery did not lift his chin in defiance afterward, but just hung his head, grinning sardonically.

"Indeed, that *would* be required to leave your hands untainted by innocent blood!" Rhaelion roared in his face, nearly spitting. "In leaving such a requirement unmet, you have taken life on the assumption that your supposed attacker would take your own, though no proof of such intent existed. Until your assailant sheds your blood, you are not acting in defense of your life by drawing your weapon; rather, you are branding yourself the assailant in doing so."

Naexa was too angry to even laugh at the absurdity. The heat of her magick was licking at the palms of her hands, begging to be released in any form, and she granted its wish. Channeling it all toward the two Elves before her, she willed them to leave the Faery be and return to Crielune. Mind-speaking had never been her strongest skill—Amogasanes had not wished to waste time training her on something he was expert at himself—but she had some practice in the art. She just required verbal supplementation to urge her magick to take root.

"This man has done nothing wrong. Release him, leave his blade, and return to Crielune to report your execution of a Titian on the charge of attempted murder of an innocent traveler."

She stared unblinking into Rhaelion's dark eyes, willing him to take her command. His Boon wasn't powerful, but it was enough to make his spirit-light yellowish-green, which made it easier for him to resist her. For a moment he stood there uncertain, looking like he was going to attack her, then she pushed her magick a little deeper and his eyes suddenly glazed over. When he straightened, all traces of anger were gone.

Nikaros was easier to convince. He looked down at the Faery, suddenly confused as to why he was holding him hostage, then released his arm and stepped away. Rhaelion silently pulled the man's blade from where he'd tucked it into his quiver strap, and dropped it on the ground. Then he and Nikaros turned to walk back into the city. Naexa willed some of her magick to go with them, but she knew it would dissipate quickly. Long-term suggestion took constant energy to maintain. Soon they would recall exactly what had transpired and return to arrest both her and the Faery.

Thankfully, he had enough sense to gather up his sword and silks and run into the wood in the direction of the Fae kingdom, Aisathas. *Perhaps he will remain there.* From what she had heard, it was one of the only remaining kingdoms that was not tainted by the corruption which the others were nursing. *Sichan must be doing something right.*

When the guards were distant enough, she leaned back against the tiche she'd punched and sighed, closing her eyes. Then she let her body melt back into its natural form, save for the one alteration which she always kept, no matter how drained she was. It was as much second-nature to her now as good posture was. When you first began practicing it, you felt every strain of every muscle being used to stand tall. But over time, those muscles were still being used, only you didn't feel the strain anymore. It was this way with the transfiguration of her back.

As she was resting, listening to the shuffle of the retreating Faery's footsteps on fallen leaves, she heard another whisper of sound as well. Only this one was nearer.

She whirled around and pushed aside the thicket of marigolds from which the sound was coming. Crouched on the other side of it, between her and the path, were two young Elven boys. They stared up at her with wide brown eyes. One boy had a short and straight mop of hair, while the other boasted a single thick braid. The former looked like a mouse discovered by a wildcat, but the latter had a defiant spark in his eyes.

I wonder if that is how my eyes looked as a child, Naexa thought randomly.

"Children, what are you doing crouching amidst marigolds?" She squatted down to meet them at eye level as the Wielder boy stood.

"Nothing to concern you," he said, sticking his little chin out.

"We want watch what you say to the Faery!" the younger, loose-haired one piped up.

Naexa almost smiled as his brother glared at him. "And why is that?" she asked.

The littler one shrugged slender shoulders. "Mama tells us we no play games and…she no want talk much. All can we do is play in the plants at…close to path? This is play in the plants, yes?"

Naexa grinned at his broken speech. She had automatically continued speaking in the Fair Tongue after talking to the guards. Half of her wanted to continue listening to the boys struggling along in their third language, perhaps help them even, but the other half was still impatient and ruffled. She switched to the common tongue of Elt, which she typically used on the road.

"I think it is. Your Fair Tongue is quite impressive, boys, but I admit I am out of practice. Do you mind if we speak the Known Tongue or Elven?"

"You can speak Elven?" the little one exclaimed with a grin.

"Indeed I can."

The older brother looked halfway between dragging his sibling away and asking Naexa a question himself. She tilted her head at him, trying to look inviting, as he chewed the inside of his cheek. Finally he gave in to the insatiable curiosity that drove all children.

"Why did you make those guards let that Faery go?" he asked in the Known Tongue.

"And how?" the little one added, earning an elbow from his brother.

"Because he was innocent and did not deserve the punishment they were bringing against him. Whenever possible, you should encourage other people to do the right thing. That includes stopping them from doing the wrong thing."

The older boy rolled his eyes. "You sound like Mother."

"She must be a wise woman. You should heed her."

"But *how* did you do it?" the small one asked. "They're city guards and you're just a common woman!"

Indeed, and it could not have been accomplished without sorcery.

Despite the age-old frustration his remark stirred, she made herself smile. *"Magick."*

Both of the boys' eyes widened, and they shared a grin.

"I don't see tangles in your hair. Are you a mage?" the little one said.

"Can you keep a secret?" she asked. When they nodded, she leaned in. "I'm a sorceress." Then she held out her palm and procured a small purple flame for them. She could see it reflected in the boys' eyes as they leaned in to admire it. Then grins split their faces and the small one broke out in fits of giggles. She was surprised to find herself smiling.

The older boy's face suddenly grew stern. "Well, I have *real* magick, and I'm going to use it to help Mama and bring Papa back."

He held onto the tail of his one braid almost protectively, and it was all Naexa could do to keep the sadness out of her smile. It was not right for such a small child to have so much responsibility placed on him. She knew all too well how it robbed them of the joy all children deserve.

"That is very noble of you…what may I call you?"

The boy regarded her suspiciously for a moment. "I'm Helexios'Therakles of one braid, eight years into my first century."

"And I'm Kostas'Therakles, five years into my first century!" the little one added.

"You may call me *Asta* Naexa. Our meeting is fair, *V'* Helexios, *V'* Kostas," she said, then performed the informal Elven greeting to each in turn. Helexios returned it, looking proud to be included in an adult ritual, and Kostas copied his brother through fits of giggles.

"Why are you on the road, boys?" she asked.

Helexios looked over his shoulder. A Titian woman dressed in a commoner's clothing was walking up the road, eyes scanning the sides. She did not look concerned, but her thorough searching marked her as their mother.

"Traveling," Helexios said curtly.

Kostas clearly didn't understand his brother's desire for secrecy. He leaned forward eagerly. "Mama said we're looking for a new home. The old one was no good anymore, I guess."

Helexios glared and elbowed his brother.

Kostas cried out and frowned. "Don't be mean, Helexios!"

"You think that was mean?" he asked, and shoved his little brother out of the marigolds.

Their mother had crossed the remaining distance by then and ran to her sons. "Kostas, what have we spoken about? Do not provoke your brother!"

Naexa stood, brushing marigold dust off her cloak. "Pardon my intrusion, fairlady, but Kostas did nothing wrong. He never raised a hand to his brother."

The woman finished dusting Kostas's flowing trousers off then stood, tucking loose, short hair behind her pointed ears.

"Certainly not, but he knows that calling his brother such things only makes him angrier…pray your pardon, but do I know you?" She seemed to realize then that she was divulging private family matters to a stranger.

It was surprising the woman noticed at all: Naexa was still oozing compulsion in an effort to keep the guards convinced of her story, and it would have a second-hand effect on all those without strong mental fortitudes—such as children and the Boonless.

Naexa made herself smile, all the while wondering why she continued delaying her journey east. Perhaps she wanted more evidence for her cause, more examples to convince her future followers with. The theory was sound, but she couldn't say whether it was true or not. She only knew that she felt just as compelled to speak to this woman as she had to stop the guards. The first thing her master had taught her was to heed her intuition, and so she did.

"I was just speaking with your boys. I am—"

"This is *Asta* Naexa," Kostas said, already having forgotten his scuffle with his brother.

His mother drew him in and tried to do the same with Helexios, but the older boy dodged her and stood straight beside her. The woman's eyes roved Naexa for a moment, either deciding whether to trust a stranger on the road or trying to determine Naexa's status, she could not say.

"You may call me *Ai* Althira," she said after a moment.

Naexa's flames snapped at that. The woman wore no braids, and the brightness of her eyes marked her as undoubtedly younger than Naexa. To place her at an equal status was insulting to anyone who knew the ways of Elves. But Althira was a Titian through and through, and they thought themselves to be above all others. Most believed their race alone placed them at equal status with anyone who wasn't Titian, even if the foreigner was centuries older and countless times more powerful.

Naexa tried to receive the insult with grace. "As you say. The boys were telling me you are leaving Crielune—"

"*I* didn't say anything, Mama, *I* said we were traveling, just like you told us to!" Helexios butted in. He pointed accusingly at his brother. "It was Kostas."

Naexa smiled. "Might I ask why you left? I was considering taking up residence there myself, but if it is in some way unfavorable…"

"Apologies, but we must be on our way. I pray you find what you are searching for," Althira said, beckoning to her sons.

Frustration prickled at Naexa's palms. How dare this woman not only assume they were of equal status, but now blatantly refuse to answer her question! She should have let them be on their way, but the disrespect was too great an insult. Instead, she summoned her magick for a third time.

Ascending just slightly into the spiritual realm, an act which she envisioned as the head of her spirit just peeking out from her body, the family's spirit-lights immediately became visible. Althira's and Kostas's were the weak, corporeal color of red, as Naexa had suspected. The Boonless often had weak minds and lights alike. Even Helexios's single braid was enough to give him a spirit-light of red-orange, which might have been surprising if not for his strong character which belied his young age. He would have taken slightly more of her power to affect, though not nearly as much as the guards had. Yet she would not need to target him in her compulsions, only the powerless mother. This would make things much simpler for Naexa.

She focused on Althira's mind and pressed some of her own energy into it. The woman immediately stopped in her tracks, and Naexa grinned. It was hard not to when seeing how easily her influence could be exerted over someone. Now *tell me that we are equals.*

"Fairlady, I ask only out of necessity," Naexa said again. Her voice was full with her power.

Althira slowly turned. Her boys, each holding a hand, turned with her, eyes wide with curiosity. Then Althira smiled upon seeing Naexa.

"Certainly. How rude of me to have denied you before."

"Mama?" Helexios asked, but his mother ignored him. Her sole priority now was fulfilling Naexa's request.

"Why did you leave?" Naexa asked again, and Althira sighed.

"Crielune is a beautiful town. My family has lived there for many centuries, since my grandfather traveled from Titian to settle in a smaller area. My *koréno* and I were joyful at the opportunity to raise our boys in such a lovely place as well. We had a house to be proud of, he found good work," she said, absentmindedly stroking Kostas's hair. "I am certain you would find a lovely home in Crielune. We would return if we could."

"You left against your will?" Naexa asked, willing Althira to continue.

At this, she hung her head, her shame radiating off of her and greying out her spirit-light.

"*Viie,* the capital's guardsmen have been making rounds visiting the towns surrounding Titian. They do not say why. Small towns like Crielune have never required guarding, and none of them stay permanently, but most assume they visit to maintain order. I suppose we should be grateful, but…"

"Yes?"

"Go on and play, boys. Mother will be just a moment," Althira said, and pressed her children toward the trees. Helexios looked at her dubiously for a moment, but with a poke in his side and a grin, Althira had him running off after his brother.

She turned back to Naexa and her face grew somber. But she needed no more mental prompting. Some part of her wanted to tell this story, the part that her Titian pride kept chained tightly in her subconscious, yet which longed for interpersonal connection and perhaps even pity.

"Do you speak the Fair Tongue? I am far from proficient, but I should not like my children to hear. They have seen enough sorrow already."

"I understand," Naexa said in the language of the wellborn fairfolk.

"When they come to our house, they see the disrepair it is in," Althira said, frowning in concentration over the unfamiliar language. "They order me to repair it, and when I tell them I cannot afford a Wielder from the capital, and that nobody in the town has a Boon good for working the needed elements, we are ordered to leave our house and Crielune too. The guards say it is unacceptable for such an ugly building to represent the Kingdom of the Wood. That King Caprius be ashamed to see such disrepair in his territories."

Althira was a tall woman with strong features, and carried her head high despite her low class which the limpness of her ears, opacity of her *kta,* and lack of proficiency in the Fair Tongue betrayed. Yet now tears glistened in her green eyes. She lifted her chin so they wouldn't spill, and Naexa admired her somewhat for this.

"What caused your home to fall into such disrepair to begin with?"

Althira scoffed. "When I say my *koréno* has find fair work around the town, it is because he is the only Wielder with a strong enough Boon to repair any damages to the buildings and houses in Crielune made by the weather and creatures and things. Now that he is gone, there is nobody to repair the eaves that are blown off by spring winds, or fix the leaks after the sky water.

"I am certain other townspeople are soon finding a similar fate coming to them like the one that came to my family. But our home is one of new make, and it is made out of more wood than opal, so it takes on damage more faster. But it never matters in the past time. Icarion can fix anything in just a few moments, so talented he is." Althira shook her head, chuckling darkly. "In the end, it is his talent that has leads us to our ruin."

Naexa placed her hand on Althira's arm. "Where did your *koréno* go?" *Koréno* meant "king of my heart" in the Fair Tongue, and once the union ceremony was completed by two lovers to mark them as *koréne*—or rulers of each other's hearts—they were bonded for life. Unlike humans, immortals did not take union lightly, and Naexa knew that Althira's man would not have left her and their family without good reason.

Althira checked to ensure her boys were still out of earshot. When she saw they were chasing Pixies in the tall grasses, she leaned forward. Her dark green eyes were wide and somber.

"That is just the thing. He is summoned to the capital to serve King Caprius once his talent is discovered. We are robbed of the person who can fix our problem, and then punished for it. Still, I am now thankful. We may have no home, but if then Icarion refuses to obey, now we are still being homeless, only he is being banished as well."

Indeed, Naexa mused. Althira was strong enough to see their grim reality as a blessing.

"*Mama, Mama,* look what we found!" Kostas said, running to tug on the long sleeves of Althira's *kta.*

"*We* didn't find it, *I* did," Helexios corrected. But he was grinning as well as Kostas showed their mother a brilliant pink mouse.

Althira threw her head back to laugh, and as she did, she stealthily wiped the lingering tears from her eyes.

"How incredible is this!" she cried in her people's language, bending to peer at her boys' discovery. "See what happens when you work together?"

Helexios scowled. "I told you—he didn't help me at all."

Althira just tugged on his braid, causing a small smile to peek through his frown.

Naexa watched it all as hot rage built in her chest. If she had not expended some of her power already, her flames would have erupted from her palms before she could control them. Thankfully, her store of power was somewhat drained—not nearly empty, but at least not overflowing as it typically was—and the fire remained trapped in her veins.

"Thank you for your time, *Ai* Althira," Naexa murmured, then she stalked away before the family could see the rage on her face. Needing to release her building anger, she pushed one more command toward the Titian woman: *when the time comes, search for the sorceress with the hair of a cloud and eyes of violet.*

She poured enough of her power into it that her anger was constrained to her mind and released from her body, then she went further up the path to where the dead Titian lay. Ensuring the boys were distracted, she quickly dragged the Elf's cooling body into the bushes. She had no time to bury his body and return it to Elt; even if she had, that sounded like a lot of energy to expend for the sake of a criminal's dignity and a few trees' sustenance. The creatures of the forest would see to it that his flesh was not wasted.

Once the body was out of sight from the path which Althira and her boys would soon be walking, Naexa threw up her hood again and strode away from Crielune, Titian, and the cruelty of Elt's monarchies.

The injustices of the world had been gnawing at her like infection at a wound for many years, but now that infection was worsening to fever. So cruel the world was to punish a man for attempting to prevent his own death, simply because he hadn't stood by and allowed himself to be critically injured first. So cruel it was that the victims of violence were chastised for mentioning the brutalities they faced, simply because it upset their attacker. But more than any of it, she was in disbelief at the fact that a king would summon away a town's only means of upkeep, and a family's only source of income, and then punish them for their lack of it. Especially when the king made it clear that refusal of his summons would be admonished severely, possibly with banishment from the kingdom.

This was what was wrong with Elt. Once, it had been a realm governed by kindness and justice. Though in the majority of the world's history, so prevalent was the kindness that justice was not even needed. No Spiritkin would think to say an unkind word to another, no matter their race or status, let alone draw a weapon. Townspeople would not pay to have their homes repaired, because such was the abundance of Wielders that all of them were happy and willing to help whoever they could, whenever they found the opportunity.

In an ideal world, everybody would be selfless; gemdrops would be abolished because goods would be traded for favors and favors traded for goods. A woman would not have to be paid to grow and harvest food, rather she would share it with as many people as she was able. In return, her neighbor would provide her with eggs to cook with, or loomfly silk to be sewn into clothing. Unfortunately, Naexa's ideals were not shared by the people in power, and they were disappearing from the citizens as well. The only way forward was to establish a system which punished injustice and celebrated righteousness.

If Naexa had her way, each criminal would be punished with the crime which they had committed. A thief who stole eight emeralds from a woman would be fined eight emeralds. If they did not have the funds, they would be made to work until they came up with them. A criminal who stabbed an innocent would be stabbed in the same location in return. The Faery that had been detained would never have faced trouble with the guards, who were supposed to protect people like him—innocents subjected to the cruelties of corrupt Spiritkin.

The only problem is, as Kostas so kindly mentioned earlier, is that I am but a woman who no longer holds a position of power. If the world was to be fixed and her perfect system of justice put in place, she would need power once more—enough power to influence the entire realm. *No, not just influence, control.* Unfortunately, she had little reason for anyone to willingly place themselves under her rule. She was nothing but a lone sorceress, traveling between the kingdoms, earning enough knowledge to fuel her schemes and enough gemdrops to keep her alive and clothed. The only ways in which she could gain influence were to firstly create a problem great enough to need solving, after which she could come to the people of Elt with a solution; and to secondly remove the power from those who already held it.

She had been uncertain of her plans to correct the injustice of the world by uprooting and replacing the entire system of rule. Now, she had just witnessed all the evidence she needed in order to remind herself and her future followers of why what she was doing was necessary. And so, after years of gathering information and growing her magick, she had headed east, to what would be the birthplace of her plan to conquer Elt.

Some days after her encounter with Althira and the guards, Naexa entered Thymenos. She had made good time, reaching the Border town before the sun had peaked in the sky. With its brilliant pink rise, her dress stuck uncomfortably to her sides, slick with sweat. She would have preferred the Elven clothes in all their scantiness, but in these territories, that would be more conspicuous than wings growing from her back. But even wearing her inconspicuous dress, even in the safety of the town, she didn't drop her hood. She couldn't risk being noticed, being watched; she had come to be the watcher.

So, she kept her chin tucked and her brilliant gaze on her booted feet as she sidled through the crowd, swinging her basket of fruits and flowers out in offering to anyone who looked her way. The proposition usually scared them off with muttered curses about gemless spinsters. Naexa tried not to smile while they hurried past her.

The streets of Thymenos were narrow, dusty, and slow. People of every race were about, hands busy with the mundane tasks of daily life, but they were in no rush. They had not the energy for such effort. They worked on their dull tasks almost lifelessly; their eyes were the only quick thing about them, always scanning the people who came close enough to be a worry. A woman in a faded apron stood at a corner stall, scraping burnt crusts from loaves of bread before setting them out for sale, her eyes darting nervously toward any passerby who might inspect them too closely.

Further down, Naexa caught sight of quicker movement: a group of children ran between carts, their faces smudged with dirt, laughing as they chased a wooden hoop through the throng. Their laughter was the only evidence of joy in the little town, but Naexa did not blame the residents. Life was hard in the Border, even if things were cheaper.

The market of Thymenos, if it could be called that, was a dismal affair—rickety stalls selling trinkets, worn tools, and salted meats of questionable origin. Some rumored that even Beast flesh was sold for eating past the Border, and Naexa wouldn't have placed a bet against anyone who said so. Rules were either nonexistent or unenforced this far east of the Valley. Bartering was the preferred currency here, with drops scarce, and most deals were struck over a drink of fermented venom, a favor, or a handful of dried herbs.

She walked by peddlers shouting half-heartedly from makeshift stands, their wares laid out on patched cloths or crooked tables: tarnished trinkets, faded scarves, and jars of dubious salves. She brushed by one to inspect a scarf on display, but the peddler shooed her away with a broom. She and her basket of fruits would be seen as competitors, as meager as her offerings were. She scowled at the Goblin who chased her off and he sneered right back, but instead of searing his hair off she made herself move along.

Harpy-loving wretch. I could kill you, should I wish it. But she did not, if only for risk of spoiling her plans.

The town square was a little more crowded. Here, people seemed to linger—tradesmen haggling over worn tools, mothers dragging reluctant children toward the few vendors offering fresh vegetables. A thin cloud of smoke from a nearby blacksmith's forge curled into the air, carried on the faintest breeze. He wouldn't have enough drops to purchase raw materials from the Orcs—and certainly not the Dwarves—to work into any new weapons or tools; instead, he would work to repair old blades and arrowheads. The clanging of steel on steel mixed with the soft hum of voices and the occasional whistle of a pet bird. Someone coughed loudly behind her, a wet, hacking sound, but Naexa did not turn. She focused on keeping her movements slow and her basket swinging casually at her side.

A crumbling fountain stood at the heart of the square, its stone edges worn smooth by years of use. People milled around it, drawing water into buckets or simply resting on its edge, wiping their brows beneath the growing heat of the day. As she neared the throng of people, a man stopped to pluck the bundle of flowers from her basket. He was a dull-looking Faery, with pale hair and a deep scar that ran down the side of his face. He placed a small, chipped opal the shape of a raindrop into her basket in exchange for the flowers.

"For the wench," he grumbled.

A lucky woman to receive such a gift, she thought. But she didn't let her sarcastic thoughts show. Naexa just dipped her head slightly in acknowledgment but kept her gaze low, not meeting her buyer's eyes.

Her attention was elsewhere, trained on the crowd around her. She shifted closer to the shaded alleyways where the more private conversations took place—quick dealings in hushed tones, promises of stolen goods or whispered plans about secret movements.

Despite its dreariness, there was a certain energy to Thymenos, born from its precarious position at the edge of fairfolk civilization. The Border towns were often places of transition, where secrets exchanged hands as often as goods. Rumors always flowed faster (and more commonly) than water in these parts, and Thymenos was no exception. Whispers of the shifting power in the Valley were common around the taverns and teahouses, where patrons kept one eye on their drink and the other on the door, wary of trouble but always hoping for a stroke of luck.

And that was exactly why Naexa had sought it and its neighbors out. She found her victims before she could sell another item from her basket.

A group of men was seated beneath the eaves of a splintery teahouse. One of them, a russet-haired man, was speaking in low, controlled tones, though his eyes were sharp. His pointed ears twitched as he spoke. Though he wore the rough and modest clothing of the Borderfolk, Naexa knew at once that he wasn't from these parts. He carried himself too proudly, his posture just a little too sharp, his features a little too bright. Fae, judging by his height and the unnatural sharpness of his movements.

Though low-born fairfolk were common in the Border towns, ones who acted like it were not. But rather than shunning him for his pride, the men around him leaned in close, their expressions tight with focus. It was people like the Faery she had come for, those who had felt the effects of living in the Valley and were the worse for it—not the others, who only knew to complain because someone else told them they ought to.

Naexa crept closer, silencing her breathing and her footsteps. It would have been quieter to shift her feet into the silent pads of cat paws, but she wouldn't risk someone sensing her magick here. It would convolute her plan, her journey. So she slunk closer to the group on her Spiritkin feet while her eyes drifted to the throng of townsfolk shuffling on the road beside her. Her posture and careful movements painted a picture of a poor beggar woman, uninterested in anything but the next drop tossed her way.

"—been a long time coming," the Fae man was saying. He leaned back indolently in his chair, only confirming his foreign origins if his dialect had not. "The Central Kingdoms have held sway for centuries now, long enough to breed discontent among their *subjects*. Particularly those dwelling in the Valley."

One of the men across from him, with skin the color of burnt copper, scoffed his agreement. "That, and it seems that the only powerful Wielders being born of late are within Caprius's walls. And if they're born in our towns, the Titian sharp-ears cart 'em away before they can do the work that really needs to be done here. All we're left with are the Boonless, or Wielders with a single tangle, if that. When's the last time a new house has even been built past the Border?" He gestured emphatically at the buildings around them. "Look at this griffin-dung, going to the Void faster than the cursed."

While the homes of the Border towns were small and ugly, the dishevelment was not obvious upon first glance. All the buildings stood sturdily; none had fallen down, or if they had there was no longer evidence of it. Yet upon closer inspection, it was obvious that all the walls were sun-bleached, and the cracks in the stone ran deep into the foundation. Tile repair was a daily chore, thoughts of insulation and cooling stones were things to be laughed at, and summers killed just as often as the cold of winters. She wondered if this was what Althira's home had looked like to cause Caprius's guards to demand either its repair or her family's eviction.

The other men grunted in agreement, all likely thinking of the repairs that needed to be done to their own homes, most of which they were powerless to do. Nearly all in the little group were Boonless, with no tangles of any type in their short hair. One of the men wore either a braid or a twist, but from Naexa's vantage, it was impossible to discern which one had been woven into the curly hair. Either way, his magick was so little that it was more of an embarrassment than a Boon.

This one leaned in, frowning. "You mean to say *none* of the kingdoms of the Valley should have power? King Sichan is strange, to be sure, but he's a fair ruler. And I've gotten no trouble when visiting the other Elven cities."

"Just too-polite smiles and hesitant greetings," snorted another man. He was blue-skinned but ugly, and could only be a crossling. One half was definitely Goblish, but the other was debatable. Most likely Dwarven, judging by his bulbous nose.

"Oh, it's an evil to be polite now, is it?" muttered the curly-haired Wielder, but he leaned back to nurse his drink.

Faery-boy looked fed up with the other men already, and waved a hand as though to shoo away any words still hanging in the air.

"Nobody seeks to overthrow *all* the Central Kingdoms—it was merely an example, for spirits' sakes. The people are unsettled, that's my point. And restless folk can prove dangerous, should they begin to think that some among the monarchs are not attending to their duties as they ought." He shrugged, smirking. "That's all I am saying."

The Wielder nodded, but still looked uncomfortable.

He shouldn't be here. He didn't look like the snitching type, but he would have no ear for what she had to say, if he didn't even like what the Faery spoke of. And she had no time to waste convincing those who didn't already share her beliefs. Thankfully, she was not desperate enough for such measures.

"Yai, but the sharp-ears are holdin' on tighter to their power than a Nymph to a lost traveler," the crossling grunted. "Speakin' of Nymphs, 'member when they tried to claim themselves as one of the Central Kingdoms to get more protection from those leerin' cave trolls? The leaf-lovers practically laughed at them."

"They are, though. One of the Central Kingdoms, that is," said the Wielder.

Copper-Skin snorted. "Nymphs don't have a kingdom, boy. You think all those clusters of springs count for one?"

"You're thinkin' of them bein' fairfolk or not," the crossling added. "And ain't nobody gonna try and say Nymphs ain't fair."

The men all smirked, chuckling. Naexa's fingers prickled with power.

"Well, I should still think they deserved aid in the matter of the trolls, Central Kingdom or not."

"Yai, but the sharp-ears don't give a whit, that's the whole point. Are you not hearin' us? I feel like you aren't hearin' us," said the blue half-Goblin.

The Wielder glared at the crossling's remark.

"The others gave a whit, though. The other kingdoms, I mean. Even Caprius's allies. Don't you remember? The heralding Pixies had even the Border abuzz with the news, talking of the Crowns' decree that travelers should take it upon themselves to defend Nymphs from violent visitors." Copper-Skin picked at something in his teeth, raising his eyebrows pointedly. "Half of us were wondering why they'd even bothered to tell us, when we didn't know there had been a debate about it in the first place."

"And when we don't have hardly more than one Nymph to an inn," the crossling grunted. "Hardly affects us."

Copper-Skin nodded. "But they made a right big deal out of it. Then that half-mad Goblin—ah, no offense, Riktus—came to tell us the tale of it, and it turned out to be kind of interesting. Don't you remember?"

Their Fae leader sighed and scrubbed at his bare face. "How many times must I tell you? I am not concerned with the other kingdoms."

Copper-Skin glowered flatly at him. "If even Caprius's allies grow tired of his games, then perhaps those '*dangerous people*' you mentioned might be left unhindered for a time."

"Maybe we should be concerned with the other kingdoms anyway," the crossling, Riktus, added. His companions turned dubious gazes to him. "Zarah is so cursedly greedy that she works everyone in the kingdom halfway to death, then keeps eighty percent of the profit for herself and the Ring!"

"Yes, but everyone knows Goblins are greedy. You can't expect your queen not to be," the Wielder said.

"Riktus is right. Don't even get me started on the Dwarves. No offense, Riktus. They pretend to be above the troubles of the Valley, set apart in their precious mountains, but they're as much a Central Kingdom as the others. And their queen manages to fit a lot of haughtiness into her short body. I mean, refusing to even sell materials to anyone other than the fairfolk? As though Orcen metal is even half the quality of Dwarven steel. It's like she thinks we'll taint the Crowns' reputation just by touching her ores." Copper-Skin scoffed and folded his arms, which were corded with muscle. Naexa could see now that the tips of his fingers were blackened as well, the clear mark of a smith.

Riktus turned to the Wielder. "Come on, Cirrus, you gotta have somethin' against one of the kingdoms. Did they take your woman? Leave you in poverty? Refuse to treat your kid's fatal illness 'cause you were an emerald short?"

"Yai, there's got to be something," Copper-Skin added. "You don't end up past the Border because things went well for you in the Kingdoms."

Cirrus pulled at the hem of his tunic, eyes darting between his companions. Riktus and the smith were watching him eagerly, but the Faery was brooding with his arms crossed, looking into the distance. She wondered why he didn't want them talking of troubles outside of Titian. What did he have against Caprius that he needed all the negative attention focused solely on him? The Kid King was certainly a large contributor to the injustices of Elt, but not the sole supplier. Naexa could not think of a single monarchy (other than the Druids, but they were so uninvolved in politics that many forgot about them when considering the Central Kingdoms) that was not corrupt.

Finally Cirrus gave in. "Well, it could be said that King Sichan is the reason I'm here."

"I knew it!" Riktus exclaimed. He and the smith shared a grin. "Go on, then, get it off your chest. Tell us what kind of a shade the Fae king is."

Cirrus's ears colored purple. "King Sichan isn't a shade himself, it's just the laws that are in place in Aisathas." He clenched his jaw, the muscles there bulging, then downed the drink in front of him before leaning forward. "One of the city guards had his way with my sister—"

"Meanin' to say he violated her?" Riktus clarified, and earned a deadly glare from Cirrus.

"Yes, Riktus, he violated her! He violated her, and so I followed him one night. He was patrolling the capital's eastern border, and when he went around the back of some of the houses there, I went too. I snuck up behind him and roughed him up a fair amount."

"Atta boy, Cirrus," Copper-Skin said.

"I didn't use a weapon, but I bloodied his face and kicked him hard enough that he wouldn't have the ability to do to another woman what he had done to my sister. The thought of her, helpless and alone..." Cirrus slammed his slender fists on the table, making his companions' drinks jump out of their cups.

"He was supposed to be alone, too. But he wasn't. Another guard found us and pulled me off of him. He punched me in the mouth and broke my tooth, then took me in to receive justice from the wing overseeing the matters of the capital. I didn't go to the king's court, but where I went was just below that. I told them what had happened to my sister, and she was brought in to testify.

"In the end, I was imprisoned for three decades for assaulting a guard of the capital, and my sister's attacker was transferred to another unit for 'bad behavior.'" Cirrus scoffed and shook his head. "The son of a harpy never even saw the inside of a cell, except when he came to mine to taunt me. When I got out, I had not a gemdrop to my name, and…well, the rest doesn't matter. I'm here now. You going to drink that?" He pointed to the smith's half-full cup of what Naexa assumed to be manticore venom. When he shook his head, Cirrus took it and downed it.

"See? They're all shades, Voidtoers, sons of harpies…Every one of them. Maybe they all *should* be overthrown, Rivlon. You have that in you?" Riktus sniggered as he nudged the red-haired Faery. He was one frown line away from a scowl.

Naexa was watching the other men nod contemplatively when she felt the dip of a hand in her basket. A small girl had snatched a larkfruit, scampering away without leaving a gemdrop in its place. Hot rage ignited in Naexa's chest, but she forced it back into hiding. Even when the girl turned to smirk at Naexa, as though she actually wanted to be lit aflame.

Cursed harpy spawn, she seethed inwardly, but she dragged her eyes away from the child's dirty back and returned to her careful eavesdropping. This conversation was more important than revenge on a thief. It was hard to stop herself from imagining the many ways in which she could enact her vengeance, but Rivlon was talking again.

"It would never work. The Titians have eyes everywhere; they are likely watching us even now. They would surely mark any growing assembly long before it could pose any true threat to *multiple* kingdoms."

The men fell silent at their leader's dismissal of the idea, drinking deeply from their cups to hide their disappointment or shifting to watch the crowd that walked by them. Cirrus, however, seemed almost relieved. Now that he had received their sympathy, he wanted nothing to do with talk of revolution—of change. Certainly, things were bad as they were, but that was better than something new. Standing, and with some excuse of mending a bucket with a hole in it, he left. The others watched him go, looking sullen.

He may have hardly enough magick to stir up the dust in the corners of his home, but he likely still feels an allegiance to both his homeland and to Caprius, since he's made such a fuss over Wielders as of late. The poor kid probably thought there was still a chance, or would be if things got bad enough, to be recruited to work in Titian. He would never be so hopeless as to revolt against the capital when that was the case.

"What do you propose we do, then?" Riktus asked when Cirrus was out of sight.

A challenge. One for the leader to prove his worth. But the Faery didn't make to speak, just cleared his throat and glanced aside. Now was her chance. This was the opportunity she had been watching for, listening for. She pocketed the single opal she'd earned and set the basket in the dirt, not even minding that she left it in the middle of the road for all its fruit to be stolen. This group of men were her true purpose for coming to the town, though she had no idea who they were. That did not matter. All that mattered was that they would know her soon enough.

She had been prowling the cities on the outskirts of the Valley for some time now. At first, she had simply listened, doing the work of discerning if there was any discontent in the people of Elt; discerning if anyone shared her opinions. She'd become a regular patron at several teahouses and inns, both those underground and those in the eye of (somewhat) polite society. There, she'd gathered the beginnings of rumors and followed whispered trails to meet men who were self-proclaimed *revolutionaries.*

She had disguised herself as a common Fae man—a woman wasn't to be corrupted with such dirty information, even at the Border—and learned of their plans. Most had none, only the idea that something ought to change, beginning with Titian and its king. Naexa had hardly been able to stop herself from grinning when she'd heard this. She had been invited to revolutionary meetings, but after attending one and seeing it was only a group of five or six men getting drunk and whining about King Caprius's unfair taxes and unspoken laws, she'd given this up as a fruitless effort. That hardly mattered, though. She already had what she needed: knowledge that there were others of a like mind with her. Others, ready and waiting to become followers.

The revolutionaries themselves would not do, she'd decided. They were rough men, raised by rough times, and they would not think it to be a woman's work, revolting against the King of the Wood. They would certainly not think it a woman's work to *lead* a revolution against the king, certainly not to lead an army of men. Dirty work such as that was a man's duty, lest it disgrace the ancient Mothers and the sacred gentleness of femininity.

Naexa found that to be griffin-dung. She did not care to be a gentle and nurturing woman. She had been born with such a spirit, to be sure, and once, her desires had aligned with it. But circumstance had seen to it that her gentleness had been hammered into a fierce cruelty, and she harbored no such spirit nor desire any longer. Now she wished to fight, and now she was more capable of it than most men, they with their masculine spirits of aggression and boldness. The thought alone coated her palms with heat. She channeled that magick elsewhere: with her targets in sight, it would not do to slip up now.

The followers (the warriors) she truly wanted would be the ones who were already looking for a leader. They would not mark themselves as revolutionaries, as the cocky but ultimately craven men of the taverns did. No, these men would not even reveal their secret desires, lest someone else reveal theirs first. And so, Naexa had set traps for them. Like a basilisk luring lost chicks from their mother hen, she laid her trail of breadcrumbs and waited for them to come to her.

She'd done so in the form of letters. For weeks, perhaps months, she spied on the men she thought to fit this description, in towns all throughout the Border. Once she'd found her targets, she had written a vague message about a revolutionary's meeting and copied it onto several dozen leaflets. The hardest part had been finding leaflets outside of the Valley, but she had managed to meet an off-market seller and acquire some for ten times their worth. Then she slipped one under each target's door, ensuring to mention that it was a private meeting, invitation only, lest they be scared off by the idea of exposing themselves.

She had already primed them before this of course, meeting with each of them individually in her disguise and pretending to spill her secret desires while drunk off filtered manticore venom. She'd then mentioned her plan to gather others like them. If she sensed thoughts of interest, she marked them as a target.

She was only able to set up and execute one such meeting. She had found her targets, primed them, and delivered their invitations with directions to meet her in an abandoned home on the fringes of the Border, the outskirts of the outskirts. Few had come. She had shifted into her true disguise then, the form that her followers would know her as. But as soon as they saw her change, they had fled. Some, the ones with one or three Wielder tangles in their hair, had even tried to attack her. Whether it was because of her trickery, her use of sorcery, or the fact that she was a woman, she did not know. Mostly she chided herself for not having expected such a reaction. But she'd learned from that experience, even if she did not gain her first followers as she'd hoped. And now, she knew to always be in disguise when meeting with her potential followers. From the moment of their introduction, and every moment after that.

And so, as Naexa neared the Faery, the crossling, and the bronze-skinned foreigner, she shifted her hair to a halo of pure white curls that caught the sun even beneath her cloak. They shone against her skin, which seemed almost to glitter in the light. Her figure shifted from slim to full and curvy; attention-drawing. She had wished to go unseen before, but now, she needed to be memorable. Her disguise needed to be one that nobody she spoke to would forget. As she finished shifting, she threw back the hood of her cloak and straightened to her new, tall height. Only one of her own features remained: her purple eyes. At the ignition of her magick and the brilliance of her new appearance, all the men she headed for swiveled their heads to look at her.

Gawk was more like it.

She was certainly a sight to be seen now. Where before she had been beautiful, now she looked ethereal. Even compared to the copper-skinned man, who she now saw was fair in every way, she was the picture of elegance. Riktus smoothed his wrinkled clothes, and the Faery sat straighter, his too-tall ears perking up and blushing purple. As she grew close enough to see the details of their faces, she prepared to extend them her offer: join her in her overthrow of the kingdoms, back her as she conquered Elt, kneel to her as the Empress of the World, the *Empress of All.*

But just as Naexa's greeting was leaving her lips, something cold and fog-like slid over her mouth, around her waist, and across the back of her knees, deliberately enveloping her body. When it reached her eyes, her field of vision became coated in black. She saw only hazy buildings and men of shadows. Then the ground disappeared from beneath her feet, and she was floating in something intangible yet cold, and dark, and misty.

She didn't bother screaming, but that familiar rage erupted in her ribcage, and she began to thrash against her restraints, against this *thing* trying to control her, as though anything had the right to stand in her way. But her anger did nothing to free her, and though her mind was on high-alert, she could not detect what presence was encasing her, so she did not know how to fight her enemy. And so, she pooled her magick into her core, and then unleashed it all at once.

THE TWENTY-FOURTH

Naexa

Naexa's magick erupted from each of her channels in a paroxysm of violet fire: it gushed from her palms, her mouth and nostrils, the ends of her hair, and even her eyes, until her spirit-light had been ignited like lamp oil and she was encased in a shroud of purple flames that ripped away the false magic which had ensnared her. Once its shadowy ropes had been burned off, her own power faded, revealing the pink light of day. The pale sunlight was such a stark contrast to her dark flames that she almost grinned; she would have, if not for the remnants of anger still twisting within her. The light had revealed two things: her outburst's aftermath—an ogre-sized scorch mark on the wooden wall she had apparently been lashed to—and a large, sash-covered man cowering before her.

Naexa stood panting and glaring at the man. He gazed up at her in awe for a moment before he noticed the few purple flames still sticking to the walls boxing them in, and hurriedly beat at them with one of his tangerine sleeves. The fire didn't fade until she silently willed it to, though the man surely thought it was his own doing that stopped its destruction. He seemed the cocky type, if he was arrogant enough to attempt to disarm and capture her. The fact that he had managed to carry her away, even if it was just into one of Thymenos's many dead-end alleys, angered her even further. It was only the fact that one of the main streets ran behind them, crowded with witnesses, that she dampened the flames beginning to flicker in her chest once more.

Her assailant wore a dark, thick beard that contrasted sharply with the gaudiness of his silken sashes, all draped seemingly absent-mindedly across his broad shoulders and respectably sized torso. She wasn't certain which culture that manner of dress came from, only that she didn't like it. Naexa regarded the man suspiciously; she had learned not to trust crosslings—the offspring of two different Spiritkin races—as they were almost always outcast from the societies of both parents and therefore developed wrathful grudges against the world which hated them.

This one appeared to be some strange mix of Elf and Orc. His heritage was given away by the small, barely-discernible tusks jutting from his lower jaw, and the pointed ears poking up into his thick bun. The ears were tall and stiff; he must have been descended from a high class of Elf—nobility, though…certainly not royalty. All of Elt would have heard had an Elven royal bred with another race. Such an abomination might even call for death or banishment to the Wilder when committed by a monarch. Though the crossling's appearance was made quite fearsome by his size and ugliness, the strength of his ancestors halted at the physical; she could sense weakness hiding beneath his silks, lingering between folds of fat.

The sight of him made her realize that her own appearance had changed with the eruption of her magick. In her loss of control, she had burned away her disguise. She didn't bother to shift back into it, but faced the man with her true beauty, no longer hidden by the hood of her cloak. As she watched, he dropped to one knee and bowed his head.

"Most powerful sorceress, tales of your magick have been told all throughout the Border towns, and I have sought you for countless moons. I am Odepie, somatic mage of potions, and I beg the gift of your audience now."

The man did not lift his eyes as he spoke, and Naexa took some pleasure in that. So much so that she wasn't quite listening when he told her his name. Though it wasn't truly important.

"Rise, Pie," she said.

He rose swiftly, locking his hands in front of himself.

"It is Odepie, my great sorceress," he said through an ugly smile, and Naexa just stared at him. She knew the force of her magick burned furiously in her eyes. Realizing she would not amend her mispronunciation, the mage dipped his head again.

His attempt to correct her would earn him the punishment of a new, lesser name. *What a fool. He is fit to be named after a dessert. Perhaps he will be mine tonight,* she mused to herself. But she would not kill him yet. Some intuition halted her from doing so, and she had just received a lesson in why trusting it was so vital.

She scanned the mage's gleaming sashes, noting that they bore not a single tear in the rich fabric. His wrists and fingers were laden with golden rings and bracelets, and even his feet and their thick Orcen toenails looked supple, betraying the life of comfort he surely lived. He was not of the Border towns, to be sure. For all his assaults against her (both physical and visual), the anomaly of the man was almost enough to stir her curiosity—but not quite.

She had learned in her years that every person was driven most heavily by a single emotion, whether that be gratitude, sympathy, loneliness, depression…hers was, and had been for centuries now, rage. It burned away all other distractions and fueled her toward whatever purpose it decided she ought to pursue. Now it made her lip curl by a complimentary drive, something like jealousy, as she took in the riches the crossling wore from within the discomfort of her own ragged cloak and dress.

Naexa didn't blink as she stared at Pie.

"It seems you've interrupted the beginnings of my conversation," she said. The anger honed her voice into something delicate but sharp, like a needle. It poked into the soft flesh of her opponents, threading them with whatever insults her fire—not the flames of her magick, but the flames of her mind—had forged specifically for them.

"Ah, yes…to that end, you have every apology my heart can muster. Yet, if I might be so bold, those men are ill-suited to purposes as grand as yours, sweet sorceress." Pie stood tall with the combined height of both Orc and Elf, but his fawning words betrayed his lack of power. Naexa could detect only wisps of it curling off him, like steam. He was a pie, indeed.

"And what leads you to assume that you know my designs, or who is fit to be a part of them?"

Now his dark, beady eyes alighted with excitement. "I have kept a keen eye upon your travels through these barren lands. I observed you as you lent ear to the whispers of Valley defectors, and I saw you introduce yourself to them, well-disguised. Your talents for shifting are truly the finest I have yet encountered. Having watched you so closely, my sorceress, I daresay I have come to understand something of your intentions—and so, I offer myself to you, zealous and eager, as your first follower."

Naexa hardly noted his humble offering. His first few words had halted her listening almost completely, and she'd been contemplating them as he babbled on. *I have kept a keen eye upon your travels…I have observed you…* How had someone tracked her without her noticing?

Naexa's eyes narrowed. "I never noticed your presence."

"This is a high compliment coming from you, sorceress."

"How did you do it?"

"Come along with me, and I shall show you," he said, retreating a step into the shadows at his back. "You may regale me with your brilliant scheme, and I shall reveal how I managed to observe you without ever being detected."

Pie's face was distorted with a grin. She realized then that he was much younger than he appeared, and was likely wearing a disguise of his own. Only, his hadn't been seared away by her magick as her own was, so it must have been born of one of his mage's concoctions. The thought of made magic only increased her repulsion. She wished to singe his very presence away as she did with the giant slugs which had sometimes trailed her in the Orcen marshes, but she did not allow herself. His tactics must first be revealed to her, then his punishment for using them could be doled out. Her fingers twitched at the prospect.

Upon ensnaring Naexa, Pie had taken her into a small alley, just the space between two houses; the cobblestone path of the town had turned to dirt, and the crumbling eaves sheltered them from most of the sun's sight.

The alley was narrow, but houses of the Border towns were built long and squat; if they were erected with too much height, the dry storms and screeching summer winds would cause more damage than the Borderfolk could afford to repair. And so, the alley was deep, its farthest end mostly hidden by thin grey shadows.

Behind them, the townspeople continued their meandering, taking no notice of the exchange that went on in the shadows. It was not that they would have no interest in such a dealing. The people of Thymenos and other Border towns alike were so nosy that she was certain a few generations of evolution would see to it that their descendants would be born with noses the size of an ogre's, to better sniff out the gossip. Yet still, none turned to look at the sorceress and the mage, or the blackened bit of wall she had left behind. It was almost as though they *couldn't* see the two of them. Naexa turned back to face Pie and his insufferable grin with a scowl.

All mages are this stupidly arrogant. Amogasanes had told her as much. When her power writhed within her at the thought of the man, she blocked it from her mind. Only Pie deserved her anger—first for foiling her plans, then for capturing her, and finally for using his magic so brazenly. Not only did he dare touch her with it, but he also used it to hide her away from the sight of the townsfolk. If his power wasn't false magic sourced from potions, spells, and sacrifices to spirits, she might have been impressed, even grateful that he'd shielded her and her magick from sight—for though it was true and lived in her blood, she had not been born with it and so it was treated as blasphemy. But as it was, she held no gratitude for the mage. She was beginning to wonder if her anger had burned away not only the emotion of gratitude itself, but also her capacity for it.

And what of the men? They had seen me when Pie stole me away. How did he deal with them and their loose tongues? Perhaps they would be too frightened to say something to anyone else. In all likelihood, their own skeptical and fearful minds would ensure their silence. Even in Elt, where magick abode, the unnatural struck such a fear in people that they would rather convince themselves it was all imaginary than face what its reality might mean. The mage probably knew this, too. She didn't have much knowledge of mages' training, only what her master had taught her, but she knew that their interaction with the spirits and study of the metaphysical often gave them wisdom beyond their years.

Pie was beckoning to the shadows that half-veiled him, grinning foolishly. Naexa just glared at him with all the force of her power. She did not like to be bargained with.

"You will show me this gift and tell me of your techniques *now*," Naexa said.

But the mage did not back down. "Come with me, sweet sorceress. Come and see the delicious gift I have ensnared for you."

And then he disappeared into the shadows.

Naexa felt her power licking at her fingertips and scorching her tongue. It wanted so desperately to shoot into the darkness, wrap around the mage, and cook him until he burst like an over-baked pie and told her of his secrets as he screamed and steamed. But something had her pausing, calming her sudden rage. For curiosity had once again sparked within her belly, curiosity not only at this gift he spoke of, but also at his previous offer—to be her first follower. And a follower would be no good to her dead. So, she stifled the embers of her magick and stalked into the shadows, hating how desperate she was.

As soon as the darkness enveloped Naexa, the ground gave way to a steep staircase. She stumbled over the first step and onto the second, her hands flailing out to grasp at the cold walls on either side of her. As she clutched at the cobblestone, her power jumped from her palms in tiny sparks. She had to dig her nails into the cracks to balance herself, cursing softly at her clumsiness and the unease that had wormed its way into her stomach from the blunder. It wasn't often that she felt nervous, and just the rarity of it doubled the feeling. Naexa was just thankful that the shadows were there to hide her stumble from the mage. After regaining her balance and evicting the feeling of unease, she summoned a soft lavender flame to her fingertips to illuminate her path. Then, holding her hand up like a torch, she descended into the darkness.

After stepping through a short wooden door held ajar by a stone, Naexa found Pie standing in the middle of what seemed to be an abandoned winery. They had been common across all of Elt, before the intoxicating effects of fermented nectar had been discovered, and their popularity had remained beyond the Border even after they had become all but non-existent in the Valley. But hard soils and harder times left the Borderfolk to turn from wine to filtered manticore venom and fermented minotaur milk, which were easier to obtain and easier still to get drunk off of. It had been years since Naexa had seen a true winery.

Here, dusty casks were scattered along the short walls, and a couple of tables filled the small room, decorated with long-forgotten clay jugs. One of the wine casks was squeaking. Judging by the size of the room, it looked to be made for Fae, back when the separation of the races had been even greater than it was now. Naexa eyed the mage, noticing how he had to stoop to fit inside.

"Why don't you sit?" she asked before Pie could speak. Slouching disgusted her. There were no chairs in the room, but the tables seemed sturdy enough to support his broad frame.

Pie just glanced over his shoulder at the tabletop behind him. "I should rather not soil my robes. Besides, I am bound to deliver the gift I promised you." The mage moved toward the cask that seemed to house the squeaking.

Mutant mice were common here. She hoped such a creature was not the "gift" he intended to present her. If he had truly watched her for as long as he'd said, he would know that she preferred the taste of predatory creatures. And, best of all, the brown foxes which grew so fat they could not run.

"First you will tell me how you spied on me without my realizing."

Pie just paused to smile at her before continuing to the wine cask. Naexa had half a mind to singe the sashes covering his backside. This was twice he had disobeyed her instruction. She was not looking to acquire followers that did not conform to their purpose—*following.*

"The answer is in the gift, my sorceress," Pie said. Naexa sniffed, but secretly she perked up at that.

But when he reached into the cask and pulled out a plump red, spotted bunny, Naexa found herself again displeased.

"Your gift to me is a day's worth of food?" she asked stiffly, eyeing the bunny's round belly. She called it so, for though it was a hare of Elt, it had the softness and size of a bunny from the human world. At Naexa's remark, the bunny began to kick and squeak furiously from the mage's grip on its scruff.

Pie seemed surprised at her comment as well. "If you are inclined to make a meal of her, she is yours to cook, my sorceress. Yet, I have it on fair authority that her ilk is rather unpalatable."

"What do you mean 'her ilk?'" Naexa asked.

The mage fumbled with something around the rabbit's neck. It appeared to be a copper cord in the fashion of a collar, like those which the mortals made their dogs wear. It was as Pie grunted and cursed and fidgeted with it that Naexa noticed the diamond shape of the rabbit's pupils. It appeared only as a strange distortion of the light unless you knew what it meant. Naexa did.

"Is that—" she started, and then the plump animal began to transform.

Her kicking hind legs lengthened to touch the ground, and her paws shifted into humanoid feet with the long ankles of a deer. As her torso stretched and filled out and her front paws lengthened into arms and hands, the spotted fur shrank and distorted into reddish-brown skin. The scruff became a tangled mane of brilliant auburn hair, full of autumn leaves and marigolds. Then her muzzle shrank into the round face of a young girl, and her bunny ears shifted into the droopy ears of a fawn. When she had finished her shift, the rabbit's squeaks had turned into protests in the Known Tongue, and Naexa was staring at a short, plump Druid girl.

"Let go of me! Let go let go let go let—" she was saying.

"Does this gift please you, my sorceress?" Pie asked, round eyes gleaming and hopeful.

Naexa didn't glance at the mage as she stepped toward the Druid. The girl immediately quieted. The copper collar around her neck had grown with her, and Naexa saw that it extended into a leash held by Pie. The girl did not struggle against her restraints as Naexa neared, but she began to shiver. She wasn't clothed by anything but the curtain her red hair made around her shoulders, and feathers over her chest and hips typical of her kin. And by her small stature, it was obvious that she was still a youngling. Naexa cursed at the sight.

"I took an inordinate amount of time to capture her, to be sure," Pie was saying. "But once I tracked her in her hare form for some time, she proved most simple to ensnare. Quite the surprise, I must say, for I had heard Druids were formidable Beasts—"

Naexa slapped him. The action surprised her as much as it appeared to surprise the Druid and the mage alike, but by then she had already cranked her arm back and struck his rough cheek with the back of her hand, and her shock was burned up by her fury.

"Where are her clothes?" Naexa snapped. She could feel the heat of her power leaking onto her tongue. The sight of the little girl, trembling and leashed, was enough to ignite hot, wild sparks in her fingertips.

Pie paused his blabbering, open-mouthed. His hand went to his face, as slowly and dimly as he was blinking. "I was under the impression Druids had little fondness for clothing. She wore not a stitch when I happened upon her."

"Yes, in the Dell of Druids, among wildlife and others of her kind! But *now* she is bound to a strange *man,* probably being towed through towns and on public roads!" It was a feat to keep her rage to a simmer.

Pie was frowning and rubbing at his cheek. The slap had been forceful enough to have an initial numbing effect, but the pain would be setting in now. There would be a bruise later. She found this pleased her.

"Why, I keep her in animal form at all times, lest anyone catch sight of her…feathers. She is far less troublesome that way, I assure you. But speaking of attire, I have brought along some silks for you—another little token for my dearest sorceress." He was speaking distantly, and she wondered if she had somehow sent him into a shock. It sounded almost like he was rehearsing a script. He certainly had not expected this reaction to his gift.

"Give them to me. *Now.*"

The mage just nodded, the tips of his ears blushing golden-brown. He made his way toward another of the casks in the room, fumbling with the copper leash as he moved. He tugged on the cord as he walked so that the girl would follow him, and the act made Naexa bristle further.

"Oh, just leave her there. She won't run." At Naexa's glare, Pie obeyed, dropping the leash.

The Druid girl did not move, just shifted her hair to cover herself better.

Pie hurried back with a handful of purple silken clothes, and Naexa immediately pulled off her own cloak and gown. Pie walked past her, ears flushed and gaze downcast, muttering something about closing the door for her privacy. When Naexa had slid into the new silks, she knelt wordlessly by the Druid, holding her old gown up, measuring. She drew a blade she kept hidden in a secret belt and deftly sawed through the skirts. When they had been shortened, she pulled the dress over the child's head.

Naexa was not much taller than the Druid, who as an adult would stand taller than her, but she still found herself bending to meet her round, scared eyes.

"What is your name?" Naexa asked. Some of her rage had stilled now that the girl was clothed, but she avoided Pie's gaze so her flames would not surge again. He had picked up the leash once more.

The Druid straightened in front of Naexa, though her fuzzy ears flattened to her head. "I do not have one." Her eyes dropped. "I do not yet know my people."

Naexa nodded, but her jaw clenched. "And are you hurt?"

The girl felt at her collar, but shook her head no. "Just annoyed," she muttered. Naexa felt a smile twitch at her lips.

She straightened then to look at Pie, who was still stupidly slouched beneath the low ceiling of the cellar. He fiddled with the leash.

"You used her to spy on me?" Naexa asked. He nodded. "How?"

"I knew full well that with your great power, you would sense someone trailing you—so I bade her take the form of a hare on some days, a mouse on others. Her transformations are somewhat limited, so I had not a great many to choose from. I instructed her to follow whenever you ventured into town or set upon the road, though I kept her well out of sight in the woods. I feared, should you spot her in the forest, you might do her some…unintended harm." Pie finally sat on a cask, apparently tiring of his constant stoop.

"And how did you keep her from running off while you weren't with her?"

The mage perked up then, eyes brightening. "This is a cord imbued with magick. She is now bound to me and must heed my command, else it shall tighten about her neck. Even Beasts may be taught with a touch of…incentive."

The girl shot a hot glare at Pie, but said nothing. The rage was evident, however, in her brown eyes.

"The leash is for what, then? Show?"

"One might put it such a way, though it serves as more of a reminder. When she grows too spirited, I merely shorten the leash, so to speak, to remind her of her station."

"Clever," Naexa said flatly.

Pie smiled. "Now that my secret stands revealed, will you accept my offer, sweet sorceress?"

"Which one would that be?" Naexa could recall a few offers he'd made, none of which had been particularly appealing. Some had, however, sparked her interest, which was something of a feat. At her age, little could entice her, for she had possessed all there was to be enticed by already, courtesy of her husband and her family alike.

"I am most eager to hear of your schemes to lay claim to the Valley of Kings. The Druid has shared murmurs of it, though the Beast is cursed with a rather poor memory. You know you have my faith, my sorceress, but I should be most pleased to learn more of your ingenious plans. Pray, how do you mean to accomplish your feat, precisely?"

Naexa couldn't help but roll her eyes at the stupid mage. Besides his few magic tricks, she couldn't see how he'd be able to contribute anything to her army. But after many fruitless moons of trying to gain followers, here she stood with none. Perhaps Pie was a gift from the spirits, however meager such a gift might be. His treatment of the Druid was base at best, but she didn't sense any perverted intentions in him, only the prejudice courtesy of his Titian heritage.

I'll have to discern what other abilities or skills he has to offer me, she decided. *But perhaps, in the beginning, mere support will be enough. It may be that he will simply serve to draw in other followers, my true soldiers. Like the coins eternally displayed on the church's collection plate, he need only be proof that my cause is worthy of following.*

Instead of answering, she turned to the door. "I'm hungry."

"Me too!" the Druid said, eyes shining.

"I suppose we should find some food for us both, then," Naexa said, but she glanced at the Druid doubtfully; by the looks of her round belly, it seemed that she was never without food long enough to be hungry. In this way, she and Pie were a match written in the stars themselves.

Pie seemed to have guessed Naexa's thoughts. "Ah, you are too generous, my dear sorceress," he said laughing. "You need not trouble yourself over the whims of Beasts. Besides, do look at her—missing a meal or two might do her some good."

The Druid did not see the humor. Her ears flattened again, and she muttered something. Pie yanked on the leash, but Naexa glared at him and he loosened it again.

"What did you say?" she asked the girl.

"I said, we are not *Beasts*." The Druid turned to glare at the mage.

"Oh spare me," Pie scoffed. "You shift into every manner of creature in Elt, and you look more animal than person even when in Spiritkin form."

"I am more Spiritkin than you," the girl muttered. Naexa couldn't help the laugh that burst out.

Pie bristled, yanking on the leash. The girl yelped and grasped at her collar. "I can kill you with a twist of this cord, *Beast,"* the mage seethed.

Naexa's fingertips were once again alight with lavender flame. Her power had grown irate in her veins. "Enough," she said flatly.

When Pie continued jerking on the cord, she sent a small ball of fire out to the sashes on his neck. By the time he noticed the growing flame, he was yelping and he had dropped the leash. Once half his beard had been singed away and Naexa had grown tired of his pleading, "Sorceress, help!" she bid the flames to turn to smoke. The ashes of his magically-grown beard dusted his clean toes, and Naexa smiled slightly.

"Spiritkin of true power do not need to resort to brute force to make their points," she told the mage hotly.

Pie just grasped at his remaining beard as he stared between Naexa and the Druid. Somehow, she had managed to make him look even more imbecilic, and his apparent anger did not help the case. "Yes, my sorceress," he finally murmured.

"Remove the leash."

He did as he was told.

"Which form do you prefer for travel?" she asked the Druid.

"I would feel most comfortable as a hare while we are around other people," she mumbled.

The mage twisted at her collar again, and then she shrunk back down to the round bunny. The dark freckles which had covered her face and shoulders became spots on her fur. She ordered Pie to carry the girl's clothes, which were shed in her transformation, and he scooped them up wordlessly.

"Now, let's go find some dinner."

THE TWENTY-FIFTH

Sada

Sada's mind was numb with the weight of knowledge. After waking her with a pile of colorful fruit that she'd devoured in what felt like seconds, Dedrei had schooled her relentlessly on the Druidic tricks for discerning if a type of foliage was edible or not. While all of the fruit in the Dell was safe to eat, the leaves, roots, and flowers of the plants required more discernment. Sada had listened intently, eager to absorb the information, but when Dedrei had asked her to repeat the information back, the knowledge had suddenly evaded her. Now she sat stupidly in front of the Druid, trying to avoid those big eyes staring at her unwaveringly.

"Um…" Sada said, cringing at how ignorant she sounded. "It is edible if it is vibrant in color, but poisonous if it is marked by patterns."

"Yes," Dedrei said curtly, "but which manner of patterns?"

Sada bit into her lip, frowning at the colorful grass she knelt in as though she could find the answer written between the blades. Dedrei had just told her the answer to this question minutes ago. But she had also told her the number of mushrooms in a bunch that marked the severity of its poison, and that the food of four-eared hares could be eaten, but not that of two-eared hares. Or was that the single-tailed versus twin-tailed squirrels?

There had been so much information, and all front loaded into her mind. Now this particular bit of knowledge about colors and markings was lost amongst the rest. Sada plucked at the grass, nervous in her ignorance. Mr. Pérez had often spoken of her "incredible ability" to retain knowledge of herbs when he had taught her alongside Jezebel. But now she felt as stupid as a dog trying to learn its letters.

It's no doubt because I have hardly eaten as of late. How can I expect to think properly when even reaching my arms above my head to stretch is a chore? And it had become one. Even standing had. Whenever she got to her feet, she saw black and her head pulsed for a few moments before her vision returned to normal. In addition to that, she was constantly weak, and all movement was a momentous effort unless she got herself into a rhythm of it. Walking continuously was okay, but going from sitting to standing felt like the hardest thing possible. Especially since her legs were so stiff and sore from sprinting from the chimydra. Over-exertion in combination with starvation made for a weak body, and, it seemed, a weak mind.

"I don't—" she began, when she felt a brush of curls on her hand and suddenly the knowledge was in that new space of her mind. "Small spots and thick stripes!" Sada exclaimed. Sarana's tail flicked off her fingers as suddenly as it had appeared.

Dedrei frowned at the caelicorn, finally breaking her stare at Sada. "You cannot use Sarana to cheat."

Sada's cheeks flushed. "It wasn't my intention to do so," she said. "How can it be a fault of mine that she gave me the answer unbidden?" A lack of food had also introduced a new sense of both frustration and willfulness to her arsenal of emotions, and they came on in sudden waves whose intensity surprised her.

Dedrei just grunted. "Does she always eavesdrop?"

"She's sitting with us; we can hardly expect her not to listen." Sada glanced at the filly lying just behind her, cerulean flanks stretched across the damp grass where they sat. Dedrei, leaning back against a thick pine, merely closed her eyes and grunted again in reply. It was one of her favorite responses as of late.

"If Lady Bl—I mean, if *Sarana* is already well-versed in which fruits I may and may not partake of, why should I not seek her counsel when I am curious? Now that I know I am able to converse with her, that is."

"You did not know this already?"

"Well..." Sada hesitated, uncertain how best to reply. "I wasn't entirely certain it was real, or if it was a figment of my mind. I'd been so exhausted, and without food for so long, that it seemed altogether possible I was imagining things."

Dedrei opened one eye, fixing her with a stare. "You do not believe that."

"Well no, not entirely. But I was afraid that if I allowed myself to believe it, then...Why, I can't say I'm certain what I was afraid of. I only know that I was reluctant to consciously believe what I'd suspected to be true."

"Your mundane mind wished to deny the existence of magick."

At that, Sada laughed brightly. "My *mundane mind?* I've encountered talking foxes, horses adorned with wings and horns that can read thoughts, and women with antlers who can shapeshift into feathered wildcats...if after seeing all of this I still tried to deny that magick is real, then I fear I would not only have a mundane mind, but an insane one."

"Hmm," Dedrei said. Sada had expected her to make a joke about her insanity, but she fell silent after that. It was strange, the mood she had been in lately.

But Sada had learned earlier on that speaking of it did no good. She'd inquired about it once before, and that had only resulted in Dedrei snapping at her. So now she kept silent and joined Dedrei in leaning back against a nearby tree. Hers was the smooth trunk of a birch. She closed her eyes, listening to the distant melodies of the forest and humming along. As she did, she patted a rhythm on her shins, which were drawn up against her chest. They felt strange, and she began to poke at them.

"Feel this, DeeDee," Sada said. Dedrei lazily opened one eye, which darted down to where Sada pointed.

"Feel what?"

"My shin bones."

"I have no desire to feel your bones, Sada."

"But they feel strange! What if something is amiss with them?"

"What do you expect me to do if they are?"

"I'm sure I don't know, you're the healer!"

"And so are you from what I have been told," Dedrei scoffed, but she reached over and squeezed along Sada's shins as she'd asked.

"Only an apprentice, with half the training," Sada mumbled. Then, "See? They feel uneven."

"Indeed they do."

"Well?" Sada asked as Dedrei leaned back against her tree.

The Druid stared blankly at her, her large brown eyes making her look even more like a doe than usual. "Sada, you are the first human I have had the pleasure of meeting. I am certain I do not know what your *shin bones* are and are not supposed to feel like."

Sada smiled sheepishly then. "Oh. I suppose you are correct on that account."

Dedrei shook her head and closed her eyes again. "Allow me a moment's rest before we continue on. I slept fitfully this past night."

"Oh, of course! I ought to rest as well," Sada said, and mirrored Dedrei. "I'd quite forgotten how sleepy eating makes you."

"Mm."

The sun had snuck its way through the mist of the Dell to fall on her face and chest, and the warmth of the pink rays on her skin and the weight of food in her belly had her feeling drowsy. It reminded her of lazy summer days in Centerton, when the household staff and Jezebel alike were busy, and she'd needed to find her own entertainment. Sometimes she'd drawn, other times she'd sang, or pestered passing servants with questions. But mostly she liked to go up to her rooms, find a great slab of warm yellow sunlight on the ground, and lie in it. It was always the perfect temperature, and she would fall asleep almost immediately, feeling like one of the queen's fat and lazy cats, just content to bathe in yellow.

"Sarana will not be with you forever," Dedrei said suddenly, and Sada's eyes flew open. The filly was still stretched out beside her, tail flicking happily. "You would do well to learn which foods are dangerous and which are safe in preparation for the inevitable day that she decides to leave you. Once her horn solidifies and she can hunt for herself, or when her *Hédras* calls to her, she will have need of you no longer, girl."

Sada frowned at her friend's words, unwilling to believe that Sarana would leave her. Had they no bond between them, it might be something she could accept. But considering the nature of their connection, it did not seem right, or even possible. She'd grown very used to the filly's company and the easy way they could communicate. She met the caelicorn's eye and somehow knew that Dedrei was wrong, that she and Sarana would not part for a long, long while.

Sada just chalked the comment up to her friend's odd mood. She had been acting strangely, no doubt from reawakened grief over Shiual, and who could blame her? She had revisited a dark memory, one she'd probably spent months, if not years, attempting to hide away, to chain down in the recesses of her unconscious mind where it could not hurt her. Of course she would not be in lively spirits now that it had been brought to her attention again. Sada reasoned that it was these thoughts of her lost daughter that spurred Dedrei to say such things, and act in such a way. She just wished for her friend's sake that she could find her spirit again; that unique liveliness which manifested in her as bone-dry humor and sarcasm as thick as pudding.

She dismissed the idea of Sarana leaving, but curiosity still pricked at her mind at Dedrei's last words. "What do you mean, once her horn solidifies? It appears rather sturdy to me."

Sada suddenly wanted to poke at it, but Sarana was out of reach, and moving seemed like far too much effort.

"It only appears that way to deter predators while she is still young and vulnerable. But she cannot yet use it to kill. This is why caelicorn foals seek out their *Hédras* in their early years—they need someone to hunt on their behalf. As we have discussed before, you have become that interim guardian."

But Sada's mind was instantly filled with the sight of the nine-tailed fox speared on Sarana's horn, the blood staining its fur.

"She killed a fox the very day I met her," Sada said. *And when I washed her in the Nymph's springs, her horn was sturdy as a hoof.*

Dedrei just nodded as though the information was utterly unsurprising. "She is of royal blood. Royal caelicorns are more equipped to defend themselves than most others of their kind. In moments of dire peril, it is said their horns become enveloped in magick, rendering them solid enough to be wielded as weapons. In such a life-threatening situation, it is most probable that Sarana's magick allowed her to protect herself."

Sada found herself being drawn back to the memory again, the sight of the fox's bloodthirsty eyes drilling into hers, its fangs inches from her face as it raked its claws down her sides. Her hand drifted to her ribcage at the thought, resting atop the scars that hid just below the surface of her dress.

"Is something wrong, girl?" Dedrei asked, staring where Sada's hand rested.

Sada shook her head. "Not a fig. Just reliving the past." The Druid continued eyeing her side, but said nothing further.

There were still a few small pieces of fruit left over from breakfast, and Sada nibbled on them in hopes their sweetness would distract her from the bitter memories. As she ate, she watched Sarana. She was still lying next to the women, but her eyes were open, staring into the sky. The pale purple reflected across her golden irises, like two of the finest silks overlaying each other. Sada held a berry out to her muzzle, stomach tight with the hope that she might eat. Sarana just snorted at the offering and shifted her muzzle away from the food. Sada's heart clenched with worry for her.

"Sarana has eaten but once since she has been in my company. I know you disapprove of her diet, and her ways," she said, casting a glance at the Druid's tight-lipped expression, "but I am growing quite concerned for her. She is only a baby after all, as you yourself have said."

Sarana's feathered wings typically hid most of her body from view, but seeing her laid out in the grass, wings stretched out above her, Sada couldn't help but notice the angles of the caelicorn's hip bones, the way her stomach curved up sharply beneath her rib cage. The hound master would have proclaimed her to be the perfect weight if she were a dog, but horses were supposed to be nice and round. Indeed, she was neither animal, but she was certainly more similar to a horse than a hound. Sada wanted desperately to fatten the filly up.

Dedrei stood then, gathering her staff. "I will permit no killing in the Dell," she said firmly. "Caelicorns are resilient, and we are almost out of my people's domain. She can survive without bloodshed until then." Sada cringed at the harshness of the words, but nodded. There was naught to be done if Dedrei would not change her mind. And it was wrong of Sada to ask her to disregard the rules of her home. "Stand now, and come with me. It is better to learn with your hands than your ears."

Sada obeyed, scrambling to her feet, but still cast a worried glance at Sarana dozing in the sun. The filly had chosen Sada to be her protector, to hunt for her and feed her, and yet she was only foraging for herself.

Dedrei noticed and, with a begrudging sigh, she moved to crouch beside the filly. When Sarana raised her head up to sniff at Dedrei's face, she gently pushed her neck so that she was lying down again, murmuring in Druidic. Sarana accepted this and went back to napping. Dedrei then ran her hand down to the filly's ribs, feeling beneath the thick fur. Sada could not see what Dedrei's countenance revealed, and she worried her lip as she waited for her friend's verdict. Once her examination was complete, Dedrei stood.

"All is well, girl. Caelicorns can survive months without food if they must."

"Even the babies?" Sada asked, not taking her eyes off Sarana.

Dedrei's silence was enough of an answer. The worry was a pang in Sada's heart, and she tried to transfer it to her lip with her teeth. As she watched the caelicorn's chest rise and fall rhythmically, resolve washed over her in a cold and steely wave. She decided then that if her filly had to go without, then she would as well.

"Are you ready?" Dedrei asked.

So stealthily that Sada had not noticed her movement, Dedrei had moved to perch on a branch in a nearby tree like a wildcat. Crouching there, she seemed a creature of the forest. Her eyes, almost identical in color to the trunk, glowed brightly amidst the leaves. Her antlers intertwined with the branches, and Sada could not discern where the flowers began growing on the tree and stopped growing on the Druid. The only thing that distinguished her from the tree was her light olive skin, and Sada wondered if she could change its color the way she could change its form.

They left Sarana to sleep and guard Dedrei's staff, and Dedrei led the way from amidst the trees. Sarana had not been speaking to Sada much as of late, but she seemed content enough to stay. Both those things worried her. The filly wasn't exactly talkative, but she would typically respond if Sada asked a question or wondered strongly enough about something. And Sarana was typically full of energy, always eager to run ahead and practice flapping her wings. Sada tried to remind herself that since she was only a foal, she was likely exhausted from their trek through the forest. Even Sada wished to sit and rest for a day, and she was a woman grown. It was small wonder a foal needed extra time to recover from the constant traveling.

Dedrei, on the other hand, seemed to have regained some of her old liveliness once they set out. The Druid leapt between trunks, her well-muscled legs propelling her from one branch while her nimble hands sought purchase on the next one. Sometimes those long, sharp claws Sada had seen upon their introduction would appear in order to dig into the bark, then disappear as she swung off the branch and to the next. With each leap, the Druid's tall body stretched to its full extent, spine arching and feathered chest flaring as if she was shaped by the wind. No matter the distance between the trees, Dedrei was able to span it with little effort. It was beautiful, and near breathtaking. As Sada watched, she saw a huge grin spread across Dedrei's face. Sada couldn't help but smile herself at the sight.

As Dedrei moved among the trees, her pace increased, and she became little more than a light blur against the leaves. Sada found herself running to keep pace, and was delighted to discover that it was incredibly easy. She, too, began to smile as she moved through the Dell, relishing in the forgotten strength that food had brought her. Dedrei had been trying her best to fatten her with fruits. She still felt lightheaded when she rose from sitting, but that was a little thing. For now she no longer felt as though her arms were dead weights at her side, and after a few minutes, even the stiff soreness in her legs disappeared. She ran with what felt like the strength of one hundred horses as her legs propelled her across the moss and leaves and grass.

She came upon a sandy boulder, and instead of slowing to climb over it, Sada leapt as Dedrei was doing in the trees. She began to soar over the stone, but quickly realized she had overestimated her strength and agility both. Her toes caught on the face of the boulder, and she squealed as the rest of her body careened into the ground on the other side. The moss cushioned her fall, but barely.

"Oh, fffff*iddles!*" she cursed, barely managing to restrain her tongue from saying worse.

Sada pulled herself off the floor of the Dell and stretched her legs out in front of her, spitting out moss. Then she shook out her forearms, which had taken the brunt of her fall and were now aching and tingling. But it was her shins that made her cringe. They were half numb, throbbing, and bloody, and she sucked in a hiss of air, grasping just below her knees in any attempt to relieve the pain. The twin wounds on either leg were jagged and gruesome. Perhaps she should show Dedrei so she could see what human shins were *not* supposed to look like.

During my time in the forest, I have seen more blood on myself than I have in all my years of life. As the warm liquid ran off her legs to soak into the floor of the Dell, Sada realized with a jolt that she hadn't bled at *all* before coming to Elt. There had been many others who she had seen bleed, though. She glanced around for something to stop the bleeding with, but of course there would be nothing sanitary in the woods. Though, she reasoned, it was Elt, the world without dirt and with caelicorns who had healing saliva. And Dedrei, who was a healer both by nature and by trade, had used absorbent moss to bandage the wounds on her shoulders. That must mean it was clean for use. She should find some of that.

At least I can say I cleared the boulder, Sada thought as she stood. But the pain in her shins and the nausea in her belly dulled the sense of victory.

Putting weight on her legs made her shins scream with dull agony. Looking at the stone now, she realized it was nearly level with her belly. There was no way she ever would have made that jump without stumbling. Sada brushed the leaves and moss off her dress, letting her skirts fall to cover her wounds and praying that none of the dirty fabric stuck to the gashes. She eyed the new rips and stains that decorated the delicate dress. The poor thing had never been made to leave the city. Had she known she would be embarking on this adventure, she would have worn something better suited for travel.

Truly? What clothing do you have that would be suited for travel? She owned only dresses upon dresses. Dresses with lace, and dresses of silk; expensive dresses and slightly more expensive ones. Dresses of white, dresses of gold, dresses of sapphire. She owned no pants as men wore, nor the rough-spun cotton dresses of the commonfolk. It was a blessing that her father was not here now, or he would have thoroughly punished her for ruining this slightly-more-expensive dress.

Her chest constricted at the thought of her father, and she made herself continue limping through the great bushes and ferns to distract herself. The pain in her shins was a welcome diversion.

She hadn't seen Dedrei since she'd fallen, so without a guide, she decided to continue on straight. Hopefully her friend would find her. She thought it was strange that she hadn't already. Though she was always talking about how strangely faint Sada's scent was. Dedrei had found it odd that she'd only encountered one Beast in the forest. Then the Druid had admitted that even she hadn't scented the "mortality" on Sada at first. Perhaps her friend would have trouble tracking her, then. Though Groll certainly hadn't.

He is *the Mudhands' best tracker.* She smiled at the memory of the sweet little Trell people.

Now that Sada wasn't crashing through ferns and panting louder than a dog as she ran, the Dell had grown quiet. She heard the music without origin floating through the trees and the mist again. In the Dell, it sounded like flutes and harps, and perhaps chimes as well. As Sada walked, she sang along to the music. She sang no song from memory, but let new melodies come to her as she created music with the forest. Sometimes she thought the hidden instruments sped up or slowed down as she spun new verses, also rising in crescendo when she did, growing soft when her voice dropped. She sang a song of the wonders of beauty, of colors, of sweetness, and of friendship.

Sada had become so absorbed in her song that she hadn't noticed the throng of animals that had gathered to watch, and then begin walking alongside her. Normally, they kept their distance from her, watching from the safety of far-away trees or thickets of brush. But now, they slowly closed in, creating a wall of fur, and horns, and tails on either side of her as she walked. Sada sang freely, and loosely. She didn't notice the birds raise their own voices in song with her, how they flitted between branches above to keep pace. She didn't hear the elk snorting softly, or the hares thumping their feet in time with her tune. Lost in thought as she was, she assumed it was another bodiless source of music.

Sada let the melodies fill her, and then flow out of her. She was a *Vaisse* for music, a medium of the song. So she didn't notice either when one of the great elk, antlers covered in flowers where its kin sported only bare tines or vines, stepped away from the throng of creatures and into the weeping willow that Sada headed for. She didn't notice until she reached out to move the curtain of the willow and the elk stuck its great, shaggy head out from the drape of leaves and lowered its brown eyes to stare into hers.

Her voice abruptly faltered. For a moment, the creatures of the forest stayed where they were, waiting for Sada to resume her melody. Then the great, dark elk stretched its muzzle out and blew a soft breath onto her face. It smelled of hay and cut grass. Her hair blew back, and her chest tightened at its nearness. She couldn't help but glance at the huge antlers spanning as long as her body on each side. She saw the vines wrapped around their prongs, growing on them, and couldn't help but wonder if her intestines would soon decorate them alongside the blooming greenery. She took a stumbling step backward, and then the animals around her scattered.

Sada's head whipped to the surrounding trees at the sudden burst of movement, wide eyes taking in the mass of creatures that were running away from her, the crowd so thick they had to line up single-file in places to escape. Then Sada's eyes darted back to the elk towering over her, tall enough to graze from the hair on her head, and wondered if this creature was what the others were running from. Her apprehension stuck in her throat and tickling her belly, Sada backed away again. The elk stepped forward and her heart fluttered in her chest. The pain of her legs was forgotten in her nervousness.

Then the elk was shrinking, shaggy fur receding, and when its head matched Sada's height, it stood on its hind legs. The tail disappeared, then the huge hooves turned into olive-toned hands. The antlers and ears remained, though they shrunk smaller, and as the muzzle receded, Dedrei's grinning face was revealed.

For a moment, Sada was still too shocked to speak, to do anything but stare, one hand braced on a nearby trunk. Then the Druid laughed, and Sada found herself grinning as well.

"*DeeDee!*" Sada exclaimed as Dedrei laughed, antlers thrown back. She batted her friend's shoulder. "I should have known it was you! I cannot say why, but I had thought you might reserve your animal forms for…well, special occasions, or something of that nature."

"I would argue that playing a trick on you *is* a special occasion. You should have seen yourself—you should have *smelled* yourself! The scent of your fear was so thick, I am surprised it took the others so long to flee."

Sada was just shaking her head at the absurdity of it all. The pain in her shins had been forgotten in her encounter with Dedrei's elk form, but now they throbbed again with a vengeance. She lowered herself to sit on the roots around her feet.

"You had quite the gathering, I must say. The elk told me that they follow you when you sing. All of the animals gather around you to listen. Some even join in."

Sada just blinked in surprise. "Truly?"

"You have not noticed? I know this is not the first time you have sang in the forest." Dedrei took up a seat on a root beside Sada.

Sada smiled. She often sang both loudly and beneath her breath when she and the Druid weren't talking. Dedrei had grumbled about it in the beginning and so Sada had stopped, but the Druid had confessed later that night that truly she liked to listen to Sada sing, almost as much as she liked to needlessly complain. And so Sada had happily continued to do so from then on.

"I have noticed as much, though they do not usually venture so near. And ever since Sarana began traveling with me, they have not come much at all. I had almost forgotten it was their usual habit. How many were there?" Sada asked, surveying the undergrowth. Only a few animals dwelled there now. "I was far too preoccupied with the Giant of an elk before me to count." She grinned, poking at Dedrei's side.

"A Giant of an elk, truly?" her friend exclaimed, matching her smile. "There were nearly a hundred. It is indeed unfortunate you did not notice it. It was like nothing I have ever seen before..." Her feathered brows furrowed.

"What is it?" Sada asked. Dedrei looked deep in thought, her deer ears flicking.

"Nothing," she said, then met her eyes, her brown ones studying Sada's. "It is only...this morning—when I woke, there were animals sleeping with you. Some had piled up beside me as well. But most of them were gathered around you, Sada. Beside you, on top of you, curled around your head. When I left to find food to break our fast, they all scattered immediately. As though they did not want to be seen sleeping with you. But I have never heard of wild creatures gathering around a human to sleep. Nor a Spiritkin for that matter."

"It was indeed a shock the first time I woke to the sight, but I merely assumed the creatures of your wood are friendlier than those in mine. Yet you say this is strange?" Sada asked.

"I often wake to animals sharing my sleeping space, even if I did not lay to rest beside them. But I am a Druid, I take the forms of Elt's creatures; in some ways, I am an extension of Elt and a representative of all its creatures. The fact that you are human and they did the same..."

At Sada's frown, Dedrei blew out a sigh of air. "Many decades ago, Woia told us a legend about a...person. Animals did not shy away from their presence, but were drawn to them. And their voice called to the creatures, as though it transcended the barrier of our languages."

As a child, it had been Sada's dream to commune with animals. Hearing about someone who had made her dream a reality made her chest grow full.

"Who was it?" Sada asked in awe.

"They were known by many names," Dedrei said, her accent growing thicker as she spoke. "The gift is ageless, passed down through bodies, though it manifests in a vessel only once every few centuries. In some respects, it bears similarity to the phenomenon of the Kindreds. It is called the Accent. Each vessel is a new person, bearing a different name. Yet, the one who possesses the gift is ever known as the Bewitcher of Beasts."

Hearing Dedrei's story made her entire body alight with a burning desire to know more. As she'd listened, Sada's *instincts* had flared to life in her left hand's fingertips. Dedrei stood, apparently too restless to sit. She prodded at nearby bushes with her staff, moving the leaves aside to peer in, frowning. She seemed distracted, but Sada couldn't stop the questions that flowed from her.

"By 'beasts,' do you refer to mere animals, or the other creatures which you told me of before?"

"I speak of both. The Bewitcher of Beasts possesses the power to commune with all creatures of Elt through his or her song, whether the creatures be simple animals or magickal Beasts. And should the powers of the Accent be in perfect accord with its host, they may even command these creatures to their will."

"Do your people not possess a like ability to converse with animals?" Sada asked. Once, in response to one of Sada's many inquiries about her people, Dedrei had told Sada that she spoke the language of the woodland animals. It was an ability all Druids possessed. "You said the elk spoke to you just now."

"That is somewhat different. I can speak with elk because I know their form. The same is true for every other animal form I am able to assume. As Druids walk through life, we continue to learn the forms of new creatures. It is a process that requires time—a great deal of time spent in the company of Elt's creatures. Only when we understand their ways may we take their form, and only when we know their form may we speak their tongue."

Dedrei looked to the trees for a moment, wide eyes scanning the branches. "Look there—do you see that squinch?" She pointed to one of the small, fuzzy creatures Sada had played in a puddle with, early on in her journey. It was standing high up in one of the trees, tottering on a branch as it tried to find its balance.

She grinned at the sight of the animal with the fur of a wish flower. "Is that their name? How silly. Though they are quite silly creatures, are they not?"

"Yes, very quaint. Do you wish to hear the answer to your question or not, girl?"

"Indeed, my apologies. Please continue," Sada said sheepishly.

"Hmph...Then as I was saying, I do not know their form. I cannot shift into a squinch, and thus their language remains beyond my grasp. All I hear is the same meaningless gibbering you do."

"What might happen if you attempted to take the form of a squinch?"

Dedrei did not respond, but she held one of her hands away from herself, still staring at the squinch in concentration. Her skin began to visibly vibrate, like sand bouncing off a hard surface, or water bouncing up from the surface of a lake after a handful of small rocks was thrown in. Patterns of swirls and squares appeared, seeming to lift out of her skin before melting back into it. Then her skin began to bubble, some of the bubbles growing so large that they popped. It looked painful and Sada winced, but Dedrei only continued to stare at the little animal, jaw clenched, and eyebrows worked into a hard frown. Finally dark fur began to grow from the burst bubbles in small, fine tufts. Sada's eyes were wide as Dedrei's hand fell to her side and she dropped into a crouch, panting.

"My body does not know what shape to assume," Dedrei explained, "for I am unacquainted with the creature's ways. If I were to learn how it lives and what its habits are, the places it rests, the purpose of its fur and shape, then I could take its form. But both my body and I remain ignorant of such things, and thus I can but attempt to imitate it. Yet that is the manner of magick-users. Druids do not merely imitate; we *become*."

Sada was grinning at her friend's display of power. Even when it failed, it was beyond what she ever could have imagined a person to be capable of, even one of the fantastical Spiritkin.

"You are indeed incredible, DeeDee."

Dedrei's ears flattened, and she looked aside. Her cheeks became colored with a shade like amber, and—

She's blushing! Sada hadn't known the Druid was capable of it.

"It is no achievement for which I may claim any glory. It is merely the way of my people. But you have led me astray from my point once again, child. As you can see, a Druid's abilities are quite different from those of the Accent."

"I confess, I feel a touch of envy toward you both. This Bewitcher sounds remarkable as well."

Dedrei's lips drew into a thin line, her lids shadowing her eyes. "There are some who believe it was the last Bewitcher who incited the caelicorns to revolt and turn so bloodthirsty."

In contrast to Dedrei's shadowy feelings on the matter, Sada brightened at this revelation. It gave fuel to her argument about Sarana's nature, that the caelicorn was not inherently wicked but had indeed healed her due to the bond they shared. Or perhaps it was simply an act born of the purity of her soul. But certainly not a selfish motive as Dedrei believed.

"Then Sarana—" she began.

"It is but a rumor, unsupported by any records or knowledge. The caelicorns are dangerous Beasts, and no justification should be offered for their actions." Dedrei's big eyes had narrowed to dark slits. There would be no convincing her.

Sada sighed. "As you say," she murmured.

"Let us speak of this no more, for neither of us ever come away satisfied when the topic is caelicorns. And be glad—you will now learn the secrets of foraging."

Dedrei led Sada through what felt like leagues of undergrowth, pointing at the odd tree or piece of fruit and naming it if Sada deemed it a species she did not recognize. For every plant and tree she did know, there were three she did not. It seemed every species of vegetation and foliage grew in the Dell, and when she mentioned this to Dedrei, she confirmed it. She said that the Dell of Druids was home to all of Elt's plants, and a sanctuary to each of its creatures. Her people were representatives of its animals and Beasts, and guides to its people. The Dell was representative of its flora.

Dedrei would pause every so often to ask Sada if the leaves of a vibrantly-colored bush appeared edible. More often than not, if Sada nodded and reached for the leaves, Dedrei would knock her staff against her knuckles, chiding her for not remembering her lessons. A few knocks had Sada wishing that Sarana was there to guide her. When she thought of the caelicorn, that space in her mind would fill with a gentle tingle, but no whispered words of guidance came to her. So she would store the images of the inedible leaves and flowers in her mind for later inquiry, the sting on her knuckles imprinted in the memories.

They came to a small bush with velvety, purple leaves. Dedrei paused beside it, pointing with what Sada had come to think of as her Scolding Staff. She reminded her greatly of Governess Brown today.

"Scent it," the Druid instructed.

Sada obeyed, holding back her tangled hair as she bent and smelled the leaves. She wished to keep it in a braid so it would not grow matted beyond repair, but early into their time together, Dedrei had noticed the braid she wore and suggested she take it out. She would not explain all of the reasoning, but said that if she planned to ask for help from the Elves, she ought not upset them by wearing her hair braided. It was a strange comment, but Sada wasn't one to argue. So upon hearing this, Sada had planned to just let her hair down when she drew near to the city, but as the days passed, she'd grown more nervous that she'd run into the king or some of his men in the wood again without warning, and so she'd let it down.

It had quickly tangled, and she spent much of her time walking trying to comb out the knots with her fingers, but she was quite unsuccessful. Somehow, Dedrei's own loose hair never seemed to tangle, but she'd noticed Sada's distress and each night she sat down to work through her hair until it was somewhat neat again, using twigs held between her knuckles as a makeshift comb. Now, just after a day of walking again, the knots had returned. She missed the neatness of having her hair done, but she would not risk upsetting the people she planned to ask the aid of, and so she suffered through it.

Hair gathered in hand, Sada smelled the leaves. The aroma was pungent but pleasant, and made her mouth water. She had to close her lips to keep the saliva from spilling out, muttering, "Pardon me," as she did so.

Dedrei rolled her eyes. "You stand in the forest, clad in more grass stains and blood than clothing…attempting to maintain propriety will gain you nothing here." Sada just breathed deeper, recalling her time in the apothecary. It made her heart ache dully. "The scent made you salivate: What does this signify?"

"Umm…That it will not harm me?"

A coy smile spread across Dedrei's lips. "Then eat one."

Sada hesitated, unsure if the Druid was trying to trick her into the wrong answer so she could rap her knuckles again. She was in quite the trickster mood today.

Dedrei sighed, ears twitching. "Here," she said, swiftly plucking a few leaves from the perfectly spherical bush.

Her friend stuck her amber-colored tongue out and placed a leaf on it. Sada watched as the leaf slowly dissolved, turning to a shapeless blob of purple. She offered the remaining leaves to Sada, eyebrows raised invitingly. Wide-eyed at the demonstration, Sada took the leaves from Dedrei's hand and placed them on her tongue as the Druid had. They were soft and light, and after a few seconds, she felt them begin to melt. A mouthwateringly-tart taste spread through her mouth as the leaves softened to goo. When she swallowed, her throat buzzed deliciously.

"What *are* those?" Sada asked.

The leaves reminded her of childhood days spent sneaking down into the kitchens to steal sugar cubes when the cooks and maids had gone to bed. Yet if she went too late after midnight, the cooks would be preparing for that day's breakfast. It had to be timed perfectly. She plucked a handful of the leaves from the bush and chewed them greedily.

"It is called an azkria, or sweet-leaf, bush. The leaves themselves are not particularly nourishing, but they are a favorite treat of Druid younglings."

Dedrei plucked another leaf, her eyes closing as she savored its taste. "If you catch the scent of a leaf, root, mushroom, or a flower within the Dell of Druids and find your mouth watering, it is safe to eat. Should your nose begin to run, or your eyes start to water, it is deadly. If there is no reaction at all, it is meant for the animals."

Sada's mouth gaped. "That is all? That is the only rule?"

Dedrei grinned as she plucked a few handfuls from the bush and tucked them into a small bag tied around her waist. Sada wondered how she had not noticed it on the Druid before, but when it was filled, she slid it around so that it was hidden behind the curtain of her hair once more, her feathers hiding the rest of the strap.

"That is the only rule."

"That is delightfully simple to recall!" she exclaimed. "But then, why did you spend the entire morning instructing me on spots, bumps, and brightly-colored stems?"

Dedrei shrugged, but turned away, focusing on the purple bush. "All Druids learn the specific properties of each plant in the Dell, and what each marking means. Since you spilled blood here, I thought it only fair that you learn the knowledge its inhabitants have to."

A shameful blush crept over Sada's cheeks at the memory of the hare. The way she'd pinned it against the earth, how her fingers had wrapped around its neck almost against her will, how the foreign desire to just *kill* had filled every part of her. Even the forest seemed to still at the memory, and Sada grew cold, wrapping her arms around herself. Never again could she hunt, even once she'd left the Dell.

But Sarana…

"When I saw how earnestly you strove to learn all that I endeavored to teach you," Dedrei said, "attempting to commit to memory in a day what Druid younglings spend much of their childhoods learning, I realized it was not a just expectation. And neither was any form of punishment fair—you had no one to guide you in the ways of this Dell, of this world. And as wrong as it may seem to me, I could see that your intent in hunting that hare was born of goodwill, not malice. So, I offer you my apologies."

Dedrei smiled at Sada then, though it didn't reach her darkened eyes. "I cannot permit you to hunt within our Dell, but Sarana will fare well enough until we make our way out. Once you return to the forest of the Elves of the Wood, however, you must hunt for her. She chose you to protect and provide for her, and she did so with purpose. It is never wise to act against the will of Elt."

Half of Sada felt relieved that Dedrei had made the decision for her, and it took away a weight in her belly she hadn't wholly realized she'd been carrying with her. She tried to force herself to smile back, but the memory of the hare still tainted her mind, making her shrink into herself.

"I do not know if I will be able to," she whispered at last.

"You will. For you are good, and you are a protector. A healer does not only make poultices and tend physical ailments; we are also protectors of peace, and relievers of anguish. Many times you have done the latter for me. You are not Druidic by birth, but you match us in nature, healer.

"I know you will see to Sarana's safety, whatever the cost. It is not wrong to kill out of need, Sada, only out of want. And if there is anyone in these lands who would not kill out of mere desire, it is you. Of this, I am certain." Now Dedrei's smile truly filled her eyes, making them gleam.

Sada smiled back. But something inside her writhed at the wrongness of the words. When she'd held that hare down, she had wanted to kill it simply to kill. Not to feed Sarana, or to feed herself. But to see the light flee from the creature's eyes, to hear its squeals as it suffered. There had been a morbid and cold curiosity to know what it would look like to cease breathing, then to cease living. A shiver ran down Sada's entire body when her *instincts* began to alight in her left palm. She clenched her fist to silence them, to trap them. She didn't want that desire for death to become a part of her. She wanted to run from it, to cut that piece out of herself.

"What troubles you?" Dedrei asked.

Sada hadn't realized she'd gone quiet, or that the leaves in her palm had melted into sticky purple goo. She blinked suddenly, wiping the mess on the grass.

"Oh, pardon," Sada said, refusing to meet the Druid's eyes. "I was only thinking of Sarana."

She couldn't bring herself to tell Dedrei the truth, that there was a piece of her that wished to kill out of desire alone. She wasn't sure how her friend would view her after hearing a truth so disgusting it made even herself squirm. So she hid the feeling behind a bright smile.

"Will you show me some more plants?" she asked.

Dedrei stared at her for a moment, as though she saw right through the mask Sada had put up, but then she nodded.

"We shall find some flowers for lunch."

Sada and Dedrei didn't return to their makeshift camp in the grass until the sun's rays were little more than tendrils of pink on the floor of the Dell, and the sky was a deep reddish-purple. Dedrei carried the flowers and herbs they'd harvested in the pouch around her waist, and fixed others into her hair. The vines intertwined with her locks had even curled around the flowers Dedrei presented to them and held them in place as she walked. By the time the two of them were finished foraging, she had a mane of flowers, and her hair could barely be seen through the flora decorating it.

Sada had tried the same with her hair, but any knots she tied to weave the flowers in quickly slid undone, and she couldn't even make them stick behind her ears. So she had tied her cloak into a satchel—she always wore it in the Dell, the mist made the air cold—and filled it with countless assortments of fruits, some big and light, others small and heavy. Once they reached their camp between the half-circle of trees and rocks, her neck and shoulder had gone numb. She'd barely set the satchel of fruit on the grass before she collapsed beside it. She'd never had to carry something so heavy in her life, if anything at all. Gabriel had always been there to carry it for her.

Something squeezed her heart at the memory of the tall guard, the way he'd been so gentle with her, but so harsh with anyone who'd so much as look at her wrong. She knew her father paid him to stay by her side, but she had considered him a true friend. Perhaps now he'd be her only friend if Jezebel was still angry with her.

The thought of Jezebel was worse to bear. Sada lifted a hand to feel at the little cuff on her ear. Her only reminder of her dearest friend. If Jezebel were here, she'd be studying Dedrei with scrutiny, trying to determine which species of flora besides tulips grew in her hair and on her antlers. Then she'd force the Druid to stick out her tongue until she'd determined what exactly made it orange. She might even suggest a remedy to turn it pink like a human's. Jezebel had never been very accepting of people's differences. Though Sada's chest was tight, the thought made her chuckle. She thought Jezebel and Dedrei would get along well. They had a similar fire to them, though it showed in different ways. Jezebel in her hard bargaining, Dedrei in her pride for her people and land.

A gentle snorting made Sada look up from her place on the ground. She found Sarana standing a few feet away, muzzle to the grass. Her glittering eyes were locked on Sada, and she couldn't help but smile at the sight of the caelicorn.

"You've returned!"

The filly hadn't been at the camp when she and Dedrei had arrived, but seeing her now erased almost all of the sorrow from Sada's chest and throat. Something tickled in the shared space of their minds, and Sada reached out a hand to Sarana in a silent invitation. The caelicorn pressed her muzzle against her fingers and her *instincts* flared as their connection came to life, made strong enough for communication through touch.

Something doth trouble thee, Sarana stated.

I'm well enough, Sada said, but she felt the caelicorn's unbelief of the words in her own body, and realized Sarana could probably sense better than anyone that something truly was wrong. *I was remembering my friend,* she relented.

Understanding washed over her, followed by a sense of curiosity.

Reveal it unto me, Sarana said, and Sada frowned.

How?

Picture thine companion, and I shall see.

So Sada closed her eyes and let the image of Jezebel's face clarify in her mind, the way her brows always seemed to be scrunched together in concern, then the wild smiles that would grace her face to erase them. She saw her pinecone eyes and dark hair. She tried to focus on the good memories, like their younger days when Mr. Pérez taught them together. Or when Jezebel would make the journey up to the manor and they would spend the day feeding the horses, playing with the barn cats, and begging the cooks to make them tarts. But she found her mind returning to their last encounter, of Jezebel storming out of the shop knocking over stacks of papers and bundles of herbs in her wake. She felt the sorrow and confusion creep back into her throat.

The guilt.

Then, as suddenly as they had appeared, the feelings were gone. A sense of calm and acceptance filled her chest and enveloped her mind. Sada's eyes flew open to meet Sarana's as the caelicorn sent her those feelings of tranquility.

I see, Sarana said into her mind. *Then, thou desire not to hear this, but it was Jezebel who hath wrought ill. She is envious, yet thou will not suffer thyself to accept this truth. Thou art virtuous, yet blind, and until thou dost open thine eyes to see the flaws of others, thou shalt continue to bear them upon thyself and be harmed by them.*

Sada felt her protest growing in her mind and on her lips alike, but then the caelicorn was lifting her muzzle from her hand, and the space between their minds grew vacant again.

"Sada," Dedrei said, her voice flat.

"Yes?" Sada sat up quickly, something like embarrassment warming her cheeks. She felt almost as though she'd been caught stealing an extra pastry, though she could not think why. It was not wrong to speak to Sarana, and it was no secret that she could.

Dedrei flicked her eyes between Sada and Sarana. "I have been calling you."

"My apologies, I did not hear you. I was—"

"You were communicating with the caelicorn," Dedrei said stiffly. "There is no use in denying it. But do try to listen with both your ears as well as your mind. If you allow yourself to be so entranced when speaking with her, you leave yourself exposed to the dangers of the real world."

The heat intensified in Sada's cheeks, but the Druid didn't comment on her conversation with Sarana any further, just tossed her a square, pink fruit.

"Eat."

Sada made to catch the fruit but missed, and it rolled to her feet. She picked up the strangely shaped fruit, a diceberry as Dedrei had called it, and eyed it before tossing it back to the Druid. A claw extended from one of her hands and pierced the fruit mid-air. Dedrei raised an eyebrow at her questioningly.

"The flavor may change with each bite, but I think you will like it," Dedrei said. Sada just shook her head. "Would you prefer to try some of the flowers we picked instead? We have quite an array to choose from." She gestured at the immense pile of fruit between them, head tilted like a cat.

Sada glanced at the caelicorn fanning her wings, now a distance away. Her hip bones were definitely too sharp, her ribs too pronounced, even beneath her thick fur.

"I can't. I mean, I won't. I've decided…" she bit at her lip, not wanting to go on. Somehow, she knew Dedrei would disapprove. "I've decided I shall not eat until Sarana is able to." She dropped her eyes. She didn't want to see the disappointment in Dedrei's eyes, or the anger. She was certain they would reflect one of the emotions, if not both.

Dedrei didn't say anything for a moment.

"Why?" she finally asked.

"It isn't fair. She chose me to provide food for her, yet I am unable to do so here. It feels wrong for me to take my fill while she goes without." Sada stole a glance up at Dedrei's face, finding it as still as the trees around her. "It does not sit well with me."

Dedrei just nodded and started piling the fruits up in the roots of a tree she sat by. "Admirable," the Druid said.

Sada hurried to help her with the food, gathering the huge but delicate flowers in a separate curl of the roots. Her stomach was already twisting with apprehension. She did not like the way Dedrei was speaking; it sounded too familiar.

"You might have informed me of your decision *before* we robbed the Dell and its creatures of so much of their bounty." Dedrei looked at her from beneath her eyelashes as she worked, and Sada found herself unable to meet her eyes. She somehow felt as though if she looked up, she'd find her father's cold gaze looking back at her from Dedrei's face.

"I know, my apologies. I wasn't thinking," Sada said quietly. The words were automatic. Already she felt as though she existed more in her mind than in reality, both her lips and her hands moving without her having to instruct them.

Though she tried to suppress it, the Duke's voice filled her mind at Dedrei's reprimand. *You wasted my time and effort, yet again.* He'd said it to her so many countless times, over so many different things. Over situations just like this one. Her hands froze around the flowers as she was sucked into her mind.

No, she thought desperately to herself. *Please, not in front of Dedrei,* she begged.

But her body didn't listen, and neither did her mind. As the Duke's steely voice filled her head, the paralysis traveled from her hands to her chest. She couldn't even close her eyes, and was forced to stare at the flowers she knelt before as her lungs stopped moving, as her last breath froze in her chest, worthless to her. She began her count of heartbeats, but the Duke's cold words were on repeat in her head, leaving no room for the numbers that would save her.

Everything I do is for you, yet you show no appreciation for any of it, he'd tell her when she refused a gift from him that she hadn't requested. Like the bouquet of flowers that wouldn't stop making her sneeze, or his invitation to a ball on Jezebel's birthday. Sometimes he said it even when she truly did enjoy the gift, but he either hadn't heard her repeated thanks, or she'd stopped them too quickly, or did not thank him for the correct thing. One day he wanted to be recognized for the effort he took to choose a color she liked, another day for the effort he put out to earn the money for it.

Why do I even trouble myself with you? he would say next. *Your mother ought to have taken you with her when she left me.* He wouldn't stop until she was on her knees, crying and begging for his forgiveness, pleading for him to allow her to accept the present, no matter how much pain it caused her. Like the crop she'd refused to take to her horse, then begged her father to let her use so he wouldn't marry her off to their ugly neighboring earl in Ettedon. Or disown her from the family. She wondered if Beron ever found himself in the same situation, begging his brother not to disown him.

Would Dedrei refuse to help her now? *You would deserve it, after wasting her time, after being so disgustingly ungrateful.*

She wasn't sure how long her lungs had been robbed of breath, but they'd begun to burn. She felt her heart thundering in her chest, climbing to her throat. Anxiety prickled like stinging ants on her forehead and hands. Dedrei had stopped piling up the fruit and was now calling to her.

"Sada?" she asked. "Sada, what happened?"

But Sada couldn't move her lips to respond. She couldn't even lift her eyes to meet the Druid's. All she could do was stare at those horribly beautiful flowers that she'd ungratefully refused. That she'd robbed from the Dell without reason. The colors began to blur into a single rainbow blob as tears pooled in her eyes. She felt one fall from her lashes. Her lungs were screaming at her to breathe, just *inhale.*

But she couldn't. She couldn't do anything. She was worthless.

Sada.

Sarana's voice was suddenly pooling in her mind, in that shared space between them. Were they touching? She didn't think so. Sada registered her voice, but she couldn't respond. All she could hear was her father: *Why do I even trouble myself with you?*

Then Sarana's presence surged, filling the entirety of their Mindspace until it overflowed into Sada's own head. And then the prickling of her skin was soothed, the rampant beating of her heart stilled. Slowly, the words of her father were drowned out by Sarana's tranquil presence.

Thou hast done naught amiss. Recall what I spoke unto thee, Sada. Remember my words.

Sada searched her mind for what the caelicorn was hinting at. But it was empty. The Duke's voice had chased away all of her own thoughts, all of her own memories. What had Sarana told her? She knew it had been when they were talking about Jezebel, but what was it? Suddenly the words filled her mind again, the memory bright and clear as though it had been handed to her.

…until thou dost open thine eyes to see the flaws of others, thou shalt continue to bear them upon thyself and be harmed by them.

Good, Sarana said to her, her voice ancient and soothing and sure. *This differs not. Thine kindness is not a thing that ought to be met with chastisement, Sada. Bear not their faults as thine own. Now, draw a breath.*

At the caelicorn's command, Sada's chest suddenly heaved back into motion, and she gasped. She filled her lungs with the misty air of the Dell, for once grateful of its coolness, and she fell back against the nearest tree trunk, panting. Sarana was lying pressed against her leg. Blinking the tears from her eyes, Sada glanced at Dedrei who had moved to her side opposite the filly. The Druid was holding her hand, though Sada wasn't sure when she'd grabbed it.

"Sada, are you well?" Dedrei asked, eyes bright with concern.

Sada nodded, embarrassment threatening to color her cheeks.

"My…apologies," she said between gasps of air. She was terrified that if she stopped breathing even for a moment, her lungs would constrict again. "Sometimes I simply…I don't know…I freeze, and I find myself unable to breathe."

"I caused this?" Dedrei asked softly. She had never seen the Druid look so concerned, so hurt.

"No, Dedrei, of course not. It is but a failing of my own, something I must work upon."

Sada explained to Dedrei what had happened in her mind, how the Duke's voice had taken over every thought of her own. The Druid's grip tensed around her hand when she mentioned how Sarana had pulled her out of the trap her mind had laid for her, but she listened intently until Sada was done explaining.

"I understand," Dedrei said. She dropped Sada's hand, but stayed crouching next to her. "I apologize for speaking harshly to you. It is very gracious of you to wait for Sarana to eat before you take anything for yourself. I was not being understanding, and a Druid ought always to show compassion for other Spiritkin—or humans," she amended, a touch sheepishly. "In that moment, I brought shame upon my kind, and I deeply regret having hurt you."

Sada just shook her head. "No. You are right. I ought to have told you of it before we gathered so much fruit. I thought perhaps you might be able to…No, that's not right, is it? I hardly thought of the ramifications at all. Sometimes I forget that in real life…Well, that's not important. Just know that I am sorry, Dedrei."

"Hush, child. Do not apologize for your kindness. It is a rare quality in these times. You must preserve it. And I should help you do that…as your friend."

Sada blinked up at Dedrei in surprise, a smile spreading across her lips.

"You're my dearest friend in Elt, DeeDee," she said. The Druid turned away, but Sada could see a hint of a smile on her face as she did.

She took a deep breath and expelled it in that shuddering way that happens after you cry, as though releasing the bad thoughts one by one. She wiped her tears, careful to avoid the corners of her eyes where her powder was. She would need to reapply it once Dedrei slept.

"I must confess, Sada…I was not entirely truthful with you earlier. I told you that my thorough instruction on plant properties was given as a form of punishment. This is indeed true, and for that I am ashamed. But there is a selfish part of me…that wishes you not to reach Titian."

"What? Why?" Sada frowned, studying her friend's face. She could not believe that Dedrei would purposefully sabotage her.

Dedrei sighed. Her brown eyes were troubled, her cheeks brushed with amber. "I suppose I fear you shall not find what you seek there. Perhaps once you might have, but as Titian stands now…I dread what that city and its people might do to someone as kind and pure as yourself, Sada. Thus, I have delayed our journey as much as I could. For this, I apologize, though I will not be so selfish as to ask your forgiveness."

Sada laid a hand on her friend's arm. "There is naught to forgive. It is not the city I am in a hurry to find, though I do wish to reach it. My haste is borne only out of concern for Sarana and her diet. But I do understand this was not done out of ill intent. If we might proceed with more haste now, however…"

"Certainly. I shall delay us with lessons and detours no longer."

"Thank you. I worry for Sarana, that is all. And I do wonder why you speak so ill of Titian, though I fear I cannot let it alter my course. Your counsel as my friend means much to me, but Titian is my only hope. I must return home, and King Caprius is the sole person I know who might hold the knowledge of how to get me there." Sada smiled. "All shall be well, my friend. I only wonder what might have become of me had you not found me, or decided not to offer your aid."

Dedrei grinned. "I would not call it 'offering my aid' so much as yielding to a young human woman's persistent pleas."

"Yes, well…" Sada returned her friend's smile. "I have always been determined not to be stubborn, but now I am grateful I was—I would be utterly lost without your help and guidance. And in more ways than one."

"Indeed." Dedrei nodded. "Though I am certain you would have found someone else to charm into assisting you. Speaking of being lost without my help, the bandage on your shoulder will need to be changed tonight. Wait here while I collect more herbs for a fresh poultice."

Dedrei took up her staff and slipped into the forest.

Sada smiled as she went. Dedrei never seemed livelier than when she was practicing her art of healing. Sarana was still lying beside her, and Sada stroked the curls of her mane, murmuring to the filly what a good friend she was. She had her head lain across her lap, and was staring intently at Sada with her human-looking eyes. Her pupils were large in the darkness, and she looked more like a baby than ever. But she had spoken with the wisdom of a mother and given her the comfort of a friend.

Thank you, Sada thought.

The pleasure was mine own, Sarana murmured. The power of the caelicorn resonated throughout their Mindspace even in that simple sentence, and Sada's *instincts* brightened in response to it.

Sada had laid her cloak out to sleep on and was staring up at the sky when Dedrei returned. She would have slept directly in the grass as the Druid did—the floor of the Dell was indeed nearly as cushioned as a featherbed—but the grass was wet with dew nearly all of the time, and *cold.* Sada slept on the cloak to keep the moisture off her skin.

When Dedrei joined her, she gathered some ferns to use as pillows. The Druid did not pluck fresh ferns or collect only fallen ones, because leaves rarely fell in Elt. Instead, she would take hold of a frond she wanted and murmur something in Druidic to the plant, and it would give up its frond to her. She did the same with flowers and fruit, holding her palm beneath one and asking the plant to give it up for her, and it would fall into her palm. And so their time foraging together had really been Sada following Dedrei and watching her forage. As a human, she did not have the ability to convince plants to give up pieces of themselves for her.

Dedrei fanned the huge fern fronds until they were dry and arranged them for pillows. Then the Druid crouched beside Sada once more.

She had come back with more plants to make a new packing for her shoulder, and these Sada had seen before. But also in Dedrei's hands was a chunk of soft, orange moss, dripping with water. It was thick and stringy, with miniature flowers sprouting throughout it. It looked like the pulled candy Sada sometimes ate in Ettedon when the foreign confectioners—the candymen as she and the other ladies called them—set up their booths for festivals.

"What is that?" Sada asked.

"It is called Pixie's hair. It is recognizable by its color, and it grows only in water—thus, you will find no sand or leaf litter upon it." Dedrei held up the dripping clump for Sada's inspection. It was indeed free of any sand, unlike the moss growing on the roots and trees. "This species of moss is used for light healing. I noticed you had injured yourself."

"You have been tending to my shoulder for days, yet only now do you notice there was an injury there? I admit, Dedrei, that is quite worrisome."

Dedrei rolled her eyes. "On your legs, child—those shins you fretted over so. I may not know the precise anatomy, but I am quite certain they ought not to be encrusted with blood."

"Oh!" She shifted her dress to check the wounds; she'd forgotten them. Her skirts must have come up earlier when she was moving around, giving Dedrei view of the injuries. The blood was now dried and crusted on her skin.

"Thank you," Sada said, and she felt it with every bit of herself.

She reached for the clump of moss, but Dedrei shook her flowery head. Some of the blossoms that remained in her hair from their foraging fell to the ground as she did, releasing their gentle perfume.

"Allow me. Druids are healers."

Sada smiled, understanding. Dedrei had said she'd disgraced the name of her race with her earlier actions. Now she probably felt as though she needed to make up for it. Sada knew the feeling. It would not do to try and convince her there was nothing to be made up for. She knew how willful the Druid could be. Carefully, she unwound herself from Sarana where she was curled up against her, leaving a hand on the filly's neck, and straightened her legs.

Dedrei pressed the wet moss to Sada's shins, and she braced for the pain. But the pain never came, only the coolness of the water. Perhaps the moss also had pain-relieving properties, or it was the magick Dedrei had mentioned. She watched as her friend wiped away the blood encrusting her skin. Maroon ran in streams to the grass. Sarana stirred beside her. Dedrei had started slowly, but with each swipe of the moss, her motions became more rapid. A frown formed between her brows, the feathers almost knitting together with the intensity of it.

"What's wrong?" Sada asked, worry sparking in her belly. Then her *instincts* flared to life in her palm and shot all the way up to her elbow as

Dedrei wiped away the last of her blood, and Sada could see exactly what was wrong:

There were no cuts on her shins beneath the blood. Only smooth, unsplit flesh, as though the blood had been splashed onto her legs. But Sada had felt the rock slice open her skin, had winced at the sight of the torn flesh. Yet now there was no proof of her injury. Only perfectly undamaged skin.

And Sarana had not touched the wounds to heal them.

THE TWENTY-SIXTH

Caprius

In the twilit glow of King Caprius's council chamber, the air lay heavy with incense and ambition. Caprius of Pyrtoxos blood, his youth a stark contrast to the ancient wood from which the room had been grown, sat enthroned amidst the murmurs of his council, some young but many old, and all declared to be wise enough to advise him. His eyes were alight with the fervor of untested power. They swept over the gathering. They were his to command: Boon Wielders, strategists, advisors, various masters of various trades, even an acolyte of the all-but-faded art of sorcery…and one person who had given up her royal title, yet commanded the respect it wielded all the same: his sister, former crown princess to the Titian throne and now future Grand Priestess, whose gaze pierced deeper than the arrows of their ancestors.

It was typically Kaji'Attilore, Master of Trade, or Sebben'Desvar, his oldest and supposedly wisest advisor, who called for these meetings of the council. And it was typical that Caprius did not attend them, instead opting to remain in the upper levels of his palace and absorb himself in his studies, or aid his sister in preparing for her Profession. Yet today he had decided to join the selection of advisors who now sat in audience to him at the long, rectangular table.

Once, it had been round. But soon after his coronation, he had decided that there was no need for anyone to question who was leading the discussion. Caprius believed that the reminder they received when seeing him at the head of the table, or even his empty chair sitting there distinctly when he chose not to attend, was quite valuable. It was the symbolism, the principle of it. Now, he lounged in that golden-trimmed seat, tapping one of the rubies in the side of his crown.

He was quite bored, as he had known he would be. They all believed they were here to proffer up their various reports—

(Yes, the shipment of Dwarven steel and blades will soon arrive in Verdelore, though the new, imbued arrow tips have been delayed and will not reach the capital for a fortnight yet, Your Majesty, deepest apologies—)

or

(Certainly, the smallfolk continue their complaints, but they are dealt with readily enough…Though should Your Majesty consider holding just one audience…)

—and he had yet to tell them the true reason for their summons. He was beginning to wonder, however, if their presence today was necessary at all. Today's meeting had apparently not required the attendance of all of his council. Only six were present (he did not know how many people made up the entirety of his council, but he was certain the total number was greater than six), and based on their positions, it seemed this meeting would be concerning matters of finance, military, and more general or social issues. He only truly cared for the advice of one attendee, his sister. The others would be of no use other than to slow him down and annoy him. But now that they were already here, he supposed he would tell them his news, if only to see the reactions on their aging and drying faces. Not yet, however—but soon.

He leaned forward onto the table, clasping his hands. They were warm with the flames idling beneath the surface of his skin. But they would not reveal themselves until he released them to summon tongues of flame or the bow of fire that he and his ancestor, the first Pyrtoxos, were known for. He allowed the heat to grow until he held a ball of it in his hands, practicing shifting the output from his left hand to the right, and feeling the heat increase and decrease accordingly.

"*V'* Airedez, do you wish to be the next to offer a report?" Old Sebben asked. Though he looked as young as Caprius, he was the eldest in the room; the paleness of his eyes—once chocolate but now dusty—betrayed him. Both he and others had stopped attempting to count his years once he had passed his eighth century. It was a wonder his Boon had not gone wild yet, and that his hair remained neatly plaited in its dozens of brunette braids. Caprius had immediately recognized, though, that if he ever wished for a suitable reason to dismiss Sebben'Desvar from his council, he need only say that his age was a liability—that it would not do to have a member of the king's council at risk of becoming Surrendered to his magick.

Airedez'Dephrylus sighed and resettled his chair on the ground from where it had been balancing on its two hind legs. "If I must. The younglings are cursin' troublesome this century. They are not only being born with greater Boons, but with greater arrogance to match. It seems they do not believe archery to be a necessary skill when they can summon an army of sparrows, my king."

The corner of Caprius's mouth twitched in amusement.

One of the servants leaned forward from the shadows to whisper in Airedez's ear. He grunted and amended, *"Your Majesty."* Then, "Where did such a title come from, anyway? Are you no longer a king? I have never before heard of a 'majesty.'"

Immediately, Caprius's magick swelled, eager to singe the smirk off the arrogant man's face. Instead, he forced his smile to remain plastered to his face, though his eyes cooled just a fraction.

"It is a mark of respect, *V'* Airedez, and a symbol of the new order I now establish. I suppose its novelty may well confuse some."

How perplexing it must be to switch from calling your ruler "my king" to calling him "Your Majesty!" he thought bitterly. *How understanding I am of this terrible struggle.*

Caprius had appointed the young Elf as Bow Master to bring strength to his kingdom, to slowly replace the weakness that his father had surrounded himself with, calling it "wisdom" and "conscientiousness." Truly, it was the self-righteousness of old men and women who refused to change with the age. Airedez was not scared of bringing forth a new future for the Kingdom of the Wood. He was not scared of anything, and that was a quality a Bow Master ought to have. But there was one thing he should be afraid of: Caprius. If he did not learn how to control his tongue and fear his king, he would quickly find himself stripped both of his bow and his title of Master.

Airedez grinned, chuckling lightly, but bowed his head, fully displaying his braids to show his respect. When he straightened, Caprius held his brown stare for a moment longer before settling back into his seat. His palms had grown hot, and the scent of burning wood joined that of the incense. He moved his hands away to reveal the fresh char marks on the table.

Let them see. Perhaps it will remind them that the only thing which spares them from my flames is my will, and my will alone.

"Spirits be with me," Kunak muttered. He was no advisor, but apprentice to Sorcerer Amogasanes. Caprius officially kept him as a ward, but all involved in politics—and Kunak himself—knew that truly he was collateral used in a meager attempt to keep Amogasanes in check.

The sorcerer was not in open battle against the Kingdom of the Wood, nor any kingdom so far as Caprius knew, but he was as unpredictable as a Beast. Caprius held little respect for his practice, but everyone across Elt had to admit that the man was incredibly powerful—more powerful than most Boon Wielders, who used true magick—and ought to be regarded in a manner which reflected this. It was only by chance that Caprius had happened upon Kunak, and by greater chance still that his Spymaster had been with him to inform him that the young man in their markets was apprentice to Elt's last true sorcerer. It had been easy to apprehend him after that, though the youngling had indeed put up a fight. If not for his healers, Caprius would have been left with a scar from the encounter.

Caprius rubbed at his wrist absentmindedly where the apprentice had attempted to splinter his bones. Looking at Kunak, one would not guess he held such power. He was an Elf, but short for one, with little muscle to boast of his heritage. His ears were short and limp, the mark of low-born fairfolk, and hardly at all hidden by his free dark hair. Upon apprehending him, Caprius had immediately ordered it sheared and cropped close against his head. Nobody without the gift of a Boon, without *true* magick, was allowed the privilege of wearing their hair long. It was a disgrace to the spirits and the gift they had bestowed upon the Wielders. Now the apprentice sorcerer stared at Caprius through his bangs. And was that a smirk playing on his lips? That cursed Voidgoer.

"Hush, all of you," Caprius's sister said before he could reprimand Kunak next.

Old Sebben cleared his throat. "Do you find the younger generation in need of…shall we say, a touch of correction? I wonder only whether this matter warrants His Majesty's royal attention, rather than that of the priestesses."

Indeed, Caprius thought dryly. But outwardly he just chuckled, as though to say, "Nonsense!"

"If it is a priestess's attention you seek, then it is a priestess's you shall have." His sister had risen silently and was standing, hands folded before her, eyes roving the room. She was a sharp woman, seemingly carved of citrine itself, with her light yellow hair and her light green eyes. If not for her tan skin, she would not appear Titian at all, though even that was paler than most of their people's.

Caprius clenched his jaw. If she had an idea, it was not like to bode well for the rest of them. Atarah seemed to blame both he and his entire court for her impending Profession to the priestess order, and everything she did seemed an attempt to force them to repay a debt that was not owed to her.

"Atarah," Caprius began, but she shifted her glare to him, and he clamped his mouth shut. Priestesses were not supposed to be called by their given names—certainly not Grand Priestesses. Atarah was not yet Grand Priestess, and the kingdom knew her name since she was formerly the crown princess, but the slip-up was enough to quiet him. He did not like to embarrass his family.

"A festival," the former princess said. "Let the people gather in celebration—of Boons and magick, of the kingdom's prosperity…of the Seam's enduring presence in Titian. We might restore a sense of purpose to the capital. The Seam has blessed us with its gifts and deserves our honor, lest it slip from our grasp through want of proper gratitude."

"The Seam, hmm?" murmured Kunak. "I had thought you to be keeping quiet about that as of late."

Caprius felt a prickle of anger. It was no secret that the Seam's presence in Titian had extended well beyond what was considered natural; the restless portal usually drifted across Elt every few decades, changing hands of guardians and settling in one city or another, stoking the magick of its people before moving on. Yet for reasons that Caprius and his sister only half-understood—and certainly would not disclose—it had lingered in Titian. The people noticed of course, and the Titians called it fate, a divine blessing. Those outside of his kingdom claimed Caprius had invoked unnatural powers to chain the portal to his woods. In reality, there was no divine will involved, nor unnatural powers; only *his* will, *his* power. Wasn't it a sign that the spirits, perhaps the Creator or the Kindreds themselves, had cast favor upon him as a king? Wasn't it a sign that he ought to continue drawing all the magick-Wielders of the Valley to his capital to serve him?

And what does its disappearance signify? a dark voice whispered in his mind. *Disapproval.* Either at the actions he had taken, or at the fact that he had not yet taken the right ones. Or that the subjects outside of the capital, outside of the Valley, were right in their whisperings. That it was unjust and cruel of him to lure all the Wielders to work in Titian, leaving few magick users to the other cities of Elt. He tried not to dwell on these thoughts. They had plagued his mind since his men had reported the Seam's disappearance, the morning after they had escorted—

(*Sada, the sweet, fair Sada—she who makes a man feel like a king*)

—the human girl to the portal. He and his sister had devoted much of their time since then to investigating the mystery, and much of their resources to drawing the people's attention from it. The merchants had been angered beyond belief when they had been summoned to the throne room, only to be met by Caprius's guards holding their wares and the sudden decree that no more trading was to take place along the Road of Ages. Several handfuls of gemdrops had been required to assuage some of this anger, and more importantly, to buy their silence on the matter. Yet still, people whispered, and Caprius heard.

So did his sister.

Atarah might only have suggested the festival to strike one of Caprius's nerves, but the suggestion was not entirely unwelcome. A festival could distract the populace, he thought, from their whispering unrest. The Seam granted them great power and summoned magick-Wielders to the city, and the recent dissipation of that extra magick had made people uneasy. They did not know, of course, that the portal itself had disappeared. But they wondered why he had suddenly closed the merchant stands, especially so soon after installing them. They wondered if there had been an accident, if someone had managed to wield the power of the Seam or perhaps had journeyed through the portal. He could see it in their eyes, hear it in the market where muttered conversations ended abruptly at the sight of a guard. They feared the Seam's power was waning, or worse, being hoarded.

The former was true, in a way, but only he and a few others knew that it had disappeared from their woods. The people only sensed that their heightened magick was gone, and they wanted their power back. This was one sentiment he shared with his subjects.

"Yes, a festival," Caprius said, raising his chin to the assembled council. "And I, their king, shall demonstrate true archery, for *V'* Airedez claims my people have forgotten both its meaning and its power."

There were approving murmurs around the table. It had been decades since he had last wielded his infamous bow of fire in public, decades since he had shown them that there was nothing another Boon could grant that surpassed his mastery. The last time had been at his coronation. After the Grand Priestess (the ancient woman his sister would soon replace) had placed his golden crown on his head, he had summoned and drawn his bow and lit the night sky over Titian with hundreds of arrows, each crafted from one of his flames.

Now they will see again. They will know beyond a doubt that there is yet a power in Titian they ought to fear and heed, even if the Seam has grown silent. They will stay. They will remain mine.

Issachar'Zaelis sniffed disdainfully, and Caprius saw the old man's lips curl. He was another of the elder advisors, nearly as old as Sebben, and he was not so shy about making his disdain for the new age known.

"A show, then, Your Majesty? Shall the smallfolk not grumble that we offer them mere cakes and games, while their lives shrink about them? They already murmur of harsh taxes and unjust governance. Will this not serve to confirm their suspicions? In your father's day—"

"My father is *dead*," Caprius snapped.

Issachar flinched, as though the late monarch had not been in the ground for over two decades already. King Aphredys had been close with all of his council, and even many of his subjects—as many as his schedule allowed. Issachar, though obstinate and self-righteous, had been one of his father's dearest friends, along with Sebben. But as dearly as they'd loved Aphredys, they were not his family. Not his son. What right did they have to act as though their grief was greater than his? He would speak of his father's death if he wished.

"Let them witness the weight of true skill," he continued. "The people wish not to see the tricks of a Savvy, calling forth rodents and sparrows. In this day, they need see the reason for their kingdom's strength…" *And let them see that the bloodborne gifts which fuel it burn brightest when that blood is royalty.*

The Master of Coin had been silent thus far, save for a few murmured comments in response to questions from the other advisors. Now Aurelian'Varre leaned forward, his foxlike eyes gleaming. "They are eager to involve themselves in the affairs of the kingdom, yearning to taste but a morsel of the glory His Majesty enjoys each day. What better way to display to them the power and majesty of our good king than a festival? Perhaps it shall quell their grumbling over taxes, if only they are reminded of the wealth they are so privileged to live amongst, and if they are given opportunity to see the gifts it goes toward fueling."

"As for the concerns of the smallfolk," Sebben added, "a festival would indeed assuage some of their anxieties. In days past, whenever spirits were low, kings would call for a celebration to remind their people of the good still to be found in the kingdom, and in the world."

Issachar settled back into his chair, muttering something about "doubtful minds." Caprius ignored him. The old advisor's complaints would have little impact on the outcome; most of those assembled had already accepted Aurelian's and Old Sebben's words with nods and murmurs. Kunak looked disinterested and Airedez's narrowed eyes were unreadable, but their opinions mattered not. There would be a festival.

"It is settled, then. I trust you shall inform the proper individuals to see the arrangements made," Caprius said, addressing no one in particular. When Sebben gave a nod, he clapped his hands briskly. "Very good. What is the next matter? Come now, unless your king's time is held in such low esteem that you are content to squander it so?" He laughed, as though it was all just one great joke how readily they wasted his time.

"Oh, certainly not Your Majesty," Sebben began.

Aurelian stood, a smile playing on his lips. It seemed he was always smiling, but not in a cheerful way. Rather an impish way. Caprius would have thought the Master of Coin to be half Fae if he did not know better—no crosslings were allowed residency in his kingdom, and certainly not in his small council. Someone—he did not know who—vetted each of his staff and council members to ensure this remained so.

"I would offer my report next, should it please Your Majesty," Aurelian said. Caprius nodded his assent. "To begin with favorable news, in our last debriefing I informed Your Majesty that the profits from the amethyst mines have reached an unprecedented height. This delightful trend continues apace. However, as Your Majesty may recall, a modest cache of amethyst was recently unearthed in the eastern reaches of the Blue Dunes. Upon learning of it, I coordinated with Captain Silvanys to dispatch a company of Nymphs to retrieve these gems for the Kingdom of the Wood, supported by a unit of guards for their protection.

"The extraction commenced well enough, though the idle tendencies of the Nymphs slowed the process somewhat. Rest assured, however, that this matter has since been properly remedied—"

Caprius forced a smile. "Proceed to the point, *V'* Aurelian."

Aurelian smiled thinly, dipping his head. "As Your Majesty commands. Regrettably, the Blood Elves caught wind of our enterprise, and a band of them descended upon our camp a few days past. Our archers managed to…eliminate the threat, but alas, one of the reavers managed to escape with a sack of amethysts."

Hot smoke streamed from Caprius's nostrils in two thin jets. *"To* Torteuir *with it!"*

Aurelian hurriedly bowed and took his seat, smoothing the blue silks of his shirt and avoiding Caprius's stare. The other council members followed suit, save for Kunak and Atarah, who both studied Caprius with narrowed eyes.

"How much did the guards allow to be taken?" he asked.

Aurelian cleared his throat again, evidently uncomfortable, but dragged his vibrant eyes up to meet Caprius's. "The head guard estimated around five stones' worth in weight, or fifty uncut amethysts."

He forced himself to draw in a deep breath, then released it in a hot cloud of smoke.

They were incompetent fools, the lot of them. What was the point of sending a team of guards if they only watched as his gemstones were taken unlawfully? Did he not equip them with the finest bows in the Valley, in all of Elt? Did he not provide them with the greatest training across the continent? Did he not implement strict training regimens, focusing on both Wielding and archery? He would like to dismiss them all from their positions, from their *privilege* of serving in his ranks, but if he did that, they would be recruited to another kingdom or run back to their villages where their Boons would go to waste. Instead, he would have to punish them, and hope that it was enough to fix their imbecilic brains.

The flames were building up beneath his skin, turning his palms red with heat. He released just a flicker of their might and allowed them to coat his hands and run up his arms. He shivered at the release, then forced his magick to retreat into his blood once more. Adjusting his crown, he took a deep breath and leaned forward onto his table.

"Why was this unlawful thief not pursued until he was forced to return the gems which he stole?" Caprius asked when he was calm enough that the words could come out without a coating of flame.

Aurelian looked to Airedez, but the Bow Master just frowned and shrugged his huge shoulders. "How should I be expected to know? Does it appear to you that I am the Captain of the Guard?"

Aurelian clenched his slender jaw. "It is my understanding that you stand here on behalf of *Vi* Silvanys."

"You are correct in that bit of your understanding, but mistaken in the bit that assumes I took his knowledge along with his place in this conference." Airedez shook his head, exasperated, and leaned his chair back onto its hind legs once more.

"It would serve us all, *V'* Airedez, if you might cease behaving like a child," Atarah said coolly. "*V'* Aurelian, if you would be so good as to provide a report in place of the Captain, to the best of your understanding."

Aurelian shifted his glare from Airedez, composed himself with a sigh, then smiled at Atarah. "As you wish, my princess." If he noticed her flinch at her former title, he did not make amends for it. "As I understand it, the raider was pursued until he vanished beneath the dunes. Captain Silvanys believed there to be a Sunken City either near to the cache or directly below it. Had it been possible to follow him into the City, I am certain our guards would have done so without hesitation."

Our guards? I think you mean mine.

Airedez grunted a laugh, grinning crookedly. "Those shifty shades. The leeches have little to recommend them, but I must admit they are crafty. They knew full well they would be shot down if they flew off on their bats, so they went somewhere they knew our guards would not follow. What is that saying? 'The enemy of my enemy is my friend.'" He chuckled again. "Well, it is no secret that the Surrendered are our enemies."

Airedez might have found the situation humorous, but Caprius was disgusted. "Do my men so fear the Surrendered that they dare not leave the safety of sunlight to uphold the king's justice?" He smiled in a paltry attempt to disguise the insult. They had enough names for him already. He would not have them name him cruel, as well. Despite the fact that they were too imbecilic to even understand the true meaning of the word. They would call a crow pecking a scarecrow cruel, these lot.

"I do not believe that to be the cause of their brief pursuit, Your Majesty," Aurelian said carefully.

Caprius began to explain what a ridiculous notion it was to fear the Surrendered, who weren't even strong enough to control their own magick, when the sorcerer's apprentice spoke.

"The narrow man is right. The Dunes are wild things to begin with, as I'm sure Your Majesty knows. They also serve admirably in concealing every entryway into their depths, where the Sunken Cities and the Surrendered may be found. Generally, these cities may be discovered by only three sorts of persons: he who already possesses knowledge of their entrances, he who has been trained in the fine art of seeking and discerning such hidden ways, or he who chances upon them by mere accident."

Kunak had put up a finger with each statement—thumb, pointer, middle—and now curled them into a fist. When he opened his hand, a pile of brilliant blue sand was sitting upon his palm. It trickled through his fingers onto the table. For some reason, the sight made gooseflesh rise on Caprius's arms, and he looked away from the sorcerer-in-training. Airedez blew the sand off his side of the table where it had fallen. Atarah regarded it with something like disgust, and flinched away when a few grains bounced toward her.

The apprentice grinned. "Unless your archers have been trained in the art of locating the city gateways, the cause was doomed from the very start."

"And am I to assume, then, that you are trained in this 'art'?" Issachar asked. He squinted at the apprentice. Like Sebben, his appearance betrayed nothing of his age. "How convenient for us."

Kunak shrugged. "Had I been trained, I daresay I should have forgotten all I once knew by now. My memory could perhaps be revived, though, if offered a sack of amethysts. But then, you might as well leave the gems with the Surrendered—far less trouble for us all, and no fewer jewels for you."

Caprius scoffed and waved his hand. "Your folly wearies me, apprentice. You may leave us."

Kunak grinned and stood, then left with a bow.

"And take your cursed sand with you," Airedez grunted. The apprentice did not.

"Filthy," Atarah said, lip curling.

"Indeed," Issachar agreed. It was perhaps the first time Caprius had ever heard the donkey of a man agree with anyone.

Caprius sighed and pushed his crown back on his head. It had a habit of slipping. He had never realized until his coronation, when the crown had first been placed upon his braids, how massively large his father's head had been.

"Is there aught else that requires my attention, or might we proceed to matters of greater importance?" Caprius said.

He met all their eyes in turn. His sister shrugged lightly, still more focused on the sorcerer's sand than anything else. Airedez muttered that there was nothing from him, and that he would like to go to a nectarhouse if it was all the same to the rest of them. Caprius said it was not, and then looked to Issachar who shook his head and grumbled something unintelligible. Aurelian said that there was nothing more for him to report on, and Caprius was beginning to grow excited that he might finally get to make his announcement when Sebben opened his mouth.

"Well, there is one other matter, Your Majesty." The old Elf exchanged a glance with Issachar, who heaved a sigh.

"Oh, yes. The people."

"What of the people?" Caprius asked.

"There have been complaints—" Sebben began.

"As I *said* would happen," Issachar added roughly.

"—that your subjects are being taxed for naught, Your Majesty. These grievances have arisen with the recent increase in levies."

"As I said they would," Issachar grumbled.

"Silence yourself, old man, or you will quickly find yourself without a place amongst this council!" Caprius snapped. Orange flashed over his vision, the shocked faces of his advisors vanishing for half a second as flames coated his eyes. He should not have said that, but it was too late as it was. "And *you,* old man number two, tell me why the idiotic low-born say such imbecilic things!"

For a moment, Old Sebben could only gape in shock at Caprius's blatant disrespect of his elders, but he was smart enough not to reprimand his own king, elder and advisor or not. After he had recovered, he looked to Atarah, but she said nothing and only dipped her head slightly.

Sebben tangled his fingers in his lap and licked his lips. "With tensions mounting across the realm, Your Majesty has shown great wisdom in increasing border patrols. Additionally, as our kingdom gains in might, so, too, does your military swell in numbers. It is well understood among those with any political sense that Boon Wielders must receive a larger stipend, both for their rigorous training and their dutiful service in your guard and military. Their power is greater and their service more valuable than Boonless archers, and thus it is only fitting that their recompense should reflect such distinction."

"I thank you, *V'* Sebben, for recalling to me my own policies and the reasoning behind them." He tried to chuckle, but he feared it came out sounding maniacal. "But what of them? Do the people wish me to reduce the wages of my archers? Are they so eager to clutch at every coin that they would see their king descend to unjust rule?"

"Not quite, Brother," Atarah said.

"As the priestess says," Old Sebben continued, "it is somewhat more nuanced than that. The smallfolk do not believe the guards are paid too handsomely; rather, they question whether the guards serve any…purpose."

"They believe them to have no purpose?"

Sebben licked his lips, hesitant, but Issachar spoke up in his stead. "Whispers of rumors have begun to stir within the kingdom—whispers that, beyond our borders, have swelled into open cries—that there are no true threats left for the guards to defend against."

"Are they truly unaware of the Beasts that prowl the forests about them? Have they not heard tell of drifters, of thieves like the two I so recently apprehended, of vandals and those lawless creatures who call themselves Spiritkin?" Caprius scoffed.

"Oh, they do, Your Majesty," Issachar said, nodding. His dark braids moved with him as he bobbed his head. "They are simply convinced of their own ability to manage these threats unaided."

For a moment, Caprius was silent, scanning the gaunt face of his advisor to ensure he had not heard him incorrectly. Then he laughed. He threw his head back so far that his crown toppled off his braids, falling over the top of his throne to clatter onto the floor. He laughed until glittering tears streamed from the corners of his eyes, and he laughed so hard that he hardly noticed when a servant returned his crown to him. Atarah took it from the girl and placed it upon his head when he had finally settled enough to sit up straight again, though he continued on giggling for a few more moments.

"Oh, what a delight this gathering has proven to be. I am most pleased I chose to attend. First, we were treated to magick tricks from our sorcerer-in-training, and then to jests from my venerable advisors." Caprius let out another wheezing laugh, dabbing at his eyes. "Ah, what joy indeed. The people believe there exists no threat they cannot vanquish on their own? How fitting a segue, then, into the true purpose of my presence at this meeting."

His advisors blinked at him, then exchanged glances.

"Your Majesty?" Aurelian asked.

"Please tell me the king has not yet lost his wits," Airedez groaned.

Still grinning, Caprius waved a hand dismissively. "By no means. Indeed, I am beginning to suspect that I am the sole person of sound mind in the entire realm!"

He sighed, gathering himself, and wiped the last of the moisture from his cheeks. Then he straightened his back and his crown, and solemnly regarded his council. They were supposed to be his most trusted members of his kingdom, and yet he already knew that they would immediately try to dissuade him as soon as he spoke. He also knew that he would completely disregard all that they said to stop him.

Still, he told them. And when he did, the looks of absolute horror on their faces were enough to erase all apprehension he might have felt.

✧✧✧

"Caprius, please—"

"My king, are you certain—"

"Did you—do you mean—are you—"

They all spoke at once: Sebben, who was in such a state of shock that he had forfeited use of Caprius's formal title; Issachar, who was in such a state of shock that all self-righteousness had been erased from his voice; and Aurelian, who could hardly speak at all, and was mostly gaping at him, wide-eyed and open-mouthed. Caprius only watched them all, grinning, but did not respond—until his sister spoke.

"Are you out of your *forsaking mind?"* she asked. "Has your Boon melted all remaining semblances of a *brain?"*

Her voice, normally low and cool, had risen to a near shout and she stood from her seat, hands braced on the table, glaring at him. For a moment, he thought he saw a flicker of flame on her tongue. But that was impossible.

When she spoke, the grin faded from his face and all laughter died on his tongue. For it brought to his attention the fact that his council members were not shocked, but scared. The old men looked as though they had each gained a millennium to their age and were staring death in the face, the servants were whispering amongst themselves where they stood along the walls. Even Airedez looked apprehensive, his frown deep and his eyes bright as he studied Caprius's face, trying to determine if his announcement had been a serious one, or simply a poor jest.

There were many races of Spiritkin whom inhabited Elt, but not all were organized into kingdoms. Some remained as familial tribes, others as clans, others still choosing to live as nomadic individuals or couples. Seven were organized into monarchies, and therefore held influence in Elt. The Valley of Kings was named so due to more Spiritkin kingdoms being gathered there than anywhere else in the realm. Not all called the Valley home—it was too small for that. But the other kingdoms were spread out across the continent, and so it was only logical that the Valley be named the location for the Seven Crowns to meet. The only reason this was necessary was because while the realm was divided, the kingdoms still stood together. Elt was a world of peace. The Spiritkin were wise enough to recognize that warfare was a barbaric solution to problems, and avoided it at all costs.

Yet sometimes it was necessary:

To banish the mortals from Elt when it was made clear that they would cause only havoc.

To kill the magick-user who had turned a king of old into a Beast, causing the realm to descend into chaos.

To put another kingdom in its place.

The Blood Elves were one of the Seven Kingdoms in name, but not in alliance. They had to be recognized because they boasted the most extravagant and magick-filled military in Elt, and because their power was greater than many of the other monarchies' combined. But they attended no Meetings of the Monarchs, they aided no neighbors, they did not participate in partnerships or trade alliances. Instead, they attacked their neighboring kingdoms, raiding and stealing from the people's homes, making mock of the kings and queens who ruled there.

Yet the Spiritkin did nothing, in the name of peace. Caprius seemed to be the only one who realized that sometimes, meekness only exacerbated the enemy's violence.

Not long ago, the Blood Elves docked their warships in Myriad Wood waters and raided one of Caprius's cities. Unfortunately, this was nothing of great news. Liytara was a small seaside city within the Verdant Vale, and the Blood Elven reavers spent most of their time on the waters, sailing between islands, continents, and kingdoms to pillage and slaughter. Liytara was not an uncommon target. This time, they took his people's fish and nectar, stole their stores of gemdrops, burned and cut down buildings, and even went so far as to capture their women. The reavers who had been a part of this particular raid must have been acutely arrogant, for they made the mistake of capturing the daughter of Verdelore's Master of Sword, who had been visiting the coastal city.

He saw, and he pursued, and he cut down the Elf who had taken his girl. All could have proceeded as usual—the Blood Elves retreated with their loot, they went on to pillage another peaceful city, and the Liytarans got to rebuilding and preparing for the next raid—but another reaver had seen the Master of Sword kill his comrade. Bloodthirsty as the name of his race suggested, the Blood Elf declared battle. It was the first battle that had been openly declared in Elt in millennia. And it terrified not only the Liytarans, but also their neighboring cities, neighboring kingdoms, and kingdoms across the continent. They wondered if it meant worse than simple battle. If it would lead to outright war, perhaps another Realm War.

They were right.

Caprius faced his sister squarely, staring her down as fiercely as she stared at him. "The Blood Elves have taken advantage of our good nature for too many centuries. They make sport of our peaceful ways, knowing they may raid our lands without fear of reprisal. They laugh at our military, for we do nothing to check their insolence. They scorn all our people when they abduct our women to serve as their chattel. And they mock me most of all, robbing Liytara's goods with impunity, confident that its king will raise not so much as a finger in resistance.

"I do not put our harvesters to work to cultivate and gather easy feast for the Blood Elves! Their labor is meant to feed *my* people, not to fatten the bellies of thieves. And perhaps the low-born are not mistaken in whispering that our military is a needless expense. Reavers darken our shores, and yet we are idle as they plunder at will! Why should our people pay for a legion of archers whose sole occupation is to look on while our enemies ransack our lands?

"I have long declared that my rule shall usher in a new era for Elt, with our kingdom leading the charge. I shall see my people defended, and I vow that their taxes shall be put to proper purpose. Ours shall be the first kingdom to rise against the reavers and deny them their vile spoils and amusement. And though I know it vexes you, I shall accomplish this by declaring an official war upon the Blood Elves."

"Caprius…" Atarah whispered. Her anger had melted into some horrible expression. It wasn't grief or disappointment; that he could bear. This was simple neutrality, blankness, as though the mere thought of war had detached her from reality. He wished to comfort his sister, but he could not display such weakness in front of his council. Instead he clenched his jaw and looked away as she sunk back into her chair, defeated.

Before long, it shall be our enemies who lie defeated. Then, dear sister, you shall see the wisdom in my decision. For now, you must only trust me.

"King Caprius, I wish not to voice such disrespect—" Airedez began.

"But you will."

"—and yet, I must confess, I am of a mind with your sister in questioning your sanity. You mean to declare not merely a battle, but open war? Against the most formidable military force in all the realm?" He gave a wry laugh. "Please, tell us this is but a jest, my king."

"Your Majesty," Aurelian corrected under his breath. He also looked distant, removed from his body. His eyes were glazed over; the reflection of the lights bobbing around the room in their little glass bobbles was bright in his pupils.

Caprius ignored the both of them. "I care not a whit for your tyrannical remarks. Servant, summon for me a scribe at once."

"Pray, tell me you do not intend to do what I believe you intend to do," Sebben said gravely.

"And what does he intend?" Airedez snapped.

Sebben regarded Caprius with troubled dusty eyes. "The king means to call upon his allies."

Caprius tried to ignore the heat of embarrassment that was beginning to surface in the tips of his ears and his cheeks. He had known his advisors would disapprove of his decision, but he had not thought that their reasons for disapproval might actually have basis. It wasn't as though his decision was rash—he had pored over tomes of both Eltic and human history, studying the wars and reasons behind them, the outcomes of the fighting. It was horrid, to be sure, and the damage often took generations to repair. But eventually, the change it wrought was good. It was the same way a forest fire looked at first to be nothing but char and dead wood. Then years later, new trees and foliage would sprout and grow even greater than their predecessors, made strong by their ashes. This was the way of war.

Not all of Caprius's allies were among the Seven Crowns, but a society did not have to be organized into a kingdom to be considered a potential alliance for the Kingdom of the Wood. They only needed to be great enough to have influence in the realm. With these Spiritkin fighting alongside him, he thought the war would be a swift thing, if not an easy one.

But doubt was beginning to flicker, and as desperately as he fought to crush its spark, it continued to grow, fed by the frowns on the faces around him.

"They will make mock of us," Airedez said. Caprius did not like his tone. It was no longer disrespectful, but desperate. And somehow that was worse. "They shall name you a fool, and they shall call you weak. Have you not already heard what they say of you?"

"V' Airedez," Atarah warned. But it was only a whisper.

"They name you the Kid King, as though you were naught but a goat. The Young King, the Kingling, as though you have yet to see your first century. They whisper that you are greedy for power, that you would even snatch the throne from beneath King Aphredys's very—"

"They believe me to have killed my own father?" Caprius asked. His voice was hardly a whisper.

"V' Airedez!" This time it was Sebben and Issachar both who reprimanded the man. He had the grace to look ashamed, and sunk back in his chair, but the words had been said.

There was something heavy in Caprius's chest that he did not like. He had heard already of the titles they gave him. They had angered him in the beginning, until he had read in one of the ancient scholars' texts on mortals a quote from a human warrior*: Let them talk; mystery feeds power, and every whisper, even those unfavorable, keeps you fixed in their minds.* Since he had adopted that standpoint, he had not minded their mockery of his name. But to imply that the fires which had killed his parents had been by his own hand…

The scribe had arrived, and was standing beside the page who had summoned her, looking nervously between the faces of Caprius and his advisors. She was a young girl, still a child. Still fit to do the work of a servant. She held a stack of pale leaflets to write on in the crook of one slender arm, and in her other hand she held several chunks of wax in the colors of his kingdom. He beckoned her forth and she hurried to his side, her long garbs swishing as silently as she stepped.

"All of you are dismissed," Caprius said to his advisors. He did not look at them. When Aurelian, who sat nearest to him, was slow to stand, Caprius stood and jerked the man's chair out away from the table, then pointed to the door and roared, "OUT!"

He and the others obeyed. The poor scribe was nearly trembling, and he forced himself to become calm when he faced her. He offered her Aurelian's empty chair, then sat adjacent to her in his own gilded seat.

"My apologies that you had to witness such a thing, my dear girl. Now, if you please, gather your leaflets and prepare to write as I direct. I shall have but one letter, yet require a total of eight copies, each with a different address and signature. Do you understand?"

She nodded hastily and immediately scrambled to ready her first leaflet. She nearly knocked over the entire stack along with her lumps of wax which she would use to seal the scrolls.

"Caprius?" Atarah had not left. She stood by the door, regarding him quietly, and with an expression he could not read. It looked something like solemnity, but he could not meet her eyes long enough to tell.

"I thought I had told you to leave," he said quietly.

"You did. I only…" She squeezed the fingers of her right hand in her left. It made her look like a little girl again. "Are you quite certain this is what you wish to do? This single decision could alter the course of all Elt and may very well be remembered in history as one of its most calamitous events. I am aware you have likely spent every night since the battle in deep consideration, but…I merely wished to ask you myself. I cannot depart without that assurance."

Caprius wanted to go to her and hug her, to press his forehead against hers and assure her that he had not forfeited his sanity; that what he did was not out of rash and selfish motive, but for the good of their kingdom. But he could not bring himself to stand. Instead he looked at his fists, and the smoke seeping out from between his fingers.

"You are soon to be the Grand Priestess, while I sit here as king. Tend to matters of the spirit, and I shall attend to matters of rule and monarchy. Now leave me, priestess. History cannot be written if the man who shapes it cannot confer in peace with his scribe."

Atarah left, and Caprius instructed the scribe what to write.

It grieves me to report that Liytara has recently suffered a violent assault by the Blood Elves. My people fought fiercely, yet a band of these foes remains, engaged in battle with our swordsmen and unwilling to withdraw from our sacred land even as I write. For centuries, Elt has known peace, driven by the common belief that iniquity—thievery, pillaging, murder, abduction—is a barbaric and ancient practice far below Spiritkin nature. This peace has been broken only by the Blood Elves, and no domain of Elt has not been scourged by their wicked touch.

Thus far, we have met this blemish upon our name with naught but peace and meekness. Yet, like an infection of the flesh, our disregard has only allowed it to fester and spread.

It is with a heavy heart yet unbending resolve that I, King Caprius, write to call upon your aid in a grievous matter that threatens the peace we have long strived to uphold. Lend us your strength, that together we might drive back this darkness and lay waste to these foul invaders. Men, weapons, provisions—whatever aid you may spare, I beg you to send with all haste, for time is of the essence, and the heart of Liytara beats ever slower with each passing hour of conflict. To this end, I appeal to you, my trusted allies, in the name of our bond and for the sake of the harmony we all cherish.

Let us stand as one, united by a common resolve, as we have stood against all manner of foes. May the Blood Elves come to know the power of our united peoples, and may their dark purpose be pierced as a boil of the flesh; shattered as a wave upon the cliffs.

In the name of peace and prosperity,
Caprius "the Drake" of Pyrtoxos Blood, King Over the Elves of the Wood and Guardian of the Seam

The letter was copied seven times, as the scribe had been instructed. One scroll went to each of Caprius's eight potential allies in the realm. Carried by Pix messengers, they arrived at each ruler's doorstep all at different times, in order of how near the domains were to the Kingdom of the Wood. The first letter was sent to Sichan Avredeil, Fae King of Aisathas, the Fated Kingdom.

THE TWENTY-SEVENTH

The Rulers

King Sichan lounged soaking in one of his gilded hot springs with three of his four sisters. He and the eldest two allowed their wings to rest in the water, but the youngest present, Sapphira, had yet to realize that the effort it took to keep them dry was not worth the benefits. She was certain that soaking your wings led to long-term damage *(That is what the Druids say, Sichan, I am simply repeating it,* she would say*)* and so took pains to hold them up out of the pool's deadly clutches. There had been some teasing over this as there always was but now, thankfully, all his sisters were quiet for once.

They had just finished arguing over which color gowns they would be wearing to the ball he planned to throw. Sichan had suggested early on, and again today, that they each claim a signature color and be done with it. It would be easy, too, if they simply matched the color to their wings. But they had all adamantly refused. They all loved every color so much; they could not possibly resign themselves to wear just one or two for the rest of their lives. At this, Sichan had shrugged and told them they ought to get used to it if they ever hoped to become queen one day. All fairfolk monarchs dressed only in the colors of their kingdom. He had long since learned to love purple, though it used to make his heart ache for what had been lost.

He was just about to suggest that they ask a Savvy to determine which colors would lend them the most success in their royal affairs, when a high-pitched buzzing sounded in his ear. He whipped his head to the side, prepared to freeze the intruder in place, but his eyes landed upon a Pix messenger, and he relaxed back against the rim of the hot spring again.

"What is the meaning of this interruption?" Sichan asked. The Pixie was so out of breath that he could hardly speak, and just hovered there. He was clutching a small scroll and drooping dangerously close to the water.

"Oh, you poor thing," Sapphira murmured. His sisters had also roused with the interruption, and now the second-youngest moved to the Pix man's side, holding out a hand for him to sit on.

Sichan thought that if he were a Pixie himself, the indignity of sitting upon another Spiritkin's hand would be so horrible that he would find the offer alone insulting. Yet the little man did not seem to share the sentiment, and collapsed onto Sapphira's outstretched palm immediately.

Nimbia and Perísa joined her to take turns fussing over and interrogating the messenger. Sapphira offered him a crumb of a cake they had been eating, now sitting forgotten on the grass, while Perísa listed a string of questions for him to answer:

"What has you flying with such haste? Could your message not wait until we had finished with our soak? Who was it that sent you?"

Two wingless Fae servants had come running up behind the Pixie and now bowed to Sichan at the edge of the hot springs. He asked them Perísa's latter question as his sisters tried to glean information from the panting messenger.

"He bears the mark of the King Over the Wood's messengers, my king," one of the servants responded. Though a lowborn servant, she was still beautiful, with hair the color of fire and eyes the color of frost. He wondered how he had not noticed her before, but her reply sent all thoughts of her beauty fleeing from his mind.

"Caprius?" he asked, frowning. "What business has he with me?"

The other servant, a black-haired young man, just shook his head. "He has not been properly received, my king. He flew past our noses before we could stop him, saying only that the message was urgent. I managed to catch sight of his origin marking, then he slipped by us." He dropped into a low bow, nose pressed to the grass, and the girl did the same. "You have my deepest apologies, King Sichan. I gladly accept any resulting punishment."

Sichan just rolled his eyes and waved them off, then turned to the Pixie. His sisters had formed a ring around the poor man, and with their wet, dark hair, they looked almost like sirens, or Elves of the Deep.

"What have you gleaned from him?" Sichan asked. Nimbia moved aside to allow him a view of the messenger.

"Little," Perísa scoffed. "The man can hardly breathe, let alone speak. And Saph keeps stuffing his mouth with crumbs."

Sapphira shot her a glare. "What I've *done* is receive our guest with kindness, as a princess ought to."

"Speak properly now, Sapphira," Nimbia said softly.

Sapphira's lips tightened but she heeded her sister's advice.

Turning to Sichan, she said, "I offered him some Dell dew and cake, so perhaps now he will have recovered enough to answer your questions."

"My servants tell me you bypassed the reception process, you were in such haste to deliver to me this message. What, then, urges you on so?" Sichan asked.

The Pixie had been sitting in the grass, but he stood now, wiping crumbs from his tunic of leaf. He swiped the sweat from his miniature forehead, bowed, and unrolled his scroll. "Good king, the message I bring you is from His Majesty Caprius."

"His Majesty?" Nimbia murmured.

Sichan motioned to her to be silent. "Continue please, messenger."

"Very well." He began to read the scroll, glancing up at Sichan every so often, but before he had gotten through even the introductions, he threw the leaflet down and looked up, shaking his head. "You have my apologies, but I can't bring myself to drag this message on knowing what I do."

"Tell us, tell us now!" Sapphira said. She and his other sisters were leaning forward, clutching their hands as though they watched a performance rather than a messenger performing his duty.

"Please, go on," Sichan said, as gently as he could. But his heart had begun to pound quicker in his chest, and something tightened in his throat. He did not like the feel of this situation.

The Pixie drew in a breath, started, then stopped. Finally, gravely, he said, "King Caprius has declared war upon the Blood Elves, and he invokes your alliance to call upon your aid."

The princesses gasped, but King Sichan said nothing for a moment. He could feel the stiffness of his wings contrasting with the warmth rising from the water.

"I see," he said after a moment. His voice sounded utterly normal. "Please read the entirety of the scroll."

When he had, Sichan dismissed the messenger, thanking him for his service, and sent his servants away along with the man. Then he turned and settled back into the pool.

His sisters, who had only moments ago been bubbling with excitement, now stared between each other and the steaming waters, silent with solemnity. Looking at them now, he realized how young they all were. Eulila, his youngest sister, had only just celebrated her second century. But of the three gathered, even Perísa, the eldest, was just under five-hundred. They had heard of war, of course. Perhaps it would have been better had they not, but fate had seen a different future in mind for the Avredeil siblings.

He had heard that the mortals believed if history was not remembered, it would be repeated. He had always thought this way of thinking to be flawed. In this case, should it not be that the good bits of history—the successes, the victories, the monumental moments—were never to be spoken of, so that they *would* be repeated, and the people would see success again? Then only the bad bits—the losses, the warfare, the iniquities—should be written down and recorded, resurfaced and taught to children so that they learned what *not* to do. Instead, the humans taught both, almost as if they did not want any of history to repeat itself, not even the good parts. Were they so terrified of change that they did everything they could to prevent ushering it in? Did they not know that nothing could grow without change?

Sichan had always been of the mind that if you did not want the new generation to repeat a past iniquity, then you should not teach them the very philosophy which had led to it, or recount to them in detail how it had been executed in the past. It seemed like planting a seed that otherwise never would have found its way to soil, then watering it when it otherwise would not have felt rain.

The example that came to mind was the slavery the humans of the past had forced the early generations of Spiritkin into, resulting in their banishment from Elt. The mortals had learned it from their own culture, but the Eltics had never even considered the idea of forced servitude until the humans taught them of it. But after having been introduced to the idea, they employed it themselves.

It was for this reason that the former rulers of Aisathas—Sichan's mother and father—did not require the history of Eltic war to be taught to younglings. The only reason he and his sisters knew of the wars was because when Sichan had been taught the history of Spiritkin lineage, he had grown curious about what had happened to the humans. His tutors had taught him of the First War, the Banishing, when humans had been banished from Elt after they had enslaved the meeker Spiritkin. The Orcs had nearly been banished along with them, for they had taken to the idea of indentured servitude and implemented it within their own kingdom. But after the war, they had agreed to end the slavery (of Spiritkin, at least, though Beasts were another mess altogether) and so they remained in Elt. Knowledge of this war had led to Sichan asking if there had been other wars in their realm, until he had been taught the entire history of Eltic warfare. Then, having been a child who had not yet decided upon the philosophy that iniquity not be taught to people, he had informed his sisters of what he had learned.

His tutors had taught him of the reasons for the wars, and they had all certainly seemed necessary to the people waging them, but Sichan had come away from it thinking that it all seemed utterly imbecilic. It was nothing more than slaughter, and he could not support slaughter. All this ran through his head upon hearing that Caprius wished to begin another war, this time with another race of Spiritkin. The Blood Elves certainly did not contribute to the peace of the realm, but they did not deserve death for it. And the other kingdoms did not deserve to witness death or experience it themselves because Caprius was selfish enough to shed blood over stolen fish.

These thoughts made Sichan suddenly angry, and he yelled for a scribe to be brought to him.

"What are you going to do?" Sapphira asked. Her dark blue eyes were wide, and he saw fear there. It only enraged him even further. The war was yet to begin, and already his family suffered for it.

"I will tell Caprius that he is being rash, and firmly urge him to reconsider his options," Sichan said through gritted teeth. "He is but a child, unfit for rule. Does his council not advise him? Did he dismiss the entirety of them along with the Fae members?"

He still remembered the day, only a week after Caprius's coronation, when all the Fae who had been serving in Titian to advise or work alongside King Aphredys had been sent back to Sichan. The new king did not want them, the Faeries said, if they were not Elven. It had angered Sichan then, and it angered him even more greatly now. Evidently, the young king did not do so well without the advice of those outside of his own circle of supporters. *Who would have thought it? Certainly not every other ruler—save for the Orcs—who had offered up subjects from their own kingdoms to join Caprius's court and advise him.*

"He requires a rational mind to guide him. He may be able to send away my highborn advisors and elders, but I would like to see him send away family."

"You mean to send Eryus to Titian?" Perísa asked. "Do not do that to the poor man."

"Hush, Perísa. This is no time to be offering me your many opinions. We must act now if we wish to halt this impending war."

"Do you truly think it will happen?" Sapphira asked softly.

Nimbia rolled her eyes, irises grey as fog. "Of course not. There is no chance in *Torteuir* that a single ruler will agree to lend Caprius aid." She sounded sure, almost arrogant in her surety, but when she met Sichan's eyes she was frowning, as though begging him to confirm that what she said was true.

He thought she was right, but he could not be certain. He also could not bring himself to lie to his sisters, even if it was unwittingly. "Let us hope that it is so," he muttered. "Until then, we must show Caprius that we will not support his decision in any form. Girls, you must not visit Titian or the Gilded Streets until this talk of war is over, whether it be for—"

"Sichan!" Nimbia cried. "You cannot be serious."

"Take these foolish words back, *now,"* Perísa demanded.

"You speak to your king so?" Sichan asked. The fury was hot in him. "You will not set one toe within the bounds of Caprius's city or market. I will offer him not a single drop that might go toward funding this imbecilic war of his. Am I clear?"

He glared at them all in turn—grey eyes, blue eyes, and golden-brown ones—and, satisfied that they would obey, summoned a servant for a towel.

"We are princesses, you know. How do you expect us to perform our duties to the crown if we cannot even purchase gowns to perform them in?" The voice was deep and bold—Perísa's.

Sichan whipped around, unable to restrain his rage. "Then I will hire for you the greatest seamstresses in the realm! Now, if any of you so much as *look* in the direction of Titian, your title as princess will *immediately* be revoked. Am. I. Clear?"

They blinked at him for a moment, utterly disbelieving of what he had said. Sapphira's blue eyes filled with tears. But the three of them nodded. He tried to crush the guilt welling up within his belly at the sight of his sisters crying because of him, but it was an impossible task. He left the springs with a heavy heart and a heavy mind. But he was firm in his decision. He made for his palace to write his own letters.

The second letter found its way to the Nymphean domain, which was really just a society of sisters and cousins. Even though they lived spread out amongst several dells and springs, their great number and partnership in Caprius's gemstone harvesting deemed them an ally. Adolai was one of the eldest sisters, and had been one of the first Nymphs to agree to work alongside Caprius to mine the caches of amethyst which were so numerous in their territory. And so it was she who was named delegate.

Upon having Caprius's message read to her, she hissed animalistically and threw a handful of water onto the Pixie and the scroll in what seemed like an attempt to drown the very message itself, then retreated into a jewel-adorned cave.

It took three days for her sisters and a visiting Elven woman to coax her out in order to have her reply written back to Caprius. She did so fervently, still looking like a cornered animal, then used a fang to prick her thumb and signed the scroll with a thumbprint of her blue blood before vanishing back into her cave.

The third letter was received by the Mother of Druids, Woia of Winter. She sat on an earthen throne surrounded by foxes, deer, songbirds, birds of prey, moles, hedgehogs, and all other manner of creatures. Had there been a stream or brook leading into the clearing in which she sat, there would have been fish attending her as well. But as it was, there were so many animals that an onlooker would hardly be able to discern Woia from their flocks and herds, despite her being in her Spiritkin form.

With ravens and hummingbirds perched along the vast spread of her holly-adorned antlers, she greeted her Pix messenger with a smile. He had flown a short distance, but he did so swiftly and without rest. Still, he rushed to deliver to the Druid queen the message he bore. Woia refused to listen to a word he had to say until he was rested. She fed him Pixie-sized berries, and a robin lent him the shade of her wing. As he rested, Woia made conversation with him. They spoke of his family, most of whom the queen had met at one time or another and remembered; they spoke of the lovely spring they had been blessed with, and of the showers of rain and blossoms to come; they spoke of magick and dreams and wonderful things.

Finally, when the messenger was rested and calm and had nearly forgotten his very reason for being there, Woia gently asked if she might be read the message now. At this, the Pixie stiffened from his place on her antlers, but he obeyed. Woia said nothing as he read the scroll, and only shifted to stroke the head of a badger who had come closer to vie for her attention among the other animals.

"Oh, my dear Caprius," she murmured when the messenger had fallen silent. "What great things you have yet to accomplish. Will you forfeit them so soon?"

She stood, then, and accompanied by her family of animals and the Pix messenger, she walked through the trees in search of a birch tree. When she found one, she asked it to give her one of its paper-thin sheafs of bark. It complied, and she lengthened her nail into the claw of a cat, then heated it with the flames of a salamander and began her response to King Caprius.

The fourth Pixie went to Queen Zarah of Malachite blood. She sat upon a throne of pure gold, fashioned to look as though it was melting. Embedded in its armrests were the silky green gemstones of her family line, like the irises of Elt. She stroked one of them with a gold-encased nail, long as a talon, as she received the Pixie who came to her. The messenger hovered before her, jittery and out of place in the throne room's dark, glimmering splendor, a small slip of parchment clutched in his miniscule hands. Zarah narrowed her eyes, her gaze traveling over the Pixie. His kind rarely wandered into Goblin lands willingly; only a summons as urgent as this one could compel one to make the journey.

"Read it aloud," she commanded. Her voice was soft and magnetic, yet tinged with the unhurried confidence of one who knew her own power. The Pixie cleared his throat, wings buzzing as he unrolled the scroll.

He read the scroll quickly, glancing up at her every so often. "King Caprius wishes to 'stand as one, united by a common resolve,' as you together have 'stood against all manner of foes.' He says that in this way, the Blood Elves may come to know the power of your 'united peoples, and their dark purpose may be pierced as a boil of the flesh; shattered as a wave upon the cliffs,'" he finished.

The messenger glanced up, hopeful, as if Zarah might at once leap to join the child king's crusade. But she remained silent for a time, her eyes cold as she reclined in her throne.

Eventually, she said, "Does he now?"

Her gaze fell to the intricate rings adorning her fingers, each one meticulously crafted by the artisans of the Ring, the guild of Goblins who organized and oversaw trade between Goblish jewelers, merchants, and other customers. Caprius's call to arms, gallant as it may have sounded, held little sway over her. She knew what he wanted; the young king believed that his war against the Blood Elves would be easily won if he could marshal every ally willing to stand with him. Yet, he clearly hadn't considered the delicate web of necessity and fear that bound her kingdom to Liege Tempest and his Blood Elves.

"Tell me, messenger," she began, "does your master truly understand what he asks?" She leaned forward, eyes flashing. "The reavers may be bloodthirsty savages in his eyes, but they are also my kingdom's finest patrons. They bring us the rarest gems in all of Elt, harvested from foreign seas and distant dunes. Gems our guildsmen cut and polish with reverent hands."

The Pixie quivered, hovering lower, fearful of her wrath. Zarah's lips, painted with her own black blood, curved in a smirk. "And in exchange for our artistry, they leave us to our own devices. No pillaging, no burning of our villages. My people can work their craft without fearing the shadow of a dagger at their back. Caprius's cause is not worth that peace, however noble he disguises it to be. If I were to lend aid to him, Liege Tempest would turn on us in an instant. He has the numbers and the fury to raze my cities to ash. My jewelers' hands would be shattered—our wealth ground into dust."

The Pixie stammered, "B-but, my queen, surely you see that King Caprius means to end the Blood Elves' reign of terror—"

"Reign of terror? The Blood Elves bring no terror to my borders."

A quiet pause hung between them as the Pixie struggled to find words. Zarah rose, her movements fluid as shadows, her rings and chains chiming faintly. "Tell Caprius this, little messenger," she said, her tone glacial. "I am not his ally, nor his enemy. I am the Queen of Goblins, and I have my own bargains to uphold. Should he wish to declare war upon the Blood Elves, he is welcome to try his fortune without the aid of my people."

She turned as he bowed, disgusted by the sight of the little man. Servants lay sleeping around her, comatose from the sheer amounts of food they had gorged on throughout the day. Only the guards remained alert; the help had grown soft beneath her rule, knowing she would not punish them with death as her uncle had before her. Unlike him, she preferred to actually have subjects to rule over. She awakened one with a kick to his round belly and he scrambled to his feet, belching. She requested a scribe (not entirely certain that they possessed one) and he rushed off to find one. When he returned towing along a young Faery girl, she had the servant write a response to Caprius.

When it was done, Zarah crossed her throne room. Her gown was long and silken, and followed her like a green shadow, rippling over the floor. Unlike most Spiritkin, she preferred to cover herself in riches, from her bare feet to her slender wrists. The humans of the past had left sketches of their clothing designs behind when they were banished, and after making some modifications to fit the lithe proportions of the Goblins, her people had adopted these styles. Now, standing before the Pixie in a brilliant gown of thick silk with a flared skirt and sleeves lined with jewels, she was pleased to see he nearly cowered in her presence.

"Take this to your king, along with the message I voiced to you. And tell him that until he comes with gifts or payment for his debts, I wish not to see any aspect of him or his kingdom, including his Pix servants."

She dismissed the messenger with a flick of her hand. As the Pixie flitted out of the throne room, Zarah turned her gaze back to her precious collection, the glittering symbols of her kingdom's hard-won prosperity. The goblin artisans would continue to craft in peace, for now.

Escera'Thalphoros, Queen Over the Elves of the Deep, was regarding the ocean when the fifth Pixie found her. She did not spend much time in her throne room, preferring instead to bask on the shoreline or simply float on the waves. Like the Nymphs, the Elves of the Deep were truly just a great clan of sisters, cousins, daughters, mothers, aunts, and nieces. Though unlike the Nymphs, there were a few men among them, and they were organized into a true kingdom. Her palace was situated on a short and wide peninsula poking into the smooth waters of the *Ll'isse.* The city where her people resided was hidden beside it in a large and lush cove. The Elves of the Deep were adept swimmers and had features to reflect their aquatic lifestyle, but they could not breathe the ocean as sea life did, and so their dwellings were above ground.

Escera sat overlooking the city of Selkala. It was beautiful, grown from arches of pearl, pillars of sea crystal, and lattices of mangroves. Though it was twilight, her sisters' eyes were adept at seeing in dim lighting, and it was as active in Selkala as though it was midday. They did not sleep throughout the night like most Spiritkin, or throughout the day like the Blood Elves, but instead slept for short periods of time throughout the day and night alike, and swam or played or practiced their magick in between. She could see her sisters below, all black of hair and adorned in the garb of the ocean. Some rode tiger sharks or swam alongside giant jellyfish and seahorses in the channels running through the city. Others merely sat on the arches and talked, legs swinging and hair dripping.

Escera sighed. How she wished to be down there with them, playing and gossiping instead of ruling.

"They are so beautiful, are they not?" she murmured. The Pixie had arrived quite a while ago, but must have noticed Escera's dim mood, for the messenger girl had not spoken. Now she flitted near-silently to rest on the rocky clifftop beside Escera's bare thigh. Her bright green head was a stark contrast to the grey of the rock and the white of Escera's skin. At just a glance, she looked like a clump of moss.

"Indeed, good queen," the Pixie agreed. "Fair ladies in a fair city. I'd greet them, but I think only the ocean would wave back."

Escera smiled lightly. "I daresay you may have the right of it, Pixie. My sisters are adept at looking down into the depths of our ocean, yet seldom do they cast their gaze upward. For them, there is naught to be found in the sky, as there is for you." She turned to face the messenger. "Come, what news have you brought? I can scarce imagine it shall be of the pleasant sort. Fair tidings are in rather short supply in this realm of late."

"Your words are true; true as the water is blue."

Escera sighed. So dark this world had become. "Speak it, then, that I might grieve and be done with it all the sooner."

The Pixie told her and Escera listened numbly. When the girl was done, Escera ran her hand over the clifftop until her fingers met a loose chunk of stone. She picked it up, held it in her palm, and willed it to Morph. As soon as she had the thought, it began to stretch and flatten until it was a small rectangle, small enough for a Pixie to carry. Then it became twice as light, in both color and weight. A second before, she had held a rock. Now a rectangular sheet of dried, yellow leaf sat on her palm. She pinched it between her fingers before it could be carried off by the breeze.

Escera looked to the Pixie once more. "I see you wear your hair in braids. Have you the Boon of a scribe, or are you merely a messenger?"

"I transcribe as well as travel."

"Very well. I can use my Boon for etching, though I care little for it. The task is dreadfully tiresome."

"Very good, Your Majesty, very good, very bright."

Escera lifted her eyebrows. *"Your Majesty?'* What a peculiar title."

The Pixie immediately flushed pink. "Oh—my apologies. It is what King Caprius wishes us to call him. I had grown so used to it—forgive me, my queen."

"No…I think I am quite taken with it. It carries with it a royal bearing, does it not?" Escera handed the Pixie the leaflet she had Morphed and told her what to transcribe. When it was done, the messenger nodded, as though she had expected nothing less, bowed with another "Your Majesty," and winked away into the night.

Escera remained on her cliff, bare legs hanging over the edge and dancing with the salty breeze, and looked west toward Liytara. The city stood on the opposite side of the continent, but she imagined she could see its pale shores and silver trees. She wondered if there was more silver blood being spilled there, or gold.

She prayed for the former.

When the sixth Pixie had flown across the continent, over a span of the *Ll'isse* Sea, and onto the Isle of Centaurs, she landed on the pale grey flank of Chieftain Starskipper. He was one of the eldest Spiritkin rulers, nearly a millennium old, but his braids were only just starting to look frayed. He was also a very large Centaur, with a thick equine chest made strong by years of galloping, and huge arms plated with muscle from throwing spears and wrestling the wind. He could have killed the Pixie who landed on his flank with a swish of his white tail or a slap of his great hand, but he merely turned and asked for the messenger's name.

She had been buffeted by the harsh winds of the plains which had fought her for the last span of her journey and when he tried to answer, she collapsed unconscious instead. Starskipper gently picked the young girl up and, holding her safely against his chest, carried her to the nearest building. It was one of the great libraries for which the Centaurs were known, and he was greeted by a gust of warmth, the familiar sight of wise eyes, and the scent of dried leaves and freshly-singed pages.

The Pixie woke beside the warmth of a flame-filled glass orb, and she immediately told the Chieftain her news. Starskipper listened calmly, and then instructed his head scribe to fashion his response. Only those he trusted most greatly would hear of this dark news.

The messenger was given rest in the library for the remainder of that day, then took to the breeze with the rise of the moon. Starskipper watched her go, wishing ardently and praying to the Creator that the other rulers would have the same response as he did. If they did not, the entire realm might find itself destroyed.

Warlord Odeon Skull-Caver crushed the Pixie delivering his letter immediately upon her arrival. Laughing, he turned back to his feast of raw hog flesh, nearly eating the Pixie in his gluttonous haste.

Standing at his shoulder was an Elven girl by the name of Adina. She was ostensibly a servant (for political purposes), but the warlord often reminded her that her payment was the breath in her lungs which he allowed her to keep. She had seen the miniature scroll the Pixie had been carrying, and, thinking it might be a letter offering ransom for her release (as though her lowborn family were wealthy enough to pay a ransom—ha!), she swept it into her belt when she refilled Odeon's skull of fermented goat blood. It was the Orc warlord's eleventh cup within the hour, but still he was not drunk. Thankfully, he was well enough distracted by the combination of the feast and the Orcen women before him that he did not notice as Adina read the letter, squinting to see the Pixie-sized script.

When she'd finished reading, the scroll fell from her hand as her heart sank in her chest.

"What that was?" The rough voice caused Adina to jump, and she looked up to see one of the warlord's women staring at her. She was chewing on a mouthful of hog flesh, and dark blood gushed around her tusks and over her fat lower lip as Adina watched. She could hardly hide her disgust, but she reasoned that even if it showed, the Orc was likely too dumb to notice.

"Huh?" Odeon asked, swinging his massive head around to look at the woman. "You be sayin' sumfin to me's?"

"Nuh-uh. Hers." She swung her slab of a chin at Adina, flinging droplets of blood and spittle as she did so. Odeon absentmindedly licked a speck off his lip where it landed. "Dropped sumfink from her baby hand, she dids."

Adina began to tremble. The she-Orc saw this, and she laughed.

"You be showin' it to me's now," Odeon said. He didn't look at Adina, but gestured with a hand twice as big as her face for her to move forward. Shakily, she bent to retrieve the scroll, and did what her master bid her.

"Here," she whispered. Despite the suffocating heat of the room (only surpassed in vulgarity by the stagnant stench of Orc farts and rotting meat), her fingers were cold and stiff. She fought to uncurl them from the scroll and let it drop into Odeon's hand.

He took the paper, not even as big as his pinky, and tried to unfurl it, but to no avail. "You's thinks me's can read this bitty thing? Elves supposed to be smart, with the brains, no? Maybe me found meself a stupid Elf. Maybe you's is a Troll wearin' Elf skin, no?" He laughed and flicked the scroll in her face. She flinched. "You be readin' it to me now."

She bent once more to pick the scroll up from the ground, dodging to avoid the gas which the warlord expelled in her direction, then read it aloud.

"This be from the little king?" Odeon asked when she had finished. He laughed. "Maybe all the Elves have the stupid brains after all. If the boy be thinkin' me's gonna make an enemy out of the bleeders, the boy be needin' to think again. Tell him me said this, or me's gonna have it carved into your little belly instead."

Laughing, the warlord sent her to do his bidding. She thought that he might forget about his order before she could track down a leaflet and a scribe. Orcs were as good as Boonless, with how much physical strength they had, and so her only hope of finding one would be among the slaves they kept. It would take time, and his memory was short. But she did not want to risk his wrath, for he was a master who followed through with his threats. If he said his words would be carved into her skin, they would be.

It took her the entirety of the day to find what she sought, though she would be lying if she said she had made haste to put herself back in Odeon's stinking tent. When she finally found a Dwarven slave with a Boon for scribing, he was hardly conscious enough to transcribe what she instructed him. A few slaps to the face from his guard woke him up. With his own sooty blood dripping down his nose, he etched the Orc warlord's message.

Adina watched miserably, wishing the note had been for her ransom instead, and daydreaming that the next one might be.

The eighth and final Pixie flew for the greatest length of time in order to reach Queen Sook, daughter of Forge, deep in her mountainous kingdom. She was surrounded by her council of priestesses when the messenger found her. Though short and round, she looked entirely regal with her thick hair freshly oiled and woven into a masterpiece of intricate knots. She wore garb unlike any other the Pixie had seen in Elt, as well. Where the fairfolk of the Valley often opted for light clothing made of soft things like silk or petals, the Dwarven queen wore a tunic and pants of pure silver. The garb was thin as a leaf, and fashioned to look like hundreds of scales. It moved as easily as the finest silk, and gleamed with a dozen rainbows when touched by lava light.

The Pixie immediately bowed before the queen when she saw her and was noticed by those dark Dwarven eyes.

"You may rise," Sook said. When the Pixie looked up, her fair face was decorated with the reflection of rainbows.

"My queen," the Pixie breathed.

"What matter is so pressing that you would intrude upon the queen's sacred time?" asked one of the priestesses. She had the black eyes of the Order, and the Pixie could hardly look upon her white face, let alone that gaze, to answer her sharp inquiry.

"A message from the King Over the Elves of the Wood," she replied, looking at the stone.

"Cayprius sends word to me?" Sook murmured in her thick accent. "Beggin' yah forgive the Elder Priestess. She knows the 'portance o' spir'tual affairs, but as queen I ought to know how to balance matt'ers o' politics and matt'ers o' spirit. Read to me this message from my young friend."

The Pixie did, and after consulting with the furious priestesses, Queen Sook sent her reply as the others had done before her, signed with a thumbprint of sooty red blood.

Eight letters bearing the golden thumbprint of Caprius'Pyrtoxos had been sent to eight kingdoms, each calling upon their existing alliances or seeking to forge new ones.

Eight letters had returned to the young Elven king, each signed by a matching thumbprint, each in the unique color of the ruler's blood who had signed it.

And each signature resided beneath the same reply. Some were condensed into a single word, others were surrounded by meaningless chivalries, others still were stretched into paragraphs of repetitive nonsense. But all said the same thing:

No.

Caprius and Atarah looked upon all eight of the unfurled scrolls resting on the rectangular table where his original letters had been etched. The weight of them filled the council chamber, now empty save for the siblings and the floating lights. And, of course, the scrolls.

The rejections.

To Atarah, they were letters of hope. She had slept fitfully—if at all—since the day Caprius had sent his requests for aid to the other rulers. She dreamed of bloodshed and battle beneath her brother's rule, of a ruined kingdom no longer in need of a king because its subjects had been slain at his command. Not directly, but still, by his decree. Now, she no longer had to worry about bloodshed. Even Caprius, as young as he was, would know that an open war with the most powerful Wielders in the realm would destroy them with no allies at their side. The Elves of the Wood were powerful, but not as powerful as the Blood Elves, and not nearly as numerous. With these rejections, she thought she could finally sleep again.

But she was wrong.

When Caprius looked upon the letters, his fury roared. He had been so certain his alliances would prove strong—he controlled the second-largest market on the continent, his city was the capital of the Valley of Kings, and his palace served as the meeting place for all the monarchs of the Central Kingdoms. And yet they had refused to come to his aid. They mocked him, as Atarah had said they would. And now they would learn exactly why he was not to be mocked.

His subjects in Liytara had already commenced battle against the Blood Elves. Were he to surrender now, he would admit his weakness to both his enemies and his former allies. Surrender was not an option, and if he were to continue the battle without escalating it to war, it would continue to bloody his shores for years, perhaps centuries, wasting his resources with no end. And such a small fight, little more than a border skirmish, would leave the majority of the Blood Elf reavers free to continue ransacking Eltic cities as they pleased.

No, the only option was to obliterate them. Now, the other rulers trembled at the thought of such open conflict. But once he demonstrated the might of his military alone, they would see that the war was not a lost cause and flock to his side to end the Blood Elves' lawless reign. His people wished for an enemy to be protected from—he would give them one. His people wished for their taxes to go toward a useful cause—he would create one. And perhaps, when it was made clear to all of Elt that the Titians were constantly expending magick for a noble cause, the Creator would see and return the Seam to his wood, returning his increased power along with it.

A sliver of something dark and new twisted in the recesses of his heart at his bloody thoughts. *There is yet more. Elt enjoys peace for thousands of years at a stretch, but in time, such peace is ever broken. And when that break comes, the Kindreds return, ushering in a new era of prosperity for Elt, and a time of heightened magick for its people. Another war may be precisely what is required to herald their return. Yes…a war amongst all the kingdoms, all the Boon Wielders, all the races.*

Indeed, a war might be necessary to strengthen Elt as a whole. And Caprius would be the one to make this sacrifice for the good of the realm. With this in mind, he began to summon scribes and messengers.

And then he declared the first Kin War in eight hundred years.

THE TWENTY-EIGHTH

Naexa

Naexa needed followers in order to conquer a realm.

She tried to remind herself of this as she listened to Pie tell her—again—just how he would be of great use to her. Other than this increasingly unconvincing opinion and tireless examples (*Who else can kill an entire army with the poisoning of a single water source?* he'd ask, seeming to forget that there were Wielders whose Boons would allow them to slaughter an army without nearing any well or stream), he offered up little other conversation. Naexa considered repeating the questions she'd already asked, inquiring as to his homeland and heritage, or the source of his knowledge, but thought better of it. He had either stubbornly refused to respond or danced his way around the questions whenever she raised them. She'd have to try a new angle if she wished to learn anything from him.

Like the angle of a dagger's blade, she thought irately. If only. The mage was desperate, and it was easiest to get the desperate to do what you wanted by adding a taste of fear to their frenzy. But she thought that physically harming the first subject of her empire would probably not bode well for her future. All was well, though. She had other means of invoking fear.

"—certainly, this is a skill any common fellow might acquire," he was saying, "yet do you know what ability a mage possesses that no other—not even a sorcerer or a Wielder—could hope to acquire? Why, I shall tell you—"

Naexa clenched her jaw, steeled her gaze, and stared at Pie through the smoke of the fire he'd started until he stopped talking. It took a moment, but eventually he sensed the cold fury emanating from her direction and he trailed off, his soft chins doubling up on themselves as his jaw slackened mid-sentence.

"If you will not reveal the origins of your magic to me now, you may soon find yourself without a sorceress for whom to perform the grand abilities you speak of," she snapped.

Pie's dark eyes seemed to bulge out of his sweaty head at that. When combined with the half-singed facial hair still clinging to his left cheek and the fading hand-shaped bruise on his right, his look was that of a fool. She wanted to add a matching mark to the other side and burn the rest of the beard off. He had assured her that his face would soon be bare (though he neglected to say how this would happen, as though she didn't already know it was a disguise wrought from some spell or another), but it couldn't happen soon enough. The sight alone disgusted her, and his jowls folding down around his pitiful tusks only repulsed her further.

"No, I beg your apology!" he cried suddenly. "But my sorceress, it is shameful! *Skies,* it is mortifying!"

"Go on then."

Pie stared at her a moment longer as though trying to make certain she wasn't going to change her mind. When he saw that she was determined, he sighed, swiping the sweat off his forehead with a flash of his palm as he'd been doing consistently since she'd met him. Being fat, she knew, was sweaty work. She'd had to assume an overweight form only a few times in her life, but even that had been too many. The feeling of the fat rolls along her back pressing into each other when she walked up a hill or stairs was terrible, as was the chafing of her thighs, but the worst was the sweating. When you were fat, you were hot. Being skinny came with its own vices—the constant cold, having to wear long sleeves even in warm weather. But it was preferable to being encased in a layer of your own fluids at all times.

Pie flicked his sweat into the fire, then stared into the embers, wringing his damp hands.

"If I must tell you, then I shall," he said. He cracked his fingers, wrung his hands again, took up the stick he was using to tend the fire. Stalling, in simpler terms. Naexa sighed her frustration through clenched teeth as she watched him add another log to the orange flames.

What an ugly color for fire. An ugly color in general, she thought, catching sight of Pie's orange sashes.

But it was his color, whispered some part of her mind that belonged to the past.

Well, she conceded, *I suppose orange is certainly not as wretched as blue.*

Another sigh from the mage brought her mind to thoughts of the night before. She, Pie, and the Druid girl had returned to the cabin which Naexa had taken sanctuary in before visiting Thymenos. She didn't much like sharing it with them, though there was no reason for her to hide it from the mage or the girl. It held nothing of value (any longer) and the Druid had almost definitely seen Naexa leaving it the morning before, so in that case Pie would already know of it. But she was possessive of her belongings, and she'd begun to think of the cabin as hers from the moment she had laid eyes upon it. Just as she'd thought of Elt as hers from the moment she'd decided to conquer it, and as she was beginning to consider the mage and the Druid hers. Now, as the sun's blushing rise signaled the onset of morning, the three of them encircled a small fire chewing on its final embers.

Well, "encircled" was generous. Truly, she and Pie sat across from each other, her glaring and him babbling and wiping at his sweat. The shiftskin girl sat to the side in her rabbit form, her back to them and her face to the trees as she had been the entire night. Naexa had come to think of her simply as the Girl, though she spent more time as a bunny than a Spiritkin child. She'd only shifted once or twice in their time together. Most recently had been the night before, when she morphed to berate Naexa for the fistful of quail she'd returned from the woods with. The Girl was babbling on so furiously that her cheeks had flushed amber, but had stopped abruptly when Naexa, suppressing a smile, revealed the pocket full of crabapples she'd collected for her.

After they'd eaten the dinner she gathered (Pie cooked his, and the Girl turned her nose up in disgust while she munched on her apples), Naexa had begun her interrogation of the mage. She didn't bother trying to frame the questions as sly or indirect. She was neither a sly nor indirect person. Instead, she outright asked Pie which races his parents were, how young he'd been when he was outcast by his people—things of that nature. He had either avoided or ignored each question. Those questions she'd only asked out of simple curiosity. The ones of importance, however, concerned his magic.

Mages did not possess their own magick, but channeled the powers of the world and the unseen spirits residing in it through means of spells, potions, and rituals. They were considered revolting by the rest of the realm because they were not truly gifted, but instead borrowed or made their own false magic. Naexa could stomach working with a mage, even if his craft was pathetic. But there were many types of mages. Most broadly, there were those who worked with spirits of darkness, and those who worked with spirits of light.

In this way, they were somewhat similar to sorcerers, whose powers originated from one of these sources or the other. Naexa's morals could only be considered questionably grey at best, but she refused to work with someone who consulted with and stole power from dark, evil beings. It wasn't a question of righteousness, but of trust. It was downright idiotic to place your devotion in an evil being, when evil remained loyal only to itself. And so it was absolutely crucial she learn the origins and nature of Pie's magic before considering his proposal to serve her any further.

He had avoided these questions concerning his magic as well, until now. With the Druid asleep and the food long eaten, there was nothing for Pie to place his attention on other than her and the threat she'd given him.

"If I must tell you my tale, I shall start from the beginning," the mage said.

Naexa listened intently as Pie told her how his mother's family had rejected him upon birth. As she'd suspected, he was half Orcen and half Elven. He spoke of the former half of his lineage with barely concealed disgust, and of the latter with the arrogance of a full-blooded Titian. His father's folk, the Elven folk, were a proud bunch. Upon having the crossling child delivered to their doorstep in Titian, they'd immediately gone to their relatives in Verdelore and abandoned baby Pie with his father's aunts. The Verdelorians were still as kind as all Elves had once been, and raised the little boy to be plump and loved—if hidden from society. It seemed that his father had forgotten about him and all would be well. Then, when he was old enough to talk and read, his father returned in the night to his aunts' home. Covered in a cloak of silk and of moonlight, he snuck in and stole Pie away. The child was then sold to a mage his father had met in the Gilded Streets.

The mage lived on the southern coast near the sirens, and it was there that Pie learned his spells and potions.

"And what is the nature of the spirits your master worked with?" Naexa asked.

"They were kind spirits of the light. Spirits of beauty, of luck and love. Some even claimed to be angels." Pie shrugged. "I never laid eyes on them myself, but they asked for offerings of cakes and nectar rather than blood and flesh. And I saw no hint of wickedness in my master or his work, if that is what you wish to know."

"You've never even seen a spirit for yourself? How far into your training had you gotten before you left?"

Pie's cheeks flushed a horrid mixture of gold and brown. "I know how to craft potions, fashion altars, and make offerings to spirits. I have a book of spells, and a good many herbs and items required to complete them," he said, speaking in a rush. "Here, allow me to show you—"

"No, stop that," Naexa snapped. He had been fumbling with his clothing, trying to find something hidden in the folds of silk, and she rushed to stop him. "I don't need to see your trinkets of death. Now tell me if I have this clear: You have yet to convene with spirits or even look into their realm. I would also assume that you have not the strength to act as a medium or brew curses, either. You don't even have a familiar, for spirits' sake!" She couldn't help the grimace that curled her lip at the talk of false magic alone.

"My master departed this life before I could complete my apprenticeship—right in the midst of a ritual to summon a familiar of my own, in fact. It had naught to do with his craft," Pie hurried to add, catching Naexa's skeptical glance. "The cause was entirely natural. His heart simply ceased to beat; he fell face-first into the salamander ashes, and thus ended my master, my ritual, and my training in one fell stroke."

"You were trying to summon a *salamander* familiar?" Naexa scoffed. The Beasts were magickal but small, and had little power. The best they could do was light a bush on fire, or singe a tree cat's tongue. "Such lofty goals you had."

Pie's entire face now turned that sickly muddy yellow color as he blushed. "It was by my master's command that I began with a creature small in both size and strength," he defended hotly. "Had the choice been mine alone, I might well have chosen a basilisk or some such formidable Beast."

Naexa snorted derisively. "I should rather like to see you master a basilisk. As it is, I've no need for magic that does not flow through one's very blood—least of all from an apprentice not yet halfway through his lessons." She leaned down to toss dirt onto the fire.

"Perhaps not, my sweet sorceress—but you shall yet have need of my other talents!" Pie reached over the flames to grab her wrist mid-toss, nearly singeing his huge sleeves as he did so. Naexa slapped his hand away with a glare, but settled back onto her log to listen.

"I am not wholly convinced you have any talents to begin with," she muttered. "But go on. I shall reserve my judgements until after you've spoken."

"Thank you, my fair sorceress." Pie grinned around his tusks. "When I was but beginning my apprenticeship, my master oft sent me to the nearby towns to trade on his behalf. In so doing, I honed a keen eye for reading people—not as the Savvies do, mind you. I delve not into their minds, but observe their expressions, their gestures. With but a brief conversation, I can uncover the desires of a person's heart and know precisely what to offer to bend them to my will."

"Interesting," Naexa murmured. She wondered what he'd make her desires out to be.

"You need to gather allies, do you not? Indeed you do." He swiped at the sweat on his brow. "But you shall need a proper cause to bring them to your side. People are loath to disturb their habits; they shall not do so without a cause they find most compelling. Your power is formidable, already I have seen as much, but it requires a channel—one to direct its course, to guide it where it shall do us good and leave all else untouched, as it were.

"Sorceress, *I* am that channel. I shall seek out those who will lend their support to your cause, and I shall murmur to them precisely what they wish to hear. Some of the spells I have acquired allow me to forge guises for myself. What better emissary could you ask for? And if matters take a turn against us, neither of us shall be recognized by sight."

Divine wrath—he might be right. Pie had transformed before her. Still he was fat and sweaty, for it wasn't his physical appearance that had changed, but the way he held himself—straighter, bolder—and the way he thought of himself. This man wasn't the ashamed, barely trained mage who had just been sitting across from her. Here was a young, arrogant half-Elf, overly confident in his abilities. Yet his confidence might not be based in falsehoods. Naexa *did* need an envoy. She just didn't trust that this mage could be that person. Not yet.

He seemed so young, so untested—especially with that pathetic excuse for a beard stuck to his face. It sat there like a dead animal on his chin, like he'd borrowed it from a costume-dancer's trunk. She would need to learn more before she agreed to anything. Taking a page out of her master's tome, she decided she ought to do that through a test of sorts.

"Your proposal is an interesting one. Who would you have us first approach?" she asked.

Pie nodded, pleased with the question, as though he were the master and she the student. *Idiot.*

"We must first gather the smallfolk who bear a grievance against their kingdom and the present rule, preferably current or former citizens of Titian. These should be people of little consequence in the political sphere, that we might avoid word reaching those of influence." Naexa had, of course, anticipated as much. "An army requires foot warriors, yet one begins with Masters and Lords of War. We shall seek out those figures whom others might naturally follow. Once they are 'trained,' if you will, we may then gather the rank and file, the ordinary folk. They may be anyone. Yet our first recruits must be those blessed with spirit-gifts."

"You speak of Wielders." At Pie's vigorous nod, she added, "And do you have anyone in mind?"

Naexa expected Pie to come up short then, but to her surprise he did not.

"Of course I do," he scoffed. He swiped at his head. "I would hardly expect a woman of such wit and cunning as yourself to place her faith in mere empty promises. And I would not wish to follow such a fool. In any case, there is an old acquaintance of mine in a city not far from here; a distant neighbor to Thymenos. You have taken pains to avoid large cities, I know, yet that is where most of the spirit-gifted tend to dwell. This one is a kingdom defector with a power that is strong—and most advantageous."

"What, is he a Conjurer?" Naexa asked. She'd meant it sarcastically—the Boon of Conjuring was the rarest and most powerful type of magick a Wielder could possess. She meant to have several leading her armies eventually, but it was naïve to wish for such a powerful person to join her so early in her quest. And so, when Pie confirmed that the person he spoke of was indeed a Conjurer, her spirits jumped up along with her eyebrows.

"Is this a trick, mage?"

"Certainly not. He is a Conjurer of illusions."

Visions of a conquer that took months instead of years had begun dancing through her mind's eye at his initial words, visions of a Wielder who Conjured in the Eltics' hearts a desire to bow to Naexa, or of a man who grew deadly blades into her enemies' very spleens and spines. Then she registered what Pie had just said, and her spirits and hopes alike dropped. Illusionists most commonly held positions as entertainers for royalty, or for nobles who'd earned their titles because of the immense strength of their Boons. Conjurers of illusions weren't considered particularly skillful themselves, and were typically of the lowest ring within their branch of Wielding.

"And that will be *useful?"* Naexa scoffed, now scowling.

Her disappointment was immediately transformed into rage by her flames, and she released some of it into the campfire at her feet. The orange flames hissed and recoiled as they were devoured and overtaken by her beautiful purple ones. For a moment the two colors fought, curling around each other like battling serpents, stretching high into the dawn sky before falling back to the earth. Then she dismissed her magick and the mundane flames settled happily back over their embers again with a puff of smoke. They seemed to look at her almost smugly.

Pie had flinched back from the sudden heat and now waved away the smoke which was billowing into his face, coughing dryly. That, at least, brought her some joy. When he was done choking and had found a new place further down on his log where he could escape the smoke, he dried his brow and faced her again.

"Of course it will be useful—" he coughed again, "—dear sorceress."

"Oh, certainly. What will he do, create an illusory army to convince my new followers that I have strength and numbers? Or will he Conjure a dragon from the clouds to roar and belch fog at them? What will happen when the illusion fades and my enemies realize I have nothing but a meager entertainer?"

Pie waved his hands again as though her words were mere smoke to be fanned away. "You are considering how best to expand your influence, are you not? Indeed. For such an aim, we shall need schemes. And who better to bring those schemes to fruition than an illusionist?"

She continued to pin him with a glare, but relented to listen. "Go on."

"What possession is common to all military lords? A model of the terrain. And what is it that you lack, my dear sorceress? A model of the terrain. And what, pray, might a Conjurer provide you with? A—"

"Yes, yes, a model of the terrain," she snapped.

Pie merely smiled, and she thought she could see a bit more of his chin beneath that beard of his. The stubble seemed to be retreating back into his skin; his spell of disguise must be fading.

"And so you begin to see his worth."

"That is a generous statement, mage. But at the very least, I would do well to be able to say I have a Wielder as one of my earliest followers. It will entice others with Boons to my ranks."

"So wise you are. Yet for our Conjurer to do such a thing for you, you must first confide in him your plot. That demands a measure of trust, which you have not yet granted even me, your first and most loyal follower. Perhaps you might begin by sharing with me your designs, sweetness?"

Naexa physically recoiled. "Sweet sorceress" was a bad enough name to be called. That particular kind of groveling made her nauseous already, but to be spoken to like a lover, by a man so grotesque he was hardly fit to be a servant…

"Do *not* call me that." The words came out accented by black smoke.

Pie dipped his head, dark topknot bobbing, though he didn't even have the grace to look ashamed.

"But…your plan? I will have you know I hold the utmost faith in your abilities. Yet I should feel far more at ease championing your cause, were I assured that your scheme held the promise of something more substantial than mere murmured notions repeated to me by a hare."

Naexa's power heated her tongue at Pie's words. He was bordering on skepticism, and it made her seethe. Her master had doubted her as well, and so she'd proved to him just how capable she was. Did this mage wish to be shown a demonstration of her competence as well? She had no doubt he would be just as unhappy with that outcome as Amogasanes was.

Though she desired to scorch him, she forced her flames to recede and stood, kicking dust on the fire. Pie began to protest but she silenced him with a glare.

"We'll speak inside the cabin."

The sputtering of the fire paired with Pie's noisy shuffling woke the Girl, and Naexa invited her into the cabin. She just shook her furry head, still in bunny form, and settled back into the dry grass. Pie told her that the Druid preferred to sleep outside. She said that she felt uncomfortable being "disconnected from Elt" when sleeping on flooring made of "Elt's bones and trees' corpses."

Most folk of the Valley, which was where the Girl had come from, agreed that nature should not be killed unless necessary, and never permanently altered. And so, they opted for using magick to shape the trees and stone and leaves of Elt into the necessary structures rather than cutting planks of wood and melting sand into glass as the humans and Borderfolk did. Even the latter might implement the Valleyfolk's manner of craft, had they the magick necessary to build the way the Valley-goers did. But as it was, they did not, and so their buildings were made of tree corpses.

Naexa thought the Girl was being a bit austere, but didn't care enough to talk her out of her decision. She just confirmed with Pie that the Druid would not be able to escape, and then led him into the cabin when he ensured that the collar would prevent it. The Girl knew too much now to be safely released. The greatest threat to Naexa's scheme would come from word of it being spread to those who might try to stop her, and she had no doubt the Druid would do just that if given the chance. Shiftskins were impressively self-righteous, and loved to meddle in ethical affairs that didn't concern them.

Inside the cabin, Naexa transferred a small piece of her flame to the stub of candle on the single wooden table in the room. The house was dusty and small, as all buildings past the Border were. It had only two rooms—the foyer they stood in and a bedroom, which contained a splintered bed frame and a grass-filled mattress that had been slashed open by countless knives and claws. There was not even a bathing room or water-room; the bedroom held a chamber pot, and it seemed that was the best the previous owners had been able to afford.

Pie startled once the room was introduced to light, and she noticed him staring at the skeleton slumped in the room's single chair. Its yellowed bones became brown when bathed in the lavender of her fire, looking well-rotted and delightfully grotesque. Naexa smirked to herself and beckoned the frightened mage.

"Ah, sorceress, would you care for me to remove the skeleton for you? You ought to rest in comfort, after all."

Naexa raised her eyebrow as she leaned back against the table. Its well-worn surface scratched softly against her palms. "What makes you think that I'm not comfortable?"

She had always found bones to be beautiful. They were the Creator's sculptures, hidden during life to be revealed only after death. Those given the chance to see the secret works of art ought to consider themselves lucky. Pie did not agree. He spared Naexa a glance at her comment, but continued to eye the skeleton warily as he joined her in the center of the room.

She sighed as she prepared herself to trust this man with her most valuable possession: her plan. Her scheme. She'd known the day would come when she would finally find a follower and reveal to them her design in order to recruit them. She just hadn't expected that follower to be ugly. And a crossling mage, at that. She'd never trusted any of those three types.

"Every tale told of Elt is one of peace and harmony and beauty. Fairfolk find great joy in talking about how Elt loves its creatures, and its creatures love Elt. That indeed may be true, but the creatures no longer love each other. They pretend to, and hide behind niceties, but after living here long enough you start to see the truth: the rulers despise each other's power, and each race finds reason to hate those that are not of their blood. Wielders look down on the Boonless, and the Boonless are envious of Wielders.

"There has been talk of de-throning the Elves of the Wood; they have found too much power. There was a time when each race's leader ruled with equal influence. But now that the Titians are guardians of the Seam, more of their people are born with their hair tangled by the magick of Boons. And the power has gone to their braid-covered heads. It seems that they believe the Kindreds favor them more than others because of their abundance of Wielders. They used to love all creatures equally, and now they are some of the most arrogant fools I've met.

"Something must give way. And indeed, it shall. Such upheavals are most often stirred by war—it is inevitable. And since it must come, I'll not allow the chance to slip through my fingers." Naexa looked at her hands, noting the faint wisps of smoke curling from her palms, and calmed the storm within herself. Thinking of the state of the realm always angered her.

"And what makes you think you should stand at its helm?" Pie asked.

At once, the smoke rekindled. "I beg your pardon?"

"Assuming war does come—which, I am inclined to agree, seems certain—new rulers shall rise. Perhaps fewer than before, or perhaps more. Why not permit this revolution to run its natural course? Perhaps, for once, the people may wish to choose who rules them."

"They *will* choose who rules them," Naexa snapped. "They will choose *me*. Or else they will be left behind and *destroyed* by the embers of the fallen realm." Her smoke had turned to hot flame.

Pie's eyes were bright with delight, and he grinned fiendishly. "Yes, my sorceress. Indeed, they shall," he whispered eagerly. "You are, without question, the most powerful sorceress in all of Elt. I daresay your power surpasses even that of most Wielders. But mark me now—those you gather will challenge you. I learned as much in my time under my own master. You must be prepared to show them that you are every bit as worthy as we both know you to be."

Naexa's annoyance calmed slightly at that, but she still didn't like being tested; it spoke of underestimation, and she had been doubted enough. Especially by men. They'd all thought they'd known better than her—her father, her brother…even her late husband, in the end. That one broke her the most. It didn't hurt so badly to be let down by your family—you didn't choose them or shape them. But when a lover disappointed you, it spoke to a greater sorrow. Because it meant that perhaps something was wrong with you for picking them, and putting your trust in them. Perhaps your love wasn't great enough to transform them. But regardless of whether she'd chosen them or not, they had all questioned her, trying to suppress her and, in turn, make her doubt herself. To sense those old patterns forming again with Pie's words made her want to slap him in the jowls and banish him from her presence.

Unfortunately, he was right. She made herself nod. She would need a speech, and have answers prepared when they challenged her with questions. She could not form an army if she killed or dismissed anyone who doubted her when she'd given them no evidence that she was not to be doubted.

"After this war, new rulers would certainly rise to power," she began. "Perhaps they would be the sons and daughters of current monarchs who will be killed in the fighting, or perhaps entirely new faces. They would take over with vows to change the ways of the kingdoms on their lips. These would be promises to stop taxation, to lower market prices, to lend the kingdom's Wielders out to its villages for repairing houses and erecting new buildings. But this would not happen. The new kings and queens would find that they liked having power and full coffers and bejeweled spoons and undergarments, and they would realize why their predecessors ruled in the way they did. They would continue to make promises of change, but as they did, they would grow accustomed to the thrones beneath them and halt all progress toward that change.

"After so much fighting, so much war and pain and bloodshed, the rulers who sat upon the thrones would be different, but the rule would remain the same."

Pie's gaze had become reverent. He was staring at the violet glow now encompassing her, unable to take his eyes off of it. "And how, my sweet sorceress, can we trust that you will not do the same?"

Naexa's jaw flexed at the memories his comment brought—of her time as royalty. "Because I have already had my taste of power. I had someone to feed me, to dress me, to carry me to the water-room and to dry me after. I could have anything I wanted with the point of a finger. People would have danced at my command. They would have killed at my command. And they did. I spent my early life with power—but I want it to end with me as a protector."

It wasn't entirely true that her cause was born from high morals. She did not much care personally for all the people wrongly imprisoned, for all the women robbed of their men, children robbed of their fathers. Rather, she despised the imperfect system which birthed and nursed such injustices. It was so simple to create a form of rule which was fueled by logic and rationality rather than randomness and arbitrary customs. Yet all those in power refused to take the action that would be needed to create and enforce such a system. She knew what was necessary for Elt to operate at its most efficient, which would in turn abolish all the inequalities of the realm, and that made it her duty to implement it. If she didn't, it would be a waste of her power and intelligence alike.

Naexa realized she was gripping the table so hard her fingers were numb. In her fervor, she hadn't noticed the scorch marks she'd left there.

She peeled her hands from the divots she'd burned into the wood and then finished relaying her scheme to Pie. He watched her worshipfully the entire time, and she knew he was transfixed by her purple spirit-light. It was one of the first aspects of her magick to develop. Typically, you had to be trained in the art of sorcery to be able to see spirit-lights, those halos of color which surrounded every person. But for a reason neither she nor Amogasanes knew, hers spontaneously became visible to all at random times. When she'd begun talking, it had been a gentle halo—now it was a violet inferno. It only grew as she spoke.

"Soon, the world will be mine, Pie. I will dethrone the current kings and queens, warlords and lieges. I will destroy those who stand in my way. And once I have collected every land and its people, I will be Elt's empress."

Pie's eyes were wide, and in their darkness, her flame was reflected. As she'd spoken, the mage had transformed (physically now), his spells worn off. He was still round as a pie, but the once-sharp features of his face were now wide as well. His nose and face were broad like that of an orc, and his eyes had become big and deep-set. The tusks were still small, but once his beard fully disappeared, they seemed more prominent. The dark hair atop his head had fallen from its knot and now hung short and straight. It framed a dust-colored face which was youthful and reverent.

As she looked on, he dropped to his knees and bowed deeply, tusks scraping her toes.

"Hail the Empress of All," Pie whispered. Naexa's flames crackled pleasantly at the sight. "Oh, hail you, most powerful sorceress, the Empress of All."

Naexa watched through the cabin's single dirty window as Pie tied the Girl to the tree she slept by. It was full daylight now, and the trees were sparse this near to the barren lands of the Wilder, so they offered little shade. Still, she slept, as Naexa and Pie soon would. They had stayed awake through the night and a good part of the morning talking, and would now sleep through the day. The Druid hardly glanced at the mage as he worked before going back to sleep. Such strange creatures, Druids were. They cared so greatly when their moral code was infringed upon, but here one sat enslaved, and did nothing to escape. Were their values only of importance when in regard to others?

How meddlesome.

She had bathed once their conversation had faded and Pie had come out of his reverie. The day had left her dirty, and while she did not so much dislike feeling dirty, she did despise looking it. She'd gone to the single bedroom and found a small washbasin and matching bucket, which she'd had Pie collect pond water in. She heated the water until it was nearly boiling to kill any nastiness that might have wormed its way in.

Then she dumped it over her head. The basin was intended for taking baths in, for sitting and lounging in, despite its rusting rims, but the thought alone made her lip curl. Baths were intolerable. Sitting on dirty metal and touching her bare skin to disgusting wet surfaces that other people had touched was insufferable. Instead, she stood in the basin and poured the water over her head. Even the slimy and slippery texture of the tub on her bare feet alone was abhorrent and she subconsciously stood on the sides of her feet to avoid touching it as much as possible. She worked quickly, and once finished she immediately heated the skin of her feet so she wouldn't have to stand on slippery and soggy wet wood next.

Now, warmed by her flames, she watched her mage and her Druid.

Pie had finished his task and was shuffling back to the cabin, swiping at his forehead. He tucked loose strands of his hair behind his heavily decorated ears as he entered the room. Naexa marveled again at the sheer size of those pointed ears. They were tall with the mark of Elven nobility, but like the rest of his Orcen features, they were big and broad and flat. They reminded her of the Blood Elves' bats, only his were covered with gold rings and glinting gemstones of orange and yellow. Titian colors.

He still wears them, though he was banished from their kingdom before he could see what it looked like. How pathetic.

"You told me that the Druid was bound to you. Why, then, are you tying her up?"

Pie jumped at her voice, and she realized she was cloaked in shadow, the candle having gone out. She stepped into the moonlight.

"Ah, sorceress! I had thought you retired for the night. Pray, forgive my intrusion." He swiped at his forehead with a sleeve.

"I first wanted assurances on the girl."

Pie nodded. "She is bound to me, and time does not weaken the magick, imbued in the collar as it is. I merely rest easier at night knowing she is secured both in body and in spirit. Call me old-fashioned, if you like." He smiled. The sight was repulsive; his tusks jutted out too far, causing his lower lip to protrude with the expression.

Naexa tried to hide her grimace. "It is less traditional, and more a reflection of inner uncertainties," she muttered.

"Pardon?"

"If you feel the need to use a rope to bind her, it means that you do not trust your own magic. Why should I?"

"It is not my own spellcraft, my sorceress, and I apologize if I caused such an impression. The collar is of Dwarven make, imbued with a Boon. And it is not the magick I mistrust, but rather the changeling herself. Should she flee my grasp, it would mean her demise—yet I cannot be entirely certain that even the threat of death would dissuade such a Beast from seeking her freedom." Pie smiled distortedly and swiped his head again, then wiped it on his robes. They were stretched taught over his belly.

Naexa nodded. It was an acceptable answer. "We may need to kill her anyway."

She shifted to look out the window at the once-nameless Druid. After her conversation with Pie, she had returned to the forest to hunt. The fat mage had eaten most of her quail when she wasn't paying attention, and she'd hardly gotten two birds to herself. Before she'd left, she stopped beside the girl.

She was too young to have been given a name; Pie had captured her before she could be fully raised by the forest and return to her tribe. Naexa had studied the ways of all races during her time under Amogasanes. His methods were not traditional, and she thought that half of the things he'd made her do had been for naught but his own entertainment, but some of his lessons had stuck with her deeply. Such as the teaching that knowledge of people offered control over them.

That night Naexa had used her knowledge of the Druids for what may have been control, but what she also believed was kindness.

"I knew a Druid once," Naexa said. The Girl had been looking into the forest, but turned to her with wide eyes to listen. "She was wise, and stringent but kind. No, not just kind—gentle. She was old, but still, you remind me of her. You had no chance to be named by your people, and so I will give you your name, the same she had. In the language of your people, you are *Giver of Gifts.*"

And so the Girl had become Brinwyx. Naexa had gone into the forest before she could respond. She wasn't certain if she would accept the name, but Naexa didn't truly care. She was tired of referring to her as "the Girl" or "the Druid" or "the shiftskin." Too many words annoyed her. She preferred conciseness. Efficiency was beautiful.

Now, as Naexa looked on from the cabin, Brinwyx the bunny seemed to be sleeping peacefully. She could just glimpse the copper cord Pie had used to tie her to the tree.

"Sorceress?" Pie's voice was laced with unease. "She is your gift to do with as you please, but…do you truly mean to dispose of so valuable an asset so swiftly?"

"I hold little trust for the Druids. A race with no allegiances is a race with no loyalty except to themselves. They're raised up with the griffin-dung 'we are one with Elt' mindset. You're right in thinking that Brinwyx would likely end her own life before allowing herself to be an accomplice to the conquer of Elt. But suppose that instead, she encounters another of her kind while spying for us. Outside of their shifting, Druids have powers little understood by the rest of us. I don't fully trust that they wouldn't find a way to free her of the collar's binding. Considering the nature of the magick, could they potentially do this?"

Naexa turned her gaze to Pie. He was swiping furiously at his forehead. He knew this was a test; it wasn't only metaphysical abilities she sought in her followers. They ought to at least have brains in their skulls.

"Not by any power, no. The magick's hold may only be broken by death—either the changeling's, or my own."

He won't lie to please me, then. The rational part of her was contented by this—people grew strong in objectivity. But the irrational bit of her mind which lived nestled in the embers of her magick snapped its jaws. He should want to please her so desperately that he would do and say anything to achieve that end, including lie. She silenced her magick and killed that line of thinking. She hated irrationality, especially when she recognized it in herself. It was the weakness her husband had used to control her.

"Druids despise killing. But they might deem it acceptable if it came to freeing one of their own," she mused. She'd seen it happen before. *Giver of gifts, and taker of life.*

She began summoning a flame to her finger and putting it out. It was a habit she'd picked up from Amogasanes. There had been so many reminders of him, though she hadn't seen him in years. Why was that?

He would tell me it means something. Perhaps I will be seeing him again soon. She wasn't sure how she felt about that.

"Yes, yes, indeed," Pie was saying. "Only, if you will permit me, I believe the shiftskin may yet serve us well. We might employ her to spy upon the Elves, and any others who might dare oppose us. While it is vital to gather allies, it is equally important to keep a keen eye upon our foes."

The mage was right. Of course, she'd already thought of this.

"I don't doubt that she would be beneficial to our cause. I simply don't trust that she won't find some way to escape or communicate our plans to another Druid. Is that included in the imbuement? A ban on communication between anyone other than you and I?"

Pie pressed his tusks into his upper lip. "No, sorceress. It is not."

Naexa sighed and crossed the room to the former owner and their seat. Grabbing the rough back of the chair, she dumped the skeleton onto the floor with a jumbled clatter and sat in its place. Pie grimaced, edging around the bones as he shuffled to join her.

"You'll need to find a Dwarf who can do so now, of course. Or, if your own magic allows it, place a spell upon either the girl or the collar that meets the requirements."

"Yes, yes…" he swiped at his head, glancing through the window. "I shall do as you wish, though you must know I should bitterly lament the death of the shiftskin. Many days' labor it took to secure her, and twice that time to find such a collar to bind her. To see all my toil cast to naught would grieve me deeply."

Naexa summoned a flame to her finger then banished it. She did it again. Pie swiped his forehead. She had half a mind to burn the Druid just to demonstrate to Pie that his desires were not important to her. She didn't want her first follower, or any of them, thinking they held sway over her. But Naexa didn't like unnecessary death. And in any case, the girl would be useful; it would be a waste to kill her. This was a rare opportunity Naexa was presented with. The ability to spy on her enemies so inconspicuously sent a thrill of warmth through her skin.

"Do you think you can manage a necessary spell?" Naexa asked.

Pie nodded eagerly. "It will be hard, but I believe it can be done. Certainly, sweet sorceress."

Her fire blazed upon hearing the nickname again. "I'm not sweet," she snapped. "And I am certainly not *your* sorceress."

"Apologies my—" Pie cleared his throat. "Apologies, sorceress. I learned much about you from the changeling, but one thing she was not able to glean was your name."

Naexa set her mouth. Her name was one thing she would not give up to any of her followers. That, and her appearance. They would only see her in a disguised form, and they would only know her by an alias. She had made a mistake with Pie when she'd allowed her magick to slip upon her entrapment. Just the remembrance of the event made her skin heat. She still wasn't certain if he would be allowed to survive, having seen her in her true form. The others would see only her disguise, one she had perfected over the moons to convey exactly what she wished: reverence and fear. The name, however, was one thing she had yet to fabricate. It needed to be powerful, yet short and memorable.

She thought back to the power she'd felt coursing through her upon seeing Pie kneel at her feet. *Hail the Empress of All,* he'd said. *Hail the Empress of All.* The phrase had been delicious in her ears.

Empress of All.

Empress of All.

Naexa met the mage's eyes, and felt the violet glow encircling her again.

"I will not kill the Druid if you can cast a spell making her unable to speak to anyone besides you and me. I care not what the conditions are, as long as assurances are in place that my plans will not be spoiled by her." Pie dipped his head and made to leave. "And Pie," she said, allowing her violet spirit-light to grow. "You may call me Avahl."

The mage knelt again, black eyes gleaming. Then he raised his arm, forming a circle with his hand.

Naexa touched her fingers to her thumb, mimicking the Orcen gesture, the one used between a warlord and his warriors. Naexa would not be a queen like Escera of the Elves, nor a warlord like Odeon Skull-Caver. She would be something new entirely. She must be something new, if she were to transform the very realm.

As she officially accepted Pie into her service, she saw herself reflected in his black eyes, standing tall in her new robes.

She looked powerful. Sovereign.

"Hail the Empress Avahl," her mage murmured.

The first empress of Elt.

THE TWENTY-NINTH

Sada

When Sada awoke, Dedrei was gone.

The mist of the Dell had thickened and descended to roll across the woodland floor overnight, casting an ominous look to the trees veiled in fog. They seemed like quietly observing Giants, the nature of their motives unbeknownst to those whom they watched. Sada shivered as she sat up through the thick clouds of mist, patting the cold ground to find her cloak. Her shoulder didn't hurt so badly when she moved it now. Where before it had ached deeply, almost as if her very bones were crying out, now she felt only a dull throb. She was ever thankful for the healing, but thoughts of her shoulder led to thoughts of her shins, which led to thoughts of Dedrei, and thinking of her made Sada's mood as dismal as the weather.

She and Dedrei hadn't spoken much after they'd discovered Sada's miraculously healed wounds.

"I must take you to the Mother of Druids immediately," Dedrei had said upon seeing her unbroken flesh and confirming that Sada had indeed split open her shins earlier that day and had not been healed by Sarana.

Sada had asked why they weren't going to find the Elves of the Wood anymore—weren't they the ones who could send her back?

The Druid had just stared at her grimly for a moment then said, "I am afraid it is no longer possible for you to return to the human realm, girl." So Sada had fallen asleep with worry pricking at her belly and the sound of Dedrei muttering her prayers to the Creator in her ears. Though they weren't in any language Sada could understand, those prayers had seemed more frantic last night.

Now Sada rubbed the grains of fitful sleep from her eyes, cloak protecting her from the chill, and stood to stretch her stiff muscles. Though the floor of the Dell was thickly padded with moss and long grasses, sleeping on the ground was not something her body was used to. Sada longed to return to her down feather bed and silk sheets, always warmed at night by a great fire in her room. But Dedrei's words haunted her.

Why am I no longer able to return home? Merely because my legs healed with unusual speed? With the way Dedrei had been agitatedly praying, squeezing her eyes shut as she chanted, Sada hadn't dared to pester her with more questions. But now they flowed unbridled through her mind. A few must have leaked into the Mindspace she shared with Sarana, because the caelicorn was suddenly in front of her. Her horn parted the mist eerily, like the figurehead on a ship's bow sailing through thick fog, warning all who spied it of its potentially deadly presence. But despite her initial shiver at the sight, Sada was glad for the company of her friend.

"Oh, how glad I am to see you, Lady Blue," Sada sighed. She held out a hand and the filly pressed her muzzle against her palm, though she did not speak. "Only a friend's company can comfort me now—Dedrei's words have my mind a mess. I know she means no harm, yet the way she spoke last night set my nerves on edge. Do you truly think I won't be able to go home now?"

Sarana just stared at her for a long moment, hypnotizing Sada with her gaze. Her irises, like molten gold, seemed twin to the silver of the Seam and Sada wondered if the portal had anything to do with the reemergence of her species, which had been thought to be extinct. Sarana did not answer this question, but she did respond to Sada's previous one. Her voice, altogether ancient and infantile, tickled Sada's mind.

Thou were never destined to return unto thy home, Sada.

Those dreadful words in combination with Sarana's otherworldly voice sent a shiver across Sada's entire body. She half expected her *instincts* to flare to life in her hand, yet they remained calm. Somehow their silence only discomforted her further.

"But DeeDee said…" Sada started. She found that her voice failed her, however, and she stopped trying to speak aloud when her throat closed on itself. She fought tears forming in her eyes as she thought to Sarana, *She said she would deliver me to the Elves of the Wood. The king…he was going to send me back.*

The image of King Caprius as she had last seen him filled her mind. His hair had been like molten copper, tamed only by a hundred braids. His eyes were twin embers. He had been so sure that the Seam would deliver her back to her realm, and her guards had been as well. They had been so certain, in fact, that they hadn't bothered to wait to ensure her successful crossing. What would they and King Caprius say when they realized she was still here, disgracing their realm with her mortality? Would she receive the same punishment as the brothers? Perhaps they would share a dungeon cell.

Are they even alive? The thought was sharp and unwelcome, and it stirred her belly. She could not believe that the king, as fiery-tempered as he was, would punish trespassers with death. Certainly not accidental trespassers like Kartinar and Drath claimed to be. She tried to soothe herself with thoughts of them walking free in Elt, side by side as brothers should walk. In this vision, she saw them with new clothes that were free of tears, clean skin, and cheeks ruddy with laughter. It almost made her smile. Perhaps, if she really was trapped in Elt, she would be able to find the two of them and join them in their travels. She would have to convince them to stop thieving, but she didn't think that would be too hard a task. They were good people. Their eyes told her so.

And what did Caprius's eyes tell her? *That he holds within himself a tremendous temper, and a tremendous power to match.* Whether that came from his position as king, his otherworldly grace, or some inner ability she had not yet seen, she didn't know. But she was certain it was a power great enough to lend her some sort of aid. If not in restoring the Seam, then in finding its new location, as *Om' Modir* had said might be necessary. For the entirety of her journey, she'd put her hope in the distant king, filling her mind with daydreams of their reunion. Even the thought of it brightened her skin with gentle tingles. Would she never have her chance to see him again? Could he truly help her no longer?

Sarana sensed her thoughts and pressed against her side to comfort her. *King Caprius may well serve as the guardian of the Seam, yet it lies no longer within his power, nor within the power of any other, to return thee from whence thou came.* Sarana stopped speaking to Sada then, but she felt another thought graze their shared space of mind. It was fleeting, and Sada sensed only the vaguest whisper of it before it was quickly drowned out by another.

Perhaps...the caelicorn had thought, then, *no—the peril is far too great.* It was as though Sada had heard the caelicorn's private thoughts, not meant to be conveyed to her through their bond.

"What is it?" Sada managed to whisper through that block in her throat, the kind which only formed from great sorrow or pain. "If there is any other way for me to return home, I must know of it."

Sarana just snorted dismissively, though her brilliant eyes seemed to show pity. Sada was almost certain the filly could feel her pain.

Dost thou truly yearn for thy world so greatly? For millennia, mankind has sought to cross the Seam, hoping to find this realm. The multitude of thy kin would gladly trade places with thee in but a moment, were they granted such an opportunity. Yet thou seek to depart...pray tell, why? She sounded utterly perplexed.

"I..." Sada started, but the words wouldn't come.

Why did she wish to return home so badly—to the rules and fears? In the coming years she would surely be arranged into a marriage, be destined to live an idle life filled with children and the abundant joys of court politicking. How many guards would she be forced under the protection of then?

Yet she had grown up viewing this future with excitement; she had always looked forward to her inevitable marriage in hopes of finding love there. Beginning with her childhood crush on Gabriel, all her own attempts at discovering love had failed her in one way or another, and she thought that at this point the Duke would certainly know best which nobleman or royal would be the best match for her.

And while her father terrified her, and marred her, and suppressed all of her into what to him was the perfect daughter…she still loved him. When her mother had deemed her unworthy of love and disappeared from her life, and when her Centerton friends had abandoned her for the sake of their reputations, and even when the other noble ladies had made mock of her, her father had always been waiting at home. It was with a stern countenance and cold eyes, but still—he was there when she was otherwise alone.

Their relationship reminded her of a poem she had heard in Ettedon's markets. It was being read aloud from one of the middle stalls, one of the utterly unmemorable ones which most passed by and never thought of again. But she'd stopped then, and listened to the woman read. Her voice was as wrinkled as the tan skin of her face, but somehow the words had made it beautiful:

I shall love as the sun does
(unpredictably, sporadically)
in hopes that you will never grow used to me and push me away.
Perhaps I may scorch you, but so long as you wish me to remain, I shall call it worthwhile. You may curse my name, yet still wish me near.

At times, I confess, I fear to love
because I know that mine is so bright.
I dread the thought of you closing your eyes against me.

Look upon me as I burn you.
Watch me as I love you.
And then I shall leave,
and you will plead for my return.

And then I will shine.

She'd had the idea then that the Duke loved like the sun. Maybe he'd even heard the poem himself and applied its philosophy to his life. Maybe the poem had been written about him by one of his past friends or lovers.

She couldn't say whether the philosophy was true. But she did know that while the Duke's moments of kindness and fatherly adoration stood years apart, she longed for them with every wisp of her soul whenever she faced him, or thought of his new-ice eyes.

When she had escaped into the woods to journey to the festival, she had left her estate thinking she'd return that night, albeit to devastating punishment and a raging father. After unexpectedly being away from home and her only family for so long, her longing to be back had begun carving a pit into her heart.

And can you forget Jezebel so easily? Her favorite friend; her only true friend. Yes, she had her Gabe, but he was paid to love her. Sada owed Jezebel a debt that could never be repaid, a debt she constantly tried to alleviate through invitations to balls and gifts of expensive dresses; a debt whose payment was always rejected. With each rejection, that bond had further frayed. She hadn't realized it, but Jezebel had begun to act in heart-wrenchingly similar ways to the ladies who mocked Sada behind gloved hands. Somehow her care for Jezi had blinded her, but now she saw. When she didn't rely on her friendship as an escape from her station, she saw.

Sada absentmindedly reached up to touch the worn cuff still stuck on her ear. The metal was cool beneath her fingers. As cool, she realized, as her heart felt thinking of Jezebel.

Yes, she was now certain she wanted to return home, and not to see Jezi, but to see the Duke. Because no matter how many switches he used on her back, no matter how many times he yelled at her, he was still her father, and he didn't leave her.

But how would she be able to put all of those feelings into words that Sarana would understand?

I see, the caelicorn said. Sada glanced up at the filly, watching her eyes. She realized her own were filled with tears and squeezed her eyes in a hard blink to force them out. They ran coolly down her cheeks, chilled by the mist.

Did you hear what I was thinking?

Nay, I felt it. Longing, loss, love. Never have I been granted the chance to know these emotions, save through the memories of my mothers. I thank thee for sharing them with me.

Sada just nodded, still unable to speak. *And you are certain I can no longer return?*

Sarana's lids lowered and Sada took that to be a reluctant yes. *There exists a slim chance that such remains technically possible. Yet it is most probable that the Seam has been laid to ruin and must be restored, should thou wish to make use of it once more. Yet there are none within the Kingdom of the Wood who possess the necessary ability.*

But there is someone elsewhere who does? Sada asked hopefully.

Perhaps…someone.

Is it the Mother of Druids? Whom Dedrei mentioned?

Nay.

Then why bring me there?

The Mother alone possesses knowledge which surpasses that of the Elves of the Wood in regard to the portal. And I venture to say, if thou seek one to restore it, perchance the

Mother knows where such a soul might be found, Sarana said thoughtfully. *Though the likelihood be but slight. I perceive thy hope; thou ought not to nourish it.*

Sada thought that was an impossible request.

'Tis most probable that Dedrei intends to bring thee unto the Mother in pursuit of answers for her own sake, and of sanctuary for thee. She is well aware the Seam cannot return thee…indeed, this truth she has known for quite some time.

Sada felt alarmed curiosity light up in her chest. *Dedrei has known I'd not be able to return since before she saw my wounds heal?* Sarana snorted in confirmation, and Sada asked, *For how long?*

I believe since the very moment she first laid eyes upon thee. Or rather, the first time she laid eyes upon the remnants of Seam marking your gown.

And yet, she assured me she would take me to the Elves of the Wood. If she knew they could offer no aid…why, then, would she have deceived me? Sada felt deflated. Besides the filly, Dedrei had been her one friend in Elt. Was this how her entire life would be spent? Making friends only for them to turn on her, or disappear from her side against her will?

This is erroneous. Druids possess not the ability to speak falsehoods. Thou must not consider Dedrei to be untruthful. Sarana was incredibly uneasy from Sada's words. The feeling flowed in sharp spurts through their bond like the shock of static electricity. The discomfort translated so strongly to Sada that she physically flinched at the feeling.

"Okay!" she blurted, frantic to stop the feeling which was both entirely mental and entirely physical. "I won't think in such a way. I understand she did not deceive me." As soon as she said it, the feeling of distress faded from her mind. She relaxed, the stiffness melting from her limbs and belly. "I know she was unsettled by my tale of the portal from the very moment I shared it, yet I remain quite at a loss—Dedrei has known what transpired for days now. What has changed?"

Thou conjoin within thy mind two events that bear no true connection. The ruin of the Seam accounts for thy physical incapacity to use it to return unto the mortal realm; yet the mending of thy wounds speaks to a graver matter, one which would constrain Dedrei to prevent thy departure, bound as she is by the Druids' sacred code which she must keep from violating.

Sada stared blankly at Sarana. "My friend, I fear I've no idea what you've just said. Whatever do you mean?"

The matter henceforth concerns not technicality, but rather—

Might there be a simpler way to put it? Sada interrupted. Sometimes their communication was in emotion alone, or bursts of images, but now Sarana spoke directly into her mind. She felt as though she was listening to a philosopher or playwright of old, and she had to translate each sentence as Sarana said it.

Now it is I who take not thy meaning, Sarana said. *Playwrights speak of fiction, but what I say now is truth.*

"Oh, I do not mean it in that way, it's only that...as I mentioned before, your manner of speech is so old-fashioned."

Sada laughed as the filly shuttered her eyes and snorted. *Verily, I do well recall thy saying so. I cannot alter the manner in which I speak—for I have learned my speech from the memories of my foremothers, written upon mine own heart.*

Then this is simply the way you speak? Sada asked. *I mean no offense—*

*I understand. I sense thy curiosity. Ever does it dwell with perked ears in thy heart, yet now it does lift its bright gaze upon me. As for thy question, the answer is not so plain. I wonder...*Sarana stopped speaking and Sada realized how empty her mind felt when the caelicorn's resonant voice was not filling it. The absence felt like the hollowness of a lock empty of its key. But that feeling was quickly replaced by a sudden understanding that when a caelicorn bonded with her *Hédras*, she adopted the Spiritkin's way of speech to better communicate with them. Her very thoughts and tone were shaped to suit their mind. Yet, beneath this realization came a feeling like troubled waters—like the stillness of a pond shattered by splashing feet or the scatter of thrown stones. Confusion was there too, a foggy frustration that seeped into her chest from Sarana's own.

I see, Sada said. As she spoke, Sarana's emotions began to fade from her chest, like receding waves pulling back from the shore, and in their absence, Sada's own sadness was exposed. She hadn't realized how deeply she disliked speaking of the filly's future Rider. Every mention of that figure—someone unknown, and yet still despised—reminded her of the day she would be replaced, of a bond that would outlast her own claim on Sarana. A Rider would forge something permanent with her friend, something sacred that Sada knew she could not match.

And I will be as I have been all my life. Pushed aside. Left behind. The sorrow was not pure; it was tainted with a bitterness that curdled within her. Jealousy, sharp and raw, stirred at the thought of losing Sarana, and along with it, a dark, selfish urge to keep the caelicorn for herself, to deny her friend what was hers. The shame of it settled thickly on her, and she shifted away, unwilling to let her twisted feelings brush against the filly's innocent mind.

"Go on, then," Sada said. She wished to think of their eventual parting no longer. "I can understand your speech, ancient as it is." She tried to lighten the moment, attempting a playful wink, but it felt awkward and heavy. Her attempt at humor hung there, flimsy and transparent, and even to her own ears it sounded forced.

Sarana regarded her for a moment before Sada realized she needed physical contact to speak, and she had just broken it. Guiltily, she put a hand on her friend's neck. A sense of peace returned to her, subtle and steady, as their connection reformed. Sarana waited, her patient presence filling the silence between them.

I shall attempt to match thy—your—speech. Only consider that one day, your manner of speaking shall be deemed "archaic" and "old-fashioned" as well. Her joke translated much better; laughter bubbled up from Sarana's mind into Sada's, and any awkwardness was washed away. Sarana continued on, speaking slowly, and her concentration was palpable.

The matter at hand is no longer one of mere technicality, but of principle. Dedrei and her kin serve as protectors of Elt's creatures. Indeed, she likely surmised that the Elves of the Wood might have offered you shelter, or perhaps held the power to mend the portal; thus, she escorts you now. Yet upon seeing your wounds begin to heal, the Druid perceived that such an undertaking no longer lies within what she could permit, though it may yet be physically possible—which, I should add, is by no means certain.

"I understand the difference you speak of, but—"

Do you? I cannot sense this.

Sada chuckled. "Yes, I do. An example comes to mind: should an apothecary possess the means to ease a patient's suffering with a potent draught, he may yet refrain, for fear the patient may come to depend upon it. This is much the same, is it not? The question is not one of capability, but of principle." When Sada felt Sarana's silent assent within her mind, she pressed on. "But I fail to understand why matters have changed so. I understand that swift healing is uncommon—even here, it seems, where magick abounds—but should it not be cause for rejoicing? I simply wonder…why does my recovery mean the Druids cannot permit me to depart from Elt?"

*I cannot…there are no words…*Sarana snorted and stamped her hoof, irritated. She couldn't communicate in clear thoughts what she wished to say. Instead, she sent Sada an idea. It moved like fog into her mind, coalescing into a clear notion, a concept. One that didn't form in words, but partially in pictures, and partially as a simple understanding. She felt that something within her had shifted, possibly when she went through the portal, or maybe afterward. Maybe even when Sarana had cleaned her wounds. This part of the idea presented itself as a visual memory from Sarana's eyes, and she saw her pink tongue running across the gashes along Sada's ribs. Half a breath later, the fragment of memory was gone, and she understood that she was now a part of Elt, and part of the change that was rippling through it. She had become connected to something far greater than herself and her own personal journey home. Now her presence in Elt, and her departure from it, had the potential to affect all of the realm. She could not leave until…

Sada frowned. The knowledge she had been given trailed off there. It was like she had been following a road in her mind, and now it led into a wall of fog. When she stepped in, she was met only with a frustrating mixture of confusion and nothingness. She could almost see the thought forming within the tendrils of mist, but when she reached out to grasp it, it flitted away and only darkness was revealed.

"What is the rest?" Sada asked.

Sarana held her gaze and shook her head. She could not say more. Sada felt that it wasn't because of any desire the filly had to withhold information from her; she simply couldn't access the information herself. They shared in their confusion, and each of their personal portions of it bled through the bond to mingle with each other's.

Annoyed, Sarana stamped her hoof and paced the little clearing. When she broke their contact, some of Sada's irritation dissipated. She breathed deeply of the Dell's fresh air. She felt as though the rainbow-filled mist cleansed her very lungs.

Oh, very well. I suppose I shall either learn of it, or I shall not. I doubt it shall alter my circumstances much, yet how curious I am to know! She thought that Sarana was more upset by her inability to tell Sada the whole of it than Sada herself was. Watching the filly pace, each snorted breath sending the mist swirling away from her muzzle, Sada decided that what she had said earlier was right. Most humans probably *would* trade places with her if given the chance. Since she was here, she wouldn't squander the gift with her grief at being away from home, or her frustration at not knowing the full explanation for her being stuck in Elt. She would appreciate the magnificent beauty of the magickal realm while she had the chance to.

"You have the right of it, as usual," she said to Sarana. She didn't so much as flick an ear. "Why is it that you do not always converse with me? At times, there are images and feelings, and at times, words. Yet sometimes when I speak or think to you, it is as though you suddenly cannot understand me."

A golden eye turned to her. *It is not that I am without understanding of you. Ever do I comprehend your words and thoughts. The trouble lies rather in my inability to respond. At times, I am able, yet only when I am in bodily contact with you. At other times, I may speak to you when we stand on opposite ends of the forest.*

You must know that I am yet young; my abilities are not fully formed. Oft do they escape me.

"I see," Sada said. She wondered how young the caelicorn truly was. She was the size of a newborn horse, but oftentimes it seemed that she was far more knowledgeable than Sada, and even Dedrei.

My body has not yet seen the passing of a single moon, yet my mind is as ancient as Elt itself. Yet be not deceived—this knowledge is not mine own… It is that of my foremothers and their mothers before them, bestowed unto me through the blood. It comes unto me but slowly…

Sarana's voice was ebbing in and out now, and sometimes only echoes of thought which Sada could not fully grasp reached the Mindspace.

Suddenly Sarana turned and scented the forest. She had the idea that Dedrei would be returning soon.

Sada…there is…aspect.

Sada frowned. *Pardon? Something about an aspect?*

Another aspect to this… a difficulty that has arisen along with the rest, owing to our change in course.

What do you mean? Before she had finished asking the question, her stomach was plagued by a sudden onset of cramping and grumbling. Her mind immediately reacted with visions of food—roast duck dripping in gravy, slabs of bread coated in yellow butter and orange honey, creamy mashed potatoes, roasted and oiled asparagus, lamb pot pies, lemon tarts and strawberry ice cream—and saliva filled her mouth. The hunger was not terrible, but it was constant in both her mind and her belly.

After a few moments, the feeling retreated and Sada was left feeling nothing but blissful emptiness. She leaned onto an almond tree, pressing her forehead against the cool bark. Now the guilt came in harsh waves to replace the hunger. She couldn't bear to look at Sarana, knowing she had failed her and continued to do so.

I'm sorry, I'm sorry, I'm sorry, I'm sorry. The phrase ran on repeat in her head. She forced it to, for fear of what else she might think of—

(a little blue foal lying stretched over the roots of a concaved tree, both dead, both skinny, both failed by the one who was supposed to nurture them)

—if the words stopped. How could she have let this happen? The poor filly, so young, so hungry. What could she do to fix it?

All will…well, Sarana thought gently. *Simply wished…bring to…attention.*

"I cannot go to the Druids," Sada whispered suddenly. "You must leave the Dell, and I've pledged to come with you and care for you. Oh, how will I tell Dedrei?"

After what Sarana had told her, she wasn't certain whether Dedrei would allow her to continue on her original course to Titian, or use physical force to bring her to the Druid Mother. Even if she promised not to go through the portal (should she even find it, and should it be fixed), Dedrei seemed so agitated, so certain in her new course, that she might be unwilling to hear any alterations to her plan.

We will take up this matter again at a later time, Sarana said. Sada forced herself to look up and saw that the filly was staring into the trees, curly tail swishing as she eyed something far away. Her wings fanned, and Sada felt a sudden, crushing desire to fly, to run, to breathe the scents of the woods.

"Go," Sada whispered absently. She hadn't realized she'd responded to the filly's thoughts, but Sarana turned to look at her as she spoke.

Sada, the caelicorn said, tickling the Mindspace like breath on the back of her neck. *I perceive that you are low in spirits. Shall I remain with you?*

The desire to feel the moss squish into the grooves of her hooves momentarily banished any low-spirited feelings. "You may go on, Sarana…I am in need of a moment's thought, in any case. Feel the forest for us both, won't you?"

The filly dipped her golden horn, curls spilling over her eyes, and pranced away with a kick and a flutter of feathers. She was going to find a place to practice with her wings, Sada knew. Then the caelicorn drew out of sight and apparently out of range, as Sada could no longer hear or feel her thoughts.

The fog had mostly cleared with the rising of the sun, and Sada found she no longer needed her cloak to keep warm. She unclasped it from around her neck and went to the small stream they'd camped near for a drink of water. In the pink light of dawn, she saw that the fruit from the night before had been moved. Dedrei must have taken it with her that morning. Most likely she was handing it out to creatures of the forest, perhaps complaining to them of how Sada had wasted the trees' bounty. She wondered if the Druid was in animal form now, prancing around as a great elk or flying as a tulip-wearing bird. Perhaps she would practice shifting into a squinch.

That had her thinking about the Mother of Druids, and for some reason she shivered. Sarana said that the Mother was the only one more knowledgeable about the Seam than the Elves of the Wood. And according to the caelicorn, they were the current guardians of the portal. The thought of meeting someone so seemingly powerful made Sada nervous. Though to be fair, there wasn't much that didn't make Sada nervous. Even now, alone again in the woods, she kept glancing over her shoulder at every rustle of wings or shuffle of paws and hooves in grass. It was just the animals, she told herself, but she wasn't convinced. However, her *instincts* weren't alight, and so she knew she was relatively safe, even if she didn't feel that way.

Still, she wished her father were with her. As tyrannical as he was, she knew she could rely on him. He'd been protecting her since she was born, whether it be with his awe-inspiring strength which had earned him the role of head commander to the king's armies, or with his words which had earned him the title of "the Duke." Even if some of those words were harsh, they had always been strong. She liked to think that some of his strength had been passed down to her through his lambastes and lashings, if not through his blood.

I miss my mother, Sada thought suddenly, then frowned, surprised at her own thoughts. Sada rarely thought of her mother, but being alone in a strange realm and a whispering forest with strange music, she found that she longed to know her. She'd always felt guilty for not missing her mother, or even loving her. But seeing as the woman had suddenly disappeared just months after Sada's birth, she didn't have much to miss or care for.

The Duke had burned every portrait of her ever painted, save for one Sada knew he kept locked away in his wing of their Ettedon mansion. She'd seen him looking at it once, and after, a hall boy had snuck into the Duke's chambers for her since Sada had been too scared to do it herself. The boy had been discovered not when he took the portrait, but when he returned it. He was released from his role at their estate in punishment, but not before Sada had seen the painting.

Thinking of that portrait, of her mother sitting atop a stone wall in their flower gardens, her eyes blazing with pale beauty and her mouth turned up in a smirk, Sada's sadness only grew deeper. She didn't even know the woman's name. Her father would never speak it. Once she'd heard a servant whisper it, and she believed it started with an *M*. But she didn't have the chance to ask because the servant was also dismissed from their estate later that night. Her father had somehow discovered her betrayal. There was nothing that could be hidden from him.

A tickle against Sada's mind distracted her from her sullen thoughts, and she wondered if Sarana had come back already. It hadn't been long since the caelicorn left, but perhaps she had grown tired of her flying practice. A brush of joy through their Mindspace erased all her thoughts as she felt the caelicorn's emotions mingle with her own.

Then she heard one word spoken into her mind that made her stomach twist:

Food.

"Sarana, no," Sada whispered.

What would Dedrei say if she realized Sarana was trying to hunt in her Dell? She'd surely leave Sada, then banish her from the Dell and tell her to never return. Or she would immediately take her to Woia to be imprisoned and punished.

I'll lose another friend, Sada thought. Then frantically, she realized that she didn't even know if Sarana had killed whatever creature she'd found yet. Perhaps she could still stop the filly.

Don't kill it, Lady Blue, Sada thought desperately. The words tumbled into the Mindspace, racing to reach her friend. *I beg you. I shall find you food beyond the Dell. We need not go with Dedrei to the Mother of Druids. Please just tell me you haven't yet shed its blood.*

Sada didn't have to wait for a response. As soon as she sent the mental plea, Sarana emerged from the bushes, amber blood dripping down her horn and onto her little face.

Sada fell to her knees.

THE THIRTIETH

Sada

Sarana whinnied triumphantly as she tossed her head and stamped her hooves. Pride circulated through their Mindspace, but Sada fought it with her own grief and dread at the sight. A great, brown hare was impaled on the caelicorn's horn, its limp body suspended halfway down the golden spear. Sarana must have been so desperate for food that her horn had strengthened into a weapon again. That made Sada grow all the more distraught.

The sight struck her like a surge, driving her to her feet. What would Dedrei say? But she stood for only a moment before her knees betrayed her, buckling and depositing her to the ground once more. She began to feel like a distant observer, half-removed from her body, looking through a slightly-distorted lens.

As Sarana bowed her horn, the limp prey was relinquished. The hare slid off, a fleshy hole drilled through its body. It twitched as it landed in the grass, as if making one final and futile dash from Sarana's dancing hooves. Her ecstatic prancing taunted it with the life she possessed, and which the hare was slowly losing. It shifted, and when it did, it ended up staring directly at Sada with big, terrified eyes.

Then it began to morph.

Sada watched in disbelieving horror as the rabbit's back paws extended into long legs, its front paws into elegant hands. The tattered torso lengthened into that of a human shape, and as it did, the creature gave a long, low moan of pain that brought a lump to Sada's throat. Sada couldn't stop herself from crying out as she watched the hare shift into a tall Druid whom she knew all too well.

Crushed tulips lay scattered around her.

When Dedrei lay before her in her full Spiritkin form, curling up pitifully around her wound, Sada ran to her friend with a cry.

"Dedrei!" Sada shrieked. Her voice sounded almost inhuman in her grief. *"DeeDee!"* she cried again when the Druid only let out another low and feeble moan.

Behind her, Sarana had stopped her prancing. Now she bent to sniff Dedrei, then slowly backed away.

Oh no…Sada—I am truly sorry, the caelicorn said. The otherworldly quality of her voice robbed the words of all emotion they might have carried, and that numb apology only made Sada cry harder. *I did not…I knew not the hare was a Druid…or thy friend.*

"She was *your* friend too!" Sada wailed.

She was afraid to touch Dedrei, worried that a simple brush of her hand might make that terrible gaping wound gush more of the translucent amber blood that was pumping out of it. It was like sap, and Sada felt that if she touched it, it would be sticky.

Sap! she thought suddenly. The thought was a burst of light amidst the shadows in her heart. *I need some sort of sap to close the injury—pine, or spruce. Birch would work, too.* Sada knew all of the medicinal plants by sight, smell, and taste. If she could find some here, perhaps among the greenery Dedrei had shown her, maybe there was hope for her friend. If any forest contained medicinal herbs, it would be the Dell of Druids, which Dedrei had said represented all the foliage of Elt. She would need yarrow or horsetail to stop the bleeding, clean moss to pack the—

(fleshy orange hole gaping out of Dedrei's stomach, like a toothless creature's maw)

—wound in her belly. The thought of it made Sada's stomach flip. She tried to stop herself from wondering how the moss would stay in place when the puncture went clear through her abdomen and back like a tunnel, just to the right of her spine. Instead she recited the rest of the herbs she would need, forcing her foggy mind to obey: willow bark or poppy for pain *(and I'll just have to hope she doesn't become dependent!* Sada thought hysterically), calendula for potential infection, St. John's wort and marshmallow root for the inflammation…

Sada's hands and legs trembled as she got to her feet, searching through tear-blurred eyes for any plants around the campsite. Still, she felt as though she was barely controlling her own body. It was like she had taken a step backward—inward—and was just one or two layers removed from reality. Sarana was saying something, but Sada didn't hear. She didn't want to, and that put up a barrier in her mind.

She stumbled over her feet as she searched the stumps of nearby trees and peered into bushes. Her fingers twisted fervently in her hair, as though she might find yarrow there. There was nothing of use in the clearing. *Skies!* What could she do? Behind her, Dedrei groaned, and Sada thought she said her name. Sada felt her chest begin to seize up, threatening to block off her airway. She pushed the feeling away. This time it wasn't just her own life that her panic would disrupt. If she let herself stop breathing, it might mean that Dedrei did the same.

Only Sada's breath would return eventually. Dedrei's would not.

SADA! The caelicorn spoke so loudly into her Mindspace that her head throbbed with the intensity.

Sada turned abruptly to Sarana. Through blurry, swelling eyes, she could see the filly's own solemn gaze. It told her what she'd already known: nothing could save Dedrei now.

"No," Sada whispered, returning to her dying friend. "There must be a way. There must be something—anything. I beg you, please." She looked up at Sarana as she said the last word, hoping the caelicorn could bestow upon her some grain of knowledge. The filly just shuttered her eyes.

I can do nothing, Sarana said.

"Are you not supposed to possess generations' worth of knowledge? *YOU did this! Why can you not FIX IT?"* she screamed. She cried out so harshly that it felt like the very flesh of her throat tore with the effort, and she broke into a sobbing cough, her head hanging.

Knowledge shall not save her, Sada. The wound is far too grievous.

"*No!* You healed me. Heal her!"

I healed you, and from that moment our bond was sealed. Now my magick does serve you alone—to others, it be naught but worthless. To Dedrei…

All anger winked out of Sada's body in that second as the final bits of hope were crushed beneath the heel of Sarana's words. Sada sagged to sit with Dedrei in her final moments. Her eyes scanned her friend's face, desperate to see every detail so she wouldn't forget a single one. She took in her broad, sloped nose, so like a doe's, and traced its curve to the Druid's feathered eyebrows. Beneath them, her dark pine gaze locked onto Sada's, but her lids wouldn't stop falling down, and she had to struggle to keep her eyes open.

Sada bit into her lip so sharply that she heard an audible crunch as she pierced the skin. Dedrei's own lips were pale, and continuously opened and closed, though she didn't say anything. Sada forced herself to see it all, though her mind fought to retreat with every sporadic breath Dedrei took. She had not been given the chance to remember the face of her mother; she would not waste the opportunity to remember Dedrei's.

Sada gently moved a vine that had come loose from Dedrei's antlers and had fallen on her paling cheek. The plant was limp and yellowing. Just as they did when Dedrei grew sullen, the leaves in her hair had wilted, and the sight brought a fresh wave of tears to Sada's eyes. The Druid's eyes were glassy as well, and held none of the fire that normally blazed there. Sada choked on her own breaths as she watched her friend's grow shallower; as she watched the life slip away from her.

"I am—so—sorry," Sada said to Dedrei, each word broken by gasping sobs. "You did not deserve this—you deserved anything but this. You were right. You were right, Dedrei. You were right." About what, Sada didn't entirely know. She just felt that it was something she should say.

Somehow Dedrei managed to smile. It wasn't a smooth curve of her lips, but happened in short, twitching motions; already her body was failing her. "I…could have told you that," the Druid said.

A pitiful noise escaped Sada's throat. She was no longer in control of her own voice.

Dedrei frowned weakly, just a shift of her eyebrows. "Shush child…shh…All is well, my darling girl…"

Are her thoughts turned now to Shiual? Does she grieve the impending loss of her own life, or does the prospect of reuniting with her daughter bring her comfort instead?

Am I the only one who is distraught?

Dedrei was smiling softly now, and looking at Sada with more love in her eyes than she'd ever been looked at with before. Sada managed to smile back at her friend, not wanting her last memory to be a sad one. Silently, she said a fervent prayer. Then, feeling as though she should do something to make her journey out of this world peaceful, Sada took Dedrei's limp hand.

As soon as she touched the Druid, her *instincts* roared to life in her left palm, shooting all the way up her arm and even into her ribs. Her vision of Dedrei was replaced by a sea of translucent red. It was like closing your eyes with your face to the sun, except she was not just looking at the color, she was standing in it. Sada whirled around, whipping her head back and forth, trying to find Dedrei and Sarana and the trees—but there was only the red. Distantly, she felt Dedrei's cold fingers gripped in her own, but looking down now, she saw her hand was empty. It was partially translucent as well.

She tried to move forward, but she couldn't feel her feet on the ground any longer and she wasn't quite certain if she was walking or floating. Her legs were moving, but it didn't feel like she was going anywhere. There was no wind against her face as she moved, nor any change in her surroundings, and neither was there that internal sense that told you when you were gaining ground, moving through the world. She was beginning to panic, beginning to wonder if she had somehow fallen unconscious or died along with Dedrei, when a sudden feeling of pain washed over her, sharp and throbbing.

"Ah—" Sada clenched her teeth and moved away from the feeling, still not knowing if her location had actually changed. It must have, though, because the pain faded. Somewhere far away, she heard Dedrei cry out. Acting on reflex, she moved forward again to stop her friend's pain. Sada's *instincts* were still a roaring tempest of icy-hot tingling, and they grew stronger as she shifted toward that feeling of agony again. This time, somehow knowing she should do something with it, she didn't shy away from the sense of *wrongness* it brought.

She could see it now; or rather, she could see its center. Again, by the knowledge she shouldn't have, she knew that the entirety of the red she stood in was the pain. But she saw before her a condensed glob of it—not quite a sphere, but almost—that was laced with the faintest traces of black. It expanded and contracted slowly and sporadically, almost as though it was breathing, or pulsing in time with—

(Dedrei's heart)

—an unheard rhythm. Sada reached her left hand through the red until her fingers settled on the pulsating mass of agony. Immediately it surged toward her like a current. But it didn't surround her or suffocate her. It seemed to flow *into* her, as though her left hand was a gateway or an open channel. The tingling in her hand and arm increased and spread as it did, then moved down into her torso and away from her fingers. It condensed into a knot of icy fire in her abdomen, the heart of it sitting just to the right of her spine.

Do not let it escape, she thought suddenly, though she wasn't entirely sure the voice in her head was her own. Neither was it Sarana's. Regardless, she listened. The events that followed did not happen because she wanted them to, but because she felt as though she needed them to.

Having what she felt like was a firm grasp on the pain, Sada drew it into herself. She didn't exactly inhale, and she didn't physically pull the pain toward her either. She just opened herself—or rather, she forced herself to stop keeping it out. It was like she was straining to hold a door closed whose lock hadn't latched, and someone was pushing on it from the other side, trying to get in, but unable to until she let them. Now she opened the door of her mind, and she willed the pain to enter her body. And like an intruder bursting through, it did.

The red disappeared to reveal blackness. With a gasp, Sada flew back into the physical realm. Her *instincts* that had migrated to her stomach faded into a dull buzz. Then suddenly, the feeling exploded into a sharp shock of pain.

OH—SKIES ABOVE—is this what being stabbed feels like? Gabriel had told her once that it felt at first like being punched, then the pain grew into a fiery rage. Sada had experienced neither of those sensations before, but she thought that what she felt now was much worse than anything Gabe had ever described. For a few moments as she lay gasping in pain on the ground, Sada was unable to see anything except a nauseating blur of color through half-slitted eyes. Then the swirling slowed and she opened her eyes, and the stabbing pain dimmed to a dull but incredibly painful ache.

Sada's breaths still came in short gasps, but it was no longer because she was sobbing out her grief. No, the pain was greedy and completely robbed her of any ability to feel anything besides it. She had no thoughts, no desires, only the basest instinct to somehow make it stop. This was a pain like nothing she'd ever have been able to imagine. Even greater than the swipe from the claws of the nine-tailed fox, or the infection in her shoulder.

Sarana was standing over her now, blowing warm breath onto her face, and Sada resisted the urge to shove the caelicorn's nose away. Even the feeling of grass and air on her skin was overwhelming beyond belief. She gritted her teeth instead, turning her face away from the filly's breathy assault. She could tell Sarana was trying to speak to her, but she heard no voice in her mind. All she felt was the agony in her belly.

Then, miraculously, Sarana's nose was replaced by Dedrei's face above her. The Druid was the picture of health, her once-wilted leaves now bright green and springy. Even an amber flush colored her cheeks. Bewildered at the transformation, Sada tried to sit up to either examine or embrace her friend, perhaps both. As soon as she moved, she immediately cried out and fell back to the moss, hand clutching at her abdomen.

"Sada? What is wrong, child?" Dedrei asked. There was concern in the Druid's eyes that Sada had never seen before.

What is wrong with me? You are the one dying! she wanted to shout. *Lie down and stop trying to look after me.* But the thought of speaking brought a wave of nausea to her throat, and Sada could only moan in pain and lift a feeble hand to push away the Druid.

"Let me examine you." Dedrei started to move Sada's gown, but she seized the Druid's hand. It was warm again.

"Your...stomach," Sada gasped through gritted teeth. Skies, the pain was terrible. "Cannot...move...you'll...die." In her condition, she had no time for niceties.

Dedrei's eyes darkened. She set her jaw and rose to her knees so that Sada could see her wound. What Sada saw instead was a bare stomach with no gaping hole or oozing amber blood marring the smooth surface. A few drops remained on the feathers below her belly button, but her skin itself was unmarked. Faintly, Sada's *instincts* tickled her hand.

"How?"

"You." Though her life-threatening wound had just been healed, Dedrei's voice was still grim.

Sada didn't register anything being said through the acuteness of the pain. Now that she saw her friend was not in mortal danger, there was nothing left to distract her from her own injury. She just squeezed her eyes shut, willing it to be gone. *"Ah—*it *hurts,"* she whined.

"I know. I felt it only moments ago," Dedrei said stiffly.

How could you possibly know? You scarcely made a sound over your injury—obviously, your pain was not as severe as mine is. And now yours is gone. It was a horrible and bitter thought, but Sada could not help it. She had no room for guilt, either, with how consumed by distress her entire being was. She did not like how this injury was affecting her mind.

Dedrei helped Sada to sit up then and propped her against a great root. She had expected the movement to worsen the pain, but it didn't much change with the transition to sitting. Sarana was nearby, eyeing Sada with worried glances. The filly couldn't stay still, dancing about on the moss and tossing her head. Dedrei tried to calm her, but she would have none of it. After a few moments of agitated prancing, the caelicorn ran into the trees with a pained squeal.

Lady Blue, Sada thought, but the filly felt distant. And Sada could make no physical effort to stop her.

"She will return," Dedrei said.

She made to undo Sada's dress and inspect the wound. Sada stopped her with a hand on her wrist. Even in unbearable pain, she couldn't stand the impropriety of undressing outside of closed doors.

"People…might see."

Dedrei fixed her with a glare. "It will matter little if you are dead."

This was indeed true, and Sada didn't have it in her to raise another argument. *Apologies, Father…Governess Brown…* Sada scanned the forest for any watching eyes as Dedrei leaned her forward to unlace the gown and the corset, muttering about the unnecessary intricacies of human clothing. But the Druid was gentle as she slid the fabric off of Sada. She pulled Sada's many layers down so that the area of the pain would be exposed.

Propriety was forgotten—the sight made the two women gasp.

Rather than the deep, bloody wound Sada had been expecting to see, there was a mark on her stomach etched in gold. It was in the precise location where Dedrei had been stabbed, identical in size and shape to the injury she had borne. Sada's mark was a beautiful mirror to the grotesque wound that had marred her friend. Now, the skin was unbroken on both women. Sada's mark was a perfectly circular shape of whorls and lines and angles: a rune in a language Sada could not read. The strange symbols made Sada's *instincts* prickle, both in her left hand and her marking. She looked to Dedrei for a translation, but she was at a loss as well.

"This is an old language," her friend said. "A language of ancient beings still worshipped in some parts of Elt. Beings you have heard of—"

"The Kindreds," Sada breathed. "What does it mean?"

Dedrei met her eyes. Their depths were dour. "They have marked you, girl. In more ways than one, but this…" Her eyes flicked to the mark. "This may be the most potent."

The Druid reached hesitantly to touch the sigil. It was flush with the rest of Sada's skin. When Dedrei grazed it with a nail, she felt a flare of *instincts,* but the pain did not worsen. Dedrei flinched backward at the touch.

"What happened?" Sada asked.

"Nothing."

She quickly situated Sada's clothing so that the strange mark no longer showed. As she did, she noticed the long, pale scars on Sada's ribs.

"Where the caelicorn healed you."

It wasn't a question, but Sada nodded anyway. Dedrei just set her mouth and deftly re-laced her gown, leaving the corset loose.

"Let nobody see that rune," she said, bending low over Sada. "It is the mark of a curse disguised as a blessing. Many will fear it and try to destroy you, and others will desire it for themselves. It is hard to say which outcome would be worse." Dedrei stood. "How is the pain?"

The dull, aching pain had not worsened, but had taken on a quality of coldness. The agony brought tears to Sada's eyes, but it was mostly uneasiness at what the mark meant that plagued her now.

"It's well," she said thickly, managing to smile at Dedrei. The Druid saw her bluff, but Sada continued before she could pry. "Does yours still hurt?"

The subsequent silence as Dedrei opened her mouth to answer was shattered by a sound like thunder. Sada flinched, hands flying to her ears and eyes darting to the sky. Their campsite was a small clearing encircled by trees and the sky above was lavender and clear; there were no rainclouds or lightning bolts. She began to ask Dedrei what the sound had been when she saw great, shadowed forms begin to circle down from the sky.

Their bodies were painted in the glow of the sun, the pink halo a sharp contrast to the monstrous wings flaring out like great leather canopies. They seemed to glow with an inner red light, each tendon a shadow, as they extended to cover the sun. Each sharp movement brought another clap of sound. As they descended on their wings in a few great flaps, the wind from their flight blew Sada's hair around her face, her dress billowing up in tandem. As she hurried to right it, Dedrei moved in front of her, crouching low over Sada's legs with her staff held at the ready. Sada noticed uneasily that the Druid's nails had sharpened into long claws again.

"What are those Beasts?" Sada asked. She couldn't keep the wavering out of her voice.

Then the looming forms dropped to the ground, and Sada realized that they weren't Beasts at all, but Spiritkin. Precisely as Dedrei growled, her voice morphed into an inhuman snarl: *"Blood Elves."*

The name and the sight mixed together into an awful knot in Sada's stomach, momentarily overcoming the pain there. Cidinen had warned her of those creatures, hadn't she? *You do not know them. What right, then, do you have to fear them?* she reminded herself. Then her *instincts* flared to life in her palm, feeling as though they might scorch her hand off, and her resolve to remain of neutral opinion grew slightly weaker.

When the Elves landed, their wings folded in, poking up over their shoulders and curling around their arms like great, collared capes. They were so long that the velvety tips trailed on the ground. There were three of them, all men, all dark beings seemingly crafted from the fabric of nighttime itself—their skin of the stars, their hair and wings of the black sky. Where the Elves of the Wood were tall and evidently strong, these Elves looked lithe and agile. They were shorter (as tall as human men) and they had less muscle, but more weapons to make up for it. And, of course, they had wings.

"Why, what a delicious surprise." The Elf who'd landed first broke off from the group, stalking toward Sada and Dedrei.

The clawed tips of his wings loomed above his head; they sheltered him from the sun's light and cast his angular features in shadow. Sada immediately knew him to be the Elves' leader, the equivalent of someone like a sergeant in her world. He wore no epaulette nor sashed sword to mark him as one, but there was a dark sigil branded into his breastplate that the others didn't bear. Besides this, he didn't walk with an arrogant swagger as the two men behind him did, but with the steadiness, the stability, of a man who was always prepared to fight and tell others when to.

"Hile and ho, lovelies!" the second of the men said when he'd joined his leader. This one had a shortbow nestled between his wings: their archer. All the Elves of the Wood had carried bows, but this man was the only one of the Blood Elves who did. Though, like the others, he also had an array of knives belted around his hips and down his leather-clad legs.

The third man fell in silently behind the first two, shaking out his great wings as he walked. A dark scowl was permanently etched onto his marble-like features, and Sada had the fleeting thought that he was not a man at all, but a dark spirit or demon materialized into the physical world. She almost felt ashamed for finding him beautiful. All three of the men wore earrings of silver and jewel as though they were women, but this one also had silver rings in his left eyebrow and bottom lip.

"What are you doing in this Dell?" Dedrei growled. Her voice was closer to animal than human.

"Ooh, you found us a feisty one, Grim," the archer said to the leader.

The dark Elf heading the trio—Grim—seemed as though he was going to ignore Dedrei, prowling around the alcove and scenting trees, mouth slightly parted. The contrasting bits of jewel and bone hanging from his clothes and hair swayed and *clinked* as he strolled. He sounded like a wind chime, stirred by a staticky breeze that warned of a storm.

The Blood Elves had similar enough features that they could be brothers, and when they shifted positions as they walked, Sada felt like she was playing a street vendor's game of guessing which of the identical cups concealed the coin. *Only in this case, it is a question of which man conceals the desire to hurt us,* she thought grimly. She also thought that none of them were doing a very good job at the concealing part.

All of the men had their short, dark locks woven into twists like Sarana's horn. Each also wore between three and six thick twists, and rubies glinted from where they had been threaded in. The men were not large, but their lithe arms were still coated in muscle that was not hidden beneath clothing. They wore short-sleeved tunics and pants of black leather, with white plate overlaying the garments. The skin left uncovered was pale as bleached bone—the only color came from the many rings, armbands, and necklaces decorating their bodies. All of it was red. And their eyes…

"The scent is as bad as I remember," the archer said, grinning over his shoulder at the scowling Elf. "So…earthy."

"Aye, and musky. I forgot how strong the smell of deer is in this place. Or maybe it's only the Beasts." He twisted at his lip rings as he looked to Dedrei.

"I believe this one asked us a question, didn't she?" Grim turned to Dedrei as well. His gaze was anything but kind. "Well little changeling, we're simply making our rounds, searching for any servants who might've strayed from their masters. Perhaps you've come across some?"

"You are surely aware that Druids do not acknowledge slavery," Dedrei said. Then, speaking low so that only Sada might hear, she murmured, "Do not trust what they say; they were drawn only by the scent of my blood."

Sada's own blood seemed to freeze at that.

"It's *servitude,* dear, not slavery. Sweet little shiftskin, getting your S-words mixed up." The archer grinned. "And in any case, your refusal to acknowledge it doesn't mean it doesn't exist."

Dedrei growled. The sound was so terribly primal it raised gooseflesh on Sada's arms and legs. "I will not stand here and play your word games, Blood Elf. Leave, *now.* We do not take kindly to blood-spillers in our Dell, as I am certain you know."

"Aw, what kind of response is that? Is the Dell of Druids not a neutral territory welcoming of all Elt's children?"

"Not for you."

"Oh, you wound me so! I am deeply hurt," Grim said, frowning dramatically. Sada noticed Dedrei's antlers had begun to lengthen and sharpen. "Now what would the Creator think of that, sweet shiftskin? What would the Kindreds say?"

Dedrei hissed immediately. "Their names do not deserve to be tainted by your tongue!"

The Elves were still spread out and examining the campsite. Sada noticed then that the armor the men wore was made of bone, pale as their skin. The Elf nearest to them, the scowler, found her cloak, lifted and sniffed it, then turned toward her with hungry eyes. They were a dark, bloody red, unsettling in their vibrancy. Dedrei had earned a chuckle from the men, but it cut off quickly as scowler stopped beside Grim, holding Sada's cloak. The group passed it between themselves, then their leader snatched it back and breathed in deeply, closing his crimson eyes.

"This smells of a woman," he said. "One from a long-forgotten land. Oh, I haven't smelled a mortal in *ages.*"

His voice had morphed into a deep hum, dripping with what seemed like a lust not for her, but for her blood. At his tone, Sada instantly revoked all remaining resolve to reserve judgment of the Blood Elves. Cidinen had been right: they were terrifying.

"Is that who you protect so fiercely, changeling?"

Dedrei laughed sharply. "You believe this girl to be human? Notice the elegance of her features, the uniqueness of her eyes."

"Oh? Then what of the scent? Don't tell me you're going to try and convince me that my own senses have failed me." The Elf grinned and his men chuckled darkly.

"We've known enough Fae women to recognize what they look like," the archer added, sauntering toward them. "And what they do not."

For the first time since he'd landed, the scowler stopped scowling. It was replaced by a grin, and that was all the more horrible. "Ah, don't be so hasty, Alibi. I don't know about you, but I don't usually see my Fae from so far away, and I use more than my eyes to get to 'know' them. Maybe if we got a little closer, it would be more obvious that she's a Faery like the changeling says."

All their bloody eyes were trained on Sada. The pain in her stomach was now laced with a deep undercurrent of fear.

"This is a special occasion indeed, for my men make a fair point. What say you, Dell dew?" Grim asked. "Will seeing you from closer up explain why there's a human scent on your cloak? Or will it only confirm that it's on your skin as well?"

Sada's *instincts* sharpened in her sweaty palm. Dedrei had worded her statement carefully—cleverly—to try and convince the Elves that she was not human. *Druids cannot lie,* Sarana had told her. But Sada could…maybe.

"It is likely to be—" her throat suddenly forced her to swallow in the way it does when you're nervous, cutting off her words. She began again. "The human scent is likely to be on me as well as the cloak. I took it from one. A human."

The Blood Elves hardly spared her a chuckle, and continued their slow advance. There had never been any hope of convincing them otherwise, she realized then. This was something of a game to them, and they had simply decided to let Dedrei and Sada play along before commencing the true start of the round. One in which the women were not players, but game pieces.

"Redbloods are as wretched of liars as shiftskins, I see. Not to worry—

you'll be doing a different sort of lying soon, and I've found that all women are suited to the kind I'm talking about. The liege would be pleased with a pretty little gift like yourself," Grim said.

Dedrei hissed viciously, and her feathers rose up like hackles. "Speak *not* to her so! She is but a child, not a *toy* for your bloody liege!"

"She looks like a woman to me. And it ain't our liege who's bloody, but the Prince," the scowler said.

"Aye, and with the Bloody Prince at sea, she can go straight to Liege Tempest. So don't worry—your human pet will be kept clean," Alibi chimed in. He'd crouched low to the ground and was slinking up on their flank. "But perhaps it'd be better if she was mussed up a bit…the Prince has got a reputation for stealing our liege's trinkets away for his own personal harem…but only the shiny ones."

"Aye, and the wild ones. Maybe he'd even like to add a changeling to his trove," the scowler observed, raking his red gaze over Dedrei.

Sada's *instincts* suddenly shot up her arm and she gasped, right as Alibi shot forward and grabbed her ankle. Long nails made into weapons by metal covers cut into her flesh. They were crafted from gleaming silver and tapered to a pointed tip reminiscent of a cat's claws. Dedrei immediately hit the archer's pale wrist with her staff, and he drew back with a grin, leaving bloody scratches on Sada's shin. Their reprieve wasn't long, as the scowler immediately darted in and grabbed a fistful of Dedrei's hair. She grunted as she threw him off then stepped close beside Sada, taking up a fierce defensive position.

"They are only toying with us now," Dedrei hissed to her. The Elves were chuckling as they watched the two women. "On my count, we run. Do you understand, child?"

Sada managed to say that she did. But before the women had a chance to enact their plan, the scowler's head whipped around to glare into the forest.

"Grim, something's—" He stopped short as something blue shifted between two junipers, and the other two Elves followed his stare.

Horn still encrusted with Dedrei's amber blood, Sarana emerged from the trees, eyes wide and nostrils flaring. She reared with a furious squeal, punching the air and fanning her wings. As she did, the golden feathers on the underside of her wings reflected the light of the sun into the Blood Elves' eyes.

The caelicorn's show did nothing to dissuade the Elves, however. Their eyes, now shaded by their hands, seemed to grow even thirstier for blood as they stared at the filly. Their angular faces were lit up with savage delight. The joy—the greed—was almost palpable.

"A caelicorn," the scowler said, pointing.

"We can *see* that, Beast brain." Grim growled audibly as Alibi hit the pointing Elf over his tall ears.

"Cursed idiot, tell us something we *don't* know! You aren't called Prophet for pointing out what all the rest of us can see," said Alibi.

"Oi, I tried to tell Grim that the Beast was coming," Prophet—the scowler—defended.

All the attention of the Elves had turned to Sarana now, Sada and Dedrei forgotten. The Druid had moved away from her and was backing around a willow to their right, beckoning urgently. Sada just shook her head, knowing Dedrei would understand what it meant: *not without Sarana.*

The Elves were now trying to grab a hold of the filly. Their attempts to subdue her were met with fierce resistance. With each of their swipes, she retaliated with a flurry of hooves or a stab of her horn. She struck Alibi in the nose with her hoof, and he fell to the ground hissing like a cat. Yet the Elves quickly realized that Sarana's most extravagant weapon was useless. Despite the danger she faced, her horn was still soft and ineffective—the magick which strengthened it in times of desperation must have been used entirely when she had stabbed Dedrei in her hare form. The one named Prophet saw this and waited for Sarana to land from her rearing, then darted in and wrapped his arms around her neck. Her horn grazed his arm, but it simply wilted like a blade of grass at the pressure, doing no damage. The Elf grinned as she squealed.

"Lady Blue!" Sada cried, scrambling to her feet. She hardly noticed the throbbing pain of her wound. If anything, it fueled her rage.

Dedrei stepped out from behind the tree. *"Divine wrath,"* she swore. "She had better not bond with any of these leeches."

Dedrei began to morph, her antlers lengthening and her canines growing into huge fangs. As she shifted, fur sprouting in tufts from her back, Grim neared. Dedrei didn't have time to complete her change before he struck her against the head with a bejeweled hand. She growled and crouched to retaliate, but before Sada could blink, the Elf's leg was swinging out in a roundhouse. His booted foot (*That's the first shoe I've seen in Elt,* she thought numbly) connected with Dedrei's temple with a loud cracking sound, and she fell limp to the ground.

Sada first thought that he had cracked open her very skull, then saw that he had snapped off a branch of Dedrei's antlers. The long, pale points fell useless in the moss, and the sight broke Sada's heart. She didn't know if it would be physically painful for her friend to lose an antler, but it was the principle of it that got to Sada. The disrespect. It was like seeing a queen's crown be knocked to the floor.

Grim kicked Dedrei again in the side, grinning.

"No..." Sada whispered uselessly.

Her fallen friend shifted back into her Spiritkin form, blood trickling from her scalp. She touched her antlers where the branch had been broken off, then turned a seething glare up to the Elf who'd marred her. When she rose up again, she managed to swipe one of Grim's booted feet out from under him, but his wings lifted him into the air before he could fall. Faster than Sada could have imagined was possible, he stepped, spun, and his foot flew up and into the side of Dedrei's neck in a crescent kick.

Their fight continued with Dedrei nearly landing a blow, or nearly morphing into a bear or some other fearsome shape, before the Elf would attack with fists, feet, and fangs. Sada was frozen with fear. Across the camp, Sarana was still struggling against Prophet, whinnying indignantly. Alibi watched, laughing and mocking either the caelicorn or his friend—which one, she could not tell. But it was evident that his aid wasn't needed in subduing the filly.

It was useless. These Elves weren't even using the many knives they had strapped to their bodies and were still besting Sada and her friends with ease. She wanted to cry, both from the constant throbbing pain in her stomach and from the terrible fate they were certain to face. What else could she do but grieve for them all? Obviously Sada herself wasn't enough of a threat to even bear the attention of a single one of the men. But as she thought it, almost as though he'd sensed her thoughts, Alibi's head snapped up to stare directly at her. He began to stalk toward her.

Oh no, now I have doomed us even further. Whatever I might have been able to do, now I—

Take ACTION, girl! Her father's voice suddenly interrupted her solemn thoughts. But what could she do? She was but a girl with no training, no weapons, no armor. She wore only a ripped dress and a painful golden rune. But something, anything, would be better than allowing herself to be restrained or knocked unconscious by the angry archer who was striding toward her.

Before Sada could form a plan, the Duke's words forced her legs into motion. A step brought her in the direction of the fight between her friend and their foes' leader. Having nothing to give but herself, Sada went to the Elven leader, who was now crouched over Dedrei's prostrate body, sneering as he trailed a silver-encased fingernail down her neck. The vines in her hair wrapped weakly around his wrist, but he sliced them away with his crafted nails.

"Take me," Sada said. He didn't hear her. *"Take me."* She held her wrists out as though he would tie her up like the guards from her world would. Realizing he'd probably just grab her, she dropped her arms. The Elf was regarding her with something like amusement.

"'Twas the plan, little red-blood." He turned back to Dedrei.

As he did, the distant feeling of a plan formed in her Mindspace and she heard a single word spoken into her head: *Lie.*

"No, take me and I shall show you where to find the rest," Sada blurted. Whatever Sarana had sent to her, her mouth had picked up on it faster than her mind.

That made Grim halt his tormenting of Dedrei. "The rest of what?" he asked, facing Sada. He still knelt on Dedrei's back, one hand pressing her face into the ground when she tried to squirm. Sada had to look away from her friend, grunting protests muted by the moss, in order to keep talking. She focused on the Elf's horribly beautiful eyes instead.

Swallowing a click in her throat, she continued weaving Sarana's lie. "The rest of the caelicorns. She is not the only one, you know. We chose her because she was the weakest…and the prettiest." *I'm naught but a foolish little girl who fancied a pretty little pet,* she thought at him darkly. *Surely that is convincing enough.* "Yet there are more."

"Where?"

Sada wove a tale of a secret wood, a safe haven for caelicorns. One past a shield of leaves and pine boughs, hidden in a mist-covered ravine like the ones where Nymphs dwelled. "There are both foals and mares fully grown, their horns gleaming like liquid gold beneath the moonlight."

The Blood Elf narrowed his eyes, then glanced back at Sarana still struggling against Prophet. He was on his feet again, now trying to pin her wings to her side. Alibi was frozen halfway between the two groups, looking between them and frowning. Sada bit into her lip, praying their plan would work. If it didn't, she had nothing.

Grim called out to his men in a rolling language, the same the Elves of the Wood had spoken. Then in the Known Tongue he said, "Alibi, secure the caelicorn and bring it along, since Prophet is clearly incapable. He'll take the changeling sow instead, and I'll take the human."

Alibi spun on his heel and took his bow in hand, un-stringing it deftly. When he'd joined his comrade by Sarana, he reached around her neck while Prophet used one arm to pin her wings and the other to hold her jaw so she didn't bite either of the men. She squealed furiously as Alibi re-strung his bow around her neck, using it like a crude collar. It made Sada's stomach turn.

Sarana chided Sada through their bond, reminding her that she must continue in her lie if they were to have any hope of escaping. Before she could even finish registering the thought, she was speaking Sarana's words again.

"If I may, the grove lies more than two days' walk in that direction," Sada said, gesturing randomly. "It might suit your plan better if you flew instead—unless, of course, you'd rather take on all the Druids of the Dell yourself. Though I'm sure a leader such as yourself has little time to waste on such an endeavor. You could leave the Beast here and return on those fully matured—the ones capable of flight." She inclined her head toward Sarana. "That one, I'm afraid, is lame."

She was thankful to Sarana for all but speaking through her, because she otherwise never could have forced herself to speak of her friend so cruelly. It was also lucky that the caelicorn was translating her archaic dialect into the more modern speech that Sada used, because she wasn't certain she would have been able to do so herself without the Elves realizing something was amiss.

"Why would you be giving me advice, girl? What's in it for you?"

"A prettier caelicorn, if luck treats me well. And if not, then perhaps a kinder fate than otherwise would have awaited me."

She tried not to show that the words were not her own, that they were complete fabrications, as she met the lead Elf's eyes. He glanced between her and Sarana, weighing the decision. He knew Sada had other motives beyond leading them to more caelicorns, but he was too greedy to risk the chance that she was bluffing entirely. Sarana knew the nature of Blood Elves, and so Sada now knew it as well. A growl rose in his throat as he considered.

"Is she lying to me, Alibi?" Grim asked.

His archer looked up from across the clearing. "I can't say, Cap." One hand was holding the bow restraining Sarana, and he used the other to tug on one of the twists in his hair. "Cursed thing goes silent when I'm distracted."

Then he truly can read my thoughts?

Their leader cursed.

"Why don't I stay here, Grim, and you and Alibi can go find the others?" Prophet asked.

Grim turned slowly to glower at his companion. "We have two prisoners now, and we'll need to ride back with at least one caelicorn, though three would be preferable. Tell me, how are Alibi and I supposed to do that alone? Even if we knock the wenches out—" he gestured toward Sada and Dedrei— "one of us would still be needed here to guard them—yes, we always guard the prisoners, and the fact that you're trying to argue otherwise is why you're not a wing leader—then one of us will have to wrestle the Beasts we find. And then who will protect that person from the other caelicorns? You know well how bloodthirsty those cursed creatures are. That foal alone already bloodied Alibi's ugly face."

Prophet glanced at his archer friend and frowned. "But Grim, why don't we make the women ride the Beasts back? Then we could deliver four of them to the liege, while I stay to guard this one. That would make not four, but *five* caelicorns in—"

"Aye, I can count. Twice-bloody idiot," Grim muttered. He shook his head hopelessly. "What did I just say, Beast-brain? Do *not* leave prisoners unguarded. That means, don't go handing them a Void-cursed mount!"

Prophet opened his mouth to contribute another spectacular idea to the discussion, but the glares of both Alibi and their leader made him think better of it.

"Let the shiftskins have this one, it's lame anyway," Grim said. "We'll take three of the Beasts for Liege Tempest instead—no more, no less. And if there aren't as many as the girl promised, then we'll see to it she draws her final breath." He grinned at Sada. "But only after finding this little blue Beastling for us again, and facing Woia's wrath in our place."

The men whooped a cheer.

Alibi removed the string from his bow once more, releasing Sarana. He darted out of the way as she lunged to bite his arm. While she was distracted, Prophet swung a kick into the back of her knee, causing her to stumble when he walked away. As the Blood Elves' attention turned to Sada, Sarana slowly backed into the forest. Her golden eyes were troubled, but Sada sent her an urgent thought to flee while she had the chance.

"You, darling, are mine," the fanged leader said to Sada. His gaze incited nausea as he dragged it over her. She wished desperately she had her cloak, though it was what had begun this trouble in the first place.

Grim stood from Dedrei's back, and when the Druid tried to follow him, he drew a blade, flipped it in the air, then slammed the hilt into her temple as he caught it again. She fell limply into the grass. Sada moved for her, but Grim's cold hand caught her arm, and he wagged a finger at her. As his two companions joined him beside Sada, Alibi wiping a trickle of silver blood from his face, she sent a silent command to Sarana.

Take Dedrei and find the Mother of Druids.

You have no hope of survival alone, Sarana responded. Her ancient voice sounded panicked, a strange dissonance from its typical emotionless tone. *You must come with us.*

Sada didn't bother with words then, just sent Sarana the knowledge that either all of them would be captured, or only she would. It was a matter of simple arithmetic. Sada felt the caelicorn's understanding brush against her mind: they both knew that two free was better than three captive. Neither of them could say if Sada would ever escape her captors, who were now discussing how long they should wait before flying to find the false haven of caelicorns. But Sada didn't feel as much fear as she thought she should. She'd spent her entire life feeling like a prisoner. These captors couldn't be much worse than her father, right?

She doubted her hopeful ideations were true at all. Sarana's thoughts confirmed this, but they were growing more distant by the second. Her focus on her task must have weakened their mental bond. Sada watched the filly nuzzle Dedrei where she lay at the edge of the clearing. She had snuck around the trees to reach her while the Elves were distracted with Sada. Dedrei slowly woke and sat up, though she hardly even opened her eyes. Thankfully, though, she recognized her need for rescue.

The half-conscious Druid managed to lean onto the filly's back with some help, and then jerkily morphed into a large squirrel. Sarana shifted so that the transformation ended with squirrel-Dedrei on her back. Lady Blue looked back one last time, golden eyes troubled. Then at a nod from Sada, the two took off running into the forest. Sarana could go no faster than a canter and had to spread her wings to keep the half-conscious Druid from slipping off, but she managed. Despite the pain in her belly and the fear also taking residence there, Sada smiled. Seeing her friends escape was a better feeling than that of freedom itself.

Unfortunately, the feeling did not last long.

"Prophet, grab the shiftskin. Come on, little red-blood, let's—" Grim had been grinning at Sada but cut off with a curse as he turned to see her friends moving away from the camp. "*Husband of a harpy!* The Void-cursed Beast is getting away with my changeling!"

Alibi grabbed her shoulders hard, causing her to cry out. "Was this your little plan all along, sow?" She couldn't answer with those sharp fangs in her face and his silver nails digging into the still-healing wounds on her shoulders. The archer's breath stank with the tang of iron. *Blood,* she realized with a shiver.

There was a series of vibrating *thunks* as the Elves flung their knives at Sarana's retreating body. They were skilled with their blades, but the caelicorn was small, and more skilled at evasion; she did not allow herself to be in the open, going only where the large trees of the forest offered cover.

"Give me that bow!" Grim shouted to Alibi. He'd run out of knives to throw. "That Beast ain't escaping with breath in its lungs!"

Alibi did as he was bid. Grim ripped the shortbow from his grasp and nocked a black-shafted arrow. Then Alibi spun Sada around so that she was forced to watch her friends be hunted. She tried to turn her head, but he grabbed her jaw in rough hands and held her gaze forward. Sarana and Dedrei were half-buried in the trees by now, but Sada's breath still caught in her throat as she was made to watch the dark Elf draw the arrow, string whining as it flexed. He waited, panting, darting red eyes tracking the flashes of the filly's blue hide.

Sarana had reached a part of the forest where opals studded the ground like Giants' fallen teeth. The gaps between the trees were larger now. Her small, winged body came into view.

Sada's breath hitched.

The Elf released the arrow.

It soared through the woods. Its black shaft flew over Sarana's bouncing hide as she swiveled to look over her shoulder, missing its mark, but instead planted itself firmly in Dedrei's left side. Upon making contact, a circular, blood-red rune spread across her friend's furry brown back. It glowed for a moment before fading into a black singe-mark. The Druid immediately began to shift back into her Spiritkin form and fell to the ground, despite Sarana's efforts to catch her with her wings. She was now just too heavy for the filly.

Sada's heart dropped with Dedrei, and she watched her friend hit the ground like a discarded doll. She stared at her unmoving shape in horror. Dedrei raised her head once, twisted to look at Sada. Her friend's blood was translucent like sap, but she could already see it bubbling at her mouth.

"Sa-da..." the word was wet and broken and heart-wrenching. Dedrei dragged herself toward Sada, her legs limp and useless behind her.

She thought of a foal that she had seen born without use of its back legs, still wet from its dam's womb and trying to stand, trying to drag itself toward her, unable to understand why it couldn't. She thought of how the mother had backed away instead of going to the foal like she should have, already knowing something was wrong. Not wanting to get attached.

Sada didn't have that privilege or that ability. She already loved Dedrei, more than she loved the mother she'd never known. Her father had been with Sada to watch the foal's birth that day. He didn't give the baby time to drag itself more than a few feet, leaving a trail of clear and bloody goo in its wake, before he'd fired a rifle into its still-wet head.

The second arrow landed just below Dedrei's left collar bone. Her mouth widened into a surprised O, she tried to crawl, then slumped to the ground. Her hand twitched madly once. Twice. Sada was nauseous. Her stomach revolted at the sight of her friend, now unmoving. Would she have to suffer the loss of her—

(mother?)

—friend not once, but twice?

And will this time be reversible?

Upon seeing Dedrei struck by the second arrow, Sarana reared and released a heart-wrenching squeal that sounded like the tear of fabric. Or perhaps a heart. *She was your friend, too,* Sada had said to her. Now she saw that the filly hadn't needed a reminder of that. Of course she didn't. She had always made her affection for the Druid clear, in the nibbling of her leaves and the snuffling in her face. Sarana landed on all four hooves again and bent to nuzzle Dedrei. Sada saw she was licking the wound in her chest. Trying to heal her.

"Sarana, RUN!" Sada screamed, seeing Grim nock another arrow. She jerked to the side, just managing to brush his arm. As she did, another black arrow streaked the sky. It brushed through the feathers on Sarana's wings,

streamed through her tail, and landed in a spruce to her right. A white feather was pinned to the trunk. *"RUN!"*

Sarana answered with another despaired whinny and a flood of anguish that drenched their Mindspace, then she wheeled on her hind hooves and did as Sada bid her. Another arrow chased her, but fell short and landed in Dedrei's calf. Her leg twitched once, but the Druid did not otherwise move. Sada cried out wretchedly and struggled against her captor, trying to run to Dedrei. Maybe she could use her strange powers, her *instincts,* again and take on this wound too. The one in her belly still ached, but she hardly noticed in her newfound despair.

"Missed," Grim cursed as he watched Sarana's cerulean flanks disappear. "These bloody bows are only good for the leaf-lovers." He threw the weapon down.

"At least you got the shiftskin," Alibi said from behind her. Their leader just grunted in response.

Sada's knees shook and then collapsed. Alibi let her fall to the grass. He seemed to understand she was too defeated to fight back. The Elves collected their knives, still staring hatefully after Sarana who had long since disappeared. Muttering angrily, they congregated and spoke for a minute, then Alibi crouched to grab Sada again. His hands were unnaturally cold, though she could have guessed that from his bone-pale skin.

"Tempest will still be happy with the redblood," Prophet was saying to Grim, as if to cheer him up.

Alibi shot to standing and tried to hit his companion over the ears, but Prophet ducked. *"Never* call him by that name alone! You always have to say his title first."

Prophet rolled his eyes. "We're standing in the middle of trees and—"

"Even alone, even out here, you can't. You'll get into a rut of it," he hissed.

Grim just grunted his agreement. "Aye, Alibi has the right of it. And the liege certainly will be happy. Of the three, the mortal has the highest value. And if we're going to assume she wasn't lying to us, we can still raid the caelicorn grove. Just be careful not to mention you ever even laid eyes on a changeling when you talk about what happened today, got it? Unless you want our liege to take the twists in your hair alongside the ones in the caelicorns' horns." Grim chuckled at his own comment.

"It ain't possible for hu-mons to lie," Prophet said. A pause followed, then his comrades erupted in laughter.

"It's *humans,* Beast brain," Alibi laughed.

"I *said* that!"

"And in any case, they very well can lie. They're just as bad as a shiftskin at it. Mortals reek of deceit when they attempt it," Grim said.

Alibi sniffed her hair. The sound was loud in her ear.

"This one smells like tulips."

Lost in her gloom, Sada couldn't even bother to wonder how she'd managed to convince them of her lie if they could smell it on her. King Caprius had scented it on the brothers; why didn't the Blood Elves have the same ability, as they seemed to think they did? But rather than those questions, all she could think of were her father's words as Alibi hoisted her to her feet from where she'd fallen to the ground.

You never take action! Why do you never take action? It seems as though all you do is sit and muse upon what ought to be done, yet never stir yourself to act.

The archer passed Sada to Grim and he slung her over his shoulder, right between his neck and the big, curved spike on the apex of his folded wing. She expected the impact to make the cold throbbing in her abdomen worsen, but it remained the same dull ache. She hardly felt it as she stared at Dedrei's limp form from her position on the Elf. She was certain he'd faced her this direction on purpose. She kept waiting for the Druid to stir, to sit up and wink at her: *I am fine, child,* she'd say. *Pretend they killed me, then we will run.*

Still, she only heard the Duke's voice: *How did I father such a failure?*

"Alright, it's time to soar boys," Grim said.

"Flap to it!" another agreed. It sounded like Prophet, but she didn't much care who it was. Though she did wish he was the one carrying her—he seemed most likely to drop her, and death would likely be a better outcome than whatever awaited her when they realized her farce.

Sada watched as the leathery wings on Grim's back began to stir. There was something fuzzy on between them, maybe a strange piece of armor. The spike atop the left wing grazed her side as they unfolded, but she was so numb in her grief that she didn't even flinch. Sada closed her eyes as Grim bunched his knees, resigning herself to her flight and her fate.

Then the Blood Elves' leader cried out.

The shriek was sharp and short, cut off by a distinct gurgling sound. She'd heard it once before when she'd ridden with her father and his knights, the day they were attacked by the angry small lord. The day she'd heard the drums. Before Gabriel had ridden off with her on his horse, she'd been introduced to the terrible sounds of war. The drums. The screams. The retching. The low moans of someone suffering a fatal but slow-acting injury had been one of them, along with the sound of someone choking on blood.

Sada had heard both today. The latter was loud in her ears now.

She felt Grim's shoulder move beneath her stomach as he fumbled at his injury. Then he collapsed, sending her sprawling on the ground. Her head hit the moss sharply. The earth beneath it was not so soft.

"Leaf-lovers!" Alibi shouted. She heard the stretch of his bowstring. "Curse the Kindreds, the Void, the Mothers—curse all of it!"

"They got Grim…Void take them," Prophet spat.

The thundering of heavy hooves quickly drowned out any other comments that may have come from the Blood Elves. As Sada forced herself to sit up, she saw through painfully swimming vision a stampede of giant elk like the one whose form Dedrei had taken. Only there were no tulip-covered antlers among these.

The grey, brown, and white elk were bigger than most horses, and had antlers spanning lengths greater than most men were tall.

Of course, the men and women riding atop the Elk were also taller than most men were. Most human men, in any case. These were Elves—Sada recognized them by their inhuman beauty and height easily enough. In her blurred and doubled vision, there looked to be hundreds of them.

At a command from one of the blonde newcomers heading the group, his elk and the others' lunged forward and toward the Blood Elves. The winged men drew their weapons, but as the riders neared, they thought better of it. Instead of attacking, both Prophet and Alibi whistled and their wings began to unfurl. Then the men jumped inhumanly high, and while they were suspended their wings *fell* off their backs, as though they'd pulled a lever and released them.

Then, magnificently, the wings began to fly by themselves and Sada realized with wondrous horror that they were horse-sized bats. The great bats swooped directly beneath their riders and the Blood Elves landed on their furry backs. Alibi squatted as he landed, and Prophet dropped to wrap his legs around the bat's sides, just in front of its wings. Sada watched in amazement as the two Elves flew off on their monstrous mounts within a rain of arrows.

They hadn't bothered to take the body of their leader with them. Sada was shocked, but she shouldn't have been. However, the fallen Elf's bat crawled off its dead rider's back and took to the air after its brothers, flapping lopsided and crookedly in their wake. Its large body was blocking any clear shots to the Blood Elves, and the Elves of the Wood stopped releasing arrows as the riderless bat flew away. Through the pain of her head, she felt faintly relieved by that.

Then, as the Blood Elves flew into the path of the sun, two more arrows were loosed in their direction, hurtling with so much power and speed that the shots had to have been fueled by more than just muscle. When the arrows found their marks in the fleeing warriors' backs, they were too far away for any groans of pain that might have been grunted to be heard. Sada watched as the leather- and bone-clad men tipped off their bats and fell to their death. The motion was achingly familiar to watch.

Head still pounding, Sada faintly registered one of the great elk blowing warm air onto her face. Her vision was blurry, her head warm and throbbing, and she recalled later thinking it was Sarana. She put a hand on the soft muzzle before she was lifted to standing by strong arms. The touch had her *instincts* roaring. Through barely-open eyes she saw beautiful people adorned in forest-colored clothing blur into a jumble of pale limbs, eyes, and braids. Her knees buckled but she didn't fall—the Elf holding her was supporting all her weight.

"Will you take the child, *Ai* Havilah?" he said.

There was a murmured assent and then Sada was being lifted into the air. It incited a wave of nausea, and she closed her eyes. The Elven man set her gently onto an elk, and before she could sway and fall off, two slender arms slid around her.

"Calm, now. All will be well, seedling," said the woman who must have been Havilah. Sada briefly felt that she should not move from this clearing, though she didn't know why. She thought she told the Elves not to take her.

"No," Sada mumbled as the elk began to walk, its shoulders rolling beneath her. She forced her eyes open and as the big animal turned, she realized why she'd been so opposed to leaving. *"No!"*

One of the Elves was bent over Dedrei, one hand lifted to the sky and the other pressed to the earth in what looked like a prayer, or some other ceremonial gesture. Then the kneeling Elf turned to the rest of her companions, the ones gathered around Sada, and shook her head: *She's dead.* Sada struggled to climb off the elk, but she found that she could hardly move her body. *Skies,* her head and stomach hurt. Sada tried to cry out again, telling the Elves to stop.

"Please," Sada was begging. "I can heal her again. Let me hold her. *NO! I can save her!"*

The Elf she rode with just began to stroke Sada's hair and hum softly as her elk moved away from the clearing, and Dedrei fell away from her view. She briefly wondered if her mother would have stroked her hair like this if she were still around, or alive. Her father never had. She felt his voice in her head one last time before her swimming vision turned black.

She couldn't hear what he said.

ACKNOWLEDGEMENTS

My acknowledgments and gratitude go first to my Lord Jesus Christ, for making all things possible. I also thank my family for supporting me unconditionally and unceasingly. I am particularly grateful to both of my parents for acting as my editors, and I give special thanks to my Dad, who has always been a mentor to me in everything.

I would also like to acknowledge you, the reader, and thank you for having grace knowing that this book was edited through peer review. My goal from the beginning has been to release to the world the most authentic version of *The Kindreds* and Sada's journey possible. That goal led me to self-publishing; however, as I'm sure you know, veering from the traditional path always comes with its distinctions.

I extend my heartfelt thanks to all who have contributed to this endeavor, and I look forward to unveiling more of Elt, the Spiritkin, and the tale of *The Kindreds* in the days to come.

Sada's journey has only just begun…

PRONUNCIATION GUIDE FOR FOREIGN NAMES

You can pronounce the names in this book however you'd like, but if you want to know the way they're intended to be pronounced, this is for you:

NAME	PRONUNCIATION
Agathon	AAH-guh-thon
Airedez	/EYE-reh-dezz/
Alcázar	ahl-KAH-thar
Aisathas	EYE-suh-thass
Aphredys	Uh-FRAY-dees
Atarah	uh-TAHR-uh
Attilore	AAH-till-or
Pyrithos	PEER-ith-ohs
Aurelian	/ah-RAY-lee-ehn/
Avredeil	/AV-reh-dayl/
Beron	BARE-un
Kostas	KOH-stahs
Caprius	CAP-ree-us
Castellor	CAH-stay-or
Chimydra	/Keem-EYE-drah/
Cidinen	SEE-dih-nehn
Crielune	KREE-eh-loon
Darius	DARE-ee-us
Dedrei	DEH-dray
Dephrylus	/deh-FRIGH-luss/
Edri	EH-dree
Phalios	FAH-lee-ohs
Eulila	yooh-LIGH-luh
Icarion	EE-kah-ree-on
Havilah	hav-IH-luh
Althira	al-THEER-ah
Issachar	ISS-uh-cahr
Helexios	heh-LEX-ee-ohs
Rhaelion	RAY-lee-on
Kaji	KAH-gee
Kartinar	KAHR-tin-ahr
Liytara	ligh-TAHR-uh
Therakles	THEH-rah-klees
Kunak	COOH-nak
Naexa	NIGH-ex-uh

Necron	/NEH-cron/
Nevroxhil	/nev-ROKS-hill/
Perísa	/purr-IGH-suh/
Pyrtoxos	/peer-TOKS-ohs/
Sada	SAY-duh
Sarana	suh-RAW-nuh
Selkala	sell-KAY-lah
Shoda	SHOH-duh
Shiual	SHE-ooh-all
Sichan	SIGH-can
Silvanys	Sihl-VAIN-ihs
Solares	/soh-LAHR-ess/
Nikaros	/NEE-kah-rohs/
Thymenos	TIE-men-ohs
Titian	TISH-ee-en
Varre	/VAHR-ay/
Vasadini	VAHS-ah-dee-nee
Zaelis	ZAY-liss

*a set of slashes around a word indicate that the R is flipped
*an apostrophe indicates an abrupt stop

P.S. I only included the names which were either foreign or difficult to pronounce. If you need help pronouncing the name "John," well…I'm afraid you're on your own for that one.

LANGUAGES OF ELT

Fair Tongue

WORD	PRONUNCIATION	MEANING
Viie	VEE-yeh	True/yes
Morók	/moh-ROCK/	Idiot
Néos	NAY-ohs	No
Asta/Vo	AH-stuh/voh	Formal title for a superior/elder
Ai/Vi	eye/vee	Formal title for an equal
A' / V'	ah'/vv'	Formal title for an inferior/youngling
Kora	KOH-rah	Girl
Koréno	/kohr- RAY-noh/	King of my heart
Koréna	/kohr-RAY-nah/	Queen of my heart
Koréne	/kohr-REH-nay/	Ruler of my heart
Koro	KOH-roh	Boy
Vaisse	VIGH-eh-suh	Vessel
Vaisse'ulism	VIGH-eh-suh' YOU-lism	We are the vessels
Andrótes	/an-DROH-tee/	Men
Te'raina	/tay-RIGH-nah/	Dread
Scrysi	/SCRY-see/	See self/self-seer
Haiséthra	/high-SETH-rah/	Blood mark
Leoteryx	/LAY-oh-tare-ix/	Feathered leopard
Hédras	/HAY-dross/	Caelicorn Rider
Antýchos	an-TEE-kohs	Immortal grandsire
En	in	Is (general)
Estora	/eh-STOHR-uh/	Morning
Arithē	/Ah-REE-thay/	Fair/good
Dēmos	DAY-mohs	Mine
Emé	EE-may	Is (personal)
Kalon	KAY-lahn	Well/good
Ei	eye	If
Sos	sohs	Yours
Tōi	toy	Then/next
Sada	SAY-duh	Eternal/life
Torteuir	TOR-tay-youhr	Hell
Selkala	sell-KAY-lah	Moonlit beauty

Jei	Zhay	Unit Lord's title
Laphi	LAH-fee	Bunny/little rabbit

*a set of slashes around a word indicate that the R is flipped
*an apostrophe indicates an abrupt stop

WORD	PRONUNCIATION	MEANING
Fakta	FAHK-tah	Fool
Gom' Brodir	GOHM' bro-deer	Old Brother
Jiie	JEE-yeh	Yes
Om' Modir	OHM' mow-deer	Old Mother

*a set of slashes around a word indicate that the R is flipped
*an apostrophe indicates an abrupt stop

ABOUT THE AUTHOR

Rayne published her first book at thirteen, and has been writing professionally since then. She is passionate about exploring human psychology, the tension between good and evil, and bringing to life the fantastical workings of dreams. It is her hope that her writing can reveal truths about humanity and God in a way that is both veracious and entertaining.

Having lived all across the country, Rayne draws on a wide range of experiences in her craft. Wherever she is, she can be found immersed in something creative, whether that be singing, drawing, or daydreaming. Always at her side is her family, steadfastly supporting her endeavors.

www.ingramcontent.com/pod-product-compliance
Lightning Source LLC
LaVergne TN
LVHW090544110826
845146LV00001B/14

* 9 7 9 8 9 9 2 0 4 0 6 1 6 *